# Daimon

A Rose and an Amaranth blossomed side by side in a garden,
and the Amaranth said to her neighbor,
"How I envy you your beauty and your sweet scent!
No wonder you are such a universal favorite."
But the Rose replied with a shade of sadness in her voice,
"Ah, my dear friend, I bloom but for a time:
my petals soon wither and fall, and then I die.
But your flowers never fade, even if they are cut;
for they are everlasting."

**Aesop**

Copyright © 2017 Linette Kasper
All rights reserved.
ISBN: 0-692-88920-5
ISBN-13: 978-0-692-88920-6

*To my husband, Greg:*
*For being my sounding board, my inspiration, and my eternal love*

*And to my daughter, Chloe:*
*For your love of the story and its characters and your eagerness to always hear more*

# Part 1

# Suppression

# Chapter 1
## Why Me?

"Do I have to go?" I questioned, dropping onto the couch.

"Of course you do. Vanessa chose you as one of her bridesmaids, and you should support her. Besides, it's just a fitting and won't take long," my father argued, sitting in his favorite chair.

"Can't she just buy the dress and call it done? Why does it have to fit perfectly?"

"This is a big deal to her; everything has to be perfect. Doing this will make her feel like you're attempting to accept her. She's really excited you're a part of this."

"Oh come on, Dad. She just told you that to get in your good graces. She doesn't care about me."

"Let's not start this now," he insisted, rubbing his temple. "You need to meet her at the bridal boutique soon. Just get it over with, and then you can go sulk in the cemetery."

"Yes, let's put on a happy face for Vanessa," I mumbled under my breath as I got up and walked away.

Ever since my mom's death four years ago, my dad became a different person. He focused more on work and less on me when I needed him most. I had to learn to move on, grow up, and solve my own problems. It wasn't until Vanessa entered his life that he decided it was time to get involved in mine again.

Vanessa, my soon-to-be step-witch and thorn in my side, was very much like the stepmothers in fairy tales – a beauty with an agenda. From the first time I met her, I knew she wasn't marrying my dad for love, but for his money. And as much as I tried to convince him of that, he wouldn't listen. He was blinded by her, and only I could see the truth.

She came from the boonies of North Carolina to attend Virginia Commonwealth University, hoping to earn a Mrs. rather than a real degree. With no luck snagging a rich husband in school, she searched outside it. As she was choosing where to intern, she researched several companies and decided to apply at the same firm where my dad worked. That was how she met him.

Quite popular in the office, she was able to learn all she could about the partners from the administrative staff while working there. Once she had the information she needed, she set her sights on my dad and focused all her attention on him. Of course, he was an easy target – widower and single father to a teenage daughter.

When she initially showed interest in him, he explained that it was too soon to get involved in a relationship. It was only about a year after Mom's death, and he wasn't sure if the time was right yet. He claimed to still be mourning, but in actuality it was the uncertainty of how long she planned to stay around. He wanted companionship but didn't want to invest a lot if she wasn't going to settle down after college. But as fate would have it, the firm offered her a position, and she became a permanent fixture in the office and his life. That was where it all went downhill.

More time in the office meant more time with my father. He called to say he was staying late or to tell me he was having a dinner meeting, but I knew something else was up. He was rarely late and never had that many meetings when Mom was alive. Instead, he was out with *her*.

After several months of keeping their relationship quiet, he decided it was finally time to come clean…by bringing her home and introducing her to me. I vividly remember the first time I met her and the impression she made on me. She came through the door acting like a caffeinated cheerleader, wearing a stretched-out baby doll tee from her high school days and too-tight, stonewashed jeans that gave her a slight muffin top. She was so wrong, so totally different from my mother.

Rushing up to me, she gave me a big hug while saying how honored she was to finally meet me, and what great friends we'd be. It all sounded so nice and promising, but the clincher was the look she gave me when my dad's back was turned. It was like she was sizing me up and preparing for the takeover.

I avoided spending any time with her because most of it was spent fighting. But now, with the wedding and her joining our family, I was being forced. I had hoped to just sit in the audience and watch as if it were a bad play. But no. She insisted I be included and my dad agreed. So here I was – frustrated, angry, and betrayed.

I fell onto my bed, the soft comforter cradling me like the mom I wish was still here. Why doesn't Dad understand? He's trying to replace her with someone who doesn't like me or want me around. And it's obvious. Maybe he just doesn't care.

I folded my arms behind my head and stared at the clouds painted on my ceiling, taking myself back to a happier time…when Mom was alive. I was about twelve, and she thought it'd be neat to make it look like my ceiling was open to the blue sky. We made a total mess but had so much fun doing it. Afterward, as we lay side-by-side on the floor admiring our handiwork, she told me how much I meant to her, and how she'd always be there for me.

My smile faded and I rolled over, pushing those memories away. I sighed as I glanced at the clock and forced myself up. It was almost time to meet the witch. Slowly staggering into my bathroom, I checked myself in the mirror and then proceeded to freshen up.

Back in my room, I threw on a pair of jeans and a light sweater and left my hair down, hoping it'd stay tame. There was no need to get all dressed up for a quick fitting. A glimpse in the mirror verified I looked decent enough. I grabbed my purse and headed downstairs.

Dad was still parked in his chair watching the news. "Headed out?" he asked.

"Yeah, don't wait up for me," I replied as I kissed his cheek and left.

The sun was nearly set, painting the sky blended shades of blue, red, and purple. I stared at the striations for a moment and then backed out of the driveway. No more delays; I need to get this over with. The quicker I get in and get fitted, the quicker I can leave and not deal with Vanessa a moment longer. But on the drive to the boutique, all the traffic lights caught me and gave me unwanted time to dwell on what to expect from the soon-to-be step-witch tonight.

What kind of dress did she choose for me? It'd have to be the same as her other bridesmaid dresses – probably something lacy and pink or short and tight, perfect for her sort of friends. Or possibly something hideous, making all of us look bad so she shines. No, I suspect she won't do that to her friends. Me, yes, but her friends, doubtful.

I tried to like Vanessa at one point, but it wasn't for her or me, it was for Dad. I'd do anything for him; he was all the family I had now that Mom was gone. I just found Vanessa and I had nothing in common, and the more I got to know her, the more I realized how much I disliked her. So I assured myself at the time it was a just a phase, and Dad would break up with her any day.

But days turned into weeks, then months, and finally years. Then one day, he came home and delivered the bad news – he proposed and she said yes. Expecting me to be happy, he was surprised when I went off on him, telling him my honest feelings and concerns, all the things I pent up over the short time they'd been together. But before he could react, I took off.

I got in my car and drove to Hollywood Cemetery to be with my mom. I always went to her whenever I had a problem. Even after death, there was something soothing about being in her presence.

Usually it was instant, but that night, I was wound up and comfort wasn't coming easily. I paced in front the crypt for several minutes, venting at the stars. Then I went in and cried as I sat beside her tomb – angry with my father for not listening to me, angry that my mom was here and not at home, angry that I didn't matter, just angry at the world.

When I was all cried out and too exhausted to do anything, I closed my eyes and went to sleep. That was when she came to me. Mom always knew how to calm me, and even in my dreams she did. I woke refreshed, clear-headed, and not as upset. But the effect only lasted so long. As soon as I got home, the issues would rise again. Dad and I argued more than I ever remembered.

I realized there was nothing I could do to change his mind, so I focused my energy on changing Vanessa's. I played sweet and innocent in front of him but did what I could to aggravate and annoy her so she'd snap. She was a tough one to crack, though, and knew how to play the game. It seemed I was in trouble more often than her.

*I just need to get through this today, and then I'll be off the hook for a while.*

I pulled into a parking space as close to the entrance as I could in case I needed to make a fast getaway. Walking through the double doors, a saleswoman greeted me and asked if I needed help. I informed her I was meeting Vanessa Wiley, and she smiled broadly.

Indicating behind her, she said she was in the back of the shop trying on her gown. I thanked her and slowly headed toward the dressing area, pausing every once in a while to look at gown styles and still wondering what was chosen for me. Well, a few more steps and I'd know.

I took a deep breath and turned into the dressing area, standing and waiting for Vanessa to come out. Still in the stall, she was praising herself on a great gown choice and raving over how she looked in it. What an egotist. But compliments turned to complaints as she started banging around and fumbling with the lock. My stomach churned as it finally slipped open.

*I can't believe I agreed to do this.*

"There you are!" she exclaimed in her country twang as she stumbled out. "What took you so long?"

"I guess I left at the wrong time…I hit all the traffic lights," I replied, looking over her dress and trying not to react negatively.

It was unbelievable, but exactly what I imagined she'd wear for her wedding – tight and white with crystals running from around the waist to the base of the skirt. The crisscross, sweetheart bodice had thin shoulder straps also covered in crystals. But the most absurd part was the slit halfway up her thigh.

"What do you think?" she asked, noticing my gawking. "It's absolutely gorgeous, isn't it? I think Jack will *really* like it," she blathered, not waiting for me to answer.

"Yeah, it fits you to a T," I replied. She was right about my dad liking it. Heck, what man wouldn't?

"I have your dress right here," she commented as she pulled a lilac, Grecian-inspired gown off the hook on one of the dressing room doors.

It was nothing like what I thought she'd pick. "It's…beautiful," I remarked, surprised, as I took it from her.

"Do I have great taste or what?" she asked as she turned to admire herself in the mirrors, hoisting her chest up to enhance her cleavage. "Now go try it on."

I didn't respond, going into the nearest stall and removing my clothes. I slipped into it and was amazed at how well it fit, and how flattering it was on me. The beaded empire waist hugged my curves as the skirt cascaded to my feet, the fabric light and wispy. The spaghetti straps showed off my sylphlike shoulders, and I thought of the ideal necklace to wear with it – a teardrop diamond pendant that belonged to my mother.

Vanessa knocked on the door and called out, "How's it look? I wanna see!"

I stepped out slowly and she squealed. Wincing, I asked, "So you like it?"

"You look *hot*! Not as hot as me, of course, but still hot! It fits nicely to your body, and I just knew your breasts would look great in it!" I blushed, more embarrassed by her comments than her compliments. She fussed with the skirt a little and looked me over a couple of times. "Yes…very nice…" she mumbled.

"This one is by far the best choice," one of the saleswomen remarked as she joined us, fidgeting with Vanessa's gown.

"Of course it is," Vanessa snapped, smacking her away. "What about hers?" she inquired.

The saleswoman, 'Irene' her tag read, turned to me and her eyes lit up. "Oh! Don't you look exquisite!" she responded, fiddling with my hair and the dress.

I glanced at Vanessa, the envy burning like a wildfire in her eyes. Then she smirked. "Yes, it does…but what do you think about the length?" she asked, moving in front of me.

"It's good for her, but once she puts these heels on, it'll be perfect," Irene replied as she handed them to me. I took the shimmering lavender strappy heels, slipped them on, and modeled the ensemble.

Vanessa looked at me and then Irene. "No, I really think I should go with a shorter style. I'm not sure my other bridesmaids would like it long. The wedding is in June after all. Maybe something about…here," she remarked, taking the skirt and raising it to my mid-thigh.

I looked at her, astonished. "There is no way I'm going to wear a dress that short. I like the longer one," I argued, pulling the fabric from her hands and letting it drop.

She placed a hand on her chest, looking appalled. "This is for *my* wedding. Besides, I'm just trying to help you get a boyfriend, sweetie. By the time I reached your age, I already had, like, ten! You've had, what, one…maybe two? You really need to step it up. I'm inviting some eligible cousins of mine. You can start there."

"I don't want a boyfriend. And even if I did, this isn't the right way to get one."

"Well, you've got to show them the goods to get them interested, and you have gorgeous long legs. Believe me, I know how a boy's mind works. We also need to work on your lack of makeup, covering problem areas and highlighting your best features," she responded, completely ignoring my argument as she lifted my chin and examined my face.

"I'm not like you, nor do I want to be," I rebuked, jerking it out of her hand and backing away.

Her smug expression turned sour in an instant. Irene became uncomfortable with the tension between us and told her she would check to see if there was a shorter option, then quickly left. I stared at Vanessa, my eyes narrowed in anger, waiting for her attack.

Her face was red and her fists tightened. "Oh believe me. You are *nothing* like me, and no amount of help I give will change that," she replied through clenched teeth.

"Thank God," I muttered under my breath as I turned to go change and get out of there. I was done with her.

"Don't turn away from me!" she yelled as she grabbed my shoulder and jerked me around. "This is for *my* wedding, and if I want you to wear a short dress, that's how you'll wear it!"

"I don't think my dad needs two whores," I responded without thinking.

"What did you call me?"

"I don't think I need to repeat what you already know."

"You ungrateful little brat!" she roared as she slapped me across the face.

I stared at her, speechless, as I held my cheek. Heat rose in my face as I gave her one last look before running through the store and out the door with the dress and shoes still on. The women at the front counter just stood with mouths agape, not saying anything or trying to stop me. I quickly climbed in my car and tore out of the parking space, angry tears spilling over my burning skin as I headed to the light.

How could she do that? How could she hit me? I expected yelling, but never that. And what will she tell my dad happened? That I instigated it? That I *deserved* it?

The light changed and I sped off, heading toward the only place I found to be my sanctuary. In the cemetery, no one disturbed me, and I could be alone with my mom. I needed her guidance, her strength. And I needed to take this time to cool off and think about what happened.

Since it was after dark, I parked my car away from the front gates and headed to my secret entrance. I climbed a tree and used the aid of a lower branch to mount the top of the fence. Carefully lowering myself, I tried my best to keep my gown clean and in one piece. I didn't need Vanessa fuming to my dad about me ruining my bridesmaid dress to spite her.

I slowly crept through the gravestones and the trees, making sure to stay away from the front gate so I wouldn't be spotted. Once I was in the clear, I connected with the main path and casually strolled farther into the cemetery, glancing at familiar tombstones and monuments as I passed. Mom, Dad, and I used to come here often when I was young. I could practically walk it blindfolded.

Most people would find a cemetery scary after dark, but I didn't have a problem with it. I felt comfortable and safe mostly due to the fact I knew nothing would harm me here. Also, there was a slim chance I'd run into anyone. Occasionally there were goth kids, but they never seemed to notice me; I've learned to be pretty stealthy.

After Mom's death, I visited every day, taking a bus since Dad was working and refused to come. But in time, it became too expensive to use public transportation that often, so every day turned into three days a week, then two, then one. Eventually, it got to a point where I only visited her once a month.

But when Vanessa became more involved in my dad's life, my visits increased again. I was able to drive by then, so whenever there was an issue, or I felt the need to get away, I would, no matter what time. Night visits were the most frequent because a majority of the upsets took place after Dad came home from work.

Some of those night visits became overnight ones as I had the tendency to fall asleep in the crypt. At first, Dad worried when I didn't come home after several hours and called to check that I was okay. But the more often it happened, the less he called.

It seemed strange, but I enjoyed staying in the cemetery overnight. Sleep was more peaceful when I did. And I usually saw my mom in my dreams. Hopefully, I would tonight.

I continued along the path, enjoying the solitude and tranquility. The moon was rising over the trees, lighting my way perfectly like my own personal lantern. It glistened on the rushing water of the James River that flowed beside the cemetery, and I stopped a moment to enjoy the view before moving on again.

Finally arriving, I climbed the few steps and slowly opened the door. It creaked slightly and reminded me I needed to bring oil to lubricate the hinges; I can't have a creaky door giving me away. I glanced around before entering and then shut it tightly behind me. Sitting in my usual spot in the corner by my mom's tomb, I stared out the small window in the door into the dark sky painted with a few clouds and a hint of stars. A slight breeze whistled tunelessly through the cracks.

I hummed quietly as I ran my fingers over her name, remembering the lullaby she used to sing when I was young. It was an old tune, one her mom sang to her. I tried to remember the words, singing them softly as they came into my mind. It had been so long since I heard it, the last time being when I sang it to my mom as she lay dying in the hospital.

Settling in the corner and resting my head against her plaque, my lids grew heavy. All the emotions from the evening were catching up with me, exhausting me. Dad would be expecting me to come home, but I knew what was waiting for me, and I didn't want to go, so I gave in and drifted to sleep.

*Mom and I were standing across from each other in what looked like mist, but it was thicker and white. It shifted constantly, but never closed in on us. We were the only two there, all alone and far away from everything. I looked into her eyes, smiled, and gave her a hug, and she smiled as she hugged back. Then I let go, though I didn't want to, and looked at her again.*

*"What do I do, Mom? Dad will be marrying this awful woman in a couple of months. She's nothing like you and trying to turn me into something I don't want to be. I thought the relationship would just blow over, like it was some mid-life crisis thing, but he's serious about her. He says she makes him feel young and happy again, but I think he's afraid to be alone. I guess it's not good enough to have just me."*

*My eyes dampened at the thought of my dad not wanting me anymore. I couldn't help that I was unable to fill the void Mom left. I was only thirteen at the time and dealing with my own grief. Why couldn't he see what he was doing to me? I lost my mom and now would lose my dad.*

*She wiped the tears from my cheek and replied, "Your father still loves you, Nut-Meg, and no one will change that. Give him time; this is his way of moving on. He still loves me and my death was hard on him, too, but he knew he had to be strong for you. He also realizes that you need a female figure in your life. Find the good in her. Don't let her upset you so much and remember, no one can change you but you."*

*"It's hard…"*

*"And you'll overcome this like you have so many other things," she assured.*

*"What about Dad? He's been so preoccupied with her, he has no time for me."*

*"Help him make time. You're still his baby girl."*

*I sighed as I gazed at her. "I miss you so much. I wish you hadn't left."*

*"I know and I miss you, too. But it was my time to go. Just know I'm happy here and can still watch over you," she replied as she swept her arm over a fluffy, white mass. The clouds parted and I could see our house. "I send my love to you every morning in the rays of sun that glance your face as you wake."*

*"I love you, Mom," I responded as she glanced back at me and smiled her warm, caring smile.*

*"I love you, too. If you ever need anything, you know where to find me."*

*"I do. I can't wait to see you again."*

*"I'll be waiting, Nut-Meg," she responded as she gave me another hug. I breathed her in, memorizing her scent as she kissed my forehead...*

I slowly opened my eyes and blinked several times, expecting to see her before me, but she wasn't. I was still in the crypt curled up against her tomb. I had been dreaming. A drop of water landed on my face, and I looked up as more dripped from the ceiling. I wiped the wetness from my cheek and forehead and then sighed. I stared a moment at her engraved name on the plaque, kissed my fingers, and pressed them against it.

Glancing out the window in the door, I found the moon higher in the sky. It was getting late. I stood up, stretched, and headed out of the crypt.

I felt a little better having seen her, though it was in a dream. But even with that, I wasn't ready to leave yet. I know I'm going to hear it when I get home, so I'll just prolong my stay and deal with the consequences in the morning.

Gently closing the door, I slowly descended the stairs and walked away. I went to the bluffs overlooking the river and watched the rushing water below. The sound carried to me, a pleasant din like the soothing roar of a waterfall. Closing my eyes, I breathed in the cool night air and let it fill my lungs.

Opening them again, I stared at the island across the river and thought back to all the times Mom, Dad, and I used to visit it. Belle Isle. Situated in the James, it morphed from an industrial hub to a Civil War prison camp to a supplemental source of electrical power, but in the end was converted into a city park.

The easiest way to get to the island was by using the footbridge over the river. As a young girl, that scalloped concrete crossing was my biggest deterrent. Cars from the freeway above growled and clanked, giving me the feeling the whole thing would collapse at any moment. Below, the river flowed fast and seemed so deep and far away.

But if I wanted to enjoy everything the island had to offer, I needed to get over my fear and cross it. Mom helped to keep my mind off the heights and noise and let me take my time while Dad guarded us from reckless cyclists. When I had to pause, she encouraged me to look down into the water, pointing out that we weren't as high as I imagined. After several visits, I was used to it and able to run or bike it without a problem.

We loved to explore the island as if we were the ones who discovered it. Mom, Dad, and I cut through the vegetation and avoided the paths, discovering new places. We played in the dilapidated buildings and ran carefree in the fields. Then toward the end of the day, we settled on a dry boulder in the river and had a picnic, watching the kayakers fight the raging waters.

Hearing a faint noise behind me, my thoughts returned to the present. I glanced around but found nothing. Returning to my memories, I stared out over the river again. It seems like so long ago, like another life. Basically, it was. And in June, I'll start my new life with a new mother, though I'll never call her that.

With the marriage, I'll be stuck living with Vanessa in the same house day in and day out. I don't know if I'll be able to stomach that much of her. Thankfully, I only have another year to get through, and then I'll be off to college. I haven't decided yet what to study or where to go, but I do know I won't be living at home during that time.

Maybe I'll go to another state, far away from Dad and Vanessa and all of my memories, good and bad. I could start a new life, maybe even change my name and who I am, who I was. That'll be fun, to be somebody else for a while or maybe even the rest of my life.

Too bad it won't happen. I can't escape myself, my life, my memories, no matter how hard I try. They will always be with me, engraved in my soul.

Plus, if I move to another state, I won't be able to visit Mom as often. To not be able to see her and talk to her, even if it is all in my head, is unthinkable. And besides, she won't want me to go. She'll want me to stay near. So I'm stuck.

I stared out over the rushing moonlit river and sighed a deep sigh.

# Chapter 2
## An Unexpected Encounter

"Do you come here often?" inquired a mysterious voice behind me.

I jerked around, gasping, "Oh! Geez, you scared me!" as my eyes scanned the darkness for whomever interrupted my reverie. But no one was there. Was I hearing things?

"Forgive me, but it's not often you see such a beautiful woman wandering around a graveyard in the middle of the night," the voice responded after a moment, moving out of the shadows. As he came into view, my heart thumped in my chest.

He was stunning, like an otherworldly being, with beguiling eyes that took me in as I was taking him in and bow lips that naturally turned at the corners into a slight smile. Tall and lean, he was dressed in khaki pants and a pinstripe shirt that opened to a fitted black t-shirt.

As he casually walked toward me, he folded his hands behind his back. His movements were so fluid, they captivated me. Feeling bashful for staring, I quickly looked down at my hands and fidgeted with them, focusing on the detail of my nails rather than him.

"I-I wasn't wandering. I'm here to visit my mother…and think."

"A strange place to think and visit one's mother so late," he commented as he moved closer, standing next to me. My blush deepened, and I tried to distract myself with something mundane like the freckle on the side of my index finger.

"It's peaceful…and on a night like tonight, beautiful. This is my favorite spot because it overlooks the river," I responded, turning my attention to the bluffs. "I feel safe here…I know that sounds strange."

"Not at all. I feel the same way," he agreed, staring over the river at Belle Isle. He was silent for several minutes as we both gazed off into the distance. "My name is David," he introduced suddenly, turning to face me.

He held out his hand and I extended mine to shake it, but instead he took it softly in his. Instantly, I felt something in his touch, soothing and safe, like we were meant to be here at this moment. I looked up into his glimmering, light green eyes as he slowly lifted my hand to his lips, gently kissing it. They were soft and warm against my skin, sending an electrical charge up my arm. Maintaining his gaze, he raised a brow.

"Oh, uh…I'm Megan." I blushed slightly, not used to being treated this way or feeling like this. I looked away quickly to hinder the further reddening of my cheeks.

"It's a pleasure to meet you, Megan," he responded, his voice smooth. The way he said my name sent a quiver through my body. He paused, smiling subtly, and then slightly tilted his head. "I don't mean to pry, but is this what you usually wear to the cemetery?" he inquired, looking over my bridesmaid dress.

"No...I...not usually," I replied, embarrassed. I must look like a fool. "It's for a wedding."

"Yours?"

"No! Does this look like a wedding dress?"

"I guess it could," he grinned and my heart skipped a beat. He had the most gorgeous smile, his dimples accentuating his bright, flawless teeth and lips. I was drawn to him, wanted to be closer to him. My head was all fuzzy as I stepped nearer. He looked away quickly, staring out over the river again, his smile gone. "I apologize. I didn't mean to insult you."

"Huh...what?" I muttered as I came out of my daze and stepped back. "No...no, you didn't insult me. It's for my father's wedding."

"Oh. Is that why you're here? You don't agree with his choice of bride?" he assumed, shifting his eyes to me.

I turned away and quickly walked off. "Vanessa and I had a...a disagreement. I just needed some air...some time to think."

Coming to a bench under a large oak tree, I sat down. The river flowed below, glistening over the rocks embedded in it. In the distance, the lights of the city glowed warmly. Why am I still here, talking to this complete stranger? Maybe it's time to go home. Dad has to be getting worried about me, though he hasn't called yet.

There was no sound from David. I glanced over at where we had been standing, but he wasn't there. I guess he left. Oh well. It was nice to have someone real to talk to for once in this cemetery. If he was real...

"Forgive me, I was being rude," he remarked, making me jump.

"Geez, you have got to stop doing that!" I gasped.

I tried to calm my heart and catch my breath as he came around the bench and sat next to me. He leaned forward, resting his elbows on his knees, with his head cocked my way and a grin on his lips. My heart thumped harder this time.

His face became solemn but was still so handsome. "It must be hard. How long ago did she pass?" he inquired as he sat up and turned slightly toward me.

I stared into his sage eyes, rapt in them. There was something alluring and hypnotic about them, but also mysterious. I broke my gaze. How rude to stare into some strange guy's eyes, no matter how mesmerizing.

"It's been about four years," I responded finally, fidgeting with the chiffon of my gown as I looked down at it. "She was really sick and suffered a long time. I should be happy she's at peace now, but it's so hard. I...I miss her so much."

My eyes welled up at the thought of Mom. I tried to stop the tears from coming, pulling back, but a few escaped. Looking down river, I discreetly wiped them away and then faced forward, hoping there wasn't any residue on my cheeks. David was quiet. I glanced at him out of the corner of my eye and spied him staring straight ahead, seemingly lost in thought.

"So…what are you doing here in the graveyard in the middle of the night?" I asked, thinking it might be a good idea to change the subject.

He didn't answer right away, staring at the rushing water below us. He sighed and turned toward me again. "Same as you. It's an ideal place to come and think, away from the living…all the noise. Generally, you're alone." He bowed his head and laughed slightly at the thought. He had a beautiful laugh, too.

"Generally," I agreed, smiling at the thought as well.

We were quiet for the moment, both looking out over the river. I stole a couple glances at him, hoping to catch him doing the same. If he was, I never noticed.

I sighed. "It's true…I don't like the woman my dad plans to marry, but he doesn't seem to care about my opinion. She's really young, barely older than I am, and nothing like my mom. I don't know what he sees in her. She doesn't even like me," I complained, throwing my hands in the air. He just sat there, watching me intently.

I stood and walked around the oak, feeling the need to cool down. He shouldn't have to hear my problems. So why am I telling him? Did I hope for a solution, or am I just happy to have an unbiased ear?

Leaning my back against the trunk, I stared into its branches. It was nice to have someone listen to me for once and not yell back. But is he really interested? I dropped my head and stared at my feet, the moonlight highlighting the ground beneath me as it shone between the twigs and budding leaves.

He came around the tree a moment later, standing right in front of me. "You're not used to talking to people about this, are you?" he inquired, cocking his head to the side and grinning. Again my heart fluttered. What was with this guy and my heart?

I looked down and made designs in the dirt with my foot, allowing my blush to wane. "No…well, except with my friend Claire, but she doesn't understand. Her parents have been married forever, together forever. Plus, she thinks it'd be cool to have a 'mom' close to your age, someone to shop and hang out with. Believe me, Vanessa is not that kind of person," I replied, pushing off the tree and walking toward the path to the family crypt.

David politely stepped out of the way and then followed a few feet behind me. He was so quiet. If I hadn't noticed him out of the corner of my eye, I never would've known he was there.

"I think my dad lost it when Mom died. He wasn't there for me much after it happened, even though I did my best to help him through it. So I started coming here to see and talk to her," I continued, dreamily climbing the few stairs to the crypt and then placing my hand next to the door and resting my head against it. "Sometimes, I fall asleep here and wake up to the sunlight shining through the stained glass window, lighting the room in a kaleidoscope of colors, and know it's a sign she's with me."

David was silent, pausing a few feet from the steps, as I stared up at my family name engraved in marble above the door. "You look lovely in the moonlight," he commented, probably trying to distract me.

"What is that...some kind of lame pick-up line?" I teased. I turned and grinned at him but quickly looked away as I saw his lip begin to curl. I can't fall for his charm. I don't know him or what possible motives he may have.

"No, not at all. Just a compliment. I see you don't get those often."

My cheeks burned. I started fidgeting with a curl and began to descend the stairs when suddenly I tripped, probably on my long skirt. I braced myself, waiting to hit the hard ground, but instead I felt warm arms wrapped around me.

I opened my eyes to David gently removing the strands of hair from my face. He held me close, a look of concern in his gaze. He smelled so good.

"Are you all right?" he asked softly as he helped me to stand.

It took a moment to register his question. "Yeah...I'm okay. Wow, you're fast! I feel so embarrassed...I'm usually not this clumsy. Must be these crazy heels...or...or you," I rambled as I stared into his hooded eyes. I felt drunk, well what I think drunk feels like. I've never had alcohol before but witnessed plenty of times what it does to people.

He smiled at me and my heart fluttered again. "Maybe you should take a moment to recover on the bench," he suggested as he tried to help me over to it. My knees went weak. "Or maybe it would be easier if I carried you."

In one swift movement, he lifted me off my feet and cradled me in his arms. Staring at his neck rather than his face, I spied a thin leather string encircling it with something small dangling right in the dip at the base of his throat. My hand slipped from his shoulder, grazing the pendant, and he looked down at me.

My heart thumped and I tucked my head so he wouldn't see me swooning, but I was that much closer to him. My head swam as he glided over to the bench and gently set me down. I gripped the front of it and allowed my head to clear, embarrassment burning in my cheeks as I leaned forward slightly.

David kneeled in front of me, softly grasping both of my arms. "You're not going to pass out, are you?" he asked, trying to look at my face.

"No, I'm feeling better," I replied, closing my eyes to avoid his gaze. "I guess the excitement of the fall made me feel faint. My head's clear now." I composed myself and looked up at him. I tried to suppress the reddening of my cheeks, but it was hard. "I am so embarrassed. I don't know what came over me," I apologized, grinning sheepishly.

"It's all right," he responded, slowly releasing his grip as he moved to my side and sat.

He rested his hand on the bench, and I felt an overwhelming urge to place mine on it. What are these emotions I'm having? I want to be close to him, to hold him. I want to be with him and only him. I shouldn't feel this way about a complete stranger, but I don't feel like he is one.

"Maybe I should go…" I whispered, hesitating.

"No, stay. I'm enjoying your company…though you seem a little unstable," he smiled, but not at me this time.

Leaning forward, he rested his elbows on his knees and turned his head to look at me. His wavy chestnut hair shined in the moonlight and moved slightly with the breeze. I bet it's soft…and smells good. I bit my lip and tried to think of something else as I looked away. The moon, the river, the cemetery…

I'm glad he doesn't want me to leave. I'm enjoying his company, too. I wonder if we'll see each other again, maybe in a more pleasant place. I wonder if he's single, not that I want a boyfriend. But what if he is single and asks me out? I'd be stupid to turn him down. I mean, look at him! So stunning and perfect…

"You've been quiet a while. What's on your mind?" he inquired with a curious look.

I turned to him, surprised by his question. There was no way I was going to tell him what I was just thinking. He continued to stare, an eyebrow arched and waiting for an answer. "You," I blurted out. "I mean, wondering if we'll see each other again," I recovered quickly.

"I think it's very possible," he replied with a grin. Another flutter of my heart.

He's so enigmatic. A burning desire to know more about him consumed me – what school he attends, where he's from, about his life in general. I stared at him as he watched the river and then blushed and looked down at my hands, fidgeting again. I have a silly schoolgirl crush on this guy! I've never felt this way about anyone before. He's so different from the guys at school.

I haven't dated a lot in my life and have never been 'serious' with anyone. The guys in school really weren't my type, and apparently, I wasn't theirs. I've never really cared either. Dating brings stress and drama, and I definitely don't need any more of that in my life. Besides, most of the time what we mistake for love is lust.

Not that I don't believe in love. I believe in a deep, intense love that survives anything. A love I thought my father had for my mother, but I guess I was mistaken. I'm a romantic, dreaming up plenty of scenarios of how my perfect guy will sweep me off my feet. Whether he's a tall, dark stranger come to take me away or Prince Charming come to rescue me, I'm waiting for that perfect love.

And as I looked at David, I wondered if he could be that perfect love.

"So," I began as I twirled a curl, "where do you go to school? I don't think I've seen you around."

"I attend the university in the city – VCU. This is my first year." I noticed him shift his eyes, trying to see my reaction.

"Oh, a college boy." No wonder he's so different from the guys in school.

"I live in a house off campus with several friends. It's nice, but it gets a little insane living with them sometimes. That's another reason why I come here. I've found it to be a great place to relax and let my mind wander."

"What's your major?" I asked, adjusting my position and leaning back on my palms.

"I am pre-Med."

"Really? That's great. What drew you to that field?"

"The desire to help people."

"How honorable," I responded, glancing at him and giving a small smile. "Are you from Richmond?"

"No, but I really liked this area. There's a lot of history here with plenty to do inside and outdoors. It's alive, but not overwhelming. A big city, but not too big."

I stared at him in wonder. The moon shone on his face just right, and I noticed his complexion, so smooth and dewy, almost unnatural. Maybe it's the moonlight. My skin looked different, but then again that could be because of the dress. I have to give my soon-to-be step-witch credit for her color choice; it really complemented my skin tone. I guess that's what David noticed earlier. I smiled slightly.

"Would you like to walk?" he asked as he rose suddenly.

"Oh. Sure, that sounds nice. Let me take these heels off first. I don't want to trip again."

"Good idea," he agreed, smiling. My heart skipped yet again.

He offered his hand, and I dreamily placed mine in his. Gazing into his eyes, I slowly rose off the bench and walked around it to the path. His smile faded, and I came out of the trance. I dropped my hand and kept pace with him. We strolled side-by-side past the graves and crypts, his hands folded behind his back and mine holding my shoes and dress.

"I wonder if anyone passing by would mistake me for a ghost," I commented, noticing the ethereal movement and luminosity of my skirt.

"I thought you might have been. You looked so forlorn and the dress doesn't help."

He was right; I probably looked like some jilted bride or dead prom queen standing in the cemetery in the middle of the night. I smiled, thinking of the stories people would fabricate. The lovesick bride left at the alter who threw herself into the river and wanders the cemetery to this day. Or the prom queen whose king murdered her because he was drinking and driving. I giggled, thinking of such stories spreading through school because of me.

"What is so funny?" David asked with a small grin, glancing my way.

I quickly looked forward. "The stories that will start circulating about the mysterious bride or prom queen."

"Sounds intriguing," he prompted.

"It'd be a local ghost story. The bride was left at the alter and was so distraught, she threw herself into the river over there," I replied, pointing to the spot where I had been standing when I first met David. "Now she wanders the cemetery, doomed to replay her horrific death over and over." I glided between tombstones and then rejoined him on the path.

"And the prom queen?" he chuckled.

"Oh, she died in a ghastly car crash at the main gates. Her date, the prom king, had been drinking – you see how this is a cautionary tale – and lost control of the car. He collided into them, throwing her through the window. People have seen her drifting through the cemetery trying to find her way home." I put the back of my hand to my forehead and looked desperately lost.

"You have quite an imagination, Megan," he remarked, shaking his head. I loved the way he said my name. His voice was soft, but strong, and there was something old about it, like from another time.

"Well, growing up an only child has its benefits, I guess." We continued to stroll through the cemetery, occasionally commenting on the tombstones or crypts we found interesting. "I've heard real ghost stories about this one," I mentioned as we came to a large, creepy-looking tomb. We stopped in front of it, and a shiver spilled down my spine.

"What are the stories?" he inquired, his interest piqued.

"They say something leaves it each night to hunt, only to return before morning. One such story claims this thing was found crouching over a man's body with a bloody mouth and two pointy teeth. When it realized it had been spotted, it ran here to this very crypt."

"Interesting. But you don't believe in that nonsense, do you?" he asked as we walked away.

"No, not really. I guess that's why I don't have a problem coming here at night. There's nothing to be afraid of. When you die, you die, and there's nothing more to it."

He looked at me with a furrowed brow. "What if there is more to it?"

"Well, not that I've experienced. Never met a ghost or vampire or anything supernatural. I've never tried to contact the dead, not even after my mom's death. I just accepted she was gone."

"What about other people's experiences?"

I thought about it a moment as I slowed my pace. "I've heard about them. Sometimes I do wonder if there are beings that are not human walking the earth. I have even secretly hoped to experience them."

"Experience them how?" he inquired, intrigued.

"When I was in my early teens, I went through a phase where I wished a vampire would 'take' me. I was a vampire fanatic – read tons of books and saw a lot of movies, no matter how bad. But I realized later they're just a romantic ideal to mislead young girls."

"Quite a theory," he commented, smiling at me.

The flutter in my heart returned. I placed my hand over it and sighed. I would have thought with all the times he smiled at me tonight, my heart would be used to it.

Then suddenly I realized what I just said. I dropped my eyes to the path, the burning returning to my cheeks. I've never told anyone about my vampire obsession and here I am, telling a complete stranger and a college guy no less. He must think I'm a total dork.

"Oh, you know how stupid young girls can be," I played it off, looking at him and smiling.

"No, enlighten me," he responded, grinning. I quickly glanced away, pretending to look at an interesting gravestone.

"They have these lofty dreams of romance as it is. Male vampires are portrayed as the perfect guy – an incredibly handsome, alluring gentleman who would give anything to have the girl, even their immortality. In the real world, it's just not that way."

"Do you know this from personal experience?"

"No. The guys at school won't even give me the time of day."

"I find that hard to believe," he commented, stepping in front of me so we were face to face.

I glanced away. "They like flirty girls or the blonde cheerleader types. I don't fall into either category."

"Their loss," was all he said. I looked down at my bare feet contrasted against the dark asphalt as I played with my hair.

We continued along the path in silence, glancing at the objects around us dimly lit by the moon and casting faint shadows. A breeze blew lightly, and I rubbed my arms for warmth. Even though it was April, it was early in the month and the nights still got cool. I wasn't expecting to be in the cemetery this late, so I didn't bother to grab a shirt or jacket from the car.

I noticed David look over at me. "Would you like my shirt? I have two and can do without one," he offered.

"Oh…" I responded, contemplating. "If you really don't mind…"

He removed the button-down and helped me into it. "Not in the least."

I pulled it tightly around me and crossed my arms to keep it closed. It was warm and soft against my bare skin. His smell was all around me, and it was intoxicating. I started to feel lightheaded and suddenly needed to sit. Noticing a bench nearby, I headed toward it.

"Are you all right?" he asked, following me.

"Yeah, I feel a little dizzy. I just need a moment," I answered, taking a seat as he did the same.

Closing my eyes, I waited for the dizziness to pass. What is wrong with me tonight? I get near him and feel faint. I put on his shirt and nearly pass out. Was it his cologne or something about him making me act this way?

Feeling it fade, I glanced at him. A cool breeze blew, but he didn't seem affected by it at all. Instead, he looked completely comfortable. He sat straight and gazed off into the cemetery, his dark fitted t-shirt emphasizing the definition of his body.

Then he shifted his eyes to me and smiled. "Feeling better?" he asked, noticing me staring at him.

"Yeah, I think so," I answered, blushing as I looked into his eyes.

"Shall we continue?" he inquired as he stood and took my hand, leading me around the bench.

I wrapped myself up again, and we resumed our walk. I fortunately didn't have another episode of dizziness since the breeze seemed to be blowing his aroma away. Good thing, too; I didn't need to constantly be drunk off it.

As we turned a corner, I realized we were near the entrance. I know I should leave, but I can't seem to bring myself to do it. This has been such an amazing night, and I don't want it to end. I looked over at David, about to tell him, when I noticed him staring at something in the shadows ahead of us.

"I think I should go," he commented, his eyes locked on it.

"Why? It's not that late."

"No, I really should go. And so should you," he suggested as he quickly glanced at me and then returned his attention to it, his jaw tightening.

"Well, okay…I guess I'll see you around."

He took his eyes off whatever mysterious thing was lurking and focused on me, taking my hand in his as he turned his back to it. "Until next I see you," he replied as he raised it to his lips and kissed it.

My heart pounded as my breath was taken away, and I fought the urge to collapse. I hope it'll be soon. "Till then," I replied instead, not wanting to sound overly anxious. He gently let go, and I turned to walk away, trying to remain calm and not look back immediately. After a moment, I glanced over my shoulder, looking for him, but he was gone.

The stroll to my car seemed so lonely and cold after spending time with David. Something in me felt different having met him. Hope? Happiness? Love?

As I unlocked the door, I glanced at my reflection and realized I still had his shirt. I have to remember to give it back when I see him again. I climbed in the car and shut the door, his scent instantly filling the interior and making my head swim. Removing the shirt, I tossed it on the seat next to me and quickly rolled down the windows. I shifted into first and took off, bearing the cold air. Soon the car and my head were clear.

It was about three in the morning when I pulled into the driveway. I quietly unlocked the front door and snuck up to my room. After changing into pajamas, I slipped into bed and listened for any signs that Dad heard me. The house was quiet. Good, I was in the clear. As I settled in and closed my eyes, my thoughts turned elsewhere and I could feel myself smiling because they were all about David.

# Chapter 3
## Details

The alarm went off, and I quickly jumped up to get ready for school. I had set my clock so I could sleep in a little later, but I was paying for it now. After a failed attempt at rushing through my shower, I dressed and gathered my things as swiftly as I could. Dashing down the stairs, I turned the corner and headed into the kitchen, expecting to see my father at the island, but was surprised to find I was alone.

I called for him, but never got an answer. It was not like him to leave for work before I went to school. Figuring he didn't want to see me this morning, I sighed and went to the fridge to grab some orange juice. That was when I noticed the note:

> Megan,
> Vanessa was really upset, so I offered to
> stay with her tonight. We'll have a family
> meeting tomorrow afternoon to discuss
> your behavior. If you need me, call my cell.
> Dad

Great, a 'family' meeting. I'm not off the hook. She better not come tonight.

This wasn't unusual for Dad. He's stayed at the witch's lair many times since the engagement, but Vanessa has never spent the night here. It was his promise to me she would not stay over while they were dating or move in until after they were married.

I didn't mind those nights he went to her place. Sometimes, I even looked forward to them. I was old enough to be alone and felt safe in our neighborhood. And I had peace and quiet without judgment.

Staring at the note, I gulped down the juice and then tossed the cup in the sink. There was no time to contemplate my fate this evening; I was running late. Grabbing my bag, I dashed out the door to my car.

Traffic was moving unbelievably slow, so I tried several shortcuts to hasten my trip. I pulled into the school parking lot with more minutes than I expected to spare and sprinted into the building and down the hall to my locker, only slowing when I saw faculty members.

"So how'd the fitting go?" Claire asked, anxiously standing by my locker.

My best friend. We met in kindergarten and hit it off right away. She knew me better than anyone and has always been there for me, through good and bad.

"Good morning to you, too," I replied, switching out my books.

"Sorry. Good morning, Megan. Nice weather we're hav-"

"It didn't go too well," I interrupted. "I called Vanessa a whore and she slapped me and then I ran away."

"She slapped you?" she questioned, her hazel eyes widening, and I nodded. "That's a little uncalled for. But she'll get away with it, probably feeding your dad this whole sob story about how horribly you treated her. I bet he wasn't too happy with you when you got home."

"I wouldn't know…it was earlier this morning when I snuck in. And he stayed the night with her."

"Went to the cemetery again?" she guessed. She thought I was a little crazy for hanging out there, but she understood why I did it.

"Yeah, but this visit was much better than any other…I met someone," I grinned, anticipating her reaction.

"What, a ghost?" she chuckled as we started down the hall.

"No, a guy. A college guy."

"That's a strange place to meet a guy. What was he doing there?" she inquired.

"Hanging out…like I go to do."

"Wow, you two are made for each other."

"Maybe," I smiled. "It was nice. We just walked around the cemetery and talked," I blushed, thinking about David.

"Sooo…what's he like?"

"Oh my gosh…so handsome and charming."

"I want to know all the details," she begged as we entered our first class.

"I'll tell you all about it at lunch," I whispered as morning announcements came on and we settled into our seats.

Almost immediately after they finished, the teacher began his lecture on cell structure, droning on and on about form and function. I watched and listened, but I just couldn't concentrate enough to take notes. It was going to be a long morning.

I couldn't stop thinking about David. I tried at times to focus on class, but I just kept replaying last night over in my mind – his appearance out of nowhere, him carrying me, the two of us strolling through the cemetery…

Then it started to bug me. What did he see that made him have to leave so abruptly? We were having a good time, and then he just cut it off. Was there something dangerous hiding in the shadows and he was protecting me? Or was it a classmate wanting to prank us? I'll have to ask the next time we meet.

I wonder when that'll be. Who's to say the next time I go, he'll be there. I should have setup a time…

"Megan, do you know the answer?" Mrs. Perry asked, looking at me oddly.

It was third period already! Where did the morning go? "I'm sorry…what was the question again?" I replied, sitting up and focusing.

"Maybe you should pay attention. Allison, the answer please," she requested from a more attentive student. I have never been this bad. I pushed the thoughts of David away and concentrated on the lecture.

As soon as the bell rang, I bolted to the lunchroom and grabbed a salad to avoid the long line at hot entree. Sitting at our usual table by the window, I stared outside while waiting for my friends to join me. A sudden spring storm had formed and as the rain fell steadily, it pelted the window occasionally with a gentle tapping. The raindrops then collected and streamed down the pane in mesmerizing patterns.

Claire dropped her tray and broke my concentration, letting me know she had arrived. "So?" she coaxed excitedly, shoving mashed potatoes in her mouth.

"Well, I was standing on the hill overlooking the river, deep in thought about the mistake my Dad is making, when I heard this voice. Its owner appeared out of the shadows and struck up a conversation with me. And as I said earlier, he was gorgeous."

"Who was gorgeous?" Erin asked, sitting next to Claire and giving her a disgusted look.

Erin was another close friend, totally crazy and always full of energy. She moved here from California right before high school, so she met me after my mom passed. The first few months after she arrived, everyone was her friend. She was fascinating and different, instantly popular. Then as the months passed, the fascination wore off and only her true friends remained

"This guy Megan met at the cemetery last night," Claire answered before taking another bite.

"Nice," Erin grinned. "Continue."

"So what did he look like? Details!" Claire begged as she continued to chow down.

"He who?" Ben inquired, a hint of jealousy in his voice.

Oh, Ben. We've known each other since grade school, and that was also about as long as he's had a crush on me. We went on a date once, but it just felt weird to me and I knew it wasn't right for us. He, on the other hand, won't give up.

"This guy Megan met last night in the cemetery," Claire repeated, frustrated.

"That's not a good place to meet someone. Did he try anything? Maybe you shouldn't go alone anymore. Maybe I should go with you from now on," he suggested.

He was protective of me as well. He once got in a fight with a guy I went on a date with because he was spreading nasty things about me around school.

"No and I don't need you to protect me. He was a complete gentleman and I didn't feel threatened by him at all," I answered.

"Sooo...details!" Claire anxiously reminded me.

"Okay, okay," I responded, smiling at her eagerness. "He's unique, not like a Ken doll model-type at all, and had the most amazing green eyes and a stunning smile. His name is David, he's a pre-med student in his first year at VCU, and lives off campus with a bunch of friends."

"Ooo, pre-med. Nice," Claire remarked. "Maybe I could meet one of his friends."

Ben snorted. "Studying to be a doctor, huh? You won't see much of him."

"Anyway," I continued, ignoring his ridiculous comment and Claire's boy-craziness, "we walked around the cemetery and just talked. He was easy to chat with and I just felt comfortable with him."

"In a cemetery...at night," Ben insinuated.

"Yeah," I replied, nodding my head and smiling slightly.

"Did you get a tingling sensation being around him?" Claire asked, on the edge of her seat. "In the movies, it's a sign of true love if you do."

I looked out the window and thought back to last night. "When he took my hand, I felt something and every time he smiled at me, I had a strange reaction. His cologne had an effect on me, too. I ended up borrowing his shirt and got lightheaded from being surrounded by his scent. Not that it smelled bad, it was...intoxicating."

"He lent you his shirt?" Erin questioned.

"He had two. It was cool out, and I was in my bridesmaid dress – don't ask," I replied, not wanting to go into the less pleasant part of my evening.

"Anything else?" Claire inquired, leaning close.

"Well...an odd thing happened when we came close to the front of the cemetery. Something in the shadows caught his eye, and he said he had to leave, telling me to go as well."

"Jealous girlfriend maybe?" Erin piped up.

"No, it was weird how he acted. He was angry at whatever it was, but protective of me."

"Probably just putting on a show. You can't trust him," Ben warned and Erin slapped his arm.

"Maybe it was a serial killer who'd been stalking you, and David noticed him as he tried to readjust his plans since your usual pattern changed," Claire suggested.

"You need to lay off those detective shows," I responded, grinning.

"So when are you going to see him again?" Ben asked, probably wishing it was never.

"I don't know, but I hope it's soon."

I played with my salad, not really feeling like eating, but I forced a forkful in my mouth when I remembered I didn't eat last night. I looked outside again and started to daydream about David. His smooth voice, his stunning smile, his alluring eyes…

"You're in love," Claire revealed with a grin.

"Sounds like it to me," Erin agreed.

"There's no way. We just met. I-I don't even know this guy."

"That's right. You should just forget him," Ben suggested. Claire and Erin shot him a dirty look.

"Doesn't matter. Why do you think your heart was acting so funny? Did you get his number?" Claire asked.

"No. Like I said, he was in a hurry for both of us to leave." Ben looked relieved. "Now I wish I had or given him mine."

"That would've been smart," Claire commented under her breath as Erin nodded.

I dropped my chin in my hand and frowned, feeling stupid for not asking. That's all right, I'll just try to meet him again. When can I go back to the cemetery? Maybe Friday?

One more day, that's all I have to wait. But what if he doesn't come then? Will I have to go every evening, hoping he'll be there? What if he never comes back? I may have missed my only opportunity at true love. Really…what else could it be drawing me to him?

The bell sounded and interrupted my thoughts. "Guess we better go," Claire stated, placing her hand on my shoulder.

"Yep," I agreed quietly as I continued to mull over what I could do to see David again.

"Ugh, I shouldn't have eaten so much," Erin announced, grabbing her stomach as we exited the lunchroom.

In the hall, Ben caught my arm and pulled me aside. "Just be careful. You don't know this guy. He's older and might take advantage of you," he cautioned.

"I know, but I'm a big girl. I can take care of myself. Thank you for your concern though. See you in English," I replied before taking off down the hall toward the gym, my thoughts turning from him and David to what lies ahead in class. Hopefully, Erin would refrain from vomiting on the lacquered floors.

P.E. was fun. We were learning to play basketball and Erin made it through without throwing up once. With all her bouncing around, I was surprised she didn't. She must have a stronger stomach than I thought.

Watching her and waiting for the inevitable thankfully kept me distracted enough to not think too much about David. And the same was true for the rest of the day. My mind stayed focused on school and nothing else. After the last bell, Ben offered to walk with me, but I declined, saying I needed to stop by my locker. He hung his head and ambled slowly toward the parking lot.

I made it to the end of the day, free of thoughts of David. But now that it was safe to think about him, my mind bombarded me with questions and suggestions. All the way to my car, I tried to decide how I could meet him again. But I was interrupted as I looked up and found Claire, Erin, and Ben huddled under a single umbrella in the rain. So much for that.

"What's up?" I asked as I unlocked my door and sat.

"Are you going to be okay this afternoon? If you need to talk, I'm available," Claire offered as they crowded in my doorway.

It took a moment to realize what she was talking about since my mind had been elsewhere. "Yeah, I'll be fine. Just a tongue-lashing, and I might get grounded." I responded, remembering the family meeting tonight.

"We're here for you," Erin interjected. "Claire filled us in on what happened," she quickly explained.

Great, Claire and her big mouth. "I'll be fine, guys. It'll blow over, like it always does." I put my feet in the car and started it. "I have to get going. I don't want Dad any angrier at me."

"Good luck," was all Ben said as the others smiled and waved.

I waved back and watched them disappear in my rear-view mirror as I pulled away. They're great friends, and I'll probably take Claire up on her offer, knowing I'll need to vent later.

As I drove farther away, my mind shifted to last night at the bridal boutique and what to tell Dad as my side of the story. Vanessa was being rude and saying offensive things to me. I was provoked and had enough of it. He can't fault me for that. But he will because she's the adult and I have a history of having issues with her.

He'll probably do the same thing he always does – lecture me and then pass sentence. And I'll do what I always do – sit there and take it, apologize (but not mean it), and then head to my room. He'll probably ground me for the rest of the night or week, maybe even a month. It's a good thing I have exams to study for and projects to do.

As I came to the main road, I considered my options. I could go home, get the yelling over with, and spend the remainder of the night in my room, or I could find more time to think over what I need to say in my defense. Maybe there's a chance I could convince him she's at fault and not me.

Deciding that working on my defense was the best option, I detoured to the cemetery to visit Mom for a moment, hoping for strength and advice. I drove through the gates and around to the crypt. With the rain still coming down, I waited a moment and then rushed up to the door to avoid getting too wet.

As I grabbed the handle, I noticed a piece of paper wedged between it and the frame. My name was written in burgundy on the outside in an unfamiliar script. I looked around to see if the person who left it was nearby, but the cemetery was empty. Entering the crypt, I sat in the corner by my mom and opened the note. My heart fluttered as I read the message:

*Megan,*

*I hope your day was pleasant. I would enjoy*

*your company at the cemetery this Friday.*

*Please meet me here at 11:00 pm.*

*Sincerely,*

*David*

A surge of excitement rushed through me. I'll get to see him tomorrow! Nothing else mattered at this moment, not even the impending doom awaiting me at home. I leaned back and gazed dreamily at the darkening sky outside as my heart continued to do tumbles in my chest.

A quiet rumble of thunder in the distance shook me from my daze. I glanced around the sky, searching for the source. It looked like another storm was about to hit, coming in from the south. I settled back against the marble and watched as the dark clouds overtook the sky.

I knew I was safe and figured I'd wait it out. Thunder grumbled overhead as the rain came down, pattering against the stained glass windows on the sides of the crypt. The sound was surprisingly soothing.

Looking down at my hands, I realized I still held the note in them. I read over it several times, tracing the words with my fingers. David had such elegant handwriting, so fluid and artistic. Is there nothing unattractive about this guy?

Soon the storm began to subside and with it, the rain. I should leave before I made Dad more furious than he probably already was with me. I tucked the note in my pocket and left the crypt, dashing to my car as rain drizzled from above.

I hopped inside and slowly pulled around the circle. The river was raging from all the precipitation, roaring as I crept past the spot where David and I sat under the oak tree the night before. Speeding up, I wound through the cemetery and headed home, ready to face my father's wrath.

He was standing at the front door waiting for me as I pulled in the driveway next to Vanessa's car. Great, the witch was here, too. I rolled my eyes as I stepped out, taking my time walking up to the house and through the door with him following behind. I knew I'd at least be able to get a few feet inside before he started yelling. He wouldn't make a scene in front of the neighbors.

He continued following me into the family room and motioned for me to sit. Vanessa was on the couch, her back to me as I entered. I sat on the other end diagonally across from her and crossed my legs, waiting for the first shot to begin the war.

"Where have you been?" Dad asked, his arms crossed tightly across his puffed-up chest.

I didn't expect it to start this way, but okay. "At the cemetery."

"You went last night and stayed till God knows when. Why would you need to go again?"

"I'm having a hard time right now and needed to visit her. Why can't you understand that?" I responded, getting louder.

"There's no need to raise your voice. I know the past four years have been difficult, but we all need to move on. Your mother would have wanted it that way."

I couldn't believe what I was hearing – Dad was already letting go of Mom! She was always supposed to be with us and he wanted to move on after just four years? I could feel the anger boiling inside me. "No, she wouldn't have," I argued through clenched teeth.

"Megan, I loved your mother, but she's gone. There's nothing that can bring her back. She would want me to be happy and move on."

"But not that soon! How could you…and with someone half your age?" I rebutted, pointing at Vanessa. She looked uncomfortable. Good, maybe this would finally scare her off.

"You don't need to go there. You fall in love with whomever you fall in love with."

"Oh I hope you feel that way when I do," I threw in his face.

"You're a different story. You're still a minor and live in my house, so you have to obey my rules."

"I can't wait to get out of here!" I yelled as I shot up and headed out of the room.

"We're not done yet!" Dad shouted as he turned to follow me, but Vanessa stopped him.

"Just let her go. She'll come to her senses," I heard her say to him as I climbed the stairs.

No, I won't.

I was so angry tears were streaming down my face. I hate it here. I hate my dad and I hate Vanessa. I slammed the door to my room and curled up on my bed. It started raining again, and I could hear the drumming against the roof. Lying in the dark, I concentrated on its calming, repetitive sound. Soon my breathing began to slow, and my tears stopped.

Downstairs, Dad and Vanessa were talking. The argument went in a totally different direction than either of us expected, and he was realizing it. I grabbed my iPod off the bedside table and listened to my rainy day mix to drown them out. The melancholy melodies permeated my ears and wrapped me in a cocoon of calm.

I closed my eyes and listened closely to the words of the song playing, reminding me of David. Soon images of him began to fill my head. His amazing green eyes gazing into mine, his soft lips whispering my name, his warm hand caressing my skin…

"Megan…wake up. I want to talk to you. Megan?"

My eyes fluttered open, and I was surprised by who I found. "Vanessa?" I questioned with a strained voice. She was sitting on the edge of the bed next to me. It was dark outside and still raining. I rubbed my eyes and sat up on my elbows, not really in the mood to deal with her. "What do you want?" I asked sharply, my voice stronger.

"Just to talk…peacefully," she replied quietly, raising her hands in surrender.

I sighed. "Okay, shoot."

"First, I want to apologize for my actions last night. It was very…juvenile of me. I've been so stressed out by this wedding and making sure the planner is doing everything I ask. It's so hard…doing it all alone. Your father has tried his best to be helpful, but work keeps him so busy…and it's not really his thing."

She leaned over, holding her head in her hands. I sat up further and watched her movements, wondering if she was putting on a front, but she seemed sincerely stressed out. So maybe I did feel bad for her and could make it a little easier.

I placed my hand on her shoulder and apologized as well. "I'm sorry for what I said. I appreciate your help, but I need to figure things out on my own. And I really do like the dress the way it is. It'll lose its beauty and mystery if it's shorter."

She blew out a breath and slowly lifted her head. "Okay, I can deal with that. The longer gown is more elegant and appropriate."

I stared at her a moment and sighed. I was probably going to regret this, but I offered. "If there's anything I can do to help with the wedding, please let me know."

She paused and looked at me, her expression changing completely. "Since you asked…there is something you can do. Can you address invitations for us? I just don't have time, and the people that were supposed to help bailed on me."

"Okay, when do they need to go out?"

"Ideally this weekend. We only have a couple months before the wedding. Can you believe it?" she asked, back to her bubbly self.

"No, I can't," I responded honestly. "I'm going to plan for Sunday so they can go out in Monday's mail."

"Great. I'll let Jack know we're cool," she replied, popping up and cheerfully leaving the room.

That quick change in demeanor made me think this was my punishment – addressing her envelopes. Well, better than more yelling and being grounded. I wonder how many I should expect. Three hundred? Four? I guess I'll find out.

I climbed out of bed and went to the bathroom to freshen up before heading downstairs to see Dad. Leaving the room and pausing at the top of the stairs, I heard Vanessa talking with him in the foyer. She didn't say anything too revealing, telling him she had some errands to run before going home. The front door shut and she was gone. I made my way down the steps, meeting Dad at the bottom.

"What's for dinner?" I asked, trying to act as if our episode earlier never happened.

"How about spaghetti?" he inquired, doing the same as we entered the kitchen.

"Mmm, my favorite. I'll throw a salad together. You are going to make your homemade marinara, right?" I questioned as I took a bowl from the cabinet and started pulling vegetables out of the refrigerator.

"Of course. You know I don't buy that canned junk."

I shredded the lettuce and cut up carrots, peppers, and cucumbers, throwing them together in the bowl and rinsing them. After draining it, I announced, "Salad's done."

He was still working on the sauce while the pasta boiled. "Can you make the garlic bread?" he asked.

"No problem," I replied as I grabbed a baking sheet from under the stove. It started to feel more like it used to – before Vanessa and even before Mom's death.

I laid out the bread, made the garlic-butter spread, and smeared it on each slice. After popping it in the oven, I went ahead and set the table without his asking. By the time I finished, the bread was done. I put it in a cloth-lined basket and placed it in the center of the table. We made our plates, sat, and began eating. It was nice to have a hot meal, having nothing last night and a measly salad for lunch.

"I'm glad you and Vanessa worked it out," Dad commented between bites.

"She seems to be having a rough time getting everything ready. I also offered to help, and she said I could address invitations."

"That was kind of you."

"I try. So, how many are we looking at…two hundred? Three?"

"Try six hundred and six…"

I nearly choked. "Wh-what?"

"She comes from a large family and has a lot of friends, but not all of them are coming."

"Dad, that's a lot of invitations to address!"

"Well, it's not like you're writing all of them by hand – just peel and stick."

"Oh my God…that'll take hours!" I exclaimed, dropping my fork.

"You're overreacting. You know, you could have received a worse punishment."

"You were in on it?" I asked, shocked.

"Not really. It was all her idea; I just agreed to it."

"Don't you see how devious she is? She came up to my room and acted like she was so distraught and overwhelmed that I felt bad for her! God, I actually felt sorry for her!"

"She really is overwhelmed. Megan, just try to like her and get along. She's going to be a part of your life."

"I don't know if I want to live if it's going to be like this constantly," I snapped back as I threw down my napkin and stormed up to my room.

# Chapter 4
## Anticipation

I woke the following morning and stared at my ceiling, recalling the previous night's argument. I know I have to accept it, but I just want him to understand what I'm going through. He'll probably want to talk about it this morning since there was no resolution last night, but I don't. I just want to forget it happened.

Turning over, I spied the folded note on my dresser and smiled. The issue with my father disappeared from my mind as the excitement of what lay ahead made my heart flutter. Tonight's the night – I'll get to see David again.

Giddy all through my shower and as I dressed, I wondered how I was going to make it until eleven tonight. I've been patiently waiting for this evening to come and had a hard time containing my eagerness as it was. But I can't show it in front of my dad; he might get suspicious. So descending the stairs, I tried to distract myself with something mundane like solving math problems in my head.

He was at the counter in the kitchen, pouring a cup of coffee. "What are you so chipper about this morning?" he asked between sips as I grabbed a banana.

Guess I didn't do too well hiding it. "Oh, just glad it's Friday," I replied as I quickly headed for the door. I wasn't in the mood to linger or talk to him, especially if he was going to bring up last night's fight.

"Wait Megan," he called, catching me before I could slip out. I sighed and returned to the kitchen, standing at the island and shifting to one leg as he glanced at the newspaper. "I was thinking about it last night, and you're right. That many invitations are too much for one person. Your friends are welcome to help, if you'd like to invite them," he offered.

I was stunned for a moment. "O-okay. Thanks," I replied.

He looked at me and smiled. "You're welcome. Have a good day at school."

"Okay. See you later," I responded, leaving quickly before he could change his mind.

I arrived at school earlier than usual and decided to sit outside and enjoy the sunny morning. My book bag behind my head, I stared into the near cloudless blue sky. After a moment of watching the few float by, I closed my eyes and focused on the sounds around me.

Rumbling buses pulled up to the curb and let tired teenagers off. Voices of fellow students echoed off the building as they entered the school. Roaring cars drove by, blaring music or revving engines. I listened harder, past all the man-made noise, and found the wind rustling the new leaves on the trees as the birds sang in different tones and scales. I focused on that sound rather than the chaos of humanity.

"Megan? What are you doing?"

I shaded my eyes so I could see who was talking to me. "Oh, hi Ben. I'm just relaxing. It's such a pleasant morning, I figured I'd enjoy it while I could."

He kneeled beside me and stared as I smiled politely. "You look nice today…happier," he commented finally.

"Thank you. I'm just glad it's Friday," I responded, remaining vague. I didn't want to reveal what I was really happy about, especially to him. I didn't need a lecture this early in the morning.

But he wasn't going to accept just that. "What's so special about this Friday?" he inquired, sitting down.

"It's been a rough week and I'm glad it's over," I lied.

"Yeah, with all the schoolwork we've been getting and then your problems with Vanessa, I can understand."

I turned my face to the sky and closed my eyes again. "I'm not going to let her bother me any longer. I have a little over a year left, and then I'm outta here," I replied with a smirk.

"Well anyway, it's getting close to time for the bell. You better get moving," he informed me as he stood.

"Okay, thanks. See you at lunch," I responded, waving him on.

I stayed on the lawn a couple minutes longer and then gathered my things, brushed myself off, and headed inside. Claire was at my locker waiting impatiently for me. She pretended to look at the imaginary watch on her wrist and then at me.

"I know, I know," I stated, quickly switching out my books.

"Where have you been? I've been waiting, like, ten minutes!"

"I was out on the front lawn reveling in the glorious morning the gods have bestowed upon us. I can't believe you didn't see me."

"My mind's a little preoccupied."

"Why? What's going on?" I asked as we headed to class.

"Well, I heard a rumor that Justin Collins is interested in me and wants to ask me out."

"That's great! You've been crushing on him for a long time," I commented as we lingered outside the room for a moment.

"But it's a rumor. Should I really believe it?"

"You know what they say, there's always some truth in rumors."

"So, do I wait for him to ask me out or do I make the first move?"

"Maybe you could strike up a conversation with him, you know, talk about something generic, like movies. Hopefully, that'll lead to him asking you to see one."

"That's a great idea! See, this is why you're my best friend," she exclaimed, giving me a hug. I just hope it works; it's not like I'm an expert on boys.

"We better get inside before we're counted tardy," I stated as I backed away and straightened my clothes.

We quickly slipped into our seats just before the bell. I prepared myself for class and for the school day ahead of me. My mind had other plans, though, as thoughts of David crept into it. I had no time for this. Suppressing them, I looked around the room to distract myself.

The teacher's back was turned as he drew a plant cell on the whiteboard while morning announcements blared over the loudspeaker. Josh was doodling to my left and in the back corner, Karen was reading a romance novel. I glanced behind me and found Claire scrolling through her cell phone, most likely looking up what movies were showing. I faced forward and smiled, glad I could help with her love life.

Feeling comfortable with the thoughts of David safe in the back of my mind as class began, I focused on the lecture and took thorough notes. I was an excellent student and needed to keep my reputation as one. Mom always stressed the importance of education, and I wasn't going to let her down.

The bell rang, and it was on to the next class. I smiled at Claire as we started toward the door, hoping to encourage her. She smiled back, still looking a little unsure. Justin was in third period with her, and I wouldn't see her until lunch, so I had to boost her confidence while I had the chance.

"You'll do fine," I told her as we walked down the hall. She hesitated and then nodded before parting to go to her next class.

I had a hard time concentrating in my classes before lunch because of Claire and her predicament and not David this time. What if my advice was poor? What if she embarrasses herself?

I was so preoccupied with worry that I nearly missed the bell for lunch. I swiftly grabbed my things and headed to the cafeteria, wanting to make sure I was there before her. I chose to get a salad again and sat at our table, bouncing my leg nervously. She entered, and I watched her expression as she went through the line. She didn't look happy, but she didn't look mortified either.

As she walked toward the table, though, it looked like she was hiding something. "Sooo, did it work?" I asked anxiously.

A wide grin broke across her face, and she squealed, "We're going to the movies tomorrow night!"

"That's awesome! I'm so happy for you," I responded sincerely.

"What are you two so happy about?" Erin asked, joining us.

"Oh, Claire has a date with Justin on Saturday," I answered.

"You've swooned over him enough," she responded, nudging her.

"I know. I'm so excited, but nervous. Hey Megan, maybe if you ever see David again, you could ask him out and we could double date," Claire mentioned, probably trying to get her mind off her nervousness.

Oh my God! I was so consumed in her issue this morning, I forgot to tell her about the note. "I'm seeing him tonight," I responded, my heart feeling as though it would burst out of my chest from the pent-up excitement.

Everyone looked at me with wide eyes, Claire's the widest. "Why didn't you tell me?" she exclaimed.

"I was going to, but you got me off track when you told me about Justin."

"Is that why you were so happy this morning?" Ben asked venomously, dropping his tray on the table. "You're meeting him again?"

"Of course. Why wouldn't she?" Erin snapped.

"Sheesh, calm down. I'm just kidding," he snapped back. But we knew he wasn't.

"So how did he do it?" Claire inquired.

"He left a note in the door of the family crypt. I found it yesterday when I went to see my mom."

"How romantic!" she exclaimed, resting her head in her hands.

"How creepy," Ben muttered under his breath as he stabbed his food. She and Erin glared at him, and he put his hands up in surrender.

"Okay, enough about my situation…Claire, tell us what happened," I coaxed.

She gave a play by play of the whole conversation and by the sound of it, Justin needed that push to get him to ask. Of course, she needed the push as well. Then she blabbed on about what she planned to wear Saturday on her date as Erin gave her pointers.

I played with my salad, pretending to listen, but instead I thought about David and our 'date' tonight. What should I wear? What are we going to do?

"So how did things go yesterday evening?" Ben asked, bored of listening to them discuss girly things.

"I survived. Dad and I had a yelling match and I stormed off. Vanessa came up a little while later and conned me into addressing her wedding invitations," I replied, anger pushing my excitement away.

"That sucks. Anything I can do to help?"

I lit up. "Yeah, there is. Hey Claire, Erin," I interrupted, "I have to address six hundred and six invitations Sunday and was wondering if you would like to help. Say about noon? I'll supply lunch," I offered as an incentive

"I will," Ben answered immediately, smiling.

"I'm happy to help, but it won't be until later," Erin responded. Ben's grin widened.

"Unfortunately, I can't," Claire declined. "I have a family thing I have to go to."

Ben's grin widened even more. Great. He's going to be alone with me until Erin shows up. "It won't be the same without you," I told her, hoping to guilt her into working something out.

"Another time?" she requested.

"No problem," I replied sadly as the bell rang. We exited the lunchroom and dispersed to our next class. Hopefully, the afternoon would go as fast as the morning had.

And it did. Before I realized it, I was in English taking a test. I plowed through it and was the first finished. On my way back from handing it in, I noticed Ben look up from his and smile at me. I smiled back, being courteous, and took my seat. I really hope Erin won't be too long on Sunday.

Now that I had time to think, I considered my date tonight as I stared out the window. What should I wear? I can't top my previous ensemble and I don't want to look desperate. My favorite dark blue V-neck shirt and tan cords would be good. Flattering, but not too fancy. And I'll wear my hair down again.

I guess we'll walk the paths like last time. Maybe I could impress him with my knowledge of the cemetery's residents. Hopefully, I'll learn more about him and he about me, though he already knows a lot. He's not much of a talker. Maybe after tonight, he'll ask me out on a real date, to a restaurant or the movies.

I need to get home quickly and take a nap so I'll be refreshed when I meet him tonight. Then it struck me – what was I going to tell my dad? I know he'll be watching me like a hawk over the next couple of days because of my behavior. He'll notice if I left that late or will bust me if I try to sneak out. I need to come up with an excuse; I wasn't ready for him to know I was hanging out with a college boy.

The final bell rang, breaking my train of thought. I grabbed my bag and headed to my locker first, Ben walking with me but not talking. As I loaded my books into it, I tried to figure out a solution to my dilemma for tonight.

He was at his locker, a few down from mine, glancing at me every once in a while as he changed out his books. I shifted my eyes in his direction, considering using him as a scapegoat. No, he'll definitely tattle on me. Who else can I use? Claire. Maybe she can cover for me. Feeling I had my solution, I shut my locker and headed out with Ben right behind me.

The afternoon sun shone brightly through the doors as I pushed them open and stepped outside. As I strolled toward my car, I spotted Claire talking with Justin and waved to them. It was better I ask now rather than call her later. Switching direction, I headed toward her. Ben gave up tailing me and started walking home, not wanting to hear anymore about either of our dates.

Justin was still with her, and Erin was just joining them as well. "Hey Justin, Erin," I greeted and then turned to Claire. "I have a big favor to ask," I inquired as I pulled her aside. "Your parents are going out of town tonight, right?"

"Yeeaah…"

"Is it all right if I tell my dad I'm spending the night at your house?"

"Sure. Is this because of your date with David?"

"Yep. Dad would never let me go if he knew the truth. If he calls, will you cover for me?"

"No problem," she replied. "What time are you meeting him anyway?"

"Eleven…"

"Eleven? Why so late?" she questioned loudly, and both Justin and Erin glanced our way.

"Maybe he has an evening class or work and he's meeting me afterward…I don't know."

"Huh…so what are you going to do until you go to meet him. You can't stay at your house until ten-thirty and then suddenly tell your dad you're going to a sleepover at mine."

She's right. What am I going to do? "Well…I could hang out with you since you can't come Sunday."

"Great idea! You can help with the monster," she smiled. That was what she called her little brother. He was nine and a total pain in the neck.

"I really appreciate this. I'll be over around seven o'clock. I'm going home to take a nap in preparation for a long evening."

"I'll have the pizza ordered and movies waiting."

"Sounds good. Thanks again!" I yelled as I jogged to my car, waving goodbye to Erin and Justin.

This is great! I'll get to have some girl time with my best friend and see David later. Hopefully, I won't have any problems with my dad going along with it. I haven't been a perfect angel lately, but he never grounded me. Besides, how can he deny me helping a friend in need?

I started the car and pulled out of the lot, hurrying to get home. Dad gets off work at five and with delays and traffic, won't be home until close to six. That'll give me a little less than three hours of sleep. Better than none, I suppose.

I pulled in the drive and quickly ran into the house, bounding up the stairs to my room. Closing all the curtains, I tried to mute the light as best I could with my sheers. I set my alarm for five-thirty and crawled into bed, closing my eyes and trying to wind down. It was hard falling asleep with the birds singing and children playing outside and my mind working in overdrive. I covered my head with a pillow and after several minutes of dull droning, I finally drifted away.

*My alarm went off and I got out of bed, heading downstairs to talk to dad. He was sitting in his favorite chair watching the news. Something about an animal attack murmured in the background as I approached him and asked if I could go to Claire's for the night. He scowled, saying I wasn't allowed because I was grounded.*

*Furious, I ran up to my room and slammed the door. He never told me I was grounded! Well, it didn't matter. I was going to see David regardless.*

*As soon as Dad was asleep, I locked my door and slipped out the French doors onto the balcony and down the tree overhanging it. Reaching the grass, I crept around to the front of the house, getting in my car and taking off for the cemetery. I arrived in no time and walked right through the front gates.*

*I ran to the crypt, but David wasn't there. Calling for him, I glanced around, but he never showed. I even walked the whole cemetery, but he was nowhere.*

*He stood me up.*

*Feeling heartbroken and dejected, I headed back to the entrance. I paused at the spot where he left me the other night and sighed. Out of the corner of my eye, I saw two red eyes peering at me from the shadows. I turned to face them but couldn't make anything out. There was a low growl and then suddenly it lunged at my throat...*

I gasped as I woke from the dream, and it took a moment to gather my bearings. I was still in bed, disheveled and clammy. There was no movement downstairs. Dad wasn't home yet. I glanced at the clock – five-twenty.

I turned off the alarm and staggered out of bed to the bathroom to tidy up before he did get home. Once I was presentable, I went back into my room and packed a small bag with things I'd need tonight – change of clothes, toiletries, makeup. I figured I'd shower and change there. I didn't want to smell like pizza when I met David.

Just as I was finishing up, I heard a car pull into the driveway. I dropped my bag by the door and ran down the stairs. Dashing into the family room, I turned on the TV and plopped myself on the couch. Regulating my breathing, I tried to look as if I had been sitting there for a while.

Dad entered and I glanced over the back of the couch. "Hey, Dad. How was work?"

He hung his jacket over the railing, and I turned back to the TV in time to see some political show with a lot of yelling. I quickly flipped the channel to something more age appropriate.

"Not good. I'm so glad it's Friday...are you watching politics?" he asked as he made his way to the family room. He stood behind me loosening his tie.

"Nah, that stuff is boring. I've been watching this music station," I replied, pointing at the screen. I really didn't like it – too many shows and not enough music videos.

"Oh. So what are your plans for tonight?" he questioned as he sat partially on the back of the couch.

I changed the channel to something I could stomach a little better and replied, "Well, Claire's parents are out of town tonight, and she was really hoping I could spend the night with her. She doesn't want to be alone with Max," I responded, looking up at him with suppliant eyes. I hope he's buying it.

"I really shouldn't let you go…but I guess watching her little brother is another good punishment," he settled with an evil smile as he stood and went to his chair in the corner.

"Great! She wants me over there at seven. Maybe you and Vanessa can have a quiet evening together," I suggested.

"Not a bad idea. She probably needs one. A break from wedding preparations and work will be good for her."

I grinned in spite of myself. He was buying it, thankfully. I turned my attention back to the TV for a moment and then out of curiosity ask-- "How do you feel about the possibility of me d-ti- ---

"Depends, are you?"

"Noooo," I drew out so I didn't feel like I was lying.

He looked at me and sighed. "As long as he's a good kid and won't get you in trouble, I'm fine with it."

"You know I'm not into the bad boy type," I responded with a grin. "I'm a romantic."

"I don't know if that's any better," he mumbled, shaking his head.

We sat in silence for several minutes, cartoons playing in the background. Well, at least I knew where he stood on that subject. I decided not to talk anymore about it; I didn't want him getting suspicious. Tired of the loud animated characters chaotically running around on the screen, I turned the channel to the news to make him happy.

"You could always talk to Vanessa about it," he suggested.

I stared back, a little shocked, but then softened my expression. I wasn't going to start a fight, not while I had him in agreement with me going over to Claire's. "I could…" I replied hesitantly. I didn't know if I wanted to go down that road with her, though it would make him happy. He was just so completely oblivious to what she really was.

I looked at the clock and saw it was only six. Ugh, time was dragging. "Oh, I'm having dinner at Claire's, too, so you're on your own tonight," I remarked, changing the subject before he could make arrangements for a girl talk with the witch.

"Hmm, maybe I'll make a meal worthy of a four-star restaurant for Vanessa…show off my culinary skills."

"You *are* quite the chef," I replied as I shook my head.

I returned to the TV and was just about to get up to grab a drink when a story caught my eye. It was a special report on several unsolved murders that had occurred around the city in the past few months. Generally, that wouldn't really catch my attention, but these were different. All of the bodies were found the same way in each case – in a park, decapitated and drained of blood.

"Sounds like a serial killer," Dad commented, and I realized he was watching, too. "Promise you'll be careful?"

"I'll just be at Claire's," I responded. But seeing his concern, I added, "I will, Dad."

"You should probably get ready to go. I'm going to call Vanessa and invite her over for dinner and a movie."

"That'll make her day," I remarked as I got up. I'll try to make this work with her, for his sake. No one likes arguing. I gave him a kiss on the cheek and headed upstairs to get my bag.

Setting it at the base of the stairs, I met Dad in the kitchen. He was looking through the refrigerator to see what he could whip up for dinner. He started pulling items out and setting them on the counter.

"Looks like it's going to be good. It's a shame I'll miss it," I commented, leaning on it.

"Don't worry, I'll save some."

"Thanks," I responded with a smile. "All right, I'm headed out. I have my cell on me, but you can always call Claire's house. Have fun tonight, but don't make too much of a mess," I teased.

Shaking his head, he waved a hand indicating for me to leave. I straightened up and headed toward the door, grabbing my bag on the way out. I felt so guilty for lying, but I'll get over it. I'm seeing David tonight.

I backed out of the driveway, watching for children still lingering in the street, and drove several blocks over to Claire's house. Just as I was about to knock on the door, she opened it and signaled for me to enter while she continued talking on the phone.

As I stepped inside, I surveyed the main level and was surprised by the changes. It's been a long time since I've been to her house. It looked more professionally decorated and less like a childproofing display. Still taking it all in, I strolled into the family room and made myself comfortable on the couch, waiting for her to finish her phone conversation.

Suddenly, Max came running into the room screaming. I jumped, concerned he was hurt, but realized he was just doing it to annoy his sister. She smacked him on the back of the head and he kicked her in the shin. Knowing he was going to get it for that, he bolted and she took off after him, phone still glued to her ear. It was comical watching brothers and sisters fight, but it also made me happy I was an only child.

Hearing part of Claire's conversation in passing, I realized she was talking to Justin. I hope this wasn't what I was in for this evening. Bored, I grabbed the remote and flipped through the channels, but really had no interest in watching TV.

I stood up and went over to the bookshelf in the corner to see if there was anything good to read, but mostly found children's books and do-it-yourself manuals. Claire's family wasn't into the classics like mine. I glanced over my shoulder at her, rolling my eyes. She turned her back to me and after a minute, hung up the phone.

"Okay, so what should we do first?" she asked.

"I thought we could start with some prank calls, followed by TP-ing the neighbor's house, and finish off the evening hanging your brother out one the second floor windows," I answered sarcastically.

"Hmm, I like the last one, but I don't think any of those are possible. How about a movie?" she suggested, heading toward the TV. "Do we want to start with a comedy or horror?" she inquired, holding up two cases.

I scrunched up my face in thought. "Let's go with the horror movie. I always like a good scare."

"Are you sure that's a good idea since you're going to a cemetery?" she asked as she inserted it into the player.

"I go to the cemetery all the time. I don't think a movie's going to make a difference."

"The guy at the movie store highly recommended it – lots of blood and gore. Hope you have a strong stomach."

"Bring it on!" I dared with a smile.

The doorbell rang and Claire hopped up to get it. "Pizza's here!" she announced as she came back with three boxes.

"Do you really think we're going to eat that much?"

"I'll probably graze all night. I am sooo nervous about my date tomorrow," she responded, taking a couple slices from the first box. "Hey monster! Come and get your pizza!" she yelled up the stairs. He quickly ran down, grabbed his plate, and then disappeared back upstairs.

I took two slices and settled into my seat. "So what's Max going to do while we watch the movie?"

"I rented a couple video games for him. He'll be occupied for hours."

She grabbed several slices and sat on the couch next to me. Pressing play, we eagerly waited for it to begin. Within the first few minutes, someone jumped out and we both screamed and then laughed at each other for a moment before continuing to watch.

The movie wasn't even half over and the body count was up to thirteen. The guy from the movie store was right, lots of blood and gore.

Nasty, gooey, grisly blood and gore. I looked down at my remaining slice and decided I couldn't eat anymore. Usually horror movies didn't bother me, but this one did. Or maybe it had something to do with the serial murders on the news.

"That had to be the grossest movie I have ever seen," I commented, taking my plate to the kitchen and disposing of it as the credits rolled.

Claire was still picking at hers. "Yeah…it was pretty bad."

I returned and dropped to the couch. "So what now?" I asked.

"We could watch the other movie," she suggested.

"Great idea. I think I need to clear my mind of all that carnage."

She switched them out and started it. From the moment it began, we were cracking up and before we knew it, it was over. "I feel much better now," I commented, and she agreed as I glanced at the clock. Realizing the time, I hopped up suddenly. "Oh, I better get ready! I don't want to be late," I announced as I dashed around the couch.

I ran up to the bathroom and took a quick shower. After dressing and finalizing my look, I returned to the family room and presented myself to Claire. She smiled and gave a thumbs-up.

"Have fun. Oh, and please wake me when you get back," she requested, handing her house key to me. "I want to know how it went."

"Definitely. See you later," I responded before closing the door behind me. For her sake, I hoped Max would stay engrossed in his games.

My phone rang as I reached for the car door. "Hey Dad. How was dinner?" I inquired, leaning against it. Why is he calling? He usually never checks up on me.

"It was delicious and Vanessa was impressed. There are lots of leftovers, so you'll get to enjoy it tomorrow. How's your evening going?"

"Good. Claire and I just finished watching a couple movies and now we're getting ready to do make-overs," I lied.

"Is Max the unlucky participant?"

"No, Dad, he's been holed up in his room playing video games," I answered, hoping he'd end the conversation soon. I needed to get going.

"Well, sounds like you're doing okay. I just wanted to check on you. I'll let you go. See you in the morning."

"Okay. Love you, Dad."

"Love you, too," and he hung up.

The feeling of guilt returned, but I suppressed it as I climbed in my car and sped off. There was no time for that; I could feel guilty later.

# Chapter 5
## First Date

I hope I'm not running late.

Shifting my eyes to the clock, I realized I was. Crap! Ten fifty-seven and I still have to park, sneak in, and run to the crypt. I hope David doesn't think I stood him up and waits just a little bit longer for me.

I found a close spot down a side street and parked, jumping out of the car and running to the bushes. Watching the caretaker's house at the entrance to the cemetery, I quickly climbed over the fence, keeping close to it and in the shadows. Sprinting into the graveyard and maneuvering between the tombstones and monuments, I worried that David wouldn' .e there. I should have left earlier.

My concern grew deeper as I ascended a hill and dashed past ` eral crypts. I really wanted to see him again, be in his presence again. y heart ached at the thought that he might not be there, that I might h e missed my chance. I slowed as I came closer, worry and fear consu .ng me. Did he really want to see me again?

Yes, he did.

My heart fluttered wildly as I came around the c ner and found him sitting on the steps staring at the river, like a classic culpture poised in thoughtful repose. I could have stood there all ni ut admiring him, so aɩɩesung in the moonlight. But the urge to join him was winning over that.

Pausing a moment behind a monument, I tried to catch my breath and calm my heart. Once both were near normal, I continued toward him. He turned and looked at me as I casually strolled up. His lips spread into a smile, and I felt my heart almost leap out of my chest.

"Sorry I'm a little late," I apologized as it beat like crazy.

"You're worth the wait," he stated as he rose. He looked over my outfit and the corner of his mouth turned up slightly. "Not as formal, I see."

"Oh…yeah, it makes it a lot easier to get over the fence," I replied, slipping my hands into the back pockets of my cords and looking down at the ground bashfully.

"You still look lovely," he complimented and I blushed brighter. "What would you like to do tonight?" he asked, stepping closer.

I raised my eyes to his, trying to think of an answer, but his closeness distracted me. He was so incredibly handsome. But as I stared, I noticed something different about him. His eyes were bolder than I remembered, more brilliant, but maybe I was mistaken the first time we met. And his skin seemed paler than the last time, but maybe it was because of his dark shirt.

"Megan?"

I looked away, tucking my hair behind my ear. "Oh, sorry..." I responded, blushing again. I quickly tried to think of an answer. "We could go for a walk again. I enjoyed that."

"And maybe you could share some more stories about the graves here," he remarked, gracefully moving his arm as he indicated for me to lead the way.

We strolled along the path in silence, side by side, his hands in his pockets and my hands in mine. I tried to think of something to say but kept coming up with nothing. I thought about my day and what happened but figured he wouldn't want to hear about that. What happened after school wasn't that exciting either. I came home, took a nap, and woke from that startling dream...

The dream! I wanted to ask him what he saw in the shadows last time. "I'm curious about something," I began suddenly.

He stiffened a little. "Yes..."

"The other night...you saw something near the gate. What was it?"

He gazed at the sky and pursed his lips, then looked at me and answered. "It was one of my roommates, Brian. He tracked me here. I didn't introduce you because I didn't want you exposed to his...charms."

"His charms?"

"Yes. He has quite a track record preying on innocent young girls," he replied with a smile. My heart thumped so loud he probably heard it. I threw a hand up to my chest. "Are you all right?" he asked as he stopped and turned toward me.

"Yeah, I'm fine," I responded, dropping my hand and holding it. "So what makes you think I'm so innocent?" I inquired, hoping to change the subject quickly as I started walking again.

"There's an air about you that gives it away. It's one of your traits that drew me to you," he replied, keeping pace with me.

"Do you prey on innocent young girls, too?"

He grinned and my knees felt weak. "No, I'm not that kind of guy."

"What kind of guy are you?"

"Old-fashion," he replied. Bowing his head slightly as he smiled, he produced a deep red rose seemingly from nowhere and handed it to me.

"That's so sweet," I commented as I took it from him. "Ow! Oh, it has thorns..."

A small bead of blood formed on the tip of my index finger. As I instinctively lifted it to my mouth, he stepped back. I stepped forward and he quickly turned away, leaning on a monument for support.

"Are...are you okay?" I asked, worried.

His hand rested on the marble, barely a shade different, as he bowed his head. "I have…a problem with blood," he responded through clenched teeth.

I cleaned the puncture and applied pressure to it, holding it for a few seconds. "It's okay now…I stopped bleeding," I assured him as I held up my finger.

He slowly straightened, took a deep breath, and turned around. "Please forgive my behavior. It took me by surprise; I didn't realize there were thorns," he whispered.

"You don't have to apologize," I replied, breaking them off as we continued strolling. He kept his distance for a while and then gradually moved closer to me. "So how are you going to make it as a doctor if you have a problem with blood?" I questioned teasingly.

"It's something I'll need to build immunity toward," he answered seriously.

I couldn't think of anything else to say and hoped I didn't go too far with my comment. I twisted the stem of the flower in my fingers, staring at the velvet petals as I waited for him to say something, but he didn't. Did I insult him?

Thinking of a way to get a response, I took the now thornless rose and slipped it behind my ear. I turned my head toward him and modeled it, getting what I wanted in the form of a smile. Instantly, my heart skipped. I needed to become immune to that.

We came upon a bench, and he signaled for me to sit. The night was balmy with no breeze and the moon was high in the sky, still fairly full. I leaned back on my palms and breathed in the warm air, a mixture floral and earthy smells mingling with the familiar smell of cemetery boxwoods.

Glancing out of the corner of my eye, I noticed him watching me. I turned my head his way, and he reached up to adjust the rose. His hand brushed my skin, and I reacted to the coldness of it.

He instantly dropped it to the seat. "The crimson is beautiful against your skin," he commented.

"Th-thank you," I responded, staring into his eyes.

I became lost in them, their color striking and hypnotic. He could tell me to do anything and I'd do it. But he remained silent. Instead, he leaned in slowly and I did the same as we moved closer and closer. I could feel his breath on my lips.

A rustling nearby broke his gaze, and I snapped out of my trance. "Wh-what was that?" I asked languorously.

"I'm not sure, but we should move on," he insisted, glancing around as he quickly stood.

He grasped my arm and pulled me off the bench, walking away with me straggling behind. Leaving the path, we cut through the graves and crypts and headed toward the bluffs. He held onto my upper arm, making sure I kept up with him.

We rushed to the mausoleum and hid in a corner on the back side facing the river. Leaning against the wall, I took a moment to catch my breath while he surveyed the area. Why was he acting this way because of a noise?

"Are you all right?" he asked, concerned.

"Yeah, I'm fine. My arm hurts a little, though," I replied, rubbing it.

"I apologize."

"Well, you're pretty strong. I hope it doesn't bruise…" I trailed off.

He reached up and tucked my hair behind my ear, gazing into my eyes. I began to fall into the trance-like state again, but then he placed his hand on my cheek. I shuddered at his icy touch and my mind cleared. He dropped it and turned toward the river.

Not knowing what else to do, I slowly sunk to the ground. I watched him for a moment, staring at Belle Isle and not saying anything. This evening was not going well.

"Why did we leave so abruptly?" I asked, breaking the silence.

He turned around and glanced at either end of the building, not answering my question. After a moment, his eyes dropped to where I was sitting. "Something wasn't right," he responded, distant, as he stepped toward me.

He sat on the concrete across from me and crossed his legs. Looking at the wall next to me, he silently read the names of those interred in the mausoleum. I watched him, curious what he was thinking. Every once in a while, he'd sit still and tilt his head just slightly like he was listening for something. When he was satisfied there was nothing, he'd go back to reading.

I couldn't take the silence anymore. "So where are you from?" I asked, giving an inquisitive look as I leaned on my knees.

He stopped reading and shifted his eyes to me, answering simply, "Massachusetts."

"That's funny; you don't sound like you're from Massachusetts."

"Not everyone speaks like what is portrayed on TV," he retorted with a grin. I felt the familiar flutter in my heart and tucked my head to hide my embarrassment. "Have you always lived here?" he asked, leaning over to look at my face.

"Yeah, in Chesterfield all my life – born and raised," I replied, pulling my knees to my chest and wrapping my arms around them as I looked past him at the river and Belle Isle.

He was quiet a moment and then spoke. "Is there somewhere else you would like to meet…for our next date?" he inquired, interrupting my gaze.

That took me by surprise. "Our…our next…date?"

He grinned and my heart pounded. "Do you not want to go out with me again?"

"Of...of course I do," I replied, blushing at the thought that he wanted to go out with me again. "You just caught me off guard," I explained.

"So?" he inquired, waiting for my reply.

"Oh...we could go to a movie."

"Hmm, that's not what I was thinking," he responded, leaning back on his palms.

"What were you thinking?"

"Somewhere much like the cemetery...maybe a park?"

"Okay...do we plan to continue meeting after dark?"

"It would be best for me if we did."

Strange, but I'm not going to judge. "Hmm, that really limits our options; all the great places close after dark."

"We could always sneak in, like we do here," he suggested with a smirk.

I had to catch my breath before I could answer. "I'm okay with coming here because I feel like I have a right. Anywhere else would feel wrong."

"I see..." he remarked, sitting up and crossing his wrists over his lap.

I'm being stupid. I don't want to discourage another date. "Well, I mean, we could. I've gotten pretty good at not being spotted all these years," I recovered, boasting.

"So where shall we meet next," he asked, leaning on his knees.

I hesitated, thinking of somewhere interesting. I looked up and it came to me. "Well, one of my favorite places is there," I answered, pointing across the river.

"That might be difficult. We'll probably be spotted crossing the footbridge. Is there another way onto the island?" he questioned, standing up to get a better look.

"There is, as long as the river's not too high. The south end of the island is nothing but rocks all the way to the bank. We might be able to do that. There's a park area we can meet at, if you'd like to cross together?"

"I think it would be best...safer."

"When do we plan to do this?" I asked.

He turned and faced me. "How about tomorrow evening, say nine o'clock?"

"Saturday night? Yeah, that'll be good. I can tell my dad that I'm going to a movie with Claire. She'll be there anyway, on a date, so it works perfectly."

"Maybe you're not as innocent as you seem," he commented, the corner of his mouth curling into a smile.

I tucked my head and tried to control my heart. Looking away, I replied, "I would do anything to see you…" I bit my lip and rested my chin on my knees as I stared off into the distance. Where did that come from, and why did I say it out loud?

He came back to me and held out his hand. I gazed up at him and placed mine in his, but I didn't flinch from its coolness this time. "I think it's safe to continue our walk," he commented as I rose. Safe? Maybe he saw the caretaker.

We strolled out from behind the mausoleum and joined the path. I looked down at our hands clasped together and then glanced at him. I liked holding his hand, even if it was a little cold. Some people naturally have cold hands. I waited for him to look at me, but he kept his eyes straight ahead except for when he glanced unexpectedly to the left or the right.

We came to a grouping of several monuments, tombstones, and statues of varying shapes and sizes. Perusing through them, we read a few of the interesting epitaphs and discussed the different designs. As we were looking at one in particular, he stiffened suddenly.

"Lovely night, isn't it, David?" a dark figure inquired as it leaned against a granite obelisk. The voice was purely sensual, and I had one guess who it was.

"What are you doing here, Brian?" he growled, backing up and moving closer to me.

"Curious what was drawing you here," he answered as he rolled around the statue into view. "Now I see…she would draw me, too." He grinned, but there was something about it that made me uncomfortable. He stepped closer to me and I inched behind David, holding onto him as I peeked around his shoulder.

Brian folded his muscular arms across his broad chest, the dark color of his shirt making them paler than they were. He lifted a large hand and ran it through his straight, black hair, letting it fall along his chin. Wetting his lips, he smirked as he stared into my eyes. The cold, unnatural silver pierced my soul, and I tried to look away but couldn't.

"You need to leave," David demanded.

"But I haven't formally introduced myself…I'm Brian," he greeted, ignoring him as he leaned to the side and put his hand out.

David moved completely in front of me, shielding. They stared at each other for what seemed like minutes and then Brian smiled, his eyes shifting briefly to mine. A chill went down my spine.

"All right, all right. I'll leave," he conceded. "See you around, *Megan*."

He turned away and disappeared into the shadows of the monuments and statues. How did he know my name? I never told him and it wasn't mentioned.

David's tension eased and I moved to his side. "Are you okay?" I asked.

"Yes. I'm just perturbed with him for doing that."

"Don't worry; I didn't find him charming at all," I assured, giving a weak smile.

"Thank you," he replied, smiling back. My heart fluttered and I let out a heavy sigh. I'll take his smile over Brian's any day.

He took my hand and I wrapped my arm around his as we continued our stroll. Leaning in closer, I rested my head on his shoulder. His scent filled my head and I started to feel faint. He noticed my sudden weakness, supporting me as my steps began to falter. I stood up straight and breathed in the warm air, slowly regaining some consciousness, then looked at him and grinned like a fool.

"There's something about your cologne...that...that makes me feel...drunk," I commented, fumbling with the words.

He gave me a sympathetic look and helped me to a bench. Sitting away from him, the fog gradually lifted from my brain. When it was clear enough, I glanced over and found him staring at the stars. Between the city lights and the light from the moon, only the brightest ones shone through. I always loved staring into the night sky, trying to find the constellations.

"There's Leo," I remarked, pointing to an area in front of us.

"I see you've sobered up," he responded, still staring at the sky. "Are you familiar with the constellations?" he inquired, turning his head slightly toward me.

"Yeah, but only a few. When I was young, my parents and I would head out to the country to find the best viewing area. So many of the stars don't show up here, and when you're out there under the open sky, you feel so small compared to the vastness of space. My backyard is a good spot, too, though not like out there. But at least it's not so far away. I like to lie in the soft grass and stare up at the speckled ceiling."

"I would like to do that with you sometime," he commented, and I turned to look at him. His attention had been on me the whole time I was babbling.

I liked the thought of us lying side by side in my yard alone, staring at the multitude of stars. I blushed and replied, "Yes, that would be nice."

We were suddenly silent, gazing into each other's eyes. He reached up and cupped the side of my face, his hand cooling the blush in my cheek. I leaned into it and closed my eyes, relishing his touch. He caressed my skin with his thumb, moving slowly to my lips and brushing across them.

I gradually opened my eyes and gazed into his, longing to feel his lips on mine. As I leaned closer, he did the same, and I closed them again. The beat of my heart gained speed as I felt his breath on my skin, and my mind began to swim again. I concentrated but hesitated for a moment, preparing myself.

"I...I can't do this," he whispered, quickly turning away, his breathing heavy.

I placed my hand on his and asked, "What's wrong? Is it me?"

"No...no, not at all. It's too soon. I...I just can't," he replied, glancing over his shoulder with somber eyes.

Why would it be too soon?

Oh...maybe he just went through a bad break-up. Now I feel terrible, leading him on though I didn't mean to do it. I hope he doesn't think badly of me now. Feeling the compulsion to do so, I apologized.

He turned to me and furrowed his brow. "Why are you sorry? You did nothing wrong."

"I don't know...I thought it was the right thing to say." Suddenly, my phone vibrated, causing me to jump. I pulled it out and saw it was a text from Claire. "Oh no..."

"Is something wrong?" he asked, eager to get the attention off him.

"My dad called Claire. She told him I was busy and my phone was charging. I need to call him before he suspects anything."

"I'll wait," he responded, bowing his head briefly.

I gave him a thankful smile and walked several feet away as I pulled up the number. It was close to one in the morning, but I was sure he'd be waiting to hear from me. I dialed the house phone and waited for an answer, glancing back at David. He was sitting so still and tall as he stared at the heavens, fitting in perfectly with his surroundings as if he belonged here.

Hearing a groggy voice answer, I turned away again. "Vanessa? Why are you answering the phone?"

"Megan? Your dad is...umm...wait a minute..." She put the phone down and got up from whatever she was sitting on. In the background, she called for him and told him it was me. There was silence for a moment and then hurried footsteps.

"Megan? Are you doing okay?" my father asked, also somewhat groggy, but panicked.

"I'm fine. Did I wake you?"

"No, we...we're watching a movie. What were you doing when I called?"

"Why?" I inquired, curious if he had a reason for checking up on me so much tonight.

"I...I just like to know."

"Dad, have you been drinking?"

"Only a little...Vanessa had some, too."

"I can tell. Listen, I'm fine. You don't have to worry about me. You should go to bed and sleep off the alcohol."

"But I need to take Vanessa home."

"I think it's best she stays there tonight. She can sleep in the guest room."

"Guest room? Yeah, yeah. Whatever you say. Love you."

"See you in the morning, Dad." I heard Vanessa in the background coaxing him to come to bed. Disgusted, I hung up and returned to the bench.

"Is everything all right?" David asked.

"My dad's drunk," I answered. "I am so glad I'm not there tonight."

"Do you need to leave?"

"No, he'll be fine. He has Vanessa, though she's drunk, too."

"Then they will have a great night together, most likely passing out in an hour. I wouldn't worry about them."

"Oh, I'm not," I responded, crossing my arms.

He watched me and shook his head, amused. "I'm glad I don't have to deal with what you're going through."

"Why? Are your parents still together?" I asked, relaxing my arms.

"No, they passed away some time ago," he answered, staring off into the cemetery.

"I'm sorry." I placed my hand on his. He glanced at me and then stood.

"I would like to walk you to your car," he remarked, offering his hand.

I hesitated and then took it. "Do we have to leave?" I questioned as I rose from the bench.

"You will see me tomorrow. There's something I need to take care of and you should get some sleep," he replied, leading me away.

"If you insist," I responded, a little disappointed.

When we reached the front of the cemetery, he climbed the fence with cat-like grace. He crouched at the top and then jumped off, landing perfectly on his feet. I took a little longer climbing, but he waited patiently on the other side. As I perched at the top and prepared to jump, I stared down into his awaiting arms.

Trusting him, I grimaced and dropped off the fence. He caught my waist and slowly lowered me with little effort. I smiled and tucked my head as he brought me closer and when he smiled back, my heart went wild.

Taking my arm in his, we strolled quietly to my car. When we reached it, he seemed a bit surprised. "This is yours?"

"Yeah…it was my dad's. When he decided to upgrade to a convertible sports car, I inherited the sedan."

"He trusts you with it? That's a lot of power for a teenager."

"Of course he does! I'm a safe driver," I responded, smacking him in the chest; it was firm. He smirked, and I fell back against the driver's side door but played it off as if I leaned into it.

"I wanted to be sure you made it to your car all right," he commented, stepping closer.

"That's very sweet of you...thank you," I responded, unsure what to expect. "I had a lovely evening and can't wait to see you again."

"Nor can I," he whispered, leaning closer and gently kissing my cheek. His lips were gelid against the warmth of my skin, but my heart thumped all the same.

He stepped back, a pained look on his face, as I reached up and touched where he kissed and half-smiled. His solemn expression faded and he smiled back. Guessing it was time to go, I clumsily reached behind me for the door handle and realized I had to unlock it first.

"See you tonight," I whispered as I opened it. He nodded and then disappeared into the shadows.

I climbed in and sat for a moment, astonished by what just happened. Grabbing the steering wheel, I rested my head against it and laughed. He kissed me! Well, my cheek, but that's something. I hope Claire is awake enough so I can tell her all about my date. I started the car and quickly drove to her house.

When I got there, I quietly entered and peeked in the family room, but she wasn't there. I crept up the stairs and headed toward her room, passing her brother's on the way. I took a step back and peeked in, finding him asleep in front of the TV with a video game still on. He looked incredibly uncomfortable, so I carefully moved him from the floor to his bed and turned everything off. I cracked the door behind me and continued to Claire's room.

Slowly opening her door, I found her asleep in bed. Sitting on the edge, I gently shook her as I whispered her name. "I'm here. Claire?"

"Megan? You're back?" she responded drowsily. She blinked and looked at the clock and then pushed herself up into a seated position, stretched, and yawned. "So how did it go?" she asked as she swayed slightly.

"Amazing. He kissed me...on the cheek," I whispered, not wanting to be too loud.

"That's better than no kiss," she replied, waking up more. "What else happened?"

"We held hands as we walked around the cemetery, and he gave this beautiful rose to me," I answered, removing it from above my ear and smelling it. Its aroma was still as vibrant as its color. "I'm going to see him again this evening, somewhere else."

"Good. I don't think it's healthy meeting in a cemetery after dark," she lectured through a yawn.

"Oh, and you know that something he saw in the shadows the last time we met? It was his roommate, Brian, who happened to show up tonight. I got to meet him."

"And?"

"Well, he's a good-looking guy, but there's something about him I don't like. David was pretty pissed that he followed him there and after a brief staring contest between the two of them, he left."

"That was pretty exciting," she responded, yawning again.

"I also learned a little more about him over the course of the evening – he's from Massachusetts and both his parents are deceased. Which reminds me…after I received your text, I called Dad. He was drunk and so was Vanessa. I am so mad at him right now."

"Aw, he's just having a good time."

"I know, but I hate to hear him like that," I responded. "So how'd your evening go?"

"The monster stayed in his room all night and I talked to Justin for two hours."

"You two aren't going to have a lot to say on your date tomorrow, I mean, tonight."

"That's okay, we'll be watching a movie," she replied, yawning again.

"Well, I'll let you go back to sleep. See you in the morning."

She nodded lazily as she slid back under the covers. I went next door to the guest room and changed into lounge pants and a t-shirt. Climbing into bed, I laid the rose on the pillow next to my head and stared at it as I waited to fall asleep. Breathing in its heavenly scent, I thought of David and our evening together as it replayed in my mind and lulled me to sleep.

# Chapter 6
## Belle Isle

Sunlight poured through the window, warming my face. As my eyes gradually opened, I stared at the rose in front of me. I smiled, delicately picking it up and rolling over onto my back. Placing it over my heart, I held it there and closed my eyes. The aroma seemed more potent. I picked it up again, smelled it, and then ran it along the cheek David kissed last night.

"What are you doing?" Claire asked, standing in the doorway and giving me a funny look.

"Oh! I-I just woke up," I answered as I hid the rose, blushing slightly.

She grinned as she sauntered toward me. "I'm just messing with you. You don't have to explain," she responded as she sat on the edge of the bed. "I know you were thinking about *him*."

I propped up on my elbows and slipped the rose behind my ear, smiling. "I really can't wait to see him tonight."

"I know how you feel; I'm excited, too, about my date. Do you think Justin will try to kiss me?"

"I guess there's a chance. Or you could kiss him," I suggested with a grin. As she contemplated it, I glanced around the room looking for a clock but couldn't find one. "Umm, what time is it?"

"Oh, almost eleven. It'd be awesome if he did…"

"Crap! I've got to get going!" I exclaimed, jumping out of bed and knocking her to the floor. I dashed into the bathroom and threw on my outfit from last night and then gathered my things and ran down the stairs. She was right behind me.

"Sorry again for not being able to make it tomorrow. I'd love to be there to put Ben in his place if he got out of line," she commented, leaning against the banister.

"Don't worry about it. I think Erin will make up for the both of you. I just hope war doesn't break out over it," I responded as I shoved my shoes on. "I'll call you in the morning to find out how your date went and tell you about mine. That reminds me…I'm telling my dad I'm going to a late movie with you tonight so I can meet David. If it ever comes up, can you cover for me?"

"Sure," she responded positively. "You know, I hope your relationship isn't always going to be in secret. Your dad needs to know about it sooner or later."

"Later would be better. I just need some more time," I replied as I stood up and reached in my pocket, handing over her house key. "Well, I better go. Good luck tonight," I commented as I gave her a hug.

She smiled weakly, and I gave a reassuring smile back. I knew she'd be fine, but she looked like she needed the encouragement. I gave her another hug and then slipped out the door, waving to her as I headed to my car. As I unlocked it, I glanced at my reflection in the window and spied the rose perched above my ear. It did look really nice against my skin, even though I looked awful. I shook my head and hopped in the seat.

I pulled into the driveway a short time later and quietly entered the house. As I guessed, Dad and Vanessa were still asleep. They'd have quite a hangover this morning, so I did my best not to disturb them.

I crept up the stairs to my room and dropped my bag on the bed, opening it and pulling everything out. Before putting it all away, I removed the rose from above my ear and laid it on my bedside table where I could look at it before I fell asleep each night. I took care of my things and then went into the bathroom to wash up.

Sitting on the edge of the bed feeling a little more refreshed, I twisted my hair into a bun as I stared at the rose and reminisced about last night. My eyes shifted to the clock – nine more hours before I'd get to see David again. What to do in those long hours before then? I scanned the room and grabbed a book off my shelf as I headed to the balcony.

The trees scattered around the backyard were in full bloom and the light fragrance of their flowers surrounded me as I stepped out into the clement air. I headed over to my chaise and made myself comfortable, ready to read several chapters, but the commotion in the garden below distracted me. I put the book down and strolled up to the railing, curious what was going on. Squirrels scurried about the yard chasing each other, and birds played in the birdbath or sat in the trees calling to each other.

My mom loved to garden so our backyard was meticulously landscaped, like what you'd see in one of those gardening magazines. She wanted it to be an escape, a magical place. And for me, it was. When I was little, I used to pretend I was a fairy princess and the garden was my kingdom.

There used to be two old stumps in the back of the yard that Mom and I used as our thrones. We could see our whole kingdom from there and would sit and watch over our subjects. The butterflies fluttered about delivering messages, the bees buzzed flower to flower gathering pollen to make honey for tea and crumpets, and the birds sang songs to entertain us on the warm spring days. It was all part of our pretend world.

No matter what the season, the garden was always brilliant. Soft pastel hues abounded in spring, covering bushes and trees and complementing the fresh young grass blades. The vibrant blooms of summer encircled the yard, climbing the fences and covering the ground as the leaves on the trees and bushes darkened to a deep, lush green. In fall, the yard became a kaleidoscope of yellow, orange, and red, first on the trees and then covering the ground. When the snow fell in winter, it highlighted the brown of the tree trunks and the emerald of the evergreens while enhancing the deep colors of the crocuses, pansies, and roses that dared to bloom.

The responsibility to care for it fell on me since I inherited my mom's green thumb. Dad kills everything he touches, so he stayed away from it. Looking at it from the balcony, I realized it's been awhile since I tended to it. What a good way to pass the time. It was a big yard and would take me several hours.

I went down to the garage, grabbed my tools, and set to work. I pulled weeds and cleared debris from all the pathways. I pruned the bushes and trees and cleaned the patio furniture. I even brought out the manual mower and trimmed the patches of grass around the yard.

I was so consumed in my work, I didn't notice Dad watching me from the patio doors. "Megan, what are you doing?" he asked.

"Oh, Dad!" I gasped, startled. "I'm…umm…just tidying up the yard. It looked like it needed some TLC."

"Why didn't you wake me when you got home?" he questioned, wincing from the sunshine as he stepped outside.

I wiped my forehead and joined him on the patio. "I figured you needed to sleep in after last night," I explained.

He was in his robe, looking like death warmed over. I motioned for him to sit while I went inside to get him a cup of coffee. Watching from the window as it brewed, I noticed how he marveled over the beauty of the garden. He rarely went in the backyard because of the reminders. I, on the other hand, embraced it and wanted to maintain it in memory of her.

Once the coffee finished, I poured a cup and quickly rushed it outside, setting it on the table in front of him. "Beautiful, isn't it?" I commented as I sat down.

"Mom would be proud, Meg," he replied, fidgeting with the cup. "Listen…I'm sorry about last night. It was such a stressful day, well week…"

"You don't have to explain, Dad. I understand," I interrupted, patting his hand.

"Did you have a good time?"

"Yeah," I answered dreamily, touching my cheek. He looked at me curiously and I dropped my hand. "Yeah, it was fun," I recovered, hoping he wouldn't ask what that was about.

"Good…good," he responded, taking a sip of coffee.

He sat quietly drinking as I glanced around. This seemed like as good a time as any to ask about tonight. "Claire wanted to know if I could join her at the movies tonight. She has a date with a guy from school, but she doesn't really want go alone," I fibbed.

"Is it a double-date?"

"No, not at all. Just the two of us and him."

"Who is she going with? Anyone I know?"

"Yeah, the Collins' youngest son…Justin."

He narrowed his eyes as he considered it and then conceded. "You can go," he replied, looking out into the yard again and taking another sip of coffee. "So, are any of your friends coming to help tomorrow?"

"Ben and Erin, but Erin will be late."

"I like Ben; he's a nice boy," he commented. Then he slipped in, "Are you two dating?"

"Ben? Nooo. We're just friends," I answered.

"That's a shame. He seems to really like you," he remarked as he put his cup down, watching me out of the corner of his eye. "Well, I'm sure you'll have fun tomorrow." I got the feeling he was trying to get something out of me, but I wasn't going to cave.

Behind us, the patio door slid open and Vanessa stepped out. Wearing a silk robe and sitting on the corner of the table rather than in a seat, she took the attention off me. I have never been as thankful for her presence as I was at that moment. I sighed and stood up.

"Where are you going?" Dad asked, breaking his gaze from her.

"Oh, I still have a lot to do," I answered, grabbing a rake.

"We're done talking?"

"Yeah, I guess so," I replied, shifting my eyes to her.

"All right then. I'm going to warm leftovers for lunch. Want any?"

"Of course. Call me when it's ready," I responded.

"Don't you have a gardener to take care of this?" I heard her ask as I walked away.

"No, Lizzie always took care of it. After she passed, Megan took over. Don't worry, we'll get someone to do it when she goes to college," he replied as he got up and led her inside.

I raked angrily for a little while and then gave up. I wasn't in the mood to garden anymore. Climbing the steps to the gazebo in the back corner of the yard where the stumps used to be, I sat on the swing and stared at the house. I could see Dad and Vanessa through the window above the sink, playing around as they fixed lunch. He looked happy, but why her?

Shaking my head, I turned my attention away from them. I stared at the open area in front of me and thought of something more pleasant, like when I used to come out here in the summer and watch the fireflies light up the yard at dusk. Then I would stay until the stars appeared, admiring them as I lay on the grass and gazed into the heavens.

My thoughts turned to David, and I replayed our conversation about the stars from last night. He said he'd like to share that with me. I stared at the grassy patch where we would lie and imagined him there beside me, holding my hand, his body close to mine. Yeah, it'd be nice to have him over. But if that were to happen, I'd need to find a time when Dad wasn't around.

Hearing my name broke my daze. I sighed and hopped up from the swing, jogging to the house. The delectable smell of the food made my stomach growl loudly, letting me know I waited too long to eat. I quickly washed up and grabbed a plate out of the cabinet, filled it with a hodge-podge of items, and started toward the patio doors. Vanessa and Dad were already sitting at the table in the breakfast nook.

"Where are you going?" he asked, putting his fork down. She continued to chow down, unconcerned with what I was doing.

"I want to eat outside in the garden," I answered, opening the door and slipping out.

"Suit yourself," he shrugged and went back to his meal.

I set my plate down and took a seat, facing the yard. I tried to enjoy my solitude, but unfortunately, I could hear them talking inside. Nothing worth eavesdropping in on, just wedding and honeymoon plans. Focusing on more pleasant sounds, I cut into the smothered chicken breast and began eating.

I didn't rush through my meal, savoring the flavors and fresh air. But once I finished, I sighed and decided to go in and get cleaned up. I was done for the day.

I took care of my dishes and then headed out of the kitchen. As I passed the breakfast nook, I caught Vanessa sitting on Dad's lap, making out with him. I rolled my eyes and continued down the hall and up the stairs to my room. Slipping into the bathroom, I quickly jumped in the shower, feeling extra dirty for having witnessed that gratuitous display.

As I showered off, I thought about Claire and her date tonight. I needed to call to see how she was fairing. She'd probably appreciate it. So after I was done and dressed, I grabbed my cell and stepped out onto the balcony, sitting on the chaise as I dialed her number. I figured I'd be safe from eavesdropping if I was outside. Of course, Dad was probably too preoccupied with Vanessa right now to really care.

"Hello?" Claire answered.

"Hey…how are you holding up?"

"Wait a minute…I need to go to my room," she whispered. I heard her climbing the stairs and then a door shut. "Okay, I'm here. I didn't want my parents to hear our conversation."

"So I take it they're home?"

"Yeah, they got in about three."

"Sooo…how are you?"

"Better. I talked to Justin not too long ago. I have my outfit laid out and I'm psyched."

"I assume you told your parents you were going on a date."

"Of course. They're cool with it. Did your dad buy your ruse for tonight?"

"He hesitated, then agreed. I need to remember to coordinate my time with when you'll be leaving the movie, otherwise he'll get suspicious. He's already asking questions. By the way, what movie are you seeing? I want to be prepared if he quizzes me."

"Umm, the one about the team of superheroes…it's based off a comic book…it's called…um…Vigilante Inc," she answered. "We're going to the nine o'clock show."

"Did you have any say in choosing the movie?"

"I picked it. I'm kinda interested in it," she replied self-consciously.

"Really?"

"So your dad's suspicious of you?" Claire asked, changing the subject.

"Yeah. You won't believe this, but he asked if I was dating Ben."

"Well, with the way he trails you like a puppy, it's not surprising. What did you tell him?"

"No, of course."

"How was your dad this morning after his wild night?"

"In pretty bad shape. They didn't get up until after two."

"They? Vanessa stayed the night? I thought your dad wasn't going to allow her to do that."

"Only if I'm there and I was at your house last night. Besides, I told him it was okay. Better than him drunk on the road taking her home."

"Ever heard of a cab?"

"He wouldn't do that to her."

"How nice of you to allow her to stay. So how are you feeling about your date tonight?" she asked, curious.

"Good. I never feel nervous about seeing him, only excited. Buuut…I've noticed something about him, something strange I can't explain."

"Like what?" she asked, intrigued.

I thought about my last two meetings with David – the way he acted, looked, sounded. "He…changes," was all I said.

"Changes? What do you mean 'he *changes*'?"

"Okay, the first time I saw him I swear his eyes were light green. Last night, they were bolder, like emerald-colored."

"You know eye color can vary according to a person's mood or what they wear or even light reflection. Just ask him outright if his eyes do that. It shouldn't be a difficult question to answer."

"Yeah, maybe," I agreed, thinking about her response. It makes sense and I could just ask him. I just hope I don't offend him for whatever reason. "You know, I like him…*really* like him, and I don't want to mess this up."

"I don't think you will. And it seems to me he really likes you, too. Oh, you never told me…where are you meeting for your second date?"

I hesitated. "Belle Isle…"

"Uh, you do realize it's closed after dark," Claire lectured. "How do you plan to get there?"

"There is a way without going on the footbridge. He says he can only meet at night and prefers being outdoors, so that limits where we can go."

"That's odd. Only at night, huh?"

"Yeah…I know. I guess it's because of classes or work." There was a pause and muffled noises. "Claire? Claaaaire?"

"I'm here. Sorry, mom wants to discuss something, so I have to go, but I'll talk to you tomorrow morning…okay? Have a good time tonight and don't nitpick him."

"All right. Have a good time, too. I hope everything goes well. Talk to you in the morning." I hung up and flopped back against the chaise.

I slipped the phone in my pocket and stared out into the yard. As the sun set behind the house, the garden seemed to take on a different guise. The solar lights lining the pathways slowly brightened, and the birds and squirrels became quiet. Beyond the trees, in the open area, the last rays of the day remained. I watched them fade away as the crickets began their nightly serenade.

I slowly stood up and left the balcony, closing the doors behind me. I pulled the sheer curtains closed and flipped the light switch. Glancing around my room, I mulled over what I should do now. Probably get ready. I headed to my closet and opened the door.

What should I wear tonight? I'll be climbing over rocks and up walls to get to the island. It needs to be something easy to maneuver in, but also attractive. I skimmed through my clothes and pulled out a pair of dark blue jeans. Red shirt? No, I need to keep my outfit dark so I'll be harder to see. My scoop neck, black shirt will work perfectly.

I changed into my stealthy attire and took my hair down. That won't work – I'll need to wear it up to keep it out of my face. Reaching in to get my tennis shoes, I spotted my hiking boots tucked away in the back. The rocks may be slippery, so they're the better option. I pulled them out and slipped them on.

Downstairs, Dad was preparing dinner. Vanessa hadn't left yet, but at least she had on more clothes. I sat at the counter, patiently waiting for him to finish.

Suddenly noticing me there, he turned and asked, "Will you be eating with us tonight or are you going out with Claire and her date?"

"No, I'm eating here. The movie isn't until later, nine o'clock, so I'll be home after eleven."

Vanessa scanned my clothes. "That's an odd outfit to wear to the movies," she commented with a smirk. He glanced at it and shrugged, not thinking anything of it.

He made a plate of food and placed it in front of me. "Enjoy," he commented, smiling.

"Thanks. It looks yummy," I replied and proceeded to dig in.

Making a plate for Vanessa and then one for himself, he went to the table in the breakfast nook and sat down. I ate in silence, finishing a lot quicker than they did. While they continued to eat, I took care of leftovers and dishes.

Not wanting to sit and talk with them afterward, I headed into the family room and glanced around for something to do other than watch TV. Unfortunately, there was nothing so I turned it on anyway. It just had to be the news.

They were reporting on a gruesome murder connected to the serial killer case involving a young woman from VCU. Her picture was posted in the corner of the screen – dark hair, fair complexion, attractive. She was found decapitated in a park outside the city, her body drained of blood. Joggers discovered her this morning and time of death was determined to be around 2:00 AM. A chill went down my spine and I became nauseous.

That could have been me.

I thought back to last night and how strange David was acting. Wait…he said he had something to do and left me before two. Could he be the serial killer? I quickly turned the channel, my stomach churning.

I stopped on a movie I hadn't seen in years and tried to watch it, hoping to get my mind off the murders and the possibility David was leading a double life, but to no avail. He's strong, persuasive, and agile. He could easily handle kidnapping and killing an adult woman without a problem. But he left me a little over a half hour before two. That really didn't give him enough time to kill her.

The more I thought about it, the more ridiculous it seemed. There's no way he's a serial killer. He doesn't seem the type to do that. He's planning on becoming a doctor, to help people. If he felt that way, he wouldn't take a human life. And he's been nothing but gentle and protective. No, I feel safe with him.

"Megan," Dad called, jarring me from my thoughts. "Shouldn't you be heading out to meet Claire?" he asked, coming up behind me.

I shifted my eyes to the clock above the TV and jumped up from the couch. Crap, it was already eight-thirty! I ran toward the door, but then screeched to a halt. Rushing back, I kissed my dad on the cheek and then thanked him as I dashed out the door. I needed to hurry since I have to go to the other side of town to meet David.

Flooring it, I made great time. I parked on a side street in South Richmond near the small park area where I told him to meet me. The moon was just starting to crest over the trees and buildings, so it was fairly dark, but luckily I didn't have far to walk.

My heart leapt as I spotted his figure perched on the back of a bench in the middle of the park, staring at the river. He glanced over his shoulder and smiled, his teeth bright in the darkness. I composed myself and walked toward him as he stood and gracefully stepped down.

"Right on time," he commented and then his lip curled at the corner. "I like the outfit; very…dark."

"Thanks. Back at you," I replied with a smile as I twisted my ponytail, looking over his svelte attire and trying to calm my heart. "Shall we?" I inquired, indicating the direction we needed to head to start our adventure.

We walked down the bike path and came to a ledge overlooking the train tracks. It was going to be difficult getting to the river, but he seemed up for the challenge. He jumped first and positioned himself to catch me. I dropped into his waiting arms, and he gently lowered me to the ground. Being close to one another, we stared into each other's eyes a moment and then he looked away quickly. Clearing his throat, we continued on our way, crossing the train tracks and heading to the boulders.

"Would you like to go first or shall I?" he asked while measuring up the obstacle in front of us.

"I'll lead, since I'm familiar with this part," I answered as I started leaping across them.

He was right behind my every step as I bounced rock to rock. "I didn't expect you to be so agile," he remarked.

I stopped and put one hand on my hip and the other in the air. "Years of dance, martial arts, and sports."

"That's quite a resume."

"I know. My parents wanted me to be well-rounded. I'm also an honor student," I boasted, continuing across them.

"Impressive," he commented as he paused and looked around. "What's that building there?" he asked as he pointed to an aged, dilapidated structure.

"Oh, that's the old VEPCO hydroelectric plant. They closed it down in the sixties," I replied, continuing to boulder hop.

"So it remains, a relic of another time."

"Yeah, I guess so." I paused and pointed to a wall in the distance. "That's where we need to go in order to get on the island."

He looked at me and grinned. I turned away and held my hand over my chest, my heart beating rapidly. I tried to focus on what I was doing, finding the right paths to take to the wall. The rocks seemed to be growing farther apart and my jumps began to falter.

"And here I thought I would have t-" he started to say, but then suddenly grabbed my waist and swiftly carried me to the next boulder as if I weighed nothing.

"What was that about?" I inquired, trembling as he set me down.

"You were about to fall into the water," he replied, holding me close. I gave him an astounded look. "You're welcome," he stated, moving away and continuing to the next rock.

"Show-off," I mumbled to myself, bounding after him. We reached the top of last boulder and climbed the ladder, taking the walkway to the trail.

"Where to now?" he asked, curious.

"Well, if we go this way, we'll reach the quarry. If we go that way, we'll come to the open field where the Civil War prison camp used to be."

"I think we should avoid open fields. What's at the quarry?"

"A pond and a rock climbing wall," I answered. "And after we're done there, we can go to the rapids on the other side and sit on the boulders."

"Sounds pleasant," he replied, smiling as he took my arm in his. I blushed and looked away as we started to walk, my heart fluttering. I felt giddy being so close to him and had to fight to keep from shaking.

It was hard to see where I was going with the little bit of moonlight that shone through the trees, but he had no problem at all. Guiding me along, he safely led us to the overlook of the quarry. As we came to the edge, I stood awestruck.

"Megan?" he called softly as he took in my enthralled expression.

"I've never seen it like this before. It's so...enchanting," I replied, staring at the reflection of the moon as it glistened on the calm water and dimly illuminated the rock wall.

"It is," he agreed, placing his hand on the small of my back and sending a tingle up my spine. I turned my face to his and gazed into his eyes, not really sure what color they were tonight. They were beautiful nonetheless. Leaning closer, I attempted to kiss him, but he quickly turned away. "Where to next?" he asked, his eyes on the quarry again.

I pressed my lips together and faced forward, staring at it as well. Across from where we stood, the observation deck sat bathed in moonlight. Smiling, I came up with an idea.

"Let's go there," I suggested, pointing to it as I started dragging him behind me.

"You should be careful. You're not able to see too well," he cautioned, digging his heels into the ground to prevent me from going any farther. I huffed and he eased up, allowing me to continue slowly.

We reached the deck and walked out to the end. The moon was higher in the sky and being out in the open, I was able to see better. Staring at

David, I clearly saw him for the first time tonight. His skin was fair and his eyes were back to being light green.

He looked at me, perplexed. "What's wrong?" he asked

"Wh-what do you mean?" I questioned, looking away.

"The way you're looking at me…is something wrong?"

I hesitated. "No…well…I mean…" I fumbled with the words.

"You can tell me. I won't be offended," he encouraged.

I debated saying anything, but then sighed and decided. "Okay, this is going to sound crazy," I began, leaning against the railing, "but I just need to know."

"All right…ask," he offered, putting his hands behind his back.

"Your eyes are light green…"

"Yes, they are," he responded, cocking his head and gazing at me curiously.

"But last night, they were emerald. They change color?"

He hesitated. "Doesn't everyone's?"

"Well, in a way, but yours are pretty extreme."

"Ahh, I see," he murmured, bowing his head and smiling. "Mine are no different than anyone else's," he explained, raising his eyes to meet mine and then turning them to the sky. "It's the moonlight that makes it appear more extreme. It plays tricks on you," he grinned, moving closer. He gently touched my chin and lifted it slightly. I grasped the rough wood, trying to control my trembling as he gazed into my eyes. "The blue of yours seems brighter tonight than last night."

My cheeks flushed and I tried to speak. "Th-that makes sense," I responded finally.

"It does," he replied, slowly removing his fingers. "Anything else?"

I tucked my head and thought about what I could ask, but then Claire's words from earlier pushed any possibilities away. "No, that's all," I answered.

I took one last glimpse of the quarry in the moonlight and nudged him to move on to the rapids. We had quite a distance to cover and little time to do it. I walked as fast as I could in the dim light and he kept up, continuing to guide me.

When the sound of the rushing water of the James grew louder, I knew we were at our next stop. "Here we are," I announced as I turned and faced a break in the trees.

We walked down to the bank and onto a large, flat boulder. Coming to the edge of it, I took a seat and he followed. The river rushed next to us, but farther down, the moonlight shimmered on calmer waters.

We sat in silence, enjoying the serenity of the night. I leaned back on my palms and crossed my legs, making myself more comfortable. Glancing over at him, I couldn't help but marvel at his magnificence. He sat with his left leg propped up and his arm resting on it. The other leg was flat on the rock, hand on his lap. He glanced at me, and I quickly looked toward Hollywood Cemetery.

"There it is, in front of us," I commented casually.

"What?" he asked, following my line of sight.

"Where we met," I replied, pointing to the bluffs of the cemetery.

"Really..." he responded, leaning toward me.

My body trembled with his closeness. "It...it's a beautiful view from...from either side of the river," I stammered, making conversation to distract myself.

"Not as beautiful as my view," he commented, staring at me.

I blushed and pulled my legs to my chest, laying my chin on my knees and looking down at the rock. I couldn't think of anything to say.

"Did I embarrass you?" he asked angelically.

I turned my head and looked at him. He had a slight smile, anticipating my answer. I breathed deep, calming my heart, and replied, "No, I just don't know how to react when someone feels that way about me. I don't see myself the way you see me."

He stood and offered his hand. I took it, and he raised me as he gazed into my eyes. Quietly, he replied, "I wish you could." He paused, just staring at me, and then asked, "Shall we move on?" I nodded and we headed back to the path.

We continued on our walk, nearing the footbridge. As we passed, I pointed it out and realized we were coming to the field. He said he wanted to avoid it, but I didn't want to go back the way we came. There were so many interesting things to see this way. Avoiding the clearing, I led him close to the trees and as soon as we were beyond it, we rejoined the path. Coming upon the remains of a factory, I stopped.

Slipping my arm out of his, I glided over to an old window opening in what was left of the back wall. The moonbeams shone on that spot as if indicating for me to stand there. I glanced back to find him watching me as I stepped inside it and leaned my back against the frame. I gazed through the trees at the moon, its cool light glowing on my face. When I turned my head to look at him, he was standing right beside me.

He moved to the other side of the opening, facing me. Stepping forward, he placed his hand on my back and gently drew me away from the frame. I felt at ease and calm in his arms as I stared into his eyes, though I was so close to him. As if being pulled by an invisible force, I leaned in.

Our lips were mere inches from each other, and my head began to swim as I inhaled his breath. His hand slipped along my jaw as he guided me closer, and I closed my eyes, waiting. He kissed me, his lips like silk as they pressed to mine and made them tingle. Then that sensation spread through the rest of my body, filling me with a something I've never felt before.

He continued unfazed, slow and soft, as he barely parted his lips, and soon my pulse quickened. The warmth emanating from his body made me more eager and I wrapped my arms around him, pressing my body to his. Then suddenly, he pushed me away.

"Careful…" he warned, looking away and breathing heavy.

"Why?" I asked, surprised by his sudden distance.

"You don't know what you are getting in to."

"I d-"

"No, you don't," he interrupted and walked away. "What is the quickest way back?" he asked as he waited for me on the path.

I stood stunned in the window. Why was he acting this way? "It's…it's this way," I replied as I stepped out of the opening and headed toward him.

I crossed my arms and hugged my body, sighing as I walked past him. We were sharing such a magical moment…why did he stop and so abruptly? Maybe it's me. Maybe I'm pushing too much, being desperate. I was too embarrassed to look at him, keeping my head hung as we walked. And he remained quiet, never saying anything more.

We continued around to where we began our adventure. Taking the walkway to the ladder and onto the boulders, we stayed silent. He seemed in a hurry and rather than let me attempt any difficult spots myself, he just took me around the waist and sprinted across them, touching me for the first time since the factory remnants.

"You're not the only one who's agile," he responded to my astonished look as he set me down. His mood seemed better.

When we reached the tracks, he helped me up the fence and then I watched as he climbed it with no problem at all. As he reached the top, he sliced his left arm on a wire that was sticking out, wincing briefly from it. As soon as he was by my side, we walked the bike trail to the park area where we met.

"If you don't mind, I would like to walk you the rest of the way to your car," he requested.

"All right," I agreed, happy to spend more time with him, even though he still seemed distant. "It's just across the street."

When we reached it, I unlocked the door and climbed in to grab the first aid kit, remembering his injury. He gave me a strange look when I turned around with it in my hand. "What's that for?" he asked.

I looked at him, a little confused. "Umm, you cut your arm on the fence back there. Here, let me take care of it so it doesn't get infected." I reached for it and he pulled back. "Let me see it," I commanded as I grabbed his arm. I pushed up the sleeve and stared at the spot where the wound should have been and then looked at him. "Where is it?" Waiting for him to answer, I looked again and even checked his right arm, in case I was mistaken. Nothing.

"I didn't cut myself," he answered as he pulled his sleeves down. I spotted the hole where the piece of fence tore through it at the exact spot I first checked. He gave me a concerned look. "I just tore my shirt."

"I could have sworn you cut yourself," I mumbled, staring at the ground.

"It's been a busy night and you should get home. I'm sure the movie is about over."

Snapping back to reality, I looked at him. Yes, I did need to go because it's bound to be getting close to eleven. "When will I see you again?" I asked eagerly.

"Soon," he replied, grinning.

My heart pounded in my chest. I looked down and fidgeted with my keys. "Do you want my number so you can call and let me know?"

He pulled something out of his back pocket and handed it to me – a cell phone. "I'll call you on this." Noticing my confused look, he responded, "It's safer this way."

I like a man with an air of mystery, but now it's really starting to bug me. I hesitated, but then took the phone without inquiring further and slipped it into my pocket. There has to be a good reason for this.

He took my chin in his fingertips and gently pulled me toward him, softly kissing my lips. Surprised he'd do that again, I stared into his eyes with a quizzical expression. He smiled and my head went all foggy. I think he likes making me befuddled! After a moment, I came out of my haze and turned to unlock the door, spotting his shirt in the back seat.

"David – wait!" I exclaimed before he could disappear. I reached in and pulled it out, handing it to him. "I meant to give this to you last time."

"I've been looking for this. I forgot I leant it to you," he responded as he threw it over his shoulder and turned to leave. "I'll call soon," he remarked, glancing back.

"I'll be waiting," I replied as I watched him fade away into the night.

I sat in my car for several minutes, unable to bring myself to start it. Closing my eyes, I took a deep breath and then slowly opened them. I fumbled with my keys as I slipped them into the ignition, finally ready to go.

As I started the engine, I glanced at the clock to see how much time I had. It was nearly eleven-thirty! I tore out of the parking spot and sped home. Weaving in and out of cars and going over the speed limit, I made it in less time than if I hadn't. I parked and hopped out, giving myself a quick once over and making sure there was no evidence of what I really did tonight.

I dashed up to the house and opened the door slowly, catching my breath as I did. Dad leaned his head over the back of the couch as I entered. "Hey, Meg. How was the movie?" he asked, eyeing me.

I closed the door behind me and stopped at the base of the stairs. "Movie? Oh, good, but not really my cup of tea," I replied.

"I'd like to hear how Claire's date went," he prodded.

"I'm really tired. Can we discuss it in the morning?" I requested, leaning on the banister.

He stared at me, in thought for a moment, and then replied, "Go on to bed; it's been a busy day. We'll talk about it over breakfast."

Pretending as if I was really exhausted, I gave a weak smile and dragged myself up the stairs. When I reached the top, I hesitated, listening for any sign of suspicion. Dad was watching the news quietly, and I assumed Vanessa had gone home since I didn't hear any remarks out of her.

I entered my room and proceeded to change into lounge pants and a tank. Before throwing my clothes in the hamper, I removed the phone David gave me and set it on the bedside table next to the wilting rose. Then I climbed into bed and stared at the clouds on the ceiling.

I replayed the evening in my mind as I tried to wind down, closing my eyes and seeing it all over again. Crossing the boulders, standing on the deck at the quarry pond, sitting on the rocks at the Hollywood rapids, the factory remains, our first kiss...

It had been so perfect, so beautiful...but then he pushed me away. I opened my eyes and tried to remember what he said and as I did, the other things he cautioned came back. His voice echoed in my head, *'Careful...you don't know what you are getting into...it's safer this way'.* What was he getting at?

Struggling to decipher his cryptic warnings, I tried to come up with the obvious. Maybe it has to do with me, that I'm moving too fast for his taste. Or maybe it has to do with Brian, that he's protecting me from him. Or what if it's he himself I should beware?

I need to push it out of my mind. I don't know if I'm scared of this budding relationship or I'm undeserving of happiness or I think it's too good to be true, but I want this to work. No doubts, no second-guesses.

I stared at the ceiling thinking of the more enjoyable parts of the evening. Soon my eyelids became heavy, and I started to drift off into sleep, those pleasant memories transferring into my dreams. Being close, the way he spoke so gentle and sweet to me, his touch, his lips on mine...

That was what lingered the most – the kiss, soft and slow.

# Chapter 7
## Punishment

I slowly opened my eyes and stared at the rose and the new phone, both reminders of David, and smiled. Then my eyes cut to the clock – it was nine. I knew I needed to get up, but spending my day peeling and sticking labels and stamps on Vanessa's invitations just wasn't motivating me enough.

I rolled onto my back and stared at the ceiling, wondering what kind of day to expect. Glancing over at the balcony doors, I found the sun wasn't shining. Good. If I had to be stuck inside most of the day, I didn't want it to be beautiful outside.

I stayed in bed a little while longer and then sighed, forcing myself to get up. No more delaying. I headed to the bathroom, not really interested in showering. But as I brushed my teeth, I rolled my eyes. I have guests coming and, after a night like last night, I needed one.

I hopped in and took my time, finally getting out when the water began to cool. After scanning my closet for something to wear, I threw on my most comfortable lounge clothes. No offense to my friends, but I was not dressing up for them. I braided my hair in pigtails and headed downstairs.

"Your Sunday best, I see," Dad commented as I entered the kitchen.

"Yep. Hope my friends don't mind," I replied as I fixed a bowl of cereal.

"I don't think you'll get any objections out of Ben," he retorted, peeking over his newspaper at me, waiting for a reaction.

"Dad, we're just friends. He knows that," I responded as I shoved a spoonful of cereal in my mouth and leaned on the counter.

He sighed and returned to his paper. "How was Claire's date last night?" he asked, remaining hidden behind it.

As I chewed, I thought of what to say. I swallowed and then answered, "Good. They really hit it off. He asked her out on a second date." God, I hope I'm right. I took another bite, giving myself more time to think if necessary.

"What do you think of him?" he inquired as he lowered the paper and looked me in the eye.

"He's a nice guy, quiet. And polite, to her and me, of course. They have a lot in common surprisingly," I answered, trying to think of my encounters with Justin and how he acted. I felt like I was being interrogated for a crime.

"Maybe he has a friend or brother you can date."

He was fishing for something, but I wasn't going to bite. "Yeah, that'd be nice. Then we could actually double date next time." I grinned, sticking another spoonful in my mouth.

He contemplated his next move as I finished my bowl of cereal. "Are any of your other friends in relationships?"

"No, Ben hasn't found the 'right one' yet and Erin's too picky."

"What's your excuse?"

I stood up and rinsed my dishes in the sink, then put them in the dishwasher. I stared out the window into the garden for a moment and thought about what it could be. "The guys at school are so immature and aren't really interested in me. I'm waiting until college." He was silent. I guess I caught him off guard with that answer. After giving him some time to think up a response and he didn't, I asked, "So what do you plan to do today?"

"Vanessa wants me to go with her to Maymont to scope out the grounds and get ideas on how things could be set up," he replied, folding the paper and placing it on the counter.

"Sounds like fun. Hope it doesn't rain."

"They're not calling for it, just overcast," he responded as he stood. "Well, I better get ready. She'll be here soon to pick me up. She's bringing the invitations, so I would appreciate some help unloading the car when she arrives."

"No problem. I need to start fixing lunch around eleven-thirty, so hopefully everything will be unpacked by then."

"I'm sure it will," he responded, heading upstairs to change.

I settled on the sofa in the family room, flipping through the channels. Sunday mornings were horrible for watching TV; all that was on were television evangelists and infomercials. I flipped to the premium channels and stopped on a movie, though I wasn't in the mood to watch it. I glanced out the window into the backyard and spied a ray of light trying to shine through, but the clouds quickly overtook it. I turned my attention back to the TV and lazily watched it.

Dad came down and joined me on the couch. "What are you watching?" he asked.

"Some comedy, though it's not really that funny. I swear, the quality of movies today isn't what it used to be," I answered, turning it off.

"Aren't we the critic…"

The doorbell rang and he quickly hopped up to get it. Vanessa was at the door with an armful of boxes, begging my dad to hurry and take them. As he did, she let out a big huff and shook her arms wildly.

"You wouldn't believe how heavy those boxes are," she complained.

I got up off the couch and joined them in the foyer. He held the boxes like they were nothing and asked, "Where do you plan to put them together?"

"I'm thinking the family room. It's large enough and close to the kitchen. Plus, we can watch TV or listen to music while we work."

He took them back while I stayed with Vanessa in the foyer. She looked at my attire and smirked. "Nice getup. Would you be a dear and help unload the rest of the invitations from the car?"

"No problem," I answered with a fake smile before heading out the door.

I grabbed as many as I could carry, which was more than Vanessa, and brought them into the house. Dad passed me at the door while she remained in the foyer watching us do all the work. I shook my head and continued into the family room. I met him as I was headed back out, and he informed me he had the last of it. I turned around and looked over what I had to deal with, sighing.

She came over to the boxes and grabbed one item out of each and then called me to the breakfast nook. Taking a seat, she laid them out in front of her on the table. She proceeded to show step-by-step how to assemble the invitations and then turned and looked at me.

"Got it?" she asked, her hand in the air and a condescending look on her face.

"Easy. I'll start separating everything so we can have an assembly line going."

"Good idea," Dad responded, looking over her shoulder at the finished product.

She was not impressed. "Well, anyway, we better get going. We're meeting the wedding planner for lunch, and I really want to get there early so I can gather some ideas to bounce off her."

As they headed out of the nook, I went into the family room and started opening boxes, figuring out what was what. Dad kissed the top of my head as I separated them. "Have fun," he whispered.

"I'll try. You, too," I whispered back, and he rolled his eyes before following Vanessa to the door. I shook my head and continued my work.

When I finally finished sorting, I glanced at the clock and realized I needed to start preparing lunch. I made several different sandwiches, cut into quarters, and stacked on a platter and then covered it with clear wrap. Grabbing a bag of chips out of the cabinet, I set it in a bowl to open later. I pulled out a container of potato salad and set it on the counter.

We needed dessert. I looked through the cabinets at what I could make quick and found angel food cake mix. I whipped it together and threw it in the oven. After setting out disposable dishware, I grabbed the strawberries and blueberries out of the refrigerator and rinsed them off. They would be good as topping or alone.

The timer buzzed and I pulled out the cake, setting it aside to cool. I did a quick once over everything and settled in the family room to wait for my helpers to arrive. The options for TV hadn't improved, so I sat and listened to music, opting for something quiet and soothing.

My attention turned to the garden. It was still dreary outside, but that didn't stop the animals from scampering among the flowers and along the tree branches. Their movement made it seem as if it was snowing white and pink as the petals shook loose and delicately floated to the ground.

As was typical lately, my thoughts turned to David. I feel like I know so little about him, but I don't want to push it for fear I may push him away. I guess I'll just have to learn about him over time. That's what you do in a relationship, gradually get to know someone.

So what do I know about him that I've observed? He only wants to meet at night, his physical appearance changes, he's incredibly swift and agile, and he has a strange effect on me. When I sum it all up like that, he sounds like something supernatural. I laughed to myself. There is no way…things like that only exist in books and movies, not in real life.

Suddenly startled by the sound of knocking on the front door, I quickly jumped up to answer it. Ben was peeking through the sidelight as I approached it. "You're a little early," I commented after letting him in.

"Not by much. What were you doing? I rang the doorbell several times," he replied, following me into the family room.

"Listening to music. I guess I was so caught up, I didn't hear it," I lied, not wanting to tell him I was thinking about David.

He paused, listening to what was playing as he sat on the couch. "Hmm, very soothing."

"I wanted calm, quiet music for a day like today," I responded, sitting cross-legged on my dad's chair.

"So is this what we're dealing with?" he asked, pointing at the boxes. "How many did you say there were…six hundred and sixty-six?"

"Ha, that would explain a lot. No, it's six hundred and six. I laid them out so we can put them together like an assembly line. It'll be quicker and easier that way."

"Where's your dad? I haven't seen him in a long time," he remarked, crouching down and flipping through them.

"He's with Vanessa at Maymont. They've been so busy with this wedding. I'll be glad when it's over, though I really wish it wouldn't happen at all."

"Still not warming up to her, huh?" he asked, glancing over at me.

"I don't think I ever will," I answered under my breath. "Sooo…would you like lunch first or dive right into work?" I asked, avoiding delving into my step-witch issues.

"Let's do lunch first. I skipped breakfast this morning, so I'm really hungry."

We headed into the kitchen and as we fixed our plates, Ben commented on the nice spread. Sitting in the breakfast nook, we occasionally talked about school or the backyard as we ate. Having our fill for the moment, we threw away our trash and washed our hands so we wouldn't get any residue from our meal on Vanessa's precious invitations. Taking our places on the floor of the family room, we began.

We had a nice rhythm going when Ben decided to interrupt it. "So how are things going with *him*?"

"Him, who?" I asked, continuing my part uninterrupted.

"David," he answered, completely stopping his work.

"Oh, good. We met up last night," I replied casually, concentrating on stuffing and sticking.

"Really. So that's two times this weekend. Are you meeting him tonight, too?" he asked as he started stuffing again.

"I don't know. He's going to call to let me know."

"So you remembered to give him your number this time."

"No…he gave me a phone." After the words came out, I could have slapped myself.

He stopped working again. "He *gave* you a phone? Why?"

"I don't know. Maybe he doesn't want to run up the minutes on mine," I answered, working faster.

"Or maybe he's hiding something. See, I told you he was bad news. He doesn't want your dad to know he's calling or he doesn't want to be traced. Is it one of those pay-as-you-go kind?"

"I don't know. And I'm the one who doesn't want my dad knowing we're dating, not him. I don't think he cares if everyone knows," I snapped.

I needed to calm down. Ben was getting me riled up and I was stuffing and sticking so fast, some of the labels could be crooked or wrong. I flipped through them and didn't find any major mistakes, so they were going out as is.

I glanced at him through my eyelashes. He was quiet and still. The song playing in the background droned on about love found and love lost.

"Do you love him?" he asked suddenly.

"What?"

"Do you like him?" he corrected.

"Yeah, I do."

"Have you…kissed?"

I felt a little uneasy answering that question, but I wasn't going to lie. He needed to know I was serious about David. "Yes, we have."

"On your first date?"

"What business is it of yours?" I asked, standing up and going into the kitchen. I poured a drink and glanced at the time. Come on, Erin. When are you going to get here?

"Hey, I'm just looking out for you," he answered, following me. "You won't tell your dad you're dating. What if something happens to you while you're with him or if he hurts yo-"

"David wouldn't hurt me," I interrupted. "And he would contact my dad if something happened. I trust him."

"You've known him, what, a week, and you *trust* him?" he asked, surprised.

"There's something about him…and the way he treats me…" I answered enigmatically.

"I bet you don't even know his last name."

Come to think of it, I didn't. "It hasn't come up yet. So what?"

"Well, if you knew it, you could probably look up some information on him. You can find out a lot about a person on the internet nowad-"

The doorbell rang and I dashed for the door. Thank God, Erin's here! I opened it with a relieved smile and gave her a hug as she entered. I think I caught her by surprise, but then she put her arms around me and hugged back. As I was moving away, I spied her looking at Ben. He was leaning against the back of the couch, arms crossed and brow furrowed.

"I am sooo happy you're here," I whispered in her ear as I shut the door. "He's been giving me hell about David."

She narrowed her eyes at him as we headed his way. He threw his hands in the air and went back to stuffing, grumbling to himself. I led her into the kitchen and watched as she fixed a plate of food, not wanting to be near him at the moment.

I followed her into the family room, and she sat in a chair while I returned to my spot on the floor. I explained the invitation assembly process while she ate so we could get moving as soon as she was done. We were thrown off schedule with his jealous inquiries.

"So Ben, causing problems?" Erin asked once she was done eating, sitting between us on the floor.

"No, I'm just looking out for Megan," he replied.

"Why can't you just be happy for her? She's met this awesome guy who seems to like her a lot and, even though he's a college boy, he's not pressuring her into anything."

"I know, but-"

"No, no 'but'. She's happy, end of discussion," she commanded. "We need to find you a girlfriend," she muttered under her breath.

I chuckled quietly and then she started laughing. Soon he joined in and the air in the room was light again. As our laughter died down, he stood and went into the kitchen to get a drink as she nudged me.

"Ow! What?" I asked, rubbing my rib where she had poked me with her pointy elbow.

"How did Friday's date go?" she whispered.

I glanced over at him and saw that he was headed to the bathroom. I guess he drank too much. "Really well. We met again last night and toward the end of the date, we kissed!"

She quietly squealed with excitement as she grabbed my hands and shook them. "That's great! When are you going out again?"

"I don't know. He's going to call to let me know." I looked up as Ben was entering the room.

"What are you two whispering about…oh, I know. Don't let me interrupt," he goaded.

"Shut up, Ben, and get back to work," she snapped.

"Erin, come on…be nice," I requested.

He sat down and resumed his duties, all of us quiet. We worked together quickly, getting a lot more done since we weren't talking or tormenting each other. We had a good rhythm going when suddenly I felt vibrating at my left hip.

"Aaa! What the heck?" I reached into my pocket and pulled out the phone David gave me and looked at the screen. His name was listed as the caller. "It's David!" I exclaimed excitedly as I answered it.

"Good afternoon, Megan," he greeted. The sound of his smooth voice caused my heart to beat faster.

"What a surprise to hear from you! I…I didn't expect a call for a couple days," I responded as I stood. I glanced at Ben and Erin and smiled apologetically as I left the family room and went out onto the patio. There was no need for them to hear my conversation.

"Do you really believe I would wait that long to talk to you?" he inquired.

I smiled and blushed, tucking my head and kicking a stray pebble. "I hoped you would call sooner, but I wasn't going to hold my breath."

"I had some free time. How are you enjoying this lovely gray day?"

"I'm spending it stuffing invitations for Vanessa with my friends," I responded, feigning excitement. I glanced over my shoulder at the door and was relieved to see that neither Ben nor Erin moved from their spot in the family room.

"Sounds delightful."

"Hardly. And on top of that, one of them, Ben, gave me grief about our hanging out together."

"He doesn't like the fact that we're dating?" David asked.

Oh my God, he admitted we were a couple! "Yeah, but it's his jealousy talking."

"So he's jealous of me. I can hardly wait to meet him."

"Why is that?" I asked, curious.

"To help him get over it. He'll see how happy you are with me, and that I treat you as you should be treated," he responded without hesitation.

"You believe meeting you will stop him from pining over me?"

"Or it could make him more jealous," he replied with a chuckle.

"It's so nice to hear your voice…" I commented dreamily.

"As it is for me to hear yours," he replied and then paused. "I would like to see you again…tonight."

My heart jumped. "I would love to go out again…but I don't know if I'll be able to get away. I don't have any more excuses."

"Then sneak out after your father goes to bed. I'll pick you up wherever you like."

"I don't know…I have school tomorrow…"

"We won't be long, just a couple of hours."

I thought about it for a minute. What the heck; it was only Monday. Most of the teachers are still recuperating from their wild weekends. "Okay…so what do we plan to do tonight?" I asked as I looked down and traced the stone pavers with my foot.

"I know of a nice lake I would like to take you to," he answered.

"A lake? Okay. When should I escape?"

"How about midnight? Your father should be asleep by then, right?"

"Yes, he should," I replied and then told him where to meet me. "Do you know where that is?"

"I'll find it. See you tonight then," he responded and hung up.

I stared astounded into the yard as I held the phone close to my chest. I'm sneaking out tonight to go with David to a lake! I wonder what he has planned. I shouldn't mention this to Erin in front Ben – oh crap! I've completely neglected them! I slipped the phone into my pocket and ran inside. They were in the family room steadily stuffing invitations.

"Sorry, guys. I tried to make it quick," I apologized as I sat in my spot and took care of the envelopes that were piled there.

"What did *he* want?" Ben asked with a sneer.

"Oh…just to talk…see how I was doing," I answered, keeping it simple.

"That's nice of him," Erin commented. "Did he ask you out on another date?"

"Umm…" I delayed, not sure what I should say. My cheeks felt hot. "Yeah, he did…for later in the week," I lied.

"Meeting at the cemetery again?" he taunted.

"No. We're going to a movie."

"On a school night?" he replied, shocked.

"Give it a rest, Ben!" she shouted and he glared at her, then lowered his head and focused on his part of the assembly process.

With the remaining pieces, we worked in silence. As we came to the end, I loaded the completed envelopes into the boxes and set them aside while they helped themselves to more food. I turned on the TV and grabbed a plate for myself, squishing between them on the couch and watching what was on the comedy channel. Soon we were laughing and the previous incident was forgotten.

"So how do you think you did on that English test Friday? I didn't get to ask you after class," Ben questioned as we cleaned up the food.

"I think I'll get an 'A'; it was pretty easy. How about you?"

"I had a hard time understanding the storyline. I'm not big on those old books; I like modern literature."

"Yeah, like stupid comic books," Erin teased, nudging him in the ribs. He grinned at her and she smiled. It was good to see we were back to our old selves.

"At least I read," he retorted.

She glanced over at the kitchen and then turned to me. "Well, I guess it's time we leave," she announced and then looked at him. "Do you need a ride?"

"No, my mom said she'd be here around three to pick me up."

"Works for me. It was fun, Megan. See you tomorrow."

"Thank you for all your help. I really do appreciate it," I replied, walking her to the door. "And thanks for diffusing the situation...twice," I whispered.

"Hopefully, he won't say anything about David in the few remaining minutes he has until his mom arrives," she responded quietly before leaving. I shut the door and went back into the family room, dreading what might happen now that we were alone.

Ben was still on the couch watching TV, not noticing that I entered the room. I sat next to him and waited to see if he'd say anything, but he stayed quiet, laughing occasionally at the program. I relaxed and watched it with him. Several minutes passed and we never said a word to each other, and then suddenly he ruined the moment.

"So when are you really going out with David?"

"Later in the week."

"I know you're lying. You blushed."

I sighed. "Tonight. He's picking me up tonight."

"When do you plan to tell your dad you're dating a college *man*?"

"I don't know...when I'm ready. He's under a lot of stress right now. I can't tell him yet."

He contemplated that for a moment. "Okay, fine. At least promise me you will after the wedding."

I hesitated, but then agreed. "I will." He didn't specifically say when after the wedding...

"You know I care about you," he whispered, gazing into my eyes. Looking into his was nothing like looking into David's. I felt something powerful in the green of his, but Ben's were brown and mundane.

"I know, but as I've said before, I'm a big girl and can take care of myself," I replied, patting him on the shoulder.

"So, what do you know about him?" he asked, fishing for more information.

"He's from Massachusetts, his parents are deceased, he's the outdoors type, and he can't wait to meet you," I threw in to rattle him.

"Really...why?"

"He wants to prove your perception wrong," I responded.

He looked ready to make a snide remark, but once again I was saved by the doorbell. "That'll be my mom," he griped, deciding to refrain as he stood. I followed him to the door, opening it when we arrived.

"Hello, Ms. Galloway. How are you doing today?"

"Oh, good. How's your father and his, um, fiancée?"

"Good, but busy. Would you like to come in and sit for a while?" I asked while Ben discreetly shook his head.

"No, but thank you. I have groceries and the twins in the car. Are you ready, Benjamin?"

"Yes, Mom," he groaned as she stepped off the porch. He hated it when people, especially his mom, used his full first name.

"Well, thank you for all your help. It's been an...interesting day."

"You're welcome," he replied, heading out the door. "Just remember what I said," he commented before turning away and jogging to the car. I waved goodbye and shut the door. Thank God that was over.

I turned off the TV and went up to my room to hang out; I was done with being downstairs. I pulled an old book off the shelf and stretched out on my bed to read it. The quietness and solitude helped me to fully delve into the story.

I loved getting lost in a good book and my mom was the same way. She preferred them to television anytime. When she was alive, we had a special night set aside each week where we all read either as a family or individually. I grew up on the classics and had already read most of the books required for school.

After several chapters, I glanced at the clock to see what time it was – almost five. Dad should be home soon. I laid the book on my bed and headed downstairs to see what we could have for dinner. As I looked through the cabinets, the phone rang. I almost didn't answer it, but then saw it was him.

"I was calling to see if you wanted to join Vanessa and me for dinner at Can Can Brasserie."

"Can Can Brasserie?" I repeated, amazed they'd go there and were inviting me to join them. "Okay. I'll be there as soon as I can. I need to change into something more appropriate."

"We'll see you soon."

I hung up and dashed up the stairs. Quickly scanning my closet, I threw on a nice skirt and top and a pair of low heels. I unbraided my hair and left it down, the molded waves cascading past my shoulders. Grabbing a purse, I slipped my phone and David's phone inside it and hung it on my shoulder. One last glimpse in the mirror and I was ready to go.

I turned on the porch light, unsure of how late we'd be, and locked the front door. Before starting my car, I prayed for a good evening. I'd do my part to try to let whatever negative things Vanessa may say roll off me. Hopefully, she wouldn't try to instigate anything. I sighed and then backed out of the driveway, heading to Carytown.

I didn't think my father had ever been to Can Can Brassiere, but I knew he wasn't too fond of French food, so this must have been her idea. Personally, I've never tried French, but I was open to the experience.

I pulled into a parking spot pretty far from the entrance; it was busy for a Sunday night. I entered and indicated that I was with a party as I scanned the dining area for them. At a table toward the back, I found my father and Vanessa. He looked exhausted, but she was as chipper as ever. I greeted them and took a seat, looking over the menu and determining what to try.

"So how did your little get-together go?" she asked, taking a sip of wine.

"It went very well and we finished before three. I put them back in the boxes, ready for you to mail in the morning, Dad."

"Good. Did you and your friends have fun?" he asked.

"Yeah, except Erin and Ben kept arguing."

"About what?" she asked slyly.

I took a sip of water to stall. "Oh…who was right and who was wrong," I answered as vague as possible.

"Right or wrong about what?" she questioned. She's too curious, but why?

"Relationships," I spilled.

"A relationship you're in?"

My dad looked at me, waiting for the answer, and she smiled. "No, not me," I responded, and he let out a relieved breath. "We've tried to get Ben to go out on a date, but he refuses. He's too picky."

"Maybe you should go out with him, Megan. I'm sure you're just his type," she commented.

"We tried that years ago. Problem is, he's not my type. He's better as a friend," I replied without hesitation and then went back to perusing the menu.

The waitress arrived to take our order and I still hadn't decided on what I wanted, so I asked for her recommendations. What she suggested sounded good, but I was still uncertain. I let Dad and Vanessa order, giving me more time to think.

He chose the roast duck breast, and she ordered the braised lamb, neither sounding very appetizing to me. I finally decided to go with the sole meuniere; that seemed like something I'd enjoy. I took a sip of water as I glanced around the restaurant.

"So how was your day at Maymont," I asked, returning my attention to them.

"Oh, just horrible!" she complained. "The wedding planner was late, and I had to traipse all over that garden in these heels!"

"Really, Vanessa, it wasn't that bad. You knew what we were doing today. You could have worn flats," he retorted, and she gave him a dirty look.

"So now you know the layout. Anything inspire you?" I inquired.

"Oh, lots of inspiration. We have so many changes now."

Dad rubbed the bridge of his nose and then signaled the waitress as she passed to refill his glass of wine. I gave him a look, but he ignored me. "So, what's the occasion for coming here?"

"It was close, and I've heard a lot of good things about this place," Vanessa answered.

She continued to discuss the ordeal she went through in detail. Thankfully, the food arrived and shut her up. As each plate was placed before us, we studied it and then each other's. Satisfied, we began eating.

We enjoyed our meals in revered silence, with only the occasional comment about the flavor or presentation. And as we neared the final bite, the waitress asked if we were interested in dessert. Everyone declined, feeling pleasantly appeased. She left the check and Dad took care of it, and then we happily headed out to our cars. They lingered at hers, but I decided to go on home, telling them goodbye as I walked away.

It was only eight when I got there. I didn't bother looking for something to do downstairs and instead went straight to my room and continued reading the book I started that afternoon. But it was hard concentrating, knowing I'd be meeting David in less than four hours.

He's taking me to a lake...I wonder where. The only lakes I know of are in the city and a few in the county. What does he plan to do there?

Midnight picnic? I guess I shouldn't have eaten so much. A hike? I should plan to wear comfortable clothes.

"Megan...I'm home!" Dad yelled.

"Upstairs!" I yelled back.

I sat up in bed as I heard him climbing the stairs. He poked his head in the door and smiled slightly. "I'm going on to bed. Today was really rough on me and I have an early morning tomorrow. Don't stay up too late reading, okay?"

"No problem. I'll probably pass out in the next hour."

He nodded and then shut the door as he left to go to his room. This couldn't have worked out any better! And with the wine in him, he'd sleep soundly.

I decided it'd be a good idea to take a nap before going so I wouldn't be too tired when I met David. I changed back into my lounge clothes from earlier, set my phone to alarm so I wouldn't disturb my dad, and curled up in bed. No sooner had I closed my eyes, I was asleep.

# Chapter 8
## The Lake

The quiet tinkling of my phone alarm woke me from my slumber. I checked the time and immediately jumped out of bed – I had thirty minutes to get dressed and make my escape. I slipped on a pair of jeans, a dark shirt, and my sneakers and put my hair in a braid. Then I headed to the bathroom and washed the sleep from my face. Before leaving, I peeked down the hall to Dad's room and listened for his familiar snore. Once I heard it, I shut and locked my door and went out on the balcony.

This wasn't the first time I've snuck out of my room. During a more rebellious phase of my life, I decided to go to a party I was forbidden to attend. It was the biggest one of the school year, and I didn't want to be the only person in my class not going. So I waited for Dad to fall asleep and then slipped out. In the end, I didn't stay long, realizing it was overrated.

Climbing down the cherry tree by my balcony and jumping the remaining four feet to the ground, I made my exit like I had that night. I checked the windows of the house to make sure Dad hadn't gotten up and seeing they were still dark, I dashed across the yard.

I scaled the fence and hopped into the neighbor's yard, sneaking across their lawn. A dog barked nearby, but I kept moving. I climbed another fence and after that, found myself on the corner of the intersecting streets where I told David to pick me up. He hadn't arrived yet.

It was dark tonight. Our neighborhood didn't have any streetlamps and clouds mostly hid the moon. I stood at the curb, pulling my sleeves over my hands and fidgeting with them as I glanced up and down the street. Where is he?

Headlights beamed in the distance, and I ducked behind a tree near the fence, not sure who it might be. Soon a black car with dark windows slowly pulled to a stop in front of where I hid. Oh no, I hope it's not one of the neighbors catching me. Pressing my back against the trunk, I held my breath and waited for it to move on.

The low rumbling of the engine remained constant as the car stayed by the curb. Curious why it hadn't left, I peeked around to see who it was. Slowly, the passenger-side window lowered, revealing David smiling at me. Letting out a relieved breath, I moved from behind the tree and walked up to the car.

"What are you hiding from?" he asked with a crooked grin.

"I…I didn't want anyone to see me," I answered as I stood at the door and calmed my heart. "Everyone knows everyone else in this neighborhood. If they saw me out this late, they would definitely mention it to my father."

"I see," he replied, raising the window and stepping out of the car.

Walking around to my side, he gracefully opened the door for me. I blushed as I climbed in and buckled up, not expecting this chivalry. He continued to smile as he shut it, and I watched as he walked around to his side and entered.

Sitting, he turned to me. "Before we go, I must do something."

I gave him a confused look as he pulled something out of his pocket, folding it several times. "Wh-what are you doing?" I asked, concerned, as he held a bandana in front of my eyes.

"It's not that I don't trust you, but rather I want to surprise you," he replied as he leaned close and tied it over my eyes.

He was all around me, his arms on either side of my head and my face close to his as he knotted it. His fingers slowly glided down and around to my chin, stopping there. Feeling his breath on my skin, my lips quivered in anticipation. He gently kissed them, and then I didn't feel him anymore.

The car began moving, and it seemed as if we were traveling incredibly fast. I sighed in disappointment and almost immediately my head became foggy, just like the first night I met him. I needed air. I searched for the window button, trying the wrong one in the process.

"What are you doing?" he inquired as I heard the doors unlock then lock again.

"I…I'd like to lower the window, please. I need air."

Instantly I felt the wind whip around me, and the fog cleared from my mind. "Is that better?" he asked.

"Yes. Now I can think clearly," I responded, attempting to look around but seeing nothing but darkness. "Umm…how fast are you driving?"

"Fast enough," he replied, shifting to a higher gear.

It never felt like he stopped, travelling in one continuous movement. How was that possible? I knew of several lights that should have caught him regardless of his timing or the direction he was traveling. "This is kinda strange. I'm not used to being oblivious to where I'm going."

"Like I said, I want it to be a surprise."

"Are we almost there?"

"A few more minutes and we will be."

I felt him downshift as the car left asphalt and turned onto a gravel road, the tires grinding the earth beneath us. Then it stopped, and a door opened and shut. The muffled sound of his shoes quietly crunching dirt moved from one side to the other. My door opened and he took my hand, helping me out.

He had tied the bandana really well; I couldn't see a thing, not even a sliver of light. Holding my elbow and my arm, he guided me to wherever he was taking me. I was putting a lot of trust in him. After numerous steps, we stopped and I felt him move behind me. He loosened my blindfold and slowly let it drop from my eyes.

Ahead of us was a small dock with a rowboat tied to it, bobbing on a glistening lake. David leaned in, wrapping his arms around my body. "I want to take you out on the lake," he whispered in my ear.

I could hardly move as I felt his body against mine, his breath flowing over my skin. A twinge of excitement rushed through me, making every inch of me sensitive to his touch. I trembled, though I tried not to. He removed his arms and stepped away from me.

"Are you all right?" he asked, still so close. Another quiver reverberated through me.

"Y-yes," I answered. "Just a chill."

He stepped to my side and looked over me. The sensation lingered a moment longer and then disappeared. "Would you like a jacket?"

I smiled slightly and replied, "No, I'm fine. Thank you."

Putting his arm around my waist, he led me to the dock. He helped me into the boat, and as soon as I was seated, he climbed in and took his place at the oars. In the faint light, I watched as he rowed with little effort out into the middle of the lake. The movement was hypnotic, seeing his arms circle as they commanded them to push through the water and his chest flexing with the force he put behind it. He smiled and I looked away, embarrassed he caught me.

The lake was peaceful and quiet. The dunking and dripping of the oars in the water, the crickets in the woods that surrounded us, and the occasional hooting of the owls were all that could be heard. It seemed as if we were in a park, but I could see a few houses hiding among the trees, though all of them were dark.

He pulled in the oars and we floated freely on the water. He stared at me for a moment, then remarked, "I thought you would enjoy this after a busy day."

"This is nice. Thank you," I responded.

His lip curled into a smile and my heart fluttered. "Ah, but even better is this," he teased, lying down in the bottom of the boat. I gave him a funny look, wondering what he was doing. "Join me," he coaxed, moving to make room. I hesitated, then carefully dropped to my knees and stretched out next to him. Gazing into his eyes, I felt an overwhelming happiness being here. "Now look up," he instructed as he turned his face toward the sky.

As I turned to look, my breath was taken away. The clouds parted and were moving out like a curtain opening to a stage, allowing the twinkling stars to shine. They seemed never-ending as they stretched into the blackness of space. Even the waning moon couldn't outshine them. I concentrated on the sky for a long time, trying to find even a single constellation, but had difficulty with all the dots running together.

"This is amazing," I commented after a moment of awe.

"I knew you would enjoy it. I see it quite a bit since I live here."

I propped myself up on my arm, turning toward him. "You live here?"

He folded his arms behind his head, raising it slightly to see me. "Well, not here exactly, but at the far end of the lake. The community is very small and we're pretty well isolated. My roommates enjoy it since they can have their parties and no one complains."

"Is your house lakefront?" I asked as I rested my head on my hands on his upper chest.

"Yes, it is, making it all the more attractive for their little get-togethers."

"Would you ever invite me to one of them?"

"No. They're not something I like to participate in," he answered, delicately tucking a loose strand of hair behind my ear, and my skin tingled.

"Oh…" I responded. "Will I ever get to see your house?" I inquired as I stared out over the water.

"Someday," he replied, removing his other hand from behind his head and holding me.

Lying still, I relished being there in his arms. I sighed happily and cuddled into him, pressing my ear to his chest. Quiet. I moved my head to the center and closed my eyes, listening again. A hollow sound and nothing else. I slid my head back and listened again. Silence. Why couldn't I hear his heart beat?

"What are you doing?" he asked suddenly as I continued to search.

"I want to listen to your heartbeat, but I can't seem to find it."

He sat up quickly, forcing me up as well. The boat rocked uncomfortably with our weight shift. "Why would you want to listen to my heart?"

"I don't know," I answered, fidgeting with my hair. "It's soothing. I thought…"

He looked at me with pain in his eyes. Why? What's so wrong with me doing that? Does he have an abnormal rhythm he's embarrassed about?

"You won't hear it through the thickness of my shirt," he finally responded.

"What about against your bare chest?" I asked, playfully grabbing the bottom of his henley.

"Megan…don't," he commanded, grabbing my wrists.

"I-I'm sorry. I didn't mean to offend you," I apologized and he released me. I scooted to the other end of the boat and stared at my hands, fidgeting.

He sighed, rubbing his face. "You didn't offend me…you just caught me off guard. I'm sorry for reacting the way I did."

Outstretching his hand, he invited me to join him. I smiled softly as I took it, sitting beside him and resting my head on his shoulder. He slipped his arm behind my back and pulled me closer.

Raising my head, our eyes connected and I reached up and touched his chin. He tilted his head down and I closed my eyes, his lips pressing against mine. I opened my mouth slightly and his kiss deepened. I became lightheaded as I breathed him in, but I didn't want to stop. Then he pulled away and turned to the side.

"Is something wrong?" I asked.

"I wasn't prepared for that," he replied, looking up at the sky.

"Prepared for what? The kiss?" I questioned, joking.

"A kiss like that," he responded, turning back and smiling at me.

My heart fluttered as I returned my head to his shoulder, staring at the water. I love being with David. I find peace and happiness when I am. I can't believe anyone wouldn't want that for me, especially after what I went through with my mom and the problems now with my dad. My friends should understand, and they do…all except Ben.

As I sat in a daze watching the ripples distort the reflection of the stars and moon, my conversation with him from earlier crept into my mind, twisting around my thoughts. I don't care if he's looking out for my best interest; he's my friend, not my father. He should support me even though it hurts him to see me dating someone else. He's supposed to be happy for me.

"Megan, why are you so tense?" David asked, noticing my sudden stiffness.

"Ben. He made me so mad earlier, meddling in my business. I don't know if I want you to meet him."

"Don't get yourself worked up over it. Take a deep breath and relax," he cajoled, massaging the back of my neck. With his calm voice and soothing touch, I couldn't help but give in to his suggestions. I closed my eyes as he continued to rub the tension away and gradually I loosened up.

"Thank you. I feel much better," I smiled softly. "I don't know why I let him get to me. It's silly," I commented, remembering his remarks. Then I paused. "But there is something he brought up that I want to ask you."

He lowered his hand, letting it glide down my back and I closed my eyes a moment, enjoying it. "What might that be?" he inquired.

"What's your last name?"

He smiled. "It's Archer."

"David Archer…what a handsome, noble name. And just so this doesn't feel unfair, with me knowing your last name and you being unsure of mine, it's Caldwell."

"All right, Megan Caldwell, if it makes you happy," he responded with a grin and my heart thumped loudly.

He got up and grabbed the oars, getting ready to row. As he put them into the water, I watched intently. I've never rowed a boat before…I wonder if I could do it.

Noticing my curious expression, he smirked. "Would you like to try?" he inquired and I nodded. "Do you know how?" he asked as he guided me to the seat.

"No, but I'm a quick learner," I responded as he sat behind me.

I felt the familiar tingling throughout my body as he showed me how to hold the oars and the motion to move forward and backward. His cool hands were holding mine to the handle, his chest against my back, his head next to mine. Without thinking, I turned and kissed him. I felt him smile, and then he pulled away.

"What?" I asked innocently.

He smirked. "Focus…I want to see you try."

"Okay…like this?" I asked as I dipped the oars into the water and circled around. The boat barely moved.

He chuckled, but then pretended to cough when I narrowed my eyes at him. He placed his hands over mine, grasping them and the handle as he again showed me how to do it. I attempted on my own and this time the boat glided a couple inches.

"Add some more power," he suggested and then grinned. "Use that anger and tension you had earlier."

He leaned back as I added more force. I was able to move the boat several feet that time. I tried again and we moved farther. Soon, I was rowing steadily. I didn't know where I was headed, but I was proud that I was at least moving the boat.

After a while, though, I started getting tired. "How…how did you…not…get tired…rowing so…so far," I panted.

He smiled. "Here, I'll take over," he offered as he helped me to the seat across from him.

He picked up the oars and started rowing with ease toward a curve in the lake. "Where…are we going now?" I asked, my breathing almost normal.

"I want to at least show you where I live," he replied, not at all out of breath.

We came around the bend into a larger area of the lake. Trees lined the shore and were so deep I couldn't tell where they ended. There were very few houses among them, maybe one or two at most. He rowed toward a small peninsula at the far end and then pulled in the oars, letting us float there.

Through the trees, deeply embedded, stood an enormous house. It blended well with the surrounding woods except for the multitude of glass windows covering the back that faced the water, all of them dark.

"This…is where you live?" I asked, astounded.

"Yes."

"Wow…" I looked at the house again and then at him. "So…no wild parties tonight, huh?"

"No, my roommates are out at the moment."

"Are you renting it from someone?" I asked as he started rowing away.

He glanced back at the house and then past me. "No, I own it. I bought it with my inheritance."

"Then why do you let your roommates have so many parties if it's your house?"

"They're good about cleaning up after themselves."

I laughed. "They force you to leave your own home and you're okay with that because they clean up after themselves?"

He smiled. "If they hadn't been having a party the night I happened to go to Hollywood Cemetery, I never would have met you."

I thought about that for a moment and then replied, "Okay, so I guess it's all right to want to lend your house for parties so you can get out and explore the area."

The rest of the trip back, I was quiet as I enjoyed the peace and beauty of the night. He didn't say anything either, seemingly caught up in it as well as we glided across the lake to the small dock where we started.

He pulled in the oars, tied up the boat, and helped me out. He jumped with ease to my side and we headed toward the car, his arm around my shoulders and my arm around his waist. He opened the car door and I took a seat, but before closing it, he crouched beside me and pulled the bandana out of his pocket.

"Wait…what's that for? I thought I didn't have to wear it again."

"Actually, I don't want you knowing exactly where I live just yet," he replied with a smirk.

I pushed out my lower lip as he tied the blindfold over my eyes. He doesn't trust me!

He kissed my puckered lip and then shut the door. I followed the sound of his footsteps as he walked around the car to his side, opening the door and climbing in. The engine growled to life and soon we were speeding down the road. I felt the wind whistling next to me from the cracked window, keeping my head clear.

"What kind of car is this?" I asked, making conversation.

"A Bugatti Veyron."

"Sounds like an expensive European sports car."

He laughed and my heart fluttered. "More or less."

"And you gave me grief about my Audi," I commented, shaking my head.

"You're only seventeen. I'm…eighteen."

"So. That's only a year difference. And I'm mature for my age."

"Sometimes," he chuckled.

I'll show him how immature I am. I started feeling around the dashboard, looking for the radio. I intentionally pressed as many buttons as possible, turning on the air conditioner and messing with his GPS, until I finally hit the right one. I stopped as I recognized Beethoven playing.

"Finally find what you were looking for?"

"Yep, but I didn't expect to hear *Moonlight Sonata.*"

"What did you expect?"

"Oh…bubble gum pop or rage music," I teased.

"Really? Well no wonder you were surprised," he responded, and I could hear the smile in his voice. "This is one of my favorite pieces by Beethoven…so beautiful and heartfelt."

"Yes, but dark and sorrowful," I responded, listening to the familiar piano chords.

"You do know it was a love song written for one of his students," he informed me.

"Really? Wow, I've misinterpreted it all these years," I replied, hearing the love in the notes for the first time. "I've always liked it, too," I smiled, looking down at blackness and fidgeting.

The car came to a stop, and I felt David's hand caress my cheek. He cupped my chin and lifted my face toward his. There was a moment's pause, and then his lips touched mine and we kissed. I could hardly control myself, but he restrained me.

"Megan, calm down. It was only supposed to be a small kiss," he chuckled.

The car was in motion again and soon I felt him making familiar turns. "You're dropping me off where you picked me up, right?"

"Yes, we're almost there."

Sadness came over me as I thought about having to leave him. Such new, intense feelings I'm having for someone I just met. But he's always on my mind and I want to be with him every day. Does he feel the same about me?

The car stopped, and he carefully removed the bandana. As his eyes came into view, I gazed into them and my heart thumped. I didn't want to go.

"Here we are," he announced and I hesitated.

"How do you feel about me?" I asked, trying to maintain eye contact.

He tucked a few strands of hair that had come loose from my braid behind my ear and ran his finger along my chin. "Exactly how you feel about me," was his reply.

"But I don't know what I'm feeling," I contended, looking down so he didn't see in my eyes what was truly in my heart.

"And neither do I," he responded, taking my chin in his fingers and lifting it. "But I think of you often and always look forward to seeing you, being with you," he continued, gazing into my eyes. "From the day we met, I felt a connection...a spark."

I was so elated to hear him say that because I felt it, too. My heart flipped in my chest, and I threw my arms around his neck, hugging him. His arms slowly wrapped around my body, his head bowing as his lips touched my shoulder. The sensation sent a shockwave through me and my heart beat fast. I closed my eyes, anticipating more, but then he lifted his head and gradually released me, the feeling disappearing.

I slowly removed my arms, not ready to let go, but knowing I had to. "Well, I guess I should get going..."

"Yes," he responded quietly before stepping out of the car.

He came to my side and opened the door, taking my hand and raising me up. As he shut it, I moved to the sidewalk. He joined me, placing one hand on my lower back and the other behind my head as he pulled me close.

I closed my eyes, waiting for his kiss, but instead he whispered in my ear. "I will be counting the minutes until I see you again." Then his lips pressed softly to mine, but he pulled away too soon for my liking.

He climbed back into the car, smiled, and slowly drove away. I stood there on that dark corner for several minutes, my heart beating fast, thinking about what he said, and I grinned.

I made my way back to the house, skipping happily across the yard and climbing the tree with ease. I felt so good, so...loved. I never thought I'd feel this way with anyone. Gliding into my room, I shut the French doors and leaned against them, closing my eyes and replaying our evening together.

After a moment, I sighed and opened them. My heart sunk as I spotted the time – two-twenty. I pushed off the doors, changed out of my clothes, and climbed into bed as exhaustion finally caught up with me.

But it was worth it.

# Chapter 9
## Plans

"Megan! Wake up!" Dad shouted, banging on my door. "You're going to be late for school! Megan!"

I fell out of bed, jarred by the abrupt noise. It took a moment to gather my bearings, but once I did, I jumped up and dashed to it. My father stood there, his fist in mid-air as I opened the door.

"Sorry, Dad. I set my alarm but must have turned it off in my sleep," I apologized hoarsely, rubbing my eyes.

"Why was your door locked? You never lock your door at night," he questioned, lowering his arm.

I played dumb. "Oh, was it locked? I didn't realize I did that."

He looked at me suspiciously and then asked, "Did you have someone in your room last night?"

My droopy eyes shot open as he pushed his way inside and started snooping around. "Dad…how could you even think I'd have anyone in my room late at night? I'm not that kind of girl!"

He was on his knees looking under my bed when he stopped and stood up. "I'm sorry, Meg. It's just you've been acting so strange lately…like you're hiding something from me."

"I'm not. Honest," I lied. It felt so wrong, but I'd rather feel guilty than have to live without seeing David. "Now I need to get ready for school," I announced, ushering him out of my room.

I closed the door and fell against it, sighing as I heard his footsteps fade away as they headed downstairs. My secret was safe. I quickly made my bed and rushed into the bathroom to shower. After a quick scrub down, I ran back into my room and threw on my clothes. Hurriedly brushing my hair, I decided to put it up in a bun so I wouldn't have to deal with it. I slipped on my shoes, grabbed my book bag, and dashed down the stairs.

Dad was at the counter in the kitchen with a glass of juice set aside for me. I grabbed it and gulped it down. "Thanks, Dad," I remarked, kissing his cheek and running to the door.

"Have a good day!" he shouted as I shut it.

I sped off in my car, really testing its power as I maneuvered through traffic to get to school. I whipped into a parking spot and sprinted into the building, entering first period just before the bell. Taking my seat, I tried to control my breathing as I pulled out my Biology book.

"Psst!" Claire quietly hissed. I pretended to get something out of my bag as I glanced at her. "Why are you late?" she whispered, doing the same.

I sat up and turned my head slightly to answer her. "Overslept," I whispered back, trying to focus on the teacher as he began his lesson. "We'll talk about it later."

That seemed to satisfy her until the bell rang for the next class. I gathered my things and rushed out the door, Claire right behind me. Five minutes was not enough time to tell her what I wanted her to know and get to class on time, so I summed it up as best I could when she asked why I overslept.

"I went out with David early this morning."

She looked at me, stunned. "This morning?"

"Well, he picked me up at midnight and I got home after two," I corrected. "Listen, I'll tell you more about it at lunch." And then I left so I could get to my next class on time.

The rest of the morning flew by, the rushed feeling still driving me through my day. I hurried to the lunchroom and grabbed a salad, sitting at our usual table by the window. Having that moment to finally slow down, I realized the sun was shining. The warmth felt good on my face as I stared into the trees on the other side of the glass.

"So you went on a date last night…how'd it go?" Claire asked, interrupting my meditation.

"I had to sneak out of the house to meet him, but it was great."

"Where did you go this time?" she inquired. "You two are so adventurous!"

"He took me out on a lake in a rowboat."

"What happened?" Erin asked as she took a seat next to me. Ben was right behind her.

"Wow, Megan. You look great," he commented as he sat across from me.

"Ugh, I think I look terrible. I didn't have time to do much of anything this morning."

"Why is that?" Erin asked, nibbling on a chicken nugget.

"I was out late last night, so I overslept this morning."

"What were you doing out so late? I can't believe your dad would let you go, especially on a school night," she commented.

I hesitated, not sure I wanted to reveal how late my date was with David in front of Ben. "Her dad didn't know…she snuck out to meet David!" Claire revealed.

He glared at me from across the table. "How late did you go out?" he asked.

"Thanks, Claire," I remarked, cutting my eyes to her.

She grinned. "No problem."

"Well?" Ben pushed and I sighed.

"Midnight. He wanted to meet at midnight."

He looked at me in shock. "What?"

"So tell them what the two of you did," she coaxed excitedly, snubbing him.

I sighed again. "He took me out on a lake in a rowboat," I answered, not as excited as her.

"What lake?" he asked, wanting to get a question in that I'd answer.

I blushed, thinking back to last night. "I…I don't know."

"Well, what was nearby? There had to be something familiar," he insisted.

My cheeks became hotter. "I didn't see anything…I was blindfolded."

"What?" all three exclaimed.

The cafeteria went quiet for a moment and I tucked my head, completely and utterly mortified. When I didn't say anything, voices began buzzing again. "It was to surprise me," I replied finally. I wasn't going to mention the real reason why he did it.

"Aww, that's sweet," Claire remarked, helping my embarrassment to wane.

"So what's so great about this lake that he'd take you to it?" Ben asked, stabbing at his food.

"It's where he lives. He has a huge lakefront home at the far end of it."

"Did you get a personal tour?" he questioned bitterly.

I can play this game. "Oh, yeah," I lied. "And it was unbelievable, especially his bed-"

"I should tell your dad what you did," he snapped.

"No, please! Look, I was just playing with you. I didn't go inside his house. David actually discouraged it. He showed it to me from a distance and then we left. Nothing more."

Erin and Claire sat with their mouths agape, surprised I'd lie like that but also give in to him. "I'm still holding you to the promise we made," he threatened, getting up to leave.

"Where are you going?" I asked.

He looked outside and then at us. "I need some air. See you in English." Then he left.

"What's up with him?" Claire asked.

I turned back to them and huffed. "Over-protective."

"Megan, what promise did you make to him?" she asked curiously.

"Oh, he just asked me to tell my dad about David after all the wedding stuff was over. I agreed to it, figuring I should be ready by then."

"That's simple enough. Oh, I forgot to get after you…why didn't you call me Sunday?" she questioned, slapping my arm. "Erin told me about your date on Saturday. I can't believe you didn't call to tell me you had your first real kiss!"

"I'm so sorry. Sunday was crazy – Ben was being a total pain, David called in the middle of the day to ask if I could meet him that night, and then Dad invited me to dinner," I explained.

"Well, we have some time now. What happened?"

"We walked around Belle Isle, talked at the pond, relaxed on the boulders at Hollywood Rapids, and then he kissed me at the factory remnants."

"Sooo, what was it like?" she asked anxiously.

"Better than I ever imagined," I answered dreamily.

"Well…" Erin encouraged.

"I was standing in the empty frame of a window staring at the sky when he came over and stood across from me. He put his arms around me and pulled me closer, kissing me. His lips were so soft and inviting…"

They sighed, longing for a similar experience. "Go on," Claire pushed.

"I kissed back, but then he stopped. It was strange..."

"Why is that?" Erin inquired.

"He told me to be careful, and when I asked why, he responded by saying I didn't know what I was getting into."

"He's just being a gentleman, Megan," Claire assured me.

"So you just went out on the lake last night and looked at his house?" Erin prodded, changing the subject back to the juicy stuff.

"No, not *just* that. Lying side by side, we floated gently on the water and looked at the stars. It's so beautiful and serene where he lives. We kissed some more and talked…oh, and he taught me how to row."

"You have the strangest dates. Will your next one be at his place since he showed it to you?" she inquired.

"I don't know. Probably not, though he said he would have me over someday."

"Any other juicy details you'd like to share?" Claire asked.

"No, not really," I responded, ready to change the subject. "So how did your date with Justin go?" I asked, trying to distract from my love life.

"We had so much fun! And we're going out again this weekend."

"That's great! Where is Justin today? I haven't seen him," Erin asked, eating her dessert.

"He apparently caught a bug. He was feeling better this morning, but not enough to come to school. He'll definitely be here tomorrow," she responded and then stared at her remaining tater tots. "Is it all right if he sits at our table?" she asked.

"Sure, the more the merrier," Erin and I agreed and she smiled. Hopefully, Ben won't have a problem with another male.

The bell rang, and we left to dump our trays and head to the next class. I walked to the gym with Erin as Claire headed in the opposite direction. I didn't see Ben but hoped he was better. I don't like when he's mad at me, but then again he has no right to treat me like a juvenile delinquent.

We changed and did some warm-ups before going outside on the field to play soccer. I was hoping we'd be able to do something fun in the fresh air. As we set up, I looked at Erin and smiled as she got psyched up for the scrimmage. I loved sharing gym with her. She was so athletic and we worked well together on a team.

Coach Riser selected us to be forwards and in the first half, we scored and assisted four goals. In the second half, we were defense and no one could get a ball past us. Coach called game six-two, our team winning. We were dismissed to the locker room to change, and then it was on to our next class.

The rest of the day was uneventful. Trigonometry was tedious as usual, but Latin was at least fascinating. We were learning about mythology. I dreaded going to English because of Ben, but when I entered the room and saw him smile at me, I felt better. Maybe it was finally dawning on him that we weren't meant to be. Maybe he's accepted my relationship with David.

I took my seat and opened the required reading for this week – *The Great Gatsby*. I started perusing the chapters before class officially began, excited to study another classic and one I hadn't read before. The teacher droned on about what we'd be focusing on and had us use the remainder of the class to read. It looked more like she wasn't in the mood to teach and wanted quiet time.

When class was over, Ben caught me as I packed my things away. He apologized for his behavior earlier and asked if he could walk with me to my car. I agreed, and we stopped by my locker before heading out to the parking lot. There wasn't a lot of talking between us as we walked, but as soon as we reached my car, he couldn't contain it anymore.

"I want to take you out to dinner…this weekend. Are you free?"

Guess he's not ready to accept David. "Ben," I replied, exhausted from his many attempts to get me to go out with him, "I'm already in a relationship. It's very kind of you, but no."

"No, no. As friends…honest. Just a casual dinner, you and me."

"I don't know. I'm not sure it's a good idea. Maybe if you invite Erin and Claire and Justin, I'll come."

"Why not David, too?" he questioned.

I looked at him, trying to figure out what he was planning. "Okay…I'll ask the next time he calls me."

Claire and Erin joined us. "What're you two talking about?" the latter inquired, leaning against the trunk.

"I was asking Megan if we could all meet for dinner. Is everyone free Friday?" he asked. I smiled at him, happy he conceded.

"I am and I think Justin is, but I'll check. It'll be nice to go out together. It's been awhile," Claire answered.

"Let me check my calendar," Erin joked, pulling out a planner. "Yep, nothing as usual."

"So…how about it, Megan?" he questioned, turning to me with an expectant look.

"Sure, it'll be fun."

"Now don't forget to invite David. We're all looking forward to meeting him," he reminded me, smiling slightly.

"David might join us? That'd be awesome!" Claire exclaimed.

"Well, we'll see. He may be busy. I'll let you know as soon as I do."

I opened my car door, hoping they'd get the hint to leave. When they didn't, I announced, "Well, I better get home. I have a lot of homework to do."

"Yeah, me, too. See you tomorrow!" Erin responded, walking toward her car.

"I'll tell Justin our plans for Friday when I call him tonight. I'll call you later, Megan," Claire commented, waving goodbye.

"You got your way. See you tomorrow," Ben remarked as he walked away.

I climbed in the car and started it, backing out of the parking space and thinking about this whole get together. I'd love for David to come and put Ben in his place, but then I wasn't sure I really wanted them to meet. Ben would probably make such a fool of himself I'd feel bad for him, though he didn't deserve my pity.

A horn honked behind me, jolting me from my thoughts. I glanced in my rearview mirror, seeing Claire smiling at me. I waved as I pulled out.

When I got home, I gathered my things and went inside. It was true I had a lot of homework to do, though I wasn't anxious to do it. Giving in, I decided to get it over with, doing it outside since the weather was so nice. Laying all my books out on the patio table, I set to work.

Between subjects, I paused and stared into the garden. I watched as the petals fell from the trees, making room for the new green leaves to sprout. White, pink, and purple blossoms were sprinkled around the yard from the many flowering trees Mom had planted. Every spring, she and I would dance in the falling petals, but now all I did was sit and watch them drop.

Not today.

I stood up and went to a small grove where the petals were falling and danced like she and I used to. It felt good to do it after all these years. I bet she was looking down on me and smiling. I wish she was here…

"Megan…what are you doing?" Dad asked, standing in the doorway.

"Dad!" I exclaimed, stopping and grabbing my chest as I faced him. "I was…I was just…dancing," I answered, embarrassed he caught me.

"Uh huh…did you finish all of your homework?" he asked as I rushed to the patio table.

I gathered up my books and papers and headed toward him. "Yeah, I just have to read the first three chapters of *The Great Gatsby*, but I'll do that before I go to bed," I replied, setting them on the kitchen table and packing them away. "So what's for dinner?"

Dad whipped together a simple meal of shrimp and spinach with bowtie pasta. As we ate, we discussed how our day went and I mentioned that Ben wanted all his friends to get together and go out to dinner Friday. He seemed okay with the idea and agreed to let me join them. Ben would be happy I have my father's blessing. When we finished, I cleaned the table and dishes.

I hung out in the family room with Dad for a while, reading my book for English and half-listening to the news. There was another reported murder by the serial killer plaguing the area. This time, it was a young man who was killed. He was a second-year student at VCU and his body was found like all the others – in a park, decapitated and drained of blood. I instantly thought of David and shuddered. I hope he was safe.

Tired of reading and listening to the news, I kissed Dad on the cheek and told him I was going up to my room to get ready for bed. As I climbed the stairs, my worry over David's safety consumed my mind. What if the killer goes after him?

Entering my room, I couldn't stop thinking about it. I picked up the phone he gave me and checked to see if he called, but he hadn't. I sat and sighed, wanting to hear from him. Then my phone rang and I quickly answered it.

"Told ya I'd call," Claire greeted.

I sighed. "How's it going? Got all your homework done?"

"Yeah. Just hanging out in my room. Is something wrong? You sound funny."

"No…well, yes. You know those serial murders the reporters keep talking about?"

"Yeah…the ones by the Richmond Parks Ghost?"

"Uh, what?"

"That's what they're calling him since no evidence has ever been found. Like something supernatural is doing it."

"Oh…well anyway, there was another victim…male this time. From VCU."

"That's a strange shift in pattern. He's keeping the cops on their toes."

"How do you know it's a guy?"

"That's the most probable. There are very few female serial killers…"

"You need to go work for the FBI or something," I muttered, shaking my head.

She laughed and then asked, "So why does it matter that the victim was male?"

"What if David is in danger?"

"I'm sure he's fine. He doesn't live on campus. It says here in the article I'm reading online that the victim lived in the dorms, as did most of the others."

She had a point. "You're right. I'm sure he's fine."

"So, tell me more about your two dates with David," she asked, thankfully changing the subject and getting my mind off my worry.

"There's not a whole lot more to tell. Just more strange things."

"That works, too."

"I thought you told me not to nitpick him."

"I know, but it's still interesting to hear about. Tell me, please."

I thought about it for a moment while she begged. "All right," I conceded. "I noticed a lot on Saturday."

"Like what?"

"To begin with, he's extremely quick and agile and has no trouble seeing in the dark."

"Maybe he has super powers..."

"Come on, Claire, be serious."

"Okay, okay. Maybe he's an athlete and ate lots of carrots. What else did you notice?"

"Well..." I hesitated, not sure if I wanted to tell her about what happened as we were leaving Belle Isle. She might think I'm crazy.

"Yeeeaaah..." she coaxed and I gave in.

"I swore he cut himself on the fence by the train tracks, but when I checked his arm, there was a hole in his shirt, but no cut."

"It was dark, right?"

"For the most part. There was some moonlight..."

"Dark enough then, with shadows? You probably couldn't see as clearly as you thought," she rationalized.

"I could have sworn..." I mumbled, the incident replaying vividly in my mind. I shook it from my head and sighed. "I feel like I want to find something. Should I be concerned?"

She was quiet. "No, I don't think so. This is your first real relationship and it's all so new to you. Don't think too much abo-"

"Oh, hold on Claire," I interrupted. "My other cell phone's ringing."

"What other cell phone?" she questioned as I answered the one David gave me.

"Good evening, Megan," he greeted, his voice silky.

"Oh David, I'm so glad you called. Can you hold a moment? Thanks!" I switched to my phone. "Hey Claire, I have to go. It's David."

"Wait! What's this other phone you have?"

"He gave it to me on Saturday. Thanks for the talk…see you tomorrow," and I hung up. "Sorry about that. I was talking to Claire."

"Oh, I didn't mean to interrupt."

"No, we were finished anyway. I'm so happy to hear from you," I gushed.

"Really…why?"

I hesitated, not sure if I should say. "Well…I heard about this murder on the news tonight…a college student…"

"I'm fine, Megan. You don't have to worry about me."

"I know…it just…scared me."

"No harm will come to me, believe me." That's an odd thing to say. "So how was school today?" he asked, changing the subject.

"Same old, same old. We started a new book in English, *The Great Gatsby.*"

"I see your teacher has fine taste. Are you enjoying it so far?"

"I'm only three chapters in, but yeah, it's good," I replied, twisting my shirt around my finger. There was nothing else really interesting that happened the rest of the day except Ben's dinner request. I wonder how David will react to that news. "Ben asked me to dinner on Friday…"

"Well, I guess we will have to make plans to go out so you can regretfully decline."

"No, it's not like that. A bunch of us are going and Ben even asked if you're able to join us. Are you free?"

He was quiet. "Yes, I believe so."

"Good. So…do we plan to get together anytime this week?"

"Are you available Wednesday?"

"Yep. What do you have in mind?"

"Hmm, nothing yet. Any suggestions?"

"The mall…a walk downtown…ooo, how about coming over to my house. My dad has a dinner date with Vanessa and her parents. We could watch a movie together or something."

"Sounds ideal. What time should I arrive?"

"Is eight good for you?"

"It would be perfect."

I gave him my address and mentally started making plans for that evening. "Well, I better get to bed. It's getting late."

"Sweet dreams, Megan. I will call again tomorrow night."

"Good night, David," I replied and hung up the phone.

I slouched down into my bed and stared at the ceiling, thinking about David and wondering if he was thinking of me. Never in my teenage life did

I think I would ever fall for someone so hard. I closed my eyes and smiled. He was coming over to my house…I could make him dinner and we could stroll in the garden afterward. I was so giddy with excitement I could barely contain it.

But I did as Dad knocked on the door and entered. "Why are you grinning ear to ear?" he asked, sitting on the edge of the bed.

"Oh, I was just talking to Claire and she was telling me a funny story," I fibbed. I was getting good at this. Too good.

"Anyway, I wanted to say good night."

"Good night, Dad," I replied hurriedly, wanting to get back to my daydreaming.

He stood up and patted my head, smiling. "Good night, Megan."

As soon as he left, I turned off my light and settled into bed, ready to sleep. I rolled over to my side, staring through the sheer curtains at the balcony. I blinked several times and soon didn't bother opening them. My mind continued running, not ready to shut down. Images swirled around and thoughts became dreams.

I woke to a faint sound outside on the balcony. I got up, a little groggy, and stumbled across the room to the doors. As I opened them, I noticed a figure leaning against the railing staring at the garden. It glanced over its shoulder at me, and I realized it was David.

I walked toward him and asked, "What are you doing here?"

He smiled and my heart skipped as it usually does with him. "I wanted to check on you," he answered, taking my hand and gently pulling me into his arms as he kissed me.

It took a moment for his response to register as I stumbled back. "Check on me? But why?" I asked, gazing into his eyes. The dim lights from the garden barely made his face visible, but I could find them easily.

"Because I wanted to," he replied, leading me over to the chaise and indicating for me to lie down. He kneeled at my side and kissed me again, gently caressing the side of my face. "I will always watch over you," he whispered. "Now sleep."

I tried to resist but couldn't fight it. His fingers continued to caress my cheek and then gradually faded away. As my eyelids slowly lowered, I saw him perched on the railing, looking back at me. I wanted to ask if he was leaving, but the words failed me. A soft thump was the last thing I heard.

# Chapter 10
## The Dinner

I woke the next morning to the loud chirping of birds and found myself lying on my chaise on the balcony. Why was I out here? I sat up and held my head, recalling last night. I heard a noise and went to the doors. David was here, on my balcony. I glanced over at the spot where he had been standing.

Was it a dream? It felt real, but it all seems so hazy. It doesn't make sense why he would come here in the middle of the night. I must have actually walked out and curled up on the chaise in my sleep. But I've never been a sleepwalker before…

I shook it off, deciding it was a dream, and went into my room, shut the doors, and got ready for school. I grabbed my things and headed downstairs to find something for breakfast. Entering the kitchen, I found Dad in his usual spot with his paper and coffee. I fixed a bowl of cereal and joined him at the island.

He put his paper down and looked at me. "You're up early," he commented, checking his watch.

"I know. I must be anxious to get to school," I replied, taking a bite.

"Did you sleep well?" he asked, making conversation no doubt.

"Yeah…except at some point, I went out on the balcony and slept on my chaise."

"You must have been having a really vivid dream. Care to talk about it?"

"Mmm, not really. There's nothing to talk about. I…I barely remember it," I responded. But I did, and David was there. "Did you sleep well?" I asked to distract him.

"Quite well. Good thing since I have a major case I'm working on."

"Oh, the exciting world of corporate law," I commented sarcastically before putting another spoonful in my mouth.

"And that will be my cue to get going," he responded, folding his paper and rinsing his cup.

"Hey, I'm sure it has its days," I conceded. I hopped down from the stool and went to the sink to clean my bowl.

"It does, but I do have to get going. I'll see you tonight."

"Okay. Have a good day," I replied as he left the room. I loaded the dishes in the dishwasher and headed out the door to school.

The day was like any other school day and dragged on too long. Lunch was interesting now that Justin was part of the group. He and Claire sat close, but not all over each other. The relationship was still in the early stages, so it made sense. I wasn't big into public displays of affection, so I'd probably act the same way with David. But when we were alone, I wanted to be close to him, holding and kissing him…

"Earth to Megan…are you there?" Erin asked, shaking me.

I turned my attention back to the conversation. "Sorry, what?"

"We were just discussing where we wanted to go Friday, you know, for dinner. Any ideas?"

"Umm…what about that restaurant in the mall?"

"Ooo, we could go shopping afterward!" Claire replied excitedly.

The boys looked at each other, rolling their eyes, and we laughed. "Don't worry, you won't suffer alone. David agreed to come. You three can have some quality guy-time together," I announced.

"That's awesome!" Claire exclaimed. "I can't wait to meet him!"

"Me, neither," Ben muttered, not as excited about it as her.

The rest of lunch was spent discussing what stores we wanted to hit while we were there. The bell rang and it was on to the next class. The rest of the day flew by, probably because my mind was so occupied with planning for Wednesday and Friday. At the end of the day, Ben and I met up with the rest of the gang as we walked out to the parking lot. Everyone was still buzzing about Friday, but I decided not to linger, saying my goodbyes and taking off for home.

It was another beautiful evening, so I decided to do my homework on the patio again. I finished earlier than last night and decided to make dinner. Dad arrived just as I was turning everything off. I filled a plate and set it in front of him, then made mine and sat.

"Looks good, Meg," he commented, digging in.

We ate in silence except for the occasional question about school or work. I cleared the table when we finished and took care of the dishes as he went into the family room and did the same thing he does every night – turn on the TV and watch the news. Not wanting to hear about the world's problems, I headed upstairs. I had three more chapters to read and David would most likely be calling soon.

I stretched out on my belly on the bed and started to read. The book was getting better, but I really wasn't in the mood. I finished the chapter I was working on and set the book on my nightstand. Deciding to read something more for entertainment purposes, I picked up the one I started over the weekend. I had read it several times, but there was always something new I never noticed before. I was deep into it when David's phone rang.

"Hello, Megan, how are you this evening?"

"Good, I'm just reading."

"Your book for English?"

"No, I wasn't in the mood for it tonight. I returned to the book I started a couple days ago – *Interview with the Vampire*."

He was quiet. "Interesting choice," he commented finally.

"I've read it about three times before now. Louis is such an intriguing character, fighting to maintain his humanity even though it's a losing battle. Have you ever read it?"

"Once. It's an interesting work of fiction, but I prefer the classics like *Dracula*."

"Hmm…I've read that, too. Fascinating use of storytelling through other means, like letters and diary entries," I responded, setting the book aside and rolling onto my back. "So enough about books…we decided where we're going to dinner on Friday. We're meeting at the mall and eating at the burger restaurant there."

"What time?"

"Five o'clock. Are you picking me up or meeting us there?"

"I'll meet you there. Are we still on for tomorrow night?"

"Yes and I can't wait."

"Neither can I," he replied and then there was silence. I could make out muffled talking and then suddenly he came back on, startling me. "I need to go. I'll see you tomorrow, around eight. Good night, Megan."

"Good night, David," I whispered, just in case my dad was nearby. I hung up and returned to my book.

Dad came by a few minutes later to tell me good night and then went to bed. I turned off the bedside lamp and stared at the wall. Again, I had trouble going to sleep. I snuggled into my comforter, hoping the warmth would cause it to come faster. It worked.

*I was in Hollywood Cemetery, running toward something, someone…*

*Maneuvering between the graves, my lilac gown flowed behind me as I dashed to the crypt. I stopped abruptly, spying him waiting for me. Standing at the base of the stairs was David, dressed elegantly in a tuxedo. He smiled at me and I smiled back, my heart racing from running and seeing him. I rushed into his arms, so happy to be with him.*

*He gently released me, taking my hand and waltzing with me to phantom music in the moonlight. My eyes remained locked on the stunning emerald of his. Then he dipped me suddenly, leaning in to kiss me, but instead he moved to my neck. His cold lips on my skin sent a shiver through me, but I liked it. I closed my eyes as I felt them part, holding my breath as my heart raced. Then he faded away and I opened them.*

*As he slowly pulled me up, his lips glistened red…*

I gasped as I woke, sitting up straight in bed. Squeezing my eyes shut, I quickly opened them again, giving them time to adjust to the sunshine pouring into my room. I rubbed my face and then glanced at the clock. Reaching over, I turned off the alarm before it sounded. Then I fell back onto my pillows and stared at the ceiling, thinking about the dream.

It must have been because of the book.

I glanced at the clock again and climbed out of bed, heading into the bathroom to get ready for school. Dressed and prepared for the day, I grabbed my book bag and went downstairs. I was surprised to find Dad missing from his usual spot. A note on the counter informed me he had to get to work early and he'd see me tonight before going out with Vanessa.

I poured a glass of juice, drinking it as I stared out the window. David was coming over tonight. My heart fluttered and I sighed. I put my glass in the sink and snatched my book bag as I headed out the door.

I met Claire at my locker and told her about my plans for the evening. She was excited for me and made a few suggestions as we entered class. As I took my seat, she babbled on about something her brother did, continuing even through the morning announcements, but then stopped suddenly when the teacher stood and walked to the front of the class.

Like yesterday, my day flew. By lunch, I was busy planning the menu for tonight and didn't pay too much attention to the conversation. I responded when asked a question, but I couldn't say what the topic du jour was. When the bell rang signaling the end of the period, I gathered my trash and quickly left for my next class.

The final bell rang, snapping me out of my daydream. Had the day gone by that fast? Ben stopped me before I could race out the door. "Where have you been all day?" he asked, grabbing my arm. I looked down at his hand and he let go.

"I've been here. Didn't you see me at lunch?"

"Not mentally, you haven't. What's going on?"

I didn't want to get into it with him right now. As we walked to my car, I told him I was distracted by my dad's wedding. He seemed to buy it, knowing how much I despised Vanessa and the fact she was marrying my father. Erin, Claire, and Justin joined us and the conversation shifted to our get together Friday.

After a half hour, I informed the group I had to leave. I told them I had a lot of work to do, which wasn't entirely a lie. The group broke up and we headed out. When I got home, I rushed through my homework so I'd at least have that out of the way. Dad arrived as I was finishing Trig.

"All done, I see," he stated, sitting next to me at the patio table.

"Reading is all I have left," I replied, packing away my books and papers.

"So what are your plans for tonight? Anything special?"

I closed my book bag and dropped it to the ground. "Nope, just the reading, maybe some TV. I'll probably call Claire before I go to bed."

"Sounds like a fascinating evening. It could be worse – you could be going to dinner with Vanessa and her parents."

"You'll have fun, I'm sure. Just don't drink too much."

He gave me a dumbfounded look. "It's a stressful situation. I've only met them twice before this. Why is that? What if they don't like me?"

"They like you," I encouraged. "If for nothing else, for your money," I muttered under my breath.

He looked away, ignoring my comment undoubtedly. "Well, I guess I better get ready. I don't want to show up late."

I followed him into the house and up the stairs and there we broke off, him going to his room and me to mine. I put my book bag at my desk, taking out my book for English, and then headed back downstairs. Stretching out on the couch in the family room, I started to read, having some chapters I needed to catch up on since I skipped them last night.

By the time I finished, Dad was coming down the stairs. He was dressed in a nice suit, ready to impress. As he headed to the door, he informed me he'd probably be late. Perfect – that will give David and me more time together.

I pushed him out, telling him he'd be fine and not to worry about me. He gave me an unsure look and then turned to leave. Closing the door, I leaned my back against it and listened for his car. As soon as I was sure he was gone, I ran into the kitchen and pulled out the items I needed to make the meal I selected.

While everything simmered and baked, I prepared the table in the formal dining room. I planned to use our best china and silver; I wanted to impress him. As I pulled the dishes from the hutch, I thought of the last time we used this room. It was after Mom's funeral. A lot of friends and family came to honor and remember her that day...

The stovetop sizzled as something overflowed, and I snapped back to the present. I ran into the kitchen, stirred the vegetables, and removed them from the burner. Pouring them into a decorative dish, I moved it to the counter to wait for the other items. While there, I checked the steaks and roasted potatoes – almost done.

Heading back into the dining room, I finished setting the table and then grabbed two crystal candlestick holders out of the cabinet and set them at either end of the table, inserting burgundy tapers into them. I'd light them right before he arrives. With everything the way I wanted it, I went back into the kitchen to finish preparing the main course and start making dessert.

It was twenty till eight when I put the last item on the table. I gave the room another once over, then ran up the stairs to change into something nicer. I slipped into the strapless red dress I wore to homecoming last year and applied a little bit of makeup to highlight my eyes and lips before letting my hair down. I dampened it to rejuvenate the curls and took one last look at myself as I put on heels and then headed downstairs.

With less than ten minutes until his arrival, I lit the candles in the dining room, turned off the lights in the kitchen, and waited in the living room by the front door. I fidgeted with the satin of my dress, smoothing it out over my thigh. Outside, the sound of a car door shutting alerted me. That has to be him.

Standing by the front door, I patiently waited, a little nervous. I listened for footsteps, anticipating his approach, but never heard any. Then suddenly, the doorbell rang and I jumped. I composed myself and slowly depressed the handle, opening the door.

David's head was bowed as I moved into the doorway. As usual, he looked dashing wearing a fitted dress shirt with the sleeves rolled up to his elbows and gray dress pants. He lifted his green eyes to look at me and froze, astonished. Of course, I blushed.

"Hello Megan," he greeted with a smile. "You look amazing."

My heart skipped a beat and my blush deepened. "Thank you," I responded as I moved out of the way, expecting him to enter, but he didn't. I looked at him a moment and then invited, "Would you please come in?"

He nodded once and entered. "This is a beautiful house," he commented as we walked through the foyer toward the dining room.

"Thank you again. I'll give you the grand tour later," I replied as I slid open the pocket doors. "Here we are…" I motioned for him to sit, but he remained in the doorway.

"You didn't have to go to all this trouble," he commented, ashamed.

"I wanted to…there's filet mignon, roasted herb potatoes, and steamed vegetables. And for dessert, I made cheesecake."

"No, really. You shouldn't have. I'm not hungry."

"Oh…" I didn't know what else to say and felt a little embarrassed.

"It's all right," he assured, taking my hand in his cool one and leading me to a seat. "You did a lovely job and I'm sure it's delicious. I'll gladly sit with you while you eat."

"Okay. We can do that," I consented, somewhat disappointed as I filled my plate. "Would you at least like a drink?"

"No thank you. Please, enjoy," he insisted, sitting in the chair at the other end of the table.

I cut into the steak and took small bites. He watched my every move, not saying anything. It felt weird eating while someone stared at you. I blushed and looked down at my plate, staring at its contents. I cooked a wonderful meal he wouldn't get to enjoy. The steak was so tender and the potatoes perfectly seasoned.

"How is it?" he asked suddenly.

"Hmm? Oh…wonderful."

He grinned and continued to stare. I quickly looked down at my plate again, hoping there wasn't too much left to go. I wasn't fond of people watching me dine. In the silence, I quickly finished, dabbed my mouth, and stood up with David standing as well. I grabbed my dishes and headed into the kitchen as he followed.

"You really do look incredible tonight," he commented, leaning next to the sink as I rinsed my dishes.

"Thank you," I responded quietly, still a little upset as I concentrated on what I was doing.

He leaned over, trying to look in my eyes. "Would you like me to clear the table?" he asked.

Seeing the concern in them, I felt bad I was being so sullen while he was being so considerate. "Yes, that'd be nice," I replied with a timid smile.

He smiled back and left, returning a moment later with several items in his hands and setting them on the island. He went back again as I started packing away the leftovers. Dad's going to wonder why I cooked such an elaborate meal, but I'll come up with an excuse later.

Setting the final items aside, he stood back and waited for further instructions. When I didn't give any, he asked, "Is there anything else I can help with? You worked so hard, it's the least I can do since I didn't partake."

I paused, looking around. "No, it's okay. I'm just about done," I replied as I packed the last bit away and put the dishes in the sink. I filled it with soap and water to let it sit.

As I turned around to face him, he moved toward me. "Is it all right if I see the rest of the house now?" he asked angelically.

"O-okay, we'll start downstairs since we're already here," I replied, leading him into the family room first.

As we strolled through each of the other rooms, I said a little bit about them. He quietly followed and observed, never saying much more than to compliment the décor or ask a brief question. Having completed the tour of the lower level, we headed upstairs. At the top, we turned and went down the hall hitting all the other rooms, saving mine for last. We looped back to the beginning where it sat on the other side of the stairs and I stopped.

I slowly opened the door and announced, "And this is my room."

He walked in and studied everything – the items on my wall and shelves, my CDs and books in my bookcase, and what I had on my dresser and bedside table. He picked up the rose and smiled to himself, then gently put it back down. He sat at the foot of my bed and slowly lay back, staring at the ceiling. Oh my God – he's lying on my bed! My pulse raced as I stood off to the side fidgeting with my skirt, a little embarrassed by the thoughts I was having.

"I like your ceiling," he commented suddenly. "It's soothing and authentic."

"My mom and I painted it several years ago," I responded, walking around to the other side of the bed.

He continued to stare at it, a longing in his eyes, and then sighed and rolled to the side closest to me, sitting up. He looked at me a moment and then at the balcony. "May I?" he asked, heading to the door. I indicated he could and walked out with him.

The night was warm and no moon graced the sky. I sat on the chaise as he walked to the edge, staring out over the garden. The solar lights dotting the yard helped to illuminate the sleeping plants. "This is my mom's garden. She planted it when she and my dad first moved here and maintained it herself. Now I take care of it for her," I commented.

He turned to me, leaning against the railing. There was something familiar about him standing there, like from my dream. "It's stunning."

"You should see it during the day, especially at this time of year. It's so colorful and alive."

He walked over and sat next to me. "I would love to, but I'll take your word for it."

"Would you like to take a stroll in it?"

He glanced out into the yard and then back to me. "Yes, I would enjoy that. But before we do, would you happen to have paper and a pencil?"

"I do," I replied as I headed back into the room and sifted through my desk. "Why?"

"It's a surprise," he responded with a smirk, taking the items from me. I narrowed my eyes but didn't get a follow-up response.

I led him downstairs and to the patio doors, exiting out into the backyard. I didn't bother turning on the spotlights; doing so would kill the ambiance. Besides, the pathway lights provided enough of a glow to see where we were going.

Strolling hand in hand along the walkway, I paused occasionally and told him about the plants Mom chose and why. As we came to the end, we reached the gazebo and sat on the swing, staring at the yard from a different angle. We stayed for a moment, admiring the quiet garden at night, but as my eyes came to the open spot in the yard, I pulled him off and took him to it.

I proceeded to lie in the grass as he watched, perplexed. "What are you doing?"

"Looking at the stars," I replied, pointing at the sky. They were bright tonight and the clouds were few and far between. "It's not like at the lake, but I am able to make out the constellations."

He lowered himself to the ground, lying next to me. It was just as I imagined it, there with him in the grass under the stars. We were quiet, taking in their beauty.

I turned my head and as his eyes met mine, I blushed. He reached up and gently touched my reddened cheek, smiling. I was hypnotized by his gaze as he rolled to his side and leaned over me. Moving closer, his lips slightly glanced mine. He lingered there and I languidly closed my eyes, waiting, but then he faded away.

When I opened them, he was sitting across from me, sketchbook on his lap and pencil poised. I sat up, my legs to the side and the skirt spread out over them. I twisted a strand of hair around my finger and stared at him, wondering what he was doing. He smiled as he cocked his head to the side, the pencil tip resting on his lip. Oh, to be that pencil...

"Stay just like that," he instructed as it began to move feverishly fast on the paper.

I snapped out of my daze. "Are you drawing me?" I questioned. He remained quiet, probably wondering why I'd ask such a ridiculous question.

I was fascinated by his expression, so intense but beautiful. He looked up from the paper into my eyes and I saw the corner of his mouth curl into a smile. My heart beat faster and my chest heaved with my quickened breaths. I wanted to place my hand over it to calm it but didn't want to move and mess him up. Instead, I closed my eyes and concentrated on my breathing. Once it returned to normal and my heart stopped thumping so hard, I opened them.

David was still, the pencil behind his ear. "Would you like to see?" he asked.

I lifted my skirt and walked on my knees over to him, sitting beside him. He turned the notebook toward me and I gasped. He captured my expression and stance perfectly and the detail of the garden behind me was amazing!

"This is incredible. You're really talented."

He gently tore the picture from the sketchbook and handed it to me. "It's for you."

"Thank you. I'll treasure it forever," I stated and he smiled.

"I think it's time we go in," he suggested, standing up.

I looked up from the picture to see his hand outstretched before me. I took it and we headed inside, going to the family room. He sat on the couch, waiting for me to join him, but instead I told him I'd be right back. I ran up to my room and stuck the picture in the side of my mirror so I could look at it every day, then ran back downstairs and sat by him.

"Would you like to watch some TV?" I asked, turning it on and changing the channel.

His attention was on the screen. "Stop...what was that? Turn it back to the news."

I flipped back and watched as they discussed the recent Ghost murder. He listened intently, furrowing his brow. Tired of hearing about it, I went in the kitchen and poured two glasses of water, handing him one when I returned. He took it without looking, but never drank.

Suddenly, he slammed it down. "Unbelievable," he mumbled. He said something else, but I couldn't make out what.

I nervously gripped my glass, still standing as I stared down at his infuriated expression. "Is...is something wrong?" I asked, not sure I wanted to know the answer.

His focus shifted to me as he rose, the anger fading from his face. "Unfortunately, I have to cut our evening short. Thank you for inviting me to your house. It was lovely," he responded graciously.

He headed toward the door, leaving me bewildered and standing in the family room. He was halfway when he turned and came back. Touching my bare arms, the coolness of his hands shocked me into consciousness as he kissed my lips lightly. Then, without a word, he showed himself out. I ran to see him off, opening the door wide, but he was already gone. Slowly closing it, I slouched against the cold wood.

"What the hell was that about?" I asked myself aloud.

The grandfather clock in the living room chimed suddenly, startling me. It was almost eleven! I shut off the TV and finished the dishes, then ran up to my room and changed quickly into lounge pants and a tank.

I curled up under my covers and nuzzled my face into the pillow. A strange aroma rose from it. It smelled amazing, even though it made me lightheaded. I closed my eyes and hugged the comforter, smelling the same scent, and soon I was deep in sleep.

A cool hand caressed my cheek and I slowly opened my eyes. The room was pitch black, as was outside. I was turned toward the balcony, the French doors sitting ajar. I knew I closed them before I went to sleep. A figure sat on the edge of the bed beside me, but I couldn't make out who it was.

"Dad..." I whispered hoarsely.

"No, he hasn't come home yet," David replied softly.

I sat up suddenly and covered myself with the comforter. "H-how did you get in here?" I exclaimed.

"I climbed the tree next to the balcony and worked the lock open," he answered casually. "It's quite easy."

"What...why are you here?"

"I didn't like leaving you the way I did. I came back to apologize and to see that you were all right," he responded, reaching up and stroking my arm.

I relaxed, letting the comforter fall to my lap. "You scared me, sneaking into my room like this..."

"Again, I apologize."

I smoothed out my hair and rubbed my eyes. "It's okay. Just warn me next time," I replied. He was quiet. "So why were you so upset?" I asked.

He looked toward the balcony. "The murders…"

I waited for him to continue, but he didn't. "Do you know more than they're showing?"

He hesitated. "Yes."

Fearing the worst, I asked, "Are you involved in them?"

He turned back to me. "Not exactly," he whispered, moving closer.

I started to feel uncomfortable. "Wh-what do you mean?"

"Don't be afraid…I would never hurt you," he whispered in my ear. He was so close to me, his breath coming out in soft bursts against my neck. He gently kissed it and then sat back.

"I…I know you won't, but what do you mean you're 'not exactly' involved?"

His shadowy figure held its head in the darkness of the room. Then he dropped his hands and looked toward me. I caught a strange glint of light in his eyes and then he looked away. "I don't want to keep secrets from you, Megan. I want you to know…know what I am."

"Are you…a…a…murderer?" I hesitated.

He laughed, but there was no joy in it. "Not anymore…" he murmured.

"David, you're worrying me…"

"Please don't," he whispered, turning to me and caressing the side of my face. I could feel my uneasiness fading away. "You are always safe with me," he continued as he coaxed me to lie down. "Release this from your mind and go back to sleep."

As my head rested against the pillow, he stood and leaned over to kiss me. He turned to go, but I stopped him. "Please…don't leave," I begged, grabbing his arm.

He hesitated. "I'll stay as long as I can," he replied, sitting on the edge of the bed by me. He caressed my face, making my eyelids heavy. I tried to keep them open, but with every stroke of his fingers, they became heavier. Finally, I gave in and fell asleep.

# Chapter 11
## Get Together

I woke as the sun came through my window and lighted on my face. I ran my hand over the space next to me, hoping to find David, but he wasn't there. Sitting up, my eyes immediately went to the balcony doors. They were shut and locked with no sign of ever having been disturbed.

Did I dream his late night visit? It seemed more real than the last time – his touch, his kiss, being with me. But how?

The alarm sounded and startled me, bringing me back to the present. It had to be a dream. There was no other logical explanation. I shut it off and climbed out of bed, going into the bathroom to get ready for school. I took my shower and dressed, not thinking of anything but what I was doing at the moment. That was until I sat down.

As I brushed my hair, my eyes wandered to the picture David drew last night and my heart fluttered. Memories of the evening with him filled my mind and I felt excited. I can't wait to tell Claire.

I went downstairs to the kitchen to get breakfast and noticed Dad wasn't there again. I grabbed a pear and headed back upstairs to check his room, not sure if he ever made it home. He wasn't there either, so I pulled out my cell and dialed his number.

"Morning, Meg. I was waiting for your call. Sorry I didn't come home last night. It was late and I figured it was best to stay with Vanessa," he explained as I stepped out the front door.

"No problem," I replied, locking it. "Did you have a nice evening?" I asked, walking down the sidewalk.

"It was surprisingly pleasant."

"See, you worried over nothing."

"I know," he responded. In the background, I heard a door shut. "I have to stop by the house to change. Are you going to be there?"

"Actually, I'm on my way to school now, but I'll see you tonight," I replied as I got in my car.

"Oh, okay. See you then," he responded and then hung up.

I met Claire in the parking lot, anxious to tell her how things went last night. "So how was your evening?" she asked as I waited at her car. She was trying to find her books in the mess that had accumulated in the back seat.

"We had a very lovely evening. I made a delicious dinner, which he didn't eat, and then I showed him the house and garden. We relaxed on the grass and looked at the stars and later he sketched a picture of me."

"He's an artist?" she inquired, still rummaging.

"Probably just a hobby. Anyway, the night turned strange when we went inside. We were getting ready to watch a movie when he spotted something on the news about the Richmond Parks Ghost and suddenly became angry."

"Maybe he doesn't like criminals…ooo, maybe he's a vigilante, with his 'super powers' and all," she commented as she loaded her book bag.

"Ha ha, you're so funny," I remarked. "I'm not sure what it was about it, but he left after that. I went to bed, since it was after eleven, and had this bizarre dream that he came back, visiting me in my room."

"Uh huh…" she responded, stopping and looking at me suspiciously.

"Not doing anything but sitting next to me and talking," I clarified. "I woke up this morning thinking it really happened, but there was no sign that it had."

"Have you been having a lot of these kinds of dreams lately?" she asked as we walked to the building.

"Actually, yes, I have. In the first one, he appeared on my balcony, saying he was there to watch over me. The following night, I dreamt I met him in Hollywood Cemetery and he drank my blood. And then, of course, last night's dream."

We stopped at my locker and Claire leaned against the others as she pondered what they meant. "You're just thinking about him a lot. I wouldn't look too deeply into it. You know, half the time the things you dream don't really mean what you think they do."

We entered the classroom and took our seats. I pulled out my book and prepared myself, even though my mind was distracted. Was Claire right about my dreams not meaning anything and that it was all because I was thinking about him so much? Or did my subconscious know something my conscious didn't? I continued to mull over it even though I really shouldn't have.

When the bell rang, I turned to Claire and remarked, "Something's really bothering me about the dreams."

She stood and gathered her things as I did the same. "Unfortunately, we don't have enough time to talk about it now, but we will at lunch. In the meantime, stop worrying about it."

We parted, and I tried to get it out of my mind. By the beginning of third period, I had stopped dissecting them, but when the lunch bell rang, it all came back, with the dream last night nagging at me the most. I grabbed something quick and sat at the table, waiting for Claire. I really wanted to talk to her about this before the others arrived.

"So what about your dreams is bothering you so much?" she asked, taking a seat next to me. She must have rushed to get here, too.

"Well, the one last night in particular. Everything about it was so real, even what I felt and saw."

"So what happened?" she inquired eagerly.

"He came back to apologize for his behavior but acted strange when I asked him if he was involved in the murders."

"What was his response?"

"That he wasn't, but something about his reaction to my question made me think he had a connection to them. When I pressed him about it, he acted like he wanted to tell me but couldn't. So I asked if he was a murderer, and he said he wasn't anymore."

Holding her sandwich in the air, she pondered it all. "Okay...you're hearing a lot about the murders, so you incorporated that into your dream. You also don't know a lot about him and have noticed weird things when you hang out, so that factored in as well. Dreams are just a product of what goes on during your day, especially significant pieces," she explained, taking a bite.

I glanced out the window at the trees, watching them sway in the breeze. "I guess so. I was just wondering if there's something my subconscious is trying to tell me."

"No, your subconscious isn't telling you anything. David's a great guy. Maybe you have a fear of commitment and that's why you're dreaming up all these things."

"Fear of commitment...that explains it," Ben commented as he sat next to me.

"For the thousandth time, I don't want to ruin our friendship. That's why I don't want to date you."

"I was just kidding. You're so sensitive lately," he huffed, biting a fry.

Claire, sensing the tension, changed the subject quickly. "So how about Friday? Everyone excited?"

"I'm so ready. I've been saving up my allowance for an occasion like this!" Erin exclaimed as she sat.

I looked at Claire and mouthed 'thank you'. Justin was the last to join as we continued our discussion about our get together. He seemed happy about going and I saw Claire give him a smile.

While everyone else talked, my mind wandered away from the conversation as I picked at my food. I thought about what she said as I stared out the window. Maybe I should talk to David about it. After all, he was the reason I was having all these dreams.

The bell rang and it was off to class. By fifth period, I decided to tell David about what I've been dreaming. When he calls tonight, I'll setup a time to meet with him. Maybe getting it out in the open will help.

As we walked to the parking lot, I told Claire and Erin in more detail about my wonderful evening. Ben and Justin weren't far behind us, but thankfully out of hearing range. When we reached our cars, we said goodbye and left.

At home, I knocked my homework out and warmed the leftovers from last night's dinner to surprise Dad. I figured I'd tell him I made it especially for him. Little did I know, he was bringing Vanessa with him. Good thing I had extras.

He thought it'd be nice change to eat in the dining room, so I set the table and brought in the food. "This looks great, Meg. What's the occasion?" he asked, filling his plate.

"Oh, I just thought you'd like it. I know how hard you've been working lately."

"That's so sweet of you, *Meg*," Vanessa commented in her saccharine voice as she prepared hers.

We sat together at one end of the table, Dad at the head and Vanessa across from me. She smirked as she took a bite of steak, expecting it to be tough, but she was mistaken. I smiled and glanced at the opposite end, thinking about last night and David sitting there watching me. Dad and Vanessa paid no mind to me, having their own conversation while I sat quietly and enjoyed my delicious dinner a second time.

"That was a great meal," he commented as he helped clear the table. She went into the family room without a word and turned on the TV, watching some sitcom.

"I'm glad you enjoyed it," I responded as I took the last of the dishes from him. He glanced at her and then at me. "Go ahead...I'll take care of the rest."

He joined her on the couch, and she immediately cuddled up to him as he put his arm around her. I finished the dishes and loaded them into the washer and went over to Dad to tell him good night.

"Why don't you join us?" he asked. Vanessa gave me a look.

"I can't...I have to finish my book for English tonight. We have a test tomorrow."

"Okay. Good night, Meg."

"'Night, Dad," I replied as I kissed his cheek. "Vanessa." She nodded and I left.

I grabbed my bag off the end of the banister and jogged up the steps to my room. Hanging it on the door handle, I pulled my book and David's phone out and laid them next to me on the bed as I sat. Leaning back against my pillows, I started reading.

As soon as I finished, I set the book aside and grabbed David's phone. Lying down, I rested my head on a pillow as I scrolled through it. No missed calls or messages. I dropped my arm beside me and sighed. David's scent still lingered on the pillow and as I breathed it in, I started feeling lightheaded. I closed my eyes to stop the room from spinning, but even as the dizziness faded, I couldn't bring myself to open them. I fell asleep, David's phone in my hand.

A vibrating sensation against my palm woke me, and I opened my eyes to see the phone light up. "Hello..." I answered, still groggy.

"Good evening, Megan. How are you tonight?"

"Asleep..." I answered, sitting up in bed and holding my head.

"Am I calling too late?"

"No, not at all," I replied, focusing on the clock on my bedside table. It was after midnight. "I...I was resting my eyes."

"Did you have a pleasant day?" he inquired.

"For the most part," I responded. I tried to remember what I wanted to ask him and then it came to me. "David...can we meet tonight?"

"Tonight? Why?"

"I want to talk to you about something," I replied, starting to wake more.

"All right. Where would you like to meet?"

"There's a playground down the street from my house. Meet me there in fifteen minutes."

"I will see you soon," he responded and then hung up.

I got out of bed and went to the bathroom, washing the sleep away from my face and making myself more presentable. Then I headed out onto the balcony, not bothering to change since I was still wearing what I wore to school. Peeking over the side at the family room window, I saw it was dark. Dad must have taken Vanessa home. I climbed down the tree and went through the gate into the front yard, then crossed the lawn and walked down the street to the playground. David was already there.

"How did you get here so fast?" I asked as I walked up to him.

"I was in the area. What did you want to talk about?" he inquired, leading me to the swings.

I took a seat on one of them, and he gently pushed me. I looked back at him, almost forgetting why I was there, but refocused. "I've been having these strange dreams lately...about you, and I wanted your opinion on what they might mean."

He started pushing harder. "All right. What was your most recent one?"

I explained it to him and he listened intently, still pushing me. When I finished, he stopped the swing and came around to the front, crouching at my feet. "Megan," he responded, his hands on my thighs. I tried not to shake with his touch. "That wasn't a dream. I did come back."

I was still. "So you...you *were* in my room last night? All those things you said...were true?"

He looked into my eyes. "Yes." I stood up and started to walk away, but he caught my arm. "Please...don't leave."

I turned to him and he let go of me. "I want an explanation."

He walked over to a merry-go-round and sat on the edge, waiting for me to join him. I hesitated, but then decided to stay. Cautiously, I sat and he turned to me, his arresting green eyes gazing into mine.

"I'm not normal," he remarked slowly.

"I gathered that from all the odd things I've noticed about you."

He cocked his head. "Like what?"

"I *know* you cut yourself the other night on the fence, but there was no wound, just a hole in your shirt. I couldn't find your heartbeat when we were on the lake. You have crazy reflexes and sometimes I can't think straight around you. You only want to meet at night. I swear, if I didn't know better, I'd think you were a…" I stopped short, taking him in as I held back my thought.

He arched his brow. "A what?" he questioned.

I fidgeted nervously with my shirt sleeve as I averted my eyes. No, there's no way. There's some other explanation. There has to be.

I looked up as he looked away and shook his head. "I want to tell you, but I can't."

"Why not?" I questioned.

He gazed adoringly into my eyes. "I don't want to lose you."

I paused a moment and let that sink in. "Wh-why do you think you'd lose me?"

"I'm afraid it will scare you away…what I am"

"It won't. David, I lo-"

He stood abruptly. "No, you can't say that. Not until you truly know me," he interrupted.

I grabbed his arm. "Let me, then."

He stopped, his head bowed. "You have to be patient," he conceded after a moment, raising his eyes to mine.

"I will," I responded, gazing into them.

He caressed my cheek as he leaned in and kissed me softly. "May I walk you home?" he requested.

"Yes, I'd like that," I replied, happy for more time. We strolled away from the playground arm in arm and went to my house. "We have to sneak in the back. It looks like my dad's home, but he must be in bed," I whispered as I led him to the gate.

We headed into the backyard and climbed the tree to my balcony. Quietly slipping in the doors, I got into bed. He sat next to me as he had the night before, watching over me as I waited for sleep. And even when it came, he remained.

The alarm woke me, and as I opened my eyes, I searched for David. He was gone and my book and the phone were next to me on the bed. I was still in my clothes from yesterday.

Did I really meet him last night?

I sat up and checked the phone to see if his call was in it, but it wasn't. He never called. I could have sworn it happened.

I remembered being woken by a phone. I grabbed mine, just in case, and checked for calls. None. It must have been a dream, just as vivid and real as the others.

I got up, took my shower, and dressed for school. It's finally Friday. I'll meet with my friends and David tonight and afterward, I can talk to him about my dreams. At least I had it all played out in my mind thanks to last night. I just hope I don't get the same answers, or lack thereof.

I greeted my dad as I grabbed breakfast, but he didn't have much to say so I didn't linger. I climbed in my car and noticed the dreary day, wishing I grabbed an umbrella. As I was getting ready to pull out of the driveway, David's phone rang.

"Hello," I answered, a little surprised.

"Good morning, Megan. On your way to school?"

"Yes, I was just pulling out when you called," I replied as I put the car in neutral and pulled up the brake. "What's up?"

"I wanted to apologize."

"For what?" I asked, taking a bite of my granola bar.

"For not calling last night…and backing out of dinner tonight."

I nearly choked. "What? You're not coming?"

"No…something has come up and I'm unable to join you and your friends. I hope you can forgive me. I would still like to meet them someday soon, though."

"Oh…okay," I responded, disappointed. Then I remembered how he reacted the other night to the news of the murder. "Does this possibly have to do with what happened after dinner on Wednesday?" I inquired.

"What?" he questioned, unnerved.

"With the murder…on TV. You got upset and left abruptly. Does it have to do with that?" I paused, recalling the dream, and then hesitantly asked, "Do you know something they don't about the Ghost?"

Silence and then a slow exhale. "No, I don't. I reacted that way because of work. I assist the Medical Examiner and we have the pleasure of seeing all the victims. I knew I would be getting a call soon and would have to cut my evening short with you. That is why I was upset," he explained.

"Oh…" I responded, my cheeks flushing.

"I apologize if I unsettled you. I didn't intend to."

"You…you didn't, really. It was just unexpected," I replied.

"That's reassuring," he remarked and paused. "Well, I need to get to class and you to school. Try to have fun tonight," he commented, reminding me he wasn't coming and instantly depressing me. "I'll call you around midnight."

I tried not to sound despondent as I said goodbye, but I really couldn't help it. Dropping my hand with the phone in it to the seat, I sat and stared at the steering wheel. How could he do this to me? What was so important that he needed to cancel on me?

My eyes slowly drifted to the clock and I sighed, realizing I needed to go. I pulled out of the drive and headed to school, wanting a distraction from my misery and hoping I could find it in Claire. But the more I thought about David backing out of our date tonight, the more upset I became. I was so distraught, I wanted to turn around and go home, saying I was sick so I could back out of going tonight, too, but I refrained. No, I was going to go and have fun.

It started sprinkling by the time I reached the parking lot and was coming down heavier as I dashed to the building. I ducked inside, my clothes damp, and met Claire at my locker. She took one look at me and knew instantly something was wrong, even though I did my best to hide it.

"What's going on?" she asked while I switched out my books. "You look like your cat died."

"David's not coming tonight," I replied, slamming my locker shut. "Something came up and he can't make it."

"Oh, Megan, it's okay. We'll still have lots of fun," she consoled, rubbing my arm.

"I know, but now Ben's going to have a field day with this," I responded.

"Don't let him get to you. Things like this happen all the time. We'll get to meet him…someday."

I started walking toward class, contemplating it. "You're right. I'm not going to let this ruin my day or my time with everyone tonight. We're going out and having the most fun we've ever had!" I exclaimed as we stood outside the classroom.

"Here, here!" she concurred, and we both laughed as we entered and took our seats.

The morning zoomed by, thankfully, and by lunch, my mood was much like it was before I got David's call. I went through the normal line and got my food, wanting something hearty. Sitting between Claire and Erin, I felt protected in case Ben started to attack me.

"I can't wait to meet David tonight," he commented, shoving food in his mouth.

"Well, it'll have to wait for another day. He can't make it," I responded, trying to show indifference.

He choked. "What? He's not coming?"

"No, something came up and he's unable to make it, but he's still interested in meeting everyone someday soon," I replied coolly. I calmly ate my food, maintaining a poker face.

"Told you he wouldn't show," he muttered to Justin.

"Things do come up, Ben, that are beyond our control. I don't think he's intentionally ditching us," I explained, losing it and instantly becoming infuriated with him. He grinned, knowing he got to me.

"Maybe he has a college girl on the side and tonight's her night to go out with him," he whispered loudly to Justin as he cut his eyes to me.

I stood up and glared at him. "I can't believe you'd say something like that! You're such a jerk!" I shouted and then stormed out of the cafeteria and into the bathroom around the corner.

As if I wasn't having enough doubts about David, Ben had to add one more. What makes me think David isn't going out with other girls or women? He's smart, handsome, charming…he could have anyone he wants. Why me?

I looked at myself in the mirror and wanted to cry, but I refused. Sucking back the tears, I took a deep breath and then washed my face. I was not going to give Ben the satisfaction of knowing I had concerns about David.

I didn't bother going back to lunch and decided to skip gym. Instead, I went to the nurse, complaining of a stomachache and asked if I could lie down. She showed me to a cot in the back of the office and turned out the light, pulling the curtain around so no one would disturb me. I closed my eyes and tried not to think about David with another woman.


I woke a little over an hour later as the sun brightened the frosted glass window above my head. Taking that small nap really helped me feel refreshed. I got up and informed the nurse I was feeling better and then headed to sixth period. Latin was already in progress when I entered, and I apologized to the teacher as I took my seat.

Seeing the sun shining outside the window helped to brighten my mood and by the time I entered English, I felt invincible. Nothing Ben could say would upset me. But instead of negativity, I got regret.

He kneeled beside my desk and apologized repeatedly for his stupidity. I was starting to get embarrassed and was thankful when the teacher told him to get in his seat. But it felt good knowing he made a complete fool of himself.

The teacher passed out the tests and I breezed right through it. After handing it in, I sat in my seat and stared out the window, but every once in a while I stole a glance at Ben. He was obviously stressing over something, either the questions or me. I smiled and turned my attention back to the window as I waited for the bell to ring.

Once it did, I dashed out of class before he could start apologizing again. I met Claire in the hall and we walked as fast as we could out to the parking lot, giggling all the way. He never caught up.

"I see you're doing better," she commented as we arrived at my car.

"I decided to not let Ben's comments bother me. I know David isn't cheating on me. Besides, I think I've been so sensitive because I haven't been getting enough sleep. I feel so much better after my nap."

"Good. Oh, here comes Ben! We better leave. See you in a couple hours," she shouted as I hopped in my car and she in hers. We both took off before he made it onto the asphalt.

I smiled all the way home, imagining the look on his face as I tore out of the lot. I pulled in the drive and went inside, not really knowing what to do with myself for the next hour and a half. I climbed the stairs and entered my room, hanging my bag on the door as I looked around.

Going to the closet, I scanned the racks as I considered changing my outfit. Maybe I should wear something sexy to drive Ben crazy. I grinned and pulled out a V-neck, button-up cardigan and a short, pleated skirt. Perfect.

After changing, I fixed my hair, leaving it down with the exception of the few pieces I pinned back. I took one last glimpse of myself in the mirror and headed downstairs to kill time. I plopped on the couch and flipped through the channels, but never found anything I wanted to watch. My cell phone rang and I saw it was Dad.

"What's up?" I asked, glancing out the window into the backyard. A squirrel chased another squirrel up the cherry tree and jolted the branch, making it drop several pink blossoms.

"I wanted to let you know since you're going out tonight, I decided to take Vanessa to dinner."

"How late will you be?"

"Oh, I don't know…eleven, maybe midnight. That doesn't mean you get to stay out that late. I expect you home by ten, ten-thirty at the latest."

"That's fine, the mall will be closed by then anyway. Have fun and I'll see you in the morning, I guess."

"Okay," he replied and hung up. I slipped the phone in my purse next to David's and glanced at the TV. It was getting close to time, so I turned it off and headed out the door.

I arrived at the mall and parked near the restaurant. As I was walking in, I saw Ben waiting at the door. I rolled my eyes and continued toward him, putting on a friendly smile.

"Wow…you look great!" he gushed, unable to take his eyes off me.

"Thank you. I decided to change into something nice for our get together," I replied with a smirk.

"Do you want to sit or wait for the others?" he inquired, still staring.

"We can sit. I think they'll be able to find us when they come in."

He told the hostess we needed a table for five, and she sat us immediately. We got a nice round booth in the corner of the restaurant, somewhat private. The waitress came by after a few minutes and introduced herself and then took our drink orders and left. We sat in silence for a while, either examining the menu or the decorations around the restaurant. Too bad it didn't last.

He put the menu down and stared at me. "What does he have that I don't?"

"Please...don't start this now," I pleaded.

"Just answer that one question and I won't bring it up again for the rest of the night."

I glanced around to see if anyone else had arrived, but it was still just the two of us. I rolled my eyes and sighed. "Fine. I'll answer that one question, but I don't know you'll like what you get."

"I'll deal with it. So what is it about him that has you so enthralled?"

"He's *different*. When I'm with him, I feel things I've never felt before. And there's something intriguing about him, drawing me to him."

"Sounds like love," he commented, looking toward the door. The waitress left the drinks and, noticing it was still just us, didn't bother to hang around.

"Maybe it is," I replied, leaning back in the seat. Wow, I admitted it...out loud and to Ben.

"Well, I really wish I could've met him tonight. I'm really interested in seeing what's so great about *David*."

"You'll be surprised," I muttered under my breath.

I looked toward the door just as Claire and Justin entered. I waved at them, and they came to the table with Erin right behind them. "Sorry we're so late. We had to pick Erin up. She took forever picking an outfit," Claire explained. "Speaking of which, check out Megan!"

I blushed, embarrassed by the attention. "Oh this old thing?" I replied.

"Old?" Justin commented, staring. She narrowed her eyes at him and I laughed.

"Sooo, what are everyone's plans for the weekend?" I asked, getting the attention off me. But unfortunately, they were more curious about what David and I might be doing. "I don't know...we haven't talked about it," was my reply. Ben seemed pleased nothing exciting was arranged.

The waitress returned and took the drink order from everyone else. We went ahead and ordered our food while she was there. I didn't know how much longer I could wait to eat. Several minutes later, she brought out the appetizers and we dug in. As we munched, we talked about our day and Erin filled us in on the things I missed in gym.

Our meals arrived and we continued talking, this time returning to the discussion about weekend plans. Erin had some game she was going to, Claire and Justin were hanging out, but hadn't decided what they were doing exactly, and Ben would be catching up on his video gaming. The waitress stopped by to check on us and see if anyone wanted dessert, but we declined.

After the check was dropped off in passing, we pooled our money together and paid the bill. Then we headed into the mall, the boys trailing behind us talking about the latest video games. David didn't seem the type to be interested in things like that and probably would have felt odd.

When we came to a store we liked, we dipped in and looked through the racks. Sometimes Justin and Ben followed us and other times, they hung out outside. Claire, Erin, and I had a blast trying on different outfits, some we would wear and some we wouldn't. Stopping in a dress shop, we looked at gowns for the Junior/Senior prom. It was coming up soon, but this was the first time it crossed my mind.

"So are you inviting David?" Erin asked in the dressing room as she tried on a skin-tight, red gown.

"I don't know. I hadn't even thought about it until now," I replied, standing on the other side.

"You should go regardless. It'll be fun. We could rent a limo together," Claire suggested. "Why don't you try on some dresses?"

"If I go, I'm wearing my bridesmaid dress."

"You should get something new for the occasion. It's special," she insisted.

"It's not special. We get to go again in our senior year. I'd rather wait until then."

"If David asks you, would you go?" Erin inquired, coming out of the stall and checking herself in the mirror.

"I don't know…maybe. But he doesn't know about it. All I've been thinking about is the wedding. Besides, why would he ask? It's my prom."

"What do you think of this one," she inquired, ignoring my response.

I rolled my eyes. "A little short, don't you think?"

"But I have great legs. Claire, what do you think?"

She peeked over the stall and smiled. "Looks pretty good to me. Do you have a date yet?"

"No, but if David doesn't go with you, Megan, would you like to go to prom with me?" she asked, batting her eyes.

"Only if I get to wear the tux," I joked.

Claire stepped out of the stall, laughing. She stopped when she saw herself in the mirror. "This is the one," she announced, turning around.

"You look awesome! That green is perfect on you!" Erin exclaimed.

"I think Justin will be floored. Has he asked you yet?" I inquired.

"No, not yet. I've been dropping hints, but I don't know if he's not getting them or if he's avoiding saying anything."

"Maybe we could say something to him," Erin suggested.

"No, don't do that. I'll just buy the dress and hope he asks. If not, I could also be your date, Megan."

"Wow, I feel so wanted," I laughed.

She changed back into her clothes while Erin tried on more gowns, searching for her perfect one, but she walked away empty handed. Ben and Justin were relieved to see us when we finally joined them. "We thought y'all might've gotten lost in there. We were about to launch a full-scale search party," Justin teased.

"We were trying to find the perfect gown," Erin responded.

"For what?" Ben asked.

"Uh, prom, duh!" she exclaimed, realizing too late what she said.

Justin looked at Claire and she went red. "Prom's coming up and you haven't said anything?" he whispered to her.

"Oh, look at that store!" I blurted out, hooking my arm around Ben's and Erin's. "Let's go check it out," I continued, walking away. We didn't need to make Claire any more uncomfortable than she already was.

"I've been dropping hints all week," she whispered back.

"Do you want to go?" he asked and we stopped, pretending to talk, but really eavesdropping.

"Of course I do, and I want to go with you."

"Okay...so we're going to prom," he smiled nervously.

She screamed and gave him a hug and kiss on the cheek. Erin and I squealed quietly with delight and Ben covered his face, embarrassed by our overreaction. She came running up, telling us what we already knew, but we pretended not to know. She was ecstatic. Justin joined us and we congratulated him. He blushed, feeling embarrassed by all the attention and the fact he was so oblivious.

The rest of the night, we couldn't separate her from him. The only time they did was when we went into a couple of stores the guys would enjoy. It was a reward for having to wait so long for us.

Having gotten our fix of the mall, we all decided to call it a night. I gave Claire a hug goodbye and whispered a thank you to Justin. Erin said goodbye to Ben and me and then they left.

We stood on the sidewalk outside the mall in silence for several minutes before he asked if he could catch a ride with me. I looked at him, knowing he did it on purpose. "Sure, let's go," I sighed, walking into the lot.

I unlocked the doors and he climbed in, breathing in the scent of my car. "It smells so nice in here. What air freshener do you use?"

"None, I just keep it clean. Or it could be a mixture of my perfume and the leather," I replied, backing out of the parking space.

He took another deep breath. "I really appreciate you taking me home."

"Um-hmm. So why didn't you ask Claire for a ride?"

"I didn't think I'd be able stomach all that lovey-dovey stuff between Justin and her. Besides, she already had Erin to drop off…I didn't want to be a burden."

"Fair enough," I replied, turning on the stereo. I switched the channel to the alternative station. I felt like listening to something angry and loud.

He stared at me as I sang along with the songs, impressed I could. After a couple of sets, he turned the volume down and looked at me. "What did you do that for?" I asked, reaching to turn it up again but he stopped me.

"Will you go to prom with me, Megan?"

I stared straight ahead at the road, not sure how to answer. My grip on the wheel and my jaw tightened as I thought about it. Part of me wanted to scream and yell at him, but the other part wanted to let him down gently. I pursed my lips, trying to decide which one to choose. I could feel him staring at me.

"Ben, I'm not sure I'm going to prom."

"Why? Are you waiting for *him* to ask?"

"Of course not. Honestly, I've been so focused on the wedding, I completely forgot about it."

"Oh…" he murmured, fidgeting with the door buttons.

I glanced at him, feeling sorry. "Isn't there someone else at school you could ask?"

"There's only one person I want to go with and she's taken."

Ugh, he's so pathetic! I tried to think of a solution as we came closer to his house. Then I remembered David mentioning his roommates. I wonder if any are female. "What if we were to double-date? If David happens to agree to go, I could see if one of his roommates or friends will go with you."

"And what if David doesn't agree?"

"Well, I already told Erin I'd go with her," I mused.

I pulled into his drive and waited for his answer. "Yeah, I guess so. That way I'll still be with you."

"Good. I'll mention it to him tonight."

"Wait…David has female roommates?" he questioned as he gave me a suspicious look.

"Don't you dare go there," I growled.

"Okay, okay. I won't. Let me know as soon as you find out," he replied, opening the car door.

"I will. See you Monday."

"Thanks again," he responded as he shut the door and skulked toward his house. I didn't bother waiting to see if he got inside okay. I was ready to go home.

# Chapter 12
## Breaking the News

It was after eleven when I pulled in the drive and noticed Dad wasn't home. Good, he wouldn't know I was out later than his curfew. As I entered the house, my phone rang. I wonder if he's checking up on me. I looked at the screen and let out a relieved sigh – it was Claire.

I could tell in her voice she was still hyper from the evening's excitement. "Just checking to see you made it home all right," she responded to my greeting.

"Yeah, I just got here. After you left, Ben asked for a ride. Seriously, I don't know if I can deal with his puppy love much longer," I replied as I headed to my room.

"Why? What happened?"

I entered and put her on speakerphone as I changed. "He asked me to prom."

"What? Why does he keep doing this to himself? I swear."

"I explained to him I wasn't sure if I was even going. Then I suggested asking someone else in school and he said I was the only one he wanted to go with," I remarked, picking up the phone and changing it back.

"What did you say after that?"

"I offered to double-date. I told him I'd talk to David and see if one of his roommates or friends would be willing to go out with him. He seemed okay with that."

"David has female roommates?" she questioned.

"Claire," I huffed, not wanting to hear it from her, too.

"Sorry…well, maybe you'll make a love connection and he can get over you already."

"That's what I'm hoping." There was a beep and I looked at the screen to see who was calling. "Hey Claire, I have to go. It's my dad."

"Okay. I'll talk to you tomorrow."

I hung up and picked up Dad's waiting call. "Hey, what's up?"

"Just calling to check on you and let you know I'm staying with Vanessa again tonight."

"Oh, okay. I was just getting ready for bed," I replied, containing my thrill.

"Did you have fun?"

"Yeah, it was a blast. And you know what? Prom is in two weeks."

"Prom? Are you going?"

"I don't know yet. If I do, I thought about wearing my bridesmaid dress. Do you think Vanessa will mind?"

"Probably not. So no one has asked you?"

"Well, Ben did, of course, but I turned him down."

"Poor boy," he mumbled, somewhat distracted. "Hey, I'd love to chat some more, but Vanessa's looking for me. See you tomorrow, okay?"

"Okay. Good night, Dad." I hung up and fell back onto my bed.

Prom…how could I completely miss it with all the posters on every wall announcing it? And now I feel pressured to talk to David because of Ben. I wonder if I should hint for him to ask me or just ask him. I mean, it is my prom.

I think I like the idea of hinting at it. I'm an old-fashion kind of girl and would like to be asked to it. Maybe I could approach it by saying Ben asked me to prom, hoping it'll make him think about it. Then again, he might not like that. I know…I could casually talk about what happened with Justin and Claire. It's a good story he'll probably find amusing.

I switched off the overhead light and turned on the bedside lamp, bathing my room in a dim glow. It was getting close to midnight and he should be calling soon. I flopped over onto my stomach and played with his phone, listening to the different ringtones and looking at the games. I was deep into solitaire when I heard a light tapping on my balcony door.

I flipped over onto my back and stared at it, not seeing anything through the sheers. Maybe I misheard. Then it did it again and I gasped.

I've watched too many scary movies to think it was a good idea to let whatever was out there into my room. It tapped again, a little harder, as I crawled backwards off the bed and hid behind it. Why won't it leave?

Then the phone in my hand rang. I answered it, my voice meek and shaky. "Are you going to open the door or not? I've been tapping on it, trying to get your attention," David stated.

"That was you?" I replied as I stood and crept to the French doors, slowly pulling the curtain back. He was standing in the middle of the balcony, a smile on his face as he hung up. My heart thumped loudly as I unlocked the door and stepped out. "Why didn't you call first?" I asked, moving closer, but I didn't give him time to answer. "You don't just show up at my house in the middle of the night and expect me to open the door because you're tapping on it!" I exclaimed, pushing his chest. "What are you doing here?"

He laughed, not moving at all from the force of my shove. "I thought I would surprise you," he replied, stepping back and leaning against the railing.

I crossed my arms. "So what came up that caused you to miss hanging out earlier?"

"Work. They called me to come in tonight because someone was out sick. I really am sorry I missed it. Did you enjoy the time with your friends?"

I paused, examining the sincere expression on his face, and then sighed. "Yeah, it was great," I responded, my anger subsiding as I took a seat on the chaise.

"I'm glad you had a good evening. What did you and your friends do?" he asked, sitting cross-legged on the floor in front of me.

"Well, we had dinner and then strolled around the mall. Claire, Erin, and I tried on different outfits and dresses while the guys waited for us."

"Did you model any of them for the 'guys'?" he inquired, raising a brow.

"No, just for each other. They didn't bother coming into the store." Now was as good a time as any to mention prom. "Claire picked out and bought her prom dress tonight, though she wasn't sure if she was going. Justin hadn't asked her, but he finally did moments after Erin's big mouth spouted off about it."

His eyes were focused on me even though I avoided looking in his. "Your prom is coming up?"

"Yeah, in two weeks," I replied, fidgeting. "I completely forgot about it because of the wedding."

"So no one has asked you yet?"

"Well, Ben did…tonight, but I turned him down," I responded quickly, hoping he wouldn't get upset.

"What if I were to ask you?" he inquired, cocking his head slightly. "Would you go with me?"

My heart beat rapidly with excitement. "Of course I'd go with you," I replied without hesitation. "But I do have a small request."

He arched his brow. "And what might that be?"

"Do you have a roommate or friend who could go with Ben? I told him we could possibly double-date…if you did."

He thought for a moment and then smirked. "I think Madeline would."

"Oh, is she a friend?" I asked as casually as possible.

He cocked his head. "Yes, and also one of my roommates," he replied.

So he does have female roommates. I don't know if I should feel threatened or not. "What's she like?"

"She's pleasant to be around. She's energetic, creative, and attractive. I think he'll like her," he responded confidently as he played with the soft, pink petals dappling the balcony.

"Sounds good to me," I remarked and then paused. "Do you have any other female roommates?" I asked hesitantly.

"Yes, but she's Brian's girlfriend," he replied, lifting his eyes to mine. "Were you concerned about how many women I had living with me?" he inquired with a slight grin.

"No…well yes…a little," I answered, looking away.

"I was helping them out," he replied sincerely. "I am only interested in you, Megan," he continued, his focus on me as I turned back to him. His lucid green eyes captivated me. A few moments of silence lingered between us and then he spoke again. "Did you pick out a dress as well?" he asked, glancing down as he continued playing with the petals.

"No, I figure I'll use my bridesmaid dress. Well…as long as Vanessa lets me."

He gracefully stood and walked to the railing, leaning against it. "What if I were to take you to purchase a gown?"

I was surprised and a little impressed by his gesture. "No, I couldn't ask you to do that. I'm sure Vanessa will allow me to use it."

"You should have something new, something impressive to wear. The bridesmaid gown is beautiful and you look magnificent in it, but you need something better."

I have a feeling he's not going to give up. "I'll think about it," I replied, joining him at the railing. He turned toward the house as I faced the garden. It was quiet and dark, no animals moving or faint lights glowing along the path. I glanced at him and smiled softly. "I really appreciate you helping Ben," I remarked.

He gazed into my eyes and replied, "I'm not helping Ben."

Placing his cool hand on my neck, he leaned in to kiss me when something must have caught his eye. He turned his head slightly and stared out into the garden, remaining completely still. He concentrated on one spot and furrowed his brow.

"What are you looking at?" I asked, trying to follow his line of sight. I couldn't see anything.

He continued to stare, his eyes moving with whatever he was focused on. "Nothing…an animal." Then after a moment, he glanced at me. "We should go inside."

Feeling a sudden chill, I agreed and started toward the door. I glanced over my shoulder and found him still watching whatever it was in the yard. Shaking my head, I sighed and headed into my room.

Sitting cross-legged on the bed, I waited patiently for him. He started toward the doors and then glanced back into the yard, pausing. After a brief moment, he continued inside. He pulled them shut and locked them. Taking the chair from my desk, he moved it in front of the glass panes and sat, glancing over his shoulder out the window.

"Is everything okay?" I asked, wondering why he was acting so strange.

He faced me and smiled. "No, everything's fine."

This reminded me of my dreams. "David, there's something I want to ask you."

"What might that be?"

"Well, I wanted your opinion on these dreams I've been having," I replied, sitting up on my knees and moving to the edge of the bed.

"That's not really my area of expertise, but I'll give it a try," he smiled, sitting back.

I looked at him, not sure if I really wanted to tell him and a bit nervous that what I dreamed happened at the playground would come to fruition. I bowed my head and sighed. "Never mind. Now that I think about it, they seem so silly."

"No, now you have my interest piqued. You have to tell me at least one of them," he requested with a grin. My heart thumped.

I tried to think of the least embarrassing one. "Okay...several nights ago, I dreamed you were out on my balcony. I joined you and asked why you were there, and you told me you were watching over me. Then you coaxed me to relax on the chaise, where I fell asleep. The strangest part was I woke the following morning...in the exact place where you left me."

He was staring at the ceiling, scratching his chin. "You feel weak and powerless. You're looking for a hero...someone to guard and protect you since your father was absent in your life after your mother's death. How is that?"

"Yeah, this really isn't your forte!" I laughed. "So how do you explain the fact that I ended up outside?" I questioned, wondering what his rationale would be for that.

"It was a vivid dream that caused you to sleepwalk," he replied smoothly.

I leaned forward and raised my brow. "But I've never been a sleepwalker before."

He leaned forward as well and smirked. "There is a first time for everything," he whispered and my heart went wild.

Then suddenly he stood, smiling as he casually strolled around the room. I couldn't think of a thing to say, still recuperating from his comment, but my eyes followed him. He looked at my bookcase again, running his fingers over the bindings of the books, and pulled out a couple, glancing at the covers before returning them.

He moved on from that, heading to the other side of the room. "Is your father out for the night?" he asked out of the blue as he opened my closet door.

"Yeah, he called earlier to let me know he wouldn't be coming home."

He peeked out. "So you're home alone tonight. Would you like company?"

I know I shouldn't say yes, but I didn't want him to go. "Sure, sounds like fun. How long do you plan to stay?"

He smiled crookedly. "All night, if you like."

My heart thumped and I started rethinking this whole idea. My boyfriend...staying the night at my house...with no parent around. "Umm...maybe? Let's see how long before I get tired. If I can make it all night, you have to be sure to leave before seven."

He exited the closet and shut the door. "I don't think that will be a problem."

"Sooo...how about a movie to start things off?" I suggested.

He opened my bedroom door, standing by it so stiff and tall like a soldier. "After you..."

I spun around and hopped off the bed, heading toward him. As I passed, I noticed him glance at the balcony before turning off the light and shutting the door. He followed me down the stairs and into the family room where we sat together on the couch.

"Should we order a movie, check what's on cable, or pick from the personal collection?"

He got up and walked over to the cabinet, flipping through the cases. He chose three and came back to the couch. "Your pick," he offered, showing me the movies.

His choices were a thriller, a horror, and a romance. I wasn't in the mood for a horror movie since I had my scare earlier, so I tossed that one aside. I really didn't think it was fair to make him sit through a romance, so I tossed that one.

"Thriller it is," I announced as I took the movie and popped it in the player. "Would you like popcorn? You can't watch a movie without it."

"True, but no thank you," he replied politely.

I decided to skip it as well and took my place next to him. Putting my legs up on the couch, I leaned into him and rested my head on his shoulder. He placed his arm around me as I pressed play.

We weren't even a half hour into it when a fog slowly crept into my brain and I started getting drowsy, but I forced myself to stay aware. I really wanted David to stay the whole night. I resituated myself several times, but he never moved. He stayed in the same position the whole time.

When I couldn't fight it anymore, I fell asleep. In my borderline conscious state, I heard him turn the movie off. I woke slightly as he picked me up, cradling me in his arms and carrying me to my room. As he set me on the bed, I tried to tell him I was awake, but the words never came out. He pulled the covers over me and then walked to the balcony doors. Was he leaving me already?

I was able to whisper 'stay', which made him stop mid-step and turn around. As he sat next to me, he gently ran his fingers over my hair and softly kissed my lips. My eyes closed and I began to drift away.

The last thing I remember is hearing, "I will see you tomorrow..."

I slowly opened my eyes to a brightly lit room. I checked beside me, finding the space where David sat empty. Was last night also a dream? I grabbed the phone he gave me and checked the log, finding his call. I let out a relieved breath as I fell back onto my pillows.

Lying there a moment, I tried to decide what I wanted to do. It was ten o'clock, but I didn't feel like showering just yet. I stared at the ceiling a moment longer and then rolled out of bed, dragging myself downstairs to the kitchen to fix a bowl of cereal. Dad was in the family room watching TV.

"Morning," I greeted sluggishly as I sat at the counter to eat.

"It's about time you woke up," he responded, looking over the back of the sofa at me.

"I wasn't tired when I came home from the mall, so I stayed up late watching a movie."

"That explains it. So what are your plans for today?" he asked, getting up and walking into the kitchen.

"Nothing, really."

"Well, Vanessa and I have some more things to do for the wedding. It's getting closer, and yet there's still so much to get ready. I can't believe it's in a little over a month."

"Are you getting cold feet?" I teased.

He smiled and answered, "No, Meg. It just seems to have come up so fast. It's like it was just yesterday when I proposed."

I got up and went over to the sink, rolling my eyes. That's because it really wasn't that long ago. "Well, you go have fun. I think I'll enjoy the sunny day, maybe go to a park," I remarked as I headed back upstairs.

Sitting at my laptop, I tried to think of where I wanted to go today. I pulled up a map of Richmond and searched for parks I hadn't visited. As I scrolled around, I noticed several communities built around lakes.

Curiosity getting the better of me, I zoomed in on a couple, wondering if I could find David's house. After checking several and coming up empty, I was ready to give up, but then I spied one that didn't have many houses. Scanning around, I found a large, dark-colored one all alone on a peninsula. That has to be it.

A twinge of guilt struck me as I grabbed a piece of paper and a pencil. I really should respect his privacy, but what would it hurt? I wrote down the directions and put them in my purse. It was my turn to surprise David. Having a purpose now, I showered and got ready. I put my hair in a braid and dressed in light clothes since it was such a warm day.

Dad was still in the family room when I came down the stairs. "I'm headed out. I'll see you later." I announced, kissing his cheek.

I went to my car and pulled out the directions as soon as I sat, memorizing them. I placed them on the seat next to me in case I did need to reference them and left the neighborhood. Rolling down all the windows, I took a deep breath of the fresh spring air flowing around me. I couldn't have asked for a more gorgeous day to take a drive.

It was a long trip out to David's house, but it was worth it just to see the look on his face when he opened the door to find me standing there. I just hope he was home. I turned into the community and drove around looking for anything familiar from the aerial map. I went in circles trying to find it and was about to leave when I spotted a driveway hidden by trees.

I turned onto it and drove a little way down, coming to a complete stop in front a large, black, wrought iron gate. How strange. Putting the car in neutral and pulling the brake up, I climbed out and stared at the spires rising above me. Creepy. I checked the fence, trying to find a way in, but it disappeared into the woods. Both ways.

I spotted a call box nearby and went over to it, pushing the button. Not much of a surprise now if he answers. Oh well. As I waited for a response, I glanced around. Ahead of me, nothing but trees lined the drive as it curved with the road with no sign of a house. He must own a lot of land. I went back to the box and tried again. Still no answer. He must be out. Everyone must be out.

My attempt to surprise him failed, but maybe I could try another day, now that I knew where he lived. I climbed back into my car and backed out of the drive, carefully pulling onto the main road. I left the community and headed to a drive-thru to grab something to eat. Going to the closest park, I took my lunch and sat at a picnic table, munching on my food as I looked around.

Nearby, moms played with their children. I smiled watching them, but then felt a pang of sadness as I remembered mine taking me to the park and pushing me on the swing or chasing me around on the playground equipment. Not wanting to remember anymore, I quickly finished my food and left the picnic area.

I still wanted to continue enjoying the beautiful day, so I headed to the trails and took my time meandering along them. The new leaves sprouting on the trees gave the forest a bright green radiance. In my awe, I walked into a spider web. I must be the first person out here today. Grabbing a twig, I waved it in front of me to catch any additional ones as I continued my hike.

I looped back to the beginning and decided it was time to go home; the sun was starting to set. I thought about stopping by David's house again but figured I should head home instead. I didn't want to look like I was stalking him. Someday, he'd invite me.

As I drove, my thoughts turned to prom. I really should get a new dress, but I don't want David buying it. I could go next weekend and pick one up without him knowing, that way he'll be surprised the night of prom when he sees me coming down the stairs. No, I'll just ask Vanessa about the bridesmaid dress. Maybe if I catch her in a good mood, she'll agree.

I pulled into the driveway and parked behind Dad's car. The red sports car he bought Vanessa as a wedding gift was parked next to his, meaning she was here as well. Maybe tonight's the night I ask her about using the dress, as long as everything went well today.

I opened the door to her smiling face. "Oh good, you're home! We need to talk," she greeted abruptly, dragging me into the living room.

I was a little worried about what kind of 'talk' we'd be having. "Oookay," I replied, sitting on the loveseat.

Her eyes were fixed on mine as she sat beside me, taking my hand in hers. "Your dad told me your prom's coming up. I want to be here for you, preparing you for the best night of your life. So, first things first – you need a date. I'm going to share the secrets of my success in snagging the perfect guy..."

I didn't want nor need her advice, so I decided to cut her off right then and there. Dad was going to have to meet David soon anyway. "Vanessa, I have a date for prom."

"But your dad said you didn't," she replied, shocked.

"And last night, I was asked...by my boyfriend."

"So you have been seeing someone! I knew it!" she exclaimed, standing up.

"Just over the last couple of days," I lied.

She narrowed her eyes as she slowly lowered herself to the cushion and then smiled. "How did you meet him?"

I had to think up something quick. "Through a friend at school."

"Oh really? What's he like?"

"He's kind and has a great personality."

"And how does he look?" she asked anxiously, scooting closer.

"He's handsome."

"Just handsome? Ya gotta give me more than that."

I glanced at her and then out the living room window, thinking about David. "He has the most amazing green eyes and his smile is to die for. He's so different and...enthralling."

"You've only known him a couple days, but you seem to be in love."

"Yeah, he has that effect," I replied, looking at her grinning face. For the first time I noticed how young she really looked – not a single wrinkle.

"Personality is great, but looks help. Do we get to meet him soon?"

"Probably the night of prom. He's pretty busy."

"Busy? Why would a high school student be so busy?"

I blushed. This truth would have to come out, too. "He isn't in high school. He's in college."

"Oh...my...God! You're kidding me, right?"

"No, he's a freshman."

"Wow…when you pick a guy, you aim high."

I figured while we were having our little bonding moment, it'd be a good time to ask about the dress. "Vanessa, I wanted to ask, since we're talking about prom and whatnot…could I use my bridesmaid dress?"

Her smile faded and her face was stern. "Absolutely not. I can't have people seeing it before the wedding."

I tried to control my temper, but it was hard. She was being ridiculous. "No one going to my prom will be coming to your wedding. Why should it matter?"

She puffed up her chest and glared at me. "My wedding…my rules."

I refuse to get into it with her. I don't need her dress; I'll go get my own and it'll be better than her stupid bridesmaid dress that's mine anyway. I glared back at her as I stood to leave, but then remembered she had something on me. I have to tell Dad before she gets to him and blows it all out of proportion.

Not giving her the opportunity to even think about it, I dashed down the hall. I barged into his office and grabbed him by the arm. "I need to talk to you – now!"

We passed her as I dragged him outside, a look of shock on her face. He apologized and asked her to give us a couple minutes. She replied with a huff as she crossed her arms and stomped into the family room, dropping herself onto the couch to be consoled by the TV.

I continued dragging him all the way out to the gazebo as he asked the whole way what this was about, but I remained silent. When we reached it, I sat on the swing and he sat next to me. Putting my hands between my knees, I leaned forward slightly. I feared this day would come, but I hoped not this soon.

"Dad, I wanted to tell you that I do have a date for prom…" I began, staring at the worn wooden boards beneath my feet.

"That's great honey. Did you change your mind about Ben?"

I turned my head his way. "No…my boyfriend asked me," I replied, bracing myself for his wrath.

But instead, he gave an astonished look. "Your…your boyfriend? How long have you been dating?"

"Not long," I replied vaguely. I wasn't going to elaborate; he was having a hard enough time with what I was already revealing.

He stared off into the yard, not sure what to say next. "So, does he go to your school or another one nearby?"

"Umm…nearby. But he's not in high school."

"Please tell me he's younger than you…"

"No! That'd be like a middle school kid. Isn't that against the law or something?" I exclaimed. Looking into his eyes, I calmed down and placed my hand on his. "He's a great guy and I really like him."

"How did you meet?"

"Through a friend at school."

He looked pained, probably because I kept it from him. "What's his name? Is he from around here?"

"David Archer and no, he's from Massachusetts. He's a freshman at VCU and is studying to be a doctor."

He was quiet, taking it all in. "Has he pressured you to do anything?" he asked, wringing his hands as he tried to remain levelheaded.

"No, he hasn't. He's not like that. Please believe me."

He paused, staring at his hands, and then faced me. "When will we get to meet him?"

"We?"

"Well, Vanessa will be your stepmother in a few weeks. She should be included."

I looked away and clenched my teeth. "Probably not until prom night. He's busy."

"Busy with what?"

"Didn't you hear me? He goes to school full-time, plus he works at the medical examiner's office."

"So he doesn't have much time for you either. When have you been able to see each other?"

What could I say to him – that I've been seeing David behind his back, sneaking out at all hours of the night, and that he's come to the house? "He's met me after school just to say hello, but we mostly talk on the phone," I lied.

It was getting darker and as I looked toward the house, I saw Vanessa pacing at the door. Dad was still trying to wrap his head around everything I confessed to him. He sighed and looked at me again. "I trust you, Megan. I can't wait to meet David the night of prom," he conceded.

"Thank you, Dad. You'll like him a lot," I responded happily, giving him a hug and a kiss on the cheek.

He gave a weak smile, knowing this day would eventually come, too. We stood up and walked back to the house, arm in arm. Vanessa backed away from the door as we entered and jumped on him as soon as he turned into the kitchen.

"What did she tell you? Did she mention her boyfriend…who's in college?" I heard her say as I climbed the stairs.

Yep, she had nothing on me.

# Chapter 13
## Preparation

As soon as I entered my room, I grabbed my phone and headed out onto the balcony as I dialed Claire's number. She had to hear about this. The phone rang several times, but she never answered. I left a message to call me back, figuring she was probably out with Justin. I re-entered the room and sat on my bed, trying to decide what to do when my stomach rumbled.

"You should eat something," a masculine voice commented behind me, and I jumped.

I turned and found David standing in the doorway of the balcony, smiling. My heart raced as I shot up and grabbed him, fear overriding the urge to get caught up in his gaze as I pulled him inside.

"What are you doing here? My dad and Vanessa are downstairs in the kitchen! They could have seen you!" I whispered loudly.

"Highly unlikely," he responded coolly, sitting on my bed. "I was nearby and wanted to stop by and see you."

"That's very sweet, but could we do this after my dad has gone to bed?"

"No, now is as good a time as any," he replied, lying back. "So, what did you find to do today?" he asked calmly as I anxiously paced back and forth, biting at my thumbnail.

"Megan! Dinner's ready!" Dad called up the stairs.

I panicked, not knowing what to do. "Tell him you're coming. I'll stay here while you eat," David suggested, propping himself up on his elbows.

I nodded slowly and cracked the door. "Coming!" I shouted.

I opened it wider and was ready to walk out when he suddenly grabbed me, giving me a quick kiss. I froze, surprised by it, and then turned. Shutting the door tightly behind me, I took a deep breath and headed downstairs.

Dad had the table set with a plate of food waiting for me. Vanessa didn't bother looking at me as I entered. But he did and there was a look of concern on his face.

"Are you okay? You seem uneasy," he remarked as I took a seat.

"Yeah...no, I'm fine," I answered, trying not to think about David...lying on my bed...up in my room.

My stomach growled again and diverted the attention away from my worried expression. "Looks like I prepared dinner a little late for your schedule," he commented with a grin, taking a bite.

The corners of my mouth twitched into a slight smile, and I began to feel less apprehensive as I lifted the fork to my lips. He doesn't suspect a thing. "That's okay. There were more important matters that needed to be taken care of."

Vanessa ate quietly while Dad and I exchanged quips. Then she picked up her paper napkin and patted her mouth. "I was thinking, Megan, since I was so harsh about using the bridesmaid dress, maybe I could take you shopping for your prom dress. How does that sound?"

Where is this coming from? Ohhh...Dad must have had a talk with her. I glanced at him giving puppy dog eyes and rolled mine. "Sure, why not," I replied, taking another bite. He smiled at me as I narrowed my eyes at him.

"Great! We can go tomorrow afternoon. This is going to be fun!" she responded excitedly, hoping to relive the best years of her life through me.

For the remainder of the meal, they discussed work and what was going on in the world as I sat and listened. I wasn't really interested, but it kept my mind occupied. As soon as I finished, I quickly rinsed my plate and stuck it in the dishwasher. I told them good night as they stood to clear their plates and then hurried out of the room before they could stop me. I rushed up the stairs, wondering what David has been doing to occupy himself while I've been away.

I got my answer as I opened the door, finding him leaning over my desk looking at my laptop. I shut and locked the door, just in case Dad came up to bother me. Walking over, I found him examining maps of the Richmond area. He never turned to greet me.

"What *did* you do today, Megan?" he asked through clenched teeth as he continued to stare at the screen, his hand resting on my scribbled directions to his house.

His tone stunned me. "I...I was looking for a new park to go to today and noticed several lake communities. Next thing you know...I found your house," I answered hesitantly. He's never acted this way toward me before. "I stopped by, but no one was home. I wanted to surprise you," I finished meekly.

He quickly turned away and stalked out onto the balcony, going to the cherry tree to leave. I followed him, briefly peeking over the edge to make sure Dad and Vanessa weren't in view. He held onto the branch and stared at me, a pained expression on his face.

"You shouldn't have done that," he scolded.

When I didn't respond or defend myself, he turned to climb down the tree. "Wait! Why?" I shouted against my better judgment.

He let go of the branch and hopped off the railing, striding toward me. "I have secrets...things I'm not ready to share with you. Coming to my house uninvited is not safe," he replied sternly, backing me against the French door.

"I'm sorry. I-I won't do it again," I responded quietly.

"Promise me you won't do it again," he demanded abruptly.

"I…I promise."

He stared silently for a moment and then strode past me into the bedroom, sitting on the bench by my closet. As I entered, a little shaken, my phone rang. I glanced at the screen, seeing it was Claire returning my call. Rather than ignore her, I indicated to David I was taking it and headed back out onto the balcony to talk.

Taking a deep breath, I answered. "How's it going?" I asked as casual as possible, peeking below to see if Dad or Vanessa noticed anything.

"Good…Justin and I were out on a date and I forgot my phone. So, what did you want to talk about?" she inquired.

"My interesting afternoon, but I'm going to have to keep it short. I have a visitor," I responded, dropping my voice.

"A visitor? Who…David?" she questioned excitably.

"Yep," I answered, glancing over my shoulder at him. He had gotten up and was strolling around the room, looking restless.

"He's there now…in your room?"

"Yes, and anxiously waiting for me to finish my call. Now can we talk about the reason why I called?"

"Shoot…"

"David asked me to prom last night and agreed to have one of his roommates go with Ben. Realizing I could no longer keep our relationship secret, I told both Dad and Vanessa about him. Now needing a dress, I asked Vanessa if I could use my bridesmaid gown. She refused to let me, but later offered to take me shopping instead," I summarized quickly.

"Your dad took it well?"

"For the most part. I didn't tell him exactly how long we've been dating and said I met David through a friend at school."

"Well, I'm glad he didn't forbid you from seeing him. Wow, this is great news! So we get to meet him at prom!" Claire exclaimed.

I felt a presence behind me, but when I glanced over my shoulder, nothing was there. David was in the room sitting on the bench again, reading a book. I turned back around, looking out into the garden.

"I should go. I'll call tomorrow to let you know how my shopping experience with Vanessa went."

"Good luck!" she replied and hung up.

I stayed out on the balcony a little longer, allowing him to cool off some more. I hope he wasn't going to be mad at me all night. How could he? It was an innocent mistake and yet he blew up. *Secrets*. What secrets could he have that were so bad my life would be at risk?

Staring at the sky for answers, I sighed. It was extremely dark tonight. I hadn't heard if we were getting rain tomorrow, but looking like this with the clouds covering the sky, it made me wonder. I continued to contemplate the weather until I felt the presence again. But this time when I turned to check, David was standing there.

He wrapped his arms around my body, holding tight. "Please forgive me. I shouldn't have gotten angry with you," he whispered in my ear. "I know you had the best of intentions, but you have to be careful."

"Okay," I responded, shocked by his sudden mood swing.

"I don't want to lose you," he continued, something oddly familiar in his words which caused my heart to flutter.

He loosened his hold and gazed into my eyes. Leaning in slowly, he pressed his lips to mine, kissing soft and slow. Then we parted, but I wasn't ready to end it so soon. I slipped my arms around his neck and brought him closer, kissing more passionately. He replied at first and then suddenly broke away.

Without a word, he went back into the room and walked toward the bench. He never looked back to see if I followed and after he sat, he leaned forward on his knees with his head down. I sat on the edge of the bed across from him and waited for him to say something. He finally looked up, but remained quiet, staring at me as if trying to memorize everything about me in that moment.

"Are you okay?" I asked quietly.

He looked away. "Yes, I am. You took me by surprise," he replied.

"Oh, I'm sorry," I apologized, blushing.

"It's all right," he responded as he stood and strolled over to my bookcase, replacing the book he had been reading earlier. He scanned the others, pulling one out and flipping through the pages.

Now that we were somewhat back to normal, I decided to let him know we were official. "I told my dad about you tonight," I commented.

"How did he take it?" he asked, slipping the book back before turning toward me.

"Pretty well. He wants to meet you, of course, but I told him it wouldn't be until prom."

He grinned. "Why wait? I could go down right now and introduce myself," he replied as he crossed the room.

I quickly jumped up and blocked his way. "Don't. You. Dare," I threatened.

"All right, I won't," he laughed. "Did you get a chance today to ask Vanessa about the dress?"

"She said no."

"The offer is still on the table..."

"I know, but I can't. She's taking me shopping for one tomorrow. Besides, I want it to be a surprise."

"Even if I buy it, I won't know what it looks like on you until that night," he retorted, trying his best to convince me.

"The answer is sti-" I started but cut myself off as I heard the front door shut. "Quick, hide!" I commanded, knowing Dad's next stop would be my room.

David dashed out onto the balcony, closing the doors behind him. I quickly unlocked the bedroom door and grabbed the book laying on the bedside table. Flopping onto my belly on the bed, I pretended to read as Dad knocked on my door.

"Come in," I requested, glancing quickly at the balcony. David peered through one of the panes, and I signaled to him to hide better. As the door handle lowered, I jerked back and perused the book. Dad poked his head in and paused, watching me read. "Yeah, Dad?" I asked, innocently raising my eyes to him.

"Nothing, just wanted to say good night and let you know how much I appreciate you going shopping with Vanessa tomorrow. It'll be good...for both of you."

"No problem...anything for you. Has she left?"

"Yep. She'll be here around one tomorrow to pick you up."

Crap. No running away this time. "Sounds good. Well, I better get some sleep so I'm in a good mood for her tomorrow. I'm sure I'll be trying on plenty of dresses," I remarked, closing the book and replacing it on the table.

"Okay. Good night," he smiled softly.

I replied as he shut the door. As soon as I heard his steps fade down the hall, I ran to the balcony doors and opened them, peeking around the side. David was leaning against the brick wall, staring out into the yard. He glanced at me as I waved at him to come back inside.

"He's gone to bed now," I informed him as he entered.

"He seems like a good man."

"Thank you...he is," I commented, sitting on the bed.

He sat next to me, leaning forward on his knees. "So other than trespassing on my property, what else did you do today?" he asked with a smile, making my heart beat rapidly.

I took a breath and stared at my hands. "Well, I went to a park nearby, had lunch at the playground, and then walked around. I've never been there before. It's beautiful."

"It is. I spend a lot of time there."

"After that, I came home and the rest is history. Oh, did you ask Madeline about going to prom with Ben?"

"I did. She agreed and is very excited, not only to meet him, but to meet you as well."

"Oh…really?"

"I was thinking, since you won't let me buy your dress, would it be all right if I rent the limousine for the group. There will be…four couples, correct?"

"Yes. I'll text the addresses to you later. That's really generous of you."

"It would be my pleasure," he responded. "We'll pick you up around eight."

Eight? Why is he waiting so late? "We're not going out to dinner together beforehand?" I asked.

"No, I have something important I have to do."

"Oh, okay. No problem. Maybe I'll have a nice meal with Dad and Vanessa. They'll like that."

"Good," he replied as he stood. "I should be going and you should get some sleep. You're going to have a very exciting day tomorrow," he grinned. My heart thumped.

He leaned down and kissed me, holding my chin lightly in his fingertips, then he straightened up and headed to the balcony. I wanted so badly to ask him to stay like he did in my dreams, but I couldn't. What I was doing behind my dad's back was bad enough.

I hopped off the bed and went to the doors, standing in the frame watching as he quietly climbed down the tree and sprinted across the yard. Once he was out of view, I closed them and turned around, leaning back against them as I sighed. Pushing off, I grabbed a set of pajamas and headed into the bathroom to prepare for bed.

As I re-entered my room, I couldn't bring myself to go to sleep just yet. Sitting on the edge of the mattress, I thought about our conversations. What a strange mix of subjects we covered tonight. And yet I felt more confused than ever.

I don't know what to do when something like this happens. It was almost scary how defensive and angry he acted. And all because I went to his house uninvited. Then just like that, he's all apologies. Everything is forgiven and forgotten and life moves on.

Forcing myself to wind down, I turned off the light and curled up under my covers. Staring at the clock numbers, I watched as the minutes passed. Before a half hour had gone by, I was asleep.

There was no sun when I woke Sunday morning. I could hear the quiet pattering of rain on the balcony and roof. I covered my face with the pillow and moaned. What a miserable day to go dress shopping!

I rolled out of bed a couple minutes later and went into the bathroom to get ready. It was only nine, but I might as well prepare now. Flipping through my closet, I searched for an easy outfit to change in and out of and finally decided on a cute cap-sleeved dress with a scalloped neckline. I put my hair in a ponytail and headed downstairs to grab something to eat.

As I reached the bottom step, I smelled bacon and pancakes. Dad was making a full breakfast this morning. I sat at the island and watched as he flipped the eggs and stirred the hashbrowns. I couldn't wait to eat.

"Good morning, Meg," he greeted cheerfully. "Did you sleep well?"

"Yes. And you?"

"Best sleep I've had in a while. So what would you like?"

I looked over what was laid out. "A little of everything, please."

"You have a big appetite this morning," he commented, loading up my plate.

He handed it to me and I took it to the nook table. It smelled delicious and I couldn't wait to dig in. He fixed his plate and joined me, giving the okay to start. It was nice to have breakfast alone with my dad.

I stared out the window at the rain as it came down harder. "Not the ideal day for dress shopping, but I'm ready," I remarked, crunching a piece of bacon.

"Just don't forget an umbrella," he replied.

I nodded as I munched my toast. "So what are your plans today? You're a free man."

"Oh, I'll probably watch a game. Nothing spectacular."

"But it's perfect for you."

"And I'll enjoy every minute," he smiled, leaning back. He must be getting full like I was. "About today…I know how Vanessa is, so don't let her talk you into anything she would wear. Not that I have a problem with her wearing it, but I would if you did."

"Don't worry, Dad, I won't. I'm looking for something classic and sophisticated," I replied, clearing the table.

I took care of the dishes and then joined him in the family room, watching as he flipped through the multitude of ministers preaching on TV. We didn't go to church, though we used to when Mom was alive. He lost his faith when he lost her. During her sickness, we prayed constantly for her to get better and when things got worse, he felt abandoned. He gave up, but I never did.

"There aren't any games on right now. You might as well give it up," I commented as he angrily flipped through all the channels again.

"Maybe I'll pop a movie in for the time being," he commented, forcing himself up.

"That's a great idea, and I'll watch it with you. I still have a while before Vanessa gets here."

He picked a comedy, I guess to brighten his soured mood. And it worked. Not a moment later, he was laughing through the whole thing. I hadn't seen him like this in a long time. I laughed, too, enjoying the time together and hoping it would stay with me through my shopping trip with Vanessa.

After the movie finished, he flipped through the channels again. He was more successful this time. I stayed with him to kill time, watching baseball though it was my least favorite sport. She should be here any moment, so I made sure I had everything I needed so I didn't keep her waiting. I made a promise to myself to try not to anger or insult her in any way so we both could have a pleasant day.

The doorbell rang and I jumped up to get it, letting her in and following her to the family room. She looked at my dad, repulsed by his slovenly appearance. I guess she's never seen him on his 'do nothing' days.

"Good morning, honey bun," she greeted sweetly as she kissed him on the cheek, the disgusted look still on her face. "Is this what you plan to do today?"

"Yep, it's been awhile since I've watched a game. Well, have fun and I'll see you later," he responded quickly, trying to rush us out. The commercials were over and the game was back on.

"Okay then, let's get going," she commanded, leading me out the door.

We took her car and headed into the city. She claimed there were a lot of exquisite dress shops where we could find something extraordinary and one of a kind. I knew it was a special occasion, but I still didn't get why everyone was making such a big deal out of this.

As she drove, she babbled on about her friends and past boyfriends – so much drama. I responded as appropriate to whatever she said, not really paying attention to the context of what she was saying. Most of the car ride, she talked and when she didn't, there was silence. I cherished those moments the most.

I was thankful when she pulled up to our first stop. The shop was an elite store with one of a kind creations made by the store owner. As soon as we walked in, I was ready to walk out. It was too stuffy and the saleswomen were arrogant. Price was not an issue, but I just about died when I saw how much one of the designer creations cost. I tried on a couple, but none were what I wanted. We left and headed to the next shop.

Store after store, I didn't find anything I liked. Vanessa was being very patient with me, but two hours in, her patience started to wane. Her last resort was a dinky little place in Carytown that carried specialty dresses. We went there and searched the racks for something. That's when I found it, the only one and in my size. It was meant to be.

I went into the dressing room and slipped it on. The fabric was lithe and the color made the blue in my eyes pop. My curly, dark brunette hair even looked great with it. I stared in the mirror and marveled at it, imagining David's expression when he saw me descend the stairs the night of prom.

It was midnight blue, almost black, at the top, fading into a dark blue toward the hem. An abundance of rhinestones accented the chest area which became sparser and more spread out as they flowed to the base of the skirt. It reminded me of the night sky with millions of tiny stars. Yes, it was perfect.

I came out of the dressing room and modeled it for Vanessa. She was delighted and relieved all at the same time. She liked how it was strapless, fit to my body, and had a nice slit to just above the knee. It was a little pricey, but not as bad as some of the other shops. I pulled out Dad's credit card and paid for it.

The lady behind the counter smiled sweetly at me. "It was made for you," she stated.

I smiled politely as I took the bag. What an odd thing to say. "Thank you," I replied.

"What a weirdo," Vanessa mumbled as she pulled me out the door.

The rain had finally stopped, but the clouds lingered, ready to open up again at any moment. We had a good distance to walk to her car, and I hoped it would hold off until we got there. As we strolled down the sidewalk, she couldn't stop talking about my gown and the weird lady at the dress shop.

Then she stopped suddenly, watching as a man on a motorcycle slowly drove by and then sped off. That was strange. We started walking again, but she didn't resume her previous jabbering. *He* was the new subject of conversation.

I didn't get a good look at him, but she apparently did. Tall and muscular riding a red and black Hyabusa (she knows her motorcycles), dressed all in black with a black helmet. She acted like a silly school girl gushing over this nameless, faceless guy.

Within a couple of minutes, we heard the motorcycle again and noticed it slowing near us. Wanting to get him to stop this time, she gave a flirty pose and grinned as he pulled into an open spot alongside us. This can't be good.

He stood tall with the motorcycle between his legs, and I started wondering when it might be a good idea to leave. Of course, I couldn't get Vanessa to budge. She held steadfast as he shut off the engine. When he removed his helmet, I gasped.

"Hello, Megan," Brian greeted, his deep voice smooth and sultry. He had his hair partially pulled back, his dark brows accentuating the piercing gray of his eyes. "I thought it was you when I first rode by. Nice to see you again." The grin he had sent a chill through me.

Vanessa looked at me and smiled. "Who's this handsome devil?"

"That's Brian…and we should really be going," I remarked, grabbing her arm and trying to walk away, but she remained.

"Why so quick to leave?" he purred, gazing into her eyes. "You haven't introduced me to your lovely friend." She smiled at him, completely still like she was stuck in the concrete under her feet. I couldn't tell if she was even breathing.

"She's not my friend. She's my soon-to-be stepmother, Vanessa."

"Huh, she looks like she could be a classmate," he replied as he kicked the stand into place and climbed off the bike, moving toward us.

I backed away, but she didn't. He came up and took her hand, bowing slightly and kissing it. She stared at it with a dumbfounded look on her face as he straightened up. I was not at all comfortable with him being here. Wary of his proximity to me, I moved closer to her and tugged on her shirt while quietly urging her to leave.

"So what are you beautiful ladies up to today?" he asked, only looking at her.

"Shopping," I replied quickly, continuing my attempt to get her to move.

"Shopping for Megan's prom dress," she answered, delayed and daze-like. I swiftly moved to her side and looked at her in astonishment. She never even noticed I was there.

"Prom? David didn't tell me you have prom coming up. Is he going with you?" he inquired, breaking his stare with Vanessa to look at me. Another chill spilled down my spine.

"Yes, he is," she replied, beating me to the answer this time.

We need to go and now. "Well, Brian, it was nice seeing you again, but we must be leaving," I announced, grabbing her and forcefully dragging her away. Her eyes never left him.

"It was a pleasure to meet you, Vanessa, and good to see you again, Megan," he commented with a smirk as he mounted his bike and put his helmet back on. It growled as he started it and then he was off, speeding down Cary Street. Making sure he wasn't coming back, I let go of her and turned as I watched him disappear.

She seemed to come out of her daze as soon as he was out of sight. "Wow, what a hottie!" she exclaimed, walking next to me as I continued toward the car. "How do you know him?"

"He's one of David's roommates."

"Oh…he has a way with women," she remarked, fanning herself.

"Yeah, he's a charmer," I responded as we approached the parking area.

The whole ride home was nothing but talk about Brian. She asked me questions, but I had nothing for her. She went on and on about his eyes and hair and how muscular he was. I was glad when we finally pulled into the drive. Quickly exiting the car, I headed into the house and to the family room to see if Dad was still planted in front of the TV.

To my surprise, he was setting the table for dinner in the dining room. "I see we came home just in time," I joked.

"Oh, hey Meg. How was the shopping trip? Find anything good?" he asked as Vanessa walked into the room.

I raised the bag and smiled. "We had a good time and I found the perfect dress, but you can't see it until prom night."

He looked at her. "You'll be pleased with it, very elegant and tasteful," she answered.

"Well, dinner is just about ready. I figured after your day-long excursion, you would appreciate it."

He brought out the last dish and set it on the table. It looked amazing. We dug in as we told him about our trials and tribulations of finding the perfect dress, but through it all, we had a good time. I could tell he was pleased to hear it. Both of us conveniently left out the part about Brian. I promised myself I would never tell him about her encounter. Let her do it.

She and I offered to take care of the dishes and leftovers as Dad went back to the family room, smiling. We worked well together, Vanessa and me, and even had a little fun. Maybe she wasn't as bad as I made her out to be. We just had to find a common ground.

"Thanks for not saying anything to your dad about Brian," she remarked casually as I put the last of the dishes in the washer.

"No problem. It doesn't hurt to look," I responded, bumping my hip into hers.

She smiled and then we joined Dad in the family room, begging him to turn it to something other than sports. He offered to buy a movie, so I let her choose. She picked a romance and as it began, she cuddled up to him. I looked at them and longed to have David by my side, holding him.

It was good, your typical sappy romance with not a dry eye between Vanessa and me. Dad was moved by it, but not teary-eyed. That was a man for you. Standing up and stretching, I looked at the time and decided to go to my room so they could have some privacy. She probably missed him and he her. I thanked her for taking me out and helping to find my dress and Dad for dinner and buying the dress before heading to my room.

I changed as I checked my phone and saw Claire called around seven. As soon as I was comfortable, I dialed her number. The phone rang several times and I almost thought she wasn't going to answer, but she did before it went to voicemail. She was out of breath, like she ran a mile to catch it.

"What took you so long?" I asked.

"I was in the other room playing video games with the monster and Justin. There was a quiet moment while the screen loaded and that's when I heard the phone. So how was your evening last night and your day today?"

"We talked about prom. He insisted on renting the limo since I wouldn't allow him to buy my dress. He plans to pick me up around eight and then everyone else after that."

"That's kind of late to have dinner."

"We're not having dinner together. He has something important going on before prom and can't do it. I'm just going to stay home and eat with Dad and Vanessa."

"And Ben's date?"

"She's busy until eight, too, so Ben's on his own for dinner."

"So how was dress shopping? Did you find anything?"

"We actually had fun, even though toward the end we were both struggling. But I found the perfect dress. David's going to love it," I replied and then remembered our unpleasant encounter. "Oh, and you won't believe who we ran into as we headed back to the car."

"Who?" she asked eagerly.

"Brian. He pulled up next to us on his motorcycle. Vanessa was fawning all over him...it was crazy."

"He rides a motorcycle? He's just a regular bad boy, isn't he?"

"Yeah, I think so. He makes me uncomfortable when I'm near him."

"That's because you're David's girl."

Ooo...I like the sound of that – *David's girl*. "No...there's something unnerving I can't put my finger on."

"Well, hopefully you won't have too many encounters with him," she remarked and then I heard her cover the phone, coming back on after a brief moment. "Okay, I better get back to the game. Justin will be going home soon. I'll see you tomorrow at school and you can tell me more about your dress."

"Bye, Claire," I responded and hung up.

Not ready to go to bed and still waiting on David's call, I decided to relax and listen to music. Turning off the overhead light, I switched on the bedside lamp and selected the classical playlist on my iPod, playing it through my stereo. I stretched out on the bed and stared at the ceiling, letting the music spark my imagination.

It started off soft and serene and I imagined lying in a meadow, gazing at the sky as the clouds slowly rolled by. As it switched to the next piece, I found myself running through the tall grass with the sun bright on my face, feeling overwhelming joy. Then the next piece changed to something darker. Standing in that same meadow, I watched as storm clouds gathered above me, turning the sky dark and sinister. My happiness was replaced with gloom and fear. I opened my eyes to make it go away.

It was close to eleven and I could feel myself getting tired. I hope David calls soon. I really want to talk to him and tell him about the dress and running into Brian. To stay awake, I sat at my laptop and played a couple of games. I had just finished Solitaire when his phone started vibrating.

I grabbed it and hopped onto the bed. "Good evening, David."

"Hello, Megan. How was your shopping experience?"

"Better than I expected," I answered, rolling onto my back. "Why are you calling so late?"

"I was working. Did you find a dress?"

"I did and you're going to love it."

"Do you plan to model it for me sometime?"

"Not until prom night. I told you I want it to be a surprise."

"I tried."

"I can't believe you thought I'd give in that easily," I responded as I twisted a curl around my finger. "So did you do anything special today, other than work?"

"No, nothing exciting. I had a very relaxing day."

"So did my dad. I think he really enjoyed having a day to himself."

"We all need those every once in a while," he responded, and I could hear the smile in his voice. "Did you and Vanessa play nice?"

"Surprisingly, yes. She was patient with me through all of it, but I could tell my indecision was wearing on her. She kept her cool, though. When I finally found my dress, she was visibly relieved and couldn't stop talking about it as we headed to the car," I replied. "Well, that was until something else distracted her."

"And what might that be?"

"Brian…he spotted us as he rode down Cary Street."

"Brian?" David questioned, his tone changing drastically. "Did he speak with you?"

"He wanted to know what we were doing, to which I replied shopping, but then Vanessa and her big mouth said it was for prom. He asked if you were going and again, she blabbed. Finally having enough, I dragged her away and he took off. That's it." He was silent. "Is something wrong?"

"No, everything is fine. So he didn't say anything more?"

"No, just that. Vanessa was quite taken with him."

"I bet she has a history of dating bad boys," he commented, a bit calmer.

"So how was work?" I asked, changing the subject.

"Good. I'm learning quite a bit working in the medical examiner's office."

"What do you do there?"

"I help with autopsies, taking samples…"

"How…morbid."

"Yes, I know it's not the most glamorous job…"

"Are you okay? You don't seem like yourself all of a sudden."

"It's been a long day; I think we both need rest. I'll talk to you tomorrow night. I promise I'll be in a better mood."

"All right. Good night."

"Sleep well," he replied softly and hung up.

I put the phone on the bedside table and turned off the stereo and light. Exhaustion catching up with me, I curled up in my blanket and closed my eyes. Falling asleep shouldn't be too hard tonight with the tiring day I had.

But lying there waiting for it, I found I couldn't. My mind had other plans. It was busy thinking about David's reaction and the questions he asked about my encounter with Brian. I mulled over it for a long time, trying to piece things together. It was the last thing on my mind before I fell asleep.

Something woke me from my slumber. I sat up and stared at the balcony doors, feeling the need to go to them. I stood slowly and staggered over, pushing down on the handle and stepping outside. In the dark, waiting by the railing, was David. He turned and looked at me, concern in his eyes.

"Meg-"

"What are you doing here?" I asked groggily, interrupting him.

"You should go back inside," he whispered, moving toward me and placing his hand on my back as he guided me.

"Why?" I inquired, turning toward him and taking his hand in mine. His skin was icy.

"Please...just trust me," he requested, gazing into my eyes. My mind went blank, and all I could see were the deep green of his irises. "Go back to bed."

I obeyed, stepping back and slowly moving away from him and toward my room, my eyes remaining locked on his. I could hear something in the background, unable to make out what it was, but it distracted David. I was just over the threshold when he turned away, breaking my trance.

He moved quickly to the railing and stared down into the yard. As my mind became more aware, curiosity got the better of me. Without saying a word, I slipped back out and to his side. As I looked over the railing, I saw Brian's grinning face and gasped.

David turned to me and grabbed my arms, forcing me inside. "I need you to stay here. I will take care of him," he whispered, then kissed me softly.

My head swam and I craved more. He tried to move away, but I wouldn't let him. My pulse raced as I parted my lips, wanting to taste his. Suddenly he broke away, breathing hard.

The desire gone, I instantly felt embarrassed, but it was soon replaced by worry when I heard Brian calling for me. "Why is he here?" I asked as David released me onto the bed and stepped away.

"You don't need to worry about that. Go back to sleep," he instructed as he slipped out the doors and shut them tight.

I stood up and rushed to them to see what he was doing. He came back and stood before me, wood and glass separating us, and slipped something through the handles. Giving me one last look, he turned and went to the railing and stood on it. I tugged on the handles, wanting to stop him from jumping, but they wouldn't budge. He glanced back, gave a soft smile, and then leapt.

I violently shook the doors, but couldn't get them open. Quickly dashing out of my room, I ran downstairs to the patio doors, scanning the yard for him. He was nowhere. Turning the latch, I started to go outside when I noticed something moving in the back part of the yard. What if it was Brian?

I pulled the door tight and watched, waiting for confirmation. The figure remained in the shadows a moment and then in a blink, it was at the foot of the cherry tree. It briefly glanced my way, and I realized it was David. He moved so fast, but how?

He started climbing, never noticing me watching from the patio doors. Then I realized I needed to get back upstairs before he discovered I was missing. I dashed up the steps and quickly ducked into my room, slipping into bed.

There was no sign of him. Maybe he hadn't made it up the tree yet. I rolled over and pretended to sleep, peeking through my lashes at the doors and expecting him to appear any moment. My eyelids became heavy as I waited and then finally I gave up. Before I was completely out, I felt the gentle caress of a cold hand and a soft, chill kiss on my cheek.

# Chapter 14
## A Mistake

My alarm woke me too soon. Slamming my hand down on the clock, I hit the snooze and rolled onto my back. Was it time to get up already? I felt like I only had a few hours of sleep.

Then I remembered what happened last night.

Did it really happen? It was all so strange – the way David acted, felt, looked, and Brian being here. It had to be a dream. There was no other explanation.

The alarm sounded the second time, making me jump. I shut it off and sat up, knowing I needed to get moving. Forcing myself off the bed, I went into the bathroom and got ready.

I arrived at school, anxious to get through the day as quickly as possible. With being so tired and the bizarre dream plaguing my thoughts, I had a feeling it was going to be a bad one. But I couldn't go home or else I'd dwell on it, so I needed the distraction of school.

I didn't have much to say to Claire before class, but she had plenty to tell me about her weekend, her parents, and her date with Justin. Don't get me wrong, she's heard enough of my stories and problems, but I just wasn't in the mood this morning. I was thankful when the bell rang, cutting her off mid-sentence.

When lunchtime rolled around, I chose to eat outside. The sun was shining, a change from all the rain the day before, and it was cooler than it had been last week. I grabbed my food and waited until everyone made it to the lunchroom, then indicated I was going out to the courtyard. I sat alone, waiting for the others to join me as I picked at my salad.

Claire came first, followed by Erin and then Ben and Justin. Their expressions were split; Erin and Justin were happy to be out in the fresh air while Claire and Ben resented the fact that I insisted on it. Oh well, they just have to deal with it. Nobody else wanted to be outside today. I was there to soak up the sun and have some privacy.

"So Megan, Claire told us you have good news," Erin commented.

I looked up from my food. "Oh, I do! For starters, I'm going to prom with David and…" I paused, turning to Ben, "his roommate agreed to go with you!" I announced excitedly.

He didn't seem happy about it. "Oh…good," he replied grumpily.

"Yay for Ben! So what else?" Erin asked eagerly.

"I found the perfect dress yesterday. Also, David is renting a limo for all of us."

"Tell them the not so good part," Claire piped up.

"Unfortunately, he has something going on before prom, so he won't be picking us up until after eight," I answered with a grimace.

"So we're not having dinner together?" Ben asked.

"No, I'm eating with my dad and Vanessa. I don't know what everyone else's plans are," I answered.

"Oh. Guess I'll eat at home since my date won't be available till then either," Ben grumbled, but then looked as if a light bulb came on. "Or…you and I could go to dinner together," he suggested.

"No," I responded. "I already told Dad I'm having dinner with them," I lied.

He angrily propped his head on his hand and stabbed at his food. "So what's my date's name?" he inquired.

"Madeline," I replied.

"Madeline," he repeated, trying her name out. "What does she look like? How long has he known her? What kind of person is she?" he questioned.

"Your guess is as good as mine. I've never met her, but David said she's lots of fun."

"Have you met any of his roommates?" Justin asked.

"Only one."

"Brian…the one I was telling you about," Claire whispered to him. He nodded, knowing exactly what she meant. I felt a little perturbed but let it roll off.

The discussion turned to dinner ideas for prom night, and Ben and I were silent as we ate or looked around. Claire and Justin went over options and times, and then Erin decided to get in the middle of it, suggesting different places.

"How was your weekend, Ben?" I asked, starting a conversation with him rather than sitting there being antisocial.

He took a moment to answer. "Okay, I guess. I played this awesome new zombie game all day Sunday."

"Well, it was a good day for it. I spent my Sunday dress shopping in the gloom with Vanessa."

"That bad, huh?" he asked.

"No…actually, it was nice. It was just the rain that spoiled it."

He paused, shifting in his seat. "With him asking you out, did you have to tell your dad?"

He'll be happy to hear that our dating is no longer a secret. "Yeah, I was talking to Vanessa Saturday night and it came out. I told Dad all about him a few minutes later."

"How did he react?"

"He was pretty cool about it. He's eager to meet him."

"We all are!" Erin exclaimed, butting in.

"So what about you, Erin? Do you have a date yet?" I asked curiously.

"I think I'll go stag. There's no one in this school that's good enough for me," she answered prissily.

"What about that hot guy we passed coming out here, with the shoulder length, curly, black hair and nice skin? I've seen him during soccer practice after school and he's good. He might actually be competition for you," I suggested.

"He is cute, but I don't date younger than me. He's a sophomore."

"Your problem is your standards are too high," Claire joked.

"No, none of the *boys* here can handle a woman like me!" she retorted. Justin and Ben looked at each other and burst into laughter. "What? What's so funny? Oh, I know…well, apparently the boys weren't doing anything for Megan either. She got herself a man!"

Justin continued to laugh, but Ben stopped. He glared at her grinning face and suddenly wrenched up his lunch tray, rushing inside. I looked at her, shaking my head, and then ran after him. He had already dumped his food and was walking quickly toward the hall when I entered the cafeteria. I continued after him, catching him by the arm in the hall.

"Ben, don't listen to her. You know Erin – when she's made fun of, she wants to turn it back around on the person who ridiculed her. And you know she knows how to get to you."

He jerked loose and stared at me. "Is it true?"

"Do we have to go through this again? You know the answer…"

"What did I do wrong?" he questioned. "Why aren't you in love with me?"

"Please. Not now…"

"Is it because of money? Apparently, David's loaded. I didn't think you were like that."

"It's not about money – I'm not shallow. We…we…there's just no chemistry between us. You're a great friend, but I don't see this ever evolving into more."

"You've never kissed me. Maybe if you kiss me, there'd be chemistry."

"No…I have a boyfriend," I replied sternly, surprised he'd go there. He was getting desperate.

"Forget about him for a moment and let's see if there's anything," he suggested, moving closer.

"You're being unreasonable. I'm leaving."

I turned to go, but he grabbed me and before I knew it, his lips were pressed to mine. Immediately, I shoved him away, knocking him to the ground. I stared in shock as he watched me, waiting for some response, but I gave him nothing.

The bell rang and the hall filled with students, some of them looking at the two of us, curious what happened. Others just passed by, in their own worlds. I shook my head and turned away, joining the masses as they headed to class. He called my name, but I ignored him. It was best he stayed away from me for a while; I might kill him.

I entered the locker room and changed quickly, wanting to avoid anyone who might have seen us. I was in the gymnasium before the other students even made it in to change and started shooting baskets while I waited for class to begin. Hopefully that would calm me down.

Shot after shot, I thought about what happened. No, I still don't feel anything for him. My heart belongs to David and nothing Ben does will change that. Maybe now he'll leave me alone.

But what if he felt something? He'll never give up, and I'll be stuck with him pining over me forever. Ugh, why does he have to be so difficult!

"What happened with Ben?" Erin asked and I jumped, missing my shot.

"God, you scared me!" I exclaimed.

"No, I'm Erin," she joked, nudging me and waiting for a laugh, but I scowled instead. "Sooo…what happened?" she asked as the gym teacher entered and instructed us to line up.

"He was so pissed about your little comment he wanted to know why I didn't want to be with him," I answered as we were told to jog to the field.

Erin trotted beside me so we could continue talking. "Why was he on the floor?"

"Because I pushed him."

"And why did you push him?"

I looked down at my distorted reflection in the shiny wood flooring, wishing she hadn't asked. "He kissed me," I mumbled.

She stopped dead in her tracks. "What?" she exclaimed.

"Miss Reed, you haven't been jogging long enough to take a break – keep moving!" Coach Riser yelled.

"Sir, yes, sir!" she yelled back, booking it to my side. "He kissed you? Why?"

"I told him we didn't have any chemistry, but he wanted to find out for himself if we did or not."

"I hope for your sake this date with Madeline forces him to get over you."

"Yeah, me, too," I replied as we lined up on the field.

We were still doing soccer, and today Erin and I were against each other. She fought hard, but in the end my team won. She joked about it as we changed in the locker room after class, saying she had all the rookies and the added adrenaline in my system gave me an unfair advantage. Competing made me feel better, being able to get all the aggression and anger out. Maybe I'd be civil to Ben in English this afternoon. Or I may just let him sweat.

I told Erin I'd see her in the parking lot later before heading to my next class. Thanks to gym, I wasn't as anxious or restless the rest of the day. When I got to English, I didn't bother looking for Ben. I went straight to my seat and opened my books, ready to start. I heard him 'psst' me several times, but I ignored him.

When the bell rang, signaling the end of school, I dashed out the door and down the hall to my locker. I quickly switched out my books and sprinted to the parking lot. Ben never caught up with me.

Claire and Justin came over to my car as I was unlocking it. "So what happened after lunch with you and Ben? Word around school is it was a lover's quarrel," she commented.

"Oh come on!" I shouted, turning around. "The rumor mill is already churning that out? Geez, people need to grow up," I vented, feeling the anger rise again.

"Claire's just teasing," Justin explained and I calmed down.

I glanced around, making sure Ben wasn't nearby. Erin walked up and noticed my scanning eyes. "He's already gone, hitched a ride with a classmate."

"So what happened?" Claire asked anxiously.

"I pushed him down because he kissed me."

"Oh, no way," she remarked. "He's desperate."

"Tell me about it."

"Didn't feel anything from it, huh?" Justin asked.

"Nope, he's like a brother. And that's what it felt like…kissing my brother."

"Ewww," Erin responded.

"Yeah, I know. I didn't bother talking to him in English and I'll probably ignore him tomorrow. I'm pretty pissed about the whole thing."

"Are you going to tell David?" Claire asked.

"I don't know. I don't want to keep secrets from him, but I also don't know how he'll react."

"I'd keep it quiet. Who knows…he may turn into a homicidal maniac if you tell him," Erin teased.

"At least that would get rid of Ben," Claire commented under her breath.

"And on that note, I think I'll leave," I announced, climbing in my car and starting it as they headed to theirs.

When I got home, the first thing I did was go through the house and open all the windows and my French doors. It was a pleasant day and the house needed airing out anyway. A warm breeze blew through it, freshening the rooms with a sweet floral scent as I headed back downstairs and outside.

I threw my bag on the patio table and quickly pulled out my books. I dove into my homework so I'd have it completed by the time Dad got home. Once it was done, I went to the gazebo and sat on the swing, gently gliding back and forth as I enjoyed the winsome spring evening.

But memories of the dream began to gnaw at me. Staring at my balcony, I remembered how real it was being there with David. The feel of his caress, his kiss, even the smell and taste of him was unmistakable. There was no way I could dream something that real, that vivid…

But how could it not be a dream? When I touched him, he was like ice even though the night was warm. He was able to control me by gazing into my eyes. His reaction and mine to the kiss. Then there was the way he crossed the yard with incredible speed.

And what about Brian? Why would he be at my house? Why was he so interested in me? He has a girlfriend, and I really don't see myself as his type. Maybe it has something to do with David. Maybe Brian likes to see if the girls David goes out with are easily swayed by him. That might explain David's protectiveness.

Continuing to swing, I returned to considering the possibility that it did happen. It wasn't too odd that David was here last night, though he did seem a little stranger than normal, like he was on edge. Maybe in my drowsy state, everything was distorted. But again, what about Brian? How do I explain his presence if it wasn't a dream?

The natural light began to fade from the yard, darkening the area where I sat. An uneasiness came over me and I decided to head in. Still trying to answer the questions I had, I grabbed up my books and went to the door, running into my dad as I crossed the threshold. They flew everywhere and I scrambled to pick them up, flustered.

"Meg…are you okay? Didn't you see me standing in the doorway?"

I stacked everything on the nook table and knit my brow. "Sorry…no. I guess I…I was preoccupied."

"Is there something you need to talk about?" he inquired, concerned. "You look exhausted. Are you having trouble sleeping?"

There's lots bothering me, but I don't need to unload it now. And he doesn't need to know about the dream, if that's what it was. "Yeah, just thinking about prom," I replied, coming up with the best excuse.

"Worried about going with David?"

"Not really, just what you and my friends will think of him," I responded, feeling some truth in my answer.

He placed his hand on my shoulder and gave a soft smile. "You're a good judge of character. I'm sure he's great."

"Thanks, Dad," I replied, appreciating his acknowledgement that I have taste. I glanced at the clock realizing how late it was. "Any ideas for dinner?" I asked, heading into the kitchen.

"Don't worry about that. Relax on the couch and I'll order in," he suggested, putting his arm around me and rubbing my shoulder.

Maybe I can grab a quick nap to catch up. "Yeah, that sounds good," I agreed, going over to it and lying down.

"Chinese?" he questioned, and I lifted my head and nodded.

He called and placed the order while I pulled the throw from the back of the couch over me, resting my head on one of the decorative pillows nearby. He joined me a moment later, turning on the TV. The newscasters droned on about the market and general business news. I started dozing, but woke when it suddenly switched to a report on the Richmond Parks Ghost.

"Another body was found this morning in a local park. Police are investigating the scene. Sources say it's a new victim of the Ghost, but police have yet to confirm. More at eleven."

"I can't believe they don't have a single lead. It's a terrible reflection on our police force," Dad commented.

I couldn't go to sleep after that. They gave us nothing – no victim name, park location…nothing. I stared at the TV, hoping something more would come across, but instead the news ended and sitcom reruns came on. Then the doorbell rang, and Dad hopped up. I turned to another channel, but it was the same thing. Sighing in frustration, I lay back down. In a matter of minutes, he was back with dinner. So much for my nap.

He set it on the coffee table and went into the kitchen to grab paper plates and utensils. Good, minimal dishes tonight. He loaded them up, handing one to me as I sat up. Watching whatever was showing on the current channel, we quietly enjoyed our meal. Eight o'clock rolled around and the primetime shows started, so he flipped through a couple of channels to find the one he watched regularly.

"Now if only our police force worked as well as these guys, they'd already have the Ghost in custody," he commented.

"Yeah, Dad. If only everything was like it was on TV," I replied.

"I see you're thinking straight…your sarcasm's back."

"I guess that short nap was enough."

I watched his show with him until nine o'clock and then decided to go to my room. I had some reading to do and I hoped David would call or visit soon. I kissed Dad good night and shut all the windows on the lower level before heading up the stairs.

I entered my room, dropping my book bag by the door and kicking off my shoes. Flipping on the light switch, I discovered a body lying on my bed and started to scream. Quicker than humanly possible, it jumped up and covered my mouth, its hand warm against my lips.

"Are you trying to give me away?" David whispered in my ear, slowly removing it.

I took a moment to calm my heart and breathe, then I laid into him. "You have got to start giving me some kind of heads up before you come so I'm not so surprised. How long have you been waiting?" I questioned as I sat on the bed.

"About a half an hour," he replied, sitting on the other side of me.

I turned my body to face him. "A half an hour? What have you been doing?"

"Lying on your bed, staring at the ceiling." Oh great, my pillows will be saturated with him. "Is that wrong?"

"No, it's okay. I just didn't expect you to break into my room."

"But I didn't break in; the doors were open," he replied with a crooked smile.

My heart fluttered and I stared at my hands, fidgeting. "Oh yeah, I forgot I did that."

"So what was the occasion?" he asked, leaning over to look at me.

"Occasion? Oh, it was such a beautiful day, I thought I'd freshen the house," I replied with a smile as I glanced at him.

"Ah, I see," he responded. "How was school? Anything exciting happen?" he asked and my eyes suddenly widened, remembering what Ben did today. "By your expression, it looks like something did."

"No...nothing exciting," I answered guiltily. "I told the gang about prom...yep, that's about it."

"Hmm...no, there's something more you're not telling me," he surmised, leaning closer. "Something to do with...Ben?"

"How...how do you know that?" I asked, astonished.

"You just told me. So what did he do today, beg you to break up with me?" he inquired, surveying my expression.

"Partly..." I replied, not wanting to divulge any details. I hope he'll stop guessing; I don't want him to know what happened. I just need to change the subject. But how could I change it? "I want your opinion on something," I began, still thinking of what and wondering if it'd work.

"What might that be?" he asked curiously.

I said the first thing that came to mind. "This strange dream I had last night...I've been trying to figure it out."

"Another one? What happened this time?" It worked; I have his interest in the new subject. I recounted it to him and he watched me intently. When I finished, he leaned forward. "That is strange. So what about the dream were you trying to decipher?"

"Believe it or not, I actually woke this morning thinking it happened. It seemed so real, but there were so many things that were just too impossible."

"Like what?" he inquired, cocking his head.

"Well, number one, when I touched you, your skin was frigid even though it was warm outside. Number two, when I wouldn't go back to my room, it was like you hypnotized me and made me move. Number three, when I was downstairs, I saw you at the back of the yard and then in a blink, you were at the cherry tree. And number four was the simple fact that Brian was there."

His brows furrowed, darkening his light green eyes. "Depending on how vivid it was, it very well could have been mistaken for reality. But those things are pretty far-fetched. Could experiencing such a vivid dream affect your sleep?"

"It's a possibility…"

He glanced suddenly at the door, signaling for me to be quiet, and then stood up and swiftly walked backward toward the balcony, his index finger at his lip. As I watched him in puzzlement, a knock sounded on my door. I got up and headed toward it, wondering why Dad would be coming to see me already. Before opening it, I checked over my shoulder to make sure David was outside.

I cracked it and to my surprise, Ben was standing there and not my dad. "What are you doing here?"

"I…I just wanted to personally apologize for today. It was wrong of me to do what I did," he replied, his head tucked.

I kept the door slightly ajar, not really wanting him to come in. "Oh, that's all right. I overreacted. We're still friends," I responded hurriedly. "Well, it was nice of you to come by," I added, quickly trying to shut it.

He blocked it with his foot and forced his way into the room. "No, I don't believe you're okay with it."

He walked around me, glancing about. "It's getting late. You really shouldn't be here."

"Your dad's okay with it," he retorted as he stared at my vanity mirror. He strolled over and pulled David's sketch off it. "Is that you? It's good. Who drew this?" he questioned, showing it to me.

I quickly glanced toward the balcony but didn't see any sign of my boyfriend. "David did."

He slipped it back into the mirror and leaned against the vanity. "So he's an artist, too," he sighed.

After a moment, he pushed off it and headed toward the balcony. "Wait Ben!" I exclaimed, dashing across the room to stop him.

"What?" he asked, annoyed, as he paused but didn't turn around.

"Okay…I was really angry with you and was going to be for a while, but I can't stay mad at you, especially when you come to my house so late on a school night to apologize," I explained, trying to distract him.

He turned and faced me. "You mean it? I still want to be friends, and I hope the kiss doesn't change that."

My eyes grew wide. Oh God, I hope David didn't hear that. "No, nothing will change. We can just forget it...like it never happened."

"Yeah, like it never happened," he agreed quietly, hanging his head.

I took that opportunity to sneak a peek outside – still no sign of David. I put my arm around Ben and led him to the door. "Thank you again for coming by to apologize. That was really sweet. I'll see you tomorrow, okay?"

He glanced at me and gave a weak smile as I opened the door. "Yeah...glad we could work it out."

As soon as he started down the stairs, I shut the door and ran out on the balcony. David was nowhere. I went to the railing and searched the dark for him but didn't find anything. I hope he didn't leave because he thought I was cheating on him. I wrung my hands as I turned to go back inside but froze when a figure dropped down in front of me, graceful and quiet. I gasped as it stood, but soon realized it was David.

"What were you doing on the roof?" I asked, passing him as I headed back into my room.

"It was just in case Ben decided to come outside," he answered, following me. "With your father being downstairs in the family room and Ben in the room with you, I had but one choice."

I sat on the edge of the bed, facing him as he entered. "I'm not even going to bother asking how you got up there."

"It's really not too hard," he grinned and my heart fluttered lightly. "So what is this about a kiss?" he asked, crossing his arms over his chest.

I stiffened as he leaned in close to me, staring into my eyes. "I...I hoped you hadn't heard that..."

"I see. *That* was the exciting thing that happened today," he responded calmly.

"It didn't mean anything and it was against my w-"

"Did he hurt you?" he interrupted, his jaw tightening.

"No...actually, I think I hurt him. I pushed him down as soon as it happened."

"Why did he do it?" he inquired austerely.

"I told him there was no chemistry between us, but he wanted to find out since we had never kissed. Please don't be mad at him. It was a stupid mistake. It won't happen again," I promised, worried David might do something.

"Did you feel anything?" he questioned, becoming less tense.

"No, nothing at all. It was like kissing a family member." I paused. "I'm not sure he felt the same way, though."

David joined me on the edge of the bed, calmer. He put his arm around me and kissed my cheek. With a grin, he remarked, "Madeline will change that."

I didn't want to know how that was going to happen but hoped he was right. He pushed my hair behind my ear and caressed my face, leaning closer. I moved to him, our lips connecting. Soft and slow, then he stopped.

"It's time I leave," he whispered as he slowly stood up. I was in a daze. "You need your rest after the night you had."

I nodded as I stood, walking with him to the French doors. He kissed me briefly and left. I locked the doors and then languidly changed into my nightclothes and crawled into bed. As I rested my head on the pillow, David's scent rose from it. Instead of fighting the fog creeping into my brain, I surrendered to it.

*I was standing outside Ben's house, wondering why I was there. The windows, the street, the sky – everything was dark. I stared at the spot where his room was and saw something move behind the curtain. Curious, I went to the front door and turned the handle. It opened, so I stepped inside. All was quiet as I made my way up the stairs toward his room. It'd been years since I'd been there, but nothing had changed.*

*I paused at his door, thinking I heard something. Slowly pushing it open, I saw a dark form standing over Ben as he slept. It turned at the sound of the creaking hinges, and I realized it was David. He looked back down at Ben, his hand over Ben's mouth and the other behind his head, ready to snap his neck. Ben's eyes suddenly opened, widening as he looked at him and then stared in horror at me as David swiftly jerked.*

"David…don't!" I shouted as I sat up in bed, yelling at the wall.

As I focused on it, I realized it was just a dream.

It was dim outside, the early morning sun trying to break through the thin layer of rain clouds. My chest heaved as I stared ahead and concentrated on calming down. It was just a dream. Ben was fine. Nothing happened last night.

I turned off the alarm and went into the bathroom to get ready. But as I did, I was bothered. Was David really capable of something like that?

I grabbed my things and headed downstairs, walking into the kitchen and pouring a glass of juice. My stomach was upset, so I didn't feel like eating anything. Dad was enjoying his paper and cup of coffee, not immediately noticing me. I sat at the counter and stared out the kitchen window into the backyard. A light rain fell, gently hitting the new leaves on the trees and causing the remaining blossoms to fall.

"Did you have a nightmare?" he asked, lowering his paper.

"Hmm? Oh, no…why?"

"I heard a yell. Maybe it was your alarm going off; some of those morning DJs are so loud."

"Yeah, I think it was," I responded as I glanced back outside. "Well, I guess I better get going," I announced as I stood to leave.

"Have a good day," he replied, going back to his paper.

All the way to school and as I walked down the hall to Ben's locker, I thought about the dream. I waited several minutes, hoping he'd show up, but he never did. No longer able to hang around, I headed to class, worried my dream really wasn't a dream. So many of them recently have seemed that way, could this one be one of them? I sat in my seat and turned to Claire.

"Where have you been?" she asked abruptly.

"Have you seen Ben this morning?" I asked in return.

"No…why?" she answered, noticing the concern on my face.

"I had this terrible dream about David and Ben…at least I hope it was a dream."

She looked at me like I was losing it. "I'm sure he's just late. Did you tell David last night about the kiss?"

The teacher entered the room and was getting ready to begin. "Ben came over late last night and apologized. David was on my balcony and overheard the conversation we were having. But he seemed okay when he left, not angry or anything."

Mr. Barton cleared his throat, signaling the start of class. "I'm sure David didn't do anything to Ben. Don't worry," she whispered. The teacher gave her a stern look, and she and I faced forward.

Easy for her to say. What a strange coincidence I'd have a dream about David going after Ben and then Ben doesn't show up at school today. How could I not be worried?

I fretted about him all through my first three classes and by the time I went to lunch, I was getting hysterical. I skipped getting any food and went right to our table and put my head down. I tried to block out all the noise in the cafeteria but couldn't. I lifted my head and looked toward the lunch line to see if anyone else had arrived, but no one had, so I turned around and hung my head.

"Hey, Megan. Why're you so down?"

I glanced up at the sound of the familiar voice as Ben took a seat across from me. I jumped up and rushed over to him, giving him a relieved hug. "Oh, Ben, you're okay! I am so glad to see you!" I exclaimed, not letting go.

"Of course I'm okay. Why'd you think I wasn't?" he asked as I loosened my grip.

"It was just a nightmare I had. Why weren't you at your locker this morning?" I inquired.

"I was having a problem with the twins earlier and they caused me to be late. Huh, it's kinda nice to see you worried about me. Does this mean you really care about me?" he asked with a grin as I released him.

I went back to my seat, instantly regretting my actions. "Only as a friend, Ben."

"Okay, I'll accept that," he replied. "For now," he muttered under his breath. I rolled my eyes.

Finally, the rest of the gang appeared and looked at the two of us as they sat. "What's up with the lunch line today? It's moving so slow," Erin commented, taking a bite of meatloaf surprise.

"So I see you made it to school, Ben. Megan was worried about you," Claire commented.

"Yeah, I know. You should've seen what she did when I got to the table," he smiled.

My face started getting red. "Ben, drop it."

"What did she do?" Justin egged, grinning.

He looked at me and then him. "She hugged me and wouldn't let go."

"You are such a jerk," I grumbled as he laughed. "And to think I was scared something happened to you. Now I wish it had."

"Aww, you don't mean that," he replied.

"Hmph," I huffed as I turned my back to him.

"So why were you late?" Erin asked, wanting to get into the conversation.

"My mom had to get to work really early this morning, so I was left to take care of the twins. They refused to get ready, fighting me the whole time. I got them on the bus in time, but I still had to get ready. That's why I was late."

"Man, you have it tough," Justin commented.

"You said it. I can't wait till I graduate and get outta there."

I looked at Ben and for once understood how hard his life really was. We all have it made, but he has to work for everything. He has to help raise his sisters and be the man his dad refused to be.

The bell rang, and we headed to our next class. Before I got too far, Ben stopped me in the hall. "What was your nightmare?"

"You really don't want to know."

"I really do. It had to be something pretty bad."

I hesitated. "David killed you."

He narrowed his eyes. "Why would he do that?"

"Because you kissed me…"

"Megan, if he's that jealous, maybe you should stop seeing him."

"Oh no, you're not doing this to me. It was just a dream. He's not the jealous type," I defended. "I have to get to class. I'll see you in English," I continued, turning into the locker room.

The rest of the day passed as normal and when English was over, I was ready to go home. I spoke briefly with everyone in the parking lot and then left. I completed my homework and threw dinner together before Dad walked through the door. We ate as we discussed how our day went, and he was relieved to see and hear I was less preoccupied than yesterday.

He took care of the dishes while I packed away leftovers. We said good night as he took his place in his chair in the family room to watch TV, and I went to my room to await David's call or visit, whichever it would be tonight. I read my chapters for English, every once in a while glancing at the balcony doors. I hoped he'd visit, but it didn't look like that'd happen.

I started to drop off to sleep when David's phone rang. I answered it with a yawn. "You're a little late tonight."

"I know…it was a busy night at the medical examiner's office. Did you have a pleasant day?"

"Not at first. I had a nightmare last night involving you and Ben and when I didn't see him all morning, I thought the worst. My fear was unfounded when he showed up for lunch, though."

"What did I do…beat him up?" he asked, laughing slightly.

"No, you killed him."

He paused. "You really think I would do that over a kiss you didn't enjoy?"

"I guess my subconscious did. It was amazing how real it was. I woke up yelling at you to stop."

He was quiet on the other end. "Megan, I'm sorry if I made you worry. I would never hurt any of your friends, even if they did something as idiotic as what Ben did."

"I appreciate that; I don't believe you would have. It's just that my friends and I were talking about it before I got home yesterday and I guess it got stuck in my head since I wasn't sure how you'd react if I told you."

"Maybe a strong talk, but I would not harm anyone unless they deserved it."

"I'll remember that for future reference. So, have you gotten a tux yet for prom?" I asked, ready to change the subject.

"Not yet. I plan to pick one up this weekend. However, I have made arrangements for the limousine."

"I can't wait to go. It seems to be taking forever to get here."

"I'm looking forward to it as well."

I yawned and looked at the clock – almost midnight. "I better go to bed. I have a test in the morning and I'm tired."

"All right. I will talk to you tomorrow. Good night, Megan," he whispered.

"Good night," I replied before hanging up. I placed the phone on the nightstand, set the alarm, and got under my comforter. Again, David's scent surrounded me and I easily slipped into sleep.

# Chapter 15
## Richmond Parks Ghost

Prom was fast approaching and I couldn't wait. And it seemed that way for everyone else, too. All the upper classmen were buzzing about it – getting a date, finalizing dinner plans, and renting tuxes or buying dresses.

David and I made plans to meet over the weekend but hadn't decided where. By Friday, I had an idea and proposed it to him when he visited that night. Dad was out with Vanessa, so he actually came to the front door. We settled in the family room and discussed plans while a movie played in the background.

"Why don't we go to Pocahontas State Park tomorrow night?"

He glanced at the TV and then looked at me. "I'm not sure that's a good idea. They're still looking for that serial killer," he replied.

I smiled sweetly. "You'll protect me."

"If you insist," he responded. "Promise me one thing, though. If I say we have to go, we must leave immediately."

"I won't argue. So I'll meet you at eleven o'clock at the entrance?"

"Would you rather I pick you up? It's easier to hide one car as opposed to two."

"True. I'll be at the same corner where you picked me up the night we went to the lake."

Straight for tomorrow evening, he turned his attention back to the movie playing. "What time will your father be home tonight?" he asked.

"After midnight. He and Vanessa are doing some more meet-and-greets. She has a never-ending trail of friends and family."

The first movie finished and we started another one, even though I was too tired to watch it. I dozed during the beginning and finally dropped off to sleep in the middle. I woke slightly as David got up and kissed my cheek, whispering good night. After replying, I fell back asleep, figuring I'd stay on the couch since I was too sleepy to go to my room.

I woke the next morning in my bed, to my surprise. Dad must have put me in it when he finally got home last night. I sat up and stretched, ready to get the day over with so I could enjoy my evening with David. Opening the balcony doors, I stepped outside to see what the weather would be.

The sun peeked out from behind some clouds and was promptly covered up. Mostly overcast, I surmised. That was okay. I have a report to complete for Biology, so it was better that the weather was drab. I didn't want to be tempted to slack off.

I took a shower and dressed, heading downstairs for breakfast afterward. Dad was in the family room watching TV rather than reading his paper, so I fixed a bowl of cereal and joined him.

"Thanks for putting me in bed last night," I remarked between bites.

"What? I didn't put you in your bed. You were already there when I got home. Are you sleepwalking again?" he asked, looking over at me.

I froze for a moment, thinking I made a major slip-up, then I smiled sheepishly. "Yeah, I guess I did."

"You've never been a sleepwalker before…maybe you should see a specialist," he suggested.

"No, I think it'll pass. Probably has something to do with everything going on," I replied.

He gave me an unsure look and then asked, "What are your plans for today?"

"I have a Biology report due Thursday, and I want to get started on it since I don't have anything major going on this weekend. And today is perfect because it's dreary outside."

"Why? Is your report on the effects of rain and a person's mood?"

"No. If the weather was nice, I'd want to be out in it instead of in my room or at the library working on my report," I responded, finishing my cereal. "Why? What plans do you have?"

"Vanessa and I will be picking out our cake. Would you like to come along instead of doing your report?" he asked eagerly.

I hadn't seen Vanessa except for once since our shopping excursion. She treated me better than usual, but I was wary of how long it'd last. "No, thank you. Like I said, I want to get it out of the way since I'm free. Who knows what next week holds for me."

"Suit yourself," he replied, turning his attention back to the TV.

I took care of my dishes and then headed up to my room to start working. Sitting at my desk, I jotted down some notes from my Biology book and one I picked up Friday from the school library. I checked the internet for any additional information but kept coming up with what I already had. Dad yelled up the stairs to let me know he was leaving and as soon as he was gone, I grabbed my bag and hopped in the car.

My report was on blood disorders – not something I chose. I honestly would have preferred any other subject, but it was the luck of the draw. I just knew I would inevitably come across what killed my mother, and I wasn't in the mood to dredge up old memories of how she suffered. So to avoid running into that dilemma, I planned to choose a rare blood disorder.

But it proved to be more difficult than I expected. I left the local library and headed into the city to VCU's library; it was bound to have more detailed information. As I scoured the shelves, I found book after book on rare disorders. I brought them over to a desk and poured through them, struggling with some of the terminology. David would be useful at a time like this. I looked at several diseases and picked the one that really interested me, building my report off it.

The library was mostly empty and dead silent. Every once in a while, I got the unnerving feeling I was being watched, but when I looked around, I never saw anyone. Several minutes passed without anything, and then I felt it again and glanced around. Nothing.

Checking my phone, I realized it was getting late. I jotted down a few more important notes and packed everything away. Gathering the books, I quickly replaced them in their proper spots.

As I tried to find a place for the last book, I heard a quiet cackle, dry and throaty. I turned quickly to catch the culprit, but all I saw was a trail of golden hair disappear beyond the end of my aisle. Beginning to feel anxious, I hurriedly scanned the shelves and slipped the book into its space. As I rushed to the stairwell door, I heard the cackle again but didn't bother looking for the source. Instead, I swiftly exited the floor.

The lamps along the street were lit, casting an amber glow over it and the sidewalks as I walked quickly down them. I glanced around nervously, hoping the owner of the creepy laugh wasn't following me. Finally approaching the car, I climbed in and took off, anxious for the safety and security of home.

I felt better as I pulled in the drive. Dad was still out, so as I entered the house, I called his cell to find out if he was going to be home anytime soon. It rang several times and then went to voicemail. I left a message asking him to call as soon as he could.

Glancing at the clock, I realized I still had lots of time before my date with David. I turned on the TV and tried to find something interesting, stopping on some new show on one of the cable networks. Not really wanting it for anything other than noise, I scanned over my scribbles, verifying I could read them. There was nothing worse than diligently taking notes and then not being able to read them later.

As I tried to decipher a symbol I drew, my phone rang. "Hey Dad."

"Hey…is something wrong? I called you as soon as I could," he responded, sounding out of breath.

"No, I'm fine. I just wanted to know what your plans for dinner are."

"Oh…Vanessa and I are eating out. Want me to bring you anything?"

"No, I'll fix something here. What time do you plan to be home?"

I heard him cover the phone. His muffled voice asked Vanessa the same question I asked him. "After midnight again, Meg. Vanessa's taking me to this club in Shockoe Bottom…said I need to loosen up."

I laughed at the thought of my dad at a club with a bunch of college kids. "Well, have fun. I won't wait up for you." He gave a nervous laugh and then said good night.

As soon as I hung up, I hopped up and did a little dance. Vanessa made sneaking out so easy! Once I got that out of my system, I calmed down and went into the kitchen, searching for something to eat and settling on a frozen dinner. As it cooked, I went back to reading over my notes and added a few things I wanted to remember when I typed up my report.

The microwave dinged and I jumped up to get my food, returning to the couch and eating it as I watched TV. It wasn't as good as a home-cooked meal, but it was at least satisfying. With the last bite, I set the dish aside and went back to working on my notes. An hour passed and I decided to call it quits, slipping the papers into my bag and heading up to my room to freshen up.

By the time I was done, I had ten minutes to get to the corner to meet David. I slipped some pillows under my comforter to make it look like a body, just in case Dad peeked in the room before going to bed, and went to the balcony doors. I taped the lock and shut them so I could get back in without Dad knowing I ever left. After quickly climbing down the tree, I dashed across the yard, over the fence, and through the neighbors' yards.

I dropped from the last fence and turned to find David leaning against his car. "Did you have trouble sneaking out?" he asked with a smirk as he opened the car door.

"No, I didn't time it right," I replied, holding my chest as I climbed in.

He shut the door and walked over to his side, pausing a moment to look around, then sat and started it, the engine rumbling like a distant thunderstorm. The wind whipped my hair around as he sped toward the park, but I didn't mind. It felt good to sneak out, it felt good to go fast, and it felt good to be with David.

He turned into a subdivision and I gave him a curious look. "We're going to park at the end of this road and walk. It's not far to the trail I prefer we take. We'll avoid the campgrounds and be on the farthest side of the park," he explained.

"Okay. I don't believe I've ever seen this part," I commented, looking at all the darkened houses.

"Remember what I told you…if I say we have to leave, we leave, no matter what."

"Agreed."

He pulled into a cul-de-sac after winding through several streets, knowing exactly where he was going, and parked the car at the curb near several trees. He stepped out and came to my side, opening the door. "Just ahead is the park. It's about two miles to the lake. Think you can handle it?" he asked as I stood up.

"Easy…I could probably run that." I answered.

"Is that a challenge?" he asked, his voice smooth and irresistible.

I thought about it for a moment, sizing him up. I could take him. "Yeah, it is," I answered as I took off. I heard him laughing as he passed me. How was he so fast?

The moon was just a sliver in the sky but gave enough light to help me avoid running into anything large. I dodged trees and thick branches just in time, but it was the little ones that kept whipping me. I ignored the pain and continued forward, determined to at least catch up to him. Farther into the woods, I came to a path that must have been the one he was referring to.

I didn't see him anywhere around and I didn't remember passing him, but I must have. I rested, waiting for him to catch up, when I heard his voice behind me. "What took you so long? I've been waiting several minutes."

"Yeah, yeah," I huffed, waving at him. "How...can you...run that fast...and not...and not be...tired?" I asked, trying to catch my breath.

"I have great stamina," he replied as he leaned against a tree. "Are you ready to walk?"

I held up my index finger and took a deep breath. "Yep, let's go. I'll beat you on the way back."

"We shall see about that," he replied with a smirk. My already racing heart beat harder.

We walked the trail around the lake, the little bit of light shining through the new leaves on the trees cast a faint green glow around us. We didn't talk much; David seemed distant, scanning the woods constantly. I guess he felt even more responsible for me since he agreed to bring me to the site of several of the murders.

I made comments every so often to break the silence, but he never added anything, so we went back to being silent until I commented again. As we moved closer to the lake, the once distant sounds of frogs croaking and chirping grew louder, and I was happy to hear something other than my own voice.

We stopped at one of the small docks and walked out to the end, the waning moon reflecting on the murky waters just beyond it. Standing in silence and gazing at it, we took in the sounds of the animals residing there as they sang a soothing night opus. David put his arm around me and went to kiss my cheek, but stopped short. He pushed my hair behind my ear and tilted my head, examining it

"You scratched yourself..."

I ran my fingers across my skin and was thankful I wasn't bleeding. "Oh, it must have been from a twig while I was running."

He glanced around, a concerned look on his face. "Let's continue around the lake," he suggested as he took my hand and led me off the dock. I looked back, wanting to stay longer, but he pressed on.

"Why are you in such a hurry?" I asked, frustrated with the way he was acting.

"I'm sorry. I feel…anxious. I'm only looking out for you," he replied, glancing around again.

"Well, you're giving me the feeling that you're expecting the serial killer to show up tonight," I commented, continuing ahead of him.

"I'm being cautious. Anything could be lurking in these woods," he retorted. A shiver went down my spine.

I slowed my pace and hooked my arm around his, holding him close. He looked at me and grinned, knowing he was right about being guarded. My feet fumbled as I stared at his amazing smile, but luckily I was attached to him so I didn't fall too far. As soon as he looked away to check our surroundings again, I was no longer mesmerized.

We arrived at the spot where we started and I grinned. "Ready for a rematch?" I asked, nudging him. He was scanning the woods as if he heard something.

His attention returned to me. "Yes, I am," he replied with a crooked smile. "I'll give you a ten second head start this time."

"Thanks. So when does it begin?"

He leaned close to me. "Now," he whispered.

I took off but paused after entering the woods to scope it out. I noticed a path nearby that was clear, so I ran to it; it was much easier than dodging trees. I was sure to beat him this time. After running awhile, I realized I wasn't getting any closer to the subdivision. Instead, it seemed as if I was heading farther into the woods. I stopped and glanced around, trying to find David. He was nowhere to be seen.

As I searched for a way back to the trail, I spotted something moving among the trees. Maybe they were campers who could direct me where to go. I moved closer and was able to make out two people slowly trudging through the brush dragging something. What in the world could they be hauling to this remote end of the park so late?

Hiding behind large trees, I crept nearer as I tried to get a better look. They continued to lumber along and then stopped suddenly. Moving closer still, I was able to make out a male and a female figure but still couldn't determine what they brought with them. They never said a thing to each other but worked quickly with whatever it was.

Gradually raising it up, the male figure held a limp object as the female grabbed the top of it. A loud crack echoed through the woods and in her hands, she held something round. As she stared at it, an eerily familiar cackle reverberated among the trees before she tossed it away. It rolled toward me, but I didn't bother checking where it stopped. I was more interested in the couple.

In a fervent embrace, they kissed as the limp thing dropped next to them. I looked away, feeling uneasy watching them in the throes of passion, and instead decided to search for the object. My eyes scanned the darkened forest floor, stopping as they came to something that didn't fit the usual flora and fauna.

On the ground, mere feet from where I hid, was a human head.

I backed away, ready to scream, when a hand covered my mouth preventing me. It pulled me close and slowly carried me away, restraining my body to the point I could hardly move. I panicked, not knowing who had me and what they planned to do with me.

"Megan, calm down...it's David," he whispered in my ear.

I tried to talk, but he wouldn't let me. He dragged me until we were far enough away from the couple and then removed his hand from my mouth, telling me to remain quiet. Holding my wrist tightly, he guided me the rest of the way through the woods until we came to a clearing – the subdivision.

"Why didn't you run straight through the woods?" he questioned abruptly, turning to face me.

"I saw the path. I...I wanted to avoid the trees," I responded, looking back into the darkened forest. "David...was that who I think it was?"

There was a mixture of fear and anger on his face as he gripped my shoulders. "Get in the car...now!"

I ran to the passenger side, quickly opening the door and climbing in. He was already in the driver's seat, shifting into gear. He whipped around and tore out of the subdivision, remaining silent and stern. I gripped the soft leather of the seat and leaned forward, trying to remember what I saw.

"Were they...the Ghost? Did I...did I just witness a...a murder?"

His hands grasped the steering wheel tightly. "No, you missed the murder. That was just the decapitation..."

"Please pull over...I think I'm going to be sick," I responded, covering my mouth and grabbing my stomach.

He found an area to park on the side of the road and quickly opened my door. Helping me out of the car, he led me to a grassy area where I unloaded my entire dinner. Staying by me, he held my hair as I vomited until I was dry. How embarrassing to see me this way.

Once I finished, he took a handkerchief from his pocket and wiped my mouth. I felt weak and unstable as he led me back to the car and helped me into the seat. I sat and buried my head in my hands, crying as he dashed to the driver's side. He got in and immediately put his arms around my shoulders, comforting me. I continued to cry and he just held me, giving me time to let it out. Then he kissed the top of my head and lifted my chin.

"We have to tell the police. I saw them...I saw the killers," I sobbed, staring at him through damp eyes.

He ran his fingers over my hair, trying to calm me. "What did you see exactly?"

"I saw…I saw a man and a woman with a…with a body."

"Did you see their faces?"

I tried to remember. "No, it was…it was too dark."

He was quiet, trying to read me. "Megan, you can't tell anyone about what you saw."

I stared at him, my eyes wide with surprise. "Wh-why not?"

"You didn't see anything…"

"Wh-what? Of course I did! How could you… how could you say that?"

"You were lost, panicked," he explained, gazing into my eyes. I couldn't look away. My memories began to alter, the images shifting and disfiguring. "The distortion of the shadows made you think you saw people, but you didn't," he continued as he caressed my face. I felt sleepy. "You didn't see anything," he whispered as they began to fade into a mist.

"I didn't see anything," I repeated in a daze.

He lifted his hand and moved it slowly over my face. The motion made me want to close my eyes and go to sleep. He gently let go, and the last thing I remember was a soft whisper in my ear, "Please forgive me. It's for your own good…"

I slowly roused, stretching as I gradually opened my eyes. I was in my room, on my bed. How did I get here? I replayed last night's events in my mind. I went with David to Pocahontas State Park and we walked the trail around a lake. We were racing back to the car, but then everything goes blank. I rubbed my face and rolled out of bed.

Grabbing a light throw, I went out on the balcony and sat on the chaise, thinking the fresh air might help. The sun was breaking through the clouds as the birds chirped happily. I stared out into the yard, trying again to remember racing to the car, but I couldn't. That's odd that I have no memory of the remainder of the evening. I hope nothing bad happened.

Deciding to take my mind off last night, I planned out my day as I reclined on the chaise. I needed to type up my report, call Claire, and pick up some accessories to go with my prom dress. That should keep me busy.

Sitting a moment longer, I enjoyed the pleasant weather until a low grumble erupted from my abdomen. I got up and then headed in to get breakfast. As I shut the doors, I noticed they clicked as they normally do. I opened them slightly and found the tape missing. I didn't remember removing it, but maybe I did subconsciously. I shrugged and left my room.

The kitchen was empty as I entered it; Dad must still be in bed after his wild night. I couldn't wait to hear how it went and tease him about it. I started to grab a bowl for cereal but decided instead to have a heartier breakfast. I didn't know why, but I felt like I didn't eat at all yesterday.

I whipped up some pancakes, sausage, grits, and eggs and brewed a small pot of coffee, hoping the aroma would make its way up to Dad and he'd join me. I was arranging the food when I heard him slowly coming down the stairs. I fixed his plate and poured a cup of coffee as he came into the kitchen, not as chipper as I was.

I placed his plate and cup on the table as he sat. He just stared at it as I fixed mine. "Good morning, Daddy! Did you have a good time last night?"

"Hmph," he answered, grabbing his head. "Why are you in such a good mood?"

"I don't know…I feel well rested, I guess," I replied sitting next to him. "Drink some coffee – it'll help wake you up."

I looked at my plate of food as its delicious bouquet drifted up to me and my stomach growled. I picked up my fork, ready to take my time and enjoy my meal, but instead I woofed it down. I was hungrier than I thought.

He looked at me and shook his head. "I thought you said you were going to have dinner last night," he commented between sips.

"I did. Must have burned a lot of calories in my sleep," I replied, grabbing up my empty dishes and putting them in the sink. He hadn't even touched his food yet.

While I waited for him to finish, I went into the family room and turned on the TV, flipping through the channels. I glanced at him every once in a while to check his progress. After about a half an hour, I heard him get up and then he joined me moments later.

"Thanks for breakfast," he remarked, a little peppier.

"You're welcome. So, would you ever go back to a club?" I asked, grinning.

"Never again," he answered. "My head's still throbbing from that loud, repetitive music."

"Did Vanessa have a good time?"

He narrowed his eyes and I tilted my head innocently, waiting for his response. "She did, until some guy spilled a drink on her."

"Was it an accident or on purpose?"

"Oh, I think it was on purpose. I almost started a fight over it."

I grinned, imagining my dad beating up some drunk frat boy. "What time did you get home?"

He closed one eye and thought hard. "Hmm, around two maybe."

I smiled as I continued flipping. Ah, the Sunday morning TV struggle. "Just so you know, my plans today are to type up my report and go shopping for prom with Claire."

"After you take care of the dishes," he ordered.

"Obviously," I replied, hopping up and handing him the remote.

I threw the pots and pans in with the other items and filled the sink with water and dish detergent. The bubbles swelled to the rim and I quickly turned the faucet off before it overflowed. As I let them soak, I stared out the window into the backyard and admired the abounding colors.

Dad cleared his throat, snapping me out of my daze, and I glanced over to find him staring at me. I grinned as I went about scrubbing and rinsing the dishes and then loading them in the washer. When the sink was empty and the counters and stove clean, I notified him I was done and going to my room to work on my report.

Grabbing what I needed for it, I went out onto the balcony and sat on the chaise, my laptop on my lap and the notes laying on the keys. I glanced over them, thinking of what to say, and then began typing. After an hour, I decided to take a break and let the laptop recharge. While resting my eyes, I called Claire to ask about shopping later. The phone rang a couple times and then finally she picked up.

"What's up?" she asked cheerfully. That's a good sign.

"I was just taking a break from writing my Biology report and wanted to see if you're interested in going shopping with me today. I need to pick up a few accessories to go with my prom dress."

"You're typing up your report already? I haven't cracked one book yet," she answered, completely ignoring my invitation. Typical Claire, she'd probably start writing it Wednesday night.

"So can you go?" I asked, plain and simple.

"Oh, yeah. All my chores are done and my afternoon's free. Do you mind picking me up?"

"I can. Let's say two o'clock? That'll give us plenty of time."

"Cool. I'll be ready."

"Well, I better get back to my report. I want to have it finished before I leave."

"Overachiever," she muttered under her breath and then laughed. "See you in a couple hours."

I hung up and went back to work. I kept typing until about twelve-thirty, figuring I should get something for lunch. Plugging up my laptop again, I left the room and headed downstairs.

"Hey Dad, I'm making a sandwich. Want one?" I asked as I entered the kitchen.

"Sure," he replied. He was still on the couch; apparently, he found something worthwhile to watch. Unfortunately for me, it was a baseball game.

Making two, I put them on separate paper plates with chips and brought them into the family room, handing one to him before sitting down. I watched the game, not really interested in it, until I finished my food. During a commercial, I told him my plans.

"I'm picking Claire up at two to go shopping. We'll probably be back around five or six."

"All right. Should I have something ready for dinner?"

"That'd be nice," I replied, getting up to throw away my trash and taking his with me. "I'm going to get ready now," I announced as I headed out of the room, noticing the game coming back on.

I dashed upstairs and into my bathroom, immediately hopping in the shower. All clean and refreshed, I threw on a tea length dress and left my hair down. I slipped on sandals, grabbed a purse, and headed downstairs to tell Dad I was going. He took his attention away from the game long enough to say goodbye and kiss my cheek.

I climbed in the car and went a couple streets over to Claire's house. She was waiting on the metal bench in her yard, a smile on her face as I pulled into her driveway. She popped up as I parked and came over to the car as I unlocked the doors. Slipping in the seat, she grinned as she looked at me.

"Did you get to go out with David?" she asked as I backed out.

"Yeah, last night."

"Anywhere interesting?"

"Pocahontas State Park. It was nice..." I hesitated as I entered the highway.

She stared at me, waiting for me to finish. "But..." she encouraged, trying to get me to continue.

"I...I don't remember the rest of the evening," I responded.

"What do you mean?" she asked curiously.

"Well, I remember everything up until we were leaving."

"Not that I think David would do it, but did he give you anything to drink last night?" she asked, examining me.

"No. We were racing back to the car and I remember running into the woods, but I don't recall ever reaching it."

"Oh...maybe you tripped and bumped your head," she suggested as I parked.

"Maybe, but I'm not usually that clumsy. As embarrassing as it is, I plan to ask him tonight when he calls," I commented as I stepped out and Claire followed. "So what store should we hit first?"

# Chapter 16
## Uninvited Visitor

I dropped Claire off at her house around six. She jogged up to the door with both arms full of bags. She was really going all out for prom. I shook my head as she put them down and waved from the front porch, signaling that I could leave. I backed out of the drive and headed home with my goodies.

As I pulled into my driveway, I noticed Vanessa's car parked next to Dad's. I pulled in behind his so I didn't block her and gathered all of my bags from the back seat. I didn't have nearly as many as Claire but still had enough for both hands. I shut the door with my hip and made my way up the sidewalk to the house.

Opening the door, a wonderful aroma floated toward me. I was so hungry and glad Dad had dinner ready. I yelled to let him know I was home and headed up to my room to put the bags on the bed for the time being. I dashed down the stairs and into the kitchen a moment later, ready to enjoy Chef Jack's special for the evening.

"Hey, Vanessa," I greeted cheerfully. I was still trying to maintain a good rapport with her. "It's so nice of you to join us for dinner."

She smiled at me, not sure how to take my exuberance. I guess she still felt the need to be guarded around me, too. "I stopped by to drop some things off and Jack asked if I wanted to stick around. I figured why not and even helped cook some of it."

I looked at him, impressed he could get her to step into the kitchen. "Well, I can't wait to try it," I replied.

He leaned close to me and whispered, "I'm glad you weren't here to see it. You would have had a field day watching her attempt to cook."

I stifled a giggle and asked her, "Did you enjoy your cooking experience?"

"It wasn't too bad, but I was more of a helper. I don't think I'm ready to take on a large meal by myself."

I pulled plates out of the cabinet and handed them to Dad. "Maybe you'll have enough practice by Thanksgiving."

By the look on her face, I could tell she wasn't interested in learning that much. Another way she was nothing like my mom. She loved cooking, whether it was alone or with Dad and me. Vanessa would be okay with helping or watching Dad for now, but probably planned to eat out all the time or hire a personal chef once I left for college.

We filled our plates and grabbed utensils and drinks before heading into the dining room to eat. They talked quietly amongst themselves about wedding issues. The sooner it was over the better; I was so tired of hearing about it. To change the subject and be included in the conversation, I told them about my shopping excursion.

"Claire and I had fun hunting for our prom accessories," I announced, interrupting a building argument.

"Ooo...find anything good?" she asked, turning toward me. He looked at me, thankful.

"A great pair of earrings and some nice heels that match my dress perfectly."

"So are you getting excited?" she inquired.

"Yeah, a little," I replied, though I was more excited about going with David than prom itself.

"Well, I can't wait to meet your boyfriend," Dad commented, gathering up his dishes and then Vanessa's and mine.

"Oh don't worry about cleaning up. I'll take care of it. You both cooked a delicious meal and should go relax," I insisted.

She gladly accepted my offer, rushing to the family room, and he followed, smiling at me before settling on the couch next to her. I piled the dishes on top of one another and headed to the sink. I stared out the window as I washed, every once in a while glancing over at them. I'm glad my dad is happy, but I wish he would have found someone other than Vanessa. They're just too different. He needs someone more like him, like Mom.

I put the last dish in the washer and told him I was heading up to my room to put my things away and get ready for bed. As I entered, I turned on the bedside lamp and emptied the bags, laying the items out on the comforter and looking over what I bought. Everything matched so perfectly with my dress, as if it was destined to be this way.

I grabbed the shoes and took them to the back of the closet to hide with the gown. On my way out, I stopped and looked through my clothes, deciding on what to wear tomorrow for school. I pulled an outfit off the rack and proceeded out the door, nearly running into David as I exited. I gasped and then sighed out of frustration.

"I think you like scaring me," I commented. "Honestly, what kind of guy likes to sneak into his girlfriend's room?"

"The kind that can't wait to see her," he replied, slipping his hand along my jaw and kissing me.

Hesitantly, I broke away. "That's sweet," I whispered timidly, placing my hand over my heart and trying to calm it as I pushed past him. "How did you get in anyway?" I asked, tossing my ensemble on the bench by the closet. I continued to the bed and paused in front of it as I faced him.

"The doors were unlocked," he responded and then grinned mischievously. "You really should check them. You never know who will come in."

Sitting on the edge, I tucked my head and let my heart slow to a normal pace as I fidgeted with my hair. I noticed the tips of his shoes as he moved closer and I shifted my eyes to him. He was looking over the items laid out next to me when he paused and picked up a small velvet box.

He opened it and examined the contents. "I like these a lot," he remarked, holding them up and showing me the earrings I picked to go with my gown. "Did you buy a necklace to match?"

I hadn't thought to get one. "No, I plan to wear one of my mom's. She has a nice diamond one that'll work."

He lifted my chin and looked at my neck, cocking his head side to side. "One that hits right at your clavicle would be ideal," he recommended, his finger glancing my skin.

My heart beat rapidly. "She might have something like that," I replied tautly as I stood and started picking the other items up, putting them away in a drawer as I let it slow. Once it was reasonable, I hung my outfit on the closet door and sat on the bench.

"So I see you had a fun day shopping for prom. Are you starting to get excited?" he asked, sitting on the edge of the bed across from me.

"Not so much about prom as I am going with you," I blushed.

He laughed lightly. "I love to see you embarrassed; the color in your cheeks is beautiful," he commented as he strolled over and sat next to me. I could feel my face getting hotter.

He reached up and touched the blush, his hand cold against my burning skin. Slowly moving to my chin, he lifted my face up so I was gazing into his eyes. I closed mine and waited.

At first, his lips gently caressed mine, barely touching, and then lingered. But I yearned for more as I breathed him in. I reached up and placed my hand on the back of his neck, pulling him closer. I kissed deeper, hungry for his lips against mine, and he wasn't denying me.

He tasted so good, felt good, and I didn't want to stop. I moved from beside him onto his lap, throwing my arms around his neck. His hands moved from my hips up my sides, stopping under my arms. He stayed there for a moment and then lifted me off, ending the kiss. He stood and without a word, walked out onto the balcony, leaving me standing by the bed vexed and confused.

I paced back and forth, wondering if I should join him or wait for his return. I can't believe I let myself go that far. That's not like me at all. I stopped pacing and sat on the edge of the bed, burying my head in my hands.

A hand alighted on my knee and I jerked my head up, finding him kneeling in front of me. I quickly stared at the ceiling. "I'm sorry. I don't know what got into me. I am so ashamed of myself."

He stood and sat next to me, putting his arm around my shoulder. "Don't be...you can't help it," he whispered in my ear.

What does he mean by that?

I lowered my head and looked into his eyes. They were a beautiful shade of green, darker than his lighter color but lighter than his darkest. As I gently touched his cheek, he closed them. Moving closer, I kissed him again.

Once more, he didn't stop me as I pushed myself further, forcing him onto his back. I was about to throw my leg over him when he blocked me and slipped away. I sat back on the bed, my hands over my mouth.

"I told you," he admonished, walking around the bed to my desk and opening my laptop. My report was open on the screen.

I twirled a curl repeatedly around my finger as I stared at my lap, still trying to wrap my head around why I couldn't control myself. Was it because it was all so new to me, these strange feelings of affection and want? I looked up and watched him read, my heart fluttering slightly as I admired his quiet beauty.

"It's not due until Thursday. I'm still working on it," I mentioned as I moved closer to him.

"You have a lot of detailed information here. Where did you find it?"

"Oh, I went to the campus library. There aren't a lot of books on rare blood disorders in normal libraries."

"Did you pick that subject?" he asked, glancing over his shoulder at me.

"No...I really didn't want it...but I wasn't going to argue with the teacher," I replied, pushing the hair behind my ear. "It's been fascinating learning about them, though. So many odd and unusual diseases..."

"Like what?" he inquired, turning the chair around to face me with a smile.

My heart rate increased and I tried to think. "Well...like the one I'm focusing on, porphyria. It's a genetic disease that can affect the skin, triggering sensitivity to sunlight which causes the afflicted person to burn easily," I responded as I fidgeted. "Also, their body doesn't produce heme like it should, causing them to crave blood. It kinda reminded me of a vampire..." I trailed off.

He closed the lid of the laptop and turned to me. "Did you enjoy our walk in the park last night?" he asked, completely off subject.

I looked at him and knit my brow. "What I can remember of it..."

He smiled slightly. "What do you remember?"

"Racing to the trail, walking around the lake, and then starting to race back to the car. It's unclear what happens after that."

He looked at me sympathetically. "You fell and hit your head. After I carried you to the car, I checked to make sure you were all right. You were groggy, but coherent. I let you sleep on the ride back and when we arrived at your house, I decided to carry you in and put you to bed."

I looked at him, nodding my head. It made sense – I must have tripped. It was a dark, unfamiliar place. "Okay, that's understandable why I don't remember," I agreed. "If I didn't say it at all last night, thank you for taking care of me."

He stood and caressed my cheek. "You're welcome," he remarked as he moved in front of the balcony opening. "It's getting late and I have to go. I'll talk to you tomorrow. Good night, Megan."

He gave me a soft but short kiss and then slowly backed away. I watched as he descended the tree and when he was out of sight, I closed the doors. At least now I knew what happened. Feeling content, I changed into shorts and a tank and climbed into bed.

The alarm woke me out of a deep sleep. Ugh…Monday morning. I looked out the window next to me at the gray, gloomy sky. I should stay home, but what would I do? I was already awake and wouldn't be able to go back to sleep now. Grumbling, I rolled out of bed and headed into the bathroom.

I jogged down the stairs and into the kitchen, grabbing a banana before saying good morning to Dad. He was in his usual spot reading the paper at the counter. "Another beautiful Monday morning," I commented as I leaned against it.

He moved the paper to the side and looked at me curiously. "Have you looked out the window yet?" he asked, glancing over his shoulder and then back at me.

"Yes, Dad, I did. I was being sarcastic."

"It's too early in the morning for sarcasm," he replied, hiding behind his paper.

"Sorry…well, I'm going to head out. See you this evening."

"Oh, I forgot to tell you. I have dinner with a client tonight, so I won't be home until about nine."

"Better than another wedding-related dinner," I muttered under my breath as I turned to leave. "All right, I'll grab something for myself after school. See you when you get home."

I was in pretty good spirits even though the day was gray. Turning into the parking lot, I pulled into my usual spot and Claire pulled up next to me as I was getting out of the car. Throwing my bag over my shoulder, I walked around to her door.

"Did you show off your treasures?" I asked as she rummaged through the back seat, looking for her book bag.

"Of course! Mom was thrilled and is so excited," she answered as she got up and turned toward me, bag on her arm. "Did you see David last night?"

"Yeah and I attacked him," I replied, blushing slightly as we walked toward the building.

"Like punched him?"

"No, we were kissing and it got a little intense. He stopped me, though."

"Wow...what a gentleman and what restraint," she commented as she opened the door.

"It was like something came over me...like a hunger. I wanted more, wanted him. I lost all sense of control."

"Huh...nothing like that has happened with Justin and me..." she mumbled as she thought about it.

"Hey, guys! Wait up!" Ben shouted from behind us. He caught up and took a deep breath. "So how was your weekend?" he asked.

I exchanged glances with Claire. "Great! We did some more shopping for prom," she replied.

He threw his arm over my shoulder. "Do anything cool this weekend other than shopping?"

"I went out with David on Saturday night."

"Oh...what hot spot did you two go to this time?" he inquired, a hint of resentment in his tone.

"Pocahontas State Park. Just a walk."

"Hmm, he likes to take you to parks at night where the two of you are alone and no one knows where you are...and you're comfortable with that?"

We stood at my locker. "Ben, what are you getting at?" I asked with my hands on my hips.

"I don't know...maybe David's the Ghost..."

I looked at him and then Claire. "Are you serious?" I laughed, turning away and heading toward class. "He's not a serial killer," I stated as I glanced back at him.

"You're so pathetic," she sneered as she turned to join me.

"Hey, I wouldn't rule it out," he shouted while we continued to walk, leaving him behind.

Nothing exciting or interesting happened all day, but of course it was Monday. Everyone, students and staff, took that first day back to recuperate from the weekend and wish for the next to hurry and arrive. Conversations in class and at lunch rehashed its glories, making storytellers and listeners alike mourn the passing of their beloved free time.

As the school day came to a close, I didn't feel rushed to get home. I was going to be alone for several hours, so I decided to hang out in the parking lot for a while with everyone. Claire was all over Justin, occasionally pecking him on the cheek. Maybe what I told her about David had her wondering if Justin had a similar effect on her. From what I saw, it didn't look like it.

We pestered Erin about getting a date, but she insisted she was still going stag. For some reason, none of us believed her. Getting tired of the harassment, she switched the discussion to me. I thanked her with a punch in the arm and reluctantly accepted her distraction as we talked about my date Saturday with David.

The focus stayed on me and my relationship as the parking lot gradually cleared. Soon, we were the only ones left. "Well, I better get going," Ben announced first and I sighed thankfully. "I'm sure the twins will be home soon from practice, and I have to get dinner started," he commented as he lifted his bag to his shoulder.

"Yeah, I should be going, too," I seconded, opening my door. Soon everyone concurred and headed to their cars.

I pulled out of the lot, watching Ben slowly stroll down the street, and felt sorry for him. He's so young and yet forced to be so responsible. Going away to college will be a blessing for him. I drove on down the road, waving at him as I passed, and then headed to grab dinner before going home.

Sitting at the kitchen table, I pulled out my homework and worked on it as I ate, making sure to keep any evidence of food off it. Once I finished, I cleaned up and packed everything away and then relaxed on the couch as I did some reading for English. After completing the required chapters, I turned on the TV.

Flipping through the channels, I stopped on a horror movie. It was the kind of evening that made it extra scary. And it was one I'd never seen before. At a really intense moment, my phone vibrated in my pocket and caused me to jump.

It was Dad. "I wanted to call and let you know I'm going to Vanessa's after my meeting. I didn't see her all day and she wants me to come over. Do you mind?" he asked.

"No, I'm fine. I finished my homework and ate dinner. And now I'm watching a scary movie," I replied as I walked into the kitchen to get a drink. Out of the corner of my eye, I spotted something large moving in the garden.

"Well, I'll let you go then. I probably won't be home before midnight," he responded as I went to the patio doors and scanned the darkness.

It was only seven, but the coverage from the full-leafed trees and overcast sky really made it dark, like it was dusk. I flipped on the floodlights, hoping to scare whatever might be out there. The beams cut through the darkness, revealing nothing.

"Megan? Are you there?"

"Yeah…sorry, Dad. I thought I saw something in the backyard," I answered as I headed back to the couch, glancing outside again before I sat.

"Is the movie getting to you? Should I come home?"

"No, no, I'll be okay. Probably a raccoon or something. Enjoy your evening. I'll see you in the morning."

"Okay…call me if you need anything," he offered and then hung up.

I went back to watching the movie, every once in a while checking out the windows. I think the lights worked, keeping whatever I saw initially away. As the credits rolled, I turned everything off, including the floodlights, and climbed the stairs to the upper floor. I entered my room and turned on the bedside lamp before changing into nightclothes. I placed both phones on the bedside table and grabbed a book, stretching out on my belly on the bed.

I went to the library while at school and picked up something new to read. The teachers have a list of books they recommend their students check out but aren't required. I picked one that stood out and started reading it between classes. It was interesting enough to keep reading and helped take my mind off the movie and whatever had been in the yard.

I was deep into it when I heard a light tapping on the balcony door. David must be here! I hopped up, excited to see him, and unlocked the door. Opening it, I expected to see his mischievous grin but didn't.

Instead, it was Brian's cold, sinister smirk. Gasping, I quickly shut and locked it. Leaning back against the frame, I searched my room for a something I could use as a weapon in case he tried to come in.

"Aww, were you expecting someone else, Megan?" he asked, his menacing voice muffled slightly by the doors.

"Of course I was," I replied. "You're the last person I expected. Now go away."

"You should be more cordial toward your guest."

"You're not welcome here."

"I just want to talk…please let me in," he begged.

"I don't want to talk to you," I responded, turning and moving away from the doors. "You need to leave, Brian."

"I won't bite…I promise," he commented. I could see his pretentious grin through the sheer curtain. "Just invite me in…I want to get to know you better."

"How do you know where I live?" I asked, continuing to back away.

"I'm extremely good at finding people. Now please, let me in so we can talk. There's something I think you should know about David before going to prom."

He goes from wanting to get to know me better to having something important to tell me about David? I'm not falling for that. "My dad will be home soon, so you better leave," I threatened.

"Oh no he won't. I know he went to see Vanessa. And I know he won't be home before midnight. Don't make this hard."

How did he know about Dad? Is he stalking me? I glanced at the clock – only ten. I tried to think of something else to say. "David should be calling anytime now. He won't be happy when I tell him you're here."

He laughed, the sound of it deep and threatening. "He's working tonight. He won't be calling for a while, giving us plenty of time to talk. Now let me in," he demanded, trying to sound calm, but his underlying irritation betrayed him.

I moved around my bed and stood on the other side. I could see him pacing back and forth like a hungry lion waiting for his prey to falter. Then he stopped and stared at me through the curtain, his pale eyes piercing through the sheer fabric. He placed his fists against the frame and waited.

"Go away, Brian," I attempted to growl, hoping to sound intimidating.

He was quiet for a moment and then another deep laugh rose out of him. I backed closer to the main door, feeling incredibly uncomfortable with this situation. Suddenly, his fists came down as he roared, "Let me in!"

I jumped and not thinking twice about it, ran out of the room and down the stairs to the front door. I grabbed the handle but turned as I heard him laughing at the patio doors. How did he get down so fast? I was frozen, trying to decide if it was best for me to stay or make a run for it. The laughing stopped and I glanced around nervously.

There was no sign of Brian anywhere. Silence filled the house and outside was eerily the same. I slowly released the handle and backed away, fearing he might be waiting for me on the other side. It wasn't safe outside, not with him out there hiding. The safest place for me was in the house, maybe in my closet, waiting until Dad came home or David called.

Several loud booms erupted from the front door and I jolted, holding my scream. I started quietly creeping up the stairs while keeping my mouth covered. Then the banging stopped and so did I as Brian's voice calmly called my name. But I didn't wait to find out what he wanted. I continued up the steps and slipped back into my room, grabbing the phones off the bedside table and hiding in the closet. I shut the door and sat in the dark, waiting.

The entire house was dead silent as I sat huddled on the closet floor, clenching the phones and hoping for a call. My mind started coming up with different reasons why Brian was here and none of them were good. I hope he leaves before Dad comes home; I don't want him seeing some strange man hanging around the house. But what if Brian attacks Dad and takes his keys? Maybe Dad shouldn't come home...

I was tempted to call and tell him to stay at Vanessa's tonight, but I couldn't come up with a good enough excuse as to why he should. I looked at the time on my phone – ten twenty-six. It was so calm in the house, but that made me worry. What if he tries to come down the chimney or work a door open? What if he's in the house, standing outside my door at this very moment? I slipped deeper into the closet.

"Meaaagan...I know you're in there," Brian's voice sang, but not from outside the door. It seemed muffled and farther away. He must be on the balcony again.

I didn't peek out the door. I didn't move at all. I stayed in my spot and listened. He called my name again in the same tone while scratching the frame of the French doors. I still didn't move. His nails dug into the wood as he called again, and I covered my ears and head.

Then silence filled the house once more.

Several minutes passed with no sound from him. He must be gone. Lying on my stomach, I peeked under the door and attempted to see into my room. The gap between the bottom of it and floor was small, but I was able to make out the legs of my bed and the base of the French doors. One side opened slowly and then shut quietly. Dark shoes softly stalked toward me, and I held my breath.

How did Brian unlock my doors? I continued watching the shoes as they passed the closet and went to the main door. I slowly let out my breath. He was leaving.

But then they paused and my fear returned. I held my hand over my mouth, trying not to scream or cry as they turned and started walking back. Quickly sitting up, my heart raced as I scooted to the back and hid among my long dresses. I covered my head and closed my eyes, waiting and hoping he'd pass by. Instead, the door creaked open.

"Megan?"

I slowly raised my head and parted the dresses slightly. David stood in the doorway, a perplexed look on his face. I jumped up and ran into his arms. "Oh, I'm so glad it's you!" I exclaimed, not letting go.

"Who else would it be?" he inquired, prying my arms from around his neck.

"Brian...he was here tonight."

"What? Are you sure?"

"Yes. I saw him, on my balcony...at my door."

"What did he want?" he asked coolly.

"To talk...talk about you. David...he knows where I live!"

He pulled me close and I inhaled deeply, instantly calmed. He smelled wonderful. I started to feel dizzy, so I closed my eyes and held him tighter. With my head resting against his chest, I heard the same hollow sound as that night on the lake. No heartbeat, just the soft hint of air passing through an object.

"What were you doing before he showed up?" he asked quietly, lifting my chin and gazing into my eyes.

I couldn't take mine off his with my mind so foggy. I didn't answer right away, the words lingering a moment in my brain as I analyzed what he asked. "I was…I was watching…a…a horror movie."

"A horror movie," he repeated, his eyes never leaving mine.

"Yes…where a crazed serial killer is harassing a young woman in her house…"

"I see," he mumbled as he continued to stare into my eyes. "Brian wasn't here tonight. You imagined it," he whispered. "Your mind was still active from the movie and you thought you heard and saw him, but you didn't," he explained in a soft voice. "It was just a dream…"

I nodded, not arguing. Really, why would Brian be here? It was my overactive imagination. I must have passed out sometime after watching the movie and dreamed it all.

"Brian was never here," I replied groggily.

"That's right," he commented, kissing my cheek.

My head started to clear as he tried to get me to release him, but I refused. I still felt scared and didn't want him to go, even if it was all a dream. "Please stay with me until my dad gets home. I don't want to be alone," I begged.

He smiled as he slipped his hand under my hair and held my jaw. "I will."

Lifting my chin, he gently kissed my lips. As I kissed back, the hunger from the other night returned. What's wrong with me? Moments ago, I was terrified, thinking something awful was going to happen to me, and then David shows up and I'm all over him?

Trying to control myself, I resisted the urge to force him onto my bed and instead placed my palms on his cool cheeks, keeping him from moving away. His hands moved from my back to my waist and I thought he was going to push me away, but he kept them there.

Lowering mine to his sides, I let them trace the contour of his body, feeling its leanness. When I reached his hips, I slipped my hands under his shirt and caressed his torso with my fingers. His skin was cool and smooth as I ran my fingertips over every indentation. I eagerly lifted his shirt, wanting to see his body. He blocked me, but I insisted. Conceding, my anticipation built as he slowly removed it. And it was worth the wait.

I stared at his perfectly sculpted body in awe, my fingers trembling as they skimmed over his chest and stomach, tracing their shape. He was like a newly finished Michelangelo's David – pale and smooth, not a single imperfection. I moved closer to hold him, wanting to feel his bare skin against my face, when suddenly he stepped back and turned away, slipping his shirt back on.

"What's wrong?" I asked as he turned back around.

He played with my hair, staring at the dark spirals in his hand. "I'm very modest," he replied.

I gazed into his amazing green eyes. "You're so beautiful..."

"No, I'm not," he interrupted, abruptly walking to the balcony and sneaking a look outside.

I sat on the bed, my back to him, and sighed. He's acting so strange, but at least he's here. *He's here...*

Then I remembered what Brian said in my dream. "Did you have to work tonight?" I inquired, glancing over my shoulder at him.

He cocked his head my way as he leaned against the wall. "I did, but they sent me home. Good thing they had," he replied with a grin.

My heart fluttered, but it quickly went away as I thought about the dream again. "Why do you think I dreamt it was Brian coming after me and not some random crazed killer like in the movie?" I asked, turning around and facing him.

He was quiet, deep in thought as he stared out the French doors. "I don't know..."

"It just seems so strange, all these vivid dreams I've been having," I responded softly and then looked up at him. "Ever since meeting you."

"I must have quite an effect on you," he replied, smiling.

Rather than a flutter, my heart thumped hard and I looked away, facing the wall across from me as I bit my lower lip and closed my eyes. All I saw was David and the same desire rose in me like before. I placed my hand over my chest as my heart pounded against it. It beat faster as I saw us kissing, his lips on mine, and then moving down my chin to my neck...

A hand alighted on my shoulder and I quickly opened my eyes. "Are you all right?" he asked, his hand running down my bare arm as he sat, taking mine in his. I trembled at his touch, but a good tremble.

"Yeah...I'm still a little shaken," I lied, facing him but avoiding his eyes.

"Why don't you lie down for a while?" he suggested, moving so I could.

I stayed above the covers, lying on my side beside him. He remained at the edge of the bed, caressing my shoulder and neck. Closing my eyes, I felt drowsier than I had a moment ago. I raised my chin as his fingers gently danced down my throat and across my collarbone toward my chest. Peeking through my eyelashes, I watched him, curious what he was doing.

He was staring at me, his expression soft and sad. His hand was paused above my chest, deciding where to go next. My breathing deepened as he lightly placed his palm above my breasts. Slowly, I felt his fingers come down one by one, relaxing. He closed his eyes and remained that way for several minutes, as if memorizing my heartbeat.

My drowsiness disappearing, I opened my eyes a little more and continued to watch him. He was completely still, not seeming to breathe. I glanced down at his hand, pale against my tan skin, and noticed that it also never moved. Slowly raising my arm, I started to place my hand over his when his eyes shot open. He quickly jerked away and turned from me.

"Please forgive me...that was uncalled for," he whispered as I moved closer.

Sitting behind him, I rested my chin on his shoulder as I ran my fingers through his hair. "It's okay...I don't mind," I whispered, slowly letting them glide down his neck. "You looked so peaceful."

I kissed it and then slipped my arms under his, holding across his chest. Resting my head between his shoulder blades, I sighed deeply. I could stay like this forever. He slid his fingers between mine, holding them there, and then sighed. But it wasn't a contented sigh like mine. Lifting my hand, he kissed my palm and then placed it over his heart. I felt nothing but his chest barely rising and falling.

"I have to go," he whispered. "Your father is home now."

He released my hand and stood, turning to me and taking my chin in his fingertips. In the background, Dad's keys jingled in the lock as he opened the front door. David tilted my head back as he leaned down and kissed me, pausing a moment before straightening up. I followed him to the balcony and watched as he climbed down the tree.

He glanced toward the family room and then up at me before completely disappearing. I ran to the edge and scanned the yard for him, but he was lost in the darkness. Out of the corner of my eye, I saw the kitchen light come on. Dad must be getting a snack. I rushed back into my room, deciding to go see him.

He was making a sandwich as I entered the kitchen. He looked up, surprised to see me, as he added the last few pieces of meat. "What are you doing up? It's after midnight," he commented as he cut the sandwich and put it on a plate.

"I was dozing when I heard your keys in the door. I wanted to see you before I fell asleep," I responded as I walked with him to the family room.

"That's sweet of you, but you do have school tomorrow," he reminded me as he turned on the TV.

I sat on the sofa as he sat in his chair. "How did your dinner go?" I asked, stalling.

"Fine," he replied and then puckered his brow. "Megan, are you all right? Is there a reason you don't want to go to bed?" he questioned.

I looked at the concern on his face. "No, I'm good. I've just been lonely tonight," I responded.

"So nothing exciting happened," he commented, taking a bite of his giant sandwich.

"Nope. Calm and quiet," I replied. "Well, good night, Dad," I remarked as I stood to leave, realizing there was no use lingering.

"Sleep well, Meg," he responded and I glanced back and smiled.

I gradually climbed the stairs and entered my room. Before getting into bed, I went over to the balcony doors and closed one side while scanning the yard again. Standing under a gnarled redbud was David. He grinned as I came to the railing, but before I could do or say anything, he disappeared into the shadows.

I smiled to myself and turned to go back into my room. Meandering toward the doors, I froze suddenly as my smile vanished, my eyes catching sight of something that shouldn't exist. Slowly, a shiver spilled down my spine as I stared at the long scratch marks marring the door.

# Chapter 17
## Countdown to Prom

"Claire…what do you know about Justin?" I asked as I played with the fruit inside my gelatin.

He was out sick today and the rest of the group hadn't arrived yet. "Umm…he really likes video games, has posters of swimsuit models on his bedroom walls, has an older brother and sister. Why?"

I sighed, not really getting what I wanted out of her. "I don't know a lot about David and can't figure him out. There's just something guarded about him."

At that moment, Ben sat at the table and Erin after him. "Having second thoughts?" he asked, noticing my troubled expression.

"No, I just wanted to know if this is normal in a relationship."

"Well, I'm having second thoughts about my date," he responded, squirting ketchup on his burger.

"You have nothing to worry about. Madeline is interested in going out with you. And if David likes her, then she must be a good person," I encouraged.

"Uh…what about Brian?" he asked.

I looked at him, stunned. "What do you mean?"

"It doesn't sound like Brian's a nice person and David likes him, right?" he asked.

"Actually, David's not really fond of him. He's just helping him out," I replied.

"What if she's beautiful…I mean, like, too beautiful for me?"

"That'd be just about every girl," Erin commented aside and Claire giggled.

"Then you'll be the envy of all the guys at school," I responded, narrowing my eyes at them. "It's going to be okay, Ben. We'll be there for support."

He glanced at the three of us and rolled his eyes. "Some support."

I went back to playing with my food and realized Ben's worry took my mind off mine. But Claire made sure to bring it back up, touching my arm to get my attention. "So getting back to what we were talking about…what brought this on?" she whispered.

"So many strange things have been going on in the last few weeks. I don't know what to think." I paused a moment and glanced at Ben and Erin, making sure they weren't listening to the conversation. "And I had this strange dream last night that Brian came to my house," I whispered.

"Were you alone?"

"Yeah, Dad was out. David was working but showed up about eleven and found me hiding in the closet."

"How did you get in the closet if you were dreaming?"

"I don't know…after watching a horror movie, I headed up to my room to read," I explained. "I must have fallen asleep while reading and didn't realize it," I mumbled.

"So you fell asleep and dreamed Brian came to your house," she surmised. "How did you end up in the closet again?"

I slipped my hand into my hair and held my head as I leaned on the table. "I…I'm not sure. I guess I was sleepwalking again," I responded, though I really wasn't sure I believed it.

"In your dream, did Brian say anything odd to you?" she asked, pulling me from the overwhelming theories boggling my brain.

"He…he wanted to tell me something…about David. He said I should know it before going to prom with him."

"What? That he's a serial killer?" Ben commented, playing with a fry.

I turned to him with a shocked expression. "Oh my God, Ben, you're totally right! Working and going to school is just a cover up. He really spends his time stalking his prey and then killing them. It all makes so much sense now," I retorted sarcastically.

"Or maybe he takes the bodies to work, cuts their heads off, and drains them there. That's why they never find any blood," Claire added.

"Ha ha…you guys suck," he responded.

"Ooo, speaking of which…did you hear about the latest murder?" Erin asked, getting into the conversation.

"There was another?" I asked.

"Yeah, the body was found in Pocahontas State Park, same way as all the rest. It was another male college student that lived on campus. Said he died Saturday night," she responded.

I looked at Claire and she looked at me. "You were there Saturday night…did you see anything?" she asked.

I thought back to that night…no, I don't remember seeing anything. "No. Besides, it's a big park and it could have happened before or after David and I were there." I looked at Ben and grinned. "So there, David has an alibi – he was with me Saturday night. He can't be the Ghost."

"Was he with you *all* night?" he inquired.

"No…but he didn't do it. There's a lot I don't know about him, but I know he's not a killer," I replied, angrily jerking my tray off the table and walking away. The bell rang and I headed to my next class without another word to him.

What does Ben know anyway? He's just trying to make me not want to be with David. Well, too bad. I really like him and Ben's not going to destroy that.

I didn't linger in the parking lot after school, but instead said my goodbyes and headed home. I took care of my homework and finished up my Biology report, then made a quick dinner before Dad came through the door. After eating, we went into the family room and watched the news. I was interested in catching the story about the recent murder.

It was just as Erin said and they had a picture of the guy on the screen. Something seemed familiar about him. Maybe I saw him on campus when I was there Saturday. Unlike the other cases, evidence was found on the body and the police were sending it to a lab. They said the time of death was around eleven on Saturday. Ha! Ben was definitely wrong – David was picking me up at eleven, so there was no way he did it.

I was ready to go to my room after that, feeling assured that my boyfriend was not a killer, even though I already knew it. I told Dad good night and headed up the stairs. As I entered, I flipped on my light, changed, and then got comfy in bed with David's phone nearby.

I was nodding off when it vibrated next to me. Drowsily, I answered it. "Did I interrupt your sleep?" he asked.

"No, I was just dozing. How was your day?"

"Peaceful...yours?"

"All right, I guess. They found another victim of the serial killer."

"Oh really. Where?"

"At Pocahontas State Park...killed the night we were there."

"Unbelievable..."

"I know. We must have missed him."

"Lucky us," he commented.

"There was some evidence found on the body this time. Maybe they'll catch him soon."

He was quiet. "Did they say what was found?"

"No, but they sent it to a lab, maybe skin cells or hair," I replied, examining my nails. "Can I ask you a morbid question?"

"All right..."

"The victims' bodies..."

He hesitated. "Yes."

"Are they as bad as they say?"

"Worse," he replied.

"I couldn't do your job for anything."

"And I wouldn't want you to."

In the brief silence of deciding what to say next, my thoughts returned to what happened last night. The dream was still bothering me and even though he assured me it wasn't real, I still had my doubts, especially after seeing the scratch marks.

"I have another question for you..." I began.

"If it has to do with the autopsies, I'd rather not respond."

"No, it doesn't. It has to do with that dream I had last night…about Brian."

"All right…what is your question?"

"Do you believe it's possible for a dream to be so vivid, so realistic, that you actually believe it happened?"

He was quiet. "Yes, I do," he responded after a moment. "I've heard of cases where a person will actually act out the dream in their sleep."

So there's a possibility *I* made the scratches on the door? "Scary…but a relief," I remarked. "So how did you get in last night?"

"The door was open," he replied simply.

Guess I did that, too. "Oh," I responded and then yawned.

"You sound tired, so I should let you go. We'll talk tomorrow."

I said good night and hung up, fatigue catching up with me. After placing the phone on the bedside table and turning out the light, I rested my head on the pillow and closed my eyes. Unlike last night, my mind was clear and I felt completely relaxed. Sleep came quickly.

I woke the next morning, refreshed and in a good mood. I hurriedly got ready and headed downstairs to see Dad and grab breakfast before going to school. I bid him good morning and then took off out the door with a pear in hand. I arrived a little early, so I sat in front of my locker and read while I waited for someone to show up.

I spoke with Ben and Erin briefly but was hoping to see Claire. I stopped Justin in the hall and asked if he talked to her. Apparently, she caught whatever he had and was out sick. It was a good thing this was happening before prom night. I went on to class and doodled while I waited for it to begin.

Lunch was pretty dull without Claire. Ben and Justin shared the latest geek gossip while Erin leaned over to the table next to us, discussing some game coming up. I ate my food and listened to their conversations, bored out of my mind.

Same as yesterday, I didn't stay long in the lot and when I got home, did my homework and made dinner. I called Claire while I was cooking to see how she was doing and let her know what she missed, which wasn't much. She sounded like she was feeling better and said she'd probably be back tomorrow. As Dad walked through the door, I told her I had to go.

We ate dinner and discussed our uneventful day. Then it turned to prom. "So are you ready?" he asked, taking his dishes to the sink.

"Yep, everything's set."

"What time are you being picked up?"

"Not until after eight. I thought I could have dinner with you and Vanessa."

"That would be nice. David's not taking you out?" he asked as he sat in his recliner.

"No, he has something to do beforehand."

"Any after prom party plans?"

"No, just going to the dance. When would you like me home?" I asked as I slipped the dishes into the washer.

He thought for a moment. "Ten…just kidding. No later than midnight is fine. It's a big night and you should enjoy it…just not too much."

I gave him an evil look as I leaned against the back of the sofa. "What are you implying?"

"No drugs, alcohol, or any of that other stuff that goes with it," he replied, avoiding saying what he was really concerned about.

"You don't have to worry, Dad. I'm not like that," I responded, moving to his side as he gave a weak smile.

With that, I figured it was time I headed up to my room. I said good night and dashed up the stairs, not wanting to have the awkward conversation about the birds and the bees with my father. I reached the door just in time to hear David's phone going off. He was calling early. I quickly grabbed it and answered, but I was too late. I set it down and paced back and forth, waiting for him to call back.

After five minutes, I went to the balcony doors and opened them, peeking out. No sign of him. I left them open in case he showed up and then grabbed a book and stretched out on the bed. I glanced at the phone periodically, but still no call. I continued reading but was restless. I readjusted several times and then rolled over to my back.

"Ahem…"

I jerked and raised my head up, looking over at my desk and finding him leaning against it with his head cocked as he stared at me. "How long have you been there?" I questioned, sitting up.

"Several minutes," he replied with a grin.

"Why didn't you say something earlier?"

"I enjoy watching you. Why didn't you answer my call?"

"I just missed it. Dad was giving me the third degree about prom."

"He's very protective of you."

"Most of the time, when Vanessa isn't distracting him. But it seems more so since he found out I was dating."

David pushed off the desk and came over to the bed, leaning over me and forcing me back onto my elbows. "What is he worried about?"

He was inches from my face, the mischievous grin I love so much on his lips. "You…I-I think," I replied, trying to remain calm.

He had one hand on the mattress supporting himself as he put his other on the nape of my neck, tilting it back. He slowly kissed along my chin, moving lower until he reached the base of my throat where he paused. "How so?" he whispered, his warm lips glancing my skin.

My breathing hastened as he moved to my clavicle. I decided not to answer since I had a feeling he knew what it was. He brushed his lips across my skin, sending a tingling sensation throughout my body. I could feel my heart pounding in my chest as he kissed above my breasts. He paused and then lifted up, sitting next to me and leaning on his knees.

I sat up and held my chest, calming my heart. Looking over at him, I caught him watching me. "What?" I asked, blushing.

"You are so beautiful," he replied, gazing into my eyes.

I looked down at my knees and smiled. "Thank you."

"So after I meet your father, will I still need to sneak into your room at night, or will I be able to come to the front door?" he inquired with a grin.

"Oh, you can come to the front door, but I don't think he'll allow us to be alone in my room. So you'll still need to sneak in at night if you plan to continue that."

"Good," he replied, looking out the balcony doors. "I should be on my way…"

"No, wait…please stay until I fall asleep," I begged, grabbing his arm.

He smiled at me and my heart fluttered. "All right."

He walked over to the other side of the bed and turned off the bedside lamp as I climbed under my covers. He came back around and sat by my side. I fidgeted with my hair and asked, "Will you lie with me?"

He didn't answer but stretched out above the covers, gazing into my eyes as he rested his head on his arm. I moved closer, nuzzling my face into his chest. I felt calm and relaxed as I breathed him in. He put his other arm around me and rubbed my back, making me think of my mom.

"When I couldn't sleep, Mom would…would rub my back just like that," I whispered drowsily. He hushed me and kissed the top of my head, continuing to rub slowly. It wasn't long before I was out.

I woke the next morning to my alarm sounding loudly. I rolled over and slapped it, then rolled back, wanting to go to sleep again. The light in my room gradually grew brighter and I was unable to continue my snooze. I rolled out of bed and headed into the bathroom.

With the shower helping to wake me up, I dressed and grabbed my things, jogging down the stairs. I said good morning to Dad as I entered the kitchen and searched the cabinet for something to eat. He folded his paper and sipped his coffee, waiting for me to sit.

I grabbed a granola bar and headed to the counter but didn't sit. "I want to get to school early. Claire was out sick yesterday and I want to catch her up on what she missed," I explained, kissing his cheek. "See you tonight."

When I arrived, I noticed her car was already in the parking lot. I rushed into the building and looked for her, finding her at Justin's locker. They were discussing dinner plans for Friday as I walked up, arguing over the restaurant.

"Megan!" she shouted as she spotted me, pulling me toward her. "What do you think – should we go to a casual restaurant or something fancy for dinner before prom?" she asked.

"Well, it is a special occasion…"

"See, we should go to a fancy restaurant, as we originally agreed!" she exclaimed.

"But that'll take all my allowance and then some," he whined.

"Why didn't you say that before? We can go half, if you want."

"Really?"

"Yeah. I know you're saving up for that new game."

They hugged and then started kissing. I turned away and looked at a nearby poster, but seeing them like that made me miss David. Justin broke away, saying he needed to get to class early to talk to the teacher. They kissed again, briefly, and then he took off down the hall.

Claire and I walked toward class in silence until I decided to speak. "It must be nice having your boyfriend in school with you."

"It has its benefits, but there are downsides. We see each other every day…a lot. That can get annoying, especially if you want to be alone. Then there are the rumors. When you're in a relationship, you're fair game, whether they want your man or not."

"That's tough. I guess I am lucky. But some days I do wish he was here."

"I'm sure you do. I don't know if I could handle a relationship like yours. I'm a pretty jealous person."

We entered class and took our seats, continuing our conversation through morning announcements. "So you're feeling better, I see."

"Yeah, just a twenty-four-hour bug, thankfully," she answered. "Can you believe prom is tomorrow night?"

"No, but I can't wait."

The teacher entered and we faced the front. Mr. Barton asked for our reports and I heard Claire panic behind me. She frantically checked her book bag as the papers were passed up. Finally finding it, she whipped it out and sighed loudly, quickly passing hers forward. The rest of class was a lot less exciting, as was the remainder of the morning.

At lunch, the cafeteria was brimming with conversations about prom. Everyone going had their dress or tuxedo and very few were still looking for a date. Plans were being finalized as groups decided who they were sharing a limo with and where they were going to dinner. And as my group joined me at the table, our discussion was the same.

"So Erin, do you have a date yet?" Ben asked, sitting by her.

"Maybe. It's a surprise," she joked. "Are you ready for your date?" she inquired, turning it back on him and making him uneasy.

"I...I think so. I mean, she's only a couple years older than me, right? Nothing to worry about," he replied nervously.

"Don't get cold feet on me now," I warned.

"I'm not. I'm looking forward to it," he replied, still not convincing me.

"So what're everyone's plans for dinner?" Erin asked.

"Justin and I are going to an elegant restaurant," Claire replied.

"Be sure to call in your reservations early," she suggested.

"I'm eating with my dad and Vanessa."

"I'm eating a frozen dinner that night since my date won't be available before eight," Ben replied, a little bitter.

"We could always go to dinner together," Erin commented.

He looked at her and laughed. "No thank you. I'll just stay home. I want to relax before going."

"How about you, Erin? Any plans?" I asked, wondering if I could get anything out of her about her date.

"Maybe a burger joint...nothing crazy," she replied with a grin. She was on to me.

I gave up attempting to trick it out of her and continued eating my food. Justin and Claire were busy trying to decide which restaurant they were going to, finally choosing a place before the bell rang. We headed out of the cafeteria and on to our classes.

In English, Ben passed notes to me, asking about Madeline and what he should say to her when they meet and at prom. I gave him the same answer with every question he asked – be yourself. When class was dismissed, I explained it to him.

"She'll like you for who you are, not who you're not. You have a great personality and you're fun."

"I'll give it a try," he replied as we walked out to the lot.

"You shouldn't try. Ben, it's going to be okay. And if it's not, so what."

We joined the others, Ben still going on about his insecurities. I leaned against my car and watched as storm clouds crept over the school. We wouldn't be able to hang out long. We talked a little while longer about final plans and then headed out. I reached the door of the house just as it started to pour.

The thunder crashed outside as I sat at the breakfast table and worked on my homework. Occasionally, I glanced outside at the sheets of rain coming down and watched as it flooded low-lying areas of the yard. The lightning flashed and the thunder cracked – the storm was right above the house. I went back to work, finishing just as Dad walked in the door, soaked.

"Did you forget your umbrella?" I asked as he shook off and joined me in the kitchen.

"I didn't think I'd need it; the weather report said there was a thirty percent chance of rain today. Usually with those odds, we don't get any."

"That's our crazy Virginia weather – fooling its inhabitants and weathermen for centuries. I guess next time you'll know better," I replied, grabbing my bag and leaving the room to hang it on the banister.

"So what do we want to have for dinner tonight?" he asked, looking through menus.

"You're not planning on making some poor delivery person come out in this, are you?" I asked, sitting at the island.

"Why not? I don't feel like cooking and I'm sure you don't either. So what'll it be – Chinese or pizza?"

"Let's go with pizza. It's been awhile."

He placed the order while I made myself comfortable on the couch. I flipped on the TV and turned it to Dad's favorite channel. He came in and sat in his chair, informing me that it'd be thirty minutes before the food arrived. I watched the storm outside rather than what was on TV, the streaks of lightning cutting through the pelting rain more entertaining than ranting commentators.

The thunder came further apart and the rain turned to a drizzle as the storm finally moved away. Dad jumped up as the doorbell rang, bringing the pizzas into the kitchen a moment later and setting them on the counter. He handed me a soda and a plate with two slices on it before taking his seat. We continued watching his program and once I finished my food, I thanked him and said good night.

I was glad to be in the quiet and solitude of my room. For some reason, I wanted silence and to be alone. I opened the balcony doors and let the rain-soaked air in, enjoying its refreshing scent. Sitting on the edge of my bed, I stared into the trees outside my room and watched as the remaining raindrops fell through the leaves to the ground, making light tapping noises and glittering in the light from my room.

I fell back on the bed just as David's phone rang. I looked at the clock and noticed it was early for him. "Hello, David. This is unusual for you to call this early."

"I'm out shopping for my tuxedo and would like to know what color vest I should choose. I would like it to match your dress," he commented.

"Oh…are there any tuxes available? I mean, this is the night before prom," I asked, concerned.

"There are plenty if you're buying them. The rentals are all gone." He covered the phone and there was muffled talking.

"Who are you talking to?" I asked.

"I'm being fitted as we speak. So what is the color?" he asked again.

"Oh, um, dark blue. Like navy."

There was more muffled talking, and then he returned. "Did you have a pleasant day?"

"Pretty good. Ben's really nervous about his date with Madeline. Is there anything more you can tell me that I can relay to him to ease his nerves?"

"Now we don't want to give too much away. The mystery is all part of the allure," he replied, and I could hear the smile in his voice.

"She will be nice, right?"

"Yes, Megan, she will. Madeline is a sweet person who doesn't like to hurt others. Trust me. They will get along great."

"Okay," I responded and sighed. "Can you believe prom is less than twenty-four hours away?"

"Are you getting nervous?"

I thought about it for a moment. Maybe I am a little nervous – nervous about Dad meeting David, nervous about my friends meeting David, even nervous for Ben. "Yeah, a little," I answered.

"There is nothing to be nervous about. Everything will be fine," he assured calmly, soothing my fears.

"You'll be there and that's all that matters to me," I responded. "This may be a silly question, but are you nervous at all?"

He was quiet. "No…you are my only concern."

I smiled to myself. "I wish I was there with you."

"Then you would ruin my surprise," he replied.

"What surprise?" I asked curiously.

"If I tell you, then it won't be a surprise," he responded, and I could almost hear a smirk in his voice this time. "Hold on a moment." He put the phone down and there was some talking in the background, but I couldn't make out what they were saying. He came back on shortly after that. "All right, I have my tuxedo. On to my next stop."

"And where might that be?" I asked, hoping to get a hint about the surprise.

"I need to pick up a pair of shoes," he replied. He was too smart to fall for it.

I heard female voices in the background commenting about him. "Are you at the shoe store already?"

"No, but it's not too much farther. Is it all right if I call you back when I'm finished?" he requested as a woman asked him a question I couldn't make out.

"Yeah…that's fine. I'll be waiting."

"It won't be for long," he responded and then hung up.

I rolled over onto my back and closed my eyes. It was too early to try to sleep, and he'd be calling back soon anyway. I hopped up and went over to my bookshelf, looking through my CDs. I slipped one into the stereo and went back to the bed, lying down and listening.

Closing my eyes, I felt the music pulse through my body, calming me. I concentrated on the words and tried to decipher their meanings as a way to keep my mind awake and aware. After listening to a couple of tracks, I hopped up and shut the doors to the balcony and closed the curtains. I changed into my nightclothes and crawled back into bed.

I was just about to fall asleep when David called back. "Where are you?" I asked, hearing wind in the background.

"On my way home."

I yawned. "So you have everything ready for tomorrow night?"

"Yes, I do. It looks like I missed a big storm while I was inside the mall."

"Yeah, it hit us earlier. Lots of rain; my backyard is flooded." I heard his car slow, then speed up only to slow down again, and then stop. A door opened and then shut. "You must be home," I commented.

"I am. Are you ready to go to sleep?" he asked.

"Not yet. I want you to talk to me some more," I answered as I yawned.

"Sounds like you're ready to sleep."

"No, just a yawn. What are you doing now?" I asked, getting him to continue talking.

"Leaning against my car and staring into the woods…I think I see a deer." He was quiet for a moment. "It seems the sky is clearing. Several stars are coming out…"

I started to drift off but woke when he called my name. "I'm here. I guess I better go. I'm more tired than I thought. See you tomorrow night."

"Good night, Megan. Sleep well," he whispered before hanging up.

I put the phone on the table by the bed and pulled the comforter around me. I thought about David's voice lulling me into sleep as the music continued to play softly. My mind quieted and my body was still. Before I realized it, I was out.

The sun woke me before the alarm did, shining brightly through the windows. I sat up and stretched, feeling a surge of excitement rush through my body. Prom is tonight!

I jumped out of bed and danced around to the other side, turning off the alarm clock before heading into the bathroom to get ready for school. Humming quietly as I brushed and washed, my heart skipped happily. I continued to dance as I went to my closet and flipped through my clothes. I pulled out a cute retro dress and heels and slipped them on.

I fixed my hair, putting it up in a bun so it'd be easy to style tonight. Snatching up my bag, I skipped down the stairs and into the kitchen, finding Dad in his usual spot. I hummed as I searched the pantry for something quick to eat. Grabbing a multigrain bar, I took a seat at the island and hummed as I ate.

He lowered his paper and looked at me strangely. "Excited about tonight?"

"Is it that obvious?" I asked with a huge grin on my face.

"Yeah, it is, but it's nice to see you this happy," he commented with a soft smile.

"Do we know what we're having for dinner?" I asked between bites.

"Would you like to stay home or go out?"

"We could go out, but I'm not putting on my gown until afterward. I don't want to ruin it," I responded to his disappointed look.

"How about the Tobacco Company?"

"That sounds good," I replied as I hopped down and threw my trash away.

"All right then. I'll call and make reservations for the three of us later," he grinned, raising his paper as I kissed his cheek. "Have a good day."

"You know I will. See you tonight."

I grabbed my bag at the stairs and headed out the door. At school, I found Claire and Justin arguing in the parking lot while Ben and Erin looked on. I walked up to him and asked what the issue was today.

"Oh, Justin forgot to call the restaurant yesterday. Claire is freaking out, thinking they're not going to get in."

"And why is everyone just standing here watching this?" I asked them.

"It's entertaining and makes me glad I don't have a boyfriend," Erin responded.

I pushed past them and went over to Claire. "Calm down. Why don't you call at lunch or during your study hall? I'm sure they're not booked up this early, but if they are, there are plenty of other options."

She took a deep breath and smoothed her hair out. "You're right, you're right. It's nothing to panic over," she agreed. "I'm sorry, Justin. I am just so stressed about tonight," she apologized as she turned and hugged his torso.

"It's okay. I'm sorry I forgot. There's just so much going on at home…" he babbled as they walked into the building.

"Look at you! Boy, do you know how to calm a storm!" Erin declared, nudging me.

"Yeah, yeah. Come on, let's get inside."

Ben grabbed my arm, pulling me back to walk with him. "I'm still unsure about tonight," he whispered, not wanting Erin to hear.

"I tried to get more out of David last night, but he wasn't relenting. All he said was that she's sweet. You'll be fine. Once you meet her, all your fears and worries will disappear."

"Do you think we'll have anything in common?"

I thought for a moment. Probably not, but I couldn't tell him that. "Look…if you need for any reason to get away from her, let me know. Cough or say that you need some air. We'll take a walk or something."

"Good plan. Thanks again, Megan."

"Well, I didn't want you to miss our first prom," I replied, patting him on the back as I stopped at my locker. "See you at lunch."

He continued down the hall to his first class, looking back at me before he turned the corner. I smiled and went into Biology, taking my seat after glancing at Claire's. She hadn't gotten there yet, and the bell was about to ring. She and Justin were probably in some dark stairwell making out now that they weren't angry at each other anymore.

Just as the bell rang, she came running through the door, telling the teacher she was in the room before it did. As the morning announcements blared overhead, Mr. Barton argued with her and then told her to take a seat. She looked over at me and grinned sheepishly.

"Where were you?" I whispered.

"In the stairwell," she whispered back, panting.

Just as I thought. "Glad you could make it," I responded, glimpsing her rolling her eyes as I faced forward and focused on the teacher.

At lunch, my joy was infectious, and nearly everyone smiled as I passed. There were those few looks of disgust or envy, but I didn't care. Let them live in their misery. I sat and waited for the others to arrive, nibbling on my salad. One by one, they came, looking at me as if I was a stranger at their table.

"Okay…is it because of prom or David?" Erin asked, looking me up and down.

"It has to be prom…she never looked like this before," Claire commented.

"Maybe it's because after tonight, she doesn't have to hide the fact that she's dating him," Ben guessed.

I looked at all of them and continued to smile. "I don't know what it is. I just woke up this morning feeling extremely happy and relaxed."

Baffled, they gave up and for the rest of lunch, we coordinated pick up times and other last minute items. Everyone was excited about the dance and David, even Ben. Erin still wouldn't tell us if she had a date or not, loving the fact it was annoying us. The bell rang, and it was on to the next class.

No one hung out in the parking lot after dismissal; we were all rushing home to get ready. I went straight to my room to put my things away, but I didn't plan to change since I looked nice anyway. Now all I had to do was wait for Dad and Vanessa.

I sat in the family room and watched TV, and as soon as they walked through the door, I hopped up to meet them. She set a large bag down at the foot of the stairs, and I looked at it curiously. Dad took my attention off it by saying we were heading out and taking my car since his was only a two-seater.

The first part of dinner was pleasant, and Vanessa and I were civil to each other. She even complimented my outfit, though she wondered why I wasn't in my gown. Dad explained the situation, and that seemed to satisfy her. As soon as the food arrived, a hush fell over us.

While we ate, Vanessa looked over at me and smiled. I tried not to think anything of it, but then she spoke. "Is it all right if I do your hair and makeup tonight?" she asked between bites.

Dad gave those same puppy dog eyes he had when she asked about dress shopping. "Okay...but the hairstyle has to be elegant and the makeup light," I replied, giving in. I've got to stop falling for them.

"No problem," she agreed. "I'll work my magic and David will be floored!"

What did I just agree to?

On the ride home, I assured myself over and over that having Vanessa do my hair and makeup would be fun. We pulled into the drive and she immediately hopped out, grabbing my wrist and dragging me out of the back seat and up the sidewalk.

"No time to waste...we've got to get to work! He's going to be here when?" she blathered as she opened the front door.

She snatched her large bag on the way up to my room. In the bathroom, she pulled up a stool and had me sit in front of the mirror as she yanked the hair band from my bun. From her bag, she pulled out all sorts of things: hair spray, curling iron, a huge makeup case, and plenty more. She played with my hair a little and then put it back up in a bun, leaving a few of my front strands loose.

She applied a cream to them and let the natural curl create neat little tendrils. She played with the leftover hair sticking out of the top of the bun and then sprayed it all down with hairspray. Turning me toward the mirror, she asked how I liked it.

"Amazing," I replied with a smile, surprised it turned out as nice as it did.

"Now on to the makeup. Let's see...the dress is a dark blue..." she mumbled as she shifted things around in her makeup box.

She pulled out various items and began working. I reminded her not to make it too heavy or dark and she assured me I'd be happy with the results.

I sat patiently as she pulled and prodded, jerking my face around and generally being rough. I hope it looks better than it feels.

She paused and checked her work, making faces as she gently turned my chin. That's not reassuring. Grabbing a couple different items from the makeup box, she touched up what she wasn't satisfied with and then paused again, examining my face. Her expression was much better this time. She smiled and moved away from the mirror to let me see.

I gasped as I saw myself. "You're incredible!" I exclaimed.

"I know. What do you expect from a girl like me? Okay...now you need to get your dress on. I'll leave you to that."

She packed everything away and left the room as I continued to look at myself in the mirror. She really did a great job. I just hope David likes it – he's used to seeing me all natural. Realizing time was running short, I hopped up and headed into my room. I quickly undressed and pulled my gown out of the back of the closet, laying it on the bed. David is going to be so impressed.

I was giddy as I unzipped the side and picked it up, my hands shaking. Stepping into it, I slowly slipped it on and zipped it closed. It felt great to be in it again.

I took the earrings out of my drawer and put them in my ears and then remembered I needed to grab a necklace. As I dashed down the hall to Dad's room, I hoped no one saw me flit by. I didn't hear my name or any comments, so they must be in the family room. I entered the master bedroom and calmed myself as I rummaged through one of Mom's jewelry boxes. I pulled out a diamond solitaire necklace and put it on, then headed back to my room to add the finishing touches.

# Chapter 18
## A Night to Remember

Running around my room, I frantically checked over everything to make sure I was completely ready before David arrived. I grabbed my clutch and glanced out the window just as a black stretch limo pulled up to the curb. That must be him.

I left the room but remained on the top step. Hiding so as not to be seen, I poked my head around the wall to watch. I wasn't ready to reveal myself, but I was interested in seeing how my dad reacted to David without me around.

The doorbell rang and Dad answered it, opening the door wide. There David stood so debonair with his hands behind his back and a pleasant smile on his lips as he greeted my father. Thank God I saw him now instead of when I descended the stairs. I probably would have fallen. My heart pounded at the sight of him, and I held my chest as I tried not to make a sound.

Dad invited him in, remaining stiff and straight-faced as he stepped aside. Glancing my way, David smirked as he entered the house and I quickly ducked behind the wall. Weird...it was like he knew I was watching.

The sound of someone dropping a glass grabbed my attention, and I peeked out again. Dad was turned toward the kitchen, shaking his head as Vanessa apologized. I grinned, imagining the look on her face when she saw my date.

"So you're Megan's boyfriend," Dad commented as he turned back around, crossing his arms and examining him.

"That would be correct, Mr. Caldwell. It is a pleasure to meet you," he replied, extending his hand.

Dad shook it and then shut the door, returning to his defensive pose as they stood for a moment in silence. "That's a pretty impressive limo for the two of you," he finally remarked.

"Megan's friends and their dates will be joining us, sir."

"Oh, well that's good," he responded. He glanced around, thinking of something else to say. "So Meg tells me you go to VCU and are planning on becoming a doctor."

"Yes, sir. I have always wanted to help people. Life is a precious thing."

"How admirable!" Vanessa cooed as she came into view, extending her hand toward him. "Hello, David. I'm Vanessa...Megan's stepmother."

He took it and bowed, kissing the back of it. She looked as though she'd faint! "It is a pleasure to meet you, *Vanessa*. I've heard so much about you."

"Oh, really?" she replied, fanning herself.

Dad stared at her, surprised by her reaction to him. "Well, I guess you two need to get going," he announced, pushing her aside. I had to stifle a giggle. "Megan! Your date is here!" he shouted up the stairs, keeping an eye on her.

I stepped back and composed myself, preparing for my entrance. I needed to take this slow and easy. As Dad called again, I stepped off the top step of the curved staircase. I took a deep breath and started down the first couple of steps, staring only at my feet. So far, so good.

Continuing down the next several, my heart tumbled in my chest with a mixture of excitement and trepidation. I wasn't used to being the center of attention and felt very intimidated by it, but I also couldn't wait to see David's reaction to me all dolled up. As anxious as I was, though, I couldn't look at him yet.

I turned with the staircase toward the front door and finally looked up, focusing on my dad. My eyes stayed trained only on him as I continued descending, smiling softly as I saw tears in his. After a moment, I felt brave enough to briefly glance at Vanessa standing beside him with her mouth gaping, and I smiled wider.

I waited until I was almost at the bottom before I looked at David. As soon as my eyes met his, my heart stopped and I was awestruck. He was even more striking up close.

"Megan," he greeted, smiling broadly and taking my hand as he led me to his side. "You look lovely this evening."

Finally able to breathe, I thanked him quietly while blushing brightly. Tucking my head, I watched as he took a corsage out and put it around my wrist. The glittering, white flower complemented my gown beautifully. I raised my eyes to his, mesmerized as he smiled at me. He kissed my cheek and then looked at my dad.

My attention on him now that David's was, Dad quickly turned away and wiped his eyes. Facing us again, he had a camera in his hands. "They're going to take pictures at prom."

"I know, but I want some here at home. Now stand at the foot of the stairs…good. Vanessa, dear, please move," he instructed as he readied the shot. "Okay…smile…"

David was a good sport as Dad took several pictures of us. But time was passing quickly and we needed to go. Realizing it as well, David politely reminded him that we had to pick up my friends. He gave a small bow to him and Vanessa as he opened the door. But Dad didn't seem ready to let me go.

"Dad, we still have to pick everyone else up. We're going to be late," I reiterated, hoping he'd listen to me.

He hesitated, continuing to stare at me as David stood patiently at the door. "All right…have a good time," he conceded finally, giving me a tight hug. "I wish your mom could have been here to see this," he whispered in my ear.

"I know, Dad. I do, too," I replied, kissing him on the cheek.

He quickly turned to David, the softness gone. "Have her home no later than midnight," he instructed.

"I will, sir," David affirmed before leading me off the porch.

We rushed down the sidewalk to the limo as the chauffeur exited and opened the door for us. David stepped aside, allowing me to enter first. I climbed in the refreshingly cool cabin and looked up to see a cute strawberry blonde sitting toward the back smiling at me. She looked like a fairy: full pink lips, creamy complexion, and petite. I took a seat near her as he entered.

"Megan, this is Madeline," he introduced, sitting next to me.

"Nice to meet you," I replied, smiling at her. Her bright, round eyes were green like his, but a different shade, more like a gray-green.

"Likewise. I've heard so much about you," she commented, her voice light and sparkling.

As the limo pulled away, I turned my attention back to him. "You look amazing," I commented, touching his lapel and grinning.

"What I said inside was an understatement," he replied. "You are breathtaking…but that necklace doesn't complement your attire," he commented as he pulled a large, velvet box from behind his back and handed it to me. "This will."

I took it from him and slowly opened it, staring at the gleaming necklace it held. It was identical to my earrings – larger diamonds at the top that gradually got smaller toward the end of each of the pendants. There were five columns in varied lengths: the outside with three diamonds each, the inside had four, and the middle one had five.

I reached in to take it out of the box, but my hands were too shaky. "Allow me," he offered as he unclasped the one from around my neck, his cool fingers caressing my skin and sending an electrical charge throughout my body. He smiled as he removed it and delicately lowered it into my hand. I promptly slipped it into my clutch so I wouldn't lose it.

Taking the new one from the box, I turned toward Madeline as he gently fastened the necklace around my neck. It was cold, but instantly warmed against my burning skin. I turned back and looked at him, curious of his response.

"Better?" I asked.

"Yes," he replied with a grin as his fingers caressed it and my chest. I tucked my head as my heart beat faster.

"It looks beautiful on you!" Madeline commented animatedly.

"Thank you," I responded, blushing. I smiled at David and then leaned in and kissed him. I wanted to prolong it but couldn't with her watching. "You really shouldn't have," I whispered.

"Think of it as stars plucked from the sky and made into a constellation just for you," he whispered in my ear before kissing my cheek. I smiled and tucked my head again as I placed my hand on the necklace. My very own constellation.

We pulled up to Claire's house and the chauffeur honked the horn, taking my attention off the gift. She and Justin exited the house, her mom following and taking pictures all the way down the sidewalk. The chauffer opened the door and Claire entered first, making her way to the middle of the limo as Justin sat next to her. She looked at Madeline and then at me and my date.

"Claire, this is David," I introduced as she waved at him, a dumbfounded look plastered on her face.

"I'm pleased to finally meet you, Claire. And this must be Justin."

She giggled and looked at her boyfriend, but he was too busy staring at Madeline to notice anyone else. Her nervous laughter stopped and she glared, nudging him in the ribs to bring his attention back to the rest of us.

"Uh, er, yeah. I'm Justin," he replied, lacking eloquence.

"And this is Madeline...Ben's date tonight," I commented.

Claire looked at me and grinned. "I think you're history, Megan."

I turned to David and smiled. "That's the plan," I responded.

He smiled back and my heart fluttered. I was caught up in his gaze until he shifted his eyes away from mine to look at Madeline briefly. Then he lowered them and smiled again.

"You look amazing, Megan," Claire commented, breaking the silence. "I don't remember you buying a necklace to go with your earrings..."

"Thank you, so do you. And I didn't," I answered, my cheeks growing pink. "David gave it to me."

She was stunned. "Really? That's so...sweet," she muttered as she stared at it, making me uncomfortable.

Then her eyes slowly wandered to him. His attention was on me, but he must have sensed her because he turned her way. Their eyes met and he smiled. It was as if her breath was stolen from her lungs.

"So, Claire, how did Justin react when he first saw you?" I inquired, taking her attention off my boyfriend.

"Huh? Oh...he was floored," she answered, laughing slightly and patting his thigh.

Coming out of a similar stupor, he looked at Claire and responded absently, "What?"

"Nothing, Justin," she replied, frustrated. "You look very handsome, David," she commented, blushing as she gazed at him while Justin stared at her.

"Thank you, *Claire.* Justin is quite lucky to have you on his arm tonight," he responded with a smile.

She didn't move or speak, her eyes glued to him. I noticed him steal a glance at Madeline, and they smiled at each other. Is there some inside joke I'm not getting? I was just about to ask when we pulled up to Ben's house. It'd have to wait. I sighed and stood up, making my way to the door.

"Where are you going?" Claire asked, coming out of her trance.

"I'm going to get Ben. I want Madeline to be a surprise." David grinned at me as I exited, and I had to regain my balance once I was outside.

I rushed to the door and rang the bell. Ms. Galloway answered it, delighted to see me. "Megan...don't you look stunning! Come in, Ben's in the living room."

I entered and followed her to the back. As I came around the corner, I spied him sitting on the floor, playing video games in his tux. His mom cleared her throat and announced my arrival.

"Megan!" he exclaimed, dropping the controller and hopping up.

"Ready to go?"

But he didn't answer me and instead just stared in awe. "Benjamin! It's rude to gawk at Megan like that," Ms. Galloway lectured as she fixed his bowtie.

"Er...uh, sorry. You just look so...so...wow," he responded, still staring.

"Thank you," I replied courteously. "We're running a little late, so we need to get going," I whispered to him.

"Oh, okay," he nodded, grabbing his jacket. "See you around midnight, Mom," he remarked, giving her a kiss on the cheek.

We headed out the door and down the drive, but then he stalled at the foot of it, staring at the rocky pavement. "I...I don't know if I can do this."

I took his hand and pulled him, forcing him to move. "You can. I'm here to support you. And don't worry, you're really going to like her," I grinned.

I climbed inside first and took my place next to David as Ben stepped in. I signaled for him to sit by me as he made his way to the back. His eyes only on me, he never saw David, Madeline, or anyone else.

As soon as he was settled, I introduced them. "Ben, this is David." He finally took his eyes off me, slowly moving them to the person sitting next to me.

David shook his hand and smiled politely. "It's a pleasure to meet you, Ben."

His eyes narrowed, examining him. "The pleasure is all mine."

"And this," I announced, motioning next to him, "is your date for the evening."

He didn't want to take his attention off David but finally did. As he faced her, he froze, bewildered. She extended her hand to him and smiled warmly.

"Hi, I'm Madeline."

He finally moved, daze-like, and took it, just holding it in his. "You're gorgeous," he stated, rapt in her eyes.

"Thank you," she giggled. "You're sweet and such a cutie!"

He grinned foolishly at her, never responding. I shook my head and turned to David, smiling at him and he smiled back. My heart fluttered and I could hardly tear myself away from his gaze, but Claire called for me.

As we headed to our last stop, we talked about what we expected at prom. David and Madeline were content staying out of the conversation, sitting back and observing us. Through the whole discussion, they never said anything to each other, but I caught them exchanging glances every once in a while.

We finally pulled up to Erin's house, and the chauffer honked the horn to signal our arrival. We didn't know what to expect with her but assumed anything. I glanced out the window and watched, waiting to see what she kept so secretive. The front door opened and she stepped out, followed by a tall, lanky guy. He took her hand and they walked together down the sidewalk, grinning.

I turned to Claire and looked at her sardonically. "I guess she managed to find a date at the last minute."

"Or she's had one all along and wanted to torture us."

"Knowing Erin, you're probably right," Ben interjected.

The door opened and all our attention turned to it, waiting for Erin and her date to enter. She climbed in, struggling with her tight red dress, and sat near Justin with her date sitting between them. "This is Tristan. He goes to school in the city," she announced as we all stared at her. "We met at a track meet a couple years ago and reconnected at a basketball game recently."

We introduced ourselves as the limo drove toward the country club. Tristan had the same reaction to Madeline as the other guys, drooling over her, and Erin was the same with David. Neither seemed affected by it. It must be an everyday occurrence for them.

It wasn't too far to the site of our prom, but that didn't stop Erin from jabbering on and on about how excited she was and her impressions of everyone. Occasionally, someone picked on her or made a joke, but it was her mouth that dominated the conversation. She was either really nervous or really excited, but I think it was more so a combination of both.

The chauffeur pulled up to the entrance of the country club, stopping right next to a bright, red carpet, and we all let out a sigh of relief. He opened the door, and we hurriedly climbed out one by one, David and I being the last to exit. Taking my arm in his, we started up the stairs leading to the main doors and followed the others inside.

They were taking pictures off to the side in the foyer and the group decided to knock ours out rather than come back later. I laughed as I watched Erin and Tristan do some crazy pose. The rest of us took it a little more seriously, standing stiff in the traditional couple pose. We waited until we were all done and then entered the main hall together. All eyes were on Ben and me, or rather David and Madeline.

It was a little uncomfortable, but then David pulled me closer and gave me a gentle kiss on the cheek, assuaging my uneasiness. My mind off the crowd's stares, I took in the setup and decorations. It was elegant, but I couldn't say what the theme was since I hadn't paid attention these last few weeks. I would guess something along the line of 'A Night to Remember' or 'Under a Starry Sky'.

Making our way into the main area, we found a table large enough for all of us and sat. I wasn't in the mood to dance to the rapid beats currently playing, so David and I stayed while everyone else went up. It was entertaining enough to watch them dance, especially Ben and Madeline. He looked incredibly awkward as he tried to move with her; she was graceful and fluid while he was stiff and clumsy.

"It's nice to have some time alone with you," David whispered in my ear, distracting me.

I turned and smiled. "I agree. I'm not used to being surrounded by so many people when I'm with you."

"Would you like to go somewhere more private?" he asked.

It was tempting. "No, we should stay. Besides, a slow song should be coming up and I want to see how well you dance."

A smile crept across his lips as he replied, "You will be pleasantly surprised."

Two girls walked up to the table at that moment and stared at him. "Hey Megan…who's your friend?" one asked.

I looked at him and then back at them, smiling politely. "Alison, Sara…this is my boyfriend, David."

Trying to hide their envy, both girls forced a smile and turned to him. "We saw you from across the room and just had to come over to meet you," Sara cooed.

"It is a pleasure. Are you friends of Megan?" he inquired, tilting his head.

"Well, Alison has Trig with her, and I'm in her Latin class."

He smiled, and Sara looked as if her knees almost gave out from under her. Alison, on the other hand, started hyperventilating. I gave him a curious look, but his attention wasn't on them or me but on the dance floor. What was he looking at?

Before I could find the answer, the music slowed and he stood and took my hand. "Please excuse us, ladies. I owe Megan a dance."

Leaving them gawking, he led me out onto the floor and held my hand in his, placing his other on my lower back and pulling me closer. Slowly, we moved together to the rise and fall of the chords. Being there in his arms felt so right. And even though there were other people around us, it felt like we were all alone.

At the climax of the song, he gracefully spun me around and then dipped me. Slowly raising me up, my eyes closed as he kissed me softly. It sounded as if the whole room let out a heavy sigh.

As I opened them, I realized we *were* the only ones on the dance floor. It had cleared and everyone was watching us. I blushed and buried my face in his neck. He chuckled as he kissed my temple, amused by my reaction.

Another slow song started, and he held me closer, taking smaller steps. I peeked over his shoulder and noticed other couples joining us, so I lifted my head and watched them. Ben and Madeline made their way over, and I saw her smile at David.

"Ben, would you like to have this dance with Megan?" he asked as they swayed next to us. I looked at David and wondered what he was up to. "I don't believe one dance will hurt," he whispered, noticing my shock.

Ben nodded curtly, trying to hide his enthusiasm, and took my hand as David waltzed off with Madeline. They looked like professional ballroom dancers as they moved across the floor, never saying a word to each other. I turned my attention back to Ben as we moved side to side, like middle-schoolers at our first dance.

"So what do you think of her?" I asked excitedly as he watched his feet.

"Madeline? Oh, she's great. She's fun and smart..."

"Do you think you should ask her out on a date?"

"I don't know. Do you think she likes me enough to go on a real one?"

They waltzed by us at that moment and she smiled at him. "Yeah, I think so," I responded.

His face was full of adoration, like she was some kind of goddess who came down from the heavens to be with him. "Okay...I will when we have a moment alone."

The song finished and David was by my side again. As we went back to the table, Ben and Madeline headed outside with Claire and Justin following. Erin and Tristan stayed, but were talking in a corner with part of the basketball team, so we were alone.

I watched the group dance for a moment and then scanned the room. There were a lot of people, some familiar, some not. My eyes caught one face in particular – a younger boy with long, curly black hair – the one I suggested Erin ask out. Guess he already had a date. He looked right at me, smiling wide with bright teeth. Weird. I didn't acknowledge him, turning my attention back to the dance floor.

"Would you like to go for a stroll?" David asked, noticing my boredom.

"I would love to. It's getting warm in here anyway."

We left the hall and headed out to the courtyard. Claire and Justin were talking by the fountain, and I waved to them before turning the corner and heading onto the golf course. There was very little light, but David had no problem seeing, just like the night we went to Belle Isle. Our arms hooked, we walked through the grass with my head resting on his shoulder.

I stared ahead, noticing something off to the side. Squinting, I tried to determine what the object was ahead of us. As we passed, I realized it was a couple making out.

"I haven't seen Ben and Madeline. Should I be worried about them?" I asked, looking back at the two people.

He glanced around the golf course and then at me, smiling. "No, there's no need to worry."

We continued our stroll until the building was a good distance away. Pausing, we listened to the music as it carried through the air. Another slow song played, its tune faint but clear.

David turned to me and took my hand, putting his other on my back and beginning to dance. But this time, it was more like how he did with Madeline. He moved faster, twirling and dipping me. I tried to keep up, but it was difficult. Then all of a sudden, he swept me into his arms.

I closed my eyes as he bowed his head and leaned closer. Our lips touched and we kissed, soft at first and then more intense. I tightened my hold around his neck, putting one hand on the back of his head. Slipping my fingers into his soft hair, I clenched it. He moved from my lips to my cheek, down my chin, and to my neck. My heart raced and I wanted more. I tilted my head back and felt his warm breath on my throat as he tightened his grip.

He lingered there, his breathing fast and erratic. I kept my eyes closed, waiting for him to continue kissing, but he never did. Instead, he loosened his hold and gently set me down, turning away. I stared at him as he looked up at the sky and held his head, wondering what happened.

"David…are you okay?" I asked, reaching for him.

He turned back around and faced me, looking deep into my eyes. "Please forgive me, Megan. I have a difficult time…controlling myself."

I moved closer, smiling softly. "It's okay…I trust you." I put my arms around his waist and pulled my body to his. I closed my eyes as I leaned in and kissed his lips. He started to kiss back, but then pushed me away.

"No, it's not all right. I don't want to hurt you."

"The only way you'll hurt me is if you leave me," I replied, wanting him to know the truth about how much he meant to me.

He smiled, but it looked pained. Taking me in his arms, he held me close, his cheek pressed to mine, and whispered, "You mean everything to me…" And with those words, my heart stopped.

But he didn't have a chance to continue or let me respond. "Megan, David…we wondered where you disappeared to," Claire commented as she and Justin walked up.

My heart resumed its usual beating as we both turned and looked at them, remaining in our embrace. "We wanted some fresh air and a quiet place," I answered.

"Uh huh," she responded, smirking. "Have you seen Ben and Madeline?"

"No…should we look for them?" I asked, my concern returning.

"That won't be necessary. They're waiting for us in the clubhouse," David responded, glancing toward it.

"How do you know that?" Justin asked.

"She sent a text message not too long ago." I gave him a puzzled look, not recalling him looking at his phone, and he smiled at me.

"Well, I guess we better join them," I suggested. I was curious how they were doing. We started walking across the green, David and I purposely lagging behind Claire and Justin so we could continue our conversation. "You were saying before we were interrupted…" I wheedled in a whisper.

"I will never leave you," he replied quietly into my ear and then kissed beside it.

"Good, because I didn't plan on letting you," I retorted.

He laughed softly, kissing me again. I saw Claire glance over her shoulder at us and then look at Justin. She intertwined her fingers with his and moved closer to him, but he removed them and instead put his arm around her shoulder. As he pulled her close, he kissed her on the cheek and then she rested her head on his shoulder.

We climbed the stone steps to the clubhouse and entered through the veranda doors. Erin, Tristan, Ben, and Madeline were all sitting at the table. They watched as we came over and ignoring their suspicious grins, we took a seat and checked out the activity on the dance floor.

"Where have you four been?" Erin asked, nudging Tristan. He laughed heartily.

"Just walking, that's all," Claire replied for all of us.

Ben looked different, more relaxed and happier. I wonder if Madeline said yes to another date. I looked at David and noticed him exchanging glances with her. She laughed her angelic laugh and turned to Ben, giving him a small peck on the cheek. I reached over and touched David's hand to get his attention.

"What's she laughing about?" I whispered.

He hesitated, looking over at her. "Ben mentioned something humorous to her." Huh, I never noticed him say anything.

"So David, what are your plans for summer? College will be getting out soon," Claire asked, leaning on her elbows.

He smiled at her. "I plan to stay around here and take classes to accelerate my degree. I hope to be in medical school the following fall."

Ben's defenses kicked in as he snapped out of his daze and glared at him. "How can you have such a heavy schedule, work a job, and have time for Megan? Do you sleep?"

"Only on occasion," he answered with a smirk. Madeline giggled, resting her head on Ben's shoulder.

"Do you go to VCU as well, Madeline?" Erin asked.

"Yes, but I'm in the art program. I have a lot of pieces at the house; David lets me display them. You'll have to come by sometime and see them," she remarked, smiling at him.

"I would love to," Justin quickly replied, gazing adoringly at her.

"Yeah, that'd be nice," Claire agreed, jamming her elbow into his side, and he turned his attention back to her. "Megan told us you have a house on a lake, David," she continued, batting her eyes at him.

He stared at Claire, grinning. "Yes, I do. We'll have to make plans to have everyone over this summer," he responded, leaning closer.

Suddenly, Justin cried out. "Ow! Let go of my leg!"

Claire shook her head and turned to him. "What? Oh, Justin…oh, I'm so sorry! Did I hurt you?"

"Uh, yeah! You dug your nails into my thigh!" he exclaimed.

David innocently played with a tendril of my hair while everyone watched them. Her cheeks were bright red as she grabbed her boyfriend's arm and dragged him away from the table. Madeline laughed as she played with Ben's collar. As I turned to say something to David, three guys walked up to our table and stood near Ben, making me lose my train of thought.

"Hey…who's your lady friend?" Jason asked.

"Oh, hey guys. This is Madeline," he answered, putting his arm around her.

"I've never seen you around school…are you from the city?" Jason inquired, moving closer.

"In a way, yes. I'm in college, though," she replied with a twinkle in her voice, getting their undivided attention.

"So where did you two meet?" Pete questioned, leaning on the table.

Ben hesitated, thinking about it, but Madeline spoke right up. "At a club. I saw him across the room and just had to meet him," she purred, caressing his jaw and kissing his neck. She paused a moment and then without reason, tucked her head. A moment later, she tossed her hair back and smiled at the guys, making them fidget and fumble.

"Would you like to dance?" Garrett asked abruptly.

"Oh, no. My date tonight is Ben," she replied politely, placing her hand on his chest as she gazed into his eyes. "Ben, dear, would you like to get a drink with me?" He nodded absentmindedly as they stood and left the table, the three guys trailing behind them.

What's wrong with everyone tonight?

Claire and Justin came back and asked where Ben and Madeline went, and we pointed to the drink table. I leaned over and told her about the scene we just witnessed. "She lied for him? Oh, that's going to get around school and he'll be the new stud on campus," she commented quietly to me.

David leaned close and whispered in my ear, "That's why she did it."

I turned toward him. "How devious."

He grinned and kissed me. They returned to the table, an empty cup in his hand and a full one in hers. She set it on the table and pushed it in front of him.

"Megan said you have other roommates, David. Do all of them go to VCU?" Erin asked, eager for his attention.

"Odette and Brian do, but Cary is working on a degree online. He is a bit of an agoraphobe." Tristan and Justin stared at him and he sighed. "He doesn't like to go outside," he clarified.

"Is Brian or Cary available?" Erin asked, blurting it out.

"Aren't you and Tristan dating?" I questioned, mortified she'd ask him that in front of her date.

They laughed. "No, we're just friends from way back."

"Brian is in a relationship, but I could see if Cary is willing to leave the house for a date with you," he replied as he winked at me. My heart thumped uncontrollably.

Seeming bored with the conversation, Madeline grabbed Ben by the wrist and dragged him out onto the dance floor. Then Claire and Justin followed. As I watched them, I noticed several girls huddled nearby staring and pointing at David. One girl volunteered to leave the group, stumbling toward us. I didn't recognize her; she must be a senior.

"Um, excuse me," she remarked to him.

He smiled, and she quickly grabbed the table to support herself. "Yes?" he inquired, tilting his head her way.

"I was wondering if…if you wanted to…to dance," she requested, shaking all over.

I leaned over his shoulder and replied for him. "No, he doesn't. He's my date."

Her jaw dropped and she stormed away. "Possessive, aren't we," he commented, watching them decide who should ask next.

"What's going on tonight? It's like there is an excessive amount of pheromones in the air."

He laughed and my frustration subsided. Another slow song came on and he stood, taking my hand. "One last dance?" he asked.

I really wasn't in the mood but gazing into his eyes, I couldn't resist. "Okay…"

As soon as we were on the floor, he held me close, moving slowly. "Prom is almost over. Was it everything you wanted it to be?" he asked quietly.

"Yes, but only because you're here," I whispered back, kissing his cheek.

The song neared the end and he dipped me, kissing my neck as I hung in his arms. Slowly raising me up, a flash of my dream in the cemetery came back to me. I jerked as I opened my eyes, but there was no blood on his lips. He looked at me with his brow lifted, wondering what came over me.

"Sorry…déjà vu," I responded.

"Has this happened before?" he asked, leading me back to the table.

"Only in a dream, but this time it turned out better."

"Good," he replied, grabbing my clutch and handing it to me. "I think it's time we leave. It's getting late," he announced to everyone.

With no complaints, we all headed out to the limo and climbed in one by one. As I entered, David paused at the door. I scooted back to my seat and noticed he didn't follow. Glancing out the windows, I searched for him and through the tinted glass, I saw his figure walk to the back of the limo as someone pulled up behind us.

No one else paid attention; they were all too busy reminiscing already about their night. I leaned closer to the glass, straining to hear what was going on. Nothing. I nudged the window button and it dropped slightly but gave enough of a gap for me to eavesdrop.

"What are you doing here?" David asked the unseen entities quietly.

"I thought Cary and I would check out the younger crowd…maybe see if anyone was interested in having some after prom fun at the house," Brian's voice replied, not as quiet. My heart stopped.

"You shouldn't have him out here. It's too dangerous."

"He's behaving. So…did you and Megan have a good time?" he inquired.

"What I do is none of your business."

"We shouldn't be left in the dark. After all, we are your *roommates*."

"Go home, Brian."

There was silence. "Okay…but we must talk later," he chided before revving his engine.

They drove off, the sound of the motorcycles fading into the night. As I tried to figure out why Brian was here and what the deal was with Cary, I closed the window and faced the group. No one noticed that little scene, not even Madeline. She was too busy feigning interest in what Ben was saying. David entered and made his way to the seat next to me, putting his arm around me and kissing my cheek.

"Where did you go?" I asked, wondering what his explanation would be.

"I thought I heard something behind the limo, so I went to check it out," he replied vaguely. I didn't know if I should press any further, but I decided not to ruin what was left of my evening.

As soon as we were settled, the chauffeur left the country club and headed to Erin's house first. David held me in his arms as I leaned back against his chest, my body alive with sensation being that close. I did everything I could to distract myself, looking around the limo at everyone.

Erin and Tristan were chatting lively about some game our school played against his and who had the better team. Madeline was leaning on Ben, playing with the hair at his neck, and Claire had her head on Justin's shoulder, her eyes droopy. David and I silently took bets seeing how long before she fell asleep.

We pulled up to Erin's house and said our goodbyes to her and Tristan. "It was nice to meet you, David," she commented, sticking her head back through the door opening.

"Likewise," he replied, smiling at her. She had the goofiest grin on her face. Tristan tapped her on the shoulder to get her attention and she came out of her daze, hitting her head on the doorframe. As she grumbled, he stuck his head in and said the same to Madeline.

"Nice to meet you, too," she replied with a smile. He gave her an equally goofy smile before Erin dragged him away.

I shook my head and then glanced at David as the limo began moving again. He looked at me, tilted his head, and kissed me. I heard Ben sigh and turned toward him, breaking away from the kiss. He quickly glanced out the window, acting as if he hadn't been watching us.

My eyes on him, I knit my brow. David gently touched my chin and turned my face back to him. He kissed my lips softly and then whispered, "Is something wrong?"

I paused, savoring it for the moment and then answered. "No...it's Ben."

He glanced over at him and smiled. "He'll be fine," he responded and kissed me again.

Next, the limo stopped at Ben's house, and I forced myself to leave David's arms. I nudged Ben to get up, but before he did, Madeline stopped him. As she gave him a hug, she whispered something in his ear and then kissed his lips. She pulled away as he gazed at her like a love-struck fool.

I grabbed his arm as I passed, dragging him out of the limo. As soon as we were outside, he came to. We started up the sidewalk and I was dying to know. "Sooo...did you have a good time?" I asked as we walked.

"Yeah, Madeline's great."

"Did you ask her out on another date?"

"Yeah..." he replied, then stopped. "I like her, but there's something strange about her."

"What did she say about the date?" I inquired, ignoring the last part as we continued walking.

"Maybe...I gave her my number, and she said she'd call."

As we reached his door, he pulled out his keys. "It's progress," I told him as he unlocked it.

"I know. Well, good night Megan. Thanks for the dance."

"You're welcome. See you Monday," I replied, hoping he'd go already. Instead, he leaned in to kiss me, but I backed away. He hung his head and went inside.

I didn't waste any time returning to my place in David's arms. He leaned close and whispered, "What was he trying?"

He had been watching me. "It's okay. I dodged him."

"He is making a bad habit out of this," he cautioned.

"It won't happen again. I'll make sure of it."

I couldn't believe prom was over. I replayed the night in my head as I looked at the remaining people in the cabin. Claire was asleep on Justin, but he was awake, gazing at Madeline who happened to be staring out the window. She looked bored and out of place.

"Has any of your work made it into a gallery yet, Madeline?" I asked, trying to make conversation.

She turned quickly and smiled at me, happy to be talked to by someone other than lovesick boys. "Not many. My pieces are...different."

"I'm really interested in seeing them."

"David will have to bring you by the house some time," she hinted as she smiled at him. He narrowed his eyes at first and then smiled back. "I'd love to show them off to people other than drunk college kids."

"So I take it you're not part of the parties he told me about."

"No, that's all Brian and Odette. I usually hide out in my studio."

I glanced at David and smiled. "Did you know David is artistic?"

She looked at him, astonished. "No, I was not aware. You never told me that!" she exclaimed, shooting a look at him.

"It's just a hobby," he answered modestly.

"I'd like to see some of your work," she requested.

"I'll sketch a fruit bowl when we get home," he grinned, kissing my cheek.

We pulled in front of Claire's house, and Justin shook her. She sat up quickly and looked around, not sure where she was. "We're home," he whispered, helping her up.

They waddled to the door and he stepped outside as Claire sat in the frame, still trying to wake up. "It was great finally meeting you," she commented to David as she tried to focus.

"The pleasure was all mine," he replied with a grin and she slipped.

Justin caught her just in time. Holding her in his arms, he peeked in and said his goodbyes. "I better get her inside and to bed. She's acting really loopy, almost like someone spiked her drink," he commented before shutting the door. I glanced at David as he grinned at Madeline.

We only had a couple of streets before my house. Madeline looked at David and me and smiled, then turned her attention back outside. With the quietness of the ride and lying against him, I started to feel tired. I forced my eyes to stay open. Not too much farther.

The limo parked in front of my house and he stepped out ahead of me, holding the door. I turned back before stepping out and smiled at Madeline. "It was great meeting you. I hope we can hang out again sometime."

She grinned, her eyes sparkling. "I'd love that. Have a good night!"

David and I walked arm in arm, quietly talking about the evening as we strolled up the sidewalk to the porch. It was a beautiful night, and I wasn't quite ready for him to leave. I pulled out my keys and unlocked the front door, getting ready to step inside when he stopped me.

"Don't you want to come in for a little while?" I asked.

"No, we have to go," he answered. He pulled me into his arms and whispered in my ear, "I will come by after you go to bed, though." Then he kissed me and left.

Standing in the doorway, I watched as he dashed to the limo and climbed inside. They drove away, and I slipped into the house as soon as they were out of sight. Dad was in the living room, waiting for me. He glanced at the clock and then at me.

"Just in time," he remarked as the twelfth chime reverberated through the house.

# Chapter 19
## Impressions

I took a seat in the living room across from my dad, anxious to hear his opinion of David. "So what did you think of him?" I asked as I fidgeted with my necklace.

"That's new…where did it come from?" he inquired, ignoring my question. "Is it one of your mother's? I don't remember it."

"No…David gave it to me tonight. Isn't that sweet?"

"Yeah…interesting gift…" he mumbled, inspecting it closer.

"Well, what did you think of him?" I tried again, folding my hands in my lap to keep from distracting him.

"Oh…he's a polite, well-spoken, handsome, young man, but…there's something I don't trust about him," he replied. I could have figured he'd say that.

"Really? He's been nothing but good to me," I defended.

"I'm sure he has, but until you know him a little better, please be careful," he requested and I nodded. "Did you have a good time?"

"Oh, it was wonderful! The country club was a great location and they did an awesome job decorating it. How was your evening?"

"Good. Vanessa and I watched a movie." He paused. "You know, she couldn't stop talking about your David."

"Really? What did she say?" I asked, leaning on my knees.

"She talked about how he made her feel and the way he looked and acted. She also told me she felt the same way when she ran into his friend, Brian, while you two were dress shopping. She described it as if her brain went foggy. Does this happen to you around David?"

"Umm…sometimes," I answered, not sure what he was trying to get out of me.

"And what about Brian? Do you have a lot of interaction with him?"

"I try to avoid him as much as possible. I don't feel that way around him. He makes me uncomfortable."

"Were you alone with David at all tonight?"

"Yeah…a couple of times. Why?"

"Did you get that 'foggy' feeling when you were and did he try anything during that time?"

"Dad! David's a gentleman. I can't believe you think he's some college sleazeball trying to take advantage of a high school girl!" I exclaimed as I stood to leave.

"Megan, don't go. Please understand I can only speculate," he responded, reaching for me.

"I need to go to bed. I've had a long day and I'm tired," I replied, jerking away from him before leaving the room.

How could he think such ill things of David? What happened on the golf course tonight was proof enough he wouldn't take advantage of me, but I wasn't going to tell Dad about that. He'd flip.

I entered my room, still angry, and was unzipping my dress when I heard a throat clear behind me. I turned to find David standing in the doorway of the balcony, in more casual clothes. "Oh my God!" I whispered loudly as I held the front of my dress up.

"Did I catch you at a bad time?" he asked with a mischievous grin.

"I…I didn't expect you so soon," I replied, fumbling my way into the closet and turning on the light. "How did you get the door open?" I asked as I peeked out.

"I didn't; it was already open when I walked up. I thought you did it," he smiled as he entered the room.

"No, I hadn't made it up here yet," I replied. Did I open it earlier and forget to close it?

"What took you so long?" he asked.

"My dad and I were talking…" I hesitated, ducking back into the closet.

"About what?"

"Oh…you," I answered as I slipped my dress off and hung it up in the back. I sifted through my clothes, trying to find something decent to wear that would also be okay to sleep in. I pulled a cotton tank dress from its hanger and threw it on.

"What about me?" he inquired as I slowly opened the door and came out. He sat on the edge of the bed, watching my every move.

I looked away and strode quickly to the other side of the room, taking off my jewelry and putting it away. I removed the band from my bun, letting my curls cascade to my shoulders and down my back. Glancing over my shoulder at him, I smiled bashfully as he stared.

"I need to wash my face," I commented timidly as I headed to the bathroom, avoiding answering him.

I pulled my hair back and rinsed the makeup off, feeling instantly refreshed and clean. I dabbed it dry and let my hair down again as I went back into the room, sitting by him on the bed. He gazed into my eyes as he reached up and gently held my cheek.

"That was a first for me," he whispered.

"What?" I asked as he moved closer.

"You took my breath away," he whispered against my lips before kissing me. I placed my hand on his shoulder and quickened his slow, soft kiss, but he pulled back slightly. Lightly touching my cheek, he kissed me one last time and then sat back. "What was it I asked you a moment ago?" he inquired casually.

"Umm...you were wondering what my father and I were discussing concerning you."

"Yes...and it was?"

"He doesn't trust you. He wants me to be careful, get to know you better."

"That's understandable."

"You think so?"

"Of course. I'm older than you, living on my own with other college students, and I am very...charming. See it as your father would."

David dating your teenage daughter would send up red flags. Not including the fact we've been sneaking out on dates or that he's been coming to my room without my dad's knowledge, but he's right – he is *very* charming. For some people, that's a dangerous thing.

"Okay. Next time, I won't be so hard on him."

"Good. Now lie back and tell me what you thought of prom," he requested as he stood.

I scooted back to the headboard and reclined against it. "From start to finish, it was better than I imagined. Truly a night I'll remember and cherish for as long as I live," I replied, watching as he strolled around the room. He resituated my candles, then turned out the light and lit them one by one.

"Keep talking," he invited as he went to the stereo and pulled up my classical music list.

I closed my eyes and listened to the soft serenade. "I enjoyed dancing with you. You're good."

"Years of practice," he replied, sitting next to me. I watched as the flames and shadows danced in unison around the room.

"What do you think your friends thought of me?"

I brought my eyes back to him. He looked stunning in the candlelight. "I think they liked you...well, maybe not Ben, but that's okay."

"Ben...ah, he's still in love with you. I can see it in his eyes. There is a longing."

"Well, he can continue to long. I'm with you," I replied, touching his hand.

He smiled as he moved closer, lounging on several pillows against the headboard. Lying under his arm, I rested my head on his chest. I slipped my hand under his shirt and ran my fingers along his breastbone to his stomach while the other arm lay useless beside me. Breathing deep, I took in the floral scent from the candles and his aroma. I closed my eyes, enjoying every breath.

Lying in silence for a long time, we watched the candles and listened to the music until I interrupted it. "Why can't I hear your heartbeat?" I inquired casually, as if it wasn't a weird question.

"What do you mean?" he asked in reply.

I lifted my head and looked at him. "Well, at the lake when I asked, you said your shirt was too thick, but there have been other occasions where that hasn't been the case, and I still couldn't hear it," I answered.

He didn't respond immediately. "It's complicated. I'd rather not go into it right now."

"Is that because it has a complex, scientific explanation…or because you don't want to tell me?"

"The latter."

Narrowing my eyes as I stared into his, I rested my upper body on his and whispered, "What are you hiding from me?"

He seemed pained by my question as he looked away. "I'm not ready to tell you yet," he replied quietly.

I don't know if I should react to that or let it go. I stared at him for several seconds and then rested my head on his chest and listened. Nothing but the hollow sound. I sighed deeply. There was a good reason why he was waiting; I just have to be patient.

He kissed the top of my head and rubbed my shoulder. I wasn't tired, but I knew I needed to sleep. I sighed again and closed my eyes, trying, but sleep wouldn't come.

"Tell me more about yourself," I requested softly.

He ran his fingers over my hair as he softly spoke, "I was born in Waltham, Massachusetts to William and Sophia Archer. My father was a quite a bit older than my mother and had great political aspirations. All my mother wanted was to have a child. After suffering several miscarriages and stillbirths, my parents were elated when I was born healthy."

"In my early years, I was very close to my mother, and even though we had people who could watch and care for me, she insisted on doing it herself. She was not used to the lifestyle my father was accustomed to and didn't want to put anyone out. But that lasted only so long."

"My father worked his way up the political ladder and when he became mayor of the town, my mother's duties changed. No longer was she able to play in the garden with me or sing while I played the piano. She now had societal duties to entertain visiting guests. I was forced to sit in the parlor with them and be a perfect gentleman."

"As my father's ambition grew, so did the strain on my family. After a successful stint as mayor, he ran for the General Court of Massachusetts and was elected. By then, my mother had become so involved in my father's world she was less and less a part of mine. I was in my early teens at the time and constantly in and out of trouble, which was difficult for my father and his career. But he was always able to get me out of it…"

David stared at the wall ahead of him, like he was remembering a distant memory. "I had an argument with my father over something I planned to do one evening. Feeling she had abandoned me for so long, my mother tried to defend me, but my father couldn't be reasoned with. She begged me not to leave, saying I should sleep on it and not go away mad. But my mind was made up and I left against their wishes. That was the last time I saw them."

He looked away, focusing on a candle, and then spoke again. "I went back years later to claim my inheritance, visiting their graves before leaving the town forever."

"You never said goodbye," I whispered, a tear making its way across the bridge of my nose to my other eye and onto his shirt.

"They received a letter from me after I left. I said my goodbyes then," he replied stoically as I wiped my eyes. "Megan, are you all right?" he asked, lifting my chin.

"I'm fine…just a little caught up in your story."

He leaned in and kissed each tear dampened cheek and then my unsuspecting lips. The simple, soft kiss grew more passionate as he turned toward me, his hand supporting my head as his lips parted. Taking in his candied breath, a strange desire came over me. I slipped my arm around him and pulled myself closer as my heart pounded. He abruptly stopped, moving his face to the side, but I continued to caress his cheek and neck with my anxious lips.

He released me and quickly got up, going to the balcony doors and starting to walk out. "David, wait…don't leave. I'm sorry if I did someth-"

"You didn't…I need some air," he interrupted, his eyes bold even in the dim light as he glanced over his shoulder before disappearing into darkness.

I sat up, pulling my knees to my chest and covering myself with the comforter. The shadows from the few burning candles that remained continued to dance to the music playing in the background. I watched the balcony doors for several minutes, the breeze lightly raising the curtains, as my heart anticipated his return. But all I saw was empty blackness.

Feeling drowsy, I curled up in the blanket and stared at the doors. I waited as long as I could for him to walk through before my lids became too heavy, and I closed my eyes briefly. When I opened them again, he was sitting next to me. He lightly touched my hair and kissed my cheek.

"I need to go," he whispered and I nodded slowly. "I will see you tomorrow night."

He gently kissed my lips and then went around the room extinguishing the remaining candles. Quietly slipping out the doors, I watched him leave as I fought to keep my eyes open. As soon as I heard the click of the lock, I was out.

"Sooo…what did you think of him?" I asked Claire as I hurriedly fixed some soup and a sandwich. I didn't get up and moving until two and I was starving. Dad was out with Vanessa all day, so I was home alone.

"Your description didn't do him justice…oh my God, Megan! Where did you say he was from? I wonder if they're all bred that way there!" she shouted so loud I had to remove the phone from my ear.

"What about him other than his looks?" I asked seriously as I poured the soup into a bowl and set it on my plate with the sandwich.

"Oh…great personality, very enthralling. I got in trouble several times last night for supposedly 'drooling' over him."

"Well, what about the way Justin was 'drooling' over Madeline?" I retorted as I sat at the nook table.

"Believe me, I got after him for that. So did David come by later?" she inquired, excitement in her voice.

I took a bite of the sandwich and chewed slowly, letting the anticipation build. "Yeeesss…"

"Well…what happened?" she asked anxiously. I slurped my soup, purposely delaying. "That's it! I'm coming over there!" she exclaimed and hung up.

I laughed as I put the phone down and continued eating. I had about ten minutes before she'd be banging down my door. But I didn't mind. I'd get to enjoy her company and talk about last night without anyone around to eavesdrop.

I finished my meal just as she impatiently rang the doorbell. "Coming!" I shouted as I jogged to the door. I peeked out the window, grinning ear to ear at her. Her hands were on her hips and her foot tapped with annoyance as she glared at me. I giggled as I slowly opened it.

"Okay…I'm here. What happened?" she asked, pushing her way inside.

"Nothing much. We talked," I answered, leading her to the family room where we sat on the couch facing one another.

"No…I want juicier details than that!"

"Honestly, nothing 'juicy' happened. What about you? What happened after we dropped you off?"

"After being out of the limo for several minutes, I wasn't feeling as dizzy or lightheaded. That happened to me a lot last night, by the way, especially around David."

I looked at her curiously. I knew he had that effect on me, but I thought it had to do with my feelings toward him. "Huh…that's strange…" I muttered.

"Yeah, well anyway…rather than go inside immediately, Justin and I went into the backyard and sat in the hammock."

"And…" I pushed.

She blushed. "We just…swung…and kissed…"

"Did you talk about anything?"

"Nooo…but we didn't get to be alone long. The Monster flicked on the floodlights and exposed us. Dad came out a moment later, lecturing me. We went inside and right on through to the front door. I said goodbye and then went to bed."

"That sucks. I got in an argument with my dad about David…if that makes you feel better."

"What…is he too good for you?" she asked sarcastically.

"No. Dad's suspicious of him, of his intentions. I understand where he's coming from, but he was being rude about it. He said Vanessa couldn't stop talking about him and that made him worry."

She stared past me, focusing on some imaginary object. "David has this thing about him…like he could've told me to do anything and I would've done it no matter what it was…" she commented, trance-like.

"Are you okay?" I asked, waving my hand in front of her face.

"Huh? Yeah, sorry. I spaced out there for a moment."

"So you experienced a strange feeling around him, too. It sounds a lot like what Dad said Vanessa told him."

I had pushed the thought out of my mind, but when she brought it back up, I started to notice a pattern. Vanessa, Claire, Erin, girls at prom, me – why do females act so strange around David? Maybe he knows hypnotism and uses it as a distraction. He must be exceptionally good to be able to do it without anything. I wonder if I go into a trance around him…

"Earth to Megan…not you, too! What's going on?"

"Oh, just pondering something." She rolled her eyes. "So, how do you think Ben's evening went?" I asked, wanting to move on from David.

"He and Madeline seemed to get along well. Even so much so that they wanted time alone. I wonder where they disappeared to when we went outside," she contemplated.

"You didn't see where they went?"

"No, I'm not Ben's keeper! He's a big boy. I'm sure they went to a nice, quiet spot and maybe kissed."

A strange feeling came over me – jealousy, maybe? I shrugged it off. I can't be jealous of Madeline; I've wanted this for so long. "I can't wait to talk to him about it. Maybe I should call," I commented just as my phone rang. I answered it, surprised to hear Ben's voice on the other end. "Are your ears burning? We were just talking about you," I remarked as I mouthed his name to Claire. Her jaw dropped.

"What are you two up to…gossiping?" he joked.

"No, just talking about last night. You should come over and hang out," I suggested as she waved her arms back and forth and shook her head.

"Really? Okay. My mom has to run some errands. I'll ask if she can drop me off. Hold on," he responded, putting the phone down.

I moved it away from my mouth and hissed, "Why not?"

"You're not helping," she hissed back.

"We can talk about Madeline and how great she is. That'll keep his mind on her," I persuaded.

Her scowl stretched into a grin. "Not a bad idea…"

"Yeah, I'm here. Oh, okay. We'll see you in twenty minutes then. Bye."

We continued talking about prom while waiting for Ben, mostly regarding the variety of gowns and which were best and which were worst. Apparently, I missed the orange monstrosity Shelley Coleman wore (thank God). We were just getting into a discussion about cutest couple, aside from ourselves, when the doorbell rang. I let Ben in and led him back.

"How was your evening?" Claire questioned, not wasting any time.

"Ben, would you like a drink?" I asked politely, narrowing my eyes at her.

"Iced tea, if you have it," he replied, sitting on the other end of the couch.

I came back into the room and handed him the glass. "What did you think of prom?"

He took a sip and looked at both of us. "I don't know…some of it's a little hazy. But what I do remember was good."

I looked at him and knit my brow. "What *do* you remember?"

"Hmm…bits and pieces of the limo ride, arriving, dancing with you…leaving, oh and you walking me to my door."

Claire and I looked at each other. "That's it?" she asked. "What about when you and Madeline danced or went for a walk…or the story she told the guys who asked where you met?"

"All foggy. Blurry images and slurred words, hard to decipher," he replied, looking off into the distance.

"Well, there goes that idea of finding out what happened on the walk," she whispered to me.

"What did you think of David?" I asked him abruptly, shaking him from his daze.

"He seems cool. Not what I expected."

"Better or worse?"

"Better, unfortunately. You know, I got this strange feeling around him, like I needed to be on guard or compete with him, but I didn't know why."

"That's not the feeling I got," she remarked under her breath.

All the guys last night seemed to be apprehensive around David, and yet the girls swooned over him. With Madeline, the girls were possessive and the men swooned. Maybe people were just intimidated by them because they're older and in college. I'd guess with the glances passed between David and Madeline, they noticed, too.

"That necklace you had on last night…was it one of your Mom's?" Ben inquired. "It was beautiful on you."

"Thank you, no. David gave it to me," I answered hesitantly.

"Really? That's quite a gift," he commented, looking at Claire. "Can I see it?"

I glanced at her and she shrugged her shoulders. "Sure," I replied as I led them to my room.

We entered, Claire immediately sitting on the bed while Ben looked around. I went over to my jewelry box and pulled the necklace out. It glistened in the sunshine as I handed it to him. He held it up to the light and then inspected it closer, flipping it over in his hands.

"What do you think it's made of?" he asked.

"I don't know…probably crystal. I can't imagine it being diamonds – that's a lot of money to wear around your neck," I replied, taking it back and putting it away.

"I don't think they're crystals…it looks like real diamonds to me."

Claire flopped back on my bed and laughed. "How would *you* know what a diamond looks like?"

"Mineralogy camp one summer," he replied casually.

"You're such a nerd," she commented under her breath.

I dropped down on the edge of the bed. "I knew he was wealthy, but I didn't think he would get me diamonds."

Claire rolled over but paused as she smelled something on my comforter. "What is that? It's intoxicating…"

I saw him furrow his brow at her while she continued to smell the cover and then my pillows. "Umm…it must be this new detergent I'm using," I fibbed, grabbing her by the wrist and dragging her off the bed. "Let's head back downstairs," I suggested, ushering them out the door.

We returned to the family room and sat together on the couch. Ben made himself at home and turned on the TV, flipping through our hundreds of channels with a disgusted look on his face. I refilled his tea and grabbed a drink for Claire and myself while they stared glassy-eyed at the screen.

"Do you really watch all of these channels?" he asked, still flipping.

I took a seat between them. "No, but Dad likes to have them for the news and sports.

Claire looked frustrated. "Would you pick something already!" she shouted.

I snatched the remote from him and put it on a music channel, turning the volume low enough to be background noise. "There."

"So…do you think Erin and her date…umm…Tristan will be more than friends?" she asked curiously.

"Probably not," he answered begrudgingly, glancing at me.

"Yeah, I don't think so either," I agreed. "She was scoping out available guys all night."

"That's a shame. They were such a cute couple. Speaking of which…what's the verdict on Justin and me? Are we a cute couple?"

"Absolutely a-dork-able," Ben responded and I laughed. She glared at me.

"You do make a cute couple," I replied, still giggling.

"I think you and Madeline made a cute couple. Did you get her number?" she asked him.

He looked at me and then at her. "No, I gave her mine."

"Has she called you yet?" she asked anxiously.

"No, but it's only the day after. No one calls that soon," he replied, pulling out his phone. "Oh man, I didn't realize it was that late. Mom'll be here soon."

He stretched as he stood and then ambled into the kitchen, putting his glass in the sink. We walked to the front door and I opened it, the sun shining directly on our faces. Sitting on the porch steps together, we waited for his ride.

"So what's next?" Ben asked.

"The wedding," I responded.

"Final exams," Claire sighed.

"Summer job," he huffed.

We stared across the yard, all deep in thought. I leaned my head on his shoulder and patted his back. "I'm sorry. We'll still try to hang out, 'kay?"

"Sure, but it might have to be late evening or early morning."

"We'll work around your schedule," I replied as Ms. Galloway pulled into the drive and he stood. "Thanks for coming over," I shouted as he dashed to the car, nodding as he sat.

I waved to them as they backed out while Claire swatted her legs and ran inside. I smacked my arm and followed her. The mosquitoes were coming out, signaling it was time to go in. With nothing more to talk about, we headed back to the family room and watched TV.

After about an hour, I heard the lock on the front door jiggling and then it opened. Dad announced he was home and brought dinner. Claire and I made our way to the kitchen to see what he had to share. It was all in take-out boxes, but not the Chinese kind, and it smelled better.

"Oh, I didn't know you had a guest. I'm not sure there's enough," he remarked as he opened the lids.

The succulent aroma of perfectly seasoned beef wafted toward us and we drooled. I stared down at an enormous piece of meat in the box. "Uh, I think there's plenty," I replied, glancing at Claire.

"It looks good. Where's it from?" she asked, leaning in for a better smell.

"The caterer for the wedding. This is what we chose to go with for dinner," he told her.

"This is nice. You're going to have some very satisfied guests," she commented.

He pulled two plates down and set them before us. "You're not eating?" I asked, confused.

"No, I ate plenty there. If I eat anymore, I won't fit into my tux and that'll make Vanessa very unhappy."

I watched as Claire filled her plate with the main course and then some of the sides. I did the same and joined her at the nook table. Dad sat with us, staring outside into the darkening backyard. No wonder we were hungry. She finished her food in no time flat and went back to see if there were more potatoes.

I left it at one plate. Leaning back against the chair, I looked at Dad and he looked back at me. Between us, there was an understanding that all was forgiven. Claire took her seat with another plateful and continued to eat, not paying attention to anything but her food. I put my dishes in the sink, rinsed them and the others that were left in there, and placed them in the washer; Claire can do her own.

"It was delicious, Dad. Good choice," I commented, sitting again.

"So what did you do all day?" he asked as Claire got up again. She glanced at the food like she wanted more but went on to the sink and took care of her dishes instead.

"Well, I didn't get up until after two. I had lunch and then Claire and Ben came over. Nothing crazy. How was your day?"

"Full of drama and excitement," he replied as she sat back down.

"With Vanessa, it always is," I remarked and he laughed.

He went to the island to see what was left of the food. "Looks like you pretty much cleaned it up, Claire."

"Sorry. I haven't been eating much lately because of prom. I wanted to be sure I fit into my dress," she answered, embarrassed.

"It's okay. I'm just kidding. I'd rather it be eaten than go to waste," he responded as he pushed it into the trash. The doorbell rang and Claire and I looked at each other. "Now who could that be?" he mumbled as he wiped his hands.

He went to the door and opened it, but I wasn't in direct view. I only heard mumbling. I turned to Claire and asked if it could be her parents, but she said there was no reason why it should be. We were discussing other possible visitors when she looked up and went silent. I turned and followed her gaze, seeing David standing in the archway with my father.

I immediately jumped up and joined his side, staring at him. "W-what are you doing here?" I asked as I stole a glance at my dad.

"I came by to ask your father if I could take you out tonight," he replied, grinning. My knees went weak, but I tried not to let it show. "Hello, Claire," he greeted, looking in her direction. She gawked and waved at him like a dummy.

"I'd offer for you to sit awhile and have dinner with us, but you just missed it." Dad commented, crossing his arms.

"That's all right. I have already eaten," David graciously conceded.

"So you're going to take Meg to a movie. Which one?" he asked and I glared at him.

"I plan to let her choose when we get there," David replied, not at all nervous or concerned with his inquiries. "What time would you like her to be home?"

"No later than eleven," he answered, looking between the two of us.

David glanced at me and smiled. "Shall we go?" he asked. I took a moment to respond, nodding absently. He turned to leave and my father chose to walk with him toward the door, quietly discussing something.

Claire was a little more aware as she came over to me, placing her hand on my shoulder. "Are you going like that?" she questioned.

I blinked and looked down at myself, realizing what I was wearing. "I have to change – I can't go out looking like this!" I whispered to her, panicking.

"That's what I was thinking," she agreed, grabbing my wrist and rushing to the stairs. "She wants to change…we won't be long," she explained briefly as we passed Dad and David standing in the foyer.

As soon as I was in my room, I hastily removed my clothes while she picked an outfit. "No, not that one…my dad will kill me if I walk out of the house in that…that's better," I directed as I grabbed the last one and threw it on. I fixed my hair, slipped on some shoes, and rushed down the stairs. "Okay…I'm ready," I announced, Claire standing behind me.

We stepped out onto the porch, and Claire and I continued off it, but Dad and David remained, stiffly standing side by side and blocking the glow from the incandescent lamps. The garage light came on and lit our way as I walked with her to her car, pausing at the door.

"Thanks for coming over. I'm glad we could hang out," I commented as she opened it.

"You have got to call me tomorrow. I want to know how your first 'real' date went," she requested, climbing inside.

I nodded and she smiled as she shut her door, waving to the men on the porch as she backed out of the driveway. When she reached the end, she flicked on her headlights and blinded me momentarily. My eyes came back into focus as she turned the corner, and I decided to wait a moment while I readied myself for what Dad really had to say about my date tonight. But before I could turn around to find out, a hand rested on my back and I jumped.

I glanced over my shoulder and saw David's grinning face. "Are we ready to go?" he asked, moving to my side. I stood mesmerized for a moment, gazing into his green eyes, and then nodded.

Dad was still on the porch watching as David led me toward an unfamiliar sleek, black sedan. "Where's your car?" I asked quietly.

"This is my *other* car," he replied as he opened the door for me. "The Bugatti is too pretentious for your father. The BMW is my casual car – not as fast, but still fun to drive."

I sat, David shutting the door as I waved to Dad still standing on the porch with his arms crossed. His eyes were intent on David as he walked around the car to the driver's side. He opened his door and paused before sitting, allowing me enough time to get a glimpse of the interior – subtle tan leather with some black accents and dark wood trim.

He started the engine and immediately rolled down the windows, letting the air flow around to clear the smell of leather and him from my momentarily befuddled brain. Putting it in reverse, he slowly backed out of the drive. Dad remained on the porch, watching even as we pulled away.

The car rumbled over the soft operatic music playing through the speakers as we exited the neighborhood. "So what did my dad say to you?"

"He was giving me advice," he grimaced.

"Advice or threats?"

"He is just being your father."

I was quiet as I stared out the open window, amazed he was so brazen. He just met David and was being so aggressive toward him. He was never that way with the few guys I went out with before him. Maybe it has to do with age or the fact he wasn't from around here.

As we drove down busy streets and past shopping centers, I realized we were in town. "You really are taking me to a movie," I commented as he turned into the theater parking lot. It was packed, though I should have guessed being a Saturday night.

"You sound disappointed," he responded as he parked under a light toward the end of the side lot.

I hesitated. "We always have such interesting and unusual dates, and then for you to take me to the movies…"

"I'm not going to lie to your father."

I sighed and stared at my hands. How noble of him. He came over to my side and opened the door, and I looked up at him as he took my hand

and helped me out. Gazing into my eyes, he asked, "Do you know what you want to see?"

My brain was all foggy, but I answered. "I...I'm not sure what's playing. I can't seem to remember."

"All right, let's go inside and decide," he responded, smiling as he took my arm in his and led me to the entrance.

I held tight to him, a goofy smile on my face as we neared the doors. Staring at the marquee, I read the movie titles while my head cleared. There weren't a lot of appropriate ones to watch with him.

"Umm...how about 'Final Dawn'? I've been curious about it," I replied, glancing at him.

"Intriguing choice. It won't be too scary for you, will it?" he asked, putting his arm around me as we walked inside.

"Isn't that the point? You're supposed to take your date to a scary movie so she'll cuddle close the whole time."

"Is that how it works?" he chuckled quietly. Several women turned and looked at him.

He bought the tickets and we headed into the theater, skipping popcorn and drinks since I had just eaten. We picked seats in the back where it was nice and dark and not near too many people. He put his arm around me and I rested my head on his shoulder as the lights went down and the previews began.

The opening to the movie was serene and pleasant, but it didn't take long for the gore to begin. I made it through the first several scenes without a problem, but for most of the rest of it, my face was buried in David's chest. He just smiled at me when I did it, rubbing my shoulder.

I was at least able to watch the end. The hero triumphantly saved his high school sweetheart from certain doom as he fought off all sorts of nasty creatures and then standing with her above all the carnage. I just wish I'd known they were going to get pulled under the pile of bodies. I screamed, jumping about a mile out of my seat, which really had him laughing. As the credits rolled, we left the theater with my head tucked into his shoulder. I was mortified.

"I don't think you were the only one who reacted that way to the ending," he commented as we entered the lobby, trying to soothe my embarrassment.

"Well, you didn't," I retorted.

"I knew it would happen. The movie was very predictable."

"Not for me..."

"Did you enjoy it aside from that?" he asked, kissing my temple.

"Only for being with you. Did you?"

"Only for being with you," he echoed, looking ahead of him.

The parking lot was still pretty full, with the late night crowd showing up for the last show. We turned the corner and noticed the lot we parked in, though, was dark and empty save for David's car. So much for parking under a street lamp.

As we came closer, a man strolled out from behind a bush and leaned against the trunk. He was large and dressed all in black, but it was too dark to see his face. I gripped David's arm tighter as we slowed our pace. He started toward us and we stopped. David moved from beside me to in front of me, but still held my hand.

"Hey rich boy, mind givin' me your wallet? I'm sure you have plenty to spare," the man demanded, his voice gruff.

Something cold and sharp pressed into my throat, and I gasped as I squeezed his hand. "Now," a voice snarled from behind me. David quickly glanced back and then returned his attention to the man in front of us.

"You don't want to do this, gentlemen. You don't know who you're dealing with," he replied coolly. How can he be so calm while I'm being held at knifepoint?

"Give us your wallet and your girlfriend won't get hurt," the first man demanded, ignoring David's threat. I whimpered as the second man pushed the blade deeper into my skin.

"Please don't hurt her...I'll give you my wallet," he conceded as he glanced over his shoulder at me. "It's going to be all right," he assured softly, letting go of my hand. He reached into his pocket and gradually pulled it out.

Lifting my eyes to the sky, I closed them and tried not to cry as I said a short prayer, hoping we'd get to leave unharmed. I breathed in and as I let it out, I felt a jerk and then was released. Hearing sounds of struggling, I slowly lowering my eyes and gasped at what I saw – both men face down on the asphalt with David standing over them.

"Get in the car," he commanded as he unlocked the doors with the remote. I obeyed, rushing to the other side and hopping in. As soon as my door was shut, it immediately locked.

I watched out the back window as he kneeled between the two men, but I couldn't see what he was doing. Maybe I didn't want to see. I faced forward and sat back, resting my head against the seat and controlling my breathing.

Hearing someone cry out in pain, I jerked around and stared out the rear window, not seeing anything. Then it happened again, but this time it sounded different. Scared, I frantically tried to roll down my window to see if David was in trouble, but the car was off. As I checked out the back again, he came into view. It must have been one of the men.

I turned around again and sat still, staring straight ahead. But my curiosity got the better of me. As I glanced back, I spotted him walking toward his door. He came closer and then stopped to pick something up.

He opened the door and sat, turning to me and placing his hand on my jaw. "Are you all right?" he asked quietly, slightly tilting my head and checking my neck.

I looked into his eyes and it all came rushing out. I tried not to cry but didn't do a very good job holding it in. He pulled me toward him, my face buried in his chest.

"I-I was so…so scared…" I sobbed as he caressed my hair.

"It's all right. I will never let any harm come to you, Megan. You are always safe with me."

Wrapped in his arms, I believed him. My sobbing receded and I sat back, moving the hair from my face and taking a deep breath. "I'm okay, I'm okay," I mumbled and took another deep breath.

Gathering I was telling the truth, he started the car and pulled out of the parking space. As he drove away, I glanced out the window, catching a glimpse of the two men on the ground writhing in pain. I was a little stunned at first, not knowing what to make of what I just saw, but then I was curious.

"What did you do to them?"

He smiled as he turned out of the lot onto the main road. "There is no need to worry. They won't be hurting anyone ever again," he replied.

"Did you call the police?"

"Yes, they're on the way," he responded as two cop cars flew by with lights flashing.

"Shouldn't we go back?"

"No, we don't have time. Besides, I gave them all the information they needed over the phone."

"How did you do it?" I inquired.

"Do what?"

"Take them both down so fast."

"A distraction – the wallet. I tossed it next to the first man and while he went after it, I took care of the one behind you."

"I never saw any of that…"

"Of course you didn't. Your eyes were closed…praying, I believe," he replied, his lip curling at the corner. He was speeding down the road.

"Why are you going so fast?"

"It's close to eleven. You can't be late."

"I'm sure my dad will understand, being that we were getting robbed."

"I'm not sure you should tell him about it," he responded as we pulled into my neighborhood.

"Why not? I think he should know. Besides, you protected me…saved me. That will show him you're serious about this relationship and not just with me for the wrong reasons."

He was quiet as we whipped into the drive. "All right, but let me tell him."

He climbed out of the car and came to my side, opening the door. We walked to the porch, his arm around my shoulder in a comforting embrace all the way to the front door. I entered, glancing at the grandfather clock as I passed, with David following. We had a couple minutes to spare and there was no sign of Dad in the living room. I called for him and he answered from the family room.

"Oh hey, David. Just in time, I see," he commented as he stood.

"We would have been sooner, Mr. Caldwell, if we had not run into trouble in the parking lot," David responded coolly.

"What happened…flat tire?" he asked, looking at my expression.

"No…we were nearly robbed, but Megan is all right, just a little shaken. I was able to subdue the offenders and call the police."

"Robbed?" he questioned, staring at me.

"Dad, I'm okay. They didn't hurt me or take any money. David protected me," I explained.

He grabbed me and held me close, kissing my head several times before turning to lay into David. "You will not take her out late at night ever again."

"But Dad!" I protested.

"No. If he wants to go out with you, it'll have to be earlier in the evening or during the day."

I glared at my father and pushed away. "You know we can't with school and work! I'll never get to see him!" I yelled.

David stood still, calm and collected. "I understand completely. It will not be a problem," he replied to my dad. "I must be going now. I will check in with you tomorrow, Megan," he continued as he leaned in and kissed my cheek. He turned to him and bowed his head slightly. "Good night, Mr. Caldwell."

Then he was gone. I shot a look at my father and then started up the stairs. "Where are you going?" he shouted after me.

Halfway up the steps, I turned and glared at him. "I was trying to make you see that David's not a bad person and wants to keep me safe, not take advantage of me."

"It's not like you won't ever be able to see him…"

"Imposing this curfew will keep me from seeing him!"

"Meg, David said he's okay with it. Calm down," he requested, starting after me.

I didn't answer, but instead climbed the remaining few and turned into my room, slamming the door in his face. I quickly changed, shut off the light, and crawled into bed. The best thing for me to do right now was sleep and not think about how angry I was at my father. I grabbed my iPod and shoved my earbuds in, turning on my rainy day mix to soothe my irritated core. I closed my eyes and slowed my breathing, eventually falling asleep after several songs.

# Chapter 20
## An Invitation

I was still angry with my dad when I woke Sunday morning. I didn't bother talking to him as we passed in the kitchen and instead of sitting at the counter like I usually do, I grabbed my breakfast and a book and went outside on the patio. Aside from my seething animosity toward him, it was another beautiful day and I wasn't going to sit inside and miss it. I read as I ate, enjoying the songs of the myriad of birds perched in the trees.

"Meg, can we talk?" Dad asked from behind me, interrupting my meditation.

I swallowed my food and glanced at him over my shoulder. "Okay…about what?"

He pulled out the chair next to me and sat. "Last night…"

"Then I don't want to talk," I replied abruptly, pushing the rest of my food away and staring at the words in the book but not reading them.

"I understand you're angry with me, but put yourself in my shoes. You're my only child and one of my biggest reminders of your mother," he continued, disregarding me. Out of the corner of my eye, I could see him staring at me. Then he sighed. "You are so much like her. I don't know what I'd do if I lost you, too."

I never thought of it that way. I lowered the book to the table but still didn't look at him. He was right to be afraid and worried, but what is he going to do in another year when I'm on my own. He can't be with me all the time.

I sighed and then turned to him. "I know you're worried and concerned about me, but David protected me and I feel he always will."

"I know…I owe him an apology for being so rude last night. I was just so mad at that moment. But when I did take the time to think about it, I realized he did bring you home safe and sound."

He stood up and kissed my forehead and then went inside. Okay, so I guess all is forgiven and maybe he won't be so hard on David anymore. I stared out into the yard and sighed again, then picked up my book and returned to reading.

I didn't do much of anything the rest of the day but lounge around the house. Dad left once or twice to grab something for Vanessa. I did call Claire late in the afternoon and told her all about my exciting evening. As usual, she wanted all the details, so I gave her a play by play.

"But you didn't see him take them down?" she asked, confused.

"No, I closed my eyes, preparing for the worst."

"Wow, that's incredible. What did he do after you got in the car?"

"I don't know…I couldn't see. He probably reprimanded them, maybe hit them a few times for good measure."

"You're so lucky…not only to come home unscathed, but to have David to protect you," she commented. There was a pause and then she said, "I have to go…Justin's calling. We'll talk more at school tomorrow."

I went downstairs and joined Dad on the couch, watching the local news. I was just in time for the report on two men who were arrested last night for attempted robbery. They were found in the parking lot of a movie theater with several broken bones. An anonymous phone call alerted the police to the crime and location, though the victims were nowhere to be found. When the perpetrators were asked to describe them, they couldn't remember.

"Are those the ones that attacked you?" Dad asked, looking at me.

"I-I'm not sure. I couldn't see them very well."

"Well that was the theater you went to last night, right?"

"Yeah…maybe it is them."

"And David did that?"

"I-I don't know," I replied, a little shocked. But what else would explain the screaming I heard?

"The police have them now; they'll pay for their crimes. They were wanted for several robberies and two deaths, so he did the right thing…albeit a little unorthodox," he assured me. I must have had a concerned look on my face.

After dinner, I decided to head up to my room. I pulled out notes from school and looked over them, getting a head start on studying for exams since the next couple of weekends were going to be busy. I also hoped they'd help me fall asleep. I was dozing off when David's phone rang.

"Did you see the news?" I asked in a perkier than normal voice.

"No, I've been at work. What happened?"

"They reported on the attempted robbery on us last night. Pretty interesting the way the men were found…"

"How so?" he asked.

I hoped he'd say something more than that. "David, what did you do to them?"

"I had to get you home, and I wasn't going to wait around for the police to show. I wanted to make sure they wouldn't be able to get away…so I broke their legs."

"You what?" I exclaimed.

"I had to do it. Otherwise, we would have been there all night waiting and answering questions. I'm sorry if that upsets you, but they were criminals and could have killed you. And this wasn't the first time they've done this either."

"I know…the police said they were wanted for several crimes, one of them being murder."

"Really…"

"Yep…they had fingerprint matches, so you made the cops' job that much easier by incapacitating them."

"Glad I could help," he responded modestly. "So other than that bit of news, how was your day?"

"Good. Dad realized he was wrong to treat you the way he did and plans to apologize the next time you come over. But I think the curfew still stands."

"As I said before, it's not a problem," he replied, pausing a moment before speaking again. "I assume your father will not let you out on a school night, so I was wondering if you would like to come to the house on Friday."

"Your house?" I asked, astonished.

"Yes. You could come over after school and stay for a couple hours. Do you think he'll mind?"

"I don't have to tell him I'm going to your house."

"What *will* you tell him?"

"That we're going to a park. He shouldn't have a problem with that."

"Are we back to lying again?"

"It's for his own good. Besides, I'm not really lying…your house is in or near a park," I rationalized.

"True…"

I glanced at the clock, surprised at the time. "It's later than I thought. I better go to bed. I'll talk to you tomorrow," I remarked and then hung up.

Rolling over, I placed the phone on the bedside table and turned out the light. The sound from the TV carried up through the cracked door. Dad was still awake, watching the news again and though he didn't have the volume high, it seemed like it was since the house was so quiet.

I tried to concentrate on something soothing to help me sleep, but my mind was too busy. I had so much to tell Claire tomorrow and the excitement made it hard. But soon that excitement turned to concern.

Seeing the report drudged up memories of the other night and I tried to imagine what David did while I wasn't looking. It took him mere seconds to bring both of them down and breaking their legs was like snapping a twig to him. They were grown men, heavier than him, and experienced in committing crimes. How was it possible to do what he did?

I couldn't explain it. There was no explanation for it. No reasonable, realistic one at least. After a half hour of mulling over it, I passed out.

"Did you see the news report last night on the attempted robbery?" I asked Claire, rushing up to her as she entered the lunchroom. She had a doctor's appointment earlier, so this was the first I saw of her.

"Yeah, what about it?" she asked, then gasped. "Those were your robbers?"

"Yep, and that was David's handiwork. But don't tell anyone. He apparently doesn't want it known we were the victims."

"No problem. I'll keep your secret safe," she responded, filling her tray.

We sat in our usual spot and continued discussing Saturday night until the others joined us. That's when I changed the subject. "So David invited me to his house…" I began, waiting for a reaction.

"That's awesome!" Erin exclaimed.

"What are you going to be doing there?" Ben asked suspiciously.

"Getting the grand tour and hanging out. Nothing special," I responded.

"Will Brian be there?" Claire asked.

"I don't know…he didn't say. Hopefully not," I replied, thinking more and more about it.

"I can't wait for him to invite us. Ooo, does he have a pool? I know you mentioned the lake…" she babbled on.

I never answered, my mind preoccupied with the thought that Brian might be there. But why should I worry? I'll be with David the whole time. He won't leave me alone with him. And maybe Madeline will be there, too. I feel comfortable around her.

"Megan…time to go," Ben commented, nudging me.

"Oh, sorry," I replied, standing up and heading out of the cafeteria.

The rest of the day went by pretty quickly and before I knew it, I was at home doing my homework. My evening was the same as usual and around nine, I headed up to my room to get ready for bed. I received another phone call from David, telling him about my day, but he didn't share much about his. He was a fairly private person, and I didn't pry.

The conversation quickly shifted to my visit to his house, since the whole question of whether Brian was going to be there or not was bothering me so much. "Who will be there Friday?" I asked, trying not to sound concerned.

"Everyone for the early part of the evening. Brian and Odette usually go out later to clubs and bars."

"Oh…okay. That's cool," I replied, trying to sound enthused.

"Brian will not try anything while I'm around. You'll be fine," he assured me. "I have to go. I'll talk to you tomorrow," he continued. I replied and hung up.

Lying there in the dark, I imagined what the inside of his house might look like. Airy and open, no doubt, and woodsy. Would Madeline's artwork be in one room or dispersed throughout? And what of the roommates' rooms? What about David's?

I fell asleep with those thoughts on my mind.

*A large wooden door slowly opened, and I was greeted by David and invited inside. It was dark and rustic, like one of those posh mountain cabins celebrities escape to when they need downtime. He took my hand and led me down a dark hall into a large open room with giant windows that faced the lake. Through the trees, I could see the sun glistening off the rippling water. I stood for a long time, stunned by its beauty.*

*He urged me to move on, taking me through the rest of the house. For being so extravagant on the outside, the interior was modest – simple furnishings and bucolic décor. It easily fit its surroundings but not David. Madeline's work hung throughout, abstract versions of lake and woodland scenes that somehow complemented it all.*

*We continued on, finally ending at his room. Windows covered as many walls as possible, displaying a panoramic view of the lake. Looking around, he had a lot of the same things any person would have – a stereo, CDs, lots of books, a chaise – but no bed. I asked about it, and he replied that he didn't need one. With school and work, he must not have time to sleep.*

*He guided me to the chaise where we sat side by side. He gazed into my eyes and gently caressed my cheek as he leaned in and kissed me. As it became more intense, I felt something sharp graze my lip. I pulled back, tucking it in. A metallic taste hit my tongue and when I looked at him, blood tinged his lips...*

I sat straight up in bed, gasping. As my eyes adjusted, I realized I was in my room. Glancing at the clock, I had several minutes before I needed to get up. Sighing as I lay down, I tried to go back to sleep, but I kept thinking about the dream. I rubbed my face, turned the alarm off, and got ready for school.

The day was like any other, as were the next two, and all were sunny and beautiful. David only called at night to talk and never came to visit. Fortunately, the weekend was only a few days away, and I couldn't wait.

Thursday morning breezed by, but at lunch everything slowed to a crawl. At least the conversation was interesting. "Have you heard the latest...Damian and Evil-Lyn, or whatever her name is, have been missing for almost a week," Claire announced as she dropped her tray on the table.

"That goth couple in our History class?" Ben asked, sitting next to her.

"Yeah...the last anyone saw of them was at prom."

"It's really not unusual for them. Once, they didn't come to school for three weeks, crashing at a friend's place and hanging out there," Justin responded.

"But this time, they're really missing. No one has seen them outside of school either," she stated.

I thought back to the night of prom and tried to remember ever seeing them. I didn't know them very well and frankly, they creeped me out, but I hoped nothing bad happened. "Maybe they ran away together," I suggested.

"Maybe you're right. I don't know much about him, but I know she didn't have a very good home life," Erin replied.

We sat quiet for a moment. Nobody else in the cafeteria seemed to be dwelling on the news as much as we were. I'd guess because they weren't the captain of the football team and the head cheerleader. *That* would be front-page news. Finally, Erin spoke up, changing the discussion to more pleasant things.

"So how about that date with David's roommate, Cary?" she inquired.

"Oh, he hasn't mentioned anything yet. Maybe Cary's really busy with school," I replied. She looked disappointed.

"Have you heard anything from Madeline?" Claire asked Ben.

"Yeah, she called me last night. We're going to a movie on Saturday."

"That's great!" I commented. But it didn't look like good news to him. "How do you feel about it?"

"Nervous. This will be our first date…alone."

"You'll be fine. What are you going to see?"

"I don't know. I'm letting her pick."

"Well, I can't wait to hear how it goes," I remarked as the bell rang.

We gathered our trays and exited the lunchroom. Erin and I headed to the gym as the others continued on to their classes. She pestered me as we changed and all through warm-ups and the softball game about getting David to convince Cary to go out on a date with her. I told her I'd try, but reminded her finals were coming up and he'd be really busy.

When I got to English, Ben was still worrying over his date. I was close to suggesting a double date but decided he needed to be a man and face it alone. Again, I told him it was going to be all right and then ignored him for the remainder of class. He got the hint and when it was over, he talked about something else on the way to my locker and car.

Once home, I rushed through my homework and cooked something before Dad arrived. After dinner and some TV, I went up to my room around nine to prepare for bed. I was changed and ready to read my latest book when David called.

"Good evening, Megan. Did you have a pleasant day?"

"Yeah. Erin asked repeatedly about her date with Cary. I told her I'd ask but cautioned that he was probably busy with finals."

"That he is. Unfortunately, he will most likely never go on a date with her. I don't think he's ready to leave the safety of home just yet."

Huh…then why was he out with Brian on prom night? Probably just an excuse to get out of dating a high school girl. "I'll let her know so she's not holding out for him. Did you know Ben and Madeline have a movie date Saturday?"

"Of course. She's looking forward to it. Is he?"

"For the most part, but he's nervous. He talked about it all day today."

"She will make it easy for him. There's nothing to worry about."

I didn't want to know what he meant by that. Changing the subject, I asked, "Hey, do you remember a goth couple at prom?"

He was quiet for a moment. "I think so. Both dressed completely in black with matching nail polish and makeup…they sat in a dark corner most of the night. Why?"

"They're missing. They actually went missing the night of prom…" I paused for a moment, thinking about what I was going to ask before I did. "I was wondering if maybe Brian knew their whereabouts."

He didn't answer right away. "What do you mean?" he inquired finally.

"I…I overheard you talking to him the night of prom. He said something about seeing if anyone wanted to have some fun at your house afterward."

"Hmm…as far as I know they never made it inside, leaving before we did. And there wasn't a party going on nor did I see anyone new when I arrived home."

"Oh…okay. I was just curious. So are you preparing for finals?" I asked, changing the subject again.

"Somewhat, but I don't have as difficult a time with them as Cary does. He's intelligent, but not a quick learner."

"So you really haven't started studying yet."

"I read over my notes every night, so I probably won't have to study at all. I have an exceptional memory."

"When will summer classes begin for you?" I asked, wondering if we'd be able to get together once school was out.

"I may have a week or two off," he replied.

"I'd like to spend as much time with you as I can."

"I know. I will do my best to make that possible."

I rolled over onto my back and stared at the ceiling. "Why haven't you come to visit me?"

"I feel guilty…for some reason."

"Because of my dad?"

"Yes…but I also feel it's wrong."

"It's not. We're not doing anything objectionable, just talking. I've heard much worse going on in school."

"I'm sure you have," he replied, chuckling.

I placed my hand over my fluttering heart as I glanced at the clock. "Well, I should go to bed. I can't wait to see you tomorrow."

"Do you remember where the house is?"

"Yeah. I'll be there around four."

"You may want to eat before you come. We dine late."

"Oh…no problem," I replied, a little confused. Maybe college throws their schedule off. We said good night and then hung up.

I was giddy with excitement, thinking about tomorrow afternoon. I rolled over and tried to sleep but couldn't. Wondering what I should wear, I pulled out my phone and checked the weather – warm with showers and thunderstorms, sixty percent chance. Great.

How am I going to convince Dad to let me go now? I can't very well tell him I'm going to a park. A study group…no, he won't buy that, especially on a Friday. Ooo…I could say that David is meeting me at the mall. That's something typical for a teenager to do on a rainy Friday afternoon.

I rested my head on the pillow and closed my eyes, confident he wouldn't have a problem with that. As I began falling asleep, my dream from the night before returned.

*We were back at David's house, in his room sitting on the chaise. He started kissing me, moving down my chin to my throat, and I tilted my head, lengthening my neck. His arms wrapped around my body, constricting me as he held me close. I gasped as his mouth opened over my throat and I felt a sharp pain. I remained still, not fighting him, and let him do what he wanted as I lay limp in his arms…*

I woke suddenly, feeling drained and tired. Looking at the clock, I was relieved to see it was only two and I didn't have to get up yet. I closed my eyes, but this time the dream didn't return. My mind drifted in and out as I did the same, finally falling into a deep sleep.

*I felt the familiar sensation of someone running their fingers over my hair. As I opened my eyes, I saw my mom sitting on the edge of the bed, gazing down at me. "Mom? Why are you here?" I questioned.*

*"Why haven't you visited me? I miss you, Nut-Meg."*

*"I'm sorry. I've been busy with school and other things," I explained and then paused. "I have a boyfriend, Mom," I replied drowsily with a smile, hoping she'd be happy for me.*

*"I know. I've been watching him from afar, curious about him. I know you really like him…but be wary – he has a dark secret," she warned, her delicate visage marred with angst.*

*"What do you mean? What's his secret?"*

*"I can't say…"*

*"Mom, it's important. I've noticed these things about him, strange things that can't be explained, and I've tried to be patient with him, giving him time to trust me with whatever it is he's hiding, but I can't be patient forever. Isn't there anything you can tell me?"*

*Her expression became solemn. "Only that you need to be cautious," she replied as she started to fade.*

*I sat up and reached for her. "No, don't go! Don't leave me yet!"*

*"I love you, Nut-Meg. Please be careful," she whispered, her fingers evaporating as they grazed my cheek. Then the rest of her did the same.*

*"Mom, don't!" I begged, but it was too late. She was gone.*

*Lying back down, I stared at where she had been sitting beside me. As if from somewhere far off, I heard the faint sound of talking. I looked around the room but didn't see anyone. I closed my eyes, trying to concentrate on what was being said, but couldn't make out anything. Slowly, it became louder and louder...*

I opened my eyes to the jabbering of the morning DJs on my alarm clock and sighed as I turned it off. Rolling over, I stared through the sheer curtains at the bleak day outside and listened to the rain pelt the windows and roof. I closed my eyes and saw a flash of my mom's worried face. Quickly sitting up and opening them, I tried to rid the image from my thoughts.

I didn't linger in the shower and dressed fairly quickly, but I took my time deciding on an outfit for my after school activity. I wanted something appropriate but still flattering. I chose a teal, three-quarter sleeve shirt and a brown, plaid, knee-length skirt that flared out slightly, pairing them with brown high-heel Mary-Janes. Slipping the outfit into a separate bag, I took it into the bathroom and added makeup and other items to tidy up after a long day at school.

Rushing down the stairs, I hooked my bags over the end of the banister and headed into the kitchen. I greeted Dad as I grabbed my breakfast, glimpsing the rain coming down in the backyard. I took a seat and bit into an apple while he continued reading the news.

"Don't forget your umbrella today," I reminded him as I stared outside.

He put his paper down and looked at me. "Don't worry, I won't."

I took another bite and chewed, remembering what I was going to tell him about my date. "David wants me to meet him at the mall after school to hang out for a couple hours tonight. Is that all right?"

"Sure, that's no problem. Hey, while you're there, can you pick something up for me?"

I wonder if he's testing me. Well, better than him going to the mall and not finding me there. "Sure. What do I need to get?"

"At the engraving store, there are two glasses Vanessa ordered for the wedding. They're supposed to be ready today. Here's the receipt," he replied, pulling a small, folded piece of paper out of his wallet and handing it to me.

"Will I need to pay for them?" I asked as I glanced at it.

"No, that's taken care of. Just check over them and make sure everything is spelled correctly and they look okay."

"All right. Well, I better get going. I'll see you around eight," I replied, knowing I had to give myself extra time to run by the mall now.

"Have fun," he commented, going back to reading his paper as I threw the remains of the apple away.

I rushed out of the room, grabbing my bags on my way out the door. In my haste, I forgot to grab an umbrella, so I got soaked as I fought to get in my car. Hopefully, it'd let up by the time I got to school.

No such luck when I arrived. Fortunately, I ran into Erin and she shared her umbrella with me as we walked into the building. I took that moment to tell her Cary was not available in the nicest way possible. She handled it well. As soon as we were inside, she headed on to class and I met Claire at my locker.

"Sooo…you ready for tonight?" she asked as I put my extra bag in it and switched out my books.

"Yeah. My dad was cool with it, though he thinks I'm going to the mall. Now I have to cut my time short to pick something up for the wedding."

"Hey, at least it proves you were there."

"True," I agreed, shutting the door. "I need to run to the bathroom to attempt to dry out. Wanna come?"

"No, I'll pass. Justin should be getting here soon. He always likes to see me before class."

"All right, see you there," I replied as I dashed down the hall to the nearest restroom.

I wrung my hair out in the sink and dried my clothes under the hand dryer. After getting as much of the rain water out of my clothes as possible, I fixed my hair and tidied my outfit so I didn't look like a ragamuffin going into class. Thank God I wasn't wearing it to David's.

Taking my seat, I stared at the clock and hoped for time to pass quickly, but it decided to drag instead. Through every single class. I was anxious all morning and it showed.

"What's with you today?" Ben asked at lunch.

"She's going to David's house after school. Duh!" Claire answered.

"Oh…right. I forgot. So are you anxious nervous or anxious excited?"

"A little of both, actually," I replied, playing with my food. I didn't have much of an appetite.

"So…going to David's house. Ooo, you should take pictures with your phone so you can show us!" Erin suggested eagerly.

"No, that would be rude. Besides, I believe he still plans to have everyone over sometime this summer."

Ben sat back in his seat and stared at me, a scheming look on his face as he contemplated our conversation. "You should see if he'll throw us a party," he suggested and then he and Justin high-fived each other.

"Oh, that'd be awesome!" Claire agreed enthusiastically. "It could just be us...and a couple hundred of our friends," she added slyly.

"Or better yet, it could be for our end-of-school party," he proposed, thinking more about it.

"That's even better! We haven't found a place yet, and I'm sure his is ideal!" Erin exclaimed excitedly.

I glared at Ben and then smiled as I considered it and putting him in his place. "All right, I'll ask him. But don't be surprised if he says yes."

I don't know how David will react to that request, especially since he doesn't seem to like parties. Maybe he'll say no. Then again, maybe he'll say yes. Wonderful – Ben just added more to my anxiety. I stared out the window at the rain streaming down the panes, trying to get my mind off it.

In the remaining hours of the day, I grew antsier. I tried to concentrate on my classes, but it wasn't working. After the last bell, I took off so quick Ben didn't have a chance to catch me. I sprinted to my locker to get my clothes and then to the nearest restroom to change.

I fixed my hair and put on a little makeup, giving myself a once over before leaving. I was stuffing things into my bag as I stepped out of the bathroom and ran smack into Ben outside the door. "What are you doing here?" I exclaimed.

"Waiting for you, obviously. Erin said you didn't have an umbrella, so I thought I'd offer the use of mine," he responded as he held it up and then hesitated. "I also need a ride."

"How perfect," I muttered, picking up the couple of items dropped in the collision.

We walked down the hall to the doors that led to the parking lot, stopping to ready ourselves for the rain. He opened the small umbrella as we stepped outside and we had to squeeze in close, but I didn't complain. I really didn't want to get wet again, especially after working so hard on my look.

When we got to the car, he graciously stood by me as I opened my door and climbed in, quickly unlocking his as he ran to the other side. He got in and shook off the umbrella before closing it. I could feel him staring at me and a quick glance confirmed it.

"You look really nice," he commented as I started the car.

"Thanks," I responded, not taking his compliment seriously. I didn't do anything spectacular. "Is your mom working late?"

"Yeah. And thank you. I really wasn't in the mood to walk home in the rain."

"Well, it's a good thing you caught me in time," I replied, pulling out of the lot.

There was a long silence as he stared out the window at the rain coming down in sheets. Then he cleared his throat and I glanced his way. "So Madeline will be there?" he asked, running his fingers along the door.

"That's what David said. Is there anything you want me to tell her?"

"No…no. I was just curious if she was going to be there."

"I'm glad she will. She seems like a nice person."

He was a little dazed for a moment. "Yeah…" he replied tentatively, returning his gaze to the rain. And he left it at that.

"We're here," I announced as I pulled into his driveway.

"Huh? Oh yeah…well, have a good time and tell Madeline I can't wait to see her tomorrow," he commented as he climbed out of the car.

"I will. Have fun on your date tomorrow."

He shut the door and stood in the rain, not opening the umbrella as I backed out of the drive. I shook my head, wondering why he remained there getting drenched, when I spotted it out of the corner of my eye. He left it for me. He was already inside by the time I realized it, so I left it alone and headed to David's house.

# Chapter 21
## Maison de la Mort

The rain came down much harder, making it difficult to see exactly where David's driveway was, but I found it finally. I turned in and pulled up to the call box, pressing the button. He answered and buzzed me through as the massive wrought iron gates creaked open. Spooky.

The road was long and lonely, but visibility was at least better. The trees lining it created a leaky umbrella effect, allowing some rain to come through, but not as much as being without them. It seemed to be taking forever to get to the end of the drive, but then I noticed an opening up ahead. As I came to the clearing where the house stood, I slowed almost to a stop, staring at the structure ahead of me.

Dark and archaic, it seemed out of place here in Virginia and intimidating in the gloomy weather. Its design was that of a French chateau meant to be perched on the side of a mountain rather than buried in the woods. There it would look majestic, but here it was menacing.

I slowly pulled around past the front door and parked, pausing a moment to ready myself. I closed my eyes briefly and saw my mom's troubled expression from the dream as her warning repeated in my head. Why wouldn't she just tell me? Why was she so vague?

I sighed, shaking it from my mind. It was just another dream. It probably meant nothing. Returning my focus to the visit, I glanced out the window and took in the house as I heard a distant rumble of thunder. Great. Now it was even creepier.

I grabbed Ben's umbrella and cracked my door, popping it open before exiting the car. Quickening my pace, I rushed up the steps as lightning flashed in the darkened sky behind the house. As I stood under the porch, I shook out the umbrella and took a deep breath before grasping the heavy, iron, scroll doorknocker on the large, wooden doors. I knocked three times and then stepped back slightly, waiting. Slowly, one side creaked open.

"Megan…please come in," David greeted graciously, a half-smile upon his lips. "You can leave your umbrella here," he indicated to a small stand outside the door.

I dropped it in and continued into the house. My heart fluttered as I stared at him, and I tried not to stumble over the threshold. "Thank you," I replied, keeping my eyes on his. I was beyond happy to see and be near him again.

We stood in the foyer staring at each other for what felt like forever, and then he smiled and my heart thumped. "Shall we join the others in the grand salon?" he inquired, offering his arm to me.

I hesitated. "Grand salon? Okay," I agreed in a daze, hooking mine around his and smiling.

Taking a deep breath and preparing myself, I took in the scent of the house – fresh and new, like he just moved in. He led me down a dim hallway, the natural light barely highlighting the subtle inlays in the oak flooring and the rich colors of the wall. On either side was a doorway that sat slightly off from the other and then mostly empty space except for a few unlit decorative sconces and a painting.

I paused a moment to look at it, stopping him in the process. It was of a moon streaked in dark red paint that dripped down and over the frame. I looked closer to see if it leaked onto the floor or wall, but it hadn't.

"Is this one of Madeline's?" I asked, pointing at it.

"It is. She calls it 'Harvest Moon'," he answered.

"She was right…her work is different," I remarked as we continued down the hall to a great, open room.

It was a large half oval with floor length windows lining the walls. A set of French doors leading out onto a wrap-around veranda were open at the end, letting in the aroma of rain-soaked woods. Off to the right, attached to the kitchen, was a morning room half the size of the grand salon.

So far, the house was nothing like in my dream.

Madeline sat in an armchair under a window reading a book. Her attire was much more casual than the last time I saw her – earthy bohemian – but fitting for her. As soon as we entered, she hopped up and came toward me, giving me a hug.

"It's so good to see you again, Megan!" she exclaimed, her cheek cool against mine.

"Welcome to Maison de la Mort," Brian commented languidly as he glanced over his shoulder at me, smirking. He lounged on an antique loveseat with his back to us, his arm laying across the backrest.

David glared at him, as did Madeline. He just snickered and turned his attention to the window ahead of him, which of course made me look. Pacing nervously on the veranda was an unfamiliar person.

David noticed my curious expression and whispered, "That's Cary. Storms make him anxious."

Brian scoffed. Ignoring him, we walked over by the morning room and sat on a different antique loveseat while Madeline returned to her chair. A woman with golden blonde hair reclined with her head on Brian's lap, her eyes closed as he stroked her tresses.

Again, David noticed who I focused on and whispered, "That would be Odette."

I turned and narrowed my eyes at him. "I figured that," I remarked.

Brian snickered. Odette, however, didn't do anything. She just remained there like a perfectly preserved corpse, not bothering to say a word or even look at me.

Examining the room, I had to admire David's taste – lots of antiques and rich, deep colors. All the furniture looked like it was from the Victorian era, fitting in perfectly with the rest of his décor. The hardwood floors were covered with elaborate oriental rugs and thick, velvet curtains cascaded down the windows.

The morning room next to us was raised and lighter in color than the grand salon, with natural wood flooring and pale walls. The furniture was more contemporary, with a few leather pieces and a coffee table. It opened to a modern kitchen with marble flooring and walnut cabinets, granite counter tops, stainless steel appliances, and a large island containing a cook top and small sink. And all of it looked brand new, as though it had never been used.

Returning to the morning room, I discovered the terrace right off it. Several French-style, wrought iron tables were scattered around like one would see at a bistro in Paris. Beyond it, I glimpsed the pool and patio.

"Are you going to show Megan the rest of the house?" Madeline asked anxiously.

"Of course, if she would like. I wanted to give her a moment to relax first," David replied, glancing at me and smiling slightly.

A loud crack of thunder jolted me. I looked over my shoulder at the lake beyond the trees as a lightning bolt struck over the water, creating another boom. Then another one farther off streaked across the sky followed by a low rumble. Fascinated, I watched the light show for several minutes.

I turned back around and was surprised to find everyone still in their original positions, as if they were posing for a portrait. Tired of the lack of conversation, I looked at Madeline and smiled. "Do you ever paint landscapes of the lake?" I asked.

"I've done one or two, but it's really not my style."

"That's a shame…I would think it'd be inspiring," I commented, glancing at it again.

"It inspires me in other ways," she smiled, and then it quickly dropped as she shot a look at Brian's grinning face.

"Where's your studio located?" I asked, remembering she mentioned it at prom.

She returned her attention to me, her expression softening. "On the second floor, across from my bedroom," she replied. "I have no problem with you showing either room to her, David," she added excitedly, glancing at him. He nodded once and then smiled at me.

"Please refrain from showing our room," Brian interjected, and he acknowledged without argument. Not like I wanted to go in there anyway.

At that moment, Cary entered and sat in a wingback chair near a set of doors, nervously bouncing his leg. He was small and slender with short auburn hair and wasn't as attractive as Brian or David, but he wasn't ugly either – just an average Joe. He seemed a lot younger than them, too.

David looked at him, and Cary returned his gaze with fear in his eyes. David's brow furrowed and then smoothed as Cary ran his hand through his hair and gazed out the window, seeming to calm a little. I glanced over my shoulder outside again and noticed the storm passing, but the rain lingered.

"So Megan...did you have a good time at prom?" Brian asked, leering at me. David's eyes narrowed and Brian grinned back. Odette remained unconcerned with anything, continuing to sleep.

"David was so handsome and a perfect boyfriend. We had a great time dancing and talking," I extolled, hoping to rile him.

"Oh really," he remarked with a smirk. "What did everyone think of your date?"

I was surprised by his question. Why did he want to know that? "Awestruck, mostly, by him and Madeline. I guess it was because nobody expected Ben and me to be with them," I responded. Brian continued to smirk and shifted his eyes to David.

They never spoke a word between them, but it looked as if they were having a whole conversation with their glances. I watched them for a bit, but then my eyes wandered to a painting above the fireplace across from me. I stood up and walked over to it, noticing Cary getting anxious again as I passed. Maybe I made him nervous.

I stopped in front of it, getting a better look. A woman was hunched over on her knees, her head hanging over hands coated in dark red. Her fire orange hair completely covered her face, the tips in the same deep red and dripping. I could make out the faint outline of her downcast expression, eyes closed.

"It's 'The First Time'," Madeline whispered and I jumped slightly.

No matter what my curiosity, I wasn't going to ask. "Oh...I was admiring the oranges and reds. They're so vibrant," I responded instead.

"Thank you. I use a special paint I mix myself. It makes the image more realistic."

As she rambled on about the medium she used, I glanced back at David sitting on the loveseat in front of the large window and admired him. No longer embroiled in a staring contest with Brian, he was looking over his shoulder at the rain falling steadily on the water. If I were any good at painting, he would be someone I'd want to immortalize.

Without a word, I left her and crossed the room to join him, feeling the urge to do so. As I passed Brian and Odette, I discreetly glanced down at her. She was unbelievably beautiful, but of course I wouldn't expect anything less for him. Her golden blonde hair had a slight wave to it and her features were soft and smooth. Up close, she looked more like a porcelain doll laying on his lap. I wonder if she was anything like him or the complete opposite.

As I neared David, he stood and I stopped, not sure what I was supposed to do. He indicated for me to sit and then sat next to me after I did, smiling and shaking his head. Madeline was back in her seat grinning, Cary was staring out the window, Brian was watching me, and Odette still hadn't moved. I turned my attention to the one conscious roommate I hadn't spoken to.

"So, Cary," I commented avidly, "David told me you're working on an online degree. What's your major?" I couldn't think of anything else to ask to get a conversation going.

He jerked his head in my direction and then shifted his golden eyes to David, panic behind them. But then a moment later, his focus was on me, not as frightened as before. "Computer programming," he replied in a voice that was not as mature as I expected. Then he returned to staring outside.

I glanced at David and he shrugged, but Brian chuckled. "Cary's not much of a talker," he remarked.

"What's above this room?" I asked David, ignoring him.

"That would be my room," he replied. "Are you ready for the tour?" he asked, noticing my tedium.

I smiled, eager to leave the stale company. "Yes, I am."

He stood and put his arm out, and I slipped mine under his. Brian's eyes followed us as we walked into the kitchen and while David talked about the room, I caught him occasionally glancing at Brian. He gave a final glare before we continued around to the side, losing sight of him.

Crossing the hall, we came to the dining room. It put mine to shame – large and bright with paler woods lining all the walls but the one with the huge window that looked out at the driveway and woods. To the right was a set of French doors that led out onto the veranda. A large table that could seat about twelve was in the center of the room and a magnificent crystal chandelier hung above it. An ornate, solid wood server sat in one corner and a similar china cabinet filled with elegant dishes sat in the other.

He slid open two large, wood panel doors, displaying the foyer. I stepped through them and he followed, leading me across to another dim hallway. The first room we entered was the guest room. It had a large walk-in closet, its own bathroom, and a squared bay window with a view of the front yard. In the center was a hand carved, cherry, king sleigh bed made up with fine linens.

We headed across the hall to what he announced as the library and I became giddy. My jaw dropped as the double doors glided open and revealed his vast personal collection. Books of all shapes and sizes lined the walls above and below.

A short set of stairs on either side of the large fireplace led up to a walkway wrapping around the room. I dashed to it and climbed one side, starting my exploration. As I flitted along the path, I glanced at the titles and occasionally pulled out a book to look at it. He had a lot of first editions and rare ones, some in other languages. One well-worn book I pulled from a shelf had a personalization in it:

*To David,*
*May you always enjoy life and the pleasure of a good book.*

I couldn't make out the signature but knew it had to be the author's. I looked at the date under the inscription, curious how old it was – 1919. "David…when did you get this book?"

He joined me and glanced at it in my hand. "I picked it up at a rare bookstore downtown a couple weeks ago. I liked the inscription," he replied casually before stepping away.

I slipped it back onto the shelf and pulled another one that didn't look as beat up and peeked at the inside cover. Another dedication with his name and the author's signature. I glanced over my shoulder at him sitting in a chair reading and then slipped that book back. I moved to another bookcase and pulled out an older looking book. Another inscription to David.

This is weird. Then again, maybe he collects books with inscriptions to that name. Everyone needs a hobby and maybe that's his. Besides, it's probably not too hard to find books signed to that name; it's popular and has been for a long time.

I stopped perusing and took in the room itself. In the center was a leather chaise and loveseat with a few armchairs here and there. Under them, the flooring had an elaborate inlay design that spread out from the middle to a few feet shy of the baseboards. Along the back wall was a row of windows that overlooked a pool, but floor to ceiling were mostly bookshelves. And where there weren't were more of Madeline's pieces.

Closest to me was a picture of an angel with her back turned, head hung, blackness all around her. Another nearby showed a dark, empty neighborhood street with a little girl standing at the end of it, all alone. And across the room was one of a man looking over a woman's shoulder, her back to the viewer, with her face downcast and neck exposed to him. He had an evil half-smile and his eyes burned right into you. I couldn't look at that one for long.

David stood and walked over to me. "I sometimes come here rather than go out when there are parties. When I'm not here, I generally keep the doors locked," he commented as he led me up one of the set of stairs to a bookcase in the back corner of the room. I didn't blame him. If I had this many expensive books in one room, I'd lock them up for safekeeping, too.

Grabbing the side of the shelf, he pulled on it, revealing a doorway leading to a landing. He indicated for me to go first, then he followed. As I paused outside the room, I spied the foyer and the front door ahead of us and an open hallway above us. We were on the main staircase!

He smiled and started up the stairs to the second floor with me right behind him. I slowed my pace and glanced back at where we came out of the library, finding only a wood paneled wall instead of a door. A hidden entrance...neat.

Before turning back, I caught a glimpse of an enormous window on the wall opposite from where we were. Rain streaked down the multifaceted, decorative panes, creating blurred images of the pool and woods. I paused a moment to watch, but then David cleared his throat and I turned back around, quickly climbing the remaining steps to catch up to him.

When we reached the top, he stopped and turned to face me, placing his hand on my cheek. It was cool but soothing. I leaned into it and closed my eyes as he moved closer.

"I'm happy you came today," he whispered and then kissed me.

It took a moment to recover as he moved away. "Me...me, too," I responded, blushing, and he smiled. I tucked my head, my face brightening even more as my heart beat fast. Closing my eyes, I did what I could to calm it, and eventually it slowed.

"Ready to continue?" he inquired, placing his hand on the small of my back and making me quiver.

I fidgeted as I nodded, hoping he didn't notice. He didn't say anything or react as he led me toward a hallway and into a disheveled room. "This must be Madeline's studio," I guessed and he grinned. My heart fluttered lightly in my chest, and I quickly looked away before having another episode.

By the door was an open closet that had every color of paint imaginable in it as well as other art supplies. Doodles and paint covered the unfinished walls and there was paint splatter on the floor and supplies spread out everywhere. Several unframed paintings were piled in a corner. It was a messy room, but what I expected of an artist.

The whole back wall was covered in windows with a beautiful view of the woods and lake. No curtains hung on them, but instead they had solid shutters that were folded back. A couple easels were set up in front of them with a half-finished painting on one and a white canvas with dark red spatter on the other.

We ventured across the hall to her bedroom, which was much tidier. She had a king canopy bed made of a light oak with thick, rose-colored curtains tied to each of the posts, and bright linens. Her dresser had all sorts of trinkets laid out on top. On the other side of the room was a vanity that contained all her beauty supplies. She had a walk-in closet and a private bath with dainty towels and floral decor. Her walls had several paintings on them, more lighthearted than the others – scenes of children playing and small town life.

David indicated the room on the back side of the house was Brian and Odette's and beside Madeline's was Cary's. Peeking inside, it was the complete opposite of hers. Sterile and cold, it also had a canopy bed, but it was made of a black wood with dark, thick curtains that were drawn. His walls were plain and along one of them, in front of a covered window, was a large desk with an elaborate computer setup on it. He, too, had a walk-in closet and private bath.

We crossed over the foyer to another hallway, but there were no rooms along it. David stopped in front of the set of double doors at the end and smiled. "I saved the best for last," he commented as he slowly opened them.

I gasped as I stepped inside, passing the huge side-by-side walk-in closets as I staggered to the center and paused, taking it all in. He, too, had a king size canopy bed, made of mahogany, with thick burgundy curtains tied back to the posts. On the right was an enormous private bath. I headed to it, more curious about it than anything else at the moment. There was a huge garden tub in front of a wall-to-wall shower and the floor and counter tops were marble with dark wood cabinetry.

I re-entered the bedroom and continued looking around. He had a dresser with a mirror, a chest, and an armoire – all mahogany. There was a fireplace across from the bed and above it was a very old portrait of a family. I paused and looked at it, thinking it was David and his parents, but they were dressed in clothes from another time period. An older man, a woman, and a younger man stood together, and only the woman and the young man smiled.

"Is that your family?" I asked, thinking it was obviously a dumb question.

"Yes…that is my grandfather," he replied, pointing to the young man.

"You look so much like him," I commented, moving closer. It was really uncanny how similar they looked.

"My mother used to tell me that all the time," he answered, staring at the portrait with sadness in his eyes.

"It's quite an impressive place you have. Nothing like what I expected, especially your room," I remarked, drawing his attention away from it.

"Oh, really? What did you expect?" he asked with his mischievous grin, leading me out onto the second story veranda. My heart fluttered excitedly.

I thought back to my dream, but I didn't want to tell him about it. "More like a college student's place…mostly empty with only the necessities," I lied.

"Well, I'm not a college student just breezing through. I plan to stay here for a while," he responded with a smile as he turned his attention to the backyard. Naturally, I did, too.

The view was more amazing than in the grand salon, giving the ability to see above the younger trees to the lake. I stared at it for a long time, unbelievably impressed with his home and his generosity toward his roommates. After a moment, I glanced over the edge, admiring the pool below, and noticed there was another level.

"What's on the bottom?" I asked, turning around and leaning against the railing.

"A game room, theater, wine cellar…"

"Will I get to see them?"

"If you would like."

I nodded and he led me through the room into the hallway, pausing to take my arm in his. We descended the stairs together and even though I could have been looking around me, my focus instead was on him. As we reached the bottom, he glanced toward the grand salon and furrowed his brow.

"I'll just be a moment. I have to check on something," he commented and then stepped away. Figuring he wouldn't be long, I stayed in the foyer.

I stared at the staircase in front of me, its dark wood and wrought iron spindle railing rising to the landing where we came out of the library and wrapping around to the other staircase leading to the second floor open hallway. Curving down to the lower floor was another set of stairs on the opposite side. Stepping back, I took in the enormous window I had seen earlier. It engulfed the entire back wall, even down to the basement.

David hadn't returned so I leaned back, trying to sneak a look into the grand salon, but I couldn't see him. I didn't see Brian or Cary either. I wonder where they went and if Odette was still on the loveseat. Maybe that was what he was checking on.

Deciding not to venture in to find out, I strolled around the foyer instead, noticing several more of Madeline's pieces. One had tree branches against a red and orange sky with coal black birds flying away. Another had what looked like a serene scene of a man and a woman walking down a tree lined path, but upon closer inspection, the woman was looking over her shoulder at the viewer, her face skeletal. The last piece was a sculpture of what looked like two abstract people holding each other.

As I examined it closer, I spied David coming toward me. "Please forgive me for being so long. I needed to talk to Madeline about something," he apologized, joining my side.

"That's okay. So I see she sculpts as well," I replied, pointing at the piece in front of me.

"Yes…it's called 'The Embrace'."

"This one I understand," I commented, smiling at him as I put my arms around his torso.

"Do you?" he asked slyly as he pulled me closer and contorted our bodies to resemble it. One hand was on my lower back and the other behind my head, my neck fully exposed to him as his lips pressed against my throat. He kissed it and then pulled me back up.

I was speechless and a little faint. I held onto him and steadied myself as I closed my eyes for a moment. When I opened them, his focus was solely on me, concerned something was wrong.

"I'm okay, just a little dizzy from the sudden movements." It didn't help I was starving.

"Are you all right to go downstairs?" he inquired and I nodded.

As we came to the bottom stair, we entered an open area which David called the game room. It looked very much like an English pub and even had a small bar. There was a pool table in one corner and a game table with six chairs around it in another.

"I bet this area is popular during the parties," I commented, playing with the billiard balls.

"Yes, for drinking and betting. Brian is exceptionally good at hustling people," David replied, grabbing a cue stick as I racked them. I backed away and watched as his one shot put most of them away.

"Looks like you could, too."

He just smiled as he returned the cue stick to its spot. I continued across the room to the French doors that lead to the patio and the pool. The heavy raindrops falling in it caused the water to look as if it was boiling. Glancing off to the right, I spotted two doors. I ventured down the stone hallway and peeked inside, finding both were bathrooms with showers in each.

As I walked back into the main room, I saw on the wall opposite me hung two dartboards. I grabbed the darts from one of them and tried my luck – two in the outer rings and one near the center. David pulled them out and tried from farther than where I stood – all three in the center.

"Show off," I commented under my breath as he put his arm around my shoulder, grinning at me. "So you said there's a wine cellar?" I asked as we walked toward what must be the theater.

"Yes, but it's not complete. We're still building the racks and unloading the wine. Brian, Cary, and Odette are working on it now."

"Oh…that's nice of them…"

"Well, they get their share of the wine," he replied, opening a set of double doors.

It was a smaller version of one of the big chain movie theaters, except the seats were better and the floor wasn't sticky. The red, black, and gold art deco theme harkened back to olden days of early movies. I walked down the aisle and paused at the second row as he motioned for me to sit. He went to the back, dimming the lights and turning on the projector. The seats were so comfortable I could probably watch a daylong marathon.

An old silent movie played on the screen as he sat beside me. "I went with whatever was in it," he whispered. "Looks like Madeline was the last to use it."

There was something familiar about it and after a moment, I realized what we were watching. "*Nosferatu*," I remarked, and he looked at me with raised brows. "When I told you about all the vampire movies I watched, I really meant I've watched a lot." I paused and stared at the screen for a moment. "He's not what I imagine a vampire looks like, though. I like the more romantic version," I commented.

"Like Dracula?" he asked.

"Yeah. How else do you expect them to lure people…not by looking like that," I replied, pointing at the disfigured creature on the screen.

He laughed and my pulse quickened. I loved his beautiful laugh. I cuddled up to him and closed my eyes, happy to be here. My head swam and as I looked up at him, he leaned closer and we kissed, slow and soft at first. Just as I was pressing further, the movie ended.

Taking that cue, he broke away and went ahead of me, turning up the lights as I made my way to the door. We headed back upstairs and into the grand salon. Madeline was still reading, but other than her, the room was empty.

She looked up and smiled as we entered. "What do you think?" she asked excitedly, jumping up from the chair and joining us.

"It's absolutely amazing. You all are so lucky."

"Yeah…we are," she replied, grinning and leaning her head back against David.

He playfully shrugged her off and took my hand, leading me out to the veranda. She stayed in the room, resuming her reading. Sitting on a bench facing the lake, we watched the rain lighten and then get heavy again. He put his arm around me and pulled me closer, and I slipped my arm behind him with my other across his stomach while resting my head on his chest.

We sat quietly, enjoying the peacefulness of the rain and seclusion. There must not be a neighbor for quite a distance. I couldn't see any houses through the trees or across the lake. It must be nice to have so much privacy. This would be a great place to have a party…and that got me thinking about what Ben asked me earlier.

"David…the gang was talking about doing something to celebrate the end of the school year. We usually have something small, but this year they want it to be bigger. Sooo…I was wondering if we could have a school's-out-for-summer party here…"

He was quiet, deep in thought. "I know I'll regret this, but all right. How many people are you thinking about inviting?"

"Maybe our whole class…a hundred or so…"

"Hmm…I'm not sure I want that many…"

"Okay then, we'll keep it fairly intimate – a few of our closest friends. Say thirty?"

"That's more manageable. When would you like to have it?"

"The second Friday in June, if that works for you."

"Yes, it does."

"Do you have any suggestions or ideas?"

"This is your party. It's probably best to work anything else out with your friends. My only request is that it be in the evening."

I was excited he was being so gracious about it. Everyone will be so thrilled Monday when I tell them. We'll need to start planning right away. I gave him a squeeze and then kissed his cheek. He turned his face so our lips met, then he stopped suddenly.

"When is your father's wedding?" he asked, raising an eyebrow.

"Oh crap…the wedding is the second Sunday in June…which means rehearsal will be Saturday night – no, I'll be okay," I replied as I thought it through.

"Sounds like a busy weekend," he commented, his lip curling at the corner.

"Yep, but after that, it'll be quiet. Especially when Dad and Vanessa go on their honeymoon."

"When is that planned?"

"Wednesday after the wedding. They're gone for a week…to the Bahamas."

"Are you going with them?"

"Yeah right. Vanessa would never let me."

"So…you'll be home alone that week?" he asked, his mischievous smile slowly appearing.

"Yeesss…" I dragged out, wondering what he was thinking.

"Maybe if you get lonely during that time, you could stay here," he suggested.

I was stunned by his offer. "W-would you like me to stay over?" I inquired apprehensively.

"Of course I would. You could sleep in the guest room."

"And you'd be okay with me being in the same house with Brian?"

He thought about that for a moment. "I could always send him away," he replied with a smirk.

It'd be nice to spend a night with him. I planned on inviting Claire to hang out one night, so I could work around that. I smiled at him, silently agreeing.

Looking back toward the lake, the sky began to darken and I knew I'd have to go soon. I still needed to run by the mall and pick up the glasses. I guess I could grab something to eat while I was there since I decided not to after I left school. I sighed, not wanting to leave.

"What's wrong?" David asked, taking my hand in his.

"I have to get going. My dad needs me to grab something for him at the mall," I commented, fidgeting with a curl.

"May I go with you?" he requested, gazing into my eyes. "I'm not fond of the idea of you going there alone."

"I guess…but I also have to get something to eat. I forgot to do it after school."

"I will gladly sit with you."

"Okay…ready to go now?"

He nodded and stood, raising me up as he did. We went back inside and he told Madeline what we were doing. "It was good seeing you again. Thank you for allowing me in your room and studio. You're so talented. Oh, and I hope you and Ben have a good time on your date tomorrow," I remarked as I hugged her.

"Thank you! I'm excited about it," she replied, following us to the door.

David smiled at her as we exited the house. I grabbed Ben's umbrella and opened it as we stepped off the porch toward my car. It was still raining, steady now with no storm in sight. I unlocked it, but he was there to open the door for me. I looked at him and smiled, knowing he was just being a gentleman but thought it was uncalled for. He went to the other side as soon as I was seated.

He was quiet as I left the drive and turned onto the main road, heading toward the mall. The radio played softly in the background making the silence not so unbearable. I noticed him staring at me out of the corner of my eye.

"What?" I asked, glancing at him as I weaved through traffic.

"You're beautiful," he replied.

I didn't think I looked particularly amazing tonight. "Really? I'm not feeling it today," I responded.

"But you are," he retorted.

I blushed and tucked my head slightly, keeping my eyes on the road. I turned into the mall parking lot and picked a spot as close as I could to the entrance I needed to be at. We got out of the car and walked arm in arm to the door.

The mall was as busy as it usually was on a Friday night. Oddly enough, when we entered, David was the center of attention. Everyone we passed stopped what they were doing and stared at him. It was as if he was famous, but no one knew why. He put his arm around me and grinned.

"Where do you need to go?" he asked, heads turning our way.

"Oh...I guess to eat first."

I veered toward the food court, but he stopped me. "No...let's go to a restaurant," he commented, and we headed to the nearest one.

He requested a table for two and we were seated immediately in a dark corner. He pushed his menu aside while I glanced through mine. The waitress came over and introduced herself, then took our drink order...well, my drink order. David sat patiently as I went ahead and ordered my food.

"So you're not going to eat...do you ever eat?" I asked, staring at him across the table.

He grinned and my heart skipped a beat. "I have a very discriminating palate."

"And you're not thirsty?"

"No, I'm fine. What is it that you have to pick up?" he asked, changing the subject.

The waitress brought my food and glanced at him. "Sure you don't want anything, handsome?"

"No, that will be all," he replied with a courteous smile. She threw her hand to her chest before stumbling away.

I shook my head and then answered his question after taking a bite of salad. "Vanessa had a pair of champagne glasses engraved and Dad wants me to pick them up. I told him we were hanging out at the mall because saying we were going to the park wouldn't be believable," I explained, quickly taking another bite so I could avoid talking.

He just cocked his head to the side and stared at me. I glanced down at my food and continued eating. I hate it when people watch me eat. The waitress came by at that moment to check on us, smoothing out her apron and playing with her hair. David slowly turned his head toward her and grinned.

"Could we have the check, please," he purred.

She grabbed the back of his chair to steady herself. "Right away," she breathed.

She turned quickly and ran into another server, making him drop several plates and glasses. The shattering clash cut through the music and conversations, jarring me for a moment. Embarrassed, she glanced over her shoulder at David as she helped clean up the broken dishes.

He returned her gaze and then looked at me, laughing quietly. What's with him? It's like he enjoys making her act this way. I narrowed my eyes and his face became solemn. After a couple of minutes, the waitress returned with the check. As I pulled the wallet from my purse and took out a twenty, he gave her a credit card.

I held up my money and glared at him while she stumbled away. "You don't have to do that…I have money."

"You're welcome," he replied with a smirk.

She returned a moment later and thanked us for coming while he scribbled on the receipt. We got up and left the restaurant, heading back into the mall.

"I hope you gave her a good tip."

"What do you mean?" he asked with a half-smile.

"You know, with the way you were toying with her."

"Oh…yes, I did."

"Is this something you like to do often?" I asked as we walked down the main thoroughfare toward the store.

"No, not really. It happens naturally."

"I've noticed a lot of people act strangely around you."

"You have? How so?" he inquired, hands behind his back and head tilted my way like he was toying with me.

"For instance, at prom. All the girls were fawning over you, but the guys kept their distance."

"There was one guy who was anxious to meet me," he commented, trying to distract me.

"Okay…a majority. And here…look over there," I directed as I pointed to a group of girls in front of a candy store. "Watch them as we pass…"

He did and all of them stared, some of them grabbing onto a friend or shaking wildly. He smiled at one so as not to make it look obvious that we were talking about them and she stood there dumbfounded. He tucked his head and laughed quietly before looking at me again.

"See? That's what I mean! And…and look at the group of guys over there at the game store…watch them."

Again, he looked as they stopped what they were doing and backed farther into the store. One boy came forward and tried to stare him down but couldn't. Like a puppy, he tucked his tail and vanished among the shoppers. Then we came near a couple ring shopping. The woman gazed at David admiringly and the man pulled her close, glaring at him.

He smiled at me and my heart fluttered. "I guess I have a certain air about me," he replied nonchalantly. Yes, he did, but that didn't dignify a verbal response from me.

We turned into the store and he stayed at the front, examining the various trinkets while I went to the counter in the back. No one was there at first, so I rang the bell and suddenly a woman appeared from behind a curtain.

"Hello, I'm here to pick up an order for Wiley…first name Vanessa," I told the lady at the register.

"Ah, yes. It's in the back. One moment," she replied, disappearing again.

I turned and searched the store for David, finding him near the silver keepsakes. A saleswoman was hounding him, but he was patient and cool with her. He smiled as he reached up and delicately lifted a pendant off her chest, examining it. I could see her heaving as she searched for something to grab hold of, knocking several items off a shelf. I giggled but stopped as his eyes lifted and peered directly at me over her shoulder. He smirked as if he was playing a game with me, and I rolled my eyes.

"Miss…miss…" the sales clerk called, tapping my shoulder.

I turned around quickly. "I'm sorry…is that it?"

She nodded and handed the velvet box to me. I opened it and inspected the two crystal glasses as Dad requested. The names were spelled correctly and the right date was on them…yep, they looked fine. I handed it back, nodding approval, and she slipped the box into a bag, passing it to me.

The saleswoman was gone by the time I joined David near the front. He smiled at me and put his arm around my waist, leading me out of the store. When we got outside, the rain was tapering off and the sky began to clear.

"What are your plans for the remainder of the weekend?" he asked as we entered the car.

I thought about it as I left the parking lot and realized I had no plans other than those my father may have for me. "Nothing, unless my dad or Vanessa needs me for wedding preparations," I responded, turning onto the highway.

"Good. I would like to see you tomorrow night…at your house," he requested.

"Do you plan to come through the front door or my balcony doors?"

"I hope the front door. I'll be there around nine, if that's all right."

"Why don't you come over earlier, spend the day? We could go to a park and have a picnic…"

"Unfortunately, I cannot. I have to go out of town for something important," he replied, staring out the window. "There's the driveway…you can drop me off here. I don't expect you to take me all the way to the house."

I pulled in and put the car in park. Turning toward him, I gazed into his eyes. "I had a great evening. Thank you for having me over and go…going to the…mall," I faltered as he leaned closer.

He gently pecked my lips, but I moved faster, putting my hand on his cheek to keep him from pulling away as I kissed him. He didn't seem to fight. Instead, he slipped his hand under my jaw, his silky lips caressing mine slowly. As they parted, I breathed him in, and my heart raced as my head swam, longing to taste him. As I readied my tongue, he stopped.

"I must go," he breathed hard. "I'll see you tomorrow evening. Good night, Megan." He exited the car and quickly disappeared into the darkness.

That was odd.

I paused a moment, then slowly backed out of the drive and headed home. It was nearly eight; I had to rush if I planned to make it on time. Traffic and lights held me up and when I pulled into the drive, it was ten after. I rushed to the door and entered quickly. The clock struck eight as I passed it on my way to the family room.

"Right on time. You're making a habit of this," Dad commented as I leaned against the back of the sofa.

I know the clock in my car said ten after. "Yeah…funny how that is," I replied. "You know, I forgot something in the car. I'll be right back," I commented as I rushed out of the room.

I realized I really did forget something – the glasses. I opened the door to my car and slipped the key in the ignition, turning the power on. Eight-twenty – my clock was fast. David must have changed it at some point. How nice of him to make sure I'd be home on time. I smiled as I grabbed the bag with the glasses in it and went inside.

I handed it to Dad and told him they looked good and there were no mistakes. He thanked me as he set them aside and invited me to sit with him. We talked a little longer about plans for tomorrow, and then I said good night and headed up to bed.

As I lay under my faux sky, I thought about my wonderful evening with David. And I'd get to see him again tomorrow night. I guess Dad would take that opportunity to apologize to him, being that he hasn't seen him since the incident.

I didn't realize how much I missed David until I saw him for the first time today. I hope I won't ever have to go so long without seeing him. Maybe I can convince him to start visiting me again after Dad goes to bed. I really miss having him stay with me until I fell asleep, being used to it lately.

I glanced at the clock and then turned over onto my side, staring out the balcony doors into the darkness. Something glimmered outside and I lifted my head to see better, but whatever it was disappeared. Laying my head back down, my lids began to droop. In between blinks, I thought I saw David's face peering in through the panes, but by the time it registered and I opened my eyes, nothing was there.

Too tired to get up and check, I decided it wasn't him. He would have called or tapped on the window to let me know he was here. And why would he stay outside rather than come in and sit with me? My mind was just playing tricks on me.

I'll fix it. I rolled to my other side and quickly fell asleep.

# Chapter 22
## Interrogation

The sun shone brightly through the windows as I entered the kitchen, watching Dad bustle around. "What's the rush?" I asked, grabbing an apple and rinsing it at the sink.

"Why aren't you dressed? We have to leave in thirty minutes!" he exclaimed, stopping and staring at me.

"Uh...did I miss something? What are we doing?"

"I told you last night...today is one of Vanessa's bridal showers."

Oops, I forgot. "One of them?" I questioned, putting my breakfast back in the fruit bowl.

He grimaced, sighing, "You've been doing so well. Please don't cause any problems now. Come on...it'll all be over soon."

"All right," I replied as I headed up to my room to shower and dress. Not really sure what to wear, I threw on a sundress, grabbed my bag, and headed downstairs. I met Dad at the door and we headed out.

We came to a plain building in downtown Richmond and entered to find Vanessa and company waiting around for us. She glowered as Dad approached and apologized for being late while giving her a kiss on the cheek. Not a moment later, the scowl was gone from her face and she was all smiles as she invited everyone to help themselves to the hors d'oeuvres lunch.

The guests grabbed their food and sat, filling the room with a chattering that increasingly became louder as they gathered around Vanessa. Dad and I decided not to join them. It was funny – the two outsiders sitting at the back of the group while she and her friends and family squawked gossip about other friends and family members. Is this what a bridal shower is usually like?

Dad and I didn't talk much, just observed, shaking our heads occasionally or rolling our eyes as we listened to the idle prattle. But when we did talk, it was about David. "So how was your date yesterday? I forgot to ask," Dad whispered to me as he finished the last of his barbeque meatballs.

"Great. Just walking around, window shopping," I half-lied, nibbling on a ham roll. "Oh, that reminds me. He'll be coming over tonight."

Dad set his plate aside and crossed his arms. "Should I expect him for dinner?"

"No, he'll be over around nine."

He stared at me with an inquisitive expression. "Why so late?"

"He's out of town for the day."

"Oh," he responded, glancing at Vanessa. She winked and blew him a kiss and he smiled slightly. "Hey, I was meaning to ask you. You said he lives off campus. Where?"

I set my plate down and took a sip of punch, giving him a curious look. Why did he want to know? "In a lake community deep in the county."

Vanessa's maid of honor cleared her throat and announced we were starting games, which thankfully dropped the conversation about David for the time being. The first one involved quite a bit of activity and kept us occupied, as did the next several. I didn't win a single one, but of course her friends and family are way more competitive than me.

It wasn't until Vanessa started opening gifts that he had an opportunity to bring it back up again. "Have you been to his house?"

I started to get a little worried, wondering if he might be more aware of my sneaking around than I thought. "No…why do you want to know where he lives?"

"Just curious. You said in a lake community out in the county…those homes are usually quite pricey."

"Really?" I replied, feigning shock. David's house had to be the most elaborate of any I saw.

"What does he do at the medical examiner's office?"

"Assists the Medical Examiner."

"Does he live alone?"

"No, he shares the house with several other people."

He paused, thinking about it a moment. "Do his roommates give him any money for staying there?"

"I don't know…why?" I responded, starting to get irritated with his questions.

"I just find it hard to believe he'd own a home like that."

"His parents died and left him a large inheritance."

"Ah…you know, a lot of lake front homes are custom built. They aren't from a predefined collection like ours."

"Dad, what are you getting at?" I asked, frustrated. I thought he was okay with David. Why was he doing this?

"I just want you to be cautious. You don't know him very well and there are a lot of questions surrounding him. He may not be who you think he is," Dad admonished, and I recalled Mom's words as well.

I tried to contain my anger, but it was hard. "I am very cautious. And I do know quite a bit about him. Maybe you should sit down with him tonight and get to know him."

He contemplated it a moment. "I think I will," he replied, crossing his arms and looking pleased with the idea as he turned his attention back to Vanessa and the group.

Ugh! I just wanted to have a nice, quiet evening with David, but he's going to turn it into a grilling session. Maybe I should call and cancel. He shouldn't have to be subjected to that. Then again, maybe this is what we need to get Dad to realize there's nothing nefarious about him. I'll just warn him when he arrives.

Having to spend the entire day with Vanessa and her nearest and dearest was extremely difficult, not to mention the frustrating quality time with my father, and I was beyond ecstatic when it was all over. Dad was equally happy, though we still weren't talking much.

He invited Vanessa to join us for dinner and questions with David. I could tell by her expression she was conflicted, but luckily she declined. She was going out with her girlfriends, thank God. It was bad enough Dad was going to ask him fifty questions; I didn't need Vanessa cooing and drooling all over him.

Our lack of talkativeness continued as we prepared dinner and then all the way up until we sat to eat. After getting a few bites in, we started joking about Vanessa and her friends and the mood lightened.

I kindly offered to wash dishes after we finished, letting Dad relax in his chair in front of the TV. I washed and watched the clock and as it got closer to nine, I started getting nervous. I wonder what questions he has for David. Hopefully nothing embarrassing.

I was settling on the couch when the doorbell rang. Quickly hopping up, I ran to the door before Dad could move. As I opened it, my heart jumped seeing David there patiently standing on the porch in all his splendor.

"Good evening, Megan," he greeted with a smile, slightly bowing his head.

My heart beat faster and I tried to calm it. "Good evening," I replied slowly. "Did you have a nice trip?" I asked as he entered.

"Trip…yes. It was surprisingly relaxing."

I glanced back into the family room and then pulled him to the side and whispered, "Okay…I have to let you know. My dad wants to ask you some questions, so beware."

He tilted his head and smiled. "I'll be fine…don't worry," he replied as he continued toward the back. But I will worry. He doesn't know my father like I do.

Dad turned and looked at us as we entered. "Hey, David. Have a seat," he directed, and David obliged once I sat.

"Good evening, Mr. Caldwell. How are you?" he asked politely.

"Doing well. Megan and I had a full day and just sat down to relax," he replied, turning off the TV. He set the remote on the coffee table and folded his hands on his lap, his eyes intent on David. "First and foremost, I would like to apologize for my behavior the other night. It was wrong of me to yell at you, especially after you protected Megan, so I thank you from the bottom of my heart," he expressed with all sincerity.

David nodded courteously. "It means a lot to me that you would tell me in person. Thank you," he responded.

I smiled at the both of them, thinking David might be off the hook, but then Dad took a deep breath. Fat chance. "So…with that out of the way, now on to what I really want to do. You know, I don't know a lot about you and you're dating my daughter. Is it all right to take some time to answer a few questions from a concerned father?"

I slipped my hand into David's and held it on my lap. "Of course," he agreed graciously.

Let the games begin.

"Where are you from?"

"Waltham, Massachusetts."

"What did your parents do?"

"My mother was a homemaker and my father was a politician."

"Politician…why didn't you follow in his footsteps?"

David turned his head slightly and stared at Dad. "I'm not like my father, so politics wasn't a good fit for me."

"What was their cause of death?"

"My father had a heart attack and my mother…committed suicide." I didn't know that. I glanced at David, his face emotionless.

Dad paused a moment. "Were you there?"

"No, I had been away."

"Do you have any other family?"

"No, I was an only child, as were my parents."

"Why did you move to Richmond?"

"I was impressed with the college and the city."

"How long have you lived here?"

"About two years."

"Do you rent the house you currently live in?"

"No, I own it."

"Did you buy it from someone?"

"I had it custom built."

"How are you able to afford your house?"

"My parents left me a substantial amount of money in their will, along with several stocks and bonds, making sure I was sufficiently taken care of. I was able to buy the house outright."

"Do you live alone?"

Oh, how sneaky of him. I told Dad he had roommates. "No, I have four roommates."

"Do they pay rent?"

"Yes."

"Do they all go to VCU?"

"All but one. He attends school online."

"What's the distribution in the household?"

I looked at Dad and then David, confused by the question. Apparently, he wasn't. "Three males and two females."

"Have you ever had a relationship with either of the females?"

I clenched David's hand, and he glanced at me and smiled. "No, never."

"Do you ever have parties?"

"Not me personally…but my roommates do. Usually, I'm not present."

"Is there ever alcohol or drugs involved at these parties?"

"Alcohol maybe…never drugs."

"How did you meet Brian?"

David paused. I think he realized Dad knew beforehand about the roommates. "I met him last year in one of the classes we shared. In talking with him and his girlfriend, Odette, he expressed the need to find a place to live since they were evicted. I told him I had plenty of room to spare and they were welcome to stay with me, as long as they didn't mind the distance."

"So he lives with you…"

"Yes."

"Why were they evicted?"

"Their previous roommate held the lease in his name and would take the money they gave him for rent and waste it gambling. They were completely unaware of it until they came home to changed locks."

"His girlfriend lives with you as well?"

"Yes."

"Do they share a room?" I wonder if David will lie.

"Yes, they do," he responded, and I tried not to look surprised.

"Are the other two a couple?"

"No. Madeline is currently dating someone," he replied, glancing at me and smiling. "Cary, on the other hand, is a very private person and isn't one to want to leave the house."

"What's the square footage of your place?" Okay, back to the house.

"Oh…about seven thousand, not including the basement."

Dad looked impressed. "I'd like to see it sometime. Maybe you can give Megan and me a tour."

"I would be delighted."

"How about tomorrow?" Dad asked without hesitation. I glared at him. Why was he so anxious?

David forced a smile and answered, "That won't be a problem. Why don't you come around seven?"

"Why not earlier?"

"I have work."

"Do you mind if I bring Vanessa?"

"Not at all. She will be Megan's stepmother, so she should know who her stepdaughter is dating as well."

"One more question…what attracted you to Megan?"

Oh boy. Please don't be superficial…please don't be superficial…

He gazed at me and smiled. "Her eyes tell of a fearlessness, that no obstacle or trial is too great. Her heart burns with an intense fire, and her will is unwavering. But her soul is pure…human," he answered, his voice soft and smooth. I gazed back with admiration deserving of an idol. Wow…that was so poetic.

"Very nice," Dad responded and David bowed his head slightly, accepting his approval. "All right, I'll leave you two alone now," he continued, turning the TV back on.

David shifted his eyes to me and motioned for me to stand as I remained fixed on him. I got to my feet and he followed, quietly indicating for me to lead him wherever it was we could go to be alone. Knowing Dad wasn't going to approve of us in my room, I led him outside to the gazebo.

We walked arm in arm down the garden path, my head resting on his shoulder. I stared at the sky, wondering if any stars were out, but it was a deep gray nothingness. More rain must be in the forecast for tomorrow.

"I am so sorry about my dad," I apologized all of a sudden.

"It's all right. He's doing his job and making sure you're safe. I hope now he'll trust me."

"I wouldn't hold your breath; we still have to get through tomorrow." I paused and looked at him. "So you're really fine with us coming?"

"Yes," he answered, but there was an edge to his tone that made me think he wasn't.

"I can't believe how honest you were with him. You could have lied," I commented, climbing the stairs to the gazebo and sitting on the swing.

"I figured if I was honest, that would be at least one admirable trait he couldn't deny me," he responded, sitting next to me.

"And what you said about me…was really how you feel?" I asked, gazing into his viridian eyes.

"Yes, Megan, it is. You make me feel different…alive," he whispered, touching my cheek.

I leaned closer. "It was beautiful…what you said."

My lips were within inches of his. I momentarily shifted my eyes toward the house, wondering if Dad was watching us, then back to David. I could smell his skin, his breath, and it was intoxicating. I pressed my lips to his and kissed with a passion I didn't expect. He dropped his hand to my throat and then slid it to my collarbone. Its coolness felt good against my hot skin.

He began kissing my cheek and then down my neck. I tilted my head back as he continued to my throat, his one hand still on my chest and the other on my hip. My body tingled with his touch and my heart raced. I reached up to slip my fingers into his hair when he stopped suddenly, getting up and walking away.

He stood off to the side of the gazebo, pacing back and forth. I watched him, wondering what was wrong. He continued to pace as I looked down at my fingers and fidgeted. Maybe he was uncomfortable with Dad being right there in view.

I glanced up at him, but he wasn't there anymore. Instead, he was crouched near the ground, facing the house with his back to me. I slowly got up and cautiously approached him, placing my hand on his shoulder.

"I'm sor-"

"It's perfectly all right, Megan," he interrupted, glancing up at me and then standing. "You did nothing wrong. I did."

"What do you mean?"

"I let my guard down," he replied as he started toward the house.

"Are you leaving?" I asked, running to catch up.

"Unfortunately, yes. I have some cleaning to do before my guests arrive tomorrow," he responded, a smile flickering across his face.

The house looked clean to me yesterday. "Oh, right."

We entered and walked over to the family room. "Have a good evening, Mr. Caldwell. I look forward to seeing everyone tomorrow," he commented, extending his hand to Dad.

He shook it and smiled at me. "I can't wait. Oh, will your roommates be there?"

David froze. "Some of them will be," he answered slowly.

"Okay, Dad, I think that's enough," I interjected, dragging David from the room. "You should leave before he starts another round of questions. He is a lawyer, you know," I remarked as we headed to the door.

David stepped outside while I glanced back into the family room, making sure my father wasn't watching us like a hawk. Confident his attention was only on the TV, I stepped out and cracked the door. As I turned to face David, he surprised me with a soft kiss.

"I look forward to seeing you most of all," he whispered, gently caressing my cheek.

I blushed and tucked my head, reeling from his unexpected attack. "Hopefully Vanessa won't make a scene," I responded, coming up with something to fill the silence.

"I'm satisfied she will, seeing the house and being in certain company," he remarked.

I kicked at the brick and glanced up at him. "So who will be there?" I asked curiously, now that he brought it up.

"Madeline and Cary. I hope Brian and Odette will be leaving by the time you arrive."

"Me, too. Well, at least Brian. I never really met Odette."

"Trust me, no loss there," he muttered as he ran his fingers over my hair.

I relished his touch, leaning into his hand. "Are you ever going to visit me before bed?" I inquired meekly.

"But I do," he replied.

I glanced over my shoulder through the sidelight. Dad was nowhere in sight. "No, I mean after my Dad has gone to bed," I asked as I moved closer to David.

He grinned. "Good night, Megan."

I guess I won't get an answer. "Good night," I replied, dejected, as he gave me another soft kiss before heading to his car.

I stood there a moment and watched him leave, then stepped inside and shouted a good night back to Dad. It was late enough and I was tired. I climbed the stairs and went into my room, immediately changing and crawling into bed.


To make the day pass quickly, I busied myself with chores. I needed to catch up on them anyway, and it kept my mind occupied so I worried less. Dad stayed out of my way, hiding in his office or lounging on the couch watching a game. I worked until five, when we had dinner, and then got ready to go.

As we sat around waiting for Vanessa, I nervously bounced my leg. I hope it goes well, but I'm not going to bet on it. Dad will be critical of every little thing and person and Vanessa will make a fool of herself. Glancing out the window, I sighed. The weather was dreary and damp, though there was no rain at the moment. Hopefully the house won't look as creepy to them as it had to me. I really would have liked a nicer day to visit.

When Vanessa finally arrived, my jaw dropped at what she was wearing. Dressed to impress, she was in a short sundress unbuttoned far enough for her cleavage to be sufficiently visible. Compared to her, I looked prudish wearing a fitted, V-neck tee and shorts. Dad glanced at her and rolled his eyes as he ushered us out the door to my car. He didn't approve, but he'd never tell her that.

"Got the directions?" he asked me as we climbed in.

"Yep, pulled them off the computer," I replied, handing them to him from the back seat.

"I wonder what style house he has. He seems like the modern type," Vanessa commented. Oh, how wrong she was about him.

She jabbered all the way there about different things, but mostly about seeing the house and meeting the roommates. Dad and I just sat quietly and listened, never able to get a word in edgewise anyway. I wish she'd stop talking altogether. I didn't know if I could take it much longer.

"Oh! There's the driveway!" I slipped out.

Dad skid to a stop, backing up and then pulling in. "How do you know where it is?" he asked. How was I going to cover this up?

"There was a sign. You must have missed it," I answered.

He nodded, seeming to buy it as he drove slowly down the drive a little way and then stopping when he came to the gates. He pressed the button on the call box and David answered, buzzing them open. Continuing slowly down the road, they took in the surroundings while I watched their expressions. Dad's mouth was agape, looking around in disbelief. Unfortunately, the same couldn't be said for Vanessa.

"Wow, look at all this land!" she exclaimed, feverishly glancing around. "I mean, wow! What does he do with all this? It's like he's surrounded by a park or something…" she babbled on. Seeing how she responded to the property, I braced myself for her reaction as the house came into view. "No way!" she screeched.

"Now that's impressive," Dad commented as he pulled around the circle and parked in front of the door. We exited, and they surveyed the grounds as I headed toward the stairs. "How many cars does he have?" he mumbled as he glanced over his shoulder at the garage.

I started up the steps as Dad and Vanessa trailed behind, scanning the exterior and estate. Stalling on the first step, they turned and stared out into the woods, guessing how far the land extended. I reached the top, but before I could knock on the door, it opened. David appeared in the doorway, grinning, and my heart pounded in my chest.

"Please come in," he invited. I moved out of the way as Dad and Vanessa rushed up the steps. They briefly greeted him before entering, and I made sure I was last so I could stay by his side.

"Your house is amazing, David," she gushed as we stood in the foyer.

"Thank you. I wanted something with a European flair," he responded as he shut the door.

Glancing around the room, I noticed different paintings on the wall. There were a lot of landscapes and some familiar pieces the likes of Monet, Renoir, and Van Gogh. Must be copycat artists. I guess he thought Madeline's work was too extreme for my father.

"Yes, very much European. Was it from a pre-made plan?"

"No, it was designed to my specifications."

"It's gorgeous," I commented, pretending like I was seeing it for the first time.

"Ah, but you haven't seen the rest," David played along, leading us into the grand salon.

As I figured, the picture above the fireplace was different, too, replaced with an unfamiliar still life. Madeline sat in the same spot as the other day, reading. I expected to find Brian on the loveseat, but thankfully he wasn't. No sign of Cary or Odette either. Well, if I was to choose who I'd like to be present, it'd be Madeline and only Madeline.

As we entered, she hopped up and glided over to us. "Hi, I'm Madeline. It's a pleasure to meet you all," she greeted in a bubbly voice as she hugged each of us. Dad was dumbfounded by her. When she stepped away, though, he came out of it.

Vanessa stood by David and I as Dad walked away, strolling around the room. "So you're Megan's soon-to-be stepmother," Madeline commented to Vanessa, who was staring at David and caressing her collarbone. She didn't respond.

Dad continued to inspect every inch of the grand salon while Vanessa made a quiet comment to David. I rolled my eyes and turned to Madeline, feeling bad she was being ignored. "How did your date go with Ben last night?" I asked.

"Oh…we had a good time. He really is sweet, brought me flowers," she replied as Dad started toward us.

"That's quite a view of the lake. Do you have a boat, David?" he asked, joining us again.

"Yes, tied up to the dock off to the right."

"Do you fish?"

"No, I just enjoy being on the water. There aren't many people living here, so it's quite serene," he responded. There was a moment of silence between them. "Would you like to see the rest of the house?" he asked.

"Oh, definitely," Vanessa cooed. He smiled at her and she melted.

"May I walk with you?" Madeline asked, slipping up next to my father.

Dad looked at her and answered quietly, almost bashfully. "Sure."

We went through the morning room into the kitchen and worked our way around to the dining room. David pointed out interesting tidbits about the design and woodwork, though Dad really wasn't paying much attention. He seemed to be battling between envy and fascination. Vanessa, however, was hanging on his every word. We crossed the foyer and went to the guest room and library, then headed to the second floor. That was where we ran into Brian.

"Oh, hey Megan… *Vanessa*. David told me he'd have guests by, but I didn't know it'd be you."

Dad moved closer to both of us, getting into a defensive stance. "Mr. Caldwell…this is Brian," David introduced, and Brian extended a leather gloved hand.

"Nice to meet you," Dad grimaced, shaking it.

"Where's Odette?" I asked curiously.

Brian turned toward me and stared, his gray eyes cold and calculating. "She's out in the garage. We were just getting ready to go for a ride," he smirked, moving closer to me. I stepped back behind David as he continued to stare at me, then he shifted his attention to my soon-to-be stepmother. "You look lovely today, *Vanessa*."

She giggled like a schoolgirl and pawed at him. "You're so sweet. Thank you!"

"Going for a ride, huh?" Dad asked in a haughty tone. "The roads are slick. You might want to be careful."

"Brian, I think you should be departing," David commented sternly, stepping between them. "Odette is waiting."

He stared at him and then conceded. "Yes, she has quite a temper if she's kept waiting too long," he sneered and then turned to Dad. "It was nice to meet you, Mr. Caldwell, and to see you two again," he remarked as he looked at us, smirking before descending the stairs.

Madeline came to the front and stood by David but never said anything. He looked at her and then at me. What was that about?

"Let's continue," he commented.

We went to Madeline's studio first, which was not the way it was Friday. The painting on the easel was a perfect replica of the lake out her window and the pile of pictures in the corner was gone. The walls were freshly painted and the floor was clean and clear. Strange.

"So you're an artist," Dad commented with a smile as he turned to her. "You're good."

Vanessa moved in between them. "Maybe I could hire you to do a portrait of me for Jack," she commented snobbishly as she rubbed on him.

"That would be nice. I have a knack for capturing a person's true self," she replied sweetly. I laughed quietly as we exited the room, thinking of how much I'd love to see that.

We didn't go into Brian and Odette's room, but did peek into Cary's. He sat at his desk, working on the computer. He never bothered to look or even speak to us. "Cary is studying for finals," David whispered as we turned and continued to Madeline's bedroom, which wasn't changed.

Heading back across the hallway, we entered through the already open double doors to David's bedroom and Vanessa gasped. I glanced around, noticing he didn't change a single thing about it either. Madeline plopped down on the edge of the bed and watched as Dad and Vanessa wandered around the room and then out onto the veranda like prospective buyers.

"I think they're impressed," I whispered to David.

He looked at me and smiled. "Yes, I believe so."

Briefly shifting his eyes to the French doors, he cupped my chin and quickly kissed me as they paused with their backs to us. I was a little lightheaded when they re-entered and looked at the three of us standing at the foot of the bed. Dad started to say something but lost his train of thought when Madeline joined him and started talking about the theater on the lower level.

Naturally, that was our next stop. We headed down all three sets of stairs, winding into the game room. Vanessa rushed over to the billiard table and racked the balls, smiling at David and Dad. "Who wants to play?" she invited. I rolled my eyes as Dad and Madeline stepped forward, but David stayed beside me.

"Not going to play, David?" Dad asked as he grabbed a cue stick.

"No, sir. I will observe."

"Well, we're odd. We need another player."

"Madeline is quite skilled. You'll be surprised," David replied as she broke the balls. They scattered everywhere, several falling into pockets.

"Looks like you have your choice – stripes or solids?" Dad asked, leaning back, impressed. Vanessa was not.

"I love solids," Madeline replied in a childish voice. She setup and shot again, getting two more in the pockets. When she went to shoot again, she was right in front of us. David purposely nudged her stick and made her miss. She glared at him and then smiled. "Your turn," she conceded to Dad.

"I'll go," Vanessa growled.

She leaned over, her breasts nearly falling out of her dress as she took her shot, and hit a striped ball in a pocket. She moved around the table and purposely stood in front of my father, bending over. She looked at David and bit her lip as she hit the ball, getting another one in. Madeline just stood off to the side and smiled, patiently waiting her turn.

The next one, Vanessa missed. Madeline's turn again. She glanced at David before shooting, and he nodded once to her. In just a few shots, she cleared the table. "Game's over!" she exclaimed as she hung her cue stick. Vanessa huffed and Dad chuckled. Poor guy – he didn't even get to play.

We strolled to the other side of the room and stopped in front of the bar. "Wanna fix me a drink, David?" Vanessa asked playfully as she leaned back against it.

"Oh, I usually don't bartend. That would be Brian's area of expertise," he replied, walking toward the theater.

He opened the doors and ushered us in. Some thriller I've never seen was already playing. Dad sat in one of the seats and reclined as Vanessa sat next to him. "Very nice. I bet the game would look great on this screen. Megan, maybe we should do something like this at our house," he suggested, glancing back at me.

I laughed. "Where? We don't have a basement."

"We could convert the garage," he remarked, returning to the screen.

David stood behind me and watched them, sneaking kisses on my neck and cheek every so often. They felt enticing, and I wanted to give in to them, but I had to focus since my dad was just a few feet from me. "We should move on," I suggested. "Otherwise, you'll never get my dad out of that chair," I added, using my father as an excuse.

Dad chuckled as he and Vanessa joined us in the aisle. We headed back into the main room and waited as David opened the French doors to the patio. We stepped out under the arbors onto it and gazed at his pool. Flowing from a tall rock formation at the far end was a waterfall. And it seemed as though something was behind it.

David, noticing my squinting, whispered, "There's a hidden grotto beneath the waterfall."

I smiled and replied, my voice hushed, "You'll have to show me sometime." He grinned and my heart instantly fluttered.

Apparently, I had taken too much of his attention. Vanessa glanced at him as she slipped off her shoes and asked, "Do you mind?"

"No, go ahead," he responded, smiling.

She faltered, and I hoped she'd fall in, but she quickly regained her balance. Sitting on the edge of the pool, she slipped her legs into the water and pulled her skirt up to the top of her thigh. "Ooo, it's perfect," she commented, leaning back on her palms and closing her eyes. Dad crouched next to her and slid her skirt down before dipping his hand in the water to test it.

He stood soon after and tapped her on the shoulder as he saw David and me walking toward the gate. She hurriedly slipped her shoes on and they rushed to meet us. No alone time for us, I guess. I looked back at Madeline, wondering if she planned to join the group as well, but she waved us on, deciding to stay by the pool since she was barefoot.

"Where to now?" Dad asked, coming up behind us.

"Down to the lake," David replied, opening the gate and ushering us through.

Dad asked several questions about the property on the way, trying to get between David and me. David graciously answered every one, even ridiculous ones Vanessa asked. He was so patient and polite. As we reached the dock, everyone stopped and gazed at the large boat in front of them.

The bottom half was black – David's color of choice evidently – with the cabin in white and the deck in a light cherry. Written on the back in white was a single word in a strange language. The boat was bigger than I expected and in pristine condition. He apparently takes excellent care of his possessions.

Dad stared at the boat, obviously impressed. "What is that, a twenty-eight or twenty-nine footer?"

"Thirty foot, 1859 Herreshoff sloop…with an updated cabin."

"Wow…family heirloom?"

"Yes. It has been in my father's family for generations. When he inherited it, he named it after my mother, Sophia."

"Oh, is that what that weird writing is on the back," Vanessa commented rudely.

"Yes, it's Russian."

"It's in amazing condition for being so old. And it's seaworthy?" Dad inquired.

"As good as she was in her heyday," he replied, looking at the boat nostalgically.

"You'll have to take me out on her sometime." He took the words right out of my mouth. David smiled and nodded, putting his arm around my waist as we left the dock and headed to the small beach next to it.

He stood behind me, his hands on my shoulders, as Dad and Vanessa stood at the water's edge admiring the lake. I wished he was closer but knew he wouldn't risk it being so near my dad. I sighed, watching the water ripple and lap against the shore. The lake was more beautiful up close and exactly as David said earlier…serene. Lifting my eyes to the sky, I noticed it begin to darken, but not because of rain or storm clouds.

"We should head back to the house," he commented.

Dad and Vanessa led the way up the path as David and I trailed a distance behind them. "I think my dad will be okay with you," I whispered to him.

"Does he like cars?"

"What man doesn't? Why?"

"I'm considering showing him the garage."

"What happened to not being pretentious?"

"That flew out the window when he asked to see my house," he replied, his lip curling at the corner.

"Yeah, you're right. Go ahead and show him," I grinned.

When we reached the patio, he led us up a set of stone stairs to the back of the garage, standing by the door as we entered. I immediately scanned the room – there was the BMW and the Bugatti, as well as a plain compact car, an old Jeep, and two motorcycles.

"Are all of these yours?" Vanessa asked, running her hand along the sports car.

"I can only claim the BMW and the Bugatti. The Hyabusas are Brian and Odette's, the Honda is Cary's, and the Commando belongs to Madeline."

If the motorcycles were here, that means Brian and Odette were back. Uneasy, I looked at David and he leaned close, whispering, "There's nothing to worry about."

"You…you have a Bugatti?" Dad stuttered as he stood beside it, afraid to touch it.

"Yes…would you like to take it for a drive?"

I thought he'd collapse. "Wh-what?"

"I insist. You can take it around the neighborhood," he replied, handing Dad the key. Vanessa squealed as she impatiently stood by the door, waiting for him to unlock it.

David hit the button to open the garage door as Dad climbed in and just sat for a moment, taking it all in. He caressed the steering wheel and then the dash, his face frozen in awe. She nudged him and he started the car. Closing his eyes, he listened to the rumble of the engine as he revved it a couple times. David smiled at him and then at me. Dad pulled out and took off, Vanessa howling all the way.

"Glad I could make his day," David chuckled as we walked to the porch.

We sat side by side on the top step and stared down the drive. "How long do you think they'll be?" I asked, leaning on my knees.

"Fifteen minutes…maybe," he replied, caressing my cheek. "I only offered to give us some time alone."

"For what?" I asked dreamily as he leaned in and then kissed me.

The door opened and we immediately separated. "You're still here!" Brian exclaimed as he walked up to us.

"What do you want?" David asked, his teeth clenched.

"Oh, just looking for you. Hey, where's your Dad and Vanessa?" he asked me.

"Out for a ride," I replied.

He glanced toward the garage and grinned. "How nice of you to let them take your ostentatious sports car. I bet that scored big points with Mr. Caldwell," he commented, putting a hand on each of our shoulders. His touch sent a shiver through me. He tightened his grip, making me wince. Crouching down between us, he turned to me and whispered in my ear, "By the way, you look delicious tonight. I'm surprised David can control himself."

I turned away in disgust. Why would he say such a thing? It's not like I'm dressed like Vanessa.

I felt him release me and glanced back. David had him by the arm, jerking him up as he stood. "Step back, Brian," he growled.

They stared at each other for a moment and then he surrendered. "Okay, okay. I was just giving her a compliment. I'll leave you two alone then," he replied with a smirk, backing into the house. David stood at the door until it closed.

In the distance, I heard a car coming down the drive. "They're back," I announced, disappointed.

He started down the steps as they pulled in front of the garage and parked, and I stood to meet them as they walked up to us. Dad shook David's hand and patted him on the back, gushing about the car and the ride. Vanessa grinned all over herself, rambling on about it as well and all the people looking at them.

"I'm glad you enjoyed it," he replied coolly.

"Well, it's getting late. I guess we should go," Dad commented, still smiling.

"It was a pleasure having you over," he responded graciously.

"Yes…thank you for having us," Dad replied and then paused, looking between David and me. "Everything checked out with you. I feel a little more at ease."

"We'll have to get together again soon. Maybe have a cookout? Your place is amazing!" Vanessa gushed, still reeling from the high of the car ride, as she hugged David. He remained stiff as he gently tried to push her off. "You smell so good…" she muttered as she clung tightly to him.

Dad grabbed her wrist and dragged her to the car. "Thank you again," he shouted as he helped her in and then got in the driver's seat.

I turned to David and tucked my hair behind my ear. "Well, I guess I have to go, too. Thank you for tonight," I commented, moving closer.

He put his arms around me. "You are very welcome."

I glanced over his shoulder and saw Dad's eyes in the rearview mirror. "He's watching…I better go," I remarked quietly as I released him.

He didn't pay any attention to me, leaning in and kissing my lips. "I'll see you tomorrow."

"O-okay. Good night," I replied in a daze as he released me and stepped aside.

I walked absently toward the car and climbed in, taking a deep breath as I sat. Then I turned and watched him out the back window as we drove away, standing so still and debonair with his hands behind his back and a half-smile upon his lips.

# Chapter 23
## Concession

I woke up happy and excited.

I get to tell Ben and the gang how my visit went and that we're having the party at David's house. I hurried through my shower and got dressed, rushing down the stairs and into the kitchen. On my way to grab a granola bar, I kissed Dad on the cheek and then dashed out the door. I wanted to get to school as soon as I could to tell everyone the good news. I pulled into the parking lot and waited impatiently by my car for Claire to arrive. She better be here today.

"Hey, Megan. Why're you here so early?" Ben asked as he walked up.

"Waiting for Claire. How was your date? Madeline told me you had a good time."

"Yeah…" he replied, not sounding very convincing as he leaned back against the trunk.

"Doesn't sound like it. What happened?"

"Well, she picked me up about nine. Did you know she drives an old truck-looking Jeep?" he asked and I nodded. "Oh…well anyway, she picked me up and took me to this rundown theater near the college. We sat in torn seats, surrounded by strangely dressed people."

"What did you go see?"

"A bunch of art films. Really weird stuff…"

"Art films like foreign films or art films like they were made by the students?"

"Definitely made by the students. It was like they were trying to get a message across, but it wasn't obvious. There was this one where someone dressed as a rabbit was crossing the road and got hit by a car…it was supposed to symbolize how the government treats its people. This guy tried to explain it to me, but it went over my head."

"So I take it you really didn't have fun."

"No…and I don't think she's my type. She's a little too odd for me."

"I'm sorry," I replied, rubbing his back. He smiled softly. "What you need is a little gamer girl," I teased as I quickly removed my hand. "Any online buddies living nearby you might be interested in?"

"Nah," he responded, moving closer.

"Well, I had a great weekend. I was able to spend lots of time with David. Oh, and his house is amazing!" I exclaimed, moving away. "And you won't believe it – he agreed to let us have our party there!" I revealed, figuring I'd go ahead and ruin his day.

He stepped back, astounded. "He did?"

"Yep. We need to start planning. It's going to be the last day of school."

"That's two weeks away. Wait...isn't that also the weekend of your dad's wedding?"

"Yeah, but it's on Sunday. I don't have a big part, so I don't have to be at every little thing."

"Are you sure you're not going to burn out? Finals, a party, the wedding..."

"I'll be fine. Besides, you and the rest of the gang are going to help plan it with me."

"Great," he responded unenthusiastically as he stared at the ground. "So other than going to the house Friday, did you do anything else exciting this weekend?" he asked as he kicked at the pavement.

"Hmmm...went to one of Vanessa's many bridal showers Saturday, had David over that evening for questioning by Dad, and then went to his house again Sunday with Dad and the step-witch."

He turned his head in my direction, a mixture of relief and worry on his face. "Oh...sounds like it was exciting. So...no trips to the cemetery?"

I gave him a funny look. "No, but..."

Claire pulled up on the other side of my car and quickly got out, interrupting my thought process. "What are you doing here so early?" she asked Ben as she rushed over to me. "You must have booked it to meet Megan when you saw her drive by. You're never here this early."

He made a face at her and she made one back. I rolled my eyes and answered her question. "Waiting for you. I was just telling Ben my good news."

"David wants to whisk you off to some foreign country?" she questioned as Justin joined her side, rolling his eyes.

Drawing my brows together and tilting my head slightly, I slowly answered, "Nooo...but he did agree to have the party at his house."

"Oh my God! Really?" she shrieked and Justin winced.

"Yep. And we have two weeks to plan it. We have to limit our guest list to about thirty, though."

"No problem – that'll make it an exclusive party. So...do any of David's roommates plan to be there?"

"I don't know, I didn't ask. Maybe."

Erin joined us then. "What's with the impromptu meeting?"

"David agreed to have the party at his house," Claire told her.

"Awesome. When?"

"Last day of school – that evening," I replied, checking my phone. "Oh, we better get inside. I didn't realize it was that late. We'll talk more about it at lunch."

We headed to our lockers, buzzing about plans for the party, and then on to our respective classes. Claire and I passed notes in Biology, bouncing ideas off each other, but in the next several classes, I was on my own. In between listening to the lectures and doing class work, I jotted down a few things I thought we might need.

At the bell, I headed to the lunchroom with tons of ideas in my head. I grabbed a salad and sat outside. It was a picturesque day and I wanted to be somewhere away from the crowd. We have such nosy people in our school and didn't need the news of our party spreading around too soon.

"What's his house like?" Erin asked as everyone sat.

"Enormous. Amazing. Gorgeous."

"Okay, nice adjectives, but what exactly do we have to work with?" Ben questioned impatiently.

"Well, he has a pool, hot tub, barbeque pit, game room with a bar, theater, veranda, terrace…"

"Okay, okay…we get it," he huffed angrily.

"So who was there when you arrived?" Claire inquired, focusing more on my visit than party planning.

"Everyone… hey, that reminds me," I responded, turning to her. I leaned in close and whispered, "I wanted to ask you since you're taking French…what does 'Maison de la Mort' stand for?"

"Uh…house of death, I believe. Why?" she replied, giving me a funny look.

What the heck did that mean, I wonder, and why would Brian call it that? "Oh, it's some new movie coming out," I lied and then turned back to the gang. "So, going back to what we were talking about…yeah everyone was there, waiting for me in the 'grand salon'," I continued, watching as everyone's eyes widened. "Cary's really strange, Brian was as he always is, and I didn't really meet Odette. She was sleeping most of the time."

"Madeline wasn't there?" Justin questioned.

"Oh, she was. And I saw her artwork…very interesting…"

"Anywaaay…getting back to the party," Ben interrupted. "Do we know who we want to invite?"

"Yeah, I made a list during study hall. Here…check it over," Claire replied, handing him a sheet of paper.

"Alison…Wyatt…Carrie? Why are you inviting them?" he asked.

"Revenge," she replied, deepening her voice.

"It should be people we want to be there. Here…mark them off," I requested, handing Ben a pen. "Anyone you can think of?"

We created a new list as everyone contributed several names. By the end of lunch, we had our invitees. As we walked to the trash cans, I asked, "Do we want to meet somewhere after school so we can continue planning?"

"Today? Umm…I have to study," Claire replied.

"Yeah, we do have finals," Ben agreed.

"How about we make it a party-planning-slash-study-session, my house, after school?" I suggested. Liking the idea, everyone agreed and then headed on to class.

As Erin and I jogged around the track, I talked to her about Cary. "Be happy you weren't set up with him," I commented. "You two have nothing in common."

"Could you at least tell me what he looks like so I'm not missing anything?" she requested.

"Reddish hair, brown eyes, short…oh, and he's a total computer geek."

"Eww…definitely not my type. Short and a computer geek – that does it right there!" she laughed.

The rest of the day flew and after the last class was dismissed, we met in the parking lot. Ben asked for a ride and I agreed, though I knew I shouldn't. My experiences of him being alone with me have never turned out good. Erin said she had to make a quick stop before coming over and Claire and Justin were following right behind me.

I rolled down the windows and turned up the music, hoping that'd keep Ben from talking. But the warm spring days had turned into unbearably humid summer ones. It didn't take long for me to decide to roll them up and turn on the air.

"There's something strange about them…" Ben commented vaguely.

"Who?" I asked, though I had a feeling.

"Madeline, David…all of them."

"Well, they are older than us…"

"Not by that much." He was quiet for a moment, staring out the window, his light brown hair moving slightly with the air from the vents. "That question you asked Claire at lunch…it wasn't about a movie, was it?"

I hesitated. "No…"

"Who called the house that?"

"Brian. Why?"

"I don't know. I just get this strange feeling about them…David's mannerisms and what I've heard about Brian. Don't you think it's odd he'd call David's place a 'House of Death'?"

"No. Brian's a jerk," I answered, though he was right; I did find it odd. "Maybe he's referring to the fact it was bought with money from David's parents' death."

"Gee, what a nice reminder."

"I think he's jealous of him," I commented.

He was quiet for a moment, hesitant. "Madeline kept nuzzling my neck during the movies and kissing me, but then she'd suddenly turn away or back off when I responded. She'd try again, getting more aggressive, and the same thing would happen."

Okay, too much information, although it sounded a lot like what happens with David and me. I tried to think of something to say, some reason why she'd do that. "She really likes you, but maybe she's worried about going too far. How did you react when she did it?"

"My heart pounded in my chest," he replied and then paused. "Come to think of it, that's when she'd turn away…" he mumbled, staring out the window.

Funny, the same happens with David. "Maybe she stops because she realizes the affect she has on you."

"Does David do anything unusual when you're together?"

Yeah, I can think of plenty, but I'm not telling Ben. "Nope."

"I just don't know if it's a good idea to have the party there. I have a bad feeling about it."

"Ben, you're the one who suggested I ask David if we could use his house," I argued.

"I didn't think you'd actually ask. And if you did, I didn't expect him to agree," he retorted.

"Well, it's too late now," I grumbled as I pulled into the driveway, my frustration with him building. Claire and Justin parked on the street, remaining in the car and talking as we got out. I rushed to the house, leaving Ben behind, and opened the front door. Entering, I instructed them on where to go. "We'll work in the family room," I directed, showing the way.

Justin had a look of shock on his face. "Wow, Megan! I didn't know you were loaded!"

"Justin!" Claire whispered loudly, elbowing him in the ribs.

"Ow! I'm just surprised, that's all. She doesn't act like a snobby, rich kid," he whispered back to her. "You, on the other hand…" he teased, but I interrupted.

"Okay, my dad won't be home for another couple hours. Let's get party planning out of the way and then study. I'll order pizza around five," I announced as everyone settled on the floor. I didn't want him coming home and hearing we were having a party at David's.

The doorbell rang and I dashed to get it. I went over the plans with Erin as I walked her back to where everyone was gathered. She sat between Ben and me, thankfully. I might hit him if he makes any remarks about David or his roommates.

"Do we want a theme?" Claire asked, kicking it off.

"How about a murder mystery dinner or a haunted house?" Ben proposed, glaring directly at me.

"What about a luau?" I suggested, glaring back. "We could make virgin daiquiris and coladas, decorate with tiki torches, lanterns, and have Hawaiian type food…"

"That sounds great!" Erin agreed.

"Much better than Ben's idea. All the girls could wear grass skirts and bikinis and the boys can wear swim trunks and Hawaiian shirts!" Claire chimed in.

"I'm for that!" Justin exclaimed, raising his eyebrows several times at her until she smacked him in the chest. "Do we want a DJ? My brother knows someone," he then offered.

"That'd be great, if you can get him. So who wants to do the shopping?" I asked and Claire's hand shot up. "How am I not surprised?" I laughed.

"What time do we plan to start?" Justin asked.

"Let's see…midnight will work for David, right Megan?" Ben inquired sarcastically.

"I think eight will be good. It'll give people time to get home and change. Plus, we can have torches burning and swim in the dimly lit pool. We also won't have to provide dinner, just hors d'oeuvres."

"That's a great idea," Erin agreed, narrowing her eyes at him. He better change his attitude; he seems to be pissing everyone off.

We discussed several more ideas, then divvied up the work. "So Justin's getting the DJ, Claire and I are shopping for decorations, Erin's handling food, and Ben's doing invitations – perfect! All right…I'm going to place the pizza order," I announced as I hopped up and grabbed the phone in the kitchen.

Erin joined me, telling me what to order while Claire turned on the TV and flipped through the channels. After she found something interesting, she snuggled up to Justin while Ben pulled out his books and sat waiting for us to return. I think he expected to start studying right away, but that wouldn't be the case.

He glanced at Claire and Justin making out and made a face at Erin and me. We couldn't help but laugh and I had to apologize to the person taking our pizza order. I guess he realized how miserable he was making everyone and decided to lighten the mood.

After finishing with the order, we went back to the family room, and Erin squeezed between Claire and Justin so we didn't have to witness their public displays of affection. I sat near Ben, pulling my books out as well just to be ready after dinner. While waiting for the pizza to arrive, we killed time watching TV.

Dad came home, and I told him I took care of dinner and that we were having a study session. He took one look at the family room and turned away. "This is why we need that theater room," he commented as he headed to the stairs.

The pizza arrived a few minutes later and I called him down to get his before we attacked it. Once he had all he wanted, we loaded up our plates and reconvened in the family room to begin studying. Dad sat at the island in the kitchen, watching the TV and us. Every so often, he threw out an answer if we were stumped. At about eight, we decided to call it quits.

Ben caught a ride with Erin rather than call his mom and Claire and Justin left pretty quickly. They wanted to have some time alone before he had to go home since Erin interrupted their love fest. I watched as they departed and then went back inside and joined Dad in the family room. He was in his favorite spot, watching his usual Monday night crime drama.

"Any big plans for the end of the school year?" he asked.

"Yeah, our usual party," I replied, cleaning up the plates and cups that were left behind. I checked the pizza boxes and packed all the leftovers into one and slipped it in the fridge. "We did all the planning before you got here."

"It's not going to be here, I hope."

"No, I wouldn't do that to you. We had a great suggestion…a friend of a friend's house," I lied.

"Any adult chaperones?"

"Of course, Dad. We always do," I replied, only this time they'd be David and his roommates.

"When is it?"

"In two weeks…the last day of school."

"Right before the wedding? Wow, you're going to need your summer vacation to recuperate," he joked.

I grimaced. "I have help and it's not like I have a huge part in the wedding anyway."

"True. Are you inviting David to the party?"

"Of course I am. He *is* my boyfriend."

"Yeah, I guess that makes sense," he replied, turning his attention back to the show.

"I'm going on to bed. My brain's a little overworked from party planning and studying for finals. See you in the morning," I commented, kissing his cheek.

"Good night," he mumbled.

As I changed for bed, my thoughts turned to David, wondering when he'd call. I have to make plans with him to set up a time to decorate. Turning out the overhead light, I switched on the bedside lamp and cuddled into my comforter with a book while I waited. After several minutes, the words began to blur and I started to doze, still holding the book in my hand.

I woke to a cool hand on my cheek and jerked, slicing my finger on the pages. "David…you startled me!" I gasped, sitting up and staring at the red line thickening on the tip. He was frozen, staring at me as I pressed my finger to my mouth to stop the bleeding.

Fixated on my lips, he moved closer until he was inches from my face. He closed his eyes as he breathed in slow and deep. Expecting him to kiss me, I lowered my hand and bit my lip, tasting something metallic on my tongue. He immediately opened his eyes and released his breath, then looked away.

"David?"

He stood and walked across the room. "I'm fine. How was school today?" he asked as he paused on the other side of the bed.

I turned around and looked at him, confused. "Umm…good. Everyone's excited about the party. We did all the planning tonight before studying for finals."

"Really," he commented, sitting on the edge.

"We decided to do a luau. Will that be all right?"

"It's your party."

"When can we come and decorate?"

"What time is it starting?"

"Eight."

"You could come after school. No one will be home, except Cary. I'll give you the code to the gate and a key to the house, but I expect you or your friends will not to wander around, especially upstairs."

"I'll tell them. We'll mainly be in the kitchen, basement, and on the patio anyway. Hey, do you mind if we use the bar to make mixed drinks?"

He looked at me, one eyebrow raised. "Mixed drinks? And I thought you were innocent," he grinned.

"No, virgin daiquiris and coladas – no alcohol," I replied, smacking him as my heart thumped.

"Oh…no, help yourself," he responded, moving closer. "At least you have the hard part out of the way."

"Yeah," I replied, fidgeting with my comforter. "I was wondering…are any of your roommates planning to attend?"

He hesitated. "Probably all of them. Brian and Odette can't pass up a party. Why?"

"Ben has this strange hang up about all of you and was concerned about them being there."

"I will make sure they're on their best behavior."

For some reason, I wasn't assured, but pretended to be. "Okay."

He caressed my cheek and smiled, causing my heart to flutter. I gazed into his eyes and realized something. "Wait…what are you doing here? I thought you weren't going to come to my room anymore."

"I couldn't resist," he purred as he leaned in.

Before I could say anything, his lips touched mine, caressing them soft and slow. I leaned back against my pillow and he followed, his arms on either side of my body and his chest over mine. My head was swimming and my heart racing. He smelled so good…tasted so good. I slipped my hands under his shirt and pulled him closer.

I felt him begin to move away, so I gripped tighter. I didn't want it to stop. He kept trying to get away and eventually broke free, stunning me. Then he immediately turned away and went to the open balcony doors, standing in the frame.

"Are…are you okay?" I asked, quickly sitting up.

"You have to be careful, Megan," he responded with his head bowed and his voice deep and shaky.

All my concerns that had been building to this point finally came to a head. I couldn't take it anymore. "Why do I have to be careful? What are you hiding?" I replied, louder than I should.

He looked up, staring out into the yard. "I'm not ready."

I climbed out of bed, slowly walking up to him. "I need some answers," I whispered, placing my hand on his shoulder.

"I don't have any good ones for you."

I moved around so I was facing him and looked directly in his eyes, taking a deep breath. What I was about to say, I've felt for a long time, but never thought I'd say it to him so soon. "David…I love you," I whispered. He looked surprised by my admission. I placed my hand on his cool cheek and his expression softened. "Please…let me in," I pleaded.

A warm tear streaked down my face as he gazed at me, pain in his arresting green eyes. "I cannot," he replied quietly, lowering them to the floor. "Not now."

I clenched my hand in frustration, wanting to walk away and give up fighting, but instead I relaxed it and wrapped my arms around his body, holding him as I rested my head on his chest. As much as it's killing me that he's hiding something, I'll give him time. He'll tell me when he's ready.

He put his arms around me and held tight, taking a deep breath. Then I felt something cold drop on my shoulder and slip down my chest. Was he crying, too?

His lips brushed the skin by my ear as he whispered, "I have to go." Then he lifted my chin and gazed into my eyes, shadows covering his face, but I could find his clearly. "Megan…I love you, too."

He gently kissed my tear-dampened lips, and then he was gone. I remained there with my heart thumping as a warm breeze blew through the open French doors. He loves me, too. I put my heart out there and he accepted it. I stared out the doors into the yard as I replayed his profession over and over.

He *loves* me...

The loud croak from a nearby tree frog brought me out of my stupor and I closed the doors, stumbling back to my bed. I sat on the edge staring at myself in the vanity mirror. My eyes were puffy and my cheeks were stained with trails of tear residue. And running from my shoulder to my chest was a dark red streak. I looked down at the strange line and dragged my fingers across it.

It was blood.

# Part 2

# Awakening

# Chapter 24
## The Truth

I woke feeling disoriented and exhausted, like waking from a bad dream. But there was no dream last night. It all really happened, though none of it made sense.

As I dragged myself into the bathroom, I tried to rationalize it. The bizarre way David reacted to my cut finger, how he forced himself away when I pulled him closer and said I have to be careful, and then refused to tell me what he was hiding. It was like what I had experienced previously in my dreams. Could it be that I was foreseeing this? Or was something trying to warn me about him?

Then there was the red streak. Staring down at the spot where it had been, I ran my fingers across my skin. The way it streamed down my chest reminded me of the way a tear falls. But it didn't come from my eyes.

I turned away from my troubled reflection and climbed in the shower, standing under the rushing water and relishing the warmth flowing around me, over my face. It was soothing and comforting, like a cocoon, and I didn't want to get out. I wanted to stay as long as I could, letting the water wash away all my worries and concerns. But eventually, I had to get out.

I need to see Mom. With all that's going on, I can't think clearly. She'll help me see or at least comfort me and give me peace for a couple hours. But it's going to have to wait until after school. I just hope I can make it through the day.

Feeling I wasted enough time, I turned the shower off, got out, and dressed. I wasn't as bothered as before, but something still nagged at me and I didn't know what it was. Sighing, I grabbed my bag and headed downstairs.

Dad was at the counter reading his paper as usual, a cup of coffee sitting nearby. I grabbed a yogurt out of the fridge and sat next to him. Briefly glancing over his shoulder at what he was reading, I decided it wasn't worth my attention and instead ate my breakfast. He turned the page and sighed.

"Anything interesting?" I asked, licking my spoon.

"More war, crime, death. Nope…just like every other day."

"I see you're in a good mood this morning," I commented sarcastically.

He put the paper down and looked at me. "Did you know Damian Thomas or Evelyn Moore?"

"I knew of them, not personally. I heard they were missing…the whole school is gossiping about it. Why?"

"They found them yesterday…in Hollywood."

"California? Wow, that's quite a distance…"

"No, cemetery. They were found dead. Double suicide."

"Wh-what?" I asked, dropping my spoon.

"You would tell me if you were having problems, right?" he asked, placing his hand on mine. It was like one of those after school special moments.

"Yes, Dad. And I don't have any problems…well major ones you should be worried about," I replied, jerking it away. I was a little surprised he thought me capable of offing myself.

"Promise you'll talk to me before you do something like this."

"Dad…I would never. Life is too precious."

He looked at me for a moment and decided I was telling the truth. "Okay," he responded. "Well, you better get to school. I'll see you later," he commented, picking up his paper again.

I kissed him on the cheek and headed out the door. All the way to school, I thought about the goth couple. I can't believe Damian and Evelyn killed themselves. They were dark and reclusive, but I didn't think they'd go that far. They must have really loved each other. Well, at least they were together.

When I got to the parking lot, I didn't see anyone. I walked into school and noticed everything was hushed. There were whispers about what happened and a few tears. How could people be so fake? Acting all depressed over someone they never took the time to get to know. Most of them probably teased them or talked about them behind their backs. And now look at them, weeping and seeking counsel. Maybe it was remorse.

As the principal went over morning announcements, he took a moment to offer condolences and let everyone know the counseling office was always open during school hours. Then we had a moment of silence. I looked over at Claire as she busily wrote things down in a journal. Documenting school life in the wake of a tragedy for posterity – why wasn't she on the school paper?

There was a heavy cloud over the school and all the students and faculty within. Classes changed and people dragged themselves wearily to their next destination. You'd think someone big in the school died with the way everyone was acting. Sadly, I hoped this wouldn't last all day.

And it didn't. It was a little livelier at lunch. The shock and sadness had worn off and the speculation began. As I passed table after table, I heard different theories about the goth couple's death: pagan ritual, forbidden love, boredom. I laughed to myself at the idiocy of some people.

"So I take it everyone heard the news," I remarked as I took a seat.

"Yeah. Apparent double suicide, like some weird ritual," Erin responded.

"They were found in Hollywood Cemetery at the grave of John Bannister Tabb. They had candles all around and were lying in each other's arms, their wrists slit," Claire elaborated.

"Wow…who would have thought? That's devotion," Justin commented.

"Devotion? That's twisted!" Ben exclaimed.

"Well, Damien would do anything for her and I guess if things were bad enough…" Erin babbled, no one really paying attention to her as she continued. "I was more shocked by the fact that he was the son of a doctor dating the likes of her."

"What's strange is they were completely drained of blood and yet there was very little found around them. Also, no suicide note," Claire mentioned.

"So, what? You think it's a cover-up for murder?" Justin asked.

"I'm just saying…it's been awhile since the Ghost struck. Maybe he changed his pattern because of the DNA sample they had."

"Yeah, but they threw it out because it was contaminated," he pointed out. "Maybe he moved on, had enough."

"Highly unlikely. No, he'd strike again. They love the attention. He was probably a spectator at the crime scene."

"I seriously hope you plan to pursue forensics as a career since you have such a sick fascination with it," I commented to her.

"But the police have ruled it a suicide. Case closed," he argued.

"They want it closed. There's a serial killer out there they have yet to apprehend, plus all the other murders unsolved in the area and now two teenagers dead – it's a bad reflection on them," she retorted.

They went on like that for the rest of lunch, arguing over that case and others. Ben, Erin, and I rolled our eyes and had our own conversation, staying out of their lover's quarrel. We were all relieved when the bell rang and could move on to something else.

Now a new concern on my mind, I thought about what Claire said for the rest of the day. What if she's right? What if it was a cover-up for a murder? Maybe there's some information we're missing that the police are keeping from the media. No, it had to be a suicide. It makes sense.

The last bell rang and Ben and I met up with everyone else, walking to the parking lot. I wasn't in the mood to talk, so I just listened. When Justin and Claire started arguing about the suicide again, I told everyone I had to go. I wasn't interested in revisiting that discussion.

I didn't tell anyone I was going to the cemetery. I seriously reconsidered it after hearing the news of the suicide, but decided it shouldn't stop me. There was nothing to fear or worry about. If the Ghost was still out there, he wouldn't strike this soon. I was safe, especially in my sanctuary.

I parked outside the cemetery, figuring I may be staying late, and walked slowly to the crypt, purposely avoiding Tabb's grave. I finally reached it and entered, taking my usual seat beside Mom. I stared out the door at the clear blue sky, watching the clouds drift by and change shape, their movement mesmerizing. I leaned my head against my mom's plaque and closed my eyes…just for a second.

But the second turned into a minute and soon I was fast asleep.

*Megan…it's not safe…you have to leave…*

I woke suddenly to the sound of an owl hooting loudly, my eyes opening to total darkness as I scrambled to my feet. I can't believe I slept that long! I searched my purse for my phone and pulled it out – the battery was dead. I looked for David's and found it fully charged. Thank goodness at least one of them was working. Checking the time, my heart sunk. It was nine thirty-seven. Dad was probably worried sick.

I stepped out of the crypt and called him, pacing back and forth in front of it. I hope he picks up, though I know he'll wonder why I'm calling from a strange number. It rang a couple more times and then he finally answered.

"Hey, Dad, it's Megan. I forgot to tell you I was going to Jessica's for a study group," I lied.

"I almost didn't pick up. The number was unavailable," he commented. Behind me, a bush rustled and I turned toward it. Nothing was there.

"Oh, sorry. My phone died so I had to borrow someone else's. We're finishing up now, so I'll be home soon," I informed him as I sat on the steps of the crypt, holding my head.

"Okay, be careful. See you when you get here," he replied and hung up.

I slipped the phone back into my purse and stared out over the river. I don't feel any better, but I don't remember dreaming about Mom either. She didn't visit me this time…or did she? I recall a voice, urgently pleading for me to leave. Was that her?

I heard the slight crunching of dry grass nearby and turned toward it, but again found nothing. Uneasiness came over me and for the first time, I didn't feel safe in the cemetery. If it was her telling me to leave, I needed to heed her warning and get out of there.

It was hard seeing in the darkness, but luckily I knew the cemetery pretty well. I headed toward the front, keeping my eyes focused on the path. Every once in a while, I heard an odd noise that made me pause and look around, but for the most part, I avoided stopping.

There's nothing to be afraid of…

My self-assurance wasn't working. I picked up the pace, feeling uncomfortable and a little scared. It seemed to be taking forever to get there. I heard a twig snap and turned to catch the culprit. Nothing again. If I believed in ghosts, I'd blame them.

I took a break, soothing my rattled nerves as I backed up to a nearby crypt and glanced around. It was eerily quiet and still, not an animal or insect making a single sound. The darkness and silence were almost suffocating.

I need to go...

There was a soft thud on the roof and a familiar cackle followed, like the one I heard in the college library. I was too scared to look. Instead, I turned and tried to open the doors, thinking I could hide inside, but they were welded shut.

Then I realized what crypt I was at – W. W. Pool's, the Richmond Vampire. A scraping sound and another dry cackle pierced the night, and this time I glanced up. Eerily gleaming eyes stared back at me, stopping my heart's rapid beating. I gasped as I backed away, bumping into a firm object.

"Good evening, Megan," the voice purred.

I turned and faced him, stumbling away. "Brian! Wh-what are you doing here?" There was a soft thump behind me and I backed into another firm object. I so don't want to know who that is.

"Is this David's girl?" a female voice snarled at my ear. Sharp nails ran along my neck, sending shivers down my spine. I tried to stay as still as possible.

Brian sauntered closer, cocking his head slightly and grinning. "That she is, Odette. Pretty, isn't she?" He reached up and held my chin in his icy hand.

"Hmph, she's okay," she replied, envy in her sultry voice.

"Is there a reason you're here, stalking me?" I asked firmly, jerking out of his grasp.

"You and David aren't the only ones who like to hang out in cemeteries," he responded, his pale gray eyes staring into mine. "And I'm not stalking you; I was waiting for you. I hoped we could talk, since we didn't have an opportunity that night at your house," he grinned.

I looked at him, confused. He was at my house? I searched my memory for his visit, but the only thing that came to mind was the nightmare I had after watching that horror movie. "What do you mean? That never happened..."

"Oh, dear. Did David erase that, too?" he remarked, feigned concern on his face.

"What?"

"I was there, at your balcony door, calling for you. I left the scratch marks on the frame."

"H-how do you know that?" I questioned, stunned. "It was a dream."

"It was no dream. I really was there," he replied nonchalantly. "I only wanted you to let me in."

I knew that night seemed too real to be all in my head. "Why?" I inquired, needing to know his reason.

"I wanted to warn you."

"Warn me? About what?"

Odette snickered as he smirked. "David, of course."

I tried to read him and all I saw was deceit. "No, you're lying," I accused.

"Why would I lie? He's the liar. He's the one hiding what he is because of your kind, because of *you*."

"You…you're wrong," I shot back, knowing David was keeping something from me, but not wanting to admit it to him.

"But he is. Why else would he cover up my visit?"

I tried to think of something. "Because you have ulterior motives," I responded.

"Maybe…maybe not."

"What do you want?" I questioned, tiring of his game.

"For him to accept what he is," he replied. He focused on me, making me uneasy. "And that starts with you."

I scrunched my brows. "How?"

He grinned. "Let him be what he was born to be."

"I am," I argued, and Odette snorted behind me.

"No, that's just a pathetic façade. Just give in to him and you'll see," he suggested as he stepped closer, his hand slithering around my waist. His eyes remained fixed on mine as he leaned in. "Or better yet, give in to me," he whispered and my skin prickled.

I shoved off him, breaking from his grasp, and he chuckled, but stopped short as he shot a look at Odette. They were embroiled in a silent argument, and I made the split decision to run. There was nothing I needed to hear from them. It was all to distract and deceive me.

I bolted, dashing up the hill and dodging graves as I went. I didn't hear them behind me, but that didn't mean they weren't following me. I saw a crypt in front of me and was just about to seize the handles when something grabbed my waist and threw me back.

It took a moment to register the impact. I rubbed my head as I stood, looking around at where I was. Brian and Odette were in front of me, laughing. Crime scene tape wrapped my arms and body, and I turned to find out what I hit. It was the grave of Tabb – where they found Damian and Evelyn yesterday. I gasped and backed away, tearing the plastic off me.

"I see you've found the site our latest handiwork," Brian commented, grabbing my arm and pulling me closer as he smelled my hair.

"Your handiwork? But it…it was a suicide…"

"We made it look that way, love," Odette responded, running her nails along the side of my face as she stood beside him. She inhaled deeply.

"Do you like the location…so very poetic," he continued as he jerked me closer to the tombstone.

I glanced at the epitaph, remembering it from all the times I had read it when I'd stroll around the cemetery. "Are…are you behind the other murders, too?" I asked as he released me. I turned to face them, backing away slowly as they moved closer.

"What murders might those be?" he inquired as she cackled.

"The…the Richmond Parks Ghost."

"Oh, yes. That would be us," he admitted, proud of it.

"W-why?" I questioned, not really sure if I wanted to know. I glanced around to see if there was a way to escape.

"The reason has to do with David," he answered coolly. Then he noticed my fevered glances. "You're not thinking of running again, are you?"

I stopped, bumping my back into a large bush as they continued toward me. "N-no. Why would you think that?" I asked, determining a way out of this.

He grinned and moved quickly to grab me, but I dodged him, slipping around the side of it. I sprinted into the graveyard and as I ran, I fumbled in my purse and pulled out David's phone. I went to received calls and hit the first number I saw. It had to be his. I just hope he had the phone on him.

Brian and Odette weren't far behind, laughing and taunting me, their voices echoing through the cemetery. I hid behind a large monument, waiting for David to pick up. My heart pounded in my chest as he answered.

"David," I whispered, panic in my voice. "I'm in Hollywood Cemetery…Brian and Odette are here. They're after me…"

"I'm on my way. Are you all right?"

"Yeah…I'm hiding behind an obelisk near Presidents Circle. Please hurry."

"I will…Megan, don't let them catch you," he warned, but not soon enough.

Brian ripped the phone from my hand and glared at me. "Too late," he growled into the receiver and hung up.

Odette jerked me up and pinned my arms behind my back with one hand while the other held my forehead. She was small, but extremely strong. "Silly girl, thinking you could outrun *us*," she cackled in my ear.

Brian tossed the phone over his shoulder and sidled up to me. "You really shouldn't have done that, Megan. Now you've ruined my plans."

"Wh-what was it you wanted to tell me?" I asked, trying to delay him.

"Do it, Brian! Don't waste any more time! She's trying to trick you," she hissed.

"No...she should still know," he grinned, moving closer

"Yes, I need...need to know. What's the truth...about David?" I begged.

He chuckled, relishing my weakness. Caressing my neck, he smirked. "He's a vampire."

My heart stopped.

But it all made sense – all the strange things I had noticed, the weird dreams, his resistance. *David was a vampire.*

And it didn't bother me. Actually, I was relieved. I knew the truth and it wasn't as bad as I thought it'd be.

Brian stared at me, grinning. "I love this part," he snickered, waiting for a reaction. But I had nothing for him aside from a placid smile.

"What's wrong with her?" Odette asked, staring at me. "Why isn't she scared?"

"Maybe this will scare her," he responded as he bared his teeth, his canines growing longer. I screamed and thrashed as he neared my neck and then suddenly I hit the ground.

"David," she gasped, backing away from me as she stared at him with fear in her eyes.

He had Brian by the throat, holding him in the air. His jaw was set as he stared silently with malicious intent. Then he dropped him and Brian scooted back, coughing. "We were just playing around," he admitted as he stood, rubbing his throat.

"Leave," David growled, not looking at me.

Odette joined Brian's side and they hesitated a moment before taking off into the darkness. The cemetery was still as David stood with his back to me. I stared at the ground, not sure what to say. I reached up and touched my neck, checking to see if Brian did any damage.

"I caught him before he did," David whispered. I looked up, finding him kneeling in front of me, and gasped, my hand automatically moving to my throat. He looked away, pained by my action.

"No, no! It's not you! You startled me," I clarified, touching his arm. "Honestly."

Raising his enthralling eyes to mine, he furrowed his brow as he tried to read me. "You're not afraid?"

"You haven't given me a reason to be," I replied, sitting up on my knees. "I love you, David, no matter what," I continued, smiling softly. He smiled back and my heart fluttered. Now I knew why.

"I feared you wouldn't accept me as I am," he whispered as he caressed my cheek, his touch soft and gentle.

"You can't get rid of me that easily," I mused.

"I never planned on it," he responded, leaning in closer and delicately kissing my lips. My head was in a fog, but as he moved away it cleared. "Are you all right?" he inquired, briefly examining me.

"Yeah…my head's a little tender from the hit, but other than that…" I responded.

"You have a small gash, but you'll be fine," he commented as he stood.

He extended his hand and I gladly took it. As he effortlessly raised me up, he brought me close to him and gazed into my eyes. There was peace in them, relief that I now knew what he was and still wanted to be with him. He kissed me again and then turned to leave.

"So wait…are all of your roommates vampires?" I asked, walking with him through the graves.

He flinched. "Yes, they are," he responded, bending down and picking something off the ground. He checked it over and then handed it to me – my phone.

Suddenly, it dawned on me. "Hold on…so you mean to tell me we set Ben up with a vampire?" I exclaimed, stopping abruptly.

He closed his eyes briefly and sighed. "Exactly," he replied nonchalantly as he urged me on. "That's why I agreed so easily to it, hoping she would make him forget about you. It worked for a little while."

"Oh, this explains a whole lot," I commented as we approached a fence.

He helped me up and I perched at the top, waiting for him. He climbed it with ease and dropped gracefully to the other side. I readied myself to jump and then let go.

Landing in his arms, he lowered me slowly to the ground as he brought me closer to his body. "You're not allowed to tell anyone," he instructed, his eyes focused on mine.

"I won't," I whispered with a smile.

He grinned and kissed me before turning around and linking my arm with his. We casually strolled to my car and when we reached it, we stood next to it with nothing to say to each other. The silence was beautiful.

Gazing into my eyes, he took my face in his cold hands. He leaned in and kissed my lips, slow and passionate. I replied, throwing my arms around his neck and pulling him closer. He stopped but didn't pull away. Pressing his forehead to mine, he separated our lips and closed his eyes. His breathing was heavy and his hands were tight on my face. Soon it slowed to almost nothing. With a gentle peck, he backed away.

"You will be safe; I'll make sure of it. If they come by your house, call me and don't let them in. They can't enter unless invited."

I nodded and turned to unlock my door. "I'm going to have a lot of questions for you the next time we meet," I remarked, glancing over my shoulder and grinning.

"And I'll be ready with answers," he replied, his lip curling at the corner before he turned and walked away.

# Chapter 25
## The Picnic

I stared out the window as Mr. McKeown droned on about the Cold War, the gray of the day making me drowsy. To avoid falling asleep, I glanced around the room at my fellow classmates and what they were doing to stay awake. Some doodled, others secretly played games on their phones, and a couple just gave in.

I turned my attention back to the teacher, but soon my mind wandered. I thought about David and how I hadn't heard from him in several days. Was he avoiding me now that I knew his secret? Or could Brian and Odette have done something to him? I started to fret, hoping neither was the case.

Okay, so maybe that was the wrong thing to think about. I discreetly pulled out the phone he gave me and checked to see if he called and by chance I missed it. No such luck. Maybe I should call him. No, I can't do that. There's a good reason why he hasn't contacted me. I looked at the clock and couldn't believe I still had another class to go. I didn't know how I made it the whole morning without worrying about him.

When I got to English, Ben instantly noticed my troubled expression. I briefly explained that it was about something else, but he wasn't buying it. He pressed further, but luckily the bell rang and the teacher immediately began handing out tests. Thank goodness I had that to focus on and not David. Of course once I finished, my worry returned.

The last bell rang and Ben and I met up with the rest of the gang as I tried to look unbothered. We grabbed our things from our lockers and headed down the hall, everyone else jabbering while I remained silent. My mind was still on David and my fear was deepening. How was I going to make it through the weekend if I didn't hear from him?

"You haven't talked about David in a while. Is everything okay between you two?" Claire asked, concerned. "We're still going to be able to have the party at his place, right? I mean, we can't change now…the invitations have already gone out and everything," she continued, not giving me a chance to answer.

"If he hurt you, so help me…" Ben threatened, breaking in before I could respond.

"Guys! Everything's fine and the party's still on. And no, he hasn't hurt me in any way. He…had to go out of town for a couple of days," I lied. Claire gave me a look, trying to read me, Erin just smiled and accepted it, and Ben grumbled to himself while Justin looked at the wall.

On the way to the parking lot, the discussion switched to how horrible the day had been and how glad we were it was Friday. It was still gray and gloomy outside, matching the dismalness of the day's events. Hopefully the weather would improve for the weekend.

I kept my eyes downcast, still wondering about David. No one seemed to think anything of it, though. They had moved on and were now discussing plans for the weekend. They were wondering about mine and if it'd involve my boyfriend when Ben suddenly blurted out, "Speak of the Devil…"

I followed his glare and was astonished to see David leaning against my car, a mischievous smirk on his lips. I stared at him, shocked he was here and out during the day. We approached the car and his smile widened as my heart thumped loudly.

"Good afternoon, Megan," he greeted as he put his arm around my waist and pulled me to his side. "Sorry I haven't called. I wanted to surprise you," he whispered in my ear. Then he gave me a small peck on the cheek. His lips were icy against the burning of my skin.

My head was swimming and I had a hard time focusing as my body shook being so close to him. I did everything I could not to let it show, forcing myself to concentrate and be steady. "I've missed you," I whispered back, my voice trembling slightly.

He smiled and then turned his attention away from me, sensing everyone watching us. "It's good to see all of you again."

No one responded. Claire and Erin just beamed ear to ear, totally mesmerized, Justin stood off to the side, not wanting any kind of confrontation, and Ben was in a defensive pose, his arms crossed and eyes narrowed as he sized up David. Now I understood why everyone had acted so strange around him at prom and in public.

"Why are you here?" Ben asked harshly. "I thought you were out of town."

"Ben!" I exclaimed, stunned by his abruptness.

David glanced at me, an eyebrow raised, and then smiled politely. "I came back early and thought I would surprise Megan," he responded coolly. Ben had no retort to that and I grinned in spite of myself.

David tightened his hold around my waist and gazed into my eyes. They were more brilliant than I've ever seen them, like a forest in early summer after a sudden shower – fresh, bright, and glistening. Caught up in them, everything shrank away, leaving him and me in silence and alone.

"We must be going. I have plans for a picnic in the park," he announced suddenly, breaking my concentration and bringing me back to reality.

"Awww, that's so sweet," Claire cooed, finally coming out of the daze.

"Who goes on a picnic in this weather? It could rain at any moment," Ben snapped.

Erin recovered from the daze as well, turning on him. "Oh, stop being so jealous," she ordered, pushing him aside to get closer to my boyfriend. "It's the thought that counts, right *David?*" she swooned.

I tried not to laugh at how they were acting. They were so enchanted with him. He could care less, though he found them just as humorous. I guess he was used to it.

From across the lot, Justin called for Claire. He must have slipped away at some point, feeling uncomfortable in David's presence. I shook her shoulder and pointed him out after she didn't respond.

"Oh, crap! I forgot I was riding home with him today." she exclaimed. She waved to him and then frowned, disappointed in having to leave. "I'll call you later, Megan," she commented and then looked directly at my boyfriend. "It was good seeing you again, David," she breathed, trying to keep her composure as he gazed into her eyes.

"Likewise, *Claire*," he purred and she nearly fell apart. I hit him in the chest and he just chuckled. I think he's purposely torturing my friends.

"See ya, Claire," I responded, hoping she'd leave before he tormented her further. She hesitated and then stumbled toward Justin's car, trying to clear her head.

Erin and Ben were still hanging around, and it didn't look like they wanted to leave either. I unlocked my door, hoping they'd get the hint as I climbed in the car. Sitting sideways in my seat with the door propped open, I quietly asked David if he was riding with me.

"No, I'll follow you home and we'll take my car to the park," he replied.

"Where is your car?" I inquired, looking around.

"I had to park around the corner. The lot was rather full when I arrived," he responded.

Ben coughed, getting our attention. "Well, I guess I'll head home. Got a long walk...hope it doesn't rain," he announced.

I knew I'd regret it, but I offered anyway. I was such a sucker. "Would you like a ride, Ben?" I asked.

"That'd be great," he replied excitedly, walking around to the passenger side and opening the door.

David arched his brow, wondering what I was doing. "It'll be fine," I whispered as I shut the door and rolled down my window. "Just keep up."

He grinned and leaned in closer. "Oh, I will," he responded. My heart went wild as his lips gently caressed mine. I wanted more, pushing him for it, but instead he pulled away slightly and paused a moment, his eyes shut and jaw tight. He took a deep breath and moved his head so he could see

Ben in the seat next to me. "It was nice to see you again, Ben. Maybe next time, I can give you a ride."

Ben grimaced, not really keen on the idea. "Yeah, maybe."

David straightened up and turned to Erin, telling her the same as the others as she giggled nervously. I've never seen her act like that. He glanced over his shoulder at me, smiling as he walked away, and then disappeared around the corner.

"Heading out, too, Erin?" I asked, breaking her concentration on him.

"Oh, uh, yeah," she replied, snapping out of her stupor.

"Well, you should get going," I suggested with a smile.

"Yep. See you later," she replied as she jogged to her car with a grin.

Figuring I wouldn't have to wait long for David, I started the car. I turned to say something to Ben but was distracted by the intimidating black sports car pulling into the spot next to mine. His jaw dropped and I just had to laugh, knowing who it was.

The window lowered, revealing David's smirk, and I lowered mine. "Are we ready to go?" he asked, revving the engine. I nodded and then took off.

He stayed on my tail as I wound through nearby neighborhoods with Ben holding on for dear life. It really wasn't a far drive to his house, but I lengthened the trip a little to see how well David could keep up. He was better than I expected. I whipped into the driveway as he pulled up to the curb and waited.

It hadn't registered with Ben that he was home. "Well...here we are," I announced as he sat hyperventilating. As my words sunk in, he straightened up in the seat and ran his hand over his hair, trying to calm himself.

He took a deep breath and turned toward me. "Megan, I want to say something to you before you go." I rolled my eyes. "Please...just humor me," he requested.

"All right. What is it?"

"I...I..." He glanced over his shoulder at David's car, searching for him. The windows were so dark you couldn't see inside.

"Yes," I coaxed, bringing his attention back to me.

"I...have a bad feeling about David. I can't put my finger on it," he continued, genuine concern in his eyes. I tried not to smile, knowing the reason why he felt that way.

"It's okay, Ben. I'm in no danger. I'll be fine," I assured him.

He started to argue, but then sighed. "Well...as always, I'm here for you if you need me," he whispered as he leaned in and gave me a hug. "For anything."

"Okay...thanks. Enjoy your weekend."

He opened the door and stepped out, pausing a moment before poking his head back in. He looked like he wanted to say something else, but instead gave a weak smile and shut it. As he walked up the sidewalk, he raised a hand, acknowledging David, and then went inside the house.

I didn't drive as crazy on my way home, with my mind being elsewhere. I understand his concern, but why does Ben feel the need to be so overbearing? He's my friend, not my father or brother. I can defend myself if I have to, though I know I don't need to with David. He's just so hung up on me that he's letting his resentment blind him.

I was so deep in thought, I didn't notice David pulling up next to me at a stoplight. He honked his horn to get my attention. "Are you all right?" he asked.

"Yeah, just preoccupied," I responded.

"I think I know my way from here. Shall we race home?"

I grinned, instantly forgetting my issue with Ben. "You're on!"

The light changed and we were off, neck and neck for a long time. But I wasn't going to let him beat me. Knowing a traffic trap was coming up, I suddenly turned down a side street and lost him instantly as I raced toward home. Screeching to a halt in the driveway, I quickly jumped out and ran to the back, leaning against the trunk as he pulled in behind me. He gracefully stepped out of his car and casually walked toward me, smiling.

"That was a bit unfair, don't you think?" he commented, putting his arm around me.

"No, because I won," I replied with a smirk.

"Fair enough," he grinned and my heart beat faster. "We should be on our way. I don't want your picnic to spoil."

He led me to the passenger side of the car and opened the door. As I sat, I was surprised by how bold the burnt orange interior was. I hadn't seen the Bugatti during the day and those times I was in it at night, it looked more on the brown side.

The mixture of leather and him was totally intoxicating. As my head swam, I propped my arm on the door and leaned into my hand, playing with my hair while I waited for him to get situated. As soon as he started the car, I rolled the window down slightly so I could clear my befuddled brain.

"Do you know where you're going?" I asked as he backed out.

"Of course. Why do you think I'm driving?"

"Sooo…where are we going?"

"Maymont," he answered, looking out of the corner of his eye at me.

I smiled, but then I was serious. "Why are you doing this?"

"You said you would have a lot of questions for me, so I thought it would be nice to answer them in a comfortable environment. I packed dinner for you in case we ran late."

"Can I ask you one question right now that's really bothering me?" I inquired.

"Let me guess…you want to know why I'm out during the day?" he replied with a smirk.

"Yeah…how did you know?"

"It would be the most obvious question to ask first. Besides, I planned it that way, wanting to debunk one of the many misconceptions about *us*."

"So there are lots of misconceptions about…vampires?" I hesitated saying the word aloud, and he flinched at the mention of it.

"Yes, but we'll get into that later. To answer your question, I can move around during the day as long as the sun isn't shining. The clouds act as a fine mesh shield, preventing the rays from penetrating."

"What happens if you're exposed to sunlight?"

"We become weak and sick and then begin to burn slowly. Not like catching fire; more like a sunburn, but very progressive."

"So that explains the dark curtains over the windows and around the beds."

"Yes. I love the view but only get to enjoy it on overcast days or at night."

I looked out the darkened window at the scenery and imagined seeing the world that way all the time. "How terrible," I commented quietly. Then I turned toward him and asked softly, "Do you miss the sun?"

His sighed and glanced at me with sadness behind his eyes. "Every day," he replied softly. He paused and concentrated on the road in front of him. "I would love to feel its warmth on my skin, lie in a meadow and watch the clouds pass over it, see the true color of flowers and trees in a garden. But instead, I have to live in a world of perpetual darkness."

"Is that why you like to lie on my bed and stare at my ceiling?" I asked, recalling all the times I found him there.

The corner of his lip turned up slightly as he realized it. "Yes, it is. I have come to miss that as well. You see, my skies are either gray or black, never blue."

I fidgeted with my hands as we sat in silence, not sure what to say. Lifting my head, I looked out the window again and watched the world fly by. We were almost at the park and I realized I needed to call my dad. I pulled out my phone and dialed his number as David parked. He never picked up, but I left a message saying I was going out to eat and I'd be home after that. As soon as I hung up, my door opened and David took my hand, holding the picnic basket in the other.

We entered through the historic estate entrance, walking arm in arm down the walkway. I was doing a little better controlling myself being so close to him, but it was taking a lot of effort. Luckily, the park distracted me. It was relatively empty, which was a good thing I guess – less disturbances. It really wasn't the kind of day most people would want to spend outside, with the threat of rain at any moment. There were a few, however, relaxing on the lawn or strolling around.

We walked past the enormous fountain by the carriage house and headed down to the Italian garden. I looked around in amazement at the beauty of it all. I was used to seeing it in bright sunlight, but this was just as remarkable.

The flowers were in full bloom, displaying a dull radiance in the grayness of the day, and everything seemed muted and at peace, as if in slumber. No birds, bees, or butterflies – just the burbling fountains and the soft roar of the nearby waterfall. It never seemed to get old; I could come here a million times and still love it as much as the first.

I led him over to the pergola and stood under the large dome at the end nearest us. "My father and Vanessa will be married here next week," I commented as my voice echoed hollow and tinny.

"It's definitely an ideal place to be married," he replied, his reverberating soft and smooth.

"Yep," I replied, meandering under the tangled and twisted greenery. The wisteria flowers were long gone, but the vines and leaves it left behind were just as attractive and created a nice canopy. "My mom and dad were married here as well, and I always dreamed I'd do the same. Now I don't want to because of Vanessa."

"That shouldn't stop you." he remarked, setting the basket down and joining me.

I sighed, getting ready to explain my reasoning when he reached up and delicately ran his fingers over my hair and then along my jaw, holding my chin in them. His touch was cold but pleasant. He leaned in slowly and gently kissed my lips, lingering for a moment and then straightening up. I had to remember to breathe as I opened my eyes and gazed into his.

A sudden desire to return to that kiss came over me. I stepped closer, my arms encircling his waist as I pulled my body to his, the coldness emanating through his clothes and mine. I pressed my lips to his and then parted them. He replied, but then resisted. I tried again and he refused. Kissing down his chin to his neck instead, I nestled my face into it and held him tight. Slowly, he lifted his arms and placed his hands on my back, holding me.

I breathed in his aroma, and a new desire came over me. I had no control over what I was doing, like invisible hands were moving me with distant voices telling me to give in. I did as I was told and moved as I was directed, tilting my head and letting my hair fall over my shoulder to expose my neck. David leaned in, his lips just above my skin and I waited, wanting to feel them on me. My heart beat faster and louder, beckoning him. He tightened his hold as his lips glanced my fervent skin.

Then suddenly he was gone.

"Wh-what happened?" I asked, coming out of the trance.

He stood several feet away in the shadows, his body turned slightly so I couldn't fully see his face as he peered over his shoulder at me. "Please forgive me…I don't know why I let it progress that far."

"Let…let what progress that far?" I inquired, bracing myself against a column as I tried to clear my head.

He turned and stepped closer, standing across from me but not looking at me. "It's my allure."

"Your…allure?"

"I let my guard down."

I held my head and closed my eyes for a moment. Why was it taking so long to go away? I tried to focus on the question I wanted to ask, the words repeating in my head. "Wh-what would happen if it…if it went further?" I inquired, finally feeling it lift. He was silent for a long time, and I wondered if I actually asked the question. "David?"

"It would never." And he left it at that. I tried to remember what had happened, but my mind was a blur.

He grabbed the basket and quickly walked off through the patterned tulip beds to the cascade fountain and down the steps. I had to run to keep up with him but slowed taking the stairs since I was still a little light-headed. When I fell too far behind, he stopped at the bamboo grove and waited for me to catch up. Then he took my hand and we continued down the path without a single word between us.

The Japanese Garden was completely empty and darker than the gardens above, either from the trees or more clouds moving in. It was quiet, too, my heartbeat drumming in my ears from our hurried steps the only sound. He paused a moment at the entrance, scanning it until he found where he wanted to go.

Continuing to hold onto me, we crossed a stone bridge and then moved cautiously over the stepping stones in the pond before stopping on the small grassy knoll by it. Reaching into the basket, he pulled out a blanket and laid it down, guiding me onto it once it was straight. As soon as I was seated, he set the basket next to me and sat on the other side.

"Are you okay now?" I inquired as I leaned back on my palms and looked over at him.

"Better," he sighed, lying back and putting his hands behind his head. "So, what questions do you have for me?"

I decided it wasn't worth wasting my time pressing for more when he probably wouldn't relent, so instead I thought for a moment about what I should ask. I have so many questions, not just about him, but vampires in general. Which to begin with? I guess I should focus on him first.

"When were you born?"

"Eighteen fifty-one," he answered without hesitation.

No wonder he's so old fashioned. "Wow, you've lived through a lot of amazing changes," I commented, astonished.

"Yes…quite a few," he reflected, staring through the tree canopy.

I sat up and tucked my hands in my lap. "How did it happen?"

"That is an intriguing story," he smiled as he glanced at me, and my heart fluttered. "It was the summer of 1869. My friends and I had recently graduated from university and wanted to have one last adventure together before heading out into the world. In school, we had heard ghost stories of a mysterious lady in white who was seen in the woods near town and wanted to see for ourselves if she was real. Before dusk, we headed out and set up camp, waiting for her to show."

"It was late into the evening and there was still no sign of her. Deciding the fire needed more kindling, I headed into the woods to find some. After gathering an armful, I set them down and took a break, gazing at the moon as the clouds moved away from it. Out of the corner of my eye, something glided past me. I looked over and saw her, staring in amazement at finding she was real and not at all what I expected."

"Young and beautiful, she was an angel in a gossamer gown with long platinum hair that seemed to float around her. Glancing over her shoulder with a smile, she enticed me to follow her. Without a word to anyone, I did. I didn't know where I was going, but it didn't matter – she could have led me anywhere."

"We came upon a small, stone house with shuttered windows deep in the woods and entered. I stood at the threshold and watched as she crossed the room, the moonlight shining on her through cracks between the boards giving her a luminous glow. She took a seat on a bed, motioning for me to join her. The room was dark and dank and smelled of death, but I complied even though something deep inside told me I shouldn't."

"As soon as I was seated, she moved closer. My eyes stayed fixed on her as she ran her long fingers through my hair, bringing her hand to my cheek and pausing there. Leaning in slowly, she gave me a gentle kiss. She smelled so good…so intoxicating. I took deeper breaths and my head became clouded."

"She said something to me, but her words didn't register. I was entranced, staring ahead and waiting for something, but I didn't know what. Her lips brushed my throat and I could feel her breath on it. Then a sharp pain jolted me. I felt woozy and weak and then blacked out."

"I woke the next day to search parties calling my name. Beside me lay a woman, and soon it all came back. The room I was in was pitch and musty, a cellar under the floorboards where I was to be kept hidden. I cried out, hoping they would hear me, but I was quickly silenced by her as they entered the house. They never found me."

"I thought I was being drugged, a prisoner held to appease her whims. I didn't know what she was or what she was truly doing to me. She kept me in a haze, waiting out the search parties, but eventually she realized I needed food. The following morning when I woke, a meal awaited me, but not her. I could have refused to eat and let myself waste away, but I chose not to do that. I was going to survive this and go home."

"That evening, she joined me as I ate and I treated her with kindness, giving her what she wanted in hopes she would release me, but even those attempts didn't help. It was that way for several days with no change. She continued to hold onto me, refusing to let me go. But I refused to give up."

"A span of time passed where my strength gradually returned. I wondered if it was a test, so I continued to go along with her desires. But each night I prepared as if it was the night she killed me. Fearing my time was running out, I decided to strike."

"I kept the knife from my morning meal and hid it by my side. At the time, I didn't know what I was dealing with, so I thought if I killed her, I would be free. As she came to greet me, I pulled it out and stabbed her, but it did nothing but enrage her. It was then I finally saw her true self. She easily overpowered me, taking all my strength."

"She cut back my meals, feeding me just to keep my body strong enough to feed her. Days, probably weeks, passed, and she kept with that same pattern. So many times, I wanted to give up hope and finally give in to death, but I just couldn't do it. I still had fight in me."

"She starved me for several days, watching my struggle and desperation to hold out so I could go home. When I was just about broken, she sat beside me and gazed down with sympathetic eyes as she ran her slender fingers through my hair. 'You are dying,' she told me, her voice as angelic as her face. 'I can help you pass without pain, or I can give you a new life, an eternal life'. I didn't have to think about it; it was an easy choice because I wasn't ready to die. I chose to live."

He paused and looked at me. I hung on his every word, anxious to know what happened next. "Sooo…" I cued.

"She nearly drained the life from me and I felt overwhelming lethargy, but before I could give in to it, she slit her wrist. The smell filled the room and my head. I wanted it and nothing else. She brought it closer and I grabbed her arm and drank, the blood flowing over my tongue cool and silky. I wanted more, but she pulled away."

"She promised something more satisfying, but first I had to lie back and let my body die. I was confused but did as she said. The pain was excruciating and lasted for hours, then suddenly it was over. As I took in my new world, she explained what I was and taught me how to hunt. On the third morning as we returned to the house, she told me she planned to leave and asked me to join her, but I refused. When I woke the following night, she was gone."

I leaned forward on my knees and tried to understand. "She just left you, a new vampire, to fend for yourself?" I questioned, agitated.

"I asked her to do it," he replied, smiling at my concern.

"Did you ever see her again?"

"No. Our paths never once crossed, nor did I try to seek her out."

"What about your family...your friends? Did you get to go home?"

"No, I found I had to stay away from them. I would have killed them on sight if I had. They tried to find me, though, still scouring the woods even after the others had given up. Instead, what they discovered was a body, a hermit, mauled beyond recognition. With no knowledge of anyone aside from me being in the woods, they assumed it was mine and had a funeral, burying him under my name."

"Your first victim?" I gulped and he nodded, ashamed. "Were you angry?"

"Yes," he responded, his jaw tightening. "About my choice, about what I had become, about everything. I thought I could go back to my old life, but that was impossible with my new one."

"What did you do to stay away?"

"At first, I hid, trying to avoid any and all human contact and the desire to give in to the bloodlust. But I couldn't avoid it for long. The hunger, the pain, was too much and I found it hard to fight when someone would wander into my woods. But I did. I couldn't bring myself to kill them – not so close to where I grew up, where I knew every person, every family, in the township."

He paused. "My only choice was to leave and go where I knew no one and no one knew me, somewhere large and busy, where people are forgotten. I left as soon as I was able and headed for Boston."

"So the hermit wasn't your only human kill..."

"No, there were many more, but I had to do it to survive. Or so I thought. I didn't find out differently until later," he sighed, closing his eyes slowly. "But I never killed an innocent soul after the hermit, only those who deserved it – vagrants, rapists, murderers..."

"Then you were a vigilante, an anonymous hero," I rationalized, trying not to find the bad in him.

He opened his eyes and turned his head, staring at me. "No, I was no better than the people I killed. A hero rids the world of the bad guys for honest and honorable reasons. I did it for selfish ones."

A chill went through me as he turned his attention back to the branches above him. I stared at him a moment and wondered how he could be that monster. No, there's no way. That's who he was, not who he is.

"So what do you survive off now? Blood bags?"

"No, animal blood. It has to be living, circulating blood."

"What about your body temperature? You're not cold all the time like I expect a vampire to be," I questioned and he twitched slightly.

"When we feed, we become warm because of the blood. Our bodies maintain the heat, but only for a while. As the days pass, the blood depletes and then it's time to feed again."

"Does that also have something to do with your eye color change?"

"In a way, yes. They become bolder when I have not fed, making it easier to lure prey."

I glanced at his eyes – brilliant green, like a glimmering, deep emerald. "So, you haven't fed recently..."

He closed them and looked away. "I know I should have, but I wanted to find out how I would behave around you...if I could resist the temptation. I realize after what happened under the pergola, I shouldn't try it again...at least not for a while."

"So what happened?"

"As I said before, it was my allure. When we have not fed, it's overpowering. You were giving yourself to me without realizing it, in a trance."

An uneasiness came over me. He could have killed me right then and there, out in the open, and no one would have known. I wouldn't have known...

His cold hand touched mine and I jerked slightly. "I would never hurt you, Megan. You understand that, right?" he asked, noticing my silence.

I glanced at him briefly and then twisted a curl nervously as I stared at the pond. He didn't kill me; he resisted. "Yes, I do," I replied finally, realizing the tremendous willpower he must have.

We were both quiet, surrounded by the soft sound of rain trickling on the water and gently sprinkling the leaves above our heads mixed with the quiet roar of the waterfall in the distance. "Is there anything else you would like to know?" he inquired, interrupting the mottled din in my ears.

"Of course...do you have any other powers, aside from your allure?"

He sat up, laughing quietly. "Incredible strength, keen senses, quick healing, extreme speed and agility..."

"Can you fly?"

"Hmm...do you consider jumping really far flying?" he asked.

"Not particularly," I replied, giving him a strange look.

"Then no, we cannot," he grinned. "We don't change into bats, rats, or fog either."

"Any other special talents?"

"Telepathy among others like me, within a certain distance. We don't have to make eye contact, but it helps to get a stronger link."

"So that explains why you and Madeline kept exchanging glances at prom…" I muttered.

He chuckled. "We had an ongoing bet to see how many humans we could enthrall. I won, hands down," he responded with a smirk and then it faded. "She was also giving me updates on how her evening with Ben was going."

"So what happened with him? He's uncomfortable talking about her now."

"I guess they're not a good match. And Ben was being difficult."

"I don't even want to know…"

"It's better that you don't."

I looked away, trying not to think about what he meant. "I noticed you don't like to say what you are. Why is that?" I asked.

He stared out into the garden. "I am an abomination…damned. I should have chosen death, but I was young and ignorant."

I placed my hand on his. "If you had chosen death, you would have never met me."

He looked at me and replied, "Maybe I would have, as someone else, as a human."

"You believe in reincarnation?"

"I believe some people have old souls."

"Really. Well, I'm glad to have met you as you, regardless of what you are."

He smiled. "You are very strange, Megan," he responded, lying down.

"Thank you!" I smiled back, tucking my hair behind my ear.

I glanced up at the sky as a dark cloud broke apart and mixed with the lighter gray ones. The rain began to slow and then stopped, leaving the residual sound of light droplets falling through the trees. A few sprinkles made their way to us, but for the most part we lucked out and stayed dry while everything else became damp or covered in a myriad of clear beads.

David stared into the treetops, watching individual raindrops slide leaf to leaf and then make their final descent to his chest. I marveled in quiet veneration, but then my stomach growled and disrupted it. My cheeks began to flush as I instinctively grabbed at it, hoping to quiet it.

He glanced over at me, arching his brow. "Hungry?" he asked. I nodded, and he indicated to help myself.

I peeked in the basket, wondering what he might have packed. I pulled out a sandwich – chicken salad on a croissant. Setting it on my lap, I looked to see what else was there: assorted cheeses, strawberries, and a dark liquid. I held it up, inspecting it.

"I know ya'll Suthaners like sweet tea," he remarked in a faux southern accent, noticing my curiosity. I couldn't resist the urge to giggle.

I unfolded the wax paper and took a bite of the sandwich, not sure what to expect. It was unbelievable – large chunks of chicken with pecans, grapes, and diced apples. "This is delicious!"

"I'm glad you like it."

That brought up my next question. "So you don't eat food…"

"No, our stomachs reject it. I don't even try."

"That's why you wouldn't eat the dinner I cooked for you or order anything when we went out," I realized.

"Correct."

I paused, staring at the sandwich and picking at the bread. "Why didn't you tell me sooner?"

"I was worried about your reaction. Some people don't take it as well as you do."

"I'm very open-minded," I replied with a smile.

"Yes you are. And astute. You were on the right track with your theories, but I couldn't let you know that. You didn't make it easy on me. It was getting progressively more difficult to redirect them," he smirked.

"Glad I could challenge you," I remarked as I reached in the basket for something else.

I pulled out a strawberry and bit into the sweet flesh, closing my eyes and savoring the flavor and fragrance. I opened them and took another bite, noticing him watching me eat and making me feel a little uncomfortable. I blushed and grabbed another one, playing with it.

"You said the other night Brian and Odette couldn't enter my house unless invited. That's old world superstition, but it's true?"

"Yes. A home is a sacred place. The first night I came to your house, I physically could not enter until you requested me to do so. Once invited, we can come and go as we please until the invitation is rescinded."

"What about other buildings?"

"As long as it's public, we can enter. Hospitals, hotels, schools…"

"What about crosses, garlic, and holy water?"

"No affect. I sometimes wonder how they came up with these ideas; we can't be deterred by such trinkets," he chuckled as he sat up.

"So do you sleep in a coffin?"

He laughed. "Not in a coffin and only occasionally."

"Only occasionally…what do you mean?"

"The sun makes us tired, though we don't need to sleep. It has something to do with the virus. If the sun never came out, we could stay awake all the time."

"What you are…it's a virus?"

"Somewhat. It's bloodborne and spreads through the body, taking over."

"Has any of your kind ever tried to find a cure?"

"There is still something numinous about my condition, something that can't be explained or treated. No, there is only one cure – death."

After being so lighthearted a moment ago, I didn't like the turn the questions were taking. "Do you really go to college?" I asked to change the subject, popping a cheese cube in my mouth.

"Yes, I do," he smiled.

"When are you able to attend?"

"In the evening and online."

"How many degrees do you have?"

"Quite a few. It's a good thing I love to learn."

Something we have in common. I sipped the tea and thought about my next question. "Do you have to go to college?"

"Not really, but I choose to. It keeps me in touch with the living and changes going on in the world. Also, when I apply for a job, people might get suspicious seeing a degree from eighteen sixty-nine."

"Good point. So you graduated from college the first time at eighteen. How is that possible?"

"Back then, you entered university at a much younger age. I was fourteen."

"Wow, that's amazing."

"Not really. The curriculum was vastly different from the institutes of higher learning today, with limited courses of study."

"What kind of careers have you had?"

"A wide variety: accountant, journalist, illustrator, chemist…"

"What, no politics for you?"

"As I said before, I'm not like my father. But also, I'd make for a very dangerous politician," he smirked. My heart fluttered and I tucked my head. Yes he would, easily swaying votes in his favor with a single smile.

"So nothing that puts you in the limelight?"

"I prefer careers where I blend in and not stand out. That way I can stay longer."

"How often do you have to move?"

"If it's a big city, I could stay for thirty to forty years. It's harder in small towns. Everyone knows everyone else and they tend to notice when you don't age."

"How long have you really lived here in Richmond?"

"About three years."

"How long have you actually known your roommates?"

He hesitated. "I've known Brian a long time…the others, not long at all. Cary and Madeline are the newest additions."

"I noticed Cary doesn't act the same as the rest of you. He's anxious around me."

"That's because he's still adjusting to the change. He's still new."

"How old are they?"

"Actual age or their age from the time they changed?"

I was curious to know what decades they were from, to get a feel for their background. "Their true birth year."

"Brian was born in 1909, Madeline in 1948, Odette in 1956, and Cary more recently."

"You said Cary's still adjusting. When was he changed?"

"Three years ago…at fifteen."

"Fifteen!" I responded, shocked.

"Yes. Most of us are changed around eighteen to twenty, but there are a few of our kind that like to change younger people. They use them for lures or other ill purposes."

"How young is young? Can your kind actually change children?" I inquired, my imagination running wild with images of vampiric little ones.

"No. Children never survive the change. Their bodies are underdeveloped and can't withstand the drastic transformation they have to go through to become one of us."

"Well that's a relief. I was imagining little demon children with voracious appetites running around and biting any and every person they came across."

"Maybe that's why the barrier is in place, because it very well could be that way if not," he responded, and a chill went through me.

"So you're the oldest among your roommates," I commented, wanting to get away from that discussion as well. "Does that make you the leader?"

"No, there is no leader."

I packed the remains of the picnic back into the basket, thinking of another question. "You seem distrusting of Brian and yet you let him and Odette stay. Why?"

"Brian has been with me a long time. I don't agree with his beliefs, but he's been like a brother to me. He found a soul mate in Odette in the seventies when he came across her in our travels. They have never been a problem before, but ever since meeting you, it's been strange between us."

Brian has Odette – it can't be jealousy. "When did you meet him?"

"In 1935, on my way to Oregon. He was new and seeking help from a more experienced being. By that time, I had given up feeding on humans and tried to teach him to do the same, though it was hard. His urges were too strong and more often than not, humans would turn up dead around us. We had to move a lot, but I continued to help him."

"Does he feed on animals now?"

"Rarely. He and Odette enjoy the human hunt and unfortunately do not discriminate. Against my wishes, they have included Cary in some of their conquests."

"He told me in the cemetery they're the ones behind the serial murders in the parks. So they didn't just kill them for fun, they drank their…blood?"

He paused. "Yes. The serial killer was a cover-up for their habit. I have tried to stop them, but they refuse to quit. They are careless and sloppy and will get us discovered if they're not careful," he replied angrily. "I can only help them so much."

"Are you more powerful than they are?"

"Yes, but they're not aware of it. Our abilities become stronger over time. And if I had continued to prey on humans, I would be even more powerful."

"Did you…change any of them?"

"No, that was someone else's handiwork. I have never changed anyone."

"So other than your roommates, have you met any more of your kind?" I asked, purposely avoiding 'vampire'.

"Yes. We're found all over, in groups and as loners."

"Is there a need to be with others?"

He smiled as he sat up. "Not really. Some think it makes survival easier while others like to have the feel of a family again. But more often than not, my kind prefers to be alone," he responded, looking up at the heavy sky. "I've done both, but I do have to say I like having company more. It makes me feel normal."

"I would think living in eternity alone would be maddening."

"It can be for some. I've met a few that have fallen victim to it and witnessed firsthand what happens to them."

I waited for him to tell me more, but he didn't. "Well…what happens?"

He paused and looked at me, his emerald eyes revealing a depth I've never seen before. "They get killed."

I stared in disbelief. "By whom?"

He leaned forward, crossing his arms and resting them on his knees as he stared at the pond. "One of our own…to avoid exposure. We don't want to be known, preferring to remain in the darkness and be the things of nightmares," he commented, his lip curling at the corner as he glanced at me.

I stared at him, my heart fluttering lightly. "I…I don't think you're a thing of nightmares."

His smile spread as he cocked his head slightly, causing my heart to pound in my chest. "You flatter me," he remarked humbly.

I quickly looked away, tucking my hair behind my ear and staring at the blanket as I tried to calm my heart. "Well…it…it's true…" I responded, playing with the cup.

I finished the last bit of tea as I glanced around the garden. It was so serene, with the faint sound of ducks quacking and the koi popping in the pond beside us. I looked back at David as he lay down again and thought of what a marvelous creature he was; a killing machine, but marvelous nonetheless. I closed the basket and stretched out next to him.

After a moment of trying to think of another question, I rolled to my side and leaned over him, inspecting his mouth. He grinned and asked, "What are you looking for?"

"Where are your fangs?" I inquired, gently touching his lips.

"You're like a child."

"Well, I'm curious."

He laughed the most beautiful laugh. "They are there, but retract farther into the gum, only growing when needed," he responded with a smile and for the first time, I noticed how sharp his canines actually were.

I stared at his mouth, expecting something to happen. "What triggers them to come down?"

"The smell of blood, sensing it pulse through the veins, feeling the heartbeat."

I lifted my eyes to his and asked softly, "Is that why it's hard to kiss me?"

He maintained my gaze, gently running his hand over my hair. "Yes. I battle with that inhuman side of me every time. I can hear your heartbeat when we're close and feel your pulse when our lips touch. But it won't always be that way. It takes time, but I can learn to control the urge. It's been awhile since I've had to deal with this."

"A girlfriend?"

"She died many years ago," he replied, staring at the trees as if he was inspecting every leaf. I waited for him to continue, but he didn't.

"Have you ever cried?" I asked hesitantly.

His eyes shifted to mine. "Yes, but not tears like yours. You have clear, sparkling streams that glisten on your cheeks in joy and sadness. Mine are rich, red streaks that only come with pain."

I knit my brow. "Red? Like…blood?" I questioned, remembering the crimson line on my chest from several nights ago.

"Exactly like blood."

"That's…different," I remarked slowly as I moved back and rested my head on my arm. "So how long does it usually take for you to get used to someone?" I inquired curiously.

He turned his body toward mine and propped himself up on his elbow, leaning closer. "It depends on my willpower and how much time I spend with that person," he responded.

I smiled. "I guess we need to try to spend as much time together as possible then."

"I don't have any objections to that," he grinned mischievously and my heart accelerated.

Reaching over, he tucked my hair behind my ear, his fingers tracing my jaw and then sliding down my neck to my chest. He rested his hand there, feeling the rapid beat of my heart. Then slowly, he leaned in and kissed me. I rolled to my back, him moving with me, and slipped my fingers into his hair as I parted my lips. His parted as well and his heavenly breath filled my head.

But it was short-lived. He withdrew slightly and rested his head on my chest, his ear pressed against my skin. The thumping of my heart gained speed, but I remained still, not sure what he was doing. Then slowly, he lifted his head and looked at me with a half-smile. He leaned in to kiss me again, but this time I forced him onto his back and took control.

"Hey! You two! Park's closing!" a voice yelled from across the pond.

I jerked my head up and found the park security officer glaring at us. Quickly sitting up, I turned away and tucked my head as my face burned with embarrassment. David raised his hand, indicating we heard, then stood up and chuckled, offering to help me to my feet. I took his hand and stood next to him, my back to the officer.

"It's all right. He's gone," he assured, amused with my humiliation. "And I was really starting to enjoy that..."

I gave him a dirty look and stepped to the side, taking the basket with me. I held it as he quickly folded the blanket and placed it inside. He put his arm around my shoulder, and we walked the path out of the Japanese Garden into the Italian Garden, and then past the carriage house as the sky darkened with the coming night. The officer was waiting at the gate when we arrived, making sure we were leaving.

I leaned my head on David's shoulder, letting my hair fall forward to hide my face as we passed. He smiled politely at the officer and continued to the car. Opening my door, I sat and held my head in my hands, totally mortified. He climbed in the driver's seat, and we left the parking lot as he continued to laugh at me.

"What? You've never been caught kissing?"

"Uh, no...never had a boyfriend," I answered, cracking the window.

He grinned and then turned his attention back to the road. It was a quiet trip home, but that was fine with me. I wanted silence to process all I had learned from him.

I stared out the window and sighed, watching as rain dotted the glass. The small droplets easily slid into each other, gathering into larger drops and flying off. David reached over and held my hand and my embarrassment gradually faded, turning into sadness knowing he'd be leaving me.

"When will I see you again?" I asked suddenly.

"Soon," he replied, turning into my neighborhood.

He pulled into the driveway and shut the car off, then turned to me and leaned close. I hope my dad wasn't waiting and watching for me. Our lips touched and I reached up to hold his face, but he caught my hands before I could and held them down.

"I will see you later," he whispered.

I pouted as I opened the door and climbed out. "Until later," I replied, crestfallen.

His eyes followed me as I meandered up the sidewalk to the house. I paused near the steps, letting the rain dampen my hair and clothes as I watched him back out and drive away. I turned and glanced at the windows, looking for prying eyes, but there were none. Stopping briefly at the door, I sighed, missing him so much already.

I headed to the family room where I found my father watching a movie. "Hey, kiddo, did you have fun?" he asked.

"Yeah, a blast. How was your evening?" I replied, leaning over the couch and giving him a peck on the cheek.

"Good. Want to watch this movie with me? I just started it – it's chock full of suspense."

"You know me so well," I responded as I sat next to him, happy to spend some one-on-one time with him and fill my loneliness.

# Chapter 26
## Stay

"What a great movie," I commented. "I never would have figured it was the cop."

"I thought it was, but I kept questioning my gut," Dad replied.

I stood up and stretched, glancing at the time. "I think I'm going to head on to bed," I informed him.

"All right. I plan to stay here and see what else might be on. I'm not tired enough yet," he responded as he flipped through the channels.

"Thanks for sharing the movie with me, Dad," I remarked, kissing his forehead.

"We should do it more often," he replied, glancing over his shoulder at me as I left the room.

I paused at the stairs. "That would be nice," I answered quietly.

I went to my room, quickly changing into my usual bedtime attire, and crawled into bed. Curling up under my covers, I closed my eyes and tried to shut everything down, but my mind refused to give in.

Rolling onto my back, I stared at the darkened sky above me. I closed my eyes again and concentrated on the sounds around me. Dad was still flipping through the channels. I searched for something more soothing. The quiet pattering of rain on the roof and balcony was ideal, so I focused on it.

As I tried to relax, my mind turned to thoughts of David. I wonder what he's doing right now. Is he hunting? Could he be at home? What if he's here watching over me? I glanced toward the balcony, hoping the latter was the case, but I only saw the occasional glimmer of raindrops falling. I rolled over to my side and tried to get my mind to give up. No such luck.

Does David plan to make me a vampire? He's never mentioned it, but I think he will. Otherwise, I'll grow old and die. I know I'd like to be with him forever, but I don't know if I want to give up my mortality for him. That's a pretty big decision. Am I willing to sacrifice my friends, my dad, everything, for him?

My heart ached at the thought of having to choose. His choice was eternal life or death. If something similar happened to me, I'd choose the same. At least there is a chance I might get to see my friends or Dad again. I would just look different. And in this day and age, I could chalk it up to plastic surgery.

I flipped over to my other side, staring at the balcony. The lights had gone out in the garden, leaving only darkness. The pattering of the rain started to fade and the lower level grew quiet. I was left with silence…and my thoughts.

I don't want to think anymore about David and becoming a vampire. I want to see him, feel him next to me, close to me, telling me he loves me. I nuzzled my face into the pillow, taking in a deep breath of him. My mind became fuzzy and dark. In no time, I was out.

*David was standing under the pergola in Maymont waiting for me. The moonlight shone on him like a spotlight, and he smiled as I approached, beckoning me to join him. Without hesitation, I took his outstretched hand and walked into his arms as I gazed into his emerald eyes. I tilted my head, letting the hair fall back to expose my neck, and closed my eyes as I felt his breath on my skin. He bit down and I gasped but held him tighter, not ever wanting to let go…*

I woke to a cool breeze blowing in from the balcony. I rubbed my eyes and focused on the opening – still dark out. Climbing drowsily out of bed, I went to the doors to shut them when suddenly I was grabbed from behind and held, a warm hand covering my mouth to keep me from screaming. I tried to get free, but whatever had me was too strong.

"Shhh…it's David," he whispered in my ear, slowly letting me go.

I jerked around and looked at him, bewildered. "What are you doing here?" I asked in a loud whisper.

He crossed the room and casually sat on the edge of the bed. "I told you I would see you later," he replied.

"What about my dad? What if…what if he finds you here? He'll probably be up soon to tell me good night," I panicked.

"It's two in the morning; he's fast asleep in his bed," he responded as he pat mine, indicating for me to sit.

I hesitated a moment, but then joined him. Leaning over, I turned on my bedside lamp so I could see him better. In the dim light, I noticed his eyes were light green.

"You fed," I commented.

"I had to before seeing you again. Resisting took a lot out of me, and I didn't want any problems tonight."

"What did you have?" I asked with a yawn, leaning back against my headboard.

"Deer, as usual."

"Do you hunt anything else?"

"Occasionally black bear, but deer is the mainstay of my diet. The downside to living here is Virginia doesn't offer a lot of large game. On occasion, I have gone to local farms and fed off the cattle and horses, but I try not to do that too often, being that those animals are the farmers' livelihood."

"How long will it last you?"

"A day or two. Animal blood is not like human blood. Since we were once human, our bodies thrive better on that blood; we are satisfied longer."

"Can you feed off a human without infecting them?"

He laughed quietly. "I suppose...they would have to be cut. The problem is stopping."

"What do you mean?"

Again he chuckled. "It's like giving a sip of alcohol to a recovering alcoholic...it's hard to control yourself. You want more and more until your thirst is satiated."

I moved closer to him and fidgeted with my shorts. "David...do you plan to change me?" He was quiet, his head bowed and turned away from me so I couldn't see his expression to know what he was thinking or feeling. "David?"

"When you are ready, if you choose."

"What if I'm ready now?"

"You're not ready; it's too soon to decide."

"Is it what you want?"

He turned toward me so I could see his face, his expression conflicted. "I love you as a human, but your human life only lasts so long. Yes...I do want you to change, but only if you so choose," he responded, softening.

I leaned against him, my head on his shoulder, and he put his arm around me. After a moment, he lifted my chin to kiss me. His lips were warmer than I've been used to lately. I slid my arm up his back and slipped my fingers into his soft hair. I grasped it and slightly pulled his head back, breaking his lips from mine and tilting my head. Accepting the invitation, he kissed down my chin to my neck and stopped there.

"Are you tempting me?" he whispered, his lips moving with the words on my skin.

I lowered my head and looked at him. "I thought it wouldn't be difficult for you."

He smiled his wicked grin. "It doesn't matter if I've just fed or not, I still hunger for it...for human blood," he replied, turning my face away and kissing my neck. My heart beat faster and my breathing increased. "You should calm down," he whispered against my skin.

I tried. I closed my eyes and thought of something else, anything, but only saw David. My heart raced like I had been running. I tried physically calming myself, but that wasn't working either. Did he have some power over me making me act this way?

He moved his hand down my throat, covering where he had been kissing, and sat back. I lowered my head, never looking at him. "I'm sorry..."

He lifted my face and gazed into my eyes. "There is nothing to be sorry about. I can't help what I am, but I can learn to control myself."

"So it will only get easier?" I inquired, remembering what he said earlier.

He smiled. "Yes. The more I'm around you, the more I grow accustom to you."

"Is that why you visit me so often?" I asked playfully.

"Yes, whether you're aware if it or not," he replied with a grin.

"Wait…you mean…" I began, narrowing my eyes at him. "How often have you snuck into my room?"

"Many times," he responded smoothly. "You caught me on a couple of those occasions."

The realization hit me. "So those vivid dreams of you being here were *real*?"

"Yes…but I had to make you believe they were dreams so I didn't reveal myself."

"Why?"

"Because I didn't want to lose you…"

"No, why did you come into my room while I was sleeping?"

He caressed my cheek as he smiled softly. "I enjoy watching you sleep…you're so beautiful, so peaceful." He paused and then stood, walking to the balcony doors and peeking outside. "I also wanted to keep you safe."

"From what?"

"Brian mostly…along with anything else," he replied, turning around and facing me.

"That's impossible. You can't stop me from getting sick or injured," I retorted, standing and walking toward him.

"I can do what I need to save you if I have to," he responded as he slid his hand under my jaw and leaned closer.

"What about during the day? You can't save me then."

"No, but I trust your fellow man will," he remarked as he gazed into my eyes.

"So you're my dark guardian angel," I responded quietly, fixed on his.

"In a way, yes," he replied with a grin, our lips nearly touching.

Without thinking, I kissed him. But it didn't take him by surprise; it was like he expected it. He kissed back, his smile gradually fading as his hand slid along the curve of my neck and rested on my collar. I parted my lips, breathing in his enticing breath as he did the same, and my head swam. I moved closer, putting my arms around his waist and pressing my body to his. My pulse raced being so near, clothes the only thing separating us.

His hand began to clench as his fingers gripped my collarbone. Before I could react, he pushed me away, holding me at arm's length, and turned his head toward the doors as he breathed fast and heavy. After a moment, his hand dropped, but his head remained tucked.

I stepped toward him, wrapping my arms around his body and resting my head on his chest as we stood in the doorway. A slight breeze blew and the scent of rain was heavy in the air. I closed my eyes and inhaled it as I listened to his breathing, since there was no heartbeat to focus on. Slowly raising his hand to my hair, he gently caressed it as he put his arm around me and held me in a protective embrace.

Suddenly, he bent down and lifted me, cradling my body in his arms. "What are you doing?" I asked, grasping around his neck.

"It's getting late and you should sleep," he replied, laying me on the bed and then lying beside me.

He reached over and turned off the lamp on the bedside table, stopping to softly kiss me. We faced each other, my head on the pillow and his propped up on his hand. I gazed at what I could make out as his face and ran my fingers along his jaw.

"How long are you staying?"

"However long you would like."

"Until morning?" I asked in a whisper.

"As long as there is no sun, I will be here when you wake."

He traced my face with his fingers as if memorizing me. I closed my eyes, becoming drowsy with the motion. "I hope it's still raining..." I mumbled as I drifted away.

I slowly opened my eyes, hoping last night wasn't just another dream. I was facing the balcony; no sun this morning. The rain pattered quietly as I glanced over my shoulder to see if David was behind me, but I was alone. I guess it was a dream.

I rolled out of bed and went into the bathroom, staring at myself in the mirror. Turning on the faucet, I splashed cold water on my face to wake up. As I pushed my hair back and opened my eyes, I jumped. Behind my image in the mirror was David! I spun around quickly, wondering if my mind was playing tricks, and leaned back against the counter.

"You're here!" I exclaimed, realizing he really was. "Where did you go?"

He smiled and stepped closer, placing his hands on my hips. "I was on the balcony. Your father came to check on you, so I had to leave."

"Is he still here?"

"No, he left," he replied, kissing my damp lips.

I grinned, happy he remained. I turned around to dry my face and then looked at he and I standing together in the mirror. He smiled at me and kissed my neck.

"Wait," I blurted, staring in front of me. "You have a reflection!"

"Why wouldn't I?" he asked, turning me around.

"Let me guess...that's one of those myths."

"Correct. Some people believe we have no reflection because we have no soul." He glanced at himself in the mirror and flicked his hair. "I guess they were wrong."

"Huh...so how long do you plan to stay today?" I asked, going back into the bedroom.

"How long do you want me to stay?"

"Forever..."

"I could do that, but you can't," he replied with his mischievous grin.

I went to my closet and grabbed an outfit and headed back toward the bathroom, standing in the doorway. "I'm going to get ready. Do you mind?"

"Not at all," he replied, standing with his hands behind his back, a pleased smile on his perfect lips.

"Could you go downstairs?" I asked impatiently.

"Oh...yes, I will," he responded, heading out of the room.

I shut and locked the bathroom door and proceeded to get ready. Anxious to join him, I hurried through everything, only slowing to check that I was presentable. Satisfied, I opened the door to leave and almost ran into him.

"Finished already, I see," he commented.

"Yes. I'm not like those typical girls who stand in front of a mirror for hours," I replied, pushing past him.

He followed me down the stairs and into the kitchen, sitting at the island while I searched for breakfast. Before opening the refrigerator door, I spotted Dad's note. He was meeting Vanessa and would be home around two. I guess that was how long David could stay.

I glanced at my options and pulled out the milk; cereal would have to do. Not my first choice, but I didn't want to take the time to cook anything, especially if it was just for me. I sat across from him and began eating, hating that he was watching me.

"Stop that," I requested.

"What?" he inquired.

"Watching me eat. It makes me uncomfortable."

"I apologize. I just enjoy seeing your response to food," he replied. I knit my brows together and he smiled. "Like when you bite into a ripe strawberry, savoring its sweet aroma and flavor, you look...blissful," he explained before turning his gaze instead to the backyard.

I stared at my milky reflection as I took a bite of cereal. I never thought I had any kind of real reaction to food, but he thinks I do. Well, that's still no excuse to stare at someone. It's just odd and obvious.

I looked up from my bowl, curious if he was watching me. Instead, his gaze remained fixed on the window. I stared, admiring his quiet beauty. He glanced out of the corner of his eye at me, raising a brow, and I quickly returned to focusing on the remains of my breakfast. I'm such a hypocrite.

"So what did you do while I slept?" I asked, talking into the bowl while playing with the last few flakes floating in it.

"I watched you dream."

"Did I do anything interesting?" I inquired, looking up to meet his gaze.

"Not really. They must have been pleasant, though. You looked happy," he responded with a smile and my heart thumped.

"Do you ever dream?" I asked, staring at my bowl again. I could feel warmth spreading in my cheeks.

"No," he replied, looking away. "Our brain process is different than yours. We need to be aware of our surroundings at all times in case of danger."

"Like if someone was trying to kill you?"

"Exactly. When we sleep, it's a shallow sleep."

I finished my cereal and got up, heading to the sink. Glimpsing the note on the fridge again reminded me I had to tell David the bad news. "My dad will be home around two, so I guess you'll have to go before then," I announced, glancing back at him.

"Or I could stay and help you study for finals. We could start around one, one-thirty," he smiled.

He must have been planning this. "Good idea…it's mutually beneficial," I responded, leaning against the sink. He nodded and returned to looking outside. "So what do we do until then?" I asked.

"Let's see…it's close to eleven. Would you like to go somewhere, maybe a museum or gallery?"

"What a lovely rainy day suggestion," I answered as I walked over to him and stood by his side. "How about the Virginia Museum of Fine Arts? I haven't been in a while and it's just in town."

"That sounds like a grand idea. Are you ready to go now?"

I nodded and excused myself, needing to get something from my room. I ran up the stairs while he remained in his seat staring at the yard. I grabbed my purse and was turning to head out of the room when I ran into him. He grasped me by the shoulders and smiled.

"You could have stayed downstairs," I commented, blushing.

"Yes…but I didn't want to," he replied before kissing me.

His lips felt amazing and I could have stayed there all day, but we needed to get moving. "Okay…let's go. We shouldn't waste any more time," I directed, slipping away.

"All right, if we must," he answered with a playful smile.

As we exited the house, the rain started coming down. I rushed to the car and hurriedly unlocked the doors as he casually walked toward it. He smiled at me as he sat and I just shook my head, pulling out of the driveway.

Our conversation on the way to the museum was generic – the weather, school, the wedding. But it didn't matter. I could listen to him talk for the rest of my life, and if his was the last voice I heard, I would die happy. But then again, he wouldn't let that happen.

During lulls, my mind wandered to our conversation last night and I thought about when I could be ready. If I chose now, could I really give up everyone, everything for him? I glanced at him as he stared out the window at the river and immediately thought yes. An eternal life with him would be bliss. Endless nights lying in his arms, sharing a thousand lifetimes, just the two of us in eternal darkness, no more sunshine, no more food I love to eat, no more friends or father...

"Megan, what's wrong?" he asked, taking in my sudden worried expression.

"Umm...nothing, really," I lied. He continued to stare at me. I sighed and relented. "I was thinking about my choice to be like you."

"Is something about it bothering you?" he questioned.

"Would I never get to see my father or friends...ever?"

"This is why I said it has to be when you're ready. Once you change, you won't be able to be around humans for a long time, if ever," he explained, his eyes sympathetic yet cold.

We were both silent. I continued to weigh the pros and cons, having a difficult time choosing a side at all. I pulled into the deck next to the museum and parked, sitting without any intention of moving for a while.

"Don't worry about this now. When you're ready, you'll know. You have time," he whispered, holding my cheek in his hand. I nodded, and he leaned in and kissed me. He was right; it was nothing to worry over now.

I opened my door, signaling I was ready to go in, and he followed. As we strolled up to the entrance, I realized how long it really had been since I'd been there. So many things had changed structurally, not just the exhibits.

Inside, we took our time exploring, hitting the permanent galleries first. Some of the pieces I remembered from when Mom would bring me on rainy days. I impressed David with my extensive knowledge of them. In turn, I was impressed with his stories about the pieces the museum had that were similar to the ones his parents owned by the same artists.

We continued through the exhibits, trying to outdo one another with how much we knew. Of course, he was worldlier than me. When it came to the modern art, though, neither of us had any facts or stories. Instead, we were left to discuss our interpretations of them.

"So is Madeline's art a direct result of what she is?" I asked as we stood in front of a piece that reminded me of something she would create.

"It's very dark, I know, but so true of our world."

"The portrait hanging above the fireplace in the grand salon, 'The First Time', was it...hers?"

"Yes. The pieces you saw in the house show her disgust, anger, and sadness. You also get a glimpse of her creator."

"The one in the library…the creepy man looking over the woman's shoulder."

He smiled. "They all tell a story."

"How old was she when she changed?"

"Sixteen."

"Oh my God, she was so young!"

"Like Cary," he commented, looking over an odd sculpture.

"Have you ever heard why they were chosen so young?"

"Cary hasn't revealed his story to me, but Madeline shared hers when we met," he answered. As we continued our stroll through the gallery, he elaborated. "For her, it was happenstance. Her maker lived in the same neighborhood and watched her, waiting for his moment. He was a vile and disgusting creature who liked to prey on young girls, and she was kind and naïve, his perfect quarry."

"He found his moment, tricking her so he could lock her away. She was his prisoner, trapped as he abused and fed on her as he pleased. For weeks she endured, but the moment she reached her breaking point, she fought back. He took hold of her, but she bit down on his neck and broke free, running for the cellar door and leaving."

"Not knowing where else to go, she ran down the street toward home. But as she reached it, she was hit with a horrible pain. She forced her body to the door, collapsing on the front porch. She thought she was dying, not realizing when she bit him, she took in some of his blood. When she reawakened, her brother's face hovered above her. She had just changed and *he* was her first kill."

"That's awful!" I gasped. A couple of people nearby looked at me and I blushed, apologizing quietly.

"Yes, I can't imagine what she went through," he remarked thoughtfully as he stared at an elaborate landscape painting. "So with nowhere to go, she left town, cutting herself off from humankind," he continued, glancing at me.

I couldn't even fathom what it would be like to be her during that time – sixteen, on her own, and a bloodthirsty vampire no less. It must have been difficult and terrifying. I had a totally new perception of her.

We ventured into another area of the museum, and I stopped before a picture of people in a room with wine glasses in hand, some dancing, but most standing around talking or watching the goings-on from the walls. It reminded me of an uncomfortably awkward party.

The party! Oh my God! I invited my friends to a vampire's house!

"David," I called, my voice shaky. "What are we going to do about the party?"

"What do you mean?" he asked, touching my arm as he stepped closer.

I looked around, making sure we were alone. "The end-of-school party next week…at your house," I responded.

"Oh…everything will be fine," he replied nonchalantly.

"It's going to be fine? You're joking…"

"Just because you know what we are doesn't mean you have to cancel. You were going to have it before you knew, so what difference does it make now?"

I looked at him, a little shocked he was being so cool about this. "What about Brian and Odette? What if they try something?" I retorted.

"As I said, I'll make sure they are on their best behavior and stay away from you as well as refrain from harassing or harming your guests," he replied, pulling me close. "It'll be all right, I promise." As I examined his expression, his eyes convinced me of it. He leaned in and we kissed in the middle of the gallery.

Someone walked by and cleared their throat, making us cease. My cheeks brightened and I tucked my head into David's shoulder as he chuckled, always so amused by my embarrassment. Rubbing my back, we continued to the last exhibit.

We finished our visit and headed out of the building, encountering pouring rain as we exited. Standing under the overhang, we debated whether to run or wait for it to pass. It let up a little, so we took that opportunity to dash to the garage, only getting slightly wet.

Climbing in the car, I didn't drive off immediately. "I hope the weather will be nice for the party," I commented, staring at the rain falling in front of us.

"I believe the rain is supposed to end early in the week and the temperature will be much hotter," David replied, saddened.

"I'm sorry," I apologized, knowing how much he'd love to see the sun.

"Why? I am what I am."

He has had over a hundred years to accept it, so I guess there was nothing to be sorry about. I started the car and backed out, realizing we were running out of time. The drive home seemed a lot quicker, though I didn't speed. I guess it was because David distracted me by talking about our visit.

As soon as I parked in the drive, he opened the door. "I'll be right back," he announced as he stepped out.

I hopped out of the car before he could get away. "Wait…where are you going?"

He turned and smiled. "I need to get my car. You don't want your father to come home and be surprised to find me here."

"Oh, right," I replied as he dashed down the street.

I went inside and immediately headed upstairs to get my book bag. I set it beside the island and fixed lunch for myself while I waited for his return. As I sat to eat, he walked in and took a seat across from me, grinning.

"What?" I asked, sandwich in midair.

"Nothing...just happy to see you."

"Awww..." I replied, taking a bite.

He laughed quietly as he leaned over and grabbed my bag, pulling out my books. "So what do we need to study?" he asked, looking up from one of my notebooks.

"Well, I have history on Monday and math on Tuesday. You could really help me with history, since you've been around so long," I teased, taking another bite. He smiled as he put all the other books away and moved my history book forward along with the binder for that class. I finished my lunch and cleaned my area so we could get started.

"I have a study guide in the inside pocket," I pointed out. "Mostly multiple choice and true/false and then a couple of essay questions."

"So how well do you know this subject?"

"I'm going to guess not as well as you do, being that you lived through most of what we learned this semester," I grinned.

"True," he replied, looking over the study guide.

"Next year, I'll be taking government. Your insight will be helpful for that class as well, since your father was a politician," I commented.

"Glad I'm so useful," he responded, lifting his eyes to mine and smiling.

I was momentarily stunned by his gaze and had to break away by looking down at my notes. As I read over them, I thought about David's past and his parents. Could it be what he told Dad was true? I raised my head to ask and found him reading my history book.

"What you told my father about your parents...was it true?"

He looked up and gave a slight smile. "Yes, it was. My mother killed herself not too long after my funeral. My father's heart attack came later...when I visited him."

"You did it to him?" I replied, shocked. "But you said the night you left was the last time you saw them."

"It was, technically. After my change, I wasn't who I used to be. I was a new being in my old skin."

"So what happened?" I asked, leaning on my elbow.

He closed the book and set it on the counter, folding his hands over it. "I wanted to know they were all right, and even though I refused to go back, I continued to watch them. But I found my 'death' was harder on them than I expected. My mother was so distraught and guilt-ridden that she couldn't bear to live with herself. So she did the only thing she knew to finally find peace."

"The deaths of his son and wife weighed heavily on my father, so it was only a matter of time before he would succumb to it as well. He had a minor heart attack after my mother's death and was deteriorating fast. Against my better judgment, I decided to visit him. I resisted the urge to go when my mother was suffering, but after she died, I had to see him."

"I convinced a servant to invite me in and then forget I was there, sending him off to bed as I entered. I found my father sitting alone in the library by the fireplace, an empty brandy glass in his hand. He looked like he was already dead, but when I touched him he jerked. Staring wide-eyed at me, he never spoke a word. I called to him, but he just gaped. Then slowly his eyes closed and he slumped in the chair. I was the last thing he saw before dying," he whispered as he stared out the window into the backyard, lost in an old memory.

"What did you do?" I whispered, astonished.

He looked at me, his brow furrowed. "I ran. I never notified anyone, just ran."

I went over to him and wrapped my arms around his shoulders, feeling the compulsion to comfort him. He probably never told anyone about what happened. He took a long, deep breath and then gently pushed me away.

"We should start studying," he commented quietly.

"You're right. Dad will be home soon," I replied, sitting back down.

We started out slow, the heaviness of what he revealed still hanging in the air. I tried occasionally to lighten the mood and eventually I succeeded. Soon he was more upbeat as he quizzed me and tried to catch me off guard. I got stuck on three questions, which was a disappointment, but three out of a hundred wasn't bad. We were working on the essays when Dad walked through the door.

"Megan, we're home!" he shouted.

"In the kitchen!" I called back.

"Vanessa is joining us for dinn…oh, hey David," Dad greeted, stopping in the doorway as he stared at us. Vanessa nearly ran into him. "I must have missed your car…" he trailed off.

David stood and turned to my father. "I came over to help Megan study for finals. I hope you don't mind."

"No, not at all. That's kind of you," he responded, the shock wearing off.

Vanessa peeked around him and grinned. "Hi David. How are you?"

He smiled back at her and replied, "Good. And you?"

She pushed Dad out of the way, moving closer to him. "Doing well…just finalizing a couple things before the wedding. Are you going to be able to come?"

I leaned over and looked at his face – cool and calm. He glanced back at me and grinned. "I have yet to be invited."

She jerked her head my way and narrowed her eyes. "Megan, why haven't you asked David to join you?"

"I…I…forgot. There's so much going on right now, it slipped my mind," I stammered, stunned he'd throw me under the bus like that.

"Well, you're more than welcome to come," she persuaded, rubbing his arm.

"Thank you for the invitation, Vanessa. I'll have to check my schedule, but I would love to attend," he responded smoothly.

She giggled, flipping her hair. That was when Dad decided to step in. "All right…these two need to get back to studying," he commented, dragging her into the family room.

David chuckled quietly as he sat back down, and I glared at him, turning away slightly. "Could you get this knife out of my back…it's killing me," I whispered angrily as I pointed to it.

"I was being honest. Besides, it's not like I'll be able to come unless it rains," he quietly replied with a half-smile.

As Dad and Vanessa jabbered in the family room while watching TV, we continued our study session. After a half hour more of history, we decided to move on to math. By five, I was ready to call it quits. Dad came to the counter and waited for me to finish the last problem for David to check.

"Would you like to stay for dinner?" he asked him as I packed my books away.

"I appreciate the offer, but I must be going. I have to work tonight," he replied, standing.

"No problem," Dad responded and then went to the refrigerator to find something to cook, probably happy he wasn't staying.

"It was good seeing you again, Vanessa," David commented as I walked him out of the room. She didn't have a chance to reply.

I hung my bag on the banister, leading him out the door and onto the porch to sit on the steps. I needed some peace from studying and the racket brought on by Dad and Vanessa. The rain finally let up, allowing us to enjoy the evening without getting washed out. Side by side, we watched as the sky grew darker with the oncoming night.

"You can never watch a sunrise or sunset, can you?" I asked after a moment.

"I could, but it wouldn't be very enjoyable," he replied with a smile.

"Hmph," was my only reply.

He turned to me and took my chin in his hand. He was getting cooler already; the deer blood must be wearing off. I could tell it in his eyes, too, as he leaned closer. But as he gazed into mine, I stopped worrying about his changing body temperature and eye color. He leaned in and as our lips touched, I closed my eyes and got lost in his slow, soft kiss.

As much as I wanted to do this all night, I couldn't. I gently broke away and embraced him instead. "Thank you for staying last night and spending the day with me," I whispered in his ear.

"You're very welcome," he replied, kissing my cheek.

Porch lights around the neighborhood began to come on, and I knew it was only a matter of time before he had to leave. Unfortunately, it was sooner rather than later. He stood and I followed, walking with him to his car. He was parked on the street, making it not as obvious. No wonder Dad missed it. And it was the BMW, which doesn't stick out as much as the Bugatti.

"I'll call you tomorrow night," he remarked as he opened his door. "The weather is supposed to be nice during the day. Get out and enjoy it for me."

I stepped around it and gave him another hug. I didn't want him to go. I kissed him again, longer than on the steps, but pulled back when I heard the front door open. Dad was no doubt checking on us.

David gave me a small peck on the cheek and then climbed in the car and started it. I walked to the end of the drive and watched as he drove down the street, a feeling of emptiness instantly consuming me with his absence.

# Chapter 27
## Moving In

I lingered at the end of the drive for a while, staring down the street and hoping David would turn around and come back to me. But he didn't and probably wouldn't with my dad fiddling around in the front yard spying on me. I sighed and slowly headed up to the house. Dinner was probably ready anyway.

Dad followed me inside and to the kitchen. I went to the patio doors and stared out into the dim backyard. The fireflies were starting to come out, dancing with each other among the sleeping plants. He called my name and I glanced over my shoulder at him.

"Hmm?"

"I said it was nice of David to study with you," he repeated as he pulled the food from the oven and set it on the counter.

"Oh yeah, it was really helpful."

Vanessa came into the kitchen and looked over Dad's buffet as I turned and faced them. "Mmmm...smells good, Jack," she commented, kissing him on the cheek. She leaned on the counter, looking at me. "So Megan...are we going to see more of David once school's out?"

I grabbed the plates out of the cabinet and set them down. "Probably not. Summer classes and work will keep him busy." Not to mention the hot summer sun that'll keep him at home asleep.

"That's too bad. I really enjoy his company," she replied, taking a plate and fixing it.

Dad was right behind her. "Does this mean more evening dates and late visits then?" he asked, putting a piece of chicken on his.

I grabbed mine and started loading it up. "Not without your permission, of course," I responded.

He smiled and took a seat at the table in the nook. I sat across from Vanessa, who was already eating. She couldn't even wait for us to get seated before starting. I took a bite and stared into the backyard, not interested in their conversation as they discussed honeymoon plans. I guess since most of the wedding stuff was done, it was time to move on to the next big thing.

"Do you have any plans for tomorrow?" she asked me out of the blue.

"No...why?" I questioned.

"Oh, Meg, I forgot to tell you," Dad interrupted suddenly. "We're going to be moving Vanessa's belongings into the house this week. I'll need you to help clear space for them."

I set my fork down and looked at him in shock. "She's moving in already?"

"The wedding's in a week and her rent is almost up."

I shook my head in disbelief, surprised time had passed so quickly. I wasn't ready for this so soon, to deal with her on a daily basis. The old feelings of deceit and betrayal came flooding back as I looked at her. She grinned, sticking a broccoli floret in her mouth. She purposely instigated this, knowing how I'd react.

"I guess I'll spend my Sunday cleaning out the attic then," I grumbled as I grabbed my half-eaten plate and went to the trashcan. I scraped it off and rinsed my dishes, leaving them in the sink. Vanessa could take care of them tonight since she wanted to be a part of this household so badly.

I didn't bother saying good night, heading straight up to my room. I was so mad I was being made to do this. Grabbing a random book off my shelf, I flipped the radio on and flopped onto the bed. I tried to concentrate on the words, but I couldn't. I was too angry, too frustrated, to concentrate. All I could think about was Dad's announcement and the fact I was being forced to make room for the step-witch I didn't even want around.

Realizing there was nothing I could do to change any of it, I decided to just go to sleep. I put the book on my bedside table and turned out the light, curling up in my blanket. In an attempt to relax, I closed my eyes and planned how to tackle the attic. There's so much up there, it'll take me all day just to get it cleared. I wonder how much junk Vanessa has. Can't be too much, living in a small apartment all these years.

Sometime while determining how much she could have accumulated over her short adult life, I drifted off.

I woke to the sun streaming through the curtains, seeing the light through my eyelids. Morning. Slowly sitting up and stretching, I tried to motivate myself to get up. I wasn't looking forward to this task at all, but it was something I've been assigned to do. And if I wanted to have a free evening to study some more and see or talk to David, I needed to get moving.

Dragging my weary body into the bathroom, I begrudgingly brushed my teeth and washed my face but didn't bother to shower since I was going to get dusty anyway. I threw on some lounge clothes and headed downstairs to grab something quick to eat. Entering the kitchen, I found Dad in his usual spot.

"Ready to get to work, I see," he commented, folding his paper.

I grabbed a yogurt out of the fridge and a spoon from the drawer. "Yep. So what am I doing exactly?"

"Go through the things in the attic and separate them into trash and donations," he replied, then hesitated. "I'll also need you to clear out your mother's closet."

I shoved my spoon into the cup and glared at him. "What?"

"Megan, it's time to move on…to get rid of her clothes and things. We don't need to hold on to them any longer."

I could feel the anger burning inside me. "And you want me to do it? Do you know how hard this is going to be?" I almost shouted.

"Please calm down. I have to help Vanessa get her apartment cleaned out and fixed up. I need you to take care of this. I know it's hard, but you'll get through it. Think of it as part of the process of letting her go…the final stage."

"But I don't want to let her go! I don't want to forget!" I shouted, tears pooling in my eyes as I stood.

He looked at me sympathetically and sighed. Standing, he moved to me and put his hand on my shoulder. "Fine…keep what you want, but a majority of it has to go. We have to make room."

"Yeah…for someone who doesn't belong here," I muttered, storming out of the room.

I climbed the stairs and stood beneath the attic hatch in the hall, still fuming. Jumping as high as I could, I grabbed the string and pulled down the hidden stairs, starting up them once they were set.

As I neared the top, I poked my head in and glanced around for a light. It was dim and humid and smelled of decaying memories. I stepped a little higher and hit the light bulb with my head, grabbing the pull and switching it on. Scanning the room, I surveyed the mess I had to sort and let out a heavy sigh.

The attic was fairly large and the clutter seemed endless. Stuck inside on such a nice day – sorry David. Luckily, the dormer windows on the front let some natural light in, though it wouldn't really be bright until late afternoon. I stepped up into the attic and went to each of them, opening them and letting fresh air in as well.

I found a clear spot on the floor and sat, dragging the closest box to me and opening it to see what was inside. Miscellaneous papers, bills mostly, from ten years ago. Nothing important. I pushed it aside and pulled another box toward me. Inside were folders labeled 'kindergarten', '1st grade', '2nd grade', and so forth until high school, though everything after seventh grade was empty. Each of the folders had several items in it like papers and artwork – things Mom decided were worth keeping.

I flipped through some of them, looking at my handwriting and drawings as a child and laughing at my terrible artwork. On through the different grades, I watched how it changed and then I reached my seventh grade folder.

Dredging up painful memories, I pulled out a story I had written about my mom being sick. My eyes welled up as I read it and a teardrop fell onto the paper. I wiped it off and replaced it, closing the box and pushing it to my opposite side to keep. I stood up and dusted off my pants and looked around for something else to go through, still wiping tears from my eyes.

I found another box, but this one didn't have a lid. It was filled with toys and miscellaneous knick-knacks. Pulling it over, I sifted through it. I took out the items I wanted and put the others in a space behind me. They'd be donations.

On and on I sorted, taking a break every once in a while to remove some of the items when it became too overwhelming. It was hard, emotional work at times, but other times it was entertaining. I came across things I'd never seen before or hadn't seen in a long time, examining and reminiscing and then deciding what to do with them.

I found the most challenging part of this whole chore, aside from moving my mother out, was deciding what to keep and what to discard. If I could, I'd keep all her things, but I knew I couldn't. Picking only a few select items that were really important to me, I trudged on until I reached the end of the attic.

Under the farthest window sat a large chest. Kneeling in front of it, I ran my fingers over the dusty, old wood. A discolored brass latch held it closed, and I tried it to see if it would open. To my surprise, it did.

I peeked inside, finding it filled with pictures, papers, and other items. Nothing too unusual. Opening it all the way, I rested the lid against the window frame and first studied the items in the tray hanging from it. There were pieces of jewelry and trinkets, old and forgotten. I rifled through them, picking up a few and examining them, and then moved on to the main part of the chest.

On top of the mass of items filled to the brim, I grabbed an album and opened to the first page, finding pictures from Mom and Dad's wedding. I flipped through each of them and smiled. Dad was so young-looking and handsome in his tuxedo, and Mom was absolutely radiant in her gown. They looked so happy in all of the photographs. When I reached the end, I closed it and sighed.

I put it aside and found another album, older than theirs. In it were photos from my grandparents' wedding. The dress my grandmother wore was the same as my mom's, and she looked just as beautiful in it. I flipped through the aging photos, never having seen them before, and sighed again.

Like my mother, my grandmother died fairly young. My grandfather remarried shortly after and has nothing to do with our family now. He started a new life much like what my dad was doing, forgetting his first true love.

I closed the album and set it on top of the other one, continuing to rummage through the chest. My mom's dried bridal bouquet was there, as were various other wedding memorabilia from her wedding and my grandmother's. When I reached the bottom, I noticed a large box. I pulled it out and set it on the floor in front of me, slowly opening the lid. A translucent plastic bag was neatly tucked inside.

I slowly unzipped it and gasped as I stared at my mother's wedding gown. With shaky hands, I pulled it out. Something tumbled down the back and rested on the floor beside me. I leaned over and picked up the tarnished silver tiara, admiring the still sparkling crystals and beautiful lace edged veil attached to it.

Setting it on my head, I held the dress up to my frame and looked down at it and then glanced around for a mirror. I knew I set a full-size one aside, and I soon found it leaning near a window. Dragging the gown with me, I stood in front of the mirror with it held up to my shoulders and smiled. I had to try it on.

I quickly peeked down the attic hole - silence. Dad must be gone, probably feeling it best to leave me alone. I quickly removed my clothes and carefully put on each piece, making sure not to harm it in any way. First was the floor-length satin slip, then the underskirt, and lastly the sheer silk and lace gown. Looking at myself in the mirror, I was amazed by how stunning it was in person. The photographs in the albums did not do it justice.

The bodice was made completely out of lace with a sweetheart neckline, cap sleeves, and satin buttons running down the back. The flowing organza skirt was accentuated by the ruffled petticoat and had a small train that spread out nicely behind me as I took a few steps and glanced back at myself in the mirror. As old as it was, it was still beautiful.

I stared at myself as I fiddled with my hair, trying different styles. When I had the one I liked, I adjusted the veil to work with it. I picked up the album and looked at the picture of my mom and then at me. It was uncanny how much I looked like her. I put it down and just stared at myself in the mirror, a big smile on my face. I'd wear this dress for my wedding day as my mom had worn it for hers and my grandmother for hers.

Then it dawned on me. Will I ever get married? I suspect it'll be to David, but will he marry me? If he did, will I remain a human or will I have to be like him? Then if I changed, could we even have a wedding?

I gazed down at the dress, feeling saddened that I may never get to wear it for him, for myself. Carefully slipping it off, I folded it and put it back in the bag with the veil and zipped it shut. I replaced the top on the box and gently lowered it into the bottom of the chest. Returning all the other items, I gently closed the lid.

Regardless of whether I ever get to wear it or not, I wanted to keep it safe, especially from Vanessa. The latch on the chest had a lock, but I didn't know where the key might be, and I didn't want to lock it and never be able to open it again. I searched through the tray but didn't find it. I checked under the lid and even felt for it under the chest itself but never found anything. Giving up, I shut it and hoped I'd eventually come across it during my cleaning.

I went back to work, organizing and sorting until the attic was straight and had plenty of space for Vanessa's junk. I climbed down the stairs and grabbed a trash bag, broom, and dustpan, and then headed back up. I might as well sweep it, too.

All tidy and ready for her, I shut the windows and carried the remaining donation and trash boxes one by one down the stairs to the hall. I left them there, since I'd have more to add after cleaning out Mom's closet. I glanced in my room at the time and decided to take a break for lunch.

After washing up, I made a sandwich and put it on a plate with some chips and then headed into the family room to watch TV. It was nice to veg out a moment and let the TV do the thinking for me. But it lasted so long. The show I was watching ended and I realized I needed to get back to work. My moment of peace gone, I sighed as I threw my trash away and headed back upstairs to reality.

I entered, pausing and glancing around the master bedroom. Dad's bed was made and his dresser was neat. Nothing looked any different than it did when I was young and would sneak in at night and lay with Mom and Dad if I had a nightmare or if there was a bad thunderstorm.

I went over to his closet and flipped on the light, peeking inside. I didn't see anything I needed to change in there, and Vanessa should have no reason to use his space. Mom's closet was big enough. I shut off the light and walked over to it.

Opening the door, I flipped on the light and just stood in the doorway. I stood and stared for a long time. I hadn't opened it in years. No one had opened it in years.

I slowly walked in and ran my hands along her clothes, stopping to smell them. They smelled like what I remember she smelled like. I closed my eyes and held them, taking a deep breath. Then I released the bunch I was hugging and stared at them, wanting to cry.

How could Dad make me do this? I don't care if this is part of letting her go; I never planned to let her go. He may have decided to move on, but I didn't.

But if I didn't do this, some stranger would. And that stranger would be Vanessa. I sucked back the tears and sighed, getting to work.

Starting in the back of the closet, I found a clothes bag and out of curiosity opened it. Inside were several of the party dresses Mom wore for Dad's various company events and fundraisers. I flipped through them and picked out the ones I liked and removed the others. Glancing through all the other outfits, I picked my favorites and put them in the bag and zipped it up. I removed it and took it to my closet, hanging it up.

Before heading back to Dad's room, I dashed down the stairs to the garage and found a large, empty box and brought it back up to the room, filling it with all the remaining clothes and shoes. I went through her dresser and emptied the clothes out of it and then dragged the box out into the hall.

For my next chore, I set about clearing off the top of her vanity. Dad left everything as it was the last day she shared the room with him, a layer of dust covering her items. Wiping them off, I picked a few of my favorite perfumes and discarded the rest.

Her jewelry boxes were spread around the room, filled with untold treasures I couldn't wait to discover. Starting with the couple on the dresser, I looked at every piece hidden inside and then replaced them neatly back in their home. I wasn't leaving them for Vanessa or donating them, so I took all of them to my room and put them on the top shelf of my closet. As I was putting the last one up, I noticed a small key taped to the bottom. I removed it and held it in my hand, grinning.

I immediately ran up the attic stairs to the chest and slipped the key into the lock, turning it with ease. I tried the lid and was unable to open it. Perfect. Now my mom's precious memories were safe and for me alone. I pushed the chest back where I found it and covered it with an old quilt. Hopefully, no one would disturb it until I was able to take it away from here.

I shut the attic hatch, feeling triumphant, and went back to Dad's room. By the time I finished, it was starting to get dark, but Dad wasn't home yet. I dragged the last of the boxes to the garage to add to the others and went to the kitchen to get a drink.

As I leaned against the counter enjoying my glass of ice water, I saw a light flash across the front of the house. That must be him. Going to the door, I opened it just in time to be greeted by Dad and Vanessa carrying several boxes.

"Hey Meg. Thanks for getting the door. Do you mind going to the car and grabbing a couple things?"

I rolled my eyes and grumbled, "Sure, why not. It's not like I did any strenuous work today."

I went out to the car, my car, and bent over to pick up a box when arms wrapped around my waist. Before I could react, I was spun around, revealing David's grinning face.

"Good evening, Megan. Would you like some help?"

I placed my hand over my heart and sighed. "You scared me half to death! What are you doing here?"

"I wanted to see you…maybe study some more," he smiled.

"Good, I could really use your company. I've had a difficult and emotionally draining day," I commented, reaching in the car for a box. I turned and handed it to him. "Here…take this and this and this."

I grabbed two boxes and headed toward the house, David following behind effortlessly carrying what I gave him. I entered and yelled for Dad, asking where he wanted them. He came jogging down the stairs and stopped at the base.

"Oh! Hey David. Perfect timing, I see. Come to help Megan study again?"

He peeked out from behind the boxes and gave a polite smile. "Yes, sir."

"You and David can take them up to my room and put them in your mo…I mean, Vanessa's closet. By the way, you did a great job."

"Thanks," I replied, heading up the stairs as David followed.

"So that's why you had a difficult day," he commented quietly.

I nodded as we reached the top and headed toward Dad's room. Vanessa was inside, already making herself at home. "Here's some more," I announced as I set them on the floor with David following my lead.

She didn't even acknowledge me. "Well, hello David. What a nice surprise! Thanks for your help," she cooed as she touched his arm.

"You're welcome," he responded, bowing his head and folding his hands behind his back as he stepped slightly to the side. There was an awkward silence and then he cleared his throat. "Megan and I must be going. We have studying to do," he remarked, taking my arm.

She smiled big and broad. "Are you staying for dinner then?"

"I have already eaten, but I'll stay until we're done."

"How sweet," she commented with a smirk.

We stopped by my room to get my book bag and then went downstairs to the table, passing Dad on the way. "I've ordered dinner…it'll be here soon," he commented and I nodded.

David and I sat at the island and I proceeded to pull out my books, but he stopped me, placing his hand on mine. He stared deep into my eyes and asked, "Do you want to talk about your day?"

I looked down. "Not now. Later," I whispered as I lifted my eyes to his. He smiled and let go of my hand, allowing me get my remaining books and folders. Then we studied until the food arrived.

I paused to fill a plate and while I ate, he asked questions. We worked for an hour more and then decided to call it quits. I told Dad and Vanessa good night and David said goodbye before following me to the door.

"I'll see you shortly," he whispered as he stood on the porch, gently kissing my lips.

"I can't wait," I grinned, ducking inside.

I skipped up to my room and decided to shower, since I hadn't taken one yet. It was refreshing, but I was just too anxious to really enjoy it. Rushing through, I finished and dried and then hurriedly dressed and sat on the edge of my bed, eagerly waiting for David to show. An hour passed and I was about to give up when he tapped on the balcony door.

"I almost thought you changed your mind," I commented as I let him in.

"I was held up with an issue at home," he explained as I crawled into bed. "So what happened today?" he asked as he sat next to me.

I placed my head on his chest and sighed. "I had to clean out the attic and my mom's closet to make room for Vanessa's junk."

"I see...how did you fare?"

"I cried a couple times. Dad said it was part of the 'letting go' process. But I didn't let it all go...I kept a lot of things – some clothes, perfumes, and all of her jewelry. And I wasn't going to let Vanessa have any of it. It's rightfully mine."

He put his arms around me and held me close. "I'm sorry you had to do that. It was unfair and must have been difficult."

I sighed again. "Thanks again for coming tonight."

"You're very welcome," he replied quietly, tilting my chin up and kissing me. "Now you should sleep. You have an exam tomorrow."

He rested his cheek on the top of my head and rubbed my back, making me drowsy. "Okay," I whispered as I drifted away.

I woke the following morning feeling well-rested and ready for the day. The sun was shining and the birds were singing. Too bad I had to go to school. I got ready, grabbed my bag, and joined Dad in the kitchen. To my surprise, Vanessa was there, too.

"Morning Dad...Vanessa," I greeted as I grabbed breakfast. "I'm surprised to see you here so early."

"Morning, Meg," he replied. She barely raised her eyes from her cup of coffee. She looked rough. "She stayed the night last night, deciding to go ahead and unpack her things, even though I told her there was no need," he answered for her, rubbing her back. She looked irritated by it.

I smiled slightly. "Well, I'm off. See you this evening," I announced as I headed out the door. The sooner, the better.

I arrived at school and sat in front of my locker, doing some last minute studying for the exam. Shortly thereafter, I was joined by Claire and Justin. They were laughing and carrying on like today was any other day. I closed my book as they sat beside me, waiting patiently.

Claire was grinning ear to ear. "How was your picnic Friday?"

Wow…so much happened this weekend I forgot about it. "Umm…it was great. I learned a lot about David," I replied, fidgeting with my book bag. More than I ever thought I would.

She eyeballed me. "Like what?" she coaxed.

What could I say? "His…history. It was very…interesting. The picnic itself was nice," I commented, trying to change the subject before she could ask anymore. "We sat on a knoll by the pond in the Japanese Garden at Maymont."

"That sounds so romantic. I wish somebody would take *me* on a picnic in the park," she harped as she glared at Justin.

"Megan, tell your boyfriend thanks for making the rest of us look bad," he commented sarcastically.

Claire and I laughed as the others arrived, and we chatted briefly until the first bell. As Claire and I headed to first period, Justin walked with her for once, kissing her cheek at the door and then dashing down the hall so he wouldn't be late. She grinned as we entered and took our seats.

The weather was so pleasant, we decided to eat outside for lunch. I was the center of attention, everyone curious how my picnic went. After I retold what I said to Claire and Justin earlier, the conversation shifted to what everyone else did over the weekend. Most spent it studying or being lazy. They saved me for last.

"David and I went to an art museum on Saturday and then he helped me study the rest of the evening," I replied, playing with my food.

"Well, that's a more appropriate activity for a rainy day than going on a picnic," Ben commented. He was in a bad mood. His weekend was spent attempting to study while watching his twin sisters.

"That was nice of him. What did you two do Sunday?" Erin asked.

"Nothing until that evening. He was busy all day and so was I," I responded and paused. "We had to make room for Vanessa, so my dad tasked me with cleaning out the attic and my mom's closet."

Claire gasped and Ben's expression softened. Justin and Erin were pretty clueless. "Why is that such a big deal?" he asked insensitively.

Claire turned to him and whispered rather loudly, "Her mom died four years ago."

"Oh…I'm sorry, Megan," he apologized. "I…I didn't know."

"How are you doing?" Ben asked, his tone dramatically different than before.

"Much better…I kept a lot of things, stuffing them in the back of my closet. I was determined not to give it all away."

"And you shouldn't," Claire agreed. "So you said you saw David that evening?" she asked, helping to get rid of the awkwardness I felt.

"Yeah…he came by to help me study and I was glad to have his company," I replied, playing with a curl.

Ben's expression changed back. "Wow, with all that *studying*, you should ace your test."

"I plan to," I replied, giving him a harsh look. Before he could say anymore, the bell rang, signaling the end of lunch.

The rest of the day breezed by like I breezed through my history exam. It wasn't as hard as I thought it'd be and knew I got an 'A' on it. I noticed a lot of my classmates didn't feel the same as I did about it, though. I guess David really helped the subject stick in my mind.

Out in the parking lot, everyone discussed the exam they took that day. Claire seemed the most worried; she had math, her least favorite subject. The rest of the gang seemed satisfied with how they did.

I put my arm around her and rubbed her shoulder. "Don't worry. I have math tomorrow."

That didn't make her feel any better. "But you're good at everything! I've never known you to fail."

I removed my arm and leaned against the car. "I'm sure you did fine. And if you didn't, maybe the rest of the class didn't either and the teacher will grade on a large curve," I commented, hoping that would make her feel better. She looked at me skeptically. "I've heard of it happening. Don't give up hope."

She finally smiled and headed to her car with Justin. Erin decided it was time for her to depart as well, leaving Ben standing with me. We were quiet for a while, then I remarked, "I'm sorry you had such a crappy weekend. Just think…this weekend won't be as bad. School ends and we have the party."

"Yeah…so begins my summer of minimum wage labor," he grumbled.

"Oh, about that…where will you be working? I don't think you ever told us."

"At a game store," he replied, kicking the pavement.

"That's an awesome job…for you, I mean. Better than flipping burgers or laboring out in the hot sun," I responded, nudging him with my shoulder.

He brightened up a little, grinning slightly. "Yeah, I guess so."

"And you probably get first peek at new games and get to try them out before anyone else. That'll make Justin jealous," I added, and his smile widened.

"Yeah, he'll be so envious," he replied, staring off into the distance and contemplating his upper hand.

Finding it the right opportunity to do so, I told him I had to get going. He didn't try to keep me, but instead said goodbye and started walking as I climbed in my car and took off. Thank goodness it was a clear day and he didn't ask for a ride.

When I got home, I threw my bag on the table in the nook. I went to the refrigerator to determine what to cook for dinner when I heard a groan coming from the family room. I looked but didn't see anything. Creeping over cautiously, I didn't know what to expect, but I prepared myself for anything.

I peeked over the couch. "Vanessa!" I exclaimed, and she sat straight up. "What are you doing here?"

"I was so exhausted, I called out today. I was watching TV, but must have turned it off before falling asleep," she replied groggily, rubbing her eyes and stretching.

I sighed. "I'm going to start dinner and study for a while. You're welcome to go up to the guest room and finish your nap, so I don't disturb you," I commented as I headed back to the kitchen.

She yawned. "No, I think I've slept long enough. I had a friend drop off a few more things, and I need to get them stored away. I'm going to put them up in the attic," she responded as she stood and stretched again. "When I was up there earlier, I made some room near that old chest. You know, the one with the quilt over it," she remarked, leaning against the couch.

Shoot, she found it. I tried to remain calm as I pulled out several pots and pans. "Oh, that old thing," I responded.

"Yeah. I tried to open it to put the quilt inside, but it was locked. And I couldn't find a key anywhere to unlock it," she continued as she watched me. "Do you know what's inside it? If it's nothing important, I'd like to use it for some of my more precious things. I've always wanted a hope chest."

My face started burning. I didn't know if it was from anger, the heat of the stove, or fear. "No, I don't," I replied as evenly as I could.

"Maybe I'll mention it to Jack tonight. He probably has the key," she remarked as she walked away.

There is no way in hell she's taking my mom's hope chest. She can go buy her own. That chest is mine. And she's purposely getting me worked up over it so she can make me break...

"Tsk!" I reacted, grabbing my finger and staring at the thin, red line getting thicker and spilling down my palm. In my anger, I inadvertently sliced my finger as I was intensively cutting vegetables. I rinsed it off and grabbed a bandage from the cabinet.

My wound securely covered and my emotions calmer, I finished prepping dinner and slipped the chicken into the oven before going to the table and opening my books. I had just started studying when Vanessa returned and then a moment later, Dad walked through the front door. When would she ask him about the chest? Did he even know about it? I played with my hair and read through formulas as he entered the room, greeting us and giving her a kiss on the cheek.

"I see you have dinner going," he commented to her.

"Oh no, not me – Megan," she admitted. She better not take credit.

He came over to the table. "Smells good, Meg. What are we having?" he asked, leaning on an empty chair near me.

"Oven fried chicken, squash, homemade mashed potatoes, and greens."

"A savory, old-fashioned southern dinner! What did I do to deserve this?"

"Nothing…it just sounded good tonight," I replied, returning to my studying.

He kissed the top of my head and then joined Vanessa in the family room. I eavesdropped as he told her about his day and the funny or annoying things that happened. Hearing nothing worthwhile, I took a break and checked on the food. The greens and squash had cooked long enough, and the potatoes were ready for mashing.

I peeked at the chicken and then pulled it out, setting it on the counter with the other food before calling Dad and Vanessa in to eat. We fixed our plates and went to the dining room since my study materials were all over the nook table. Most of the meal was quiet with some small talk, but nothing interesting. Then Vanessa asked the question I'd been waiting for.

"Do you know anything about the hope chest up in the attic?"

Dad furrowed his brow in thought. "Chest? No…what does it look like?"

"Very old, walnut, I think. I was going to put the quilt that was laying on top of it inside, but I couldn't get it open. Do you have a key?"

"I don't remember a chest up there. Maybe it was Megan's mother's or something I picked up at an auction. I'll look through my dresser to see if I might have one."

"Okay. If it's empty and Megan doesn't mind, can I have it?" she asked sweetly.

"I don't mind. Do you, Megan?"

Over my dead body. "No, not at all…as long as it's not my mom's," I replied, though I knew that was pointless to add. She'd probably trash the contents and claim it was empty to spite me. I have to make sure she never has a chance to check. I needed to get it out of the house soon.

I glanced at her and got the feeling she knew I was protecting it. And she was determined to have it. Continuing to silently eat my food, I avoided looking at her so I wouldn't blow up. She remained quiet, too, occasionally glancing at me to see if I showed any signs of animosity toward her request.

When we finally finished dinner, I took care of the dishes as Dad packed the leftovers. Vanessa just stood around and watched, her eyes on me in particular. I was working on the pots and pans when the doorbell rang.

"I'll get it!" she exclaimed as she dashed out of the room. Dad and I shrugged, thinking she was expecting someone. "Megan, David's here," she announced as I turned to see her walk arm in arm with him through the archway, her head on his shoulder.

Dad patted me on the back. "I guess he's here to help you study again. I'll finish this up."

David politely removed his arm from hers, though she didn't want to let go, and joined me at the table. As Dad worked on the dishes, I informed David of what I already worked on and what I needed help with.

"What happened to your finger?" he asked, raising his brow as I flipped the page of one of my notebooks.

"Oh…I cut myself preparing dinner," I responded.

He took my hand in his and examined the bandage. "You should be more careful," he grinned crookedly and my heart fluttered.

"Usually I am, but I was agitated," I responded quietly, looking at my papers to avoid getting caught up in him.

"By what…or whom?" he questioned with a smile in his voice.

I glanced into the kitchen and watched as Dad put the last dish in the washer and then checked on Vanessa in the family room. "I'll tell you in a little bit," I whispered, pulling several papers out and setting them in front of him. "Let's work on this for now," I replied a little louder as Dad passed, smiling at us.

David got right to it, catching my drift. Dad sat with Vanessa and watched TV while we worked. Every so often, I glanced over to check on them. As soon as I was sure their attention wasn't on us, I whispered, "I need you to store something for me."

He lifted his gorgeous, green eyes and stared into mine, smirking. "And what might that be?"

I had a hard time breaking my gaze, but I shifted my eyes reluctantly to Vanessa, checking again to see if she might be listening in. Her attention was focused completely on the screen.

"A chest…it was my mom's. I thought it'd be safe up in the attic, but Vanessa found it today and wants it. She doesn't know what's in it because I locked it and have the key."

"Is that what caused you to cut your finger?" he asked, cocking his head and smiling.

I looked down at my paper, my heart thumping hard. "Yes. She was prodding and I tried not to let her get to me, but she did," I responded, my hand firmly grasping the pencil.

He placed his on my wrist and I looked over into his eyes, calming instantly. "What can I do to help?" he asked softly.

"Throw her off a cliff?" I suggested jokingly.

"I think there would be too many questions," he smiled.

"You're right…do you think you can take the chest tonight and keep it at your house until I have somewhere safe to put it?"

He sat back and thoughtfully rubbed his lips. "It will be tricky…but I'll take care of it."

I put my hand on top of his and squeezed it. "Thank you," I whispered.

He leaned in and gently kissed my lips. "Anything for you, Megan." A feeling of relief washed over me and I was ready to move on, returning to studying for the next hour.

I packed up my things, and he and I headed to the front door, saying good night to Dad and Vanessa on the way. Checking to make sure they weren't watching us, we detoured up the stairs and into the attic. I showed him the chest and then we quietly closed the hatch and went back downstairs to the front door.

After he left, I rushed up to my room and changed for bed, though I wasn't tired yet. I waited on the balcony, scanning the garden for him. I never saw him cross the yard, so I was surprised when he jumped over the railing and took me into his arms, kissing me.

Once the shock wore off, I sat on the chaise and stared out into the backyard. "When do you plan to sneak the chest out of the house?" I asked, curious.

"After everyone is asleep, before I go home," he responded, sitting beside me.

"How are you going to do it?" I asked, scooting closer.

He laughed quietly and my heart skipped a beat. "A magician never reveals his secrets."

"That's unfair," I remarked, sitting back.

"You will know…one day," he replied and then kissed me again.

We remained outside for a while, but at my first yawn, he suggested I go to bed. I curled up under the covers while he sat next to me, still and quiet. It took longer than last night to fall asleep, thanks to my brain working overtime processing trig problems and trying to figure out how he'd get the chest out of the house, sometimes combining the two. But eventually sleep came and sooner than expected.

I woke the next morning, pleased with myself and anxious to find out Vanessa's reaction to the missing chest. My school day dragged on and so did my evening. I wasn't sure when she'd show Dad the chest, but my answer came shortly after dinner. He found several keys and they were going to see if any worked.

They went up into the attic while David and I studied for my next exam. He smiled, assuring me the chest was indeed gone. They stayed up there for a while and then I heard them coming down the stairs, Vanessa claiming it wasn't the same chest. How clever…rather than just remove it, he replaced it. I grinned at him and resumed working.

"Well, it was empty and it's yours," Dad told her, handing the key over as they entered the kitchen.

"Okay, but I could have sworn it was nicer than that. Maybe it was the lighting…" she mumbled as she plopped down on the couch.

After about an hour, they got up and he came over to the table. "Will you two be all right if I leave for a little while to take Vanessa home?" he asked.

"You know we will," I replied.

"About another hour of studying and then I expect you to be in bed when I get home," he instructed, pointing at me.

I gave him a stern military salute as he exited and then returned to my work. We did as we were told, studying for an hour longer. David moved his car and waited out on the balcony until after my dad said good night. When the coast was clear, he entered and we talked for a while, but then he had to go. He couldn't stay tonight, and it felt strange not having him there.

The next couple of days played out the same, minus Vanessa's discovery of the switched chest. David came by each evening and helped me study, with the exception of Thursday since I didn't have an exam the next day. He showed up in my room when I went to bed, though, and kept me company until I was asleep.

At school, we continued to muster through exams. Claire worried every day that she failed the one she took, while Justin's patience in convincing her otherwise was wearing thin. Erin just enjoyed picking at them and playing around, not the least bit anxious about her tests.

Ben, on the other hand, could care less what was going on with them. He was more concerned about me, asking each day what I was doing after school and what my plans were for the following evening, even though they were all the same – go home, make dinner, study with David, and go to bed.

My fellow classmates became more and more rowdy as the week wore on. But the faculty didn't care since it'd all be over in a matter of days. There was an excitement in the air, excitement over something big – for the end of the school year and the beginning of summer, for freedom, and for parties.

# Chapter 28
## Welcoming Summer

Finally…Friday.

The hustle and bustle of everyone cleaning out their lockers and making plans for summer filled the hallways. I received well-wishes and requests for yearbook signings from random classmates, regardless if they knew me or not. In class, it was obvious the teachers were glad the year was over as we spent our time watching movies or playing games.

Smiling most the day, I was excited because it was the last day of school and tonight was the party. My friends and select classmates will have the pleasure of enjoying a grand party at an exclusive location. I can't wait to see and hear their reactions. But even with all the excitement and joy, in the pit of my stomach is a fear that something might go wrong.

Brian and Odette are going to be at the party. I know David said he'd make sure they behave, but how much can he really control them? They seem uncontrollable.

The plan was to head over to David's after school and begin decorating. There was just so much to do, I hoped we could get it all finished before the guests started arriving. Claire's mom graciously allowed us to use her minivan, which was loaded with decorations and other supplies. And at the conclusion of school, it'd be used for hauling us, too.

We anxiously counted down the seconds in our last class of the day and our junior year. When the bell finally rang, everyone took off yelling and celebrating. Erin, Ben, Claire, Justin, and I met in the parking lot and piled into the minivan.

It was hotter than it was that morning and the sun was high in the sky. I drove since I knew where we were going, and Ben sat in the front seat beside me. We were both quiet, not sure what to talk about. Just as well, Claire, Justin, and Erin were doing enough for the both of us. Occasionally, I put my two-cents in, but most of the time I just listened.

"So David won't be there until later?" Ben asked out of the blue.

"Yeah, he has work."

He looked away, not saying anymore. I turned into the neighborhood and drove around to the driveway. "Okay, someone put the sign out," I called as I pulled in slightly and parked.

As I hit the button to unlock the trunk, Claire jumped out and grabbed the sign to indicate the party's location. She shoved it in the ground and hopped back in the van. "It's a good thing we got it. I'm surprised you could even find the driveway," she commented as I drove up to the entrance.

I stopped at the call box and entered the code. The wrought iron gates slowly creaked open and I pulled through. "What's with the maximum security?" Justin questioned, staring out the back window as they closed.

Ben looked at me with inquiring eyes, expecting me to explain, but I didn't. "It's for privacy," was all I said.

"Maybe he's hiding something...maybe he's CIA or in the witness protection program," Justin hypothesized, poking his head between us.

"Nope, he just likes his privacy," I repeated as I continued along the woodsy drive.

"It's private all right," Ben muttered, staring out the window.

"Look at all this land! What does he do with it?" Erin asked, shifting from one side to the other.

"It's how they sell the property here – as estates," I replied.

"Seems like he bought more than one 'estate' to make sure he had plenty of *privacy*," Ben remarked under his breath.

I glared at him and was about to respond when I was interrupted by Justin's sudden outburst. "Holy sh-"

"Watch your language!" Claire shouted, hitting him.

I didn't have to ask; I knew that reaction. And as I came to the circle, everyone else realized why he said it, all quiet with mouths agape. I pulled around to the front door and parked the van.

"We're here," I announced as I opened my door.

Everyone soon followed, shuffling to the side of the vehicle and staring at the massive house with astounded faces. Unlocking the trunk, I walked around to the back and started unloading the supplies. I grabbed several things and put them on the porch, then stood waiting for the gawkers to realize we had a job to do.

"All right, are any of you going to help?" I asked in frustration.

"Oh, yeah...sorry. It's just...unbelievable!" Claire exclaimed, grabbing a bag.

"This party's going to be sooo awesome!" Erin shrieked, shaking excitedly as she took a couple. Then the guys followed with the rest.

My irritation subsided and I smiled as I headed to the door, pulling out the key and glancing over my shoulder at them. "Wait till you see the inside," I enticed as I unlocked it.

They ran up behind me as I opened the heavy wooden door and entered one by one, each of them stunned. "Look at this place – it's crazy!" Justin yelled.

"And the paintings...how weird," Erin remarked, glancing from one to the other. I guess David didn't feel the need to bring out the normal pieces today.

"There are some rules – no touching unless it pertains to the party and no one, I mean NO ONE, is allowed upstairs. Got it?" I ordered.

"Got it," they collectively answered.

"Good. Now on to the basement…this way," I directed as I headed down the stairs to the game room.

"Oh my God, I can't believe this place! David must have some inheritance," Claire commented, following me.

"Or he's involved in something else," Ben muttered, but I ignored him.

Smiling as I descended, I delighted in their reactions and couldn't wait to see what they'd do when they got to the bottom. We turned the corner and before I could say anything, Justin and Ben pushed past me. They dropped their bags on the bar and hit the games, bouncing from one thing to the next like kids in a candy store.

"You should check out the theater," I tempted, setting the bags I was carrying next to theirs.

I opened all the French doors leading to the patio and then separated the items – decorations outside and food stuff inside. Something was missing. There was no way this was all the food. I looked around to see if I missed any bags and called for Erin. No one answered. I went to the theater and flicked on the lights to disappointed groans.

"Erin, where's the food?" I asked, perplexed. "We only have drinks and mixes."

"Oh, I decided to hire a caterer to handle it – authentic luau. Isn't that great?" she replied quickly, wanting to return to the movie.

"Uh, yeah…sure. When will they be here?" I asked anxiously.

"After six. I'm sorry…I forgot to tell you," she responded, glancing at me apologetically. "It was easier and surprisingly cheaper this way."

"No, that's great," I replied, my hand on the switch, but then I turned around and sighed. "Guys, we really need to get moving on the party…time's a-wasting."

"Sorry, we can't help it. This movie hasn't even been released on DVD yet!" Justin whined.

"I understand, but let's get to work first, then you can play," I promised. After some grumbles, they got up and joined me.

We decorated the patio and fence around the pool, as well as the terrace. The whole time, I heard comments back and forth about the house and what a great party it was going to be. And it was going to be a great party.

A little after six, the caterers arrived and set up on the patio. The DJ came shortly after that, setting up on the terrace so he could overlook the crowd. Claire and Justin disappeared, but then reappeared a few minutes later in their bathing suits.

"What? We worked hard. It's hot and that pool is sooo inviting," she defended as I glared at them. "Look at it – it's awesome!"

"I don't know if you should do that just yet. Why don't you wait for David or our guests to arrive?" I suggested.

"We want to be the first to use it," Justin imposed before diving in with Claire right behind him. I shook my head and walked away. There was no sense fighting them.

Ben was throwing darts as I entered the game room. "Hey, I'm going to disappear for a while. If anyone asks, tell them I took a walk," I informed him.

"Where are you really going?" he asked as he threw one, just barely making it onto the board.

"I'm feeling a little tired and want to lie down for a bit."

"Where?" he questioned, turning to me with arms folded.

"In the guest room," I replied. Why does he need to know the details?

"Okay...where is it? I want to be sure to wake you before eight," he offered, heading to the board and retrieving the darts.

"Don't worry about it. I'll set my phone," I responded, and he went back to his game without another word as I headed for the stairs.

I slipped into the grand salon and found Erin in the kitchen, loading drinks into the refrigerator. "Do they eat out all the time or what?" she remarked as I stopped to check on her. The fridge was completely empty.

"Huh, I guess so," I responded, trying not to smile. "Listen, I'm going to go sit in the library and read for a while. Keep an eye on Ben, okay?"

"No problem," she replied as she smiled at me, knowing exactly what I was getting at.

I went into the foyer and with the coast clear, I quietly crept up the stairs. I glanced out the window at the patio below as I passed. Ben was standing at the edge of the pool talking with Claire and Justin – good. Continuing up to the landing, I snuck down the hall to David's room and quietly opened the door.

The little bit of light seeping in from the foyer was swallowed up by the darkness, making it difficult to see anything. I entered the room and shut the door, allowing myself to be encased in the darkness, too. I closed my eyes a moment, giving them time to adjust, but it was still pitch black when I opened them. I'd just have to use my other senses to find my way to the bed.

I took a step, carefully feeling along the wall and trying to recall his room from the two tours – a long hallway and then it opened. I remembered his bed was on the right, so I turned in that direction and followed the wall. My fingers ran over the wood paneling and my feet slowly scooted across the floor, seeing the way for me and making sure I didn't run into anything. I passed over the bathroom door and then came to the veranda wall on the other side of it.

Turning and reaching out, I continued cautiously to the left, searching for anything that resembled a bed. Then I found it. Touching the soft velvet, I moved closer and let out a quiet sigh of relief. That was where he'd be.

I paused and thought about whether or not I should join him, standing there for several seconds debating it. But after spending all that time trying to get to it, why would I go back? My decision made, I slightly parted the curtain and slipped inside. I still couldn't see a thing, staring into more darkness. Bending over, I ran my hand across the covers and found them empty. Where was he?

Suddenly, I was grabbed from behind and pulled out of the bed, a hand covering my mouth to stifle any sound. "What are you doing in here?" David whispered in my ear as he slowly removed it and turned me around.

I couldn't make out anything, but I assumed he was in front of me. "I...I couldn't wait any longer to see you," I answered quietly, reaching out and touching his chest.

"Where are your friends?" he asked as he moved away, his voice weary.

"Swimming," I replied, trying to follow him as I heard him sit on the bed.

"You don't want to stay with them?" he inquired.

"No, I want to be with you," I answered as I searched for him. His hand touched mine and he guided me to sit beside him. My fingers traced his arm and glided over his shoulder to his neck, slipping into his soft hair. "Can I stay until sunset?" I asked timidly.

He was quiet for a moment, then answered. "Yes, you may stay."

He moved farther into the bed, lying down, and I followed, stretching out behind him and putting my arm around his chest. "Thank you," I whispered in his ear.

I didn't intend to sleep; I just wanted to be near him. But something about lying there in the dark silence with him changed that. As I sighed, my head became foggy and my eyelids drooped. Burying my face in the back of his neck, I drifted away.

"Megan, wake up," a voice called quietly to me.

"David?" I responded, blinking my eyes. The curtains were open and the room was dimly lit. Outside, faint tropical rhythms carried up through open windows. His face came into focus as he caressed my cheek. "Did I fall asleep?"

"I believe you did," he replied with a crooked smile. "Many of your guests have arrived. You need to get downstairs to your party."

"Crap," I whispered loudly, sitting up straight and rubbing my face. I jumped off the bed and went to the door. "Wait, how are you going to sneak out to make it look like you came home?"

"We have that covered. You just need to get downstairs," he instructed, joining me at the door. "I'll see you soon," he whispered, kissing my protesting lips before pushing me out.

The lock clicked and I turned to try the handle, but the door wouldn't budge. Below, guests were arriving in droves, and I knew I had to get down there before a search party was sent to look for me. Making sure I wasn't seen, I stayed close to the wall and slipped into the library by way of the hidden back entrance. I hung out for a little bit, hoping I didn't look like I'd been sleeping, and then left through the main door, meeting Ben in the hall.

"Where have you been?" he asked, concerned and a little angry.

"In the library. Why?" I asked in return as innocently as I could.

He looked at me suspiciously. "Around quarter till, after you hadn't joined us, I came up and checked all the rooms I could on the main level, but you weren't in any of them. When I asked if anyone had a clue where you might be, no one knew."

"I'm sorry. I changed my mind about taking a nap and went to read instead," I lied.

"Didn't you hear me knocking? That's one of the rooms I couldn't get into, so I knocked to see if you'd answer," he responded, indicating toward the library.

I briefly glanced around the foyer, wondering if David had shown up yet. "No, sorry. I must have been engrossed in the book," I lied again.

"Well, I was really worried," he remarked, dropping his head and sighing. "Just about everyone is here, even Madeline, Cary, Brian, and Odette, but David hasn't arrived yet," he added, lifting it and looking at me.

Just as I was about to comment, I heard Erin greet him in the foyer. "Hmm, looks like he's here now," I replied, leaving Ben and heading toward him.

Ben called my name a couple times, but I ignored him. All I saw was David. I joined him and gave him a soft kiss on his cool lips, hooking my arm around his and leading him into the grand salon while everyone else headed downstairs. We passed through it and out onto the terrace, surveying the party from above.

Next to us, the DJ played Hawaiian music with a modern beat. Little plastic palm trees and hula girls cast a colorful glow around the patio. The pool shimmered and danced in the dim lighting as its serene surface was disrupted by bodies splashing and cutting through it. The hot tub was filling up quickly with excited teens and already a long line snaked from the buffet.

I glanced at David and smiled, wondering what he thought of everything, and found him staring at me instead. He placed a cool hand on my cheek and slowly moved closer, our lips nearly touching. But our kiss was interrupted by a scream. I jerked my head in its direction as some guy threw a girl in the pool – our moment ruined. We laughed quietly and then went back to observing the party.

"So are you going to tell me how you did it?" I inquired after a brief moment of silence.

"Not a chance," he replied with his mischievous grin. As my heart fluttered, I rolled my eyes and started walking away.

Taking the stairs off the terrace, we joined the crowd on the patio. He scanned the area, no doubt keeping tabs on Brian and Odette. So far, they were keeping their distance from me tonight. Madeline was mingling and Cary was trying to sneak back into the house. David gave him a look and he disappeared.

"What did you tell him?" I asked as we walked into the game room.

"That it was best he goes to his room. He's having difficulty around all these people."

"He's not much of the partying type?"

"No, he's afraid he may attack someone," he grinned. "This kind of party is not like Brian and Odette's."

I gulped. "So they would feed on people at the party?" I whispered, glancing around.

He led me away from a group standing near us. "This is not the appropriate place or time to talk about this, but yes and usually only one."

"And that one person became the victim of the Richmond Parks Ghost."

"Yes," he replied quietly, looking ashamed.

"Why can't you convince them to adopt your way of living?"

"I'm trying to make Cary completely reliant on animal blood, but Brian and Odette make it challenging." I saw his eyes catch sight of someone and then he returned to looking at me. "No more talk of this now. You should enjoy your par-"

"What are you two chatting about over here?" Ben interrupted, standing beside me and staring at David.

"Just discussing the party," I covered for us. "Are you having fun?"

"No, I'm trying to avoid Madeline, but she keeps finding me," he responded and David chuckled.

"Maybe you should give her another chance," I suggested, elbowing him in the ribs.

"I don't know," Ben responded, looking at the ground.

"She's coming," David whispered to me.

"Come on…we all have our quirks. Maybe she was nervous and didn't know what you expected of her."

He looked apprehensively at me. "I doubt…" he began, but then stopped as Madeline popped up beside David.

"Hi David, Megan…oh Ben! I've been looking for you!" she exclaimed, moving to his side. "Look, I'm really sorry about my actions at prom and on our date. I tried to be someone else rather than myself. Can we try again, this time with the real me?" she inquired sweetly. David grinned at her, but Ben didn't notice. At least I didn't think he noticed.

He looked at me with skepticism in his eyes, but then turned to her and conceded. "Okay, we'll try again. Let's just take it slow this time," he suggested and then glanced around the room. "Are you up for a game of pool?"

She smiled. "That sounds fun."

He took her hand and they left, Madeline glancing at David over her shoulder and grinning wide. I turned to him and narrowed my eyes. "What did you tell her?"

"To be more like you," he replied with his devious smile. "She does like Ben, but he's so stuck on you."

"You don't have to remind me. Do you think she'll tell him she's a…you know," I whispered as we watched them play. She was acting innocent and pretending she didn't know how to shoot the ball. Ben was happy to help her out.

"Maybe…if it comes to that. We don't tell our secret to any and everyone."

"Well, it's looking better," I replied, returning my attention to him, but not for long. Someone passed with a plate of food and my stomach growled. "Ooo…I'm getting hungry. Do you mind if I grab something to eat?"

"Please…" he replied, indicating the way.

I headed into the crowd, stopping and talking to guests as I went. It seemed as though everyone was having a good time, whether they were playing pool or playing in the pool. After several stops and starts and long waits, I finally reached the buffet and fixed my plate. I was maneuvering toward a table under the arbor when I was stopped again.

"Megan! You have got to try a drink – they're fantastic!" Ashlea exclaimed, pointing to the bar.

I looked over and saw the crowd gathered around, several people deep. They must be good. I wonder who's mixing. Then I realized David wasn't with me. I scanned the patio and when I didn't find him, I headed back inside, figuring I might as well wait in line for a drink and him.

Even being inside in the line, the crowd was too thick to see who was making these 'amazing' drinks. I nibbled on my food as we inched slowly toward the bar. When it was finally my turn to order, I stood at the end facing the crowd and asked for a strawberry daiquiri as I surveyed the party, still trying to locate David.

"Coming right up, *Megan*," Brian replied. I turned and stared at his grinning face as I stepped back. He stopped what he was doing and leaned on the counter. "I thought I'd help out. This is my specialty and as you can see, my drinks are quite popular."

He was right – mostly girls and a few boys lined the bar, clambering to get closer to him. As he went back to work, I cautiously moved forward, so as not to make a scene, and leaned over the counter. "What are you putting in the drinks to make them so popular?" I asked, almost in a growl.

He continued to grin, not threatened by me at all. "Oh, just a little alcohol. It's the last day of school…I figured the crowd needed to loosen up," he replied smoothly, filling a glass and handing it to me.

"No thank you," I stated firmly and started to walk away.

He grabbed my wrist and pulled me closer. "Not so fast…we have unfinished business," he snarled as he dragged me behind the bar. With his other hand, he grabbed some random guy and told him to take over while he stepped away for a moment.

As he pushed me toward a nearby door, I frantically searched the room for David or even Madeline but couldn't find either one. He quickly opened it and forced me inside and then shut it, throwing me to the ground. The room was filled with racks of wine bottles, and I thought if I had to, I could use one in defense, though I didn't know how much damage it'd do to a vampire.

He put his hands up, feigning surrender as he crouched near me. "I worked it out to have Odette distract David, allowing me to have some time alone with you," he explained in a calm voice. I scrambled backwards and hit a rack as he moved closer. "Don't worry. I just want to apologize for my behavior last week."

Liar. "Why?" I questioned.

He cocked his head and smirked. "Because I shouldn't have treated you the way I did. You're so delicate and easily…broken," he replied, grabbing my chin.

I jerked my head out of his hand and glared at him. "Why were you so anxious to tell me what David was?"

Again he smirked. "You deserved to know the truth. He shouldn't have misled you for so long."

"He would have told me eventually, which was fine with me."

"Why aren't you afraid?" he inquired, looking over my tensed body. I felt violated.

"I know he won't hurt me, that he…loves me."

He laughed at the thought of a vampire loving a human. "He makes it so easy," he mumbled, then bent closer, closing his eyes as he smelled me. "David picked a good one this time…better than the last," he purred.

"The last?" I questioned.

He looked dead at me, his silver eyes sending a chill down my spine. "He never told you about his love before you? Such a shame what happened," he replied, shaking his head as he smirked.

Probably more lies. I tried to get up, but he grabbed my shoulder and pinned me down. His eyes bore into mine, stern and cold. He leaned close, and I turned my face away but still tried to keep my eyes on him. Unfortunately, such a position left my throat open before him.

He grinned, his fangs exposed in his smile as he ran a cool finger down my neck, tracing a throbbing artery. "There's the fear I was looking for…"

"Brian, you…you don't want to do this," I warned as I reached behind my back for a bottle.

"But you're so tantalizing," he whispered, his cool breath creeping along my throat and sending shivers down my spine. "I wonder what David would do if I got the first taste…"

I grasped the bottleneck firmly in my hand and quickly pulled it out of the holder, dropping my body to the floor as I smashed it across his face. As he bellowed in pain, I jumped to my feet and ran out the door, slamming it behind me before he could recover.

Maneuvering from behind the bar and dashing through the sea of people, I searched for David but still couldn't find him. I went outside and stayed in the open in case Brian happened to come after me. So far, he hadn't.

I felt a hand grip my shoulder and nearly screamed. "Megan, are you all right?" Madeline asked, Ben standing next to her.

I was heaving as I looked at her, wanting to cry. I hugged her tightly, thankful she was there, and continued holding her as I uttered one word so low only she could hear. "B-Brian…"

That was all it took.

She apologized to Ben and quickly led me into the house and upstairs to David's room. Not bothering to turn on the lights, she sat me on the bed and locked the door. I held back my tears as she went to the window and scanned the yard, focusing on one spot, and then in an instant sat next to me.

"What happened?"

I looked at her, still holding back the tears. "Where's David?"

"On his way. Tell me what happened."

"He pulled me into the wine cellar and was going to…to…" I couldn't finish the sentence.

"Bite you?" she completed for me.

"Ye-yes," I replied, taking a deep breath. "But I hit him across the face with a bottle of wine and was able to get away."

She rubbed my back and let me lean my head on her shoulder. The light scent of citrus and lilies emanated from her skin and I felt soothed by it. "I don't understand why Brian is being this way…" she muttered.

The door swung open, hitting the wall, and I quickly scooted to the back of the bed as Madeline stood. I peeked around the curtain and saw David rushing in, looking for me. Quickly scrambling to my feet, I ran into his arms.

"It's all right," he cajoled softly, holding me close and stroking my hair. "You're safe now. I have Odette and Brian locked away downstairs and will deal with them after the party."

Madeline didn't bother using telepathy. "He tried to bite her," she whispered to him.

He held me tighter and was silent. I felt him turn his head in her direction, but he never said anything. They must not want me to know what they're saying to each other. Probably discussing Brian and me and in all honesty, I was glad they weren't speaking aloud. Closing my eyes, I pressed my ear to his chest and listened to his hollow sound, calmed by it.

"Megan," he whispered after a long moment of silence.

"Mmhm," I answered, my eyes still closed. I felt much better being close to him.

"I need you to go back to the party."

I looked up at him and frowned. "But I want to stay with you," I pleaded softly.

"I'll join you after a moment, but right now I need you to go back downstairs," he requested.

I sighed and then kissed his cool lips. It's unfair he's making me leave, but I guess it's necessary to do what he needs to do. "All right, but don't be long."

I gave him a hug and left, closing the door behind me. I lingered outside for a second, curiosity getting the better of me once again. Getting my ear as close to the door as possible without touching it, I eavesdropped.

They were talking so low I could barely make anything out. From what I could hear, they were discussing what to do with Brian and Odette after the party. The voices faded and then were quiet. I backed away from the door, worried they knew I was listening in, and dashed down the stairs.

The party continued as if nothing happened and no one was aware of my attack. Except Ben. He came running up to me when I reached the bottom and gave me a hug.

"Is everything all right? Are you okay?" he asked frantically.

I was a little stunned by his reaction and it took a moment for me to answer. "Yeah...yeah. I'm fine."

"What happened? Why did Madeline rush you upstairs? I was really worried about you. You had this look on your face like you were scared to death."

"No...no. It was nothing. I freaked out over something silly," I lied. I tried to walk away, but he wouldn't let me.

"I know something more happened. Was it Brian? David was gripping some blonde chick's arm as he confronted him at the bar. There wasn't any yelling, but then the next thing I knew, they disappeared."

"Stop. Nothing happened...and there's nothing to worry about," I insisted as I walked away. This time he didn't grab me.

I seized my bag from behind the bar and went to one of the bathrooms to change into my swimsuit. It was time I got to enjoy that awesome pool. Maybe it'd calm me and help take my mind off what happened. I changed, stuffing all my clothes back into the bag, and headed out to the pool.

There were still a lot of people around it, but not as many in it. I put my towel and bag on a lounge chair and went to the edge, diving in. It was so humid outside and the cold water felt refreshing on my clammy skin. I did a couple of laps and then just floated.

"Hey Megan! It's good to see you enjoying the pool!" Claire shouted from under the waterfall.

I swam over and discovered, to no surprise, Justin with her. "So is this where you two have been hiding out all night?" I asked, joining them on a bench molded out of the wall.

"Yeah, it's nice and secluded," she giggled nervously. "Anything exciting going on out there?"

I considered telling her about Brian but changed my mind. "Nope, just your typical party."

"Where's David?" Justin asked curtly, peering through the cascading water.

"He had to take care of something but should be here soon," I replied, looking at the two of them. There was an awkward silence. "Well, I'll let you get back to enjoying your solitude. I should get back out there anyway, in case he's looking for me."

"Have some fun," she suggested.

I smiled before diving under the falls. I continued to swim until I reached the edge of the pool, coming out of the water as David crouched in front of me. Hanging on the side of the wall, I wiped the water and hair out of my face and gazed up at him. He leaned closer and kissed me.

"I see you're enjoying the pool finally. I thought you would have gotten in sooner," he commented.

"It's amazing. I love the hidden spot under the waterfall, as does Justin and Claire. Are you going to join me?"

He thought about it for a minute. "I could, if you would like."

"Of course I would," I responded, flicking water at him.

"I'll only be a moment," he replied with a smile as he stood. I watched as he jogged into the house and headed up the stairs.

I went back to floating around the pool, occasionally swimming back and forth, killing time. I knew instantly when he came outside because every girl was still and quiet. As I lounged against the wall on the opposite side, I watched as he strolled up to the edge across from me, his alabaster skin in the dim lighting more beautiful than I remembered.

He dove in, swimming up to me faster than I expected. When he came up out of the water, a group of girls crowded around us. He rested his arms on the wall beside me, glancing at me as they waited for him to speak to them.

"Fans of yours?" I asked, motioning my head toward my ridiculous classmates.

He grinned and I think one of them fainted. I shook my head as I pushed off the wall and dipped under the water, taking off toward the grotto under the waterfall. Claire and Justin were still there and surprised to see me again. Moments later, David surfaced and sat next to me. She stared at him in awe, like he was some kind of god.

"I hope you don't mind us sharing the grotto with you," he commented, intertwining our fingers under water.

"No...not at all," she answered breathily.

Justin looked at her like she had lost her mind. "Well, we were just leaving anyway," he remarked, a hint of resentment in his voice. He grabbed her wrist and pulled her into the water before she could say anything else.

I looked at David and shrugged my shoulders, then threw my legs up on the bench across from me as I leaned against him. He put his arm around me and put his legs up as well. "So I see you can swim, and really well," I commented.

"Did you think I couldn't?" he inquired with a chuckle.

"No, I just can't imagine you swimming, but I see you're as graceful at it as everything else you do. Did anyone dive in the pool after you?"

He smiled. "No, they stayed on the patio."

"I'm not a jealous person, but that'll be hard to get used to...having girls and women ogling you all the time."

He laughed his heavenly laugh. "You're not like me, but I worry about boys and men 'ogling' you. A bikini? I'm surprised," he teased, kissing my burning cheek as I tucked my head. I knew without looking he was grinning from ear to ear.

"I don't own any one-piece bathing suits," I lied. I intentionally wore it, curious what his reaction would be.

"You seem to be doing better," he commented, running his fingers down my neck, shoulder, and arm.

"I am," I replied, turning my body on its side and resting my chin on his shoulder. "So what do you plan to do with Brian and Odette?"

He stared at the waterfall, watching the blurry images dance and jump around. "We don't need to discuss this now. I want you to forget about them and enjoy your party," he replied, but that wasn't good enough for me.

I sat up and looked him in the eye. "This is the perfect time to discuss it. We're alone and it'll give me peace of mind," I argued.

He stared at me for a moment and then sighed, conceding. "I'm going to ask them to leave. I can't have him acting like this and putting you in danger."

"Immediately?"

"No, but as soon as possible."

I dropped my feet into the water and stared at the ripples around my legs. This end of the pool was pretty deep – a good twelve feet, I would say. Probably why a lot of people didn't venture all the way over here. Above us, someone shouted and then there was a huge splash. Through the waves, I could see a figure at the bottom swimming toward the surface.

"It seems as though someone discovered they can dive off the rock," he commented as there was another yell and splash. "And it's catching on."

"Well, I'm getting pruney anyway," I replied, looking at my fingers and toes.

He smiled and slipped into the water, staying close to the wall in case any other people decided to take the dive. I followed, swimming to the wall and pulling myself out. He was at the lounge chair drying off, his eyebrows raised as he watched me walk toward him. I grabbed my towel and began drying myself as he continued to stare.

"What?" I asked with a grin.

"Seeing you in your swimsuit," he replied, throwing the towel around his neck.

"You saw me in the water."

"Yes, but it was distorted," he grinned. "You're captivating. That shade of blue is very complementary to your...skin," he admired, tracing the contour of my side with his fingers.

My body tingled with his touch, and I blushed as I wrapped the towel around me. His reaction was better than I expected. "Yeah, I like this suit a lot when I have a tan. Good thing I laid out the other day or else it wouldn't look as nice." There was a hint of sadness in his expression. "Oh, I'm sorry," I apologized, covering my mouth.

"Don't be," he whispered with a soft smile. "Better you than me."

I looked in his eyes and teased, "Oh, I think you would look amazing with a tan. Have you ever thought about using the fake stuff?"

His smile widened as he shook his head and my heart raced. I grabbed my bag, throwing it on my shoulder, and as I turned back, several girls surrounded him. He was trying to be kind, but they were being pushy. Must be from the alcohol Brian doled out.

I parted the group and grasped David's wrist, dragging him away. "Pardon me, ladies," I commented, leading him into the house and around to the changing rooms. "I swear, they're like vultures around you," I mumbled, closing the door behind us.

I knew it probably looked suspicious, but I had to take him somewhere private. He leaned against the counter and stared at me. "And you said you're not the jealous type," he commented, his lip curled at the corner.

"Okay…we're all a little jealous. How about I'm not psychotic jealous?" I responded, readjusting my towel.

"I can accept that," he replied, moving closer and slipping his hand under my damp, stringy hair. He pulled me to him and we kissed. In the bathroom. How awkward.

I ran my hands along his bare shoulders and chest. His skin was smooth and cool and felt tantalizing under my fingertips. I didn't want to stop, but I gently pushed away. "Whoa…not like this," I whispered.

He put his hands behind his back and stood straight. "I apologize. I'm being too forward."

I find it funny how every so often he regressed to his old ways. No matter how much time has passed and how things have changed, he's still set in them. I smiled at this and he cocked his head, giving me a puzzled look.

"I would've thought after all these years you would have adapted to the changing times, but you're still as old-fashioned as ever," I responded, pulling a sundress out of my bag.

I dropped my towel and he immediately turned around, staring at the ceiling. I giggled, since I still had my bikini on, and slipped the dress over my head. As I put my hair into a bun, I noticed him peek over his shoulder at me before turning around.

"I prefer to stick to my old ways. They make me feel more human, more like the old me," he replied, opening the door.

"Where are you going?" I asked, following him out.

"I need to change as well. I'll be right back," he responded before disappearing into the undulating crowd gathered in the game room. I guess everyone decided now was a good time to dance.

I scoped out the mass of teenagers, looking for Erin, Ben, or Claire, and finally spotted Erin near the front dancing with an unfamiliar guy. I danced through the crowd toward her, being stopped by random guys, but I pressed on. As soon as I reached her, I tapped her on the shoulder and she turned, dancing with me.

"What's up?" she shouted, barely audible over the music.

"What's going on? Why the sudden dancing?" I yelled back. She had to pick a spot right by a speaker.

"Oh...the DJ decided to liven up the crowd...no more Hawaiian music," she replied. The guy she was dancing with tapped her on the shoulder, and she shrugged and went back to dancing with him.

I nodded and smiled at her, then scanned the crowd again. Claire and Justin were dancing close to the pool and Ben and Madeline were standing side by side in the back of the room bopping to the beat. I headed toward them, curious how things were going so far.

"Hey guys. Having fun?" I asked as she smiled at me.

"Yeah...just enjoying the song," she replied, though she looked like she really wanted to get out into the group and dance. "How are you doing?" she asked quietly. I noticed Ben's eyes shift between her and me.

I leaned in, whispering in her ear, "Much better. I think the fear and shock have worn off."

She smiled and rubbed my arm. "Good."

"Where's David?" Ben asked, not looking at me.

"Oh, he went up to change."

Barely a moment later, he came up from behind Madeline and stood by me, kissing my cheek. He was dressed in a sage, button-down shirt and khaki shorts. A clean aroma emanated from him.

"What took so long?" I asked.

"I decided to shower off." I felt dirty. He leaned towards me and whispered in my ear, "Don't worry, you still smell wonderful."

I looked at him, astonished. Could he read what I was thinking? He didn't mention that before. "How did you..."

"Your expression...I have quite a bit of experience reading body language," he replied with a smirk.

"What are you two so secretive about?" Ben asked abruptly.

"We were commenting on how the party is going so far," he answered just as abruptly.

Ben wasn't buying it. "Well, your house has been the talk of it," he commented, moving closer to David.

Madeline stared at him, her arm ready to hold him back if he decided to strike. I couldn't imagine him doing it, but she must have seen it. Ben stood steadfast, his arms crossed and eyes narrowed.

"Megan told me it was your suggestion to use my home."

"What a perfect place – large house, all the amenities you could want, secluded location…by the way, what's with the seclusion and high security?"

David moved closer and he backed up, finally feeling intimidated. "I like my privacy."

"Ooo, a slow song!" Madeline blurted out suddenly. "Ben, will you dance with me?" she asked, slipping between him and David. His face instantly went blank, and he nodded absentmindedly as she led him onto the floor.

David turned to me and furrowed his brow. "He's leery of me. He knows I have a secret, and he's dying to expose me."

"I already know your secret, so it doesn't matter, right?"

He glanced into the crowd, finding Madeline and Ben. "I suppose," he replied. He took my hand and gazed into my eyes. I was momentarily mesmerized. "Would you like to dance?" he asked and without realizing it, I nodded.

He led me into the ocean of slow dancing couples and finding a good spot, took me into his arms as I rested my head on his shoulder. I closed my eyes and focused on the music. My mind was blank, quiet.

Another slow song came on and we continued dancing. Good, I wasn't ready to quit. It was peaceful here with him even though we were surrounded by other couples talking and not dancing as slow or close as we were.

As the song neared the end, I looked up at David, but his eyes were on something, or rather someone, else. I followed his line of sight and unfortunately found him focusing on Ben. I sighed and rubbed the back of his neck, whispering his name. He looked at me briefly and then returned his gaze.

"David, stop. He's not a threat," I assured him as I took his hand and led him away from the crowd, away from Ben. I ushered him upstairs, wanting to get away as the DJ switched to a more upbeat dance song. I needed a quiet place.

I turned into the grand salon but found it too crowded. The veranda and terrace were too loud. I decided the library was the best place; no one would be in there. We entered and David went to the sofa, leaning against the back of it while I shut and locked the door.

"Look…I know you have a problem with Ben, but no matter how annoying he may be, you need to be nice. He's still my friend," I defended as I walked over and sat on one of the leather chairs, so cool and comfy.

He crossed his arms and stared at me. "I understand, but you have to be cautious. You need to watch what you say and do around him. He can't know, no one can know, what we are. And it will be harder now that he's getting involved with Madeline," he replied coldly.

"I know he's overly protective of me, but he has to see that I'm happy and safe with you," I responded.

"He doesn't believe it. Somehow he knows there's something dangerous about me and that is what's driving his desire to protect you," he stated.

His eyes shifted suddenly from me to the hidden back door. He furrowed his brow and stalked over to it, shutting it tight. Quickly descending the stairs, he went to the main door and opened it wide. He disappeared around the corner a moment and then came back, leaning in the doorway.

"Did you find anyone?" I asked sarcastically.

He grinned. "No, and you're right. There is no need to worry about Ben."

For some reason, I didn't believe him.

# Chapter 29
## Dismissal

David and I went back downstairs, running into Claire and Justin as we entered the game room. She looked exhausted but perked up when David came near her. Justin grumbled and looked away.

The party was dying down, but our guests lingered. They lounged in chairs or sat on the floor, chatting with each other. The DJ started packing up his equipment, as did the caterers. Madeline and Ben were coming out of the theater, joining us by the stairs. Her arm was linked with his and a smile decorated her fair visage.

"How's the crowd in there?" I asked, noticing David and her exchanging glances, the smile gone. I wonder if it was as obvious to everyone else as it was to me.

"There's several still hanging around and some are passed out," Ben answered, looking from me to David. He acknowledged him and gave a polite smile. Okay, so maybe he was telling the truth.

Erin ran up, throwing her arms over Ben's and my shoulders. "This has been the best party ever!" she exclaimed, still so full of energy.

"Glad to hear it was such a success," David commented, grinning at her.

She dropped her arm from around Ben and leaned on me, wanting to get closer to my boyfriend. "And it was all thanks to you," she cooed.

I playfully shoved her off. "So, should we start clearing everyone out? We still have cleanup to do."

"That's not necessary, Megan. I'll have a cleaning service take care of it tomorrow," he offered.

It's tempting, but I can't. "No, we insist," I replied as everyone groaned.

We split up and informed our guests it was time to go, herding them up the stairs and into the foyer. As they passed through the front door, we thanked them for coming and watched as the driveway quickly cleared. Yes, it was a successful party, though more than thirty showed up. I guess we forgot to count for dates and the inevitable party-crashers.

We started with the main floor, large garbage bags in hand as we cleared off the coffee and end tables and counters of plates and cups, empty or otherwise. I couldn't believe how disgusting some people were and was a little embarrassed by it. I hoped no one damaged any of David's furniture or other things.

For some reason, Ben decided to hang around David and me. When I was far enough away, I heard him ask, "So what happened to Brian and

Odette? They were having a great time and next thing you know, they're gone."

I had completely forgotten they were still locked up. I moved a little closer to hear David's response, hoping he wouldn't try to rip Ben's throat out. "Hmm…I hadn't noticed," he replied coolly, straightening one of Madeline's paintings. "They must have disappeared to a more secluded place," he added with a smirk.

Ben narrowed his eyes, but David just continued to smile and graciously walked away. Erin stopped him to ask where the vacuum was located and he led her across the foyer. She came back moments later, dragging one behind her. She plugged it in and turned it on, making sure to get every crumb in hopes of impressing him with her hard work.

I tied off my garbage bag and grabbed a new one, indicating to David that I was headed downstairs. He informed me that he was going to check the guest room, library, and dining room for any stray refuse. As I headed down, Claire was on my heels.

At the bottom, I stopped and turned, startling her. "What's up?" I asked as she leaned against the wall, her hand over her heart.

"Nothing…just wanted to join you. I need to get away from Justin," she replied.

"Okay," I responded as I went about picking up trash. "Why?"

She shrugged, just standing there and watching me work, and then she sighed. Oh boy, she has something big to tell me. "He's being really clingy tonight. I've barely been able to talk to anyone because he had to be right by my side the whole time."

He has been possessive of her tonight, but I have a feeling I know why. "Who were you trying to have a conversation with?" I inquired.

"Brian for a long time. He's so easy to talk to and oh my God is he hot! I couldn't tear myself away. But of course, Justin did. I was chatting with Brian while waiting for my drink when he came right up and dragged me away before I even got to taste it!" she huffed. "But it's okay for him to talk to other girls. I got after him about flirting with that blonde chick, Odette, and he snapped at me."

She followed me as I continued to clean, not bothering to help. "There's something about those two that bring out the worst in people," I commented.

"And then with David…" she began, pausing. "I don't know what it is, but I go kinda blank around him. Justin got all snippy and mean each time I was near him," she paused again, looking like she wanted to cry. "I didn't do anything wrong."

I put my bag down and sighed. No, she can't help it. I hugged her, hoping it'd help. "It's okay…Justin's just being protective," I assured her.

The faint sound of footsteps coming down the stairs caught my attention, and I looked up to find David staring at us.

"I can come back," he suggested quietly, turning to leave.

"No...we're fine," she responded, still holding me. She avoided looking at him, which was probably a good thing.

"I'll be in the theater then," he replied, smiling at me as he passed.

She let out a sobbed sigh and then slowly moved away from me as soon as he was out of sight. "So what should I do?" she asked, sitting on an ottoman.

"I think you should have a talk with him about treating you the way he did," I recommended, resuming my trash pickup. "Especially if he's guilty of the same."

She wiped her face and looked toward the theater. "Is David a jealous person?" she asked quietly.

"Hmm...not that I've noticed," I replied, standing up and stretching my back. "He knows I'm devoted solely to him."

"But you haven't been dating any longer than Justin and me. How can he be so confident you won't stray?"

I scanned the room and stopped on her. "Maybe age has something to do with it...or trust. Justin's young and insecure right now. After high school, he'll probably be more confident."

She started sniffling as she stared at the floor. "What if we don't last that long?"

Rolling my eyes, I joined her on the ottoman and put my arm around her shoulders. "Just talk to him about it. I'm sure you two will work it out."

She wiped her eyes and cheeks and then sighed again. "Okay," she conceded and stood.

Grabbing my bag, I went back to work and she joined in this time but remained quiet. Soon Ben, Justin, and Erin came downstairs. Madeline must have decided to call it a night. Justin stuck by Ben's side and scanned the room, most likely looking for David or Brian.

His eyes meeting Claire's, he noticed something was different. He came over and I separated myself from her as he asked what was wrong. "I need to talk to you...about us," I heard her say as she led him back upstairs.

Glancing around the game room, I felt I had done enough as Erin started vacuuming. Now on to the exterior. I headed out to the patio and Ben followed. I guess seeing me alone warranted his company.

"Wow, I never realized our friends were such messy people," he commented, setting his bag down as he surveyed all the trash laying around.

"Mm hm," I replied, not really wanting to talk. There was so much to do and it was getting late.

He touched my arm and asked, "Is everything okay?"

I looked up and dropped my bag, crossing my arms over my chest. What did he not understand about my lack of reply to his comment? "Yes, it is. Why?"

"You seem angry."

"Well, it's late and I don't really feel like talking, Ben," I explained as I snatched up my bag and went back to picking up party debris.

"Oh," he responded, slowly grabbing his and joining me. We worked quietly for a while, and then he decided to try to have a conversation again. "I like this Madeline better than the weird, seductive one," he remarked, looking around. I glanced at him and smiled but didn't say anything. "We're going out Friday night...wanna double date?"

Well, he found a way to get me to talk. "Sure," I answered, still keeping my reply short. I wonder if I should consult David first. Nah, I can make my own decisions. Maybe if I get them to hang out together more often, they'll learn to like each other.

"Oh...oh really? You're not going to ask David first?"

"Nope. He'll be fine with it."

"Good," he commented and then under his breath, he muttered, "I can't wait."

I tied off my bag and set it to the side. Letting him finish garbage pickup, I grabbed the pool skimmer and went over the surface of the water, trying to get any refuse floating on top. I wasn't going to do too much since David probably has one of those robot things to clean it but did just enough to make it look sanitary. After I finished walking around the pool, I turned off the bubbles for the hot tub and skimmed it as well.

Ben whistled as he picked up trash, interrupting the natural serenade coming from the woods and lake. I glanced toward the game room and spotted Justin and Claire returning arm in arm. Looks like all's well with them.

They came outside, followed by Erin, and started removing the lights and decorations. I wiped my forehead and glanced around. Everyone was here...except David. I excused myself and headed inside to the theater. It was dim and no movie played as I scanned the room. No sign of him. Calling for him, he finally peeked out from behind a curtain by the screen.

"Oh, there you are. What are you doing?"

"I was checking on Brian and Odette," he responded as he disappeared behind the velvet panel.

I waited for him to reappear and then gave him a funny look. "How are you able to do that? I thought you said they were locked up in a room down here."

He stepped out and straightened the curtain. "Secret passage," he replied, looking over his shoulder at me with a smirk.

"No seriously, what were you really doing?"

He rolled his eyes. "I was checking the screen."

I nodded and strolled to the front, waiting for him to finish. As I looked over the room, he came up behind me and placed his hands on my bare arms, his body close to mine. "Looks like they didn't make too big of a mess in here," I commented casually, trying to ignore the feelings I was having.

He leaned closer and I felt his breath on my neck. It sent tingling sensations throughout my body, and I yearned to feel his lips against my skin. He granted me that one wish as he softly kissed it, then lingered there with a smile on his lips.

His closeness, his touch, his sensuality. I couldn't stand it anymore. I turned and attacked him, my lips hungry and hands eager. As I kissed him, I reached under his shirt and touched his cool, silky skin. Wrapping my arms around his body, I pulled myself closer and threw my head back, letting him kiss down my neck. It felt amazing. I was so caught up in it all, the whole house could have collapsed and I would be oblivious. But his voice got my attention. He breathed my name, not out of ardor, but out of warning.

"Megan…David?" Claire called as she entered.

I dropped my face and turned my head in her direction. Somehow, we had moved to a dark corner of the room. I looked at him and he grinned. My heart thumped hard and I had to look away. I released myself from his embrace and headed toward her.

"We're here, Claire," I announced as she came into view.

"Oh, I didn't see you at first," she replied, looking at us suspiciously.

"We were in the back, checking the last row for refuse," he remarked smoothly, noticing her skepticism.

"Sorry," she responded, staring at him. It was hard for her to break her gaze, but she did finally, turning to me. "Umm, we're getting ready to head out. Are you ready to go?"

I looked at him and then back at her. Before I could say anything, he answered for me. "I'll take Megan home, if you don't mind. I need to discuss something with her."

She and I both stared at him, surprised by this seemingly sudden decision. He smiled at her and she giggled like a schoolgirl. "Okay, *David*, just don't keep her out too late," she cooed.

"I won't," he promised. "Please let the others know."

"O-okay."

She stumbled out of the room and before I could lay into him, Ben came rushing in. "What do you mean you're not going with us?"

"David needs to talk to me…"

"What, *David*, is it exactly you need to talk to her about?" he interrupted.

I tried to restrain my boyfriend, but it was like trying to stop a tree from falling on top of you. He moved in front of me, dangerously close to Ben. "I need to discuss an earlier incident with her," he almost growled.

"Oh, something to do with Brian?" Ben instigated.

David moved closer and Ben was obviously intimidated. I touched David's arm, hoping he'd remember to be civil. "No, something to do with Claire," he replied calmly.

Ben looked at me and I nodded, going along with it, but having no clue what he was talking about. "So you'll be fine staying?" he asked, wanting to get around him, but unsure about attempting it.

"Yeah, I'm in good hands," I replied as I went to a seat.

David blocked Ben as he tried to get closer. "I'll take her home within the hour. You're welcome to call later to see that she's all right, if you don't trust me," he offered, leading Ben to the door. He went willingly and as he glanced back, I smiled at him.

David was gone several minutes, leaving me alone in the theater. I sat back in the seat with my eyes closed, exhausted from the day's events. I could fall asleep…

Soft, cool lips caressed mine, and I opened my eyes to find him staring at me. I smiled and sighed. "You don't really plan to talk about Claire, do you?" I asked as he vaulted over the seat and sat next to me.

"No, that was to throw Ben off. I do, however, plan to continue our conversation about the parties," he replied with a smile, and my heart fluttered.

"Right…so why did you let it go on?"

"I wasn't aware at first. It was Cary who told me one evening while Brian and Odette were out, so I confronted them about it when they returned. They said it was a mistake, that they went too far, so I let it go. But then it happened again. That's why I was so upset the night I was at your house and saw the news about the serial killer."

"There were two more murders after that, one of which they left evidence. Luckily for them, I was able to handle it. I emphasized how serious it was and the repercussions of their actions. With full understanding that I would not help again, they promised to stop."

I hesitated. "Did you hear what happened to the two high school students I asked you about?"

"Your classmates…the two that went missing after prom? No, I didn't."

"They were found in Hollywood Cemetery…dead. Brian and Odette confessed to killing them, staging it as a suicide. They told me that night I found out…about you."

He was stunned. He looked toward the screen for a long time, then stood and took my arm, rushing me upstairs. We passed Madeline in the hall but didn't stop to answer her curious gaze. Or maybe he did, because she took off downstairs as we continued on to his room.

"Stay here," he directed as I sat at the foot of his bed. I watched in bewilderment as he left the room, locking the door behind him. What was going on?

I sat quietly for a long time, straining my ears to hear anything, but the house was completely silent. Tired of waiting for who knows what to happen, I decided to get up and look around. Well, snoop was more like it.

First, I went to the closet. Everything was so neat and tidy: shoes on the lower rack, pants and shirts on separate racks above each other, suits on longer racks, and ties organized by color in the back. Were all vampires this OCD? I ran my hand over the clothes and his scent wafted toward me. Feeling dizzy, I stepped out for a moment to clear my head, then went back in to continue my exploration.

The shelving above the racks had boxes and miscellaneous items on them. I glanced around the floor for a stepstool and found one near a window. Picking a good spot, I climbed up and grabbed a large, black box. As I sat on top of the stool, I set the box on my lap and slowly opened it, not sure what could be inside.

Photographs, and lots of them – old, new, in strange places with all sorts of people, David in almost every one of them. It was funny to see him styling different fashions through the years. As I reached the bottom I found the really old pictures of him and his parents. They were not as happy as the other photos. I closed it up and put it back on the shelf.

Other boxes held hats and knick-knacks from another time, but nothing as interesting as the photos. I turned off the light as I left and went to the bathroom next. I peeked in the shower at the products he used. All botanical, nothing unusual. I thought about washing off, but decided it was a bad idea, not knowing when he'd return.

There was nothing too exciting in there I hadn't already seen, so I exited and strolled around the room. I stopped at the fireplace and stared at the portrait above it. David told me the young man in it was his grandfather, but I knew better now; it was really him.

He looked handsome in his antebellum garb. I examined his parents – his father seemed stern and cold, but his mother appeared soft and kind. And she was gorgeous. I could see his father in him, but he favored his mother, mainly her eyes.

I would guess the photograph was taken the same year he disappeared. He must have picked it up when he went to claim the inheritance. I glanced around the room, wondering if anything else was from his previous life. The oil lamps on the mantle looked fairly old, as did several other items. Probably some of the knick-knacks in the closet were from his home in Massachusetts. Then, of course, there was the sailboat on the lake.

Going to his dresser next, I looked at the things he had sitting on top. There was a tray for his keys and wallet and several colognes, just for looks probably, but nothing else. I looked to the door and listened a moment for him and when I was satisfied he wasn't coming, I opened one of the bottom drawers. Jeans. In another were shorts. Moving up, I found lounge clothes. Socks were next. Then underclothes. Oops!

I quickly shut that one and moved to the top row, pulling the middle one. In it was a variety of jewelry – necklaces, bracelets, rings – all masculine of course. I pulled out a familiar piece, the one he wore the first night we met. The small object hanging from the leather string was a dappled, dark blue stone. It was so intriguing, so unique.

The sound of a key turning in the lock broke my concentration, but before I could put the necklace away, David opened the door. He closed it and walked toward me. Stopping right in front of me, he crossed his arms and stared with one eyebrow raised.

"I can explain. I got bored, so I decided to look around. I never left the room…honest," I admitted out of guilt.

He smiled his wicked grin and took the necklace from me, setting it back in the drawer. "Find anything else interesting?"

"The photos in your closet," I replied and then paused. Biting my lip, I leaned against the dresser and continued, "And you're a boxer kind of guy."

He didn't look angry, but he didn't look happy either. "Really…"

"Hey…you snooped around my room," I answered defensively.

He moved closer, taking me in his arms and gazing into my eyes. "I'm not mad, Megan."

"Oh," I replied, a little embarrassed. Okay, time to change the subject. "So what were you doing?"

"Moving Brian and Odette out."

"Wow…so soon, so quick?"

"Brian's become unstable and I can't trust him. It's been lie after lie with him and he's endangered our safety and your life. I can't have him around anymore."

"Getting all their things together would take some time…"

"They really didn't have much. The furniture is mine. All they had were clothes and small personal items. Madeline put their things in her vehicle and is following them to a hotel outside of town. They'll be leaving the state tomorrow evening."

I felt relieved, but something in the back of my mind told me not to be. Brian won't let this go. He'll be back.

"Let's hope they stay away," I remarked.

"If they're smart, they will," he responded, a hint of animosity in his tone.

It was getting late and I felt it. Sensing my weariness, he led me over to a settee near the window and sat, taking me in his arms. But I didn't want to sit; I needed to go. As I tried to stand, he forced me to stay down. I sighed and gave in, leaning on his shoulder and closing my eyes. Maybe just a moment to relax...

Instead, my brain ran a million miles a minute. I thought about our earlier discussion and the reason why he left so abruptly. I thought about Brian and Odette killing those people and setting them up as serial murders and now a suicide. And yet, there was never a mention of puncture wounds. Why didn't the police ever find any tell-tale marks on Brian and Odette's victims?

"How did Brian and Odette not leave bite marks on the people they drank from? Wouldn't you think the cops would have noticed that?" I asked suddenly, raising my head.

He chuckled, though I didn't see how it was funny. "We've had centuries to perfect the art of killing. Like a good serial killer, Brian knew not to leave any evidence of our existence. Why do you think the victims were decapitated?"

I stared at him, aghast. "To cover up..."

"Precisely. When I used to feed on humans, I had to get creative with hiding the marks as well, so as not to implicate myself or my kind."

My stomach lurched at the thought of him killing a human for food. When the queasiness passed, I realized his explanation didn't account for the cover up of the goth couple's marks. "So how do you explain what they did to my classmates? Why set it up as a suicide?"

"After the mistake Brian and Odette made with the most recent murder, the one that occurred at Pocahontas State Park the night we were there, they retired the Ghost and staged the next one as a suicide. That way, no one would be looking for a suspect and the case would be closed immediately. Quite clever of them, actually," he replied admiringly.

Huh, so Claire was right. Wait...the night we were there? "They were at Pocahontas the same night we were? Why don't I remember that?" I questioned, trying to recall what I couldn't. I looked into his eyes, my brows scrunched in confusion. "What happened that night? Honestly."

He cast his eyes to the floor and sighed. "I had to erase your memory. You saw it happen, saw them, but didn't know it was them."

"Wh-what?" I exclaimed, pushing off him.

"I had to...you were hysterical."

"So you can erase memories, too. What else have you erased from my mind?" I questioned angrily.

"Please calm down," he whispered, caressing my arms. I wanted to push him away again, but I couldn't bring myself to do it. "That was it. Anything else I manipulated into dreams." He put his arm around me and held me close. "You reacted the way I feared you would if you knew what I was."

"What did I see?"

"As we were racing back to the car, we somehow were separated, and you found your way over to where they were decapitating the victim, watching it. You apparently were unsure of what you saw because you never reacted. That was until you discovered the head and almost gave yourself away. That's when I found you."

My hands covered my mouth instinctively – out of shock or to prevent myself from vomiting, I wasn't sure which. I sat for a moment, scanning my mind for the memory of that night, but I only remembered what David had told me. I witnessed a decapitation and saw a severed human head. I guess I should be thankful I didn't remember.

And I was. "Thank you," I replied quietly, slowly removing my hands from my lips.

He took my chin in his hand and turned my face to him, gazing into my eyes. He kissed me and then whispered in my ear, "If I could take all your bad memories away, I would."

Sitting back, I tucked my hair behind my ear as I looked up at him. "So you can't erase everything?"

"No, it has to be recent," he replied, tucking the other side and caressing my cheek as he pulled away. "We can manipulate a person's short-term memory, but not the long-term. It's too complicated."

I sighed. There are a lot of things I'm going to learn about him and some will be disturbing. I'll just need to go with it and not freak out.

"So going back to my classmates, you're telling me instead of biting them on the neck, they bit their wrists and then sliced them to cover it up?"

"We don't always have to bite the neck. There are plenty of other places. It's all about preference."

A slightly uncomfortable feeling came over me talking to him about this, but I brushed it off. I was curious. "Like where?"

He gave me a funny look, surprised, I guess, that I would be interested. "Anywhere there's an artery, really."

"Is the neck preferable for blood flow? Are there any other places just as good?" I asked before I could stop myself. Where was this morbid curiosity of mine coming from?

He laughed. "Yes…the chest," he replied, tracing the arteries above my breasts. "Arm," he continued, running his finger along the underside down to my wrist. "And inner thigh," he finished, looking down but not touching.

"Oh," I responded, folding my hands over my lap.

There was an uncomfortable silence between us as I looked around the room, distracting myself and suppressing my blushing. Huh, not a single clock. I wonder what time it's getting to be. I hope Dad isn't worried about me. If he was, he would have called. I went to reach for my phone and realized I left it in my bag downstairs.

"What's wrong?" David asked, noticing my pause.

"I was just thinking I need to check my phone…to see if my dad called, but I think I left it downstairs. What time is it?"

"After two," he replied, not looking at anything.

"Is that another one of your special gifts…an internal clock?"

"No, just a good judge of time," he laughed, taking my hand and lifting me off the settee.

We headed down to the basement where I grabbed my bag and checked my phone and then went back upstairs, stopping in the foyer. "I guess I should be getting home. Dad hasn't called yet, but it may be soon," I commented.

"Yes, and I would expect a call from Ben as well," he replied, leading me to the garage.

"Oh, that reminds me. He's going on a date with Madeline next Friday and wants us to join them. I said we would. Do you mind?"

With a flat expression, he responded, "No, not at all."

That's better than the response I was expecting, so I'll take it. "Good."

We climbed in the Bugatti, waiting in silence as the garage door opened. I remembered to roll down the window so I wouldn't pass out. In my already drowsy state, it wouldn't take much. He took off down the driveway and before reaching the gate, it automatically opened and he drove through without having to stop.

"I'm sure the house is going to feel empty without Brian and Odette there," I commented, making conversation. "And no more parties."

He glanced over at me and smiled. "You could always have more. Your friends would like that."

I rolled my eyes. "Yes, I'd be the most popular girl in school."

"We don't want that now, do we?" he remarked with a smirk.

No doubt Brian's angry about being kicked out, but he did it to himself. Will he blame me? I stared out the window into the dark night, wondering if I'd be okay tonight.

"What are you thinking about?" David asked, noticing my solemn expression and silence.

I felt scared voicing my fear aloud, but I did, hoping for reassurance. "Am I going to be safe tonight?" I inquired, turning my body toward him.

"Yes, you will. I'll be staying with you as long as I can."

"What about tomorrow night and the night after that?"

"We'll guard you until we feel the threat is gone."

"We?"

"I won't be able to stay all night every night, so Madeline has offered to help."

He turned into my neighborhood. All the houses were dark and the only sound was his rumbling car. As we pulled into the drive, the light came on and Dad stepped out onto the porch.

"Oh, great," I commented under my breath as I unbuckled my seatbelt and opened the door. David did the same, joining my side as we made our way up the sidewalk to the house. Dad didn't look too happy to see us so late, but he didn't give me a curfew, so he shouldn't complain.

"Good evening, Mr. Caldwell," David greeted politely, bowing his head. "We stayed to help with clean-"

"I don't need excuses. Megan, get inside," he interrupted.

I looked at my father, astonished. "What are you so mad about? You didn't give me a curfew."

"I don't care – it's nearly three in the morning…now go!" he commanded, pointing inside.

I turned to my boyfriend, thanking him for a great evening, and gave him a kiss. I could care less that I did it in front of my dad. He was being unreasonable. David replied with a soft kiss on my cheek and then whispered in my ear, "I'll be up soon."

I smiled as I walked into the house. Before shutting the door, I looked back to see Dad glaring at him. David's eyes shifted to me, and he gave a slight smile. He'll be all right. I shut the door and pretended to go up the stairs, crawling back and hiding under the sidelight to eavesdrop. Their voices were muffled, but I could make out most of what they were saying.

"What do you think you're doing having her out at all hours of the night?" Dad asked sternly.

"I was unaware of a curfew, sir. If I had known, I would have had her home sooner. I apologize," David replied, cool and calm.

"Where was the party tonight?" Ooo, he's checking to make sure I wasn't lying to him.

"One of Megan's classmates has a house on the lake," he replied. Well played, David.

"Which classmate?"

I doubt Dad would know if he just guessed a name. "Amelia Kensington."

Good guess. Dad was silent for a moment. "They have a nice place on Gregory's Lake. Was it well attended, with appropriate chaperones?"

"Yes, sir," he replied.

"Any alcohol or drugs?"

"No, sir."

Dad was quiet again, and then he let out a heavy breath. "Well, I'm sure you're tired. Will we see you on Sunday for the wedding?" he asked, easing up.

"Unfortunately, I won't be able to attend. I've been called into work. We are short staffed in the summer." Yeah, they're calling for sunshine all day.

"That's a shame; Megan will be disappointed. Well, the rehearsal dinner is tonight, if you can come to that," he offered.

"I would enjoy that. Thank you, Mr. Caldwell," David replied graciously.

Behind me, vibrating erupted from my bag hanging on the banister. I hopped up, trying not to be seen, and caught the phone before it rang. I crept up the stairs as I answered it, wondering who was calling.

"Hey Megan, just checking on you, you know, since David suggested it," Ben commented.

I sighed. "Hey…I just got in," I responded as I entered my room and turned on the bedside table lamp. In the background, I heard our front door shut.

"So…what did David want to talk to you about?"

I tried to undress while holding the phone to my ear. I needed to change quickly before Dad or David came. "Umm…can I call you later, like in the afternoon? I'm getting ready for bed and talking on the phone is making it hard."

"Why the hurry?"

"Because I'm tired and have a long day to look forward to," I replied as I dipped into the bathroom.

"Oh…okay. Well, I guess I'll talk to you this afternoon."

"'Night Ben," I replied as my dad knocked on the door. I grabbed a towel and ran into the room.

I hung up quickly, throwing the phone on the bed. "Come in," I called, wrapping the towel around me.

Dad entered and quickly shielded his eyes. "Oh, sorry Megan."

"It's okay. I was just getting ready to get in the shower," I explained and then shifted to my left leg. "So, did you scare David off?" I asked as I took my hair down. It felt like straw that was bent out of shape.

"No, I think it'll take worse interrogations than that to run him off. Did you have fun tonight?"

"Yeah, it was great. The luau theme was as big a hit as the location," I replied, impatiently waiting for him to leave.

He noticed my agitation. "Good. Well, I'll let you get to your shower so you can go to bed. You need plenty of sleep; it's going to be a long day tomorrow and the next," he commented.

"Good night, Dad," I responded, grabbing an outfit out of my drawer.

I heard the door shut as I headed into the bathroom. Hopefully I can wash up before David arrives. I locked the door just in case and then turned on the water.

It felt good to wash away the day. After a thorough cleaning, I stepped out feeling refreshed. I dried and slipped on my clothes and fixed my hair. Humming and in another world, I unlocked the door and left the bathroom, jumping when I saw David lounging on my bed.

"I see you finally got your shower," he commented.

Holding my chest and trying to calm my heart, I replied, "Yes…and I feel so much better."

He sat up and patted the bed as I crossed the room. I sat next to him and leaned against his shoulder as he reached up and tilted my head back, kissing me briefly. "Did Ben call?" he inquired.

"Yes, while you were talking with Dad. By the way, nice name-drop. How did you know Amelia had a house on a lake?"

"Were you listening in?" he asked with a grin. I nodded. "She mentioned it tonight to some friends that her family was having a party on the lake around the same time as yours."

"How perfect…"

"Yes it was. I doubt your father will call, though."

"What's this about coming to the rehearsal dinner tonight?"

"Your father invited me, and it will allow me to keep an eye on you."

"Just be sure to feed before you come. Vanessa will no doubt have her girlfriends meeting you, and I don't want to have to beat them off with my purse."

He chuckled. "I'll do that. Are you still tired or more awake now that you had a shower?"

I turned to him and smiled. "Just little tired, but I don't want to go to sleep."

He caressed my cheek and smiled back. "But you need to," he replied.

I dropped my head, lying back. He remained sitting, reaching up and turning out the light. "Will you lie with me?" I asked, trying to find him in the darkness.

Without a word, he slid down and slipped his arm around my shoulder. I put mine across his stomach and rested my head against his chest. Closing my eyes, I focused on the hollow sound. That wonderful hollow sound, like a heartbeat, soothed me and made me feel at ease and safe as it lulled me to sleep.

# Chapter 30
## Rehearsal

I woke to the sound of Dad gently knocking on the door and calling my name. Sitting straight up, I looked around for David, but he was already gone. As I responded to my father, I wiped my eyes and stretched. He came in and sat on the edge of the bed, staring at me.

"I know...it's time to get up," I grumbled.

He looked at me sympathetically. "I let you sleep as late as I could, but now we have to get moving."

"Okay," I pouted, dragging myself out of bed and into the bathroom.

I pulled out a washcloth and wet it, washing the sleep away, and then did other mundane morning preparations. Dad was gone by the time I came back into the room. He probably still had a lot to do.

I made my bed and headed to the closet. Searching for what to wear, I scanned several outfits and finally chose a short, pale yellow sundress. Even though I didn't have to wear the bridesmaid dress, I still wanted to look nice.

I took down my bun and put my hair in a ponytail tied with a yellow ribbon and then headed downstairs to grab a quick bite. Dad was in his usual spot reading the paper and drinking coffee. I checked the fridge, deciding to have yogurt. I grabbed a spoon and sat across from him, waiting for my instructions for the day.

"We're expected at Maymont by three. We'll probably run through the wedding several times, so dinner may not be until eight or eight-thirty," he commented. He lowered the paper and looked at me and my attire. "Yeah, that'll be fine. Did David call you?"

I was a little surprised by his question. "For what?"

"I invited him to the dinner tonight and he said he would come. I hope I didn't ruin the surprise."

"Oh...yeah, I talked to him after my shower last night. I'll call him later to let him know what time and restaurant," I replied, playing in my yogurt. "That was nice of you to invite him."

He raised the paper and started reading again. "Well, it looks like he'll be around for a while. Might as well include him as much as we can."

I smiled as I went back to eating. "Are you nervous at all, Dad?"

"Not one bit. I trust you, and David seems to treat you well..."

"No, about the wedding."

"Oh...no. Been there, done that. It's all for Vanessa anyway. I just have to stand where they tell me to stand and say what they tell me to say."

I thought a moment, wondering if I should ask the question that popped into my head at that moment. I played with my ponytail, twirling it, and went ahead since I really wanted to know. "Do you miss Mom at all?"

He didn't reply right away, but then he lowered the paper and gazed at me, his eyes reddening. "Every day, Megan," he responded quietly. He stared outside and sighed. "This has been hard…remembering our wedding day at Maymont, along with clearing out your mom's things I held onto for so long." I went over to him and gave him a hug. "You are all that's left of her other than my memories, and they're slowly fading."

"It's all right, Dad. I'm not going anywhere," I promised, continuing to hold him.

Then his phone rang. I let go and sat back down as he answered it. "Hello? Oh, good morning, Vanessa…yes, we're up and ready…oh really…honey, calm down. It'll be all right…it will…it *will*…okay, we're on our way," he commented with a heavy sigh before hanging up.

"What…pre-wedding crisis?" I asked sarcastically.

"There's a problem at the park so we have to head out now," he replied, folding the paper and dumping his coffee in the sink.

I rolled my eyes and stood, throwing the remains of my breakfast away. Our special moment ruined by the witch as usual. "I'll be in the car," I commented, walking to the door.

We arrived at Maymont and dashed to the Italian garden where Vanessa was in hysterics. Dad went up to her, trying his best to calm her, but it wasn't working. She had black streaks running down her cheeks from the mascara as she cried about the florist, horses, and other things I couldn't make out of her blubbering. I covered my smile with my hand and walked away before I burst out laughing.

With nothing better to do, I strolled around the garden and watched the people plan out decorations. So much fuss over a wedding. Vanessa, dressed in her usual high heels, short skirt and low-cut top, was frantically speed walking down the pergola in the second stage of bridal meltdown, yelling at people about what they were doing wrong. Again, I reassured myself that I only have a year to deal with her before going off to college.

With some time before the rehearsal began, I wandered down to the Japanese garden and sat in the azumaya, watching the ducks glide on the pond. It was a bright, sunny day and I knew David would be sleeping, but I decided to call him anyway, just to hear his voice taking the message.

Figuring I needed to say something after the beep, I let him know dinner would be around eight-thirty and to meet us at the Bellgrade Manor House. I told him I missed him and couldn't wait to see him later, then hung up.

Not ready to join the chaos, I stayed in the garden and enjoyed the solitude, watching the water ripple slowly as the fish moved under it. I stood and walked the path to the stepping stones where I stopped to crouch and look closer at the koi. I dipped my fingers in the water, expecting a nibble, but they were shy and instead scattered, creating violent waves across the surface.

My phone vibrated suddenly, causing me to lose my balance and nearly fall in the pond. Steadying myself and standing, I quickly answered it. "Hey Megan. Did you get enough sleep?"

"Ben? Why are you calling me?"

"Well, you said we'd talk and you hadn't called…"

"I just got up an hour ago and then there was a crisis at th-"

"Do you need me?" he interrupted.

I was shocked by his question. "Uh, no. Why would I need you?"

"Oh, I don't know…maybe for company?" he replied. "When does rehearsal start?"

"Not for another hour."

"Would you like someone to hang out with until then?" he asked.

It would be nice to have a friend to talk to, but I'd rather it be anyone other than Ben. On the other hand, it might be fun to sit with him and pick at Vanessa from a distance, like we used to do to people in the mall. "Oh, all right. How soon should I expect you?"

"I'm already on my way," he replied as a door slammed in the background.

"I'm down in the Japanese garden. See you soon."

He replied and hung up. There was an excitement in his voice that bothered me. What was I getting myself in to?

I walked back to the azumaya and waited for him to arrive. As I sat staring at the pond, I devised a plan to avoid talking about David. Our discussions involving him are never civil. If he brings him up, I'll defer the conversation to something else. I wonder if I should avoid talking about Madeline, too, since it'll inevitably lead to David.

I was deep in thought, contemplating my dilemma when Ben walked up. "Whatcha thinking about?" he asked, taking a seat next to me. Before I could say anything, he complimented, "By the way, you look great."

"Nothing too important and thanks. Has it calmed down any up there?" I asked, standing and walking toward the path to go back to the Italian garden. I wanted to be in full view of everyone so he couldn't try anything.

"She was yelling at some woman with a planner when I passed. Your dad had his head buried in his hands."

"Poor guy. Well, it'll be over soon."

He walked next to me, playing with the bamboo as we made our way through the thicket. "So what did David want to talk to you about last night?"

Here we go. What lie could I come up with to cover for him? "Claire was curious about having another party later in the summer. I mentioned it to him but couldn't go into details during the party, with so much going on."

"Oh...when is she thinking about having it?"

What can I say...what can I say? "Mid to late August, you know, one last hurrah before school starts," I replied. I'm such a liar, but he seems to be buying it.

"Same as this last one, with all our friends?"

"Yeah, something like that, but Claire's responsibility completely," I replied with a smile as I sat on a wall opposite the promenade. It was a great place to scope out all the action but far enough away from it.

He sat next to me, watching what I was watching. Vanessa had not calmed down at all, continuing to run around and give everyone grief. Dad was following her, apologizing to everyone left in her wake. I glanced at Ben and he glanced back at me, a funny look on his face.

"So are you going to be this crazy when you get married?" he asked.

"No way! Vanessa's one of those girls who's probably dreamed about this moment all her life. That's not me. I'm not even sure I'll ever get married."

"What...you don't see David in your future?" he asked.

Great, back on David again. "I didn't say that. I just don't know if it's possible."

"Not possible? What's not possible about it?"

I rolled my eyes. "Nothing...just forget it," I replied, scanning the garden for something to distract him. "Oh look, here comes Vanessa again," I remarked as I watched her storm down the promenade, screaming at the top of her lungs.

"I wonder what it is this time," he commented, focusing on her as well. Good, it worked.

"Watch the people run as she heads toward them," I remarked, pointing out the scattering workers.

"Here comes bridezilla," he laughed. "She takes out whole wedding venues with one sonic shout!" I giggled, glad my distraction worked so well.

Over the next half-hour, we sat and made fun of everything going on and especially Vanessa. He got several good laughs out of me and himself. He could be fun when he didn't act like a jealous friend or overprotective brother.

After sitting for so long and still having time on our hands, we got up and walked back down into the Japanese garden and toward the animal exhibits. We talked about plans for college and the future. I hadn't thought much about school or a career. Dad wanted me to be a lawyer like him, but that wasn't really me. Ben, as I figured, was interested in video gaming and planned to go to a school on the west coast.

"California, huh? That's so far away," I commented as I leaned on the railing and watched the sleeping grey fox.

"Aww, you're not going to miss me, are you, Megan?" he teased.

"Of course I will, Ben. We've known each other for a long time and have been friends equally as long. How could you think I wouldn't miss you?" I replied, hugging around his shoulders.

He got this elated look on his face and I quickly let go. I didn't want to give him the wrong impression, but I just kept screwing up. Now I've just made it that much worse. "So what do you have planned for your date with Madeline on Friday?" I asked, hoping to remind him of his girlfriend as I started walking again.

He had a conflicted look on his face. "Oh, Madeline...yeah. Well, there's a concert in Dogwood Dell. I thought I'd pack a picnic for us and enjoy music under the stars."

"That's so romantic! I bet she'll love that," I responded, glad I could refocus his affections.

"Are you and David still joining us?"

"Yeah...yeah we are. I guess I'll pack a picnic for us," I commented, though I'd be the only one eating.

"No, that's okay. I'll pack enough for all of us," he replied with a smile.

"Thank you. It's going to be so nice," I remarked, hoping it really would.

Feeling it was getting close to time for the rehearsal, we headed back toward the Italian Garden. On the way, we talked about what we expected school to be like in the fall and the fact that it was almost over. We were coming up to the garden as everyone was lining up.

"Oh, I've got to get over there. I don't want to incur bridezilla's wrath!" I shouted as I sprinted.

He ran with me. "Mind if I stay and watch?" he asked.

Slowing down, I replied, "We'll be at it for several hours. Do you really want to hang around that long?"

"Maybe not the whole time...I'll stay as long as I can stand and be your motivational support."

I shrugged. "Okay...well, enjoy the show!" I responded with a smile, running off to join the group.

I got there just in time, falling in line with the other bridesmaids. We were instructed where to stand and how entrances would work. Vanessa watched as each of us came in with the groomsmen – I was paired up with her dorky cousin – and changed things as we went along. The coordinator wasn't too pleased with her criticism and input but bit her tongue and adjusted accordingly.

Of course, Vanessa's entrance was the grandest, putting those of the girls on *My Super Sweet Sixteen* to shame. All her girlfriends watched in awe and envy while Dad and I rolled our eyes. I glanced over at Ben, who was grinning ear to ear, but giving me a thumbs-up. I shook my head. Ever-supportive Ben.

We worked on them about twenty more times and then took a break. I grabbed two drinks and headed over to join him for a moment. Taking a seat next to him on the wall, I handed him a bottle as he smiled in the sunshine. I opened mine and took a sip as I soaked up the sun.

"It's very interesting," he commented before taking a swig.

"Yep...try being in my shoes."

He looked down at my feet and smiled. "No thanks, they wouldn't match my outfit."

I hit him and then took another sip. "I know Vanessa is a perfectionist, but I never expected this to be as grueling as it is. It's just entrances and exits!"

"Ooo...you should purposely forget to do something or trip. I mean, accidents happen," he suggested quietly, nudging and winking at me.

I smiled. It would be funny, but I couldn't do that to my dad. He'd never hear the end of how his daughter intentionally ruined Vanessa's special day. "I better stick to what bridezilla has dictated. Hey, are you sticking around for the second half?"

"No, I have to get going. Mom gave me a curfew with the car," he replied, standing up and taking a final swig.

"I'm sure it won't be any different from the entrances," I remarked, standing as well. "Thanks for keeping me company. I guess I'll see you Friday. What time?" I asked, taking his bottle to throw away with mine.

"I believe it starts at dusk, so eight-thirty, nine?"

"Sounds good," I replied, giving him a friendly hug. He hugged back, more affectionately.

I gently pushed him away and smiled, leading him to the gate. As we passed the bridal party, I noticed Vanessa watching us out of the corner of her eye while she talked to the other bridesmaids. No doubt she'll say something to me about this whole affair with Ben.

I waved goodbye as he went to his car, then rushed back to the garden to work on exits. I joined the group standing around waiting, but before we began, Vanessa pulled me aside. "Was that your friend Ben?" she asked, giving a suspicious look.

"Yeah, he kept me company while I waited for rehearsal to begin," I replied.

"The same Ben that has a crush on you, but you'll never date because he's more like a brother?"

"Yep, that'd be him."

"Did something happen between you and David?"

"No, we're still together. He's coming to dinner tonight."

"Then why are you leading Ben on?"

I looked at her, astonished. "I'm not leading him on! He was here as a friend."

"Maybe in your eyes, but he has it bad for you. How would David feel if he found out he was here?"

Pretty pissed, I'm sure. "He wouldn't have a problem. He knows Ben's my friend and has a crush on me, but he's not threatened by that."

She was quiet, giving me a skeptical look. "Uh huh," she replied and walked away.

She headed back to the group and commanded everyone to get lined up. I joined them again, falling in line and waiting for instruction. We worked on exits about as many times as we did entrances and as the sun dipped lower in the sky, we wrapped it up. Thank goodness it was all over and tomorrow would be the absolute last of it. As everyone else hopped in their cars and headed to the restaurant for dinner, Dad, Vanessa, and I hung around finalizing some last minute details.

It was close to eight when we finished and as we walked to the car, the phone David gave me rang. I took it out and hung back so I could talk somewhat privately. "Hello, David. Did you sleep well?"

"I did. I received your message and am on my way out the door now."

I glanced ahead of me, making sure they weren't listening in. "Did you feed?" I whispered into the phone.

"Not yet. I'll grab something quick as soon as we are off the phone," he replied and then laughed.

"What's so funny?"

"How paranoid you are about this."

"Well, we are talking about Vanessa and her friends, and there will be drinking going on."

"So you know, I will still be alluring to them…just not as hypnotizing."

"Great. I'll have to stay by your side all night."

"And that's a bad thing?" he questioned, laughing again.

"You're in a good mood…"

"Of course I am. I'll get to see you in less than a half an hour."

He's good. "Let me let you go so you can take care of your 'business'. See you at the restaurant."

"Till then," he replied and hung up.

We climbed in the car and Vanessa immediately looked over her shoulder at me. "Was that David calling...or Ben?" she asked with a sneer.

"David...he was letting me know he's on his way," I replied pleasantly.

"Good. He'll probably beat us there since we have farther to drive," Dad commented, pulling out of the parking lot.

She narrowed her eyes at me before turning back around. They talked as he whipped in and out of traffic, ignoring me in the back seat. I didn't care, though. I was happy to stay to myself.

When we finally arrived, we parked in the full lot and headed to the main entrance, getting there just in time to be greeted by David waiting at the front door for us. He opened it and indicated for us to enter. Vanessa thanked him, being sure to touch his arm as she passed, and then he and I entered behind them. He grinned at me as he put his arm around my waist.

"You look lovely tonight," he complimented, kissing my cheek. "Very...sunny," he smiled.

"Thank you. You're not too bad yourself. I like this look," I responded, touching the collar of his burgundy polo shirt.

We made our way back to the banquet room and were instructed to sit with Dad and Vanessa at a large round table. She made sure she was next to David as we took our seats. Her parents sat with us, along with the maid of honor and her date.

As the waiters brought the menus around, I reached under the table and grasped David's hand. He glanced at me and smiled, but that wasn't a good enough response for me. I leaned in and whispered in his ear, "How are you going to pull this off? They expect you to eat."

He lifted the menu and glanced at what was available, then turned and whispered in my ear, "What do you like?"

I gave him a funny look, wondering why he was asking. "I was thinking about getting the filet mignon."

"Order a salad; I'll get the filet mignon," he instructed.

I knit my brow. "Won't that be a waste of food?"

"No, you're going to eat my dinner," he grinned.

"I can't wait to see this," I replied.

"How do you like your steak?"

"Umm...medium."

He smiled and placed his order as the waiter came around. I ordered a salad and Dad looked at me, surprised. "You're not eating more than that?" he asked.

"No, I'm not that hungry," I lied.

He shrugged and went back to talking with Vanessa's parents. They had a lot in common since they were around the same age. Vanessa's maid of honor, Sara, sat next to me, and I could see out of the corner of my eye she was itching to ask me something about David. I turned slightly in her direction, and she took that as an indication to introduce herself and her boyfriend, Jon.

"I'm Megan, Vanessa's step-daughter," I replied, though I had met her before. "And this is my boyfriend, David," I continued as he peered over my shoulder and smiled at her.

She just stared at him. "You have the most beautiful eyes and smile…" she murmured in a daze.

"Thank you," he replied and then looked at me. She sighed, placing her hand over her heart. I know what that feeling is.

"So what do you do, David?" Jon asked abruptly.

"I work with the Medical Examiner," he replied coolly.

Both Sara and Jon gave a disgusted look. "He's studying to be a doctor," I interjected.

"Oh, a doctor," Jon scoffed.

"What do you do, Jon?" David asked politely, though he could easily guess.

"I…I work in construction," he replied.

"How nice to be outside all the time," David responded with a smile before turning toward Vanessa.

She wanted to introduce him to her parents. Even Mrs. Wiley seemed enthralled by him, but she tried not to show it. As he talked with Vanessa's father, the food arrived. The filet mignon looked delicious, and I wondered how he was going to pull this off with everyone staring at him.

I took a bite of salad and watched as the rest of the group enjoyed their hot meals. He looked at me sympathetically and cut a slice of the filet, offering it to me to try. Was this how he'd get away with clearing his plate? I smiled and bit the meat off the fork, savoring the juicy morsel. He cut another slice and prepared to eat it as Mr. Wiley asked him a question.

He lowered the fork and responded, everyone's eyes on his intently. As I listened, I took another bite of salad, but this time it didn't taste like the slightly bitter greenery I had been consuming. Glancing down, I spied a slice of meat mixed in with my lettuce. He continued cutting and talking, slipping more into my leafy greens and even adding his vegetables to my mix.

When his plate was clear, he patted his mouth and set his napkin next to it, indicating he was done. Sneaky, but it worked. He looked at me and smiled with a wink.

"How was your salad?" he whispered as I finished it.

"Delicious. That filet was cooked to perfection."

"David, how was the steak?" Dad asked, not even a moment later. "I thought about getting it but settled on the lamb chops."

"Perfect," he replied as he switched cups with me. His was still full while mine was empty. I took it and sipped, glad to have a drink.

Vanessa finished off her glass of wine and signaled for a refill. She leaned on David and grinned stupidly. "I want to introduce you to my girlfriends. I told them alllll about you," she slurred slightly.

She stood up, teetering a little, but steadied herself on Dad's shoulder. David stood to follow but turned and took my hand. He knew I didn't want him to be alone with her and her friends. We walked to the next table over and she introduced us. Well, mainly him.

"This is Megan and her boyfriend, David. He's the one with the huge house on the lake and the Bugatti!"

He nodded politely, trying not to chuckle at her drunkenness, but he couldn't help it. There was a collective sigh and then all the women scrambled to get closer to him, pushing me out of the way. I forced my way back to his side, and he put his arm around my waist, holding tightly.

They asked inane questions while flipping their hair and openly flirting with him, Vanessa worst of all. After answering something about our relationship, he leaned in and kissed my cheek as they 'awww'd. He was really working this. After a few more questions, he excused us and we left the group, to their dismay. But we didn't go far – he wanted me to hear what they had to say once we left their circle.

"Oh my God, Vanessa, he's so hot!" one woman gushed.

"Yeah, you're so lucky to have that eye candy around all the time," replied another.

"And rich to boot!" added another.

"I know. I just wish he wasn't so in love with Megan. I might have been able to lure him away," she slurred and then hiccupped.

"That witch!" I hissed. "How could she do that to my father?"

David led me into another part of the building, trying to calm me down. "Megan…that's the alcohol talking. Though I don't doubt she would try to seduce me, I don't think she could follow through. She likes to flirt and be loved by men, but in all probability she would back down if it was turned on her."

"Oh…" I responded quietly. I'm sure she would, but I don't want to test that theory.

"So now that we have some private time…how was the rehearsal?" he asked, taking my hand and kissing it.

"Grueling," I replied. "She made us redo the entrances and exits like twenty times…each. I am so exhausted."

He kissed farther up my arm, and my skin tingled. "It'll be over tomorrow."

I closed my eyes and relished it. "Then I'm stuck with her until death do they part."

"You only have a year to live with them and then you're off to college," he remarked, kissing my shoulder. I tilted my head slightly, inviting his lips on my neck.

"Yeah…I can always make excuses why I can't come home for certain holidays…"

He paused right above it. "Vanessa mentioned something to me about Ben being at the rehearsal. I told her I was aware of it to cover for you. What was he doing there?"

Crap. Why did she have to tell him that before I could? I straightened my head and sighed before briefly recapping the afternoon.

"What did you talk about?"

"We made fun of Vanessa mostly," I replied, leaning against a wall. "But we also talked about future plans and school next year."

"So what *are* your plans after graduation?" he asked, shifting the conversation.

"It dawned on me that I hadn't really given it much thought. You kinda threw a kink into everything," I responded, staring into his eyes. I leaned in closer, ready to kiss him when Sara interrupted.

"Megan, Vanessa's looking for you. You better get back to the banquet hall."

I looked at David and rolled my eyes as we returned to the room. Vanessa was standing at the front, signaling for me to join her. She put her arm around my shoulders and gave me a wet kiss on the cheek and then introduced me to the crowd as her lovely stepdaughter.

I forced a smile for the group as the smell of alcohol wafted toward me. She was even more drunk than when we left her. David grinned at me from beside my dad, who was teary eyed. She said a few more kind but hollow words and then went to my father's side, giving him a passionate kiss before plopping down on the chair.

I joined David, taking a seat as I buried my face in my hands, totally embarrassed by her, even though none of these people were my friends or family. He rubbed my back, laughing quietly. I glanced up briefly and found Vanessa lying across my father's lap and buried my head again.

"If it's any consolation, she's going to have a horrible hangover in the morning," he whispered in my ear. "The morning of her wedding."

That did help. I giggled as I raised my eyes to his. "Are you ready to go, because I am."

He smiled as he stood and without a word, took my hand and lifted me out of my chair. "We're heading out," I told Dad quietly, not wanting Vanessa to know. He gave me a wary look. "I'm going straight home," I assured him.

"Okay. I have to drop Vanessa off at her friend's house, and then I'll be home after that."

I kissed his cheek, and David bowed his head as he thanked him for a lovely evening. We headed out to the car and took off for home. Or so I thought.

"Where are we going?" I asked, noticing we didn't take the usual ramp. "I have to be home before my dad."

"Don't worry, you will," he replied as he drove to an unfamiliar place.

I looked out the windows into the darkness as we went from paved road to dirt, curious where we were. He slowed and then stopped, turning off all the lights. I held myself, feeling a little nervous there in the dark with him. My breathing was as rapid as my heartbeat as I stared at my lap and waited.

"Let your eyes adjust to the darkness," he whispered as I heard him turning in his seat. "It helps to close them for a few seconds."

He reached over and without fumbling, slipped his hand over my face as I closed my eyes. He caressed my cheek and kissed my arm as I counted the seconds in my head. How long did I need to do this and what was I doing it for?

"Now open them," he enjoined.

I slowly opened my eyes to the most magical sight I had ever seen. Facing a dense forest, I watched as hundreds of fireflies danced through the plants and trees to silent music, their dim lights intermittently disrupting the darkness. I rested my chin on my hands as I leaned on the dash and watched them twinkle.

"I came across this the other night while I was hunting. I thought you might like to see it," he commented, running his fingers down my spine.

I sat up and turned to him. I could somewhat see his face, but his eyes were the easiest to find. "It's incredible…thank you."

He slipped his hand under my chin, resting it on my neck as he leaned closer. His warm lips touched mine and I grew eager. I moved even closer, climbing over the gear shifter and straddling his lap. Opening my mouth slightly, I kissed deeper as my heart beat wildly.

He grabbed my waist, ready to force me away, but I gripped his shoulders, refusing to let him. As I kissed his face, I felt his lips on my cheek and then he started moving lower. I threw my head back, breathing hard as they parted on my skin. I could feel his breath on my throat, hot and heavy.

Then suddenly, the feeling was gone. I lowered my head, wondering why we stopped. Instead of a response, he gently guided me back to my seat. "Is everything okay?" I asked, trying to find him in the darkness. Getting no explanation, I sighed and buckled up, staring out the side window as he backed out of the woods.

"We need to be going. I'm sorry," he apologized, covering up his near loss of control.

We rode the rest of the way home without a word to each other, twenties' jazz playing softly through the speakers. He pulled in the drive and opened my door, taking my hand and walking with me to the porch. Dad wasn't there yet but could arrive anytime.

"I'll park my car a few blocks away and meet you in your room," he informed me as I unlocked the door.

I dropped my head, disappointed, and replied, "Okay."

He lifted my chin and gently kissed my lips. "I won't be long. As soon as you're in your nightclothes, I'll be there."

"All right," I whispered, and he turned to leave as I stepped inside and closed the door.

I slowly climbed the stairs to my room, delaying my loneliness as long as possible. I changed into a tank and shorts and climbed into bed, rolling over to my side and turning out the light. He'd let himself in and join me when he arrived. I closed my eyes and dozed for a few minutes.

*Being awoken by a hand on my shoulder, I tried to open my eyes. "David?" I asked as I focused on a dark figure.*

*"You'll pay for what you did!" a sinister voice bellowed, grabbing me.*

"No! Leave me alone, Brian!" I screamed, thrashing as I tried to get away.

"Megan! Stop…it's Dad!" he shouted, turning on the bedside lamp.

"Dad? Dad!" I cried as I stared clearly at his face. "Oh, God…I was having a nightmare. I'm sorry," I apologized, holding my chest as I turned and sat on the edge of the bed.

"A nightmare about Brian? Why would you have a nightmare about him?"

"No…not the Brian that lived with David. I was reading a horror story with a Brian as the bad guy," I lied.

"Oh," he replied, rubbing my back. "Wait…what do you mean *lived* with David?"

He was too quick for me, especially in my drowsy state. "He and Odette moved out a couple days ago…figured it was time to move on, get married, start a family," I fabricated.

"Well, it's probably a good time in their life. He's older than David, right?"

"Yeah," I responded. Well, technically no, but for this purpose he was.

He kissed my forehead and stood up. "I just wanted to make sure you made it home all right. I'll let you get back to sleep. You had a long day and tomorrow will be just as bad."

Ugh…thanks for reminding me. "Good night, Dad," I responded softly instead.

"'Night Meg," he replied, turning off the light and closing the door as I curled back up in my comforter.

I couldn't go to sleep as easily as I had before, so I stared at the nightstand and wondered where David was and what was taking so long. He should have been here by now. Maybe he had to check on something.

As I lay pondering what that could be, my mind turned to why I had such a vivid dream about Brian attacking me. I hadn't thought about him all day. Maybe it was because it was night and I was alone and not sure if he was truly gone.

What if that's the reason why David's late – Brian didn't go back and he's hunting him down? Brian could be here right now, waiting to get in. My eyes quickly flicked to the balcony doors. Nothing. I continued watching them, assuring myself there was no way he could unless he was invited and that'd never happen.

To get my mind off it, I tried to think of happier things, like the firefly forest David shared with me. As I replayed their hypnotic dance in my mind, my eyelids drooped and my breathing slowed. I was just about out when I felt the bed indent and a hand on my shoulder.

"David?" I whispered, hoping I was right this time.

"I'm here, Megan. Please forgive me for taking so long. Madeline came by to inform me of Brian and Odette's status," he explained.

I slowly pushed myself up on my elbows. "And?"

He ran his fingers over my hair and held my cheek. "They're gone."

I dropped back to the bed, letting out a relieved breath. "I had a nightmare he came in my room," I remarked, looking at him.

He leaned over me, gazing into my eyes. "He can't get you, Megan. You're safe."

"I know," I replied, yawning. Rolling to my side, I readied for sleep. "And you'll always protect me."

"Shhh…rest now," he whispered, and like that, I was out.

# Chapter 31
## The Wedding

Dad woke me at the crack of dawn, saying we had tons to do. The wedding wasn't until two, but I did as I was told and took my shower and then gathered my things together. He had breakfast waiting downstairs and as I sat and ate, he continued running around.

The wedding party was expected at Maymont before noon to take care of hair and makeup – Vanessa hired special people for that – and to get dressed. As soon as Dad had everything he needed, we headed to the park. He was anxious about the whole affair, but I was more curious than anything. Mostly how she faired last night after her binge drinking.

We arrived at Maymont and as soon as we entered through the gate, Dad was instructed to go in one direction and me in the other. In keeping with tradition, though it was pointless now, Vanessa wanted to be sure he didn't see her before the wedding. I, on the other hand, had to and she looked rough. Her stylists had a difficult job ahead of them.

I was ushered into another room, joining the other bridesmaids, and seated in an empty space in front of a makeup table. I glanced down the row at the other ladies, watching as they examined themselves in the brightly lit mirrors to gasps of horror and disbelief. Then the stylists entered, standing by each table, and started on our hair. They pulled and tugged and curled and sprayed, making small talk as they put us through excruciating pain. I vowed never to do anything this cruel to my bridal party.

From hair, they moved on to makeup. I didn't think it was possible, but it was almost as painful as the styling of the hair. Eyebrows were plucked, skin was scrubbed, and eyelashes were curled. Then they pulled out a palette and matched colors for lipstick, eye shadow, and blush according to the gowns hanging behind us.

I never bothered to look at myself in the mirror through the whole ordeal. I focused on other things to keep my mind off the pain. Once the stylists finished torturing us, they helped each of us into our gowns, making sure not to mess up their handiwork. It felt awkward being in my underwear in front of all of Vanessa's friends, but no one seemed to care.

It wasn't until after my gown was on that I finally looked at myself in the mirror. I stared at the strange person, not believing it was me. The makeup was a little heavy for my taste, but they did an amazing job regardless and my hair looked great. I checked out the other bridesmaids as they squealed with excitement over their new looks, appearing years younger. Ah, the wonder of concealer.

We were led out of the room and paraded in front of Vanessa, her mother, and the maid of honor. She was a completely different person from the hungover hot mess I saw when I first arrived. Her stylists had indeed worked their magic.

She wasn't in her gown yet, lounging on a chaise before us in a corset, garter belt, and hosiery with a glass of pink champagne in hand. She slowly stood up and examined each of us, smiling approvingly at the work of her hired help. She paused for a long time in front of me, grinned, and then sent all of us on our way. Once outside, we were directed to our places at the far end of the pergola. There we waited.

It was a beautiful, warm June day – perfect for a wedding. A light breeze blew, just enough to keep us cool and not affect the decorations. Birds were singing while the bees buzzed as they gathered pollen and the butterflies danced across the flowers. I imagine it was a day much like this when Mom and Dad married.

The guests flowed in, taking their places and pointing as they stared at the gardens and us. Scanning the crowd, I only recognized a handful of the attendees. There may have been a dozen of Dad's friends and co-workers, but a majority of the guests were Vanessa's.

The gentle melody coming from the string quartet was drowned out by the crowd's rising volume as more trickled in. I tried to focus on the music, tried to find peace in it. I wasn't nervous; I just wanted this wedding over and done. But it needed to begin before it could end.

I peeked around the bridesmaids in front of me and watched as my dad took his place by the minister. Finally! The groomsmen joined us a moment later and then the quartet started to play a different song, signaling our walk down the pergola. One by one, we took the arm of our matching groomsman and meandered along the path, lining up at the end as practiced.

The ring bearer and the flower girl, cousins of Vanessa, followed behind us, making everyone chortle with their antics. When they reached us, the little girl kissed the boy on the cheek and there was a collective 'awww'. I wasn't falling for it. It was probably staged by Vanessa to make her wedding memorable, not like her entrance alone wouldn't do that.

The quartet played another song, building into a crescendo as the carriage pulled up. It stopped and a shrouded Vanessa stood, taking her father's hand and stepping out. A young woman exited behind her, straightening her train and the back of her veil. When she fussed too much with them, Vanessa discreetly kicked at her. Thank goodness I didn't have that job.

Starting down the walkway, she grinned wide from the crowd's ooo's and ahhh's as she strolled arm in arm with her father toward us. She was eating this up. I glanced at my dad, curious of his reaction to her dress. Just as I thought, his mouth was agape, as were all the groomsmen and even the minister.

I rolled my eyes and stood by waiting for her to finally reach us. She handed off her enormous bouquet to her maid of honor and then faced her father. He lifted her veil and gave her a kiss on the cheek, then led her over to her place before the minister.

Vanessa and Dad glanced at each other, a big grin on her face and a concerned look on his. Once the minister had everyone's attention, he began the ceremony, speaking on undying love. I pursed my lips, wanting so badly to scoff at the thought. Yeah, the undying love of money.

But as he detailed this love, I couldn't help but think about David. Our love was deeper than this, deeper even than what Mom and Dad had. And maybe one day, we'd stand before a minister and profess our literal undying love for each other. I smiled at the thought, my happiest moment of the day.

Once the minister concluded his speech, Dad and Vanessa said their vows, exchanged rings, were pronounced man and wife, and kissed. My stomach turned as she did a full French kiss in front of God, the minister, her wedding party, and the guests.

Finally parting, the minister presented them as Mr. and Mrs. Jack Caldwell, and the wedding march played as we led the way back down the pergola. They followed but detoured into the waiting carriage at the end while we continued on and waited off to the side. Vanessa waved like a debutante as they passed the crowd and then disappeared behind the Carriage House.

The wedding party was instructed to wait in the Italian Garden for pictures while the guests cleared out and headed to a tent on the Carriage House lawn for the reception. Everyone gone, Dad and Vanessa circled back around and joined us. All the bridesmaids and groomsmen congratulated them, with the exception of me, but it wasn't like they noticed anyhow.

The photographer called everyone over and directed us on where to stand for pictures. There were several of just Dad and Vanessa under the dome in various poses, some serious and others playful. Then he took pictures of the entire wedding party, Vanessa and her parents, the bridal party with the bride and the groomsmen with the groom, the flower girl and ring bearer with the bride, and tons of the bride alone.

The last pictures taken were of Vanessa, Dad, and me. They were going to leave it at that, but I requested some shots of just my father and me. Vanessa wasn't happy I mentioned it, but Dad thought it would be nice. As the photographer snapped the final shots, the wedding party headed on to the reception with the instruction to wait for us before entering.

When we finally joined them, we entered the tent the same as we had for the wedding (minus the carriage) so Vanessa could have her grand entrance as Mrs. Caldwell with my father by her side. They walked around greeting everyone and thanking them for coming and then sat at the head table as the servers brought the food out, the bridal party being first served and then everyone else after that.

I had to sit at the far end of the table, away from my dad and next to my dorky escort. He talked to me and I politely smiled, but I could not for the life of me say what he was talking about. I was too busy people watching and wishing I was with David. I prayed for a sudden rainstorm to come along so I wouldn't have to suffer any longer, but the sun continued to shine brightly.

I pulled my phone out of my clutch and checked the time – still three more hours before I'd get to see him. I sighed, picking at my food while I continued watching the crowd as they ate. When it looked like things were slowing down, the emcee announced it was time for toasts and cake cutting and then after that, the real fun would begin. Hopefully, all of it would make the time pass faster.

The first toast was from the best man, one of my dad's business partners, humorous and full of sexual innuendos. Everyone else found it funny, but I was appalled. Next was the tear-filled toast of the maid of honor, followed by Vanessa's father, and then the microphone was opened up to anyone else. After everyone who wanted to make a toast had done so, Vanessa and Dad made their way to the cake table.

It started out sweet enough, though I knew it'd be a disaster because of the type of person she was. They cut the cake hand in hand, and he was first to feed her a piece, delicately placing it in her mouth. But then, like the tramp she was, she licked the icing off his fingers and smiled seductively.

Then it was her turn. She took a large piece and smiled innocently at him. He shook his head slightly, hoping she wasn't going to do what she was thinking of doing. The shouts from the crowd to do it became louder. Egged on by them, she took that large piece of cake and smashed it right in my dad's face. She laughed hysterically as he cleared the mess from his eyes.

But he had his revenge…sort of. He smiled deviously and went for her as she screamed. The groomsmen trapped her as he took her face in his icing covered hands and gave her a messy kiss, getting cake all over her. He laughed as he walked away, and they had to restrain her from attacking him. The maid of honor brought her a damp napkin, and Vanessa calmly wiped her face and then was all smiles. Yes, put on your fake face for your friends and family. Dad will get it later.

The emcee made some humorous remarks about the incident and then invited everyone up for cake as one of the caterers took over. After dessert was eaten, the emcee requested all the single ladies to follow him outside.

My escort nudged me and I rolled my eyes. Might as well. Not like I'd catch anything with these ravenous women competing for it. I situated myself among the group and waited for the disaster that was the bouquet toss.

Vanessa stared at the group, smirking at me before turning around. The emcee counted down and cued a drum roll. She tossed it over her shoulder and into the crowd. All the women huddled closer together, packing in around me. We raised our hands into the air, but it was mine that grasped that god-forsaken bouquet.

The women closest to me growled and grumbled and as I looked up at Vanessa with the tattered bouquet hanging from my hands, she smirked and mouthed 'you're next'. I smirked back and dropped my arm, holding it at my side and thinking, *You wish*. It's an old superstition and I'm not superstitious.

Dad passed me as he made his way toward her for the garter toss and looked surprised. "You caught the bouquet?" he asked.

"Yeah…funny, huh?" I replied, standing off to the side as the single men gathered near them. My wedding escort winked at me as he passed. Again, I wished for a sudden downpour as I looked to the clear, cloudless sky.

Vanessa called for Dad as she sat on the chair positioned in front of the group of eager men, the pale blue garter exposed on her upper thigh. She winked at me as he kneeled before her, waiting for the emcee to cue the music. I crossed my arms, glaring back.

The band played a burlesque number as he shimmied the garter down her leg. She threw her head back and laughed as she raised it up so he could remove it. He stood, showing the garter to everyone. There was a drum roll and then he shot it into the air.

The men were just as bad as the women as they dove for it. Lo and behold, the one who caught it was my dorky escort. He was grinning ear to ear, braces shining in the dimming sunlight, as he ran over to me.

"Now it's your turn in the chair," he directed, raising his eyebrows several times. I glanced at Vanessa, confused. She stood by it, smirking as she indicated for me to take a seat. What was going on?

I felt someone pushing me toward the center and then into the seat. Dad told her he didn't like this idea, but she assured him he'd stop at my knee. Stop what? I looked around at all the smiling and laughing faces as the dork kneeled in front of me, garter in hand.

"Oh, hell no," I muttered, trying to stand, but Vanessa gripped my shoulders tightly and forced me back down.

"It's all in fun," she whispered in my ear.

She cued the band to play that same burlesque song as the dork slowly slipped the garter over my foot and up my calf. He reached my knee and wanted to keep going, but I blocked him. Realizing I wouldn't relent, he shrugged and stood, facing the crowd and bowing. I was so utterly embarrassed. The crowd clapped and then headed inside.

Pausing before leaving, the dork whispered, "I'll see you on the dance floor."

Yeah right.

I remained seated, letting my embarrassment subside. As I fidgeted with the tattered bouquet, I stared at the deepening blue sky. What I wouldn't have given for a soothing, rainy day so I could have had David by my side through this trauma. Maybe I should call him.

I pulled out his phone and strolled away from the crowd down into the Japanese Garden. It was quiet...and completely devoid of Vanessa or the dork. As I ambled along the path, I stared at the phone in my hands. I should leave a message letting him know how I was doing. He'd probably be interested anyway in how things went. I stared at his number and then turned it off. No, he'd just call when he woke up.

I sat on the bench among the trees at the far end of the pond and gazed out over the water, watching the ducks. I missed him so much. I turned the phone on again and dialed his number. After several rings, his voicemail picked up and my heart beat fast hearing his voice. I closed my eyes, focusing on every word, every syllable.

Then the beep came, and I realized I needed to leave some sort of message. "Oh, uh, hey David, hope you're sleeping well and I'm not disturbing you. The wedding went well...all fanfare. The reception's in full swing now. You won't believe it, but I caught the bouquet. I think it was a setup though. My escort is annoying, thinking he's going to score a date with me...ha. I told him I was in a relationship..." I took a deep breath and then let it out. "I really miss you and wish you were here. If it's not too late, can you try to make it? I'd like to share a dance with you. Okay...hope to see you later." I hung up, feeling more miserable than I had before.

I stayed in the garden a little while longer and then decided to go back to the party. They'd probably start the dance soon, and I didn't want to miss dancing with my father. I barely reached the top before I was stopped by the dork.

"Where have you been? It's time to dance!" he exclaimed, grabbing my wrist and dragging me toward the tent. Oh, he'll be so sorry if David shows up tonight.

We entered and stood with the rest of the wedding party as Dad and Vanessa took the floor. A twangy country song obviously picked by her played as he wrapped his arms around her and gave her a kiss. She rested her head on his shoulder as they continued to sway and twirl.

Once that song finished, they danced again, but this time invited the wedding party onto the floor with them. I didn't want to go, resisting at first, but then gave in. It was one dance; I'd give my escort that at least. But

I soon regretted it. He kept stepping on my toes and tried to hold me closer than he should. Getting my mind off the pain and torture, I glanced out the plastic windows and saw it getting darker. The sun was finally setting. My heart thumped eagerly.

As soon as the song was over, they cleared the floor for the bride and her father to dance. Halfway through, Dad came over and took my hand, leading me out onto the floor. It was the best part of my evening so far.

"Are you having a good time?" he asked quietly as he turned me around. He was definitely a much better dancer.

"Not really. My feet are killing me from the stomping I endured during the wedding party dance. Vanessa's cousin is such a dork," I replied, glancing around. He laughed. "And I miss David," I confessed.

"Aw, honey, it's all right. You'll probably see him tomorrow," he commented, kissing my forehead.

"Yeah…I just wish he was here," I remarked as the song ended and the next one began.

Guests soon congested the small dance floor, and I decided that was my cue to leave, regardless of the protests from the dork. I took my seat at the head table and watched as everyone had a great time, wishing I could. I glanced out the plastic window again and noticed it was much darker. I wonder if David got my message.

The dork joined me a moment later, having nothing better to do than harass me. He continued discussing whatever inane topic he had before as I sighed and hoped for a miracle. Still being polite at least, I smiled slightly and feigned interest as I stared off into the crowd.

Noticing unusual movement out of the corner of my eye, I shifted my attention to the darkened entrance of the tent as a tall, masculine figure entered carrying a slim box. I couldn't tell who it was, but I had my fingers crossed. The figure added his present to the rest on the gift table and glanced around the room. My heart leapt as he stepped out of the shadows and smiled at me.

"Who's *that* guy?" the dork asked, following my stare.

I grinned wide and replied, "*That's* my boyfriend," as I got up and walked away.

David met me halfway, instantly taking me into his arms and kissing me. I held him for a long time, not wanting to let go. "I can tell you're happy to see me," he remarked quietly.

"You have no idea," I responded, excited to be with him and have all his attention.

But I should have known the moment wouldn't last long. Several women came up and started talking and flirting with him. Without a word, I took his arm and escorted him out of the tent, leading him into the Italian

Garden. Checking that no one followed, we sat on the wall and resumed our gazes.

"You look stunning," I commented, touching the lapel of his elegant, tailor-made, three piece charcoal suit.

"I should say the same of you," he replied with a half-smile. "Reminds me of the night we first met." I tucked my head and blushed, playing with dangling strands of hair as I looked at my feet. He reached over and gently touched my chin, lifting my face. "And that, too," he smiled and my heart thumped.

"I missed you so much today," I whispered, leaning close and kissing him.

We parted, and he caressed my cheek as he looked into my eyes. "You were in my thoughts all day, even as I slept," he responded quietly.

Leaning my head on his shoulder, I closed my eyes and listened to the distant sound of the band while the crickets and other creatures of the night played their own music in harmony with the soft roar of the waterfall. He slipped his hand under mine and lifted it to his lips, gently kissing it, and then lowered it to his lap, our fingers intertwined. I was happy to be just like this.

"You caught the bouquet?" he asked quietly, interrupting my meditation.

I opened my eyes and stared at his fingers wrapped with mine. "Yes, but I didn't mean to. Vanessa aimed right for me."

"Maybe it's fate."

"What?" I asked, raising my head. "That I'll be the next to be married? I don't believe in that superstition."

He smiled. "Would you ever want to be married?"

I bowed my head. I would, but I debated this time and time again. "I don't know. I guess it depends."

"Depends on what?" he asked, leaning forward on his knees.

I hesitated. I knew I wanted to be with him, but...

I looked down and fidgeted with my hands. "If it's possible..."

He took my chin in his cool hand and lifted it. "What's not possible? My mere existence proves the impossible possible."

"Are you saying...are you asking me to...marry you?" I questioned, gazing deep into his eyes.

He smiled and kissed me. "Maybe...maybe not," he whispered in my ear.

"Well, which is it?"

He grinned and my heart fluttered. "You will know...in due time," he answered, staring off into the sky.

"What...never mind," I sighed, figuring he wouldn't explain anyway.

I gazed at him staring at the stars and smiled. If he did ask, I would say yes without hesitation. He was definitely the one I wanted to be with forever. I squeezed his hand, taking his attention away from the heavens and focusing it on me again. As he smiled his flawless smile, I leaned in and kissed him and then rested my head once again on his shoulder.

We sat in silence for some time before deciding to rejoin the party. Things were winding down and guests were beginning to leave. The band played a slow song as he led me to the dance floor. He was a far better dancer than the dork, who looked on angrily from a nearby table. As the song neared the end, he dipped me and kissed my throat before raising me back up. Nearby, a group of women sighed enviously. I grinned and held him closer.

Then Vanessa had to go and ruin it. "May I cut in?" she asked as she tapped aggressively on my shoulder.

I didn't want to let go, but his look assured me it'd be all right. "Of course, anything for the bride," David replied as he took her hand and smiled while she stumbled and giggled profusely.

I stood alone off to the side, my arms wrapped around my body, and watched as he danced gracefully with her, though she had a hard time keeping up. The dork eagerly rushed over and asked to dance with me, and I almost took him up on it, but then Dad appeared at my side and asked. I smiled politely, accepting, and followed him to the center.

After a while, I noticed Dad making his way toward David and Vanessa. We moved closer and closer until we were circling each other and then, without a word, we switched partners and David was back with me. Dad smiled and bowed his head as David and I moved farther away. When the band finished playing, the four of us walked to a nearby table and sat.

The bandleader scanned the remaining crowd and then glanced at his watch, deciding it was time to pack it up. The caterers worked at clearing the tables and packing up as well, maneuvering around us as they did. The remaining few guests hung around the open bar and drank, enjoying all the free alcohol with nothing better to do.

Vanessa fanned herself as she leaned against Dad. "I see you made it to the tail end of the reception," he commented to David as he looked at the two of us.

"I was able to get off work earlier than I expected," he replied.

"Oh! You missed all the fun though! The ceremony, the food, the cake...Megan caught the bouquet! Did she tell you?" she blabbed.

"Yes, she did."

"And my cousin over there caught the garter," she continued, pointing the dork out. "Then he had to put it on her!" she laughed.

He glanced at me, raising an eyebrow. "I've never heard of that tradition before, but it has been a long time since I attended a wedding."

"He didn't get any farther than the top of my calf," I told him quietly as I showed the part of my leg where the garter sat. He smiled like he had an idea I didn't want to know about.

"It was so nice of you to dance with me. You're pretty light on your feet," she commented, bringing his attention back to her again.

"Thank you. My parents always had large parties and I was expected to dance with the young ladies attending, along with playing the piano for them."

She sat up and leaned on her hands as she stared at him. "Wow..." she replied in awe.

"Will you and Mrs. Caldwell be staying somewhere elegant for your first evening as a married couple?" he asked, looking toward my dad.

"We're spending the night at the Jefferson."

"I've stayed there a couple times prior to moving here. It's a marvelous hotel."

"That's why we picked it," she piped up. "Speaking of which, we should get going, sweetie," she remarked to Dad, grabbing his shoulder to help herself up.

"Well Meg, I guess we'll see you in the morning. David, thank you again for coming," he commented, shaking his hand. Then he gave me a stern look before leaving – the look of 'he's not allowed to stay the night'.

But he will, or most of it at least.

After they left, David looked around at the crew cleaning up. "Are you ready to go?" he asked, turning his attention back to me.

"Yeah, I just have to get with Rick to make sure he knows to follow me home. He's carrying all the gifts."

He took my hand and stood, raising me with him. "And I will follow him. The two of you will need help getting everything into the house."

With the dwindling crowd, it didn't take long to find my helper. He was by the bar, chatting up a young blonde. "Hey Rick, I'm Megan. You're supposed to follow me home."

He turned to me and grinned. "Oh yeah? And then what'll we do when we get to your place?" he slurred, reaching for me.

David swiftly slipped between us, grasping his wrist in mid-air. "Apologize," he demanded, twisting his arm. Instantly, he complied.

As David released him, I stepped forward and huffed. "There's no way you're fit to drive. Is there someone who can do it for you?" I asked.

He was still staring horrified at my boyfriend. As my question registered with him, he shifted his eyes to me. "Yeah...yeah. I'm supposed to take my nephew home. He's...he's seventeen. Gary...he's right over there," he replied, pointing at the dork.

Rick called him to come over, and he glanced our way and grinned. He dashed across the room and stood next to him. "Hey babe. Are you the one we're following?" he asked, disregarding my boyfriend standing there.

"Yes…and I'll be following you," David replied devilishly.

He looked up at him, instantly intimidated. "I-I-I d-d-didn't mm-mm-mean any…anything bb-bb-by it," he stuttered.

"Then let's go," David instructed, indicating they lead the way.

We reached the parking lot, and they climbed into an older model van as David followed me to my dad's car and waited while I got situated. Ready to go, he kissed me through the open window and then dashed off toward his car, stopping by the van before continuing on. As I pulled out of my spot and drove to the front, I noticed both Rick and Gary sitting completely still and staring forward. What did he say to them?

I waited a moment and then signaled that I was heading out, knowing I wouldn't have to wait long for David. My helpers kept a good distance and every once in a while, I caught a glimpse of David in the rearview mirror. He followed close behind them, keeping a watchful eye over me as well.

I pulled in the driveway and parked behind the other car so the van could pull as close to the house as possible. Standing on the sidewalk, I waited while they backed up to the garage and David parked on the street. They came around the van, keeping their distance from me and their eyes focused on where he was, staring with mouths agape at his car. As he casually strolled up the drive, he smirked as he passed and joined my side.

On our walk to the door, I asked, "What did you say to them before we left?"

He smiled deviously and replied, "I gave them some friendly advice."

I wanted to ask what kind of friendly advice but decided to drop it. I unlocked the door and propped it open, then headed back down the drive to the still gawking cousins of Vanessa. Standing in front of them, I blocked their view and waved my hands. "Hello? I don't want to be out here all night," I griped as they broke their daze and stared at me.

Gary leaned in but didn't get too close to me. "Does he really own that?"

"He sure does. Now let's get moving," I directed, heading to the back of the van.

David was leaning against the garage door, waiting for them to unlock it. Gary fumbled with the keys and shook as he pushed it into the lock and turned it. David must have said something pretty threatening…or showed them something threatening. I glanced at him, and he smirked as he pushed off the garage and grabbed several packages from the back. I grabbed several and headed inside.

He stood in the living room waiting for instruction. "I guess line them up neatly in that corner. It'll be like Christmas morning when they come home tomorrow."

He set his boxes down and left to get more. Gary and Rick brought in the next batch, setting them down beside me. I decided it was best to stay inside, out of the way, and sort them. On the second trip, Gary hesitated after setting his armful of gifts down and looked at me. When I glanced his way, he averted his eyes and took a deep breath.

"I'm sorry I was such a jerk. Vanessa put me up to it," he remarked quietly as he stood and then rushed out the door.

I figured as much.

Rick brought the last of the gifts in and apologized again for his earlier comments as he set them near me. Before saying good night and leaving, he and Gary shot a quick look at David as he came to my side. He smirked at them as he bowed his head, bidding them good night, and they stumbled nervously out the door. Okay, his reply was not satisfying me.

Curiosity getting the better of me, I turned to him and asked, "Did you show them?"

"Show them what?" he asked innocently, knowing darn well what I was talking about. I opened my mouth and pointed to my canines, and he chuckled. "No, I didn't."

I angrily scrunched up my face as he removed his jacket and crouched beside me, helping to organize the last remaining gifts. Turning my focus to sorting, I came across a tall box – the one he brought to the reception. I lifted it up and examined the expertly wrapped package.

"So what did you get them?" I asked, shaking it gently.

"Something rare and unique," he replied enigmatically.

"Oh, that's real helpful," I remarked as I shook it harder.

"I wouldn't do that," he admonished, reaching for it.

I jerked it away before he could grab it and moved it in different directions to keep him from taking it. Quickly standing up, I held it close to my chest and tried to run, but he grabbed my waist and threw me down on the couch, climbing on top of me. I laughed as I continued to keep it away from him, but then he pinned my arms and took it from me. It wasn't until then we realized the position we were in.

As I breathed heavy from the activity, we stared into each other's eyes, time standing still. Ever so slowly, he moved closer, setting the box on the floor and releasing my wrists. Supporting himself with one hand, he slid the other behind my neck and lifted me slightly off the couch. His lips touched mine, and I kissed with a hunger I never experienced before, like I hadn't felt them in days.

My hands gripping his back, I tried to pull him closer to me, but he wouldn't budge. I dropped them, sliding around to his chest and loosening his tie and then slowly unbuttoning his vest and shirt. My lips moved from his mouth down his neck to his exposed chest. Some burning desire was driving me to do it and I didn't know why, but he was allowing it to continue.

He lifted me up so I was sitting, our legs tangled together, and ran his cool fingers over my exposed arms and shoulders. I continued kissing his chest and neck, then returned to his lips. Turning my head slightly and tilting it, I offered my neck. I knew I shouldn't tempt him, but I wanted to feel them on my anxious skin. He continued to kiss me and soon his mouth was moving along my chin to my throat. It worked.

His lips brushing against my skin made my heart beat faster, thumping louder with each caress. I felt them part and then something sharp grazed my skin. Why wasn't he stopping? My breathing increased as I felt the sharpness again, and he gripped my body tighter.

With what breath I could muster, I whispered his name and he paused. His breath flowed in rapid bursts across my skin and then began to slow. Loosening his grasp, he gently kissed up my neck to my lips as he lowered me to the couch.

Gently touching my cheek as he leaned over me, he smiled softly. "I was able to resist," he whispered, kissing me again.

Breathless, I replied, "There must be something special about me."

His smile widened. "Yes, Megan. There is definitely something special about you." I beamed at that thought.

He sat back and I sat up, fixing my hair and looking at him sideways as he removed his tie and vest and buttoned his shirt. I smiled again and then looked at the pile of presents for Dad and Vanessa. It nearly filled half of the room. How ridiculous. I leaned over and picked up David's gift, adding it to the pile.

"I think it's time for me to take a shower," I commented as I got to my feet. "I can't stand to wear this makeup and hair spray any longer. Do you mind waiting?" I asked, walking toward the stairs and removing all the accessories from my hair.

"Here or in your room?"

"I would prefer you stay down here..."

"All right. Do you mind if I go into the family room?"

"Not at all. I won't be long," I responded as I jogged up the stairs.

I rushed through my shower and hopped out, changing into a tank and shorts and throwing my hair in a bun. I was just about to dart out of the room when my cell vibrated. I answered it, surprised to hear Dad on the other end.

"I just wanted to make sure you made it home all right and didn't run into any problems," he remarked.

"None whatsoever," I replied, eager to leave. David was waiting.

"So I guess you're getting ready for bed…"

"Yep, all snuggled up with the lights out, ready to fall asleep," I lied as I anxiously danced at the door.

He paused. "Okay…well, I'll see you tomorrow morning," he responded.

"Okey dokey, enjoy your evening," I replied and hung up, sighing loudly.

I dashed down the stairs and found David in the family room not watching TV like I expected but looking at photographs. I quietly crept into the room, hoping to sneak up on him, but he heard me. Or sensed me.

"Don't even think about it," he warned as he glanced over his shoulder with a grin.

"I should have known I couldn't surprise you," I replied, strolling to his side and looking at what he was holding before he placed it back on the mantle. "That's my mom and me on the beach in the Caribbean. I was nine," I commented, taking it off the shelf and staring at it. "It's one of my dad's favorite pictures."

"She was beautiful. You look so much like her."

"I'm told that a lot," I responded, putting it back. I turned toward him and put my arms around his neck, giving him a kiss. "What shall we do now?" I asked, releasing him and backing away.

"Whatever you would like," he replied.

I looked at him and bit my lip, thinking of what that might be. Coming up empty, I glanced around the room and searched for something. I wasn't in the mood for TV or a movie and I didn't think I'd be up for a lengthy conversation this late in the evening. My eyes stopped on the bookcase and I walked toward it, scanning the titles. I pulled a large, leather-bound book from the shelf and turned toward him, holding it to my chest.

"Will you read to me?" I asked timidly.

He stepped closer, stopping in front of me and smiling softly. "If that is what you desire," he replied, extending his hand to take it.

I lowered the book into his palm and went to the couch, indicating for him to lie down. He obliged, stretching out on his side and smiling up at me as he waited for me to join him. Lying on my back beside him, I gazed up at his handsome visage as he opened the book and scanned the titles. He flipped several pages and then began reading.

From the moment the first words were spoken, I was entranced. He read with such passion, varying the infliction of his tone as was necessary with the lines. His lips moved with every letter, their pronunciation pure and perfect. And his voice kept me drawn and fascinated. I closed my eyes and his words became images, vivid and clear. I was there on the shore watching the daffodils sway. I felt the happiness their presence brought.

He paused a moment and when I opened my eyes, I saw him staring down at me. "Don't stop," I whispered.

He leaned in and kissed me, then went back to reading. My eyes remained trained on him as he finished and then he smiled. He flipped several pages, and I anxiously awaited his next choice. With the first word uttered, I knew the poem right away from the opening lines – "The Raven" by Edgar Allan Poe. I closed my eyes again, wanting to see the words come to life.

I could hear the distant tapping and the flutter of bird wings, the raven's caw of 'Nevermore' as he spoke. He read with such emotion, I felt I could very well be hearing the poem from the author himself. The amusement, the anger, and the fear…I felt it all in his words.

With the last line, I opened my eyes and looked up at him. He paused before reading the next selection, flipping many more pages than the last. I readied myself, watching his expression as he began. I listened intently to the opening and then closed my eyes and smiled. This was way better than watching TV.

The moonlit sky, the horse's hooves, and the thief secretly meeting his love at her family's inn – all seemed happy, but deceit was on the wind. Someone jealous of their love informed the soldiers who had been searching for him about their meetings. The following night, they readied to ambush him, awaiting his return to retrieve her.

Hearing the distant hooves of his horse and knowing he'd arrive soon, she used the only thing she could to save him, pulling the trigger of the gun tied to her. He heard it go off and saw her slumped over in the window, realizing she sacrificed herself to warn him.

I gasped as tears dampened my eyes. David stopped and dropped the book to the floor, raising me toward him and holding me against his chest. I looked up at him and tried to apologize, but he silenced me with a kiss. Not pulling away, I slipped my hand into his hair and kissed more passionately, but then he stopped.

"Let's not press our luck," he whispered, reaching for the book.

His neck extended over my face, I couldn't resist rising up and kissing it. As my lips touched his throat, I smelled his skin, so inviting and alluring. Lying back, he grinned at me and then opened the book and waited.

"So what happened after she died?" I asked.

"Would you like me to tell you or continue reading?" he inquired.

I thought about it and responded, "Please continue reading."

This time I didn't close my eyes. I stared at the ceiling and listened, the ending sad but beautiful. After he finished, he flipped several pages and stared at the words for a moment. Turning slightly toward me, he gazed into my eyes and recited the poem without looking at the book, running his fingers along the side of my face.

His eyes were soft and adoring as he spoke the words the author had written for the one he loved, comparing her to the night in all its beauty and wonder. He spoke them so sincerely, as if he himself had written it for me. My heart fluttered as I gazed into his eyes and with the closing words, he gently kissed my lips.

He continued on to another poem and after a while, I started to get tired. I turned toward him and nestled my head in his chest, readying for sleep. He lowered his voice to a whisper, and I closed my eyes, continuing to see the words as they became part of my dreams.

# Chapter 32
## Ill-Fated Past

I rolled over, reaching for David, but he was gone as usual. I couldn't wait for the day when he'd always be by my side when I woke. I opened my eyes, expecting to see the family room, but was surprised to find myself in my bed. I smiled as I lay on my back, staring at the ceiling and deciding what to do today.

Dad and Vanessa would be coming home sometime this morning, so I needed to get up and get ready for them. I hopped out of bed and threw on a simple outfit, brushed my teeth and fixed my hair, and then headed downstairs. I glanced in the family room and spied the book David read from last night on the coffee table. Picking it up to put away, I noticed the ribbon bookmark in a different spot than before.

I opened to that page and glanced at the poems, finding one titled "Because She Would Ask Me Why I Love Her" by Christopher Brennen. My heart fluttered as I read the words, and I grinned and bit my lip in spite of myself. I held the book to my chest, my heart beating against it as I thought of him and last night.

While deep in reflection, the door opened and Dad and Vanessa announced their arrival. Startled, I quickly slipped the book on the shelf and ran to greet them. He lugged a large suitcase up the stairs as she ran to the gifts in the corner of the living room, dropping to her knees before them as if she was a four-year-old on Christmas morning. I sat on the sofa, figuring that was where I needed to be at the moment.

He came back downstairs and joined me while she rifled through the presents. She glanced over her shoulder and asked, "Megan dear, could you get a notepad and pen to write down the gifts and who they're from for thank yous?"

"Hello, Vanessa. Did you have a nice stay at the Jefferson?" I replied sarcastically as I got up and headed to the desk in the kitchen to get what she requested.

I came back and took a seat next to Dad. He hadn't moved, deciding that was the best place for him since this was all about her. Barely waiting for me to get settled, she grabbed the first gift and opened it.

"Awww…it's from John and Alice Kenner. Look, sweetie. Isn't it nice?" she posed as she held up a personalized plate with their names and wedding date on it.

I jotted the information down as she quickly moved on to the next gift, reacting the same as she did for the first. More presents, more of the same reaction. I was flipping to the second page when she gasped suddenly.

"Ooo, here's a gift from *David Archer*. 'For the many years to come…enjoy'," she read off the tag. "I can't wait to see what *he* gave us!" she remarked excitedly.

Dad leaned in and so did I, just as interested. As I wrote David's name on the paper, she slowly opened the box. She reached in and pulled out a bottle, looking at us.

"Champagne…how nice," Dad commented, sitting back. He was unimpressed.

She inspected it, checking the label for the house and year. "Champagne Henriot…1847…" she read slowly.

He sat up abruptly. "Let me see that," he requested, reaching over her shoulder and carefully grasping the neck. He examined the bottle as I glanced at the old label. It read as clear as day that it was bottled…in 1847. Dad held it in his hands like he was holding a newborn baby. "This is the oldest champagne I have ever seen. It must have cost a fortune!" he exclaimed.

Vanessa snatched it back, not being as delicate or careful with it. "So…do we save it or drink it?" she asked, turning it over in her hands.

"I guess he would want us to drink it…"

"Ooo, maybe on the first night of our honeymoon!"

I noted the champagne by David's name and urged them to move on. Dad took the bottle and stored it with his special wines on the rack in the pantry so it'd be safe. Vanessa continued with the next gift, informing us of who gave it and what it was as David's rare and unique present was forgotten.

It went on for the next hour as they received linens, china, silverware, trinkets, gift cards, and various other items. My hand was cramping by the time she finished. I handed her the list and helped Dad clean up and take the gifts away to their respective places.

The rest of the day was just as bad, making more room and getting Vanessa settled in. By dinner, we were all tired and decided to order in rather than go out or cook. Full and happy, we sat together in the family room. They watched TV while I read the poetry book.

By nine, I told them good night and headed to my room to see or talk to David. I took the book with me and stretched out on my bed, still hunting for the poems he chose last night. I was deep into my quest when the bed depressed and soft, cool lips caressed the skin between my shoulder blades, enlivening my body.

I looked over my shoulder and grinned at David sitting next to me. "Dad and Vanessa really liked your gift," I informed him.

"I figured it would be appropriate," he replied, running a finger down my arm and creating pleasant goosebumps.

"French and from 1847…that's quite impressive," I remarked, turning on my side.

"It belonged to my parents. They planned to drink it on their fiftieth anniversary."

I stared at him, stunned. "Why would you give that away?"

"It's not like I'll be drinking it," he replied with a grin.

"True," I smiled back, trying not to get caught up in him. "They were debating whether to enjoy it on their honeymoon or save it."

"They should drink it; it's aged long enough," he replied, placing his hand on my hip. My skin tingled with his touch. "Did you do anything interesting today?"

I tried to remain calm. "No…not really," I replied, fidgeting with the book cover. "Going through the wedding gifts, putting them away, and getting Vanessa settled. The height of my day has been seeing you…oh, and reading the poem you marked for me," I grinned.

"It's truly how I feel," he commented as he leaned closer.

He slipped his hand under my chin and held it as he bent down, kissing me. Wrapping my arms around him, I sat up and he moved with me as I parted my lips. That hunger from last night was there, driving me to push him further, but he wasn't up for it. He gently pushed me away and turned toward the balcony.

"What's wrong?" I asked, delicately touching his shoulder.

He glanced over and smiled. "I don't think I'm strong enough to stop myself tonight."

Leaning closer, I stared into his eyes. The green was bolder than yesterday. "It's only been a day…"

"I don't wish to press my luck," he responded, looking away again. "Maybe after several days, but not now."

"Fair enough" I conceded, scooting back. I pulled my legs to my chest and hugged them. "So how's Madeline doing? Friday's our double date. Is she nervous at all?" I asked, finding something normal to talk about.

"She's excited, especially since we'll be there," he replied, turning slightly toward me.

"Do the two of you plan to avoid eating or pretend to eat?"

He grinned. "I think we'll put on a show and pretend to eat. She doesn't want to hurt his feelings, especially if he makes a nice meal."

"How considerate of her. I can't wait to see what you do this time," I smirked.

"It'll be hard for me, but not so much for her. Ben will be scrutinizing everything I do."

"Do you still believe he's out to 'expose' you?"

"Not at all. I'm competition," he smiled matter-of-factly.

"Uh huh," I replied, stretching my legs out and lying back.

"What are your plans for tomorrow?" he asked, turning even more.

"Well, it's supposed to be really hot, so I thought about hanging out at the pool, but I have a feeling I'll be stuck inside all day doing Vanessa's bidding."

"Is there one in your community?"

"Yeah, toward the front, behind the clubhouse."

"Will you be alone?" he inquired.

"No, I was thinking about seeing if Claire or Erin will join me."

"Good," he responded, lying on his side next to me. "Hopefully, you'll get to enjoy the sunshine tomorrow. Try not to get burned," he advised with a wicked grin as he reached over me and turned out the light.

I tried to remain calm with his chest over mine, the temptation to grab him and kiss him overwhelming my every thought. I closed my eyes and bit my lip, holding my breath until he moved back. As soon as I felt his presence fade, I opened my eyes and sighed.

"Are you trying to make me go to sleep?" I questioned, thinking this was his way of avoiding any intimacy. "It is summer, you know, and I get to sleep in."

"I do know. And I don't expect you to sleep just yet. We need to turn out the light so neither your father nor Vanessa gets suspicious."

"Good thinking," I whispered, relieved, as I rolled to my side and tried to find his eyes. I reached up and stroked his hair, so silky and thick. My hand slipped from the lush locks to his face, and I ran my fingers along his jaw and then across his lips. Finding them, I leaned in and kissed him.

He broke away shortly after, lying on his back and scooting up a little. Okay, I get the hint. I rested my head on his shoulder and looked up at him, able to see a little better now that my eyes were adjusted. He stared at the ceiling, his head resting against the headboard. What could be going on behind those eyes? I scooted up a little further and kissed his neck and he sighed.

"What are you thinking about?" I asked, my fingers tracing his collarbone.

"What to do about you," he replied, glancing down at me.

"Whatever do you mean?" I inquired, feigning surprise.

He grinned. "You are trouble."

"I'm trouble? How am I trouble?"

"You've altered my plans."

I propped myself up so I was looking directly at him. "Altered your plans?" I repeated, curious what he meant.

His eyes locked on mine, he explained in a voice confident and cool. "I planned to stay in Richmond unseen for as many years as possible and then move on, as I have done in other places for the last hundred and thirty odd years. But that night in the cemetery changed that."

"I had seen you there several times before, rushing to the crypt, but usually you only stayed a little while and then left. I always kept my distance, never approaching or getting too close. But each night I was there, I looked for you, just to watch you come and go."

"That night, though, I *wanted* to get closer. So while you sat inside the crypt, I crept near. You were singing, so soft and sweet. I sat and listened, entranced by your voice, but when you stopped, I slid back and hid. I waited, wondering if I would get to see the owner of the enchanting voice up close."

"When you didn't come out, I moved from the shadows and lingered at the door, out of view but listening. You were mumbling as if you were talking to someone. I remained, but when you stopped, I hid again. This time, you came out. I was right there in the shadows next to you, watching as you descended the stairs and headed to the bluffs.

"I debated following, knowing I shouldn't, but there was something about you that intrigued me. Something about you felt right and no matter what the consequence, I needed to know you. So I slipped out and stole closer to get a better look. When I finally saw you, I was awestruck. Not sure how to approach or if I should approach, I watched you for a while, continuing to hide in the shadows before finally deciding to reveal myself."

I was speechless as I stared at him, my mind overwhelmed with his confession. Silence filled the room and my brain as he sat up and gazed into my eyes. "You're different from any human I have ever met. You stir something inside me I thought died so long ago," he whispered as his fingers delicately caressed my chin and cheek.

I did all I could to force myself to speak. "Wh-what would that be?" I asked softly, half dazed.

"Desire…a desire to be with you, protect you, love you unconditionally. It was nothing like this before…with Charlotte…" he trailed off as he sat back and looked away, breaking the trance.

"What happened to her?" I asked before I could stop myself.

He was silent for a long time, staring out the French doors. Why did I ask that? I should have bit my tongue. I started to apologize when suddenly he turned to me and spoke.

"She was the first human I fell in love with in my new life. She was kind and soft-spoken, always wearing her long, sandy blonde hair in a loose bun near the top of her head. Her eyes were big and brown and full of joy," he recalled, smiling slightly. "I met her in nineteen thirty-six while I was living in Oregon. She was a teacher at the one room school there. I was out for a stroll one evening when I happened upon her struggling with several books and papers."

"Being the gentleman I am and knowing my hunger was under control, I offered to help her. She wasn't scared or apprehensive of me, this strange man who approached her at dusk. Instead, she gladly accepted and even asked me to walk her home." He paused, his jaw tightening. "She was so naïve and trusting…" he muttered, rueful.

"Brian was with me then, as you know. We pretended to be brothers looking to start over in the small lumber town. I worked as an accountant when I could, but he had to stay in the house. He was a danger around humans, unable to control his urge, and so he remained locked up most of the time. I continued to see Charlotte, going to the schoolhouse after the children had gone for the day and walking her home. For weeks I escorted her, always meeting her and making sure she was never around him."

He was quiet for a moment, looking away again. "I still have no idea to this day how she found out where I lived, but she did. She bought a gift for me, a necklace, and wanted to surprise me with it. She went to the house that evening, but I was out. Instead, she was greeted by Brian," he continued, mixed emotions on his face.

"When I came home, I found him fretting over her body, her throat torn open like an animal had attacked her. But I knew it was him. Fledglings don't have the control that older vampires do, so the attacks are…not as clean. I ran to her side and held her in my arms, calling for her, but she was already gone."

"Oh my God," I gasped, covering my mouth with my hand. "What did you do to him? What did you say?"

He paused again, looking down at his hands. "I was angry at first and couldn't be around him, so I disappeared for several weeks, but then I realized it was my fault and not his. He didn't know who she was nor could he control himself…so I forgave him," he replied, looking away as if ashamed.

I sat up and turned to him, knitting my brow. "How can you say it was your fault?"

"I didn't protect her. I let her die," he responded solemnly. He brushed a loose hair behind my ear and held my cheek. "But it won't happen again."

I put my hand on his and leaned close, giving him a soft kiss. "I know," I whispered before resting my head on his chest.

No matter what, he'll never let what happened to Charlotte happen to me, though Brian is more in control of his hunger. Still, something about his behavior must be making David feel the need to be protective. Has Brian acted like this before?

Then I remembered the comment he made in the wine cellar. "Have there been any others?"

David looked at me, his brow furrowed as he tried to decipher what I was asking. "Other what?" he questioned when he couldn't.

"Girlfriends," I replied.

"No...before you there was only Charlotte. I decided after that incident not to get too close to humans. I interact with them, but nothing more than that," he responded and then cocked his head. "Why?"

"Oh...umm...just something Brian said to me."

He sat up, forcing me off him. "And what was that?" he asked.

"That you picked a good one this time," I replied with a yawn, lying next to him.

He asked nothing more, but instead returned to his previous position and invited me into his arms, rubbing my shoulder as he remained silent. I closed my eyes, listening to the sound of his breathing and setting my rhythm to it. As I concentrated on each breath, I slowly let go of consciousness and slipped into sleep.

*It was dusk as I climbed a hill to a small log cabin in the heart of the woods. I was excited; I was on my way to surprise David with a gift I purchased earlier that day – a leather necklace with a lapis lazuli pendant. In the shop, they told me it was good for protection, something he probably needed.*

*I knocked on the door and fidgeted with the box anxiously as I waited for an answer. When one didn't come, I knocked again and then it opened. Brian stood on the other side and greeted me with a pleasant smile. I didn't feel leery or afraid of him as I explained I was there to see David. His smile turned into a big, delighted grin and he invited me inside, telling me his brother would be home at any moment.*

*As he removed my shawl, I commented that I was unaware David had a brother and was surprised he never mentioned that before. Brian chuckled, saying his older sibling must be ashamed of him. I laughed politely as he moved in front of me, his pale gray eyes fixed on me. I introduced myself, and he asked how I knew his brother. I told him about how we met and that we had been seeing each other for several months.*

*Brian cocked his head and smirked, saying how David never mentioned he was seeing anyone, but understood why he was keeping me a secret. He moved closer and took the gift from me, setting it aside as he lifted my hand to his lips and kissed it. I blushed, tucking my head.*

*Taking my chin in his fingers, he lifted my face toward his and gazed into my eyes. I couldn't look away, completely still and barely breathing, as he looked over me and smirked. He said something, but his words didn't register. Placing his cold hand on my cheek, he slowly turned my face toward the window. A strange reflection stared back at me – a lovely, sandy blonde with brown, doe eyes. As his hand gradually slid to my throat, I looked past her and gazed absently into the darkness of the woods.*

*My heart beat faster as his hand moved over my chest to my waist, resting on it as he neared my neck and took a deep breath. He pressed his lips against my skin and I didn't move, continuing to stare out the window as my heart beat harder. His hands grasped my slender frame as he kissed more and more, his mouth opening over my neck as his tongue caressed it. He whispered something and I barely heard it...something about David.*

*Then there was a sharp pain. I came out of my stupor as it worsened and tried to fight, but he had my body constricted. I attempted to scream, but only gurgles came out. As I was lowered to the floor, I could feel my life slipping away. I clawed at my attacker, but Brian only smiled at my pathetic attempt, my blood dripping from his lips...*

I woke with a start and sat up, staring ahead of me. It was morning and I was home in my bed. I glanced at the clock – after ten. Rubbing my face as I sat on the side, I tried to make myself get up.

What a terrible dream...

Where was this coming from? Was it a warning? Was she trying to contact me like my mom does? But in my dreams, Mom appears to me. In this one, I *was* Charlotte.

I didn't know what to make of it, except that I needed to stay clear of Brian. Whether that dream was an accurate re-enactment of what happened or my own heart telling me to be cautious, I would never trust him.

Not wanting to think about it or him anymore, I pushed it out of my mind. It was just my brain's way of filling in details. I got up and went into the bathroom to get ready for whatever was in store for me today. I was hoping for an easy day, but I wasn't betting on it.

Downstairs, I found Vanessa in her robe lounging on the couch in the family room watching talk shows. I grabbed a bowl of cereal and joined her, politely saying good morning before sitting in Dad's chair. She barely acknowledged me, her focus on her show. We watched TV in silence until the commercial break when I asked where Dad was.

"Oh, he went in to the office to clear up some things about a case before we leave. He should be home around lunchtime," she replied as she flipped the channel, not wanting to sit through commercials about hemorrhoid cream or dentures. "So what are your plans today, dear?" she asked, turning it back to the original channel after she didn't find anything worthwhile on the others.

"Nothing in particular. I'm thinking about going to the pool for a couple hours."

"David's pool?" she inquired, a sly smile on her face.

"No, he won't be home. I'm going to the community pool with Claire or Erin."

"Mind if I join you?"

I do mind, but I'm not going to start a battle this early in our new familial relationship. "Sure."

"Great! It'll be fun spending some 'girl' time with you and your friends," she responded, turning her attention back to the TV.

"Great," I echoed, not as enthusiastically. "I'm going to call and see if either are available," I informed her, getting up to take care of my dishes.

I grabbed the phone and went out on the patio in case I said something offensive. It was going to be miserable enough having her along,

I didn't need her overhearing something and making my day worse. I dialed Claire's cell, taking a seat at the table while I waited for her to answer. Finally, she picked up.

"How was the wedding?" she asked instantly.

"Oh, great. Vanessa had a wonderful time being the center of attention," I replied, glancing over my shoulder into the house. I recounted the whole day to her, spending half an hour telling her all the exciting things that happened.

"Did David join you?"

"Not until almost the end of the reception. He got off work early and was on his way home when he decided to stop by," I lied.

"Was he as popular there as he was at prom and the party?"

"Well, a lot of the guests had left, but the few that remained were impressed with him."

"Sounds like you had an interesting weekend. Mine was pretty dull. Justin and his family went out of town and won't be back until tomorrow," she explained, sounding sad. "So, what were you calling me about?"

"Oh, I wanted to see if you'd like to go to the pool this afternoon. It's muggy and hot – perfect swimming weather."

"Hmm...I might be able to get out of doing some chores to come join you. Anyone else going?"

"I'm going to call Erin after I get off the phone with you...and Vanessa wants to tag along," I slipped in.

"Really. Where's your dad?"

"He went in to the office. The step-witch wants to spend some 'girl time' with us."

"Yeesh. Well, I guess we can include her. It's not like we have to pretend to be her friend."

"Just watch what you say around her and pay attention to her questions. She can be tricky."

"Okay. When do you want to meet?"

"How about one, at the pool."

"Sounds good. Now I have to go do some finagling," she remarked and hung up.

I dialed Erin's number and talked to her about going. She wasn't as much into my business as Claire, but to her credit, I haven't known Erin as long. She said her day was clear and would be happy to join us. I told her when and where and hung up.

I went back inside and told Vanessa that both of my friends would be joining us and she smiled. "Fabulous. We're going to have so much fun!"

About that time, Dad walked in and she immediately told him the good news. He was happy for us, but probably happier to have some time to himself. We ate a quick lunch and then Vanessa and I went to change and gather pool necessities. I had my little tote bag packed with my towel, iPod, sun block, sunglasses, and a book (I was still working on that poetry collection).

We told Dad goodbye and hopped in her car; there was no way she was walking to the pool. She pulled into a spot and parked, leaving the air on as we waited. Sitting there, we didn't talk much, just casual comments about the weather or how cute she looked.

Thankfully, I didn't suffer long. Claire was the first to arrive and then Erin a couple minutes later. As I swiped my card at the gate, they reintroduced themselves and we headed in.

Luckily, there weren't a lot of people there. Most were on vacation or not interested in leaving the comfort of their air-conditioned houses. We found a spot on the other side of the pool near the deep end where there were four empty lounge chairs. We each claimed one, and I made sure to put myself between my friends and Vanessa.

I applied sun block and waited a few minutes before diving in. Vanessa decided to lay out and Claire and Erin joined me in the water. We swam and talked about the wedding again and our summer plans. Erin occasionally checked out the boys hanging around the pool, debating whether or not she should approach any of them. We encouraged her to talk to one and she finally went through with it.

I decided it was time for me to lay out. I dried off and reapplied sunscreen, pulled out my book, and stretched out on my back in the sun. Vanessa peeked over at me and commented on my cute bikini. I told her I liked hers, though I thought she looked obscene, and went back to reading. Realizing I wasn't going to be much of a conversationalist, she got up and slipped into the pool.

I waited half an hour and then flipped over onto my stomach. By that time, Claire was out and dripping on me as she told me about her discussion with Vanessa. My lovely step-witch was trying to get information out of her about my relationship with David. I sighed, not bothering to lament or complain, and offered my iPod for her to use while she tanned.

I glanced over my shoulder at Erin, who was still talking to the guy, and then looked for Vanessa. She was hanging out along the wall, keeping her head above the water and hiding behind her sunglasses as she scoped out the guys in and around the pool. I went back to reading and after a half hour, flipped again. This time, I put the book away and just relaxed in the sun.

Vanessa got out shortly after that and walked over to Claire and me. "I'm going to head on home. I have a lot of packing still to do. Are you staying?" she asked while she dried off.

"Yeah, I'll walk home with Claire," I replied as I looked over at her bopping and lip-syncing to my music.

"Okay, see you at home then," she responded as she gathered her things. I nodded and she left.

Erin came over after that and was all smiles. "I got his nuum-ber. I got his nuum-ber," she sang as she did a crazy dance.

Claire removed the ear buds and looked at her. "Awesome. Maybe we can double date. Or triple date," she suggested, looking at me.

"Let me see how my double date goes with Ben and Madeline and then I'll decide if I ever want to do it again."

"Ooo…what did you get yourself into, Megan?" she asked, sitting up and turning to me.

Erin sat down next to her. "I don't know. I thought it was a good idea at the time. I'm hoping it'll help David and Ben get along," I replied.

"Like that'll ever happen," she commented.

I sat up and gathered my things together before slipping my sundress on. "Are we ready to go? I think I've had enough sun for today."

"Yeah," they both agreed and we headed out the gate.

Erin climbed in her car as I thanked her for coming. She offered us a ride, but we declined, saying it was good for the environment and ourselves to walk. She shrugged as she pulled away, and we started down the street.

"So how's everything with you and Justin?" I asked, kicking a rock ahead of me.

"Better. As you know, we talked at the party. I told him what happens to me around David and Brian and it's funny, he said the same thing happens to him around Odette and Madeline," she replied, looking at me. "I think we have an understanding."

"Good. It was too early to throw in the towel. You have to build tru-"

"I know, I know," she interrupted, tired of getting advice. "So what are you going to do while Vanessa and your dad are away?" she asked, changing the subject.

"I thought about having a wild party one night, then turn the house into a hostel to make money for all the damages from the aforementioned party…"

"No seriously."

"I don't know…hang out with you and Erin, hang around the house, have David over once or twice, that's all."

"Will he be staying the night?" she asked curiously.

I thought about telling her the truth but decided against it. "No, I can't do that. But you could stay the night," I invited.

"That'd be fun. It could be like the night you stayed with me, except you won't be sneaking out to see David…or will you?"

"No, it'll just be you and me…all night."

We turned the corner and were at my house. "Okay, how about Saturday night?" she asked at the foot of my drive.

"Sure. I'll grab movies and order pizza. See you around five?"

"Okay. Well, have fun Friday night. Hopefully, Ben'll behave."

I smiled nervously as I headed to the door. Once inside, I slipped upstairs and into my room before Dad and Vanessa caught me. After my shower, I changed into lounge clothes and went back downstairs to see what was going on. No one was in the kitchen or family room.

Huh...where could they be? I headed back upstairs to their room, stopping at the door. I tried the handle, but it was locked. I guess they didn't want to be disturbed.

I returned to the lower level and searched the cabinets for meal ideas, finally deciding on spaghetti. I busied myself making dinner, trying not to think about what might be going on upstairs. As a distraction, I turned on the stereo and worked to the music. They still hadn't come downstairs by the time it was done, so I covered it up and went to watch TV.

Half an hour later, they finally decided to show. I told them dinner was on the stove as I turned off the TV and joined them in the kitchen, pulling the plates out of the cabinet. Each of us fixed one and headed into the dining room to eat. There wasn't much of a discussion during the meal and after it was over, I offered to clean the dishes so they could finish packing.

Dishes done and leftovers put away, I headed up to my room to wait for David. I stretched out on the bed and continued reading poetry for about an hour. I glanced at the balcony, but there was no sign of him. I went back to reading, wondering when he'd show, when suddenly there was a tapping on the glass. Funny...he usually just comes in.

I went to the door and peeked out. To my surprise, Madeline was standing there. "What are you doing here?" I asked after opening it.

"David sent me. He had to work tonight but figured you wanted company, and I was free...may I come in?"

I trusted her enough to invite her. "Of course you can," I replied.

"Wow, you have a really nice room," she remarked as she stepped inside and looked around.

"Thank you. Now we have to be quiet because my dad and Vanessa don't know I have visitors after I go to bed."

"Oh, okay. I'll be as quiet as a mouse," she whispered as she slipped into my closet. "Oh my gosh! You have such cute clothes!" she exclaimed and I ran in to hush her. "Sorry," she apologetically whispered as she slipped a halter dress back on the rack.

"Why don't we sit on the bed and talk," I suggested as I took a seat and waited for her to join me.

She sat cross-legged across from me, looking very much like an oversized fairy on my sage comforter. "So...what do you want to talk about?" she asked anxiously.

"How are things going with Ben?"

"Oh so much better," she replied, leaning over and touching my hands. They were cool. "I can't wait for Friday night. Wasn't that sweet of him to suggest a picnic and concert under the stars?"

"It was. I can't wait either. So how is he reacting to the new you?"

"Great. Honestly, this is more like the real me anyway."

That brought up an interesting question. I hesitated though, remembering what happened to her. "Can I ask you something?"

"Sure, anything," she beamed.

I hesitated again. "What were you like before you changed?"

She smiled warmly. "Not much different than I am now, except more carefree and innocent. I didn't have any worries, walking down the street without fear," she replied and then her jaw clenched. "That was until I met the monster that made me what I am."

"What happened?" I asked, curious about the complete story. I think David edited a lot for me.

She was quiet a moment and then responded. "He lived nearby in a dingy, two-story hovel shrouded by unkempt trees and overgrown bushes. I walked by that house each day and it gave me the creeps every time. Kids in the neighborhood made up stories about him, but it was all to scare the younger ones. At least that was what I thought."

"When I finally had an encounter with him, I didn't think he was as scary as he was depicted in our tales. He was frail and worried, looking for his lost cat. I fell for it, helping him search for his imaginary animal. I followed him around to the back of his house where he told me to check the cellar. As I bent over the opening, he pushed me inside."

"When I saw him again, he wasn't that same frail being. He was robust and intimidating as he stood over me and grinned his creepy, sadistic grin. He was everything our stories made him out to be and more – a monster that preyed on children, destroying their minds and corrupting their souls."

"He stole me away from my family and friends, from the light of day, keeping me captive in his cellar for his own twisted amusement," she stated with a look of disgust on her face. "He whipped me, cut me, bit me…anything to make me bleed. He took my innocence, abusing and torturing me for days into weeks."

"At my wits' end, I fought back, tearing open his neck with my teeth to free myself from his grasp. When he released me, I ran from the cellar, down the street, not realizing I had ingested his blood in the process. I was nearly home when it hit. Collapsing on the porch, I died."

She hung her head and sighed. "When I reawakened, I saw my brother above me, teary-eyed and happy I returned. I threw my arms around him and held him tight, happy to be alive and home. If only I had known being that close was dangerous."

"The beating of his heart was drumming loudly in my ears and I could feel it pounding in his chest and see the throbbing veins. I couldn't control myself, my body moving on its own…" She paused, her head down and eyes closed. I placed my hand on hers and a red tear hit it. "I killed him… I killed my brother," she whispered, her voice strained.

I gave her a moment, feeling bad for making her relive it. She took a deep breath and then raised her head, looking at me with red-rimmed eyes. The blood accentuated the color of her irises, making them an eerie, bright light green.

She took another deep breath and continued. "I barely had time to mourn him when that fiend grabbed me, leaving that as the last image of my precious brother, cold and dead and alone under the incandescent lighting on the front porch of my home. I screamed and fought, but then he restrained me, carrying me back to my dungeon without anyone in the neighborhood aware of what happened."

"He threw me back in the room I knew as my prison and I sat on the mattress, crying and staring at my brother's blood staining my hands and wondering what demon possessed me to do such a thing. Then I looked up at the monster as he stood over me, grinning. I blamed him for it all, charging at him and knocking him down. I punched his face several times and then I grabbed whatever I could to disfigure that hideous grin. Then to finish him off, I took a wire and wrapped it around his neck, tightening it until his head popped off. I set the house on fire and ran away with no destination in mind."

"I wandered around for several years, never interacting with anyone or thing. But eventually I grew to hate the loneliness, so I joined this group of vampires I came across in my travels. Unfortunately, seeing that I was young and attractive, they used me as a lure. I stayed with them for a few years, but I got to a point where I couldn't take it anymore and left. They weren't too happy about it and tried to hunt me down, but I always eluded them. After a while, they gave up or found new bait."

I felt more compassion for her than I had after hearing David tell her story. I leaned over and gave her a hug. "I'm sorry that happened to you."

She hugged back and smiled. "It took a long time to forgive myself for what I did to my brother. I've made peace with him and myself, knowing I wasn't Madeline when I did it, but a monster."

What an incredible ordeal to overcome and yet she seems so level-headed, so normal. Any other person would have cracked, but she persevered over and over. I have a newfound admiration for her.

"So when did you meet David?" I inquired, curious where he fit into all of this.

"Umm…about two years ago. I snuck into some gallery soiree to get a taste of the local art scene and while mingling with the other guests, I sensed him. Glancing over my shoulder, I found a man paused at the entrance to a darkened gallery. With a full champagne glass in hand and a half-smile on his lips, he turned and disappeared inside. Curiosity getting the better of me, I followed."

"I saw no sign of the strange man, but I could still sense him. I wandered the dark room, searching for him, when I came across an old painting lit by a single light. I stood before it, examining the scene fraught with religious images. Appearing out of the shadows, he described how it was about redemption and maybe that was why I was drawn to it."

"Then he introduced himself and said he understood my struggle and pain and that he could help. He explained that we were the same and he lived with others like us. I was wary at first, fearing I would fall into the same group as before, but something in his eyes told me I could trust him. So I agreed and shortly after, we left. That's when I met Brian and Odette."

"Have you ever had any problems with them?"

"No, not really. Of course, I don't associate with them too much. We don't have a whole lot in common."

"What about Brian specifically? What do you know about him?"

"Not much about his past. I know he's intelligent, strong, and a charmer. He could get any girl he wants."

"With the exception of me," I corrected.

"Okay…almost any girl," she conceded with a smile.

"What was David's and his relationship like around the house?"

"Before you, it was fine." She paused and narrowed her eyes at me. "Why do you have all these questions about Brian?"

I thought about it for a moment. "I had this strange dream about him last night."

She leaned in closer. "What happened?"

I wasn't sure how much I should share with her, not knowing what David told her about Brian and him. I summarized the dream, leaving out the fact that it was Charlotte, and waited for a response.

Her expression was kind as she put her hand on my shoulder. "He's gone, Megan. You don't have to worry about him."

"I know, but there's something deep inside that's nagging at me, like he's not gone, at least not for good."

"Don't worry, we'll be watching over you."

"I really appreciate it," I responded as I got under my covers, yawning. "How long do you plan to stay?"

She turned out the light and sat beside me. "As long as you want."

"Maybe until I fall asleep? I've gotten so used to having David stay that long that it feels weird to be left alone."

She stroked my hair and whispered, "Okay, I'll stay till then."

I closed my eyes and tried to sleep. But before I could, I had one more question to ask her. "Do you miss your human life?" I inquired, sitting up slightly on my elbows.

She paused and thought about it for a moment. "I did at first, but now I'm able to move around as if I was a human again. It's just so easy in this day and age; no one's suspicious if you're pale or only come out at night."

"I never thought of it that way," I commented, lying back down.

I closed my eyes and rolled over to my side as she went back to stroking my hair. The sound of her fingers running over it seemed so loud in my quiet room. As if knowing it was bothering me, she started humming an old tune. It was soft and pleasant, helping me fall asleep. Within a couple minutes, I was out.

The following morning, Dad and Vanessa woke me with their frantic running around, popping in and out of my room. I covered my head with a pillow, hoping to block them out, but it didn't work. Realizing I wouldn't be able to sleep in today, I got up, showered, and dressed, then did what I could to help them.

Their suitcases were packed and by the door waiting for the taxi that was taking them to the airport. While they finished their last minute checks, I sat on the porch enjoying the morning air. All was quiet in the neighborhood, except for the faint bark of a dog in the distance.

"I want to go over a couple of rules with you before we go," Dad announced as he joined me on the steps.

"Dad, you know I'm not your average teenager. I don't need rules." I replied.

"I know that, but just humor me."

"All right, what do you have for me – no wild parties, no friends allowed, stay out of the alcohol…"

"No, I just want you to stay safe and think about the consequences before making a decision."

"Sounds reasonable enough," I commented, surprised at how lenient he was being.

"Now…there's plenty of food in the house, but I'm leaving some cash in case you want to order out. And you have your credit card for emergencies only."

At that moment, the taxi pulled up and honked the horn. Dad waved to him and stood up. "You don't have to worry about me, I'll be fine," I replied, standing as well.

"I know that Nut-Meg, but I still worry," he responded with a concerned look in his eyes. He hadn't called me that since Mom was alive.

He stepped inside and yelled to Vanessa, letting her know the taxi had arrived. She replied before rushing down the stairs, wearing a flowing, tropical sundress and a large brimmed hat. I could tell she was excited to leave. Dad smiled at her and then turned to me, giving me a big hug and a kiss on the cheek.

"Have a safe trip and be careful," I told him as he put his arm around her. They looked so awkward together.

"You be careful, too," he replied.

I hugged her and kissed her on the cheek. "Have a good time and don't wear my dad out too much," I commented. She didn't know how to take that, so I added, "By dragging him over all the islands and making him do too many things at once."

She grinned and replied, "Oh, we'll probably stay at the house or on a yacht most of the time."

I rolled my eyes and sat back down. I'm glad she's leaving. It'll be so nice and quiet in the house, just like it was before she entered our lives.

Dad took the luggage down to the car and the driver helped him load it in the trunk. As soon as everything was in, I watched them climb into the taxi. Dad stared at me from the window, the concern still there, but then Vanessa grabbed his face and began kissing him, looking at me over his shoulder. I know she wanted a reaction, but I didn't dignify her with one.

They drove off as I remained on the porch, staring blankly at the yard. It wasn't long before I decided to retreat inside, though. The temperature was steadily rising, as was the humidity. I looked at the TV in the family room and then walked away, not wanting to watch anything. I decided instead to go back to bed, heading upstairs to my room and curling up, suddenly feeling lonely and abandoned.

I woke about four hours later to my ringing phone. I grabbed it and answered, my head still under the pillow. "Megan?" Ben asked.

"Yeah?"

"Is everything okay?"

"Yeah…you just woke me up."

"Woke you up? What are you doing sleeping this late?"

"Catching up. What are you calling me for?" I asked, throwing the pillow off my head. I glanced at the clock and rolled over.

"We're still on for Friday, right?"

"Yeah…why?" I asked, sitting up.

"No reason. I just hadn't heard from you since Saturday. By the way, how'd everything go with the wedding?"

"Good. No mistakes or problems. The sacrifice pleased Bridezilla."

He laughed a boyish laugh. Cute, but nothing like David's. "And how about the reception?"

"It was fun, but my escort was really annoying. He thought since we were matched up together we should do everything together. Thank God David showed up and rescued me."

"How very knight-in-shining-armor of him," he responded sarcastically.

"So…what are you making us for dinner?" I asked, changing the subject.

"It's a surprise, but I hope everyone likes it."

"I'm sure we will. Madeline's really excited about your evening."

"I know."

"So how's everything going with you two?" I asked, wanting to hear his opinion.

"Much better. She's like a totally different person than she was at prom and the student film fest. I don't know where she got the idea that I'd want to be with a person like that."

"Experience, I guess. Hey, do I need to bring anything?"

"A blanket, maybe."

"Okay," I replied as my stomach growled. "I'm gonna go. I haven't eaten anything since last night and my stomach's not happy. See you Friday."

I hung up and put the phone in my pocket, heading downstairs to find something for lunch. I didn't feel like leftovers, so I made a sandwich. I added pasta salad and headed into the family room to see what was on TV. Soaps. I flipped to the cable channels and found an old movie to watch.

What am I going to do until eight-thirty tonight? I don't want to sit in front of the TV all day, and there's nothing to clean since I already took care of that several days ago. I could go to the pool again. My tan's not quite where I want it to be.

I finished the movie, threw my trash away, and headed up to my room to change. I filled my bag and headed out the door, deciding to walk. I left the book at home, but decided to take my iPod, listening to it on the way. The weather was hot and sticky and I couldn't wait to get in the cool water, knowing how refreshing it'd be.

I entered and picked a lounge chair that was all by itself. It was a little busier today, mostly with young children. Pulling out my sunscreen, I applied it and let it set into my skin before diving in. I swam a couple laps, then got out and dabbed the water off.

Pulling out my iPod, I stuck the ear buds in my ears and stretched out on my stomach first this time, closing my eyes. I loved laying out in the sun, feeling the warmth on my skin after a refreshing dip in the water. Occasionally, a cloud blocked it, taking my warmth away, but it soon passed.

I grabbed my sunglasses and flipped over to my back, watching the people in and around the pool. Moms gently dipped their babies in the water, smaller children splashed as they learned to swim, and older kids jumped off the side as they squealed with delight. Across from me, some guys about my age were hanging out along the wall pointing and looking at me. I turned my head to the side, hoping none of them would try to approach me.

Moments later, something blocked the sun and I knew it wasn't a cloud. I glanced up, finding one of them standing in front of me. "Mind if I sit here?" he asked, indicating to a chair nearby.

"Knock yourself out," I replied, unconcerned.

In the background of the song I was listening to, I heard metal scrapping on concrete near me. I shifted my eyes in that direction and noticed he had moved the chair closer to me. He said something, but I couldn't hear him, so I removed my ear buds and asked him to repeat himself.

"Do you live around here?" he asked, sitting on the edge facing me.

"I wouldn't be here if I didn't," I answered matter-of-factly, trying to deter him from continuing to talk to me. It didn't work.

"I'm Noah. My friends and I noticed you over here and wanted to see if you'd like to come to a party tonight."

"I'm sorry, but I have plans."

"Too bad…it's going to be the biggest in the neighborhood."

"Tempting, but no."

"Hey, if you change your mind, it'll be at the house with the giant inflatable palm trees in the front yard."

"Mm hmm," I responded, putting my ear buds back in.

I could still sense him nearby and I ventured a peek, finding him looking me up and down like I was a piece of meat. Creepy. He cleared his throat and I didn't respond. He waited a little longer, then finally got up and left.

After that experience, I was done with the pool for the day. I slipped my dress on and headed out, hoping I wouldn't be followed. I walked home a lot faster than I had to the pool and made sure to secure all the locks when I got inside. Feeling dirty, I dashed upstairs and took a shower.

Once dressed, I sat on the edge of my bed and fixed my hair as I considered going to the party tonight. It might actually be fun. I can't see it being too bad since most of the people who live in this community are pretty stuffy. And David could join me to keep any guys from trying to hit on me. On the other hand, having him go might be a bad idea considering what the girls at the party would try to do…

Okay – no party tonight.

I headed downstairs and checked the freezer, grabbing a frozen dinner and popping it in the microwave. I generally didn't eat them, but I picked up a couple last week, knowing I'd be alone this week. I flipped on the TV and watched it as I waited for my dinner to finish.

I still had a couple of hours before David arrived. A movie would help to pass the time quicker. I searched the premium channels for something, deciding on an entertaining rom-com before jumping up to get my food. I slipped it onto a tray and hurried back into the family room so I didn't miss the beginning.

Right at the most intense part of the movie, the doorbell rang. I ran to the door, unlocked it, apologized to David as I let him in, and ran back. He casually walked in the room and leaned against the wall as I sat on my knees watching anxiously as the lead actor professed his love to the lead actress. After a long, drawn out pause, she admitted she loved him, they kissed, and it was happily ever after.

"I didn't take you for the kind of girl that gets into movies like this," he commented, coming up behind me and kissing my neck. He paused, his lips still touching it, and then slowly turned his head so his cool cheek pressed against it, and he sighed. "I can feel the sun on your skin," he whispered after a moment. Then suddenly he stood up and stepped back, like he crossed the line. "Please forgive my obtrusiveness," he apologized.

"No, it's okay," I replied, turning off the TV. "You didn't do anything wrong."

He smiled and joined me on the sofa. "How was your day?" he asked, pushing a loose hair behind my ear and letting his fingers glide along my sun-kissed skin.

"Nothing too exciting. Saw Vanessa and Dad off, took a long nap, and obviously hung out at the pool. Oh, and I was invited to a party down the street."

"Who invited you to this party?" he questioned.

"Some guy at the pool. I never intended to go, honestly. I would much rather spend my evening alone with you."

"And so you shall," he responded with a smile, gazing into my eyes as he leaned in closer and caressed my cheek.

I blushed. "I missed you last night," I whispered, dropping my eyes to my fidgeting hands. "Don't get me wrong, it was nice spending time with Madeline, but it's not the same."

He lifted my chin, gazing into my eyes. "I wanted to be here, but I was needed early at work. I'll make it up to you tonight."

I leaned in, inches from his face, and forced my hands to stay in my lap. My lips quivered as I watched him move even closer. His breath invited me to give in. Without thought or restraint, I pressed my lips to his and kissed him. My heart raced as I got on my knees and forced him onto his back, bending over his body.

Reaching up suddenly, he grabbed my neck and pulled me down, my throat right over his mouth. His lips moved over my skin and my breathing increased as he kissed further down. He lowered my strap, letting it rest against my arm, and kissed my shoulder. I was so into it, but when I felt his fangs scrape my skin, I knew it had to stop.

"I'm sorry," I apologized, sitting back and looking away, embarrassed. "I let it go too far."

"No, you didn't," he replied, sitting up and continuing to kiss my shoulder and neck.

I glanced at him. "I felt..." I began, but he stopped me.

Taking my chin in his hand, he turned my face to his. "It's all right," he whispered, leaning closer and kissing me.

I closed my eyes and savored his lips on mine, my head swimming as I breathed in his breath. He pulled me closer, his hands slipping under my tank top and gently caressing my hips. My body jolted with his touch and my breath came in rapid bursts as I tilted my head back, allowing him to kiss down my throat. He moved to the side of my neck, his lips just glancing my skin. My heart thumped hard in my chest and within moments, I felt his fangs again.

"We should stop," I whispered, tucking my head.

"If that's what you want," he replied quietly, kissing my arm.

Lifting my eyes, I placed my hand on his jaw. I hesitated and then leaned in closer, brushing my lips across his. I paused and then kissed him, trying not to be as aggressive as before. He replied, but when the desire from before returned, I stopped and rested my cheek against his.

"We can't keep doing this all night," I whispered in his ear.

His lips moved across my cheek, down the side of my neck, and then back up the other side, stopping at my ear. "Why not?" he inquired seductively.

A tingle went through me and I forced myself away from him. "Because it might lead to something neither of us are ready for right now," I replied abruptly, looking down and away.

He was quiet. I slowly turned my head in his direction, finding him leaning on his knees staring at me. "Megan...I would never allow that to happen unless you say so," he commented quietly as he moved the loose hairs from in front of my face, his fingers brushing my skin. He paused, gazing into my eyes understandingly. "I could hold you, if you prefer."

I nodded as he lay back, turning on his side. I stretched out next to him and buried my face in his chest. He gently rubbed my back as I moved my head so my ear was over his silent heart and I was looking up at him.

"Have you heard from your father yet?" he asked, looking down at me.

"Yeah, he called briefly to say they landed safely and that it was beautiful there."

"Good," he replied, content.

And the conversation ended there. Lying together in the quiet of the house, we held each other. I occasionally closed my eyes but didn't sleep. I didn't think about anything either. Being so close to him, my head was in a fog and it was peaceful.

Every so often, he kissed my forehead, cheek, or arm. I was enjoying this quiet moment so much I fought off sleep, knowing when I woke in the morning I'd be alone. But eventually, sleep did come.

# Chapter 33
## Double Date

I woke the next morning in my bed, feeling utterly alone. And moving around in an empty house made me feel as though I was the only one left on earth. I turned on the TV just to make sure no natural disaster had wiped out everyone but me. It was Thursday morning and there was nothing on but old movies, preschool cartoons, and morning talk shows. Rather than turn it off, I left it on for the sheer sound of other voices.

It was a lot later than I was used to getting up. I guess going to bed so late last night forced me to sleep in longer. Instead of fixing a quick breakfast, I threw a salad together with some chicken and strawberries and sat cross-legged on the couch trying to find something worthwhile to watch. I had just settled into a show when the phone rang.

"Caldwell residence," I announced, not recognizing the number.

"Hey, Meg! How's everything going?" Dad asked cheerfully.

I leaned against the counter and stared out the window at the sky through the trees. "Good. It's quiet here," I replied, happy to hear his voice. On his end, steel drums played in the background coupled with singing. "I can tell it's not the same for you down there."

"Oh, Vanessa dragged me to some thing on the beach."

"Sounds fun. Is the weather nice?"

"Yeah…sunny, hot, not a cloud in the sky. What's it like there?"

"About the same, but there are a couple clouds."

"How did you do last night, being alone?"

"Fine. I watched a romantic comedy and talked on the phone with David for a couple hours, then went to bed," I partially lied. "What did you and Vanessa end up doing?"

"Unpacked and relaxed and then later took a walk on the beach. We had a nice dinner at the house, enjoying a glass of the champagne David gave us with our meal."

"How was it?"

"Exquisite. Please tell him so the next time you talk to him."

"I will. Have anything else planned for the day?" I asked, wanting to keep him on the phone.

"We may tour some of the other islands, go out on the yacht… who knows. I'm letting Vanessa decide," he replied.

I heard her in the background calling for him, but I wasn't ready to let him go. "Is the house you're staying in nice?"

"Really nice, but there's no TV. I guess when Warren takes a vacation, he likes to get away from it all."

"It was kind of your partner to let you stay at his place."

"Yeah, it was." There was a muffled sound and then he came back on. "Listen, Meg, I have to go, but I'll call later."

I tried to think of something else to keep him on the phone but came up with nothing. "Okay. Have fun," I replied, disheartened.

"I'll try. Love you."

"Love you, too," I responded and hung up with a sigh.

I went back to the couch and grabbed the bowl, finishing my salad as I watched some talk show about teen dating. As I rinsed my dishes, the doorbell rang. I peeked around the corner and saw a shadowy figure through the sheer curtain covering the sidelight. Maybe it was a delivery. I'm sure Vanessa still has more gifts coming. I went to the door and opened it, surprised to see Ben standing there.

"Hey Megan," he greeted, his hands in his pockets.

"Hey...shouldn't you be at work?" I asked, leaning against the edge of the door.

"I don't go in until later. I'm out running errands for my mom – she's sick – and thought I'd stop by."

"Would you like to come in?" I inquired.

He hesitated, like he was trying to decide if it was a good idea or not. "Yeah, for a little bit," he replied, stepping inside. "So what are you up to today?" he asked as we headed back to the family room.

"Lounging around, doing nothing in particular," I replied, sitting at one end of the couch while he sat at the other. I turned the volume down on the TV and then looked at him. "So your mom's sick and you left your sisters with her?"

"Yeah, well, they're all napping. It was a good time to leave."

"Oh. Where have you had to go?" I asked, propping my head on my hand against the back of the couch.

"Umm...the post office, movie store, mechanic to get the inspection done, and to drop some papers off at Mom's office."

"Geez, you've been all over the place."

"Yeah, it's nice to stop and relax awhile," he replied, running his fingers through his hair. "So, have you heard from your dad?"

"They arrived around two yesterday and spent the day settling in. He called not too long ago to check in."

"That's cool," he commented absentmindedly, like he wasn't really listening. "So what are your plans tonight?" he asked suddenly.

"Maybe read and then talk to David later," I replied.

He scooted closer. "Why don't you come to the game store and hang out with me. It's Thursday night, so it'll be pretty dead. We could play that new first person shooter game," he offered. That really didn't sound appealing to me, and he could tell. "Come on...it'll be fun," he begged.

"Sounds like it, but I better not."

His brows pulled together. "Why? David wouldn't like it?" he questioned spitefully.

"No, my dad doesn't like me out late," I responded angrily. "When are you going to get over this?"

He held his face in his hands. "I am…I'm just looking out for you," he grumbled, then paused and stared at the TV. "I was talking to Madeline the other night and when I brought up David, she changed the subject, like she's scared of him or something."

"She's not scared of him. He gave her a place to stay with her own studio and gallery, in essence. She's very grateful."

"Not from what I see," he muttered.

"Well, maybe you should look at it from another point of view and not your own."

He faced me again. "She never invites me over to the house. We always have to meet out and at night."

"Maybe she likes to be away from the house. Some people just aren't homebodies. And school's probably made her a night owl, trying to fill as many hours of her day as possible," I fabricated, trying to cover for her.

He looked away and was quiet. "I better go," he responded solemnly as he stood.

I threw my hands up. He can be so frustrating! Whatever. I walked him to the door and opened it. "Well, thanks for stopping by. I'll see you tomorrow night," I commented, trying to be affable.

He seemed to perk up a little. "Yeah, I can't wait. Don't get too bored tonight…being alone."

I smiled. "I won't."

He sighed and turned to go to the car, waving at me before climbing in. I shook my head and closed the door as he drove off. What am I going to do about him?

As I walked back to the family room, something wasn't sitting right with me about the conversation we just had. David felt at the party that Ben was suspicious of him and he was right. I'm just not sure what Ben's suspicions are. Maybe after spending some time with David tomorrow evening, that'll change.

I sat on the couch and turned the volume back up on the TV. Soap operas were on. I never watched them but decided to see if they were worth it. The good thing about them was you could pick up the storyline and character histories pretty quick. Johnny cheated on Sarah with her sister who slept with Don, the VP of the company she works for, who was planning to kill her because she was going to expose their affair. Yep, too much drama for me. I turned it off and looked for something to do around the house.

There was nothing downstairs, so I headed upstairs. I checked the hamper in my room and dragged it down the hall to Dad's room. Opening his door, a strange odor hit me. The room no longer smelled like Mom and him – it smelled like Vanessa.

Looking around, she had already made so many changes in the short time she'd been here. The furniture had been moved around and the bathroom sink was loaded with tons of beauty products. There was one picture of me on Dad's dresser along with one of Mom, but images of Vanessa overwhelmed the room.

It was a total mess, but there was no way I was touching any of it. I may disturb something I wasn't supposed to and get reamed out for it. So instead, I just took the laundry. I emptied their basket into mine and headed to the chute in the hall.

Downstairs, I started a load and then headed outside to do some yard work. After an hour of that, I went back inside, happy to have a break as I waited for the last load to finish. I sat in the family room and watched the early evening news to pass the time.

It looked like rain was coming our way this weekend through early next week. Good, maybe I'll get to spend a whole day with David. It went to commercial as the dryer buzzed and I pulled out the last load, folding them in the laundry room. I grabbed the basket and was headed to the stairs when something on TV caught my attention as I passed.

"It's been weeks since the last victim of the Richmond Parks Ghost was discovered and fears were beginning to subside, but all too soon. Today, a couple walking through the woods in Rockwood Park found the body of a young male eerily similar to the victims of the Ghost," the reporter announced.

I dropped the basket, clothes spilling out onto the floor as I stared at the TV in disbelief. There's no way...it has to be a copycat. I came around to the front of the couch and continued watching, hoping she was going to say there was evidence found at the scene or that it was the work of someone else, but there was nothing. Unconsciously dropping to the seat cushion, I curled up into a ball and stared at the screen, frozen with fear.

David found me there when he arrived hours later. He must have come in through the bedroom and got worried when he didn't see me or respond when he called. And the TV left running with the spilled clothes on the floor wasn't a reassuring sign either.

He crouched in front of me, and it took a moment to register his presence. Seeing the troubled look on my face, he caressed my cheek and asked what was wrong. I was afraid to say, fearing I was right and it was true. He asked again and this time, I relented.

"They...they're back," I whispered. "They're coming to get me..."

"Who?" he asked.

I stared into his eyes, looking for confirmation. "Brian and Odette...there was a body discovered...a victim of the Ghost."

"Impossible. He called the other day to say he left something behind and wanted me to ship it to his address in Baton Rouge," he tried to assure me. "What did they say about the victim?"

"He was found in Rockwood Park by a couple, a young man killed the same way as the others."

"It has to be a copycat. They're no longer here, Megan. They're living in Louisiana." He stroked my hair as his lips grazed the skin by my temple. "You're safe," he whispered. Then he was quiet. "He could have been one they attacked before leaving the area. Did they say how long the body had been there?"

"No..."

"It's only been a week. I'll give him a call."

I looked up at him, surprised. "You...kept his number?" I asked.

"It's a way for me to keep track of him...for your safety," he explained as he pulled out his phone and stood. "I'll be right back."

As he left the room, I scooted to the end of the couch and wrapped my arms around my legs, hugging my knees. I strained to hear his conversation, but he was too quiet. Would Brian tell him the truth?

My eyes stayed fixed on the TV, wondering if something else might come up about the murder, but they never said anymore. David came back in the room a moment later and sat beside me. "He admitted killing the man before they left. They're not here; you don't have to worry," he reassured me, rubbing my back.

I slowly released my legs and relaxed. "So they're gone...down in Baton Rouge," I confirmed, turning to him.

"Yes, they won't bother you anymore," he replied, lifting my chin and kissing me softly.

I put my arms around his neck and held him tightly. "Take me to my room, please," I whispered in his ear.

Without question, he turned off the TV and gently cradled me in his arms as he headed up the stairs. We entered the room and he set me softly on the bed, sitting next to me. He pushed the loose strands of hair behind my ear and lifted my chin, kissing me again.

"Thank you," I whispered as I pressed my forehead to his. I felt nasty, and not just because of the news, but also from taking care of the yard and not eating. I looked up at him, feeling bad I was in this state, and remarked, "I did yard work today and need a shower. I'll only be a few minutes. Do you mind?"

"Take your time. Do you need help getting to the bathroom?" he asked, rising.

"No, I'll be fine. I'm just a little weak," I replied, standing and staggering around the bed.

I shut the bathroom door and leaned against it, taking a moment to feel the relief I was supposed to after being told my fears were unfounded. I closed my eyes and breathed deep once, twice…

Everything's going to be okay. Brian and Odette are over a thousand miles away and not here. I'm safe.

Finally believing it, I pushed off the door and turned the shower on, setting it to just warm enough. I undressed slowly and climbed in, the water rushing over me as I stepped under the showerhead. I cleaned and then just stood for several minutes letting it all wash away. Refreshed and calmed, I turned the water off, dried, and then wrapped the towel around my body, realizing I forgot to bring fresh clothes in with me.

David was lying on the bed, staring at the ceiling when I came out of the bathroom. Seeing me in the towel, he quickly sat up and turned his back to me. "Sorry, I forgot to grab an outfit before going in," I commented as I searched my drawer for one.

"It's all right. Do you need me to leave?" he asked as he glanced over his shoulder.

"No, I'll dress in the bathroom," I answered, heading back to it and shutting the door.

I slipped on the tank top and shorts and then put my hair in a bun before exiting. Without saying a word, I went to the balcony doors and waited by them for him to join me. Turning toward me, he cocked his head to one side and smiled as he got up.

He followed me outside, and I indicated for him to sit on the chaise. "What are we doing out here?" he asked, confused, as I sat between his legs.

"It's such a beautiful evening, I want to enjoy it," I replied as I rested my head against his chest.

He kissed my neck. "I take it you're feeling better," he remarked.

"Much better. Seeing that on the news really threw me for a loop," I responded as I stared out into the yard at the fireflies twinkling above the newly cut grass.

"I imagine it would," he agreed, his fingers caressing my collar bone and the top of my chest.

The tree frogs and crickets serenaded us with their chirps as we sat in silence enjoying their sonata. David kissed my cheek and I turned my head slightly to kiss his lips. He placed his hand on the side of my face, holding it there as his kiss deepened. He was cooler tonight than he was last night, which means I needed to be more careful. I reached up and touched his cheek, kissing him gently, and then turned back to the yard.

As I stared, I thought about when I was young and how I imagined fairies in the garden. Seeing them among the flowers, I'd talk to them. If anyone had seen me, they probably would have thought I was insane. But was it possible I could have really seen them? Finding out about David and his kind made me rethink my vivid imagination as a child. If vampires are real, what else could be?

"David?"

"Hmm?" he replied languidly as if he, too, were deep in thought.

"In all your travels, have you ever heard of or encountered any other supernatural creatures?"

He hesitated, almost as if the answer might be too much for me to handle. "Yes…I have," he responded finally.

"Like what?" I asked excitedly, turning over onto my stomach and folding my hands on his chest as I rested my chin on them.

He smiled in relief and folded his arms behind his head. "Werewolves, ghosts, demons, shape-shifters, witches – all the things of fairy and folk tales."

I was a little stunned by the revelation that all of those things really existed. "Werewolves…witches…demons?" I exclaimed, sitting up. "Are there any around here?"

He propped his body up on his elbows and looked at me. "Yes, some. I've seen demons, ghosts, fairies, and a few others. Werewolves prefer colder temperatures, so I wouldn't worry about ever crossing their paths. I don't believe I've ever met a shape shifter, though I'm not sure I'd know it or not," he smiled crookedly.

My hand rested over my heart as it beat wildly in my chest. "As if I didn't have enough to worry about…"

He moved closer and put his hand over mine. "Most of the time, they won't harass humans. As long as you don't bother or try to expose them, they won't harm you."

"Wow…I can't believe they really exist."

He grinned. "What's so hard to believe? I exist."

I smiled and leaned toward him, forcing him to lie back. "But you're different," I replied, kissing him briefly before lying as I had before. I was just getting comfortable when I heard my cell ring inside. "Crap…that's probably my dad," I grumbled as I hopped up. Rushing into the room, I dove on the bed and grabbed the phone just in time. "Hello."

"How's everything?" Dad asked, sounding worn out.

"Good."

"I tried the house phone, but you didn't answer, so I figured I'd try your cell. Going to bed early?"

"Yeah, it's been a busy day. I cut the grass and tidied the yard and did a couple loads of laundry. Should I just set yours on the bed?"

"That'll be fine. We've been busy, too. Vanessa wanted to do all kinds of activities today. I swear I'm getting too old for this."

I laughed. "Aww, you're never too old. Do you plan to relax tonight?"

"She wants to take another walk and maybe check out a club on one of the other islands."

"I thought you said you weren't going to any more clubs."

"Well, we're somewhere special, so I figured I could go if she wants."

I shook my head. "Dad, you're…" I began but froze as I felt something touch my leg.

"Megan?" he called as I jerked around to see David's smiling face as he ran his fingers from my heel to my mid-thigh, sending a thrilling sensation through my body. "Are you there?"

Suppressing my urges, I narrowed my eyes at him and turned around. "Yeah…I am. My phone must have cut out," I fibbed.

"So what were you saying?"

"Oh, that you're too nice," I replied as David lightly dragged his fingers up my other leg, creating the same sensation as before. I turned to smack his hand, but he jerked it away too quickly, chuckling.

"I know. She's just so excited. She's never been outside the states."

I sat up and glared at him. "Are *you* having any fun at all?" I asked as he sat next to me, grinning wide. This is going to be bad.

"Yeah, just tired," he replied quietly.

David leaned closer and kissed my neck. A tingle went down my spine. I pushed him away and turned my back to him, slouching over. "Don't wear yourself out too much…this *is* a vacation."

I felt him getting close again and I tensed up. His lips touched the back of my neck and moved down my spine to the top of my tank top. "I won't. I'm hoping she'll let me sleep in tomorrow…or maybe Saturday," Dad responded.

He kissed across my shoulders and up the side of my neck. I tried to control my breathing, but it was hard. I closed my eyes and tilted my head to the side, giving up fighting. "Okay…I'm going to go now…"

"Is everything all right?" Dad asked, concerned with the change in my demeanor.

I opened my eyes and tried to focus on my father. "Yeah…I haven't had dinner yet. I'm feeling a little lightheaded."

David sat behind me and put his arm over the one I wasn't using, slipping his fingers between mine and bringing my hand to my heart. It was racing as he kissed my neck and chin. "Okay…I'll let you go. Vanessa wants to get going on our walk anyway."

I let out a small gasp with his kisses. I needed to get off the phone. "Okay…love you," I replied. Dad said the same but sounded sad.

As soon as I hung up, I threw my phone down and turned on David, attacking him. I forced him on his back and held him down. He let me pin him for a little bit and then lifted me with ease. Smiling, he stood and backed away as he looked at me.

"What?" I questioned angrily.

"You need to eat," he replied, walking toward the door.

"So do you," I growled, following him.

I grumbled all the way down the stairs and when we reached the hall, he went straight for the refrigerator and pulled out several items. I sat in the family room and let him do his thing while I sulked. He was busy, but I didn't look; I continued to brood, staring at the blank TV. After several minutes, it got quiet, but I still refused to check up on him. A wonderful aroma wafted toward me as a plate of food appeared before my eyes.

I raised my hands to take it, in awe. As soon as I did, David disappeared from behind me, getting to work on the dishes. I glanced over my shoulder at him, but he didn't notice. Setting the plate on my lap, I cut into the chicken and put a piece in my mouth. It was unbelievably juicy and bursting with flavors I never would have thought to put together.

I took another bite, wolfing it down, along with the vegetables and rice. As soon as I was done, he came over and relieved me of my empty plate as he handed a drink to me. "That was delicious," I commented, taking the glass.

"Thank you," he replied, heading back into the kitchen to clean the remaining dishes.

I turned around, sitting on my knees so I could see him. "No, thank you. I really needed that."

"I know," he agreed, drying his hands before joining me. "Shall we go back upstairs?"

"Yeah, I guess so."

We entered my room and went out on the balcony again, returning to our spot from earlier. I rested my head on his chest and put my arms around him as he put his around me. His body was cold against mine, but I didn't mind on such a warm summer's night. I fell asleep there in his arms on the chaise, feeling content, comfortable, and safe.

I woke the following morning in my bed. After a good stretch, I stood and walked to the balcony doors and stared through the panes at the outside world. The sun was shining and the backyard was full of activity. As I opened them, a burst of warm air hit me. I stepped out and headed to the railing, leaning on it and watching the squirrels and birds in the garden for several minutes. When I had enough, I went in and washed up.

I proceeded downstairs and flipped on the TV, seeing if anything interesting was going on. Same old, same old. I changed it to the weather, checking to see what tonight would be like for us. No rain and warm. I turned it off and tried to figure out what to do today. The pool would be good. It was a perfect day for both laying out and swimming. So it was settled. I packed up and headed out.

I enjoyed my time there, working on my tan and cooling off from the heat, but a couple hours was enough. When I got home, I showered and then ate a late lunch. Dad called and talked for a while, checking on me once again. After getting off the phone with him, I cranked up the stereo and did some light cleaning. As seven o'clock rolled around, I decided it was time to get ready for my double date.

I slipped on a V-neck maxi dress and put my hair in a bun to keep it off my neck and allow for maximum cooling and access for David. I applied some light makeup, choosing dark colors for the evening and to go with the teal of my gown. I slipped on heeled sandals and headed downstairs.

I still had some time to kill, so I watched TV, having nothing better to do. Every once in a while, I glanced outside and watched as the sun began to set. David would be here soon to pick me up, and I was anxious waiting to see him.

I turned my attention back to the TV and flipped through the channels, trying to find something to make the time pass. I ended up stopping on some documentary about China, which was actually interesting. Halfway through, the doorbell rang. I jumped up and dashed to the door, opening it to David's beautiful smile. My heart thumped wildly as he passed me on the way in.

"You look lovely tonight," he commented as I closed the door. He leaned in and gently kissed me.

"Thank you," I replied, blushing, as I headed to the family room to shut off the TV. I turned out all but one light and grabbed my purse. "Shall we go?"

He smiled as he opened the door. "We could skip this and go somewhere else," he suggested, waiting as I exited.

"No, they're expecting us. I don't want to disappoint either one," I replied as we started down the sidewalk.

We reached the car and he paused on the passenger side, smiling as he opened the door. "I tried," he commented as I sat. I shook my head and he shut the door.

A moment later, he was in his seat. The car purred as he started it and then he backed out of the drive, never saying a word. "Are you really okay with going tonight?" I inquired.

"Of course…why?" he asked, turning out of the neighborhood.

"You seem apprehensive."

"Not at all. I'm looking forward to spending the evening with you…and Madeline and Ben," he replied assuredly.

I glanced at him, and he smiled without looking at me. "If you say so."

We were both quiet, alternative music playing low in the background, as he turned onto Powhite Parkway and sped down the road. "What did you and Madeline talk about the other night?" he asked, no doubt making conversation now that I was suspicious of him.

"Her past mostly, but also about how her relationship with Ben is going."

"It's much better than it was, for both of them," he remarked and I nodded. At least it seemed that way. "Anything else interesting?" he asked, his eyes shifting briefly to me.

Thinking back to my conversation with her Tuesday night, a question occurred to me…and a worry. "How long has Madeline been off human blood?"

"I would say about three years," he replied as he passed through the tollbooth. "Why?"

"Does she still get cravings…for humans?"

He laughed. "We all do. I haven't fed on a human in nearly a hundred years, but you've seen how difficult it can be for me."

"Is her willpower as strong as yours?"

"No, but this exposure is good for her. At least for tonight, I'll be there to prevent her from making a mistake," he assured me as he turned off Powhite and headed toward Dogwood Dell. "She's done well these past few years, and I'm not worried about her regressing."

I stared out the window, wondering how Ben and her were doing so far. She seemed to be able to maintain her composure most of the time around him and would probably do fine. I don't know what would be different about tonight than any other night.

Scanning the area, David pulled into an open spot and parked quite a distance from the amphitheater. "I guess if we could have gotten here earlier, we'd have a better parking spot," I commented, stepping out of the car.

"You don't mind walking, do you? I could see if there's something closer."

"No, it's fine," I replied, looking around. "Oh, shoot! I forgot to grab a blanket," I realized as he joined me on the curb.

"I have one," he responded as he walked to the back of the car and opened the trunk, grabbing it.

"Impressive," I commented.

"You never know when you need one," he smiled as we started our trek to the park.

It really wasn't as long a walk as I thought it'd be. As we neared the amphitheater, we began searching for Ben and Madeline. This was where the telepathy would come in handy. And it did. David nodded slightly in her direction, the sound of tinkling bells ringing from her frantically waving wrist. Slipping his arm around my waist, he held me tight as we walked toward them, Ben glaring at him. Already not a good start.

They were sitting on a checkered blanket laid out on the grass, the two of them in the center with an old picnic basket next to him. David unraveled his lined, black and gray blanket and laid it behind theirs. I dropped to my knees and sat, letting my skirt cover my legs as he took his place beside me.

"Perfect timing…they haven't started yet," Madeline commented excitedly, looking back at David and me with a big grin.

"Hey, Megan…David," Ben greeted, turning his body toward us. She followed suit, wrapping her arm around his and revealing the source of the jingling I heard coming from her.

"That's a cute bracelet," I complimented.

She released him and held it out so we could see it better, shaking it gently to demonstrate the melodious chiming. "Ben gave it to me…tonight. Isn't that the sweetest gift?"

"It is," I responded, smiling at him. He replied with a slight twitch of his lip as he watched David.

"And it has such a nice jingle," she remarked with a grin, shaking it more vigorously.

"Yes, it does," David responded, staring at it curiously. He raised his eyes to Madeline's but didn't say anymore.

She turned to Ben and wrapped her arm around his again. "Doesn't he look handsome tonight? I love this *blue* on him!" she complimented and he blushed.

"It's a good color on you, Ben. You should wear it more often," I agreed.

"As should you," David commented, turning to me and gently running his fingers along my flushed cheek. He paused at my chin and raised it up so my eyes were level with his. I stared, rapt in his gaze as he leaned closer. Slowly, a sinister smile crept onto his lips. "Don't you agree, Ben?" he inquired, cocking his head toward him.

His cheeks were bright red now. "Ye-yeah, Megan, you…you should," he responded before turning away.

There was a dark chuckle from David as Madeline glared at him and then turned to console her boyfriend. "That was uncalled for…" I began quietly, but he stopped me.

"I already heard it from Madeline, so you can save your breath," he whispered as he leaned in. "I'll be good the rest of the evening, if you wish."

"Yes," I replied sternly.

With a crooked smile and a bow of his head, he responded, "As you command."

I rolled my eyes and looked away, searching for the stage and wondering when the concert would start. "I can't see from here...does it look like they're about to begin?" I asked either Ben or Madeline.

Ben, recovered from his humiliation, answered, "They're getting in their seats now."

"So why are we sitting in the grass and not in the amphitheater?" I questioned, curious why he chose to be so far away.

"It's more private and we can stretch out," he replied, leaning back on his palms and sticking his legs out.

"How thoughtful," David commented, slightly narrowing his eyes at him.

"So what kind of music are we in store for?" I inquired, quashing his remark.

Ben sat up and turned so he was facing Madeline but could see both us and the stage. "They're going to play some instrumental selections, classical and modern," he replied, opening the picnic basket as the orchestra tuned up.

Expecting food, I was surprised when he pulled out several thin sticks which he staked in the ground between us. "What's that for?" I asked as he lit them one by one.

"To keep the bugs away," he replied as he looked at David.

The scent was a sickening mixture of sweet and musky. I hope he didn't plan to have them burning the whole time. They might just ruin my appetite.

David raised a brow, the smell obviously reaching him. "Most people use citronella. What type of bugs are you warding off with sandalwood, myrrh, and coconut?" he inquired.

Ben narrowed his eyes. "The evil kind. Do you think it's working?"

David's eyes flickered to Madeline and she responded. "Maybe not here. Let's move them to the outside," she suggested, pulling them up and placing them around us.

I took a deep breath of fresh air. "Thank you," I remarked to her. "Honestly, Ben, they were making me sick," I explained as he looked at me in astonishment, and David smirked. Ben's face began to brighten. "So what have you fixed us for dinner?" I asked, hoping to keep him from verbally assaulting my boyfriend, who undoubtedly deserved it.

He was glaring at him, but then looked at me and blew out his breath before reaching into the basket. "Umm…finger sandwiches, fruit, cheese, vegetables," he replied quietly as he started unpacking them.

"Sounds delicious," Madeline commented, helping him spread everything out.

"It looks yummy. Did you do this all yourself?" I asked, scanning over the items.

He was much calmer, focusing on just Madeline and me. "Most of it, but Mom helped with the sandwiches. Unfortunately, I didn't have enough time to slice the cheese, so I brought the stuff with me," he replied, pulling out a small cutting board and setting the block on it.

David looked at the knife in Ben's hand and then Madeline. "Oh, that's not necessary," she insisted. "We can cut slices as we need them."

"No, I can do it now. We have time," Ben replied as he wedged it into the block of cheddar.

He cut several thick chunks and then cubed them into one inch squares. He seemed to be handling it pretty well until he started talking, getting a little sloppy. "We had this kid come in the other day asking all these questions about a new gaming system coming out…" he remarked as he looked at Madeline.

"Ben, you should really pay attention to your cutting," David warned, watching the knife get too close to his fingers.

"I can handle this," he growled, cutting faster as he glared at him. Then the knife slipped and sliced his thumb.

Blood dripped onto the board as he cursed under his breath, lifting his thumb toward his mouth, but Madeline stopped him midair, her hand on his wrist. More scarlet drops fell as she gaped at his blood-streaked hand. David stared at her, his jaw set as he tried to nonverbally talk her out of what she planned to do, but she wouldn't budge.

Her pale chartreuse eyes moved from the wound to Ben's eyes and as she got to her knees, she leaned closer and purred, "Let me take care of that for you…"

Her mouth was inches from his hand, fangs at the ready. "Madeline," David spoke aloud. "Don't. Once you start, you won't be able to stop." He winced as he said the words, trying to avoid breathing in the scent of the blood and reacting as well.

She broke her concentration on Ben long enough to glower at him, but as she stared into his pained eyes, her expression changed. Ben remained in a daze as his wound continued to drip slowly onto the board. Taking that moment to finally act, I quickly grabbed several napkins and covered it.

I watched Madeline, her fangs retracting as she sat back with a look of disgust on her face. As much as I didn't want to get her involved again, I asked her to hold the napkins over the cut while I cleaned the blood off the board. She hesitated, but then put her hand where mine was.

Soon Ben came out of his stupor, looking down at her hand tightly covering the wound. She was looking away, trying not to let the hunger overtake her, but he probably assumed she was just being squeamish. He touched her wrist and she looked at him, sadness in her eyes.

"Thank you, Madeline. You can let go now," he told her calmly. She slowly released him and he stood. "I think there's some bandages in the car. Mom's pretty good about keeping that stuff in there. I'll be right back," he commented and then walked off, something not quite right about him.

I gave her a dampened napkin to clean her hands. Finding an empty plastic baggy, I threw all the blood-soaked napkins in it, along with the one she just used. I zipped it closed and took it to a nearby trashcan. David was glaring at a worried Madeline when I returned. I sighed and sat next to him.

"I had a strange feeling something bad would happen," I muttered.

"At least we were able to stop her. Hopefully she entranced him well enough to not remember any of it," he replied quietly, his eyes on her.

"I just hope he's okay," she commented after a moment. "Maybe I should go check on him."

"No!" David and I both shouted.

"I'm sure he'll be back soon," I assured her.

Glancing over the spread, my stomach growled, but I couldn't eat just yet. To get my mind off it, I scanned the park. A few people nearby sat waiting but were thankfully not close enough to witness what just happened. Ahead, the musicians were poised to begin as the conductor made his opening remarks.

I looked over my shoulder at the road, trying to find Ben. It's been awhile; he should have been back by now. "Maybe I should go check on him," I commented, getting ready to stand, but David stopped me.

"No, I will. Stay here with Madeline," he instructed.

I crossed my arms and turned away from him as he jogged off. Ben was my friend and it was David he didn't trust. What sense did it make for him to go? I rolled my eyes and turned to Madeline, who looked at me apologetically.

"I'm so sorry, Megan. I…I couldn't help it…"

My anger subsided as my eyes connected with hers, and I could see the pain of what she was going through in them. I moved closer, giving her a hug. "It's okay. I'm sure it's hard," I consoled.

"I was only focused on the blood. David was shouting at me in my head, but I just blocked him out. Then I enthralled Ben…oh, how could I do that to him!" she moaned.

I held her closer and stroked her soft, wavy hair, a sweet citrus and coconut scent wafting from it. "Don't beat yourself up over this. He's okay;

you didn't go through with it." She looked up at me, streaks of red liquid flowing down her cheeks. Oh great, more blood. I grabbed another napkin and tidied her face. "Don't cry," I whispered as I looked around. Still no curious onlookers.

She sniffled as I dabbed the crimson tears from the corners of her eyes. "It's a good thing David stopped me when he did."

"I know…he would have never let you go through with it, no matter how much he despises Ben," I replied, getting a faint smile from her. "There, good as new," I remarked, slipping the used napkin under my plate.

The orchestra began and I glanced over my shoulder, wondering if he found Ben yet. "They're missing the beginning. What's taking them so long?"

She sat up and scanned the area. "They're on their way now. Ben had trouble finding something."

I looked at her. "What – the bandages?"

"No, David didn't say," she replied, laying her head on my shoulder.

"Well it must not be too important," I responded, rubbing her back.

Not even a moment later, they walked up, both silent. "How are you doing?" Madeline asked, keeping her distance from Ben.

"Better," he replied as he sat, holding up a bandaged hand. "David had to re-wrap it. It's hard to put one on with one hand."

I nudged David and smiled, but he didn't smile back. "Shall we eat?" he asked, looking at Ben.

"Please, help yourself," he replied, smirking.

"Do you need help with yours, Ben?" Madeline inquired.

He smiled at her. "Please."

"What would you like?" she asked, taking his plate. He pointed out what he wanted, and she placed it on the plate and then set it in front of him. I fixed mine and then she and David followed. She was the first to eat, lifting a sandwich to her lips and taking a bite. "Mmm…this is delicious," she commented.

Ben looked at her with an expression of what seemed like surprise. Why would he be surprised she was eating a sandwich? Of course, I was equally as surprised. I thought David said food makes them sick. I glanced at him, wondering how she was able to do it. Knowing what I was thinking by my expression, he nodded in her direction.

I watched closely as she wiped her mouth, discreetly spitting the pieces of sandwich into it. Then she started talking to Ben as she picked at the rest of it, making it look as though she ate more. He was completely unaware of her ruse.

David took the distraction as an opportunity to get rid of some of his food by slipping it onto my plate. As he did, he leaned in and whispered in my ear, "I hope you're hungry."

Not so much anymore, but for him I would be. I picked up one of the sandwiches and took a bite as he smiled at me. It was tasty, but I think Ms. Galloway overdid the seasoning. I stole a strawberry off his plate and ate it, wanting to change the taste in my mouth.

Through the meal, the conversation was light with our attention turning to the concert in the distance when it lulled. Ben cut his eyes several times to David, watching and waiting for something to happen, though I wasn't sure what. David was concerned mostly about Ben's scrutiny over his eating habits, but could he actually be looking for something else?

Seeing we were finished, Ben packed the leftovers into the basket and put it in the grass while I threw the trash away. Facing the amphitheater, he sat with his legs crossed and Madeline decided to join him, moving a little closer. As he leaned back on his palms, she stared at him curiously.

"Oh…what's this?" she asked as she reached for something at his neck. She delicately lifted it off his skin and held it in her fingertips. When did he start wearing a necklace?

"Oh, just something my mom gave me years ago. I wear it all the time."

"Huh, I never noticed it before," she remarked, pretending to examine it closer as she let it dangle from her fingers so David could see. Hanging from the chain was a silver cross. "It's beautiful," she commented, slipping it back into his shirt.

"Do you go to church?" he asked, sitting up again.

"Not since I moved here. I haven't found the right one yet," she answered, glancing back at David. "Do you?"

"Not anymore. Mom's too busy and my last experience left a bad taste in my mouth."

"So why do you wear the cross if you don't believe?"

"I never said I didn't believe; I just don't like the hypocrisy of the people."

Feeling comfortable with the conversation they were having, I turned my attention instead to David. I was not satisfied with the way we were sitting so I scooted closer and got between his legs. With my back resting against his chest, he put his arms around me and kissed my neck and then leaned back. I moved with him and watched the two silhouettes in front of us. Ben turned his head and looked back, but I couldn't see his expression.

David kissed my neck again and paused above it, his breath cool against my skin. I reached back and slipped my hand behind his head, turning so I was looking up at him. I kissed him, and though I wanted to prolong it, I couldn't with them sitting directly in front of us. Turning on my side, I rested my head against his chest and closed my eyes, listening to his breathing in one ear and the music in the other.

After a few selections, I opened my eyes and caught Ben looking back again. As soon as he noticed me, he turned and moved closer to Madeline. Putting his arm around her, he took her chin in his other hand and turned her face toward his. David sat straight up, startling me.

"She's panicking," he whispered.

"Why? It looks like he just wants to kiss her," I whispered back.

"With the blood still fresh on her mind, she's worried she might do something she shouldn't."

I could see her tensing up as his lips neared hers, but David waited to see what would happen before reacting. Ben hesitated and then gave her a gentle peck before quickly facing forward. She glanced over her shoulder at us, shrugged, and rested her head on his shoulder. David relaxed, laughing quietly.

I looked up at him and asked in a whisper, "What's so funny?"

"I guess she expected something more passionate."

I shook my head and rested against him, getting comfortable again. Above us, the stars peeked through the spaces between the leaves. The moon was slowly rising behind us, casting faint shadows on the ground. It was a picturesque night, and I was where I wanted to be.

As I stared toward the sky, David's fingers glided along my throat to my chest. He placed his hand over my heart as he kissed behind my ear and down my neck. It began to beat faster and louder. I could hear it in my ears and feel it against his hand. His lips brushed my skin and I turned my head, our lips touching.

In one graceful movement, he turned on his side and lowered me to the ground, his hand on my chin as he continued kissing me. Now I didn't care that Madeline and Ben were right there or that other people were nearby. It was as if he and I were the only ones in the park.

But it ended too soon. "Hey, Megan," Ben called without looking back. David stopped abruptly and rested on his side, propping his head on his hand. Lying on my back, I composed myself while deciding to answer. "Megan?" he called again, this time glancing over his shoulder at me. David smirked.

I propped myself up on my elbows and glared at him. "Yeah," I answered.

"I played that new shooter game I told about yesterday."

Why is he telling me this? I really don't care. "Was it fun?" I asked, trying to be nice.

"Yeah, the graphics are awesome. The blood and gore is so realistic," he replied, sneering as he shifted his eyes to David.

"Realistic? Ben, have you ever seen a dead person?" I questioned, sitting up.

"Well, no, but it looked like what you see in the movies," he defended.

"Yeah, okay. Glad it was graphic enough for you," I replied, lying back down and rolling on my side facing David. "Sorry for the interruption," I whispered to him.

He looked down at me and smiled, caressing my cheek. "He was making sure you were all right. Besides, it was probably good he did interrupt us," he responded quietly.

He leaned down and kissed me, lingering for a moment. Putting his free hand over my heart again, he closed his eyes. It had calmed significantly but started to beat faster. He smiled and removed it, moving back to his side. Intertwining his fingers with mine, he gazed at me as I gazed back at him.

"When do you think you will be able to stay at my house?" he questioned softly.

"Oh...I forgot about that. Claire's coming over tomorrow night...what about Sunday, Monday, or Tuesday?"

"Would it be too much to ask for all three days?" he inquired with his wicked grin.

"Not at all," I replied, kissing him.

Hearing movement in front of us, I lifted my head to see what was going on. Ben was lying down finally, inviting Madeline to lie against his chest, but she refused. Instead, she chose to recline next to him, his arm under her head, and stare at the tree branches above.

I relaxed and returned my attention to David, putting my arm around him as I nuzzled my head into his chest. I closed my eyes and enjoyed the music and being there. But then I felt his grip tighten around me and soon I knew why.

"What are you two lovebirds doing?" Ben asked, staring down at us. Madeline was next to him, holding his hand and smiling.

"Meditating on the complexity of the orchestration," David replied, somewhat perturbed by the question.

I looked up, leaning back. "Heading out already?" I asked.

"No, we're going for a little walk. Madeline hasn't seen this area before," he replied with a smile. David sat up and looked as though he wanted to say something out loud but must have opted to say it directly to her because her smile disappeared at that moment. Ben looked from him to her. He noticed. "Are you ready?" he asked.

She looked unsure of what to do, but then answered, "Yes, I am."

He smiled triumphantly and then glanced at me as they walked away, arm in arm. I sat up and watched as they talked quietly to each other. "Are they going to be okay?" I asked, turning to David.

He furrowed his brow, but then it smoothed. "They'll be fine. She's going to make sure he doesn't take her too far, just in case."

"If she's worried about going too far, why would she ask to see the park?" I questioned, a little confused.

With a half-smile, he answered, "It wasn't her idea, it was Ben's."

I started to feel uneasy. "What?"

"He knows we are not who we pretend to be. He knew it at the party, and the incident tonight added to his suspicions."

It dawned on me then why I'd never seen Ben wear it before. "The necklace…was that what you caught him searching for?"

David looked away. "Yes. But it wasn't just that. He's been experimenting on us since we arrived…with the bells, the blue shirt, incense, and garlic."

I stared at him in astonishment. "What's all that for?"

He smiled. "Protection against evil spirits and beings."

"If he has a theory about you two, why would he want to be alone with her?"

"Another test, I suppose, or asking her questions away from me. So far, none of them have been significant," he replied, tilting his head slightly. "When he saw Madeline eating and later touching the cross, it threw him. But he's more suspicious of me than her, like I'm controlling her."

"He did say something about that the other day. So what are you going to do if he does realize what you are?"

"Well, we either tell him the truth and make him swear to never tell anyone or erase as much as we can from his mind," he replied, lying back and folding his arms behind his head. He closed his eyes and then smirked. "Hmm…it seems Madeline chose the latter."

I looked around and then down at him. "Just now? She did it just now?"

"Yes. They're on their way back."

A moment later, she walked up with Ben staggering next to her. She led him around to the blanket and helped him to sit. His face was blank as he stared straight ahead. I got to my knees and crawled closer, looking from her to him.

"Ben?" I called.

"He can't hear you yet, but he'll come out of it soon," she whispered as she removed the necklace and slipped it into her pocket. "I had to do it. He was asking all sorts of questions and my answers weren't satisfying him."

I looked at David, still lying on his back with his eyes closed, and then at her. She leaned in close to Ben, whispering something I couldn't hear in his ear. She kissed his cheek and sat back as he closed his eyes and then slowly opened them, blinking several times. He turned to her and smiled.

"Huh…I must have dozed off. Did I miss anything?" he asked.

"Just an overture or two," she replied with a sweet smile.

"Guess I'm not much of a classical music lover," he commented, facing the front again. I stared at the two of them, dumbfounded. He was like a totally different person.

"It was what was best for all of us," David whispered, appearing at my side.

"Geez! You're too quiet," I gasped softly as I jumped, throwing my hand to my chest.

"I apologize," he replied, kissing my shoulder.

I watched them and then looked at him. "If she erased everything recent, how is she going to explain the gash on his thumb?"

He smirked. "It's not just about erasing memories but recreating them as well. You'd be surprised what a manipulated person will believe."

I thought back to my own experience. I willingly trusted what he told me happened the night I saw Brian and Odette in the park. "I guess you're right," I replied quietly, looking down.

He took my chin in his fingers and turned my face toward him. "Please understand, this is not something we do a lot. It's for protection and survival."

I gazed into his eyes and smiled softly. "I do understand."

He smiled back and then kissed me. I rested my head on his shoulder and he put his arm around me as we listened to the last set of songs. Ben and Madeline were in the same pose in front of us. Aside from all that happened, it still was an enjoyable evening.

Once the last note played, everyone clapped and then started packing up. I thanked Ben for inviting us while David folded the blanket. I gave Madeline a hug and then joined him. He politely shook Ben's hand and thanked him as well before heading to the car.

It was late and I was getting tired, but my mind was busy as we walked in silence. Ben will go home and remember only what Madeline decided he should remember or whatever false memory she planted and be none the wiser of what happened tonight. But it's for the best, as David said. Maybe now Ben won't be such a nuisance about him.

When we got to the car, I heard my phone chime and reached in my clutch, pulling it out. Crap, I missed a call from Dad. I asked David to hold on a moment while I called back.

"Hey, what's up?" I asked when he answered.

"Oh, just checking in. Where were you?" Dad inquired.

"I was on a date…with David and Ben and his girlfriend. Remember? I told you about it earlier," I responded, a little perturbed.

"Are you still on this date? It's close to eleven, you know."

"Yes, I know," I replied wearily. "We are just about home," I lied.

"Did you have a good time?" he asked and I rolled my eyes. The corner of David's lip curled.

"Yeah, it was fun. Couldn't have asked for a better night."

"Good. Well, I'll let you go since you should be home by now. Say your good nights to David and then off to bed," he directed.

"Yes, sir," I returned. "Good night, Dad."

He replied as David opened my door. I climbed in, staring out the windshield as he shut it. All of these check-ups in two days since they left. I sat back as the car started and sighed, gazing out the window as he pulled away. The ride home seemed long, feeling more drawn out even though there was less traffic on the road.

By the time we reached the driveway, I was half asleep. As he softly opened the car door, I glanced wearily up at him. I stood, a little unstable on my feet, but steadied myself and walked slowly to the porch with his help. I unlocked the front door and started up the stairs. I couldn't wait to fall onto my soft bed and go to sleep.

David noticed me struggling, so he lifted me into his arms and carried me the remainder of the way to my room. Gently laying me down, he carefully pulled the blanket from under me. After tucking me in, he left the room for several minutes. When he came back, he turned out the light and stretched out next to me. I put my arm around him and nuzzled my head against his chest.

"Where did you go?" I asked with a yawn.

"To make sure everything was locked up," he whispered.

My eyes closed, and I felt safe and secure once again in his arms. Morning would be another story, but that was hours away. No need to worry over it.

He rubbed my back and I drifted further and further into sleep.

# Chapter 34
## Figment

The loneliness returned when I woke the following morning. Not wanting to spend the day by myself, I decided to call Claire to see if she was interested in hanging out earlier. "Sure...want to go to the pool?" she asked.

"We're supposed to get rain," I responded, watching the weather on a local news channel as I lounged on the couch.

"There isn't a cloud in the sky. The sun's shining bright and it's a perfect day for swimming," she retorted.

"All right, you convinced me."

"Good. I'll be over shortly and we can walk together."

"Works for me. Thanks for rescuing me from my isolation."

"Hey, you're rescuing me from my boredom. I don't think I can stand another minute of public television."

"Why are you watching public television?" I asked, thinking there was no reason she should be.

"It's Mom's punishment for the monster. Anytime he wants to watch TV or is in a room with a TV, it has to be tuned to something educational. His report card was really bad, so it's nothing but that all summer. Unfortunately, she's also punishing Dad and me by doing this."

"That sucks. Well, anytime you want to watch mindless dribble, you can always come over here," I offered, turning the TV off and getting up.

"I'll definitely be taking you up on that," she laughed. "Okay, I'm going to get ready. I'll be over soon."

"See you then," I replied and hung up. I changed and packed my bag and then sat on the porch waiting for her.

The neighborhood was filled with the usual sounds of summer: sprinklers, children's laughter, lawn mowers, katydids, and music from nearby yards floating on the warm breeze. It was nice to just sit and listen, watching my neighbors go about their lives as if there was nothing more to it.

I sighed and glanced at my phone, figuring Claire should be here by now. Fifteen minutes had gone by and there was no sign of her. I stood and glanced down the street but didn't see her. Sitting back down, I stared at the sky. There were only a few clouds. I guess the forecasters were wrong; so far it didn't look like anything would happen.

I was pulling my phone out of my pocket to check the time again when I heard Claire shout from the street. "Come on, let's go! I don't want to get rained out!"

I jumped up and ran down to meet her. "What took you so long?"

"I had to finish up some things and then picking the right suit and outfit..."

"Uh huh," I replied, looking over her attire as we hurriedly walked down the street.

"Sooo...how'd your double date go?" she asked, getting right to it.

Good, bad. It had its moments. "It was interesting," I summed up.

"Interesting because of the double date...or interesting because of Ben?"

"No, Ben did well. Madeline kept him distracted."

"She's so pretty and sweet...how could he not like her?"

"Well, we know all too well how he is."

"A big pain..."

I laughed. "Not all the time," I defended. "He was great before David came along, acting more like a concerned friend and only stepping in when necessary. But now it's like an alpha thing with the two of them, always trying to best the other."

"But David always wins hands-down, huh?"

"I have different feelings for him than I do Ben, so of course he wins. And he's so much more tactful than Ben."

"So, have you done anything with David while your dad and Vanessa have been away, other than the double date?"

Spent every night with him. "No, just talking on the phone," I lied as we approached the entrance. She faked a yawn and I bumped her with my hip, both of us laughing as I swiped my card.

We picked two chairs in the corner and laid everything out, then undressed and jumped in the water. It felt so refreshing after walking and working up a sweat. We stayed for a long time, swimming and hanging out along the wall commenting on the young trophy wives sunbathing in tiny bikinis and the teen boys drooling over them.

When we were waterlogged enough, we took to the chairs and stretched out. The clouds started moving in as we flipped to our stomachs, getting occasional bursts of warmth. But when the cool lingered longer than it should have, we decided to head out.

When we got back to the house, we changed and hopped in my car, heading out to get movies and pizza as heavy, gray clouds covered the sky. Stopping at the movie store first, we walked up and down the aisles picking out what we wanted to watch. Claire convinced me to choose thrillers and horror movies because 'it was that kind of night'.

As I glanced at the cover of a potential one, I noticed out of the corner of my eye a woman staring at me. Odd. I turned her way to see if she wanted something, but she was gone. Maybe she was looking at something else. I shrugged and resumed my search.

I moved to another rack, looking at the movie selections there, when I heard a familiar cackle, deep and dry. Quickly skimming the store, I found no sign of who I feared it might be. It had to be my imagination, just thinking I heard her, or maybe it was from the movie playing on the TVs. Checking a nearby screen, I realized it wasn't that. Some kind of serious war drama was showing.

Slipping down the next aisle, I brushed it off and continued looking for Claire-approved movies. Reading the back of a particularly gory one, I heard the cackle again. And this time, it was closer to me. I casually raised my eyes from the words on the case and caught a swathe of golden blonde hair as it passed in front of me. When I lifted my head to get a better look, I found no one there or anywhere near me.

"Whatcha got there?" Claire asked, popping up next to me and making me jump.

"Oh geez!" I gasped, throwing my hand up to my chest.

"Sorry, didn't mean to scare you. Must be a good one," she commented, looking at the back.

"No, not really," I responded as I briefly glanced at the case again before setting it back on the shelf and scanning the store. "Hey, did you see a woman with blonde hair standing near me?" I inquired.

"Uh no," she replied, putting a movie she grabbed back and picking up another one.

"Oh," I responded, glancing around again.

"So these are what I found...any sound good?" she asked, showing them to me.

I was still distracted, trying to find Odette or the person who looked and sounded like her, so I could assure myself it wasn't her. "Yeah, they look good," I responded.

"Megan, you didn't even look at them," she complained.

"Oh sorry," I replied, taking them and shuffling through each one. "Maybe these two?" I suggested, not sure if they were what she was looking for.

"That one definitely; the other one, not so much," she remarked, taking them back. "What have you found so far?"

I handed her my selections, giving up the search for someone who wasn't there. "No...no...yes...no...hmm maybe...no," she replied, handing me the no's. "See what they have up front that were just turned in," she instructed.

I went to the counter and peeked at the movies laying behind it. As I was reading the titles, I got the eerie feeling someone was staring at me. I raised my head and looked out the window in front of me as a large group of people walked by. Through the crowd, my eyes connected with mahogany ones set in a porcelain face, and a chill spilled down my spine.

But as soon as the group passed, she disappeared with them. I dashed around the counter and out the door, looking up and down the sidewalk, but found no sign of her.

I went back inside, holding my head as I scanned the store. Nothing. Turning around, I glanced back outside as several more people walked by, but none of them looked like her. This was weird. I fidgeted with my hair and looked away, anxious to leave.

I asked the guy at the counter for a couple of the movies to take back to Claire and quickly headed her way. "What about these?" I questioned, trying not to sound bothered by the fact I kept seeing Odette.

"Ooo…this is a good one…and this. Okay, I think we're ready to go," she announced, holding up four movies.

Beyond ready, I headed to the counter with her and checked out. I tried not to act apprehensive, but I couldn't help occasionally glancing around, even as we left and walked to get dinner. We grabbed the pizza from a small restaurant several stores down and then headed home, ready to eat and enjoy our movie selections. And get my mind off Odette.

The rain started coming down as we left the lot and was pouring by the time we reached the house. Both of us forgetting umbrellas, we used the pizza boxes as cover as we ran up to the porch, but then we had to hurry and get them out of the soaking wet containers and onto a platter.

Claire popped a horror movie in while I grabbed napkins and plates. The phone in my back pocket vibrated and I jumped. As I answered, I calmed my heart.

"Did I take you by surprise?" David inquired, a devious grin in his voice.

"Yeah, a little. I wasn't expecting a call until later," I responded.

"I had time at the moment. What are you two up to tonight?" he asked.

"Watching scary movies and eating pizza. Girl stuff," I replied, throwing two slices onto my plate while Claire did the same.

"Hi David," she greeted as she walked by.

"Tell Claire I said hello," he responded. "By the way, you look radiant. Did you go to the pool again today?" he questioned and I glanced out the window, the rain still coming down in sheets.

"Where are you?" I whispered into the phone.

"Hanging from the balcony. I saw you through the patio doors as I walked up to the house."

I looked but couldn't see him. "What are you doing here? You know it's Claire's night."

"I wanted to see you regardless."

I smiled as I tucked my head and played with a curl. "How long are you staying?"

"Long enough for a kiss," he replied.

I glanced over at Claire on the couch. "I'll be right up," I whispered and hung up. I slipped the phone in my pocket as I came up behind her. "Hey, I forgot something in my room. I'll be right back."

She gave me a funny look. "Okay, but hurry. You're going to miss the beginning."

"Lickety split," I responded, dashing out of the room and up the stairs.

And there he was, waiting by the open balcony doors as the smell and sound of rain filled my room. He was damp from being in it, wavy lines of hair hanging in his face and his clothes clinging to his body. He was stunning.

My heart thumped as I stared at him. Noticing me, he smiled as he started toward me and it thumped harder. As I met him, he placed his hand on my cheek and gazed into my eyes. He was even cooler tonight; I'd have to keep my mind focused on not losing control. Leaning in slowly, his lips gently caressed mine, but soon he parted them. My heart beat wildly and he moved to my chin and then down my neck. No, this was where I needed to stop it.

"I have to go," I breathed, pulling away.

"I know," he whispered, staring into my eyes. "So do I."

Calming myself, I asked, "Call me later?"

"Of course," he replied with a smile.

I walked with him back to the balcony, giving him a soft, simple kiss before he climbed down the tree. Sighing, I watched as he disappeared into the pouring rain. In the distance, a rumble of thunder shook the earth. I shut the doors and locked them, then headed back downstairs to join Claire.

"I went ahead and paused it. What did you forget?" she asked as I sat down next to her.

"Oh, David reminded me that I needed to charge my phones. I'm so forgetful when it comes to that."

"Sweet of him to remind you," she replied, starting the movie.

"Yeah. Oh, and he said hi."

There was a flicker outside and another crash of thunder; the storm was closer. But what better atmosphere for a scary movie. Hopefully, we won't lose power. The rest of our night of movie watching will be shot.

Just as we were getting into it, the house phone rang. "Maybe it's Dad," I commented, getting up to answer it. The number was unavailable.

"Hello, Caldwell residence."

No answer.

"Hello? Is anyone there?"

Still no answer.

"Hellllooo?"

Click, dial tone.

"Who was it?" Claire asked, looking back at me.

"I don't know. The number was unavailable and there was no reply on the other end," I responded, sitting back down.

We finished the movie uninterrupted and before putting in the next one, I headed to the kitchen to take care of leftovers. The storm was calming outside with just heavy rain falling now. As I headed back to the couch, the phone rang again. I picked it up and looked at the number – unavailable again.

"Hello, Caldwell residence," I commented.

No answer, same as before.

"Look if you're not going to say anything, please stop calling," I requested.

This time there was breathing, a click, then a dial tone.

"Same weirdo?" Claire asked.

"I guess so, but there was breathing this time," I replied, putting the phone up and sitting on the couch.

"Creepy...like in the horror movies," she mumbled as she started the next one – a thriller.

Halfway through, the phone rang again. "Just don't answer it if it's unavailable," she suggested.

"It could be my dad," I replied, getting up and grabbing it. Again, no number was listed.

"Hello?"

Nothing.

"This isn't funny. Stop calling," I stated firmly.

There was a deep chuckle and then a click. A shiver went down my spine.

"That creep again?" Claire asked.

"Yeah," I replied, hanging it up and walking stiffly to the couch.

"Maybe they're done for the night," she commented, turning her attention back to the screen.

"I hope so," I mumbled, trying not to let the calls bother me.

Just before the end of the movie, the phone rang again. "Seriously, don't answer it. Let them leave a message," she suggested.

I hesitated, thinking I would let it go, but I couldn't. I got up and rushed to the phone as she stared at me in bewilderment. "No, I'm going to tell him off this time," I responded, seeing the same unavailable as I answered it.

Nothing again.

"If you don't stop this, I'm calling the cops," I threatened.

Silence, then a voice. "Megan? Is everything all right there?"

"Dad!" I exclaimed, relieved it was him. "Yeah, everything's fine. Someone's been prank calling the house, that's all. Is something wrong with your phone?"

"It's these pay phones...they never work right," he responded.

I leaned against the counter and let out a breath. "So what's up?"

"Well, I just wanted to check on you and make sure everything was fine." Checking on me again. I guess it'll be every day.

"Yep...everything's good. Claire and I are watching movies and eating pizza."

"Sounds fun," he remarked and paused, like he was waiting for me to say something else. Vanessa must be busy at the moment and not demanding his attention. "Well...I'll let you get back to your girl time," he continued after I didn't.

"Okay, talk to you later," I replied. He dittoed and hung up.

On my way back to the couch, lightning flashed and lit up the yard briefly, grabbing my attention. Lovely...another storm was starting. I stared out the window through the pouring rain, spotting an unusual figure near the gazebo. It didn't look like David and there was no reason it should be him. I paused and watched as my heart beat fast, waiting for the next flash and wondering who it could be.

In a burst of flickering light, I saw it again, standing in the center of the yard this time. Tall and slim with a sinister grin and burning mahogany eyes peering through stringy, yellow hair...was Odette. To prove what I was seeing wasn't a figment of my imagination, I quickly switched on the floodlights and instead found the yard empty.

"Something wrong, Megan?" Claire asked, looking at me strangely.

"I thought I saw someone in the yard, but it must have been my imagination," I replied, disquieted as I sat back down.

"Are the movies getting to you?" she inquired.

Then the phone rang.

I jumped up and checked the number – unavailable. Maybe Dad was calling back about something. "Hey Dad, did you forget something?"

No answer.

"Hello?"

Still no answer.

"Okay, I'm calling the police."

There was a deep, threatening laugh.

"I...I'm serious..."

"Megan," the voice growled.

"Who is this? You need to stop calling."

There was silence and then the voice hissed, "I misss you."

I stood frozen, the phone slipping from my hand. Claire turned at the sound of it hitting the wood floor and jumped up, grabbing it. She put it to her ear and then hung up.

"No one's there," she commented, handing it back to me. "Did they answer you? Was it someone you know?"

I have an idea, but I don't want to say it out loud. Besides, if he is calling, that's all he can do. He's in Baton Rouge and so is Odette. My mind's just in hyper drive. I'm safe like David said.

"No, they didn't. Probably some boys from school who thought I was home alone," I replied, putting the phone in the cradle and sitting down. "So what's the next movie?"

"Horror or horror-comedy?"

Something lighthearted would be good right now. "Horror-comedy, I guess."

"Okay," she replied, popping it in.

I sat and tried to enjoy the movie, but it was hard. With my overactive imagination seeing Odette all evening and Brian possibly calling, I couldn't concentrate. "Claire, I need to make a phone call," I commented as I stood and grabbed the house phone. I went into the living room and pulled out David's phone as soon as I was out of view.

Waking it, I stared at his number. Should I really bother him with this? He's going to tell me the same thing as the other day. My thumb above the button, I was about to press it when the house phone rang. Crap, Claire will realize I lied. I glanced at the number and saw that it was unavailable again. I answered it but didn't say a word.

"Hello Megan," the voice purred.

"Brian?"

"Ahh, it's so good to hear you say my name. How have you been?"

"Quit the chit chat. Why are you calling me?" I demanded, trying not to be too loud.

"Just wondering how you're doing. When David called the other day, I thought something might be wrong."

"They found your most recent victim."

He snickered. "Up there maybe..."

"I need to go. Please don't call again," I abruptly demanded.

"Is David going to be there soon?"

"That's none of your business."

"Okay, fine. I'll never call again, but maybe we'll see each other in the future."

"Doubtful," I replied and hung up.

Now I'm going to call David. He picked up immediately, but he sounded like he was in the middle of something. I don't want to know.

"Is something wrong?" he asked.

"Yes, Brian called." He was quiet. "And I think I've been seeing Odette."

"What did he want?"

"He said he was checking on me."

He was quiet again and then responded. "I'm at work now, but I'll ask Madeline to come over, if you like."

"Yeah, that'd be good. She doesn't have to stay the whole time."

"She'll stay as long as you need her. Please call me if anything else happens."

"I will. Thank you," I replied.

"Anything for you, Megan. I'll see you tomorrow."

I didn't want to say goodbye. I wanted to keep him on the phone, hear his comforting voice, but I had to let him go. "Can't wait," I responded. He replied and hung up, my feeling of comfort crumbling around me.

Now to tell Claire that Madeline will be joining us. I hope she doesn't mind. I went back into the family room and took a seat next to her. She left the movie running this time and it was almost over. I set the phone on the table and sat back.

"Everything okay?" she asked, glancing over at me.

"Yeah. I forgot to tell David something and I tried to call him, but his line was busy. When I hung up, Madeline called to see if she could stop by for a little bit. I said it was all right. Do you mind?"

"No, not at all. It'll be fun spending time with her. Ooo...and she can watch the last movie with us. When is she going to be here?"

"She had some errands to run and then she'll be over," I lied.

Claire nodded and went back to the movie. I wasn't sure when she'd actually get here but figured she'd check around the house first, then come to the front door. I stared blankly at the TV, not really watching the movie since I missed so much. Then it ended.

"Well she's not here yet, so what do you want to do while we wait?" Claire asked, switching movies.

"Snack time?" I questioned. She agreed and joined me in the kitchen. I pulled out what was left of the pizzas and some junk food, and we sat at the island and munched. "So, how was Justin's vacation?" I asked before taking a bite.

"Good...other than missing me. He bought me this beautiful shell necklace...gave it to me when he came over on Wednesday," she responded as she slipped her thumb under it and pulled it forward to show me.

"That was sweet of him. Did you do anything special to welcome him home?"

"No, just talked, actually," she replied, playing with her food.

"About anything in particular?" I asked as I leaned on the cool acrylic, propping my head up with my hand.

"No, just what he did on his vacation, and I told him what I did while he was away. We were completely honest with each other. You know...building trust," she answered, smiling.

The doorbell rang and I excused myself. Madeline smiled wide as I opened the door. "Hey, Megan. I checked around the house but didn't see anything," she whispered as she passed. "So, what are you up to?"

I led her back to the family room. "Snacking right now, but we have one last scary movie to watch. Interested?"

"Yeah! I love horror movies!" she replied enthusiastically.

Claire turned and looked at her as we entered, smiling. "Hey, Madeline. How are you?"

"Good. I hope you don't mind me stopping by. I was nearby and thought I'd visit."

"No, I don't mind at all," she replied.

I sat between them as the movie started. Madeline seemed unfazed by the violence and gore, but what did I expect with her history and what she was. Every once in a while, I saw her staring outside and tilting her head, but then she shrugged it off and returned to the movie.

It was about midnight when it finished. Neither Claire nor I were tired, and I didn't know when Madeline planned to leave. I guess it was like David said – until I didn't need her. I put the movie in the case and collected the others, setting them on the island so I'd remember to take them back later.

When I returned to the family room, Madeline was looking at me excitedly. "So what do we want to do now?" she asked.

I stood before the two of them. "I don't know. I'm not tired yet and we've watched all the movies."

"What do you like to do in your spare time?" Claire asked her.

"Sit by the lake and draw or paint, sometimes read," she replied.

"That's sounds nice. I didn't get to tell you at the party, but you're super talented. I'm not an artistic person. Heck, I can't even draw a stick figure!" Claire replied, laughing.

"Are you interested in drawing or painting? I could teach you."

"That's so nice of you, but I'd be a horrible student. I think I'm beyond help," she responded.

"The offer's always on the table, if you ever decide to give it a try. You, too, Megan," Madeline presented, looking at me.

"I may take you up on it someday," I replied. "So what are your plans this summer," I asked her.

"Hanging around the house mostly," she replied, playing with her hair.

"You don't go home?" Claire asked.

She looked surprised by the question at first, and then she sighed. "No, I don't talk to my parents. My lifestyle doesn't agree with them," she answered after a moment.

"That's terrible," Claire commented. "They should support you regardless."

"You would think, but it'll never happen."

"So you're not taking summer classes like David?" I asked to change the subject.

"No. It won't take long to earn my degree. I want to enjoy my time off from school while I can."

"Hey, you're free like we are. You should hang out with us, maybe go to the pool and tan. You're so pale," Claire remarked, not holding anything back.

"That'd be nice, but my skin is very fair and sensitive to the sun. I burn easily," she responded. Nice cover-up.

"Oh, that's too bad. Well, maybe there are other things we can do."

"I'd like that," she replied, smiling at me. "We can leave the boys at home and have girl time."

"A day of pampering or shopping would be ideal. Dragging Justin and Ben along the last time we went to the mall was a disaster," Claire commented.

"I can imagine. Ben can be pretty stubborn about certain things," she responded, glancing at me.

"Speaking of which, how are things going with you two?" Claire asked.

"Good. I feel like our relationship is a little more honest. He seems to like the real me."

"Yeah, I think you really scared him. He doesn't like an aggressive woman," Claire laughed with Madeline and me joining in.

"I guess not. I thought it would help, at least initially…knowing how he felt about Megan."

"We all know that story. Good luck trying," Claire replied, giving up hope he could find happiness with someone else.

"I think he's getting better about it, but there will always be a place in his heart for her," she responded, glancing at me again. Great, she had the same feeling.

"He can pine over me for eternity, but that won't change how I feel about him," I remarked, both of them staring at me.

Claire turned to Madeline and leaned in. "Do you think you two will get serious?" She looked perplexed. "Date exclusively, become intimate…" she explained.

"Oh, I'm not sure about that. I try not to look that far into the future. What happens will happen when it needs to happen."

"What kind of dates have you had with him?" Claire inquired.

"Going to the park, movies, and the mall."

"Does he ever invite you to his house?" I asked.

"No, I've never been invited to his house and I've never invited him to David's. We like to keep our relationship in the public."

"Why don't you invite him over?" Claire asked. I narrowed my eyes at her for prying into their business.

Madeline seemed okay answering her, though. "I don't feel it's right since it's not my house. He's asked to come over, but I always say no, which seems to make him upset," she replied, shifting her eyes briefly to me. She was hinting to me, but I already knew what she was getting at.

"He can be so rude," Claire muttered. "He should be happy to have a girl like you."

"That's sweet of you. I'm sure it'd be better if he wasn't so distracted."

"With work, school, his mom, and twin sisters, I can see where he's distracted," she commented. But only I knew what Madeline was really saying. "Well, speaking of boyfriend issues…I better call Justin. I told him I would before I went to bed," she announced, looking at her phone. She excused herself to the living room and Madeline took that opportunity to talk to me.

"David told me Brian called. Do you know why?" she whispered, moving closer and watching for her.

"I'm not sure. He said he was checking on me," I replied. "I also thought I saw Odette at the movie store and in the backyard."

"I haven't seen or heard any sign of her. I think it's just your imagination."

"I know. That's what I figured. So how long do you plan to stay?"

"However long you want."

"Well, I took care of Brian earlier, and since you said it was clear and all in my head concerning Odette, you could probably go whenever. I know some of Claire's questions are a little too personal."

"It's not too bad. It's nice to finally have other girls to talk to about relationships," she smiled. "But I'll probably head out in a couple of minutes. I need to hunt."

"Yeah, it's probably a good idea for Claire and I to go to bed anyway."

"She's coming back," she whispered. "So I was telling David about this new restaurant…" she made up as Claire walked in the room.

"Everything okay?" I asked, cutting Madeline off.

"Yeah. I caught him before he went to sleep."

We were all quiet, then Madeline piped up, "Well, I better get going. Thanks for sharing the movie and letting me hang out."

"No problem. I can't wait till we can do it again," Claire responded.

I walked Madeline to the door so I could personally thank her. "I really appreciate you coming over and indulging my overactive imagination," I whispered, giving her a hug.

"I'm happy to help anytime."

I opened the door and she stepped out. "I guess I'll see you tomorrow."

"Oh yeah, I forgot you're spending the next couple of days with us. This is going to be so much fun!" she squealed but tried to keep it quiet.

She gave me another hug and then skipped down the drive to her old Jeep. It roared as she started it and with a big grin and a wave, she backed out and drove off. I shut the door and locked it, meeting Claire in the foyer.

"Ready for bed?" she asked, suddenly sounding tired.

"Yeah," I replied, leading her upstairs.

She said good night and headed to the guest room as I turned into my room, leaving the door open for once. I checked the balcony doors and changed into nightclothes, then climbed into bed and was out in no time. Hopefully Claire was the same way.

# Chapter 35
## My Own Getaway

I woke the next morning to rain lightly falling outside on the balcony, and it was a beautiful sound. Would it rain all day? I sat up and checked my phone, bringing up the weather. It looked as though it'd be off and on with plenty of cloud coverage between.

I'll get to spend the whole day with David.

My heart leapt excitedly as I hopped up and headed down the hall to see Claire. She was still fast asleep, her light snoring audible as I approached. Quietly creeping into the room, I sat on the edge of the bed and tapped her shoulder as I softly called her name. She gradually roused and looked at me.

"What time is it?" she asked, her voice raspy.

I glanced at the clock on the table beside the bed. "Almost ten."

She covered her head with the pillow and moaned, "Too tired…"

I lifted it off and she groaned. "I don't understand why you're so exhausted. You went to bed the same time as I did."

"No…I called Justin after you turned out your light. He had a second wind, and we stayed on the phone most of the night."

"What did you have to talk about all night?" I questioned, perplexed.

"Stuff," she replied, sitting up. She looked horrific.

I gave her a stern look, then shook my head. "Would you like me to make you a tasty, hot breakfast?" I asked, rubbing her back as she leaned against me.

"That sounds good," she yawned in reply. "I'm going to freshen up and then I'll be down."

I smiled and helped her to her feet. As she headed to the bathroom, I headed to the hall, shutting the door behind me. I paused outside and laughed quietly as I shook my head. She's going to regret staying up so late.

Detouring to my room for a moment, I did a quick clean up and then jogged down the stairs and into the kitchen to get breakfast going. Feeling well-rested and in good spirits, I turned on the stereo and danced to the music while I prepared it. This wasn't going to be any old breakfast – I decided on a full, southern-style meal. I even brewed some coffee in case she needed it to help wake her up, though she'd probably go home and crawl back in bed.

As I fried up the bacon, the doorbell rang and I paused. I went to the door and peeked out the sidelight to check who it was, shocked to see David's back. As he turned his head slightly to the side, I quickly dropped the curtain and stepped away. I looked awful, but I couldn't change now with him waiting. I sighed and smoothed out my hair, finally opening the door.

"Good morning, David. To what do I owe the pleasure of your visit so early?" I asked, hiding behind the door as he entered.

He smiled and my heart skipped a beat. "I was anxious to see you," he responded, trying to sneak a peek at me. His smile faded and he looked toward the kitchen. "Are you burning something?" he inquired, sniffing the air.

"Oh no!" I exclaimed. "The bacon!"

I ran into the kitchen and removed the pan from the fire and quickly rinsed it under water, cooling it off so I could throw it away. He laughed at me as he opened the patio door to air out the room. I grumbled about his lack of concern while scrubbing the pan and then threw new bacon in it.

"You know I'm a better cook than this," I remarked as I started pancakes on the griddle. "I was distracted."

He smiled, sitting at the island. "By whom?" he asked innocently.

I glanced over my shoulder, narrowing my eyes at him. "Gee, I wonder…" I replied sarcastically as I flipped them.

He laughed quietly. "It could have been anyone at your door and you still would have been distracted. But I can't imagine you opening it to anyone looking like that. Your Sunday finest, I see," he smirked.

I turned, crossing my arms with spatula in hand. "Ha ha. No, I wouldn't. And I didn't think to change because I wasn't expecting company this early."

He stood, making like he was leaving. "I could come back later…"

"No, I'm just teasing. I'm happy you came by," I replied, leaning on the counter and giving him a kiss.

He placed his hand on my cheek and kissed deeper. Pressing his forehead to mine, he broke away. "I wish I could have been here last night," he whispered.

"Me, too, but it's okay," I responded, straightening up and returning to the pancakes. "Claire probably felt more comfortable with Madeline anyway."

"Speaking of Claire…where is she?"

"Upstairs getting ready," I replied as I removed them and then the bacon.

"Do you need any help?" he asked as I went to the refrigerator, took out the eggs, and grabbed a bowl.

"No, I got it. All I have left are eggs anyway."

I cracked several in it and beat them with a fork. As the music continued to play in the background, I tried to listen through it for movement upstairs. She was taking a long time just to wash up. I poured the eggs into the pan and let them cook for a little before scraping them around.

As soon as they were done, I plated them and moved everything to the island in front of David and then covered them. "I'll think I'll go check on her. She might have fallen asleep in the shower," I remarked as I put the pans in the sink.

Just as I was turning to head out of the room, she walked in. "I think I used all your hot water, so I wouldn't plan on tak-" she broke off, noticing my boyfriend as she dried her hair. "Oh, hi David!" she exclaimed, blushing.

"Good morning, Claire," he greeted as he turned around on the stool and grinned at her. She looked like she forgot how to breathe.

"David surprised me by coming by," I explained, leaning my back against the counter by him. "Oh and breakfast is ready," I added.

She snapped out of her daze and glanced at me and then him. "Are...are you eating with us?" she asked, moving toward the counter and finally taking her eyes off him.

"No, but I will sit with you," he replied, standing.

As he headed over to the table, we fixed our plates and joined him in the nook. He stood waiting behind his chair until we sat and then took his seat next to me and across from her. She seemed embarrassed to eat in front of him, taking small bites and tucking her head. But he wasn't watching her.

"This is really good, Megan," she commented after a long silence.

"I learned from the best," I responded as I cut through my stack of fluffy pancakes. David smiled and then gazed out the window.

She stared at him for a moment, admiring his quiet beauty as I like to do, and I cleared my throat, bringing her out of her awe. Blushing briefly, she turned her attention to her food and then when it passed she looked up at me with a curious expression. "What's with the music?" she asked, crunching a piece of bacon.

"Oh, I wanted something to cook to. It makes it more fun," I replied with a smile. "So did breakfast help? Are you feeling better?"

"Yeah, but I'll probably still go back to bed when I get home."

"I'm sure Justin's sleeping it off, too," I responded. I finished the last bit of my breakfast and pushed the plate away from me. As David stared out the window, Claire looked from him to me and grinned. *What?* I mouthed, wondering what she was thinking.

She didn't answer me, turning her attention to him. "So what are your plans today, David?" she asked, pushing her plate away.

He stood and picked up both of them, taking them to the sink. "I came by to see what Megan planned to do and request if I could join her," he replied, rinsing the dishes and loading them in the dishwasher.

Her grin widened as she looked at me. "I don't have any plans as of yet," I replied, trying not to mimic her expression.

He came back to the table and sat beside me, taking my hand in his and gazing into my eyes. "Well then, we can find something to do together," he responded with his mischievous half-smile. Claire stared, mesmerized by him, as he leaned in and kissed my cheek. He took that moment to stealthily whisper in my ear, "You're welcome to come to the house now, if you like."

I tucked my head and blushed, embarrassed by his audacity in front of her. She was still gawking but snapped out of it with the ringing of her phone. She pulled it out and answered, turning away from us. "Hello? Oh, hi. No, just finished breakfast...what? But...but...okay. I'll be there shortly," she answered and then hung up. "I have to go. Mom says I have to get home to watch the monster while they go to some function," she explained and then sighed. "So much for going back to sleep."

"I'm sorry," I responded, getting up.

We headed toward the living room, Claire dashing up the stairs to get her things. David caressed my hand as we stood at the bottom of the steps, staring at each other and not saying a word. A moment later, she bounded down with her bag, and he and I separated.

"Thanks for having me over and for the great breakfast," she commented, giving me a hug and then whispering in my ear, "Have fun today."

I opened the door as he stood by my side. "It was good to see you again, Claire," he commented, and she tripped over her feet onto the porch.

As I looked past her at the pouring rain, I couldn't bring myself to let her walk home in it. "Would you like a ride?" I asked.

She glanced at the sky and then at me. "Yeah, that'd be nice. Do you mind?"

"I could take her," David offered, and I looked at him, surprised. "You could shower and dress while I'm gone," he explained with a smile.

"Good idea. Do you mind, Claire?"

"Uh...no, I guess," she answered nervously, looking up at him as he passed her.

I glanced at the driveway. "Ooo, and you get to ride in the Bugatti!"

She blushed brightly as he opened an umbrella and coaxed her down the stairs, smiling over his shoulder at me. I hope she doesn't pass out in the car. I smiled back and shut the door, quickly heading up to my room. I didn't have a whole lot of time since she lived right around the corner.

I took a shower and when I got out, I dressed quickly with the thought he should be back soon. I threw on a light dress and fixed my hair, then grabbed a small bag and loaded it with numerous outfits for the next several days. I went into the bathroom and grabbed my necessities and put them in the bag as well.

As I leaned over one of my dresser drawers, a pair of arms wrapped around my waist and I froze. "I see you're getting ready to go," David whispered in my ear and my body tingled.

I turned around and faced him, trying to focus on him and not my urges. "You took longer than I expected. What happened?"

He smiled. "Claire wouldn't exit the car when I arrived at her house. I opened the door, but then had to assist her after several minutes of her just staring at me."

I stifled a laugh. "I am so sorry."

"No need. I offered."

"So did you just leave her in the driveway?" I inquired with a smile.

"No, I'm not that cruel or impatient. I walked her to the door and waited until she was inside, then I left."

"Did her parents see you?"

"No, they must have been busy at the time," he replied, leaning closer. "Are you ready to go?"

"I need to grab shoes and forward the hou...house phone," I replied slowly. He was almost at my lips. But before he could kiss me, I ducked under his arm and went to my closet. I grabbed two pairs and threw them in the bag.

He was leaning against my dresser with a smirk on his lips. Avoiding him, I turned away and headed downstairs with my bag on my arm. I detoured to the kitchen and grabbed the phone, turning it on and going through the necessary steps to forward that line to my cell. I hung it up and when I turned to leave, David stood before me. He pressed his lips to mine before I could get away this time.

"Are you ready to go now?" he asked, backing up.

"Almost...could you call the house phone to see if it worked?" I asked, leaning against the counter. He pulled his cell out of his pocket and dialed the number I gave him. Instead of it ringing, my cell did. "Perfect. Now my dad will think I'm home."

He smiled as I passed him on my way to the door. As soon as he exited, I locked up the house and started down the drive with him right behind me, holding the umbrella mostly over me. He opened the passenger door and an excitement went through me as I climbed in his car.

I'm staying with him at his house for the next couple of days!

The window was cracked, letting the tepid air swirl around the car and then flow out his window as he drove. He must have done that for Claire, knowing the effect his scent has on us humans. An old Pink Floyd song played softly through the speakers while I stared out the window. He sped down the road as I watched the scenery and the sky. The rain came down a little harder, but not enough to blur the view. He shifted gears and I felt his hand on mine, clutching it. I glanced at him, but his focus was on the road and not on me for once.

My glance turned into a stare. He was so stunning in the dim light of the cloudy sky, his eyes intense and watchful. Then they shifted to me and I quickly looked away. He chuckled quietly and my heart fluttered.

He pulled into his driveway and before reaching the gate, he pressed a button to open it. He passed through and drove the darkened road under the full leafed trees. When we reached the clearing, the dull burst of light almost hurt my eyes. The garage door opened and he pulled in, parking next to his BMW.

Before I could open my door, he was at it. I grabbed my bag and stepped out, glancing around the garage. "Madeline's not here?" I inquired, noticing her vehicle missing.

"She's out with Ben today," he replied, taking my hand and leading me up the stairs into the house.

We headed straight for the guest room so I could get settled into my temporary home. I smiled at him as I set my bag on a nearby chair and then sat on the bed. I fell back and sunk in. It was as if I was lying on a bed of feathers, light and soft.

He walked to the other side of it and into a room. "You have a full bathroom," he remarked as a light came on.

I hopped up and joined him. With both tours before, I never saw the whole room, just peeked inside. As I stood in the doorway, my jaw dropped, astonished at the size of it and what it held.

In a little cove sat a full garden tub with exotic soaps and oils and real sponges in a basket on the marble lip surrounding it. A few candles sat in the corner and a large metal sconce hung on the wall above it. In the far corner was an expanded shower with soap and hair products arranged neatly on a shelf. The sink vanity was outfitted with assorted soaps and lotions and a basket of towels and washcloths.

I guess I really didn't need to pack anything but clothes; he had everything covered. I looked at him and asked, "Is all of this for me, or is it usually set up this way?"

He smiled. "Most of it is for you," he replied, leading me out as he turned off the light.

We crossed the foyer to the other side and went straight to the kitchen. I was perplexed as to why he was taking me this way, but then he responded to my confused look. "I took the liberty of picking up some groceries for you. Please feel free to use the kitchen to cook whenever you need to eat," he commented as he showed me where everything was.

I leaned against the counter, taking it all in. "This is so sweet of you. All of it," I commented, blushing.

He touched my cheek and then kissed it. "I want to make sure you're comfortable and have everything you need," he responded softly at my ear.

I turned my head, my lips finding his, and we kissed. "Thank you," I whispered, bowing my head.

He smiled softly and took my hand. We left the kitchen and went into the grand salon, sitting in the sunroom. The view was beautiful even though it was still raining. He put his arm around me, and I leaned against him, enjoying this moment.

"Is there anything you would like to do?" he asked suddenly.

"Nope...this is good," I replied, looking up at him.

He kissed me again and then looked outside. "The rain is letting up and there's a nice breeze. We could go out on the lake," he enticed.

I perked up. "That does sound appealing," I pondered aloud. "Okay, I'm sold."

He stood and took my hand, leading me outside and down the stairs to the patio. We walked past the pool, out the gate, and down the path. It was a soothing stroll, the residual sound of raindrops falling from the leaves as the wind gently nudged the branches and the lapping of the lake on the shore filling the void of conversation.

"It's quiet on the water today," he commented as we meandered onto the dock. There was good reason for that. This wasn't usually the type of weather people like to boat in.

David helped me aboard, and I took a seat in the galley area near a wooden bar sticking out of the back of the boat while he cast off the lines. As we started to drift, he began raising the sails. I watched intently as he worked to get it all ready and then looked away, pretending to admire the lake when he hopped down to join me. His lip curled at the corner as he took the wooden bar and directed the boat as the wind caught the sails. We gradually gained speed and he guided us along until he reached the spot where he wanted to anchor.

"Would you like to go out on the bow?" he asked, standing.

"That sounds adventurous," I responded as he took my hand and helped me up.

Carefully tiptoeing to the front, I sat and waited for him to join me. I leaned back on my palms and relaxed as the boat bobbed gently on the water. The breeze wasn't as strong, and I wondered if that would be a problem for us later.

I stared into the sky, enjoying this moment of tranquility. The clouds moved slowly, twisting and winding among each other with patterns complex and beautiful. I glanced over at David as he leaned back and closed his eyes. Turning toward him, I placed my hand on his chest and moved in to kiss him. His hand quickly grabbed the back of my neck and pulled me in, his lips pressing to mine first. I pushed off and slapped his shoulder as he smiled.

Shaking my head while lying back, I closed my eyes and focused on the lapping of the water against the boat. With the lack of wind and the humidity rising, I started getting hot. All the rain we had last night didn't seem to cool the temperature at all. I turned to David and stared at him, waiting for him to realize I was there.

"Yes?" he questioned without looking.

"I think I'm going to take a dip. I feel sticky."

"Did you bring a swim suit?" he asked, sitting up and leaning forward on his knees as he cocked his head my way.

"In my bag…at the house," I realized, then quickly came up with an alternative. "But I can swim in my underwear," I replied, standing up. He raised a brow as he looked at me, trying to determine if I was serious or not. "It could pass for a bikini."

Steadying myself, I slipped my dress off. He instantly turned his face away and stared at something off to the side as I went to the edge, glancing back at him before diving gracefully into the cool, refreshing water. I swam out and then back and around the boat. He was still on the bow, sitting up and staring off into the distance.

"Don't you want to join me?" I shouted up to him as I treaded water.

I saw him smile, then get up and come to the side, grabbing the rigging as he leaned over to see better. "No, I think I'll stay up here and watch you," he replied with a grin.

"Suit yourself," I remarked as I swam out again, floating for a while.

Closing my eyes, I enjoyed the subtle rocking of the fresh water around my body. It was a shame David didn't want to join me. Wondering what he was doing, I opened my eyes and flipped upright, checking the boat. He was still sitting on the bow staring out over the water.

I swam out farther this time and treaded for a bit, getting a different view. I love water in any form: bathtub, pool, lake, or ocean. I did a couple flips and then glanced back at the boat, curious if he was watching me. As our eyes connected, I smiled. I may love being in the water, and any other time I'd stay out in it for hours, but not today. I have something more demanding of my attention.

I swam back to the boat and as I approached it, I noticed David wasn't there. Going to the rear, I glanced around, but couldn't find him. I swam to the other side, but still no sign. I finally called for him and he appeared.

"Are you ready to come up?" he asked as he crouched down and looked at me. I nodded and he dropped a small rope ladder over the side. When I got close to the top, he offered his hand and I took it as he pulled me up with ease. Once I was aboard, he looked over me and then looked away. "Yes, it could pass for a bikini," he commented with a smirk.

He grabbed a towel laying on one of the benches and handed it to me, trying not to look again. Smiling, I shook my head as I took it. I dried off and slipped my dress on as he busied himself with the sails. As I sat on the seat and rung out my hair, I noticed a cabin beneath the bow.

"What's down below?" I inquired, standing to get a better look.

"A small sanctuary," he replied as he hopped down from the bow. "Would you like to see?" he asked, opening the door.

"Of course I would," I responded, walking closer.

I followed him down the few steps into an open room with oak flooring and walls. To one side was a small U-shaped kitchen with counter space, a sink, and stove and on the other was the navigation hub with all sorts of electronics and meters. In front of us, settees with plush cushions and pillows lined both sides of the room with nooks and cabinets above and below. On the upper part of the wall, large transoms filled the space with dull light.

He led me through the room, stopping at a narrow door to the left that when opened revealed a small bathroom with a sink, toilet, and shower. Ahead of us was a wider wooden door. He slid it open and stepped aside. It was fairly dark and I couldn't make out much of anything except the oversized double bed in the center of the room. The only light came from the two small oval portholes on either side of the wall near the ceiling.

David reached over to a very old looking lamp and turned it on. But instead of flickering like a bulb, a flame appeared. The golden light filled the small room, revealing more details, like the fine linens on the bed, oak lined walls, cabinets, and shelves.

"Amazing," I commented, sitting on the cushy bed.

"Yes, she is," he replied, touching the wall as he looked at it affectionately.

"It's more like a home away from home. Have you ever taken it out on the ocean?" I asked as he turned down the lamp.

"Plenty of times in Massachusetts, for fun and for sport," he responded, taking my hand and lifting me off the bed. "I competed in a few regattas with my father, but most of the time I would take my friends out on her or she was used for family excursions."

"Sounds like fun," I responded, staring into his eyes.

"It was, most of the time," he agreed, turning away and leading me out of the room. "When my parents and I would go sailing, I would have to sleep here while they took the bedroom," he indicated as we walked back through the sitting area. We paused at the stairs and he looked at me again. "I have been up and down the east coast and even across the Atlantic in her."

"That's incredible," I muttered, lost in his green eyes.

He broke his gaze and continued outside, glancing at the sky as he exited. "It will start raining soon. We should head in," he commented.

I joined him on the deck, looking at the sky as well. The clouds were much heavier than before. He moved to start preparing to leave, but I stopped him, turning him to me and placing my hand on his cheek as I leaned closer and kissed him. I wasn't sure why I did it, but I think it was just an opportune moment to do it.

He didn't stop me, slipping his fingers into my hair and holding me to his lips. I parted mine and he did the same, intensifying the kiss. Rain began softly falling on us. I raised my face to the sky and closed my eyes, several drops splashing on my cheeks as he kissed my neck. Then he was gone.

"You should get inside before you get too wet," he suggested as he gently urged me into the cabin.

I turned to protest but gave in as he pulled up the anchor. This was the best place for me. Sitting on the steps, I watched as he went about lowering the sails. Wait…if we weren't using them, then how did he plan to get back? Paddle?

He returned a moment later and sat on the bench out in the rain next to that wood bar he used to direct the boat earlier. Grabbing a metal handle near his feet, he shifted it and an engine came on. Soon we were moving, turning around and heading back to the shore.

I remained in the doorway, watching the scenery pass for a while, and then my eyes strayed to David. He was unbelievably handsome sitting there soaked by the rain as he commanded his ship. Soon the scenery no longer held my attention – he did.

He slowed as he pulled around to the dock and shut off the engine, tying up the boat before retrieving me from the cabin. He quickly helped me off, and we ran up to the house, getting drenched along the way. We were both dripping wet as we entered, but neither of us cared. He scooped me up into his arms and kissed me.

"What have you two been up to?" a voice asked from a corner of the grand salon.

We stopped immediately and looked over to find Madeline sitting in an armchair, a book on her lap. "I took Megan out on the boat and we were caught in a downpour," David replied, gently putting me down and taking my hand as he led me out of the room.

"You should really get out of those damp clothes before either of you get sick," she teased as she raised her book and returned to reading.

He stopped at the guest room door. "You should shower, but be sure to lock the door. I'll be upstairs. When you're done, wait for me in the grand salon with Madeline," he instructed before giving me a kiss and dashing away.

I shut the door and locked it, going into the bathroom and locking that door for good measure. I wasn't sure why he insisted I do it, but I did without question. I slipped off my soaked clothes, hanging them on the side of the garden tub, and hopped in the shower.

I was curious about trying the exotic soap and hair products he bought for me. They smelled divine and made my hair and body feel so clean, especially after swimming in the lake. After I finished, I dried and put the lotion on that was in there as well and then went into the bedroom and dressed in casual wear, fixed my hair, and left the room. I joined Madeline in the grand salon as was requested.

She was still reading as I entered. "So how was your day with Ben?" I asked as I sat in an armchair next to her.

She read a little while longer, then laid the book on her lap and looked at me, smiling softly. "Not good. I took him to the student gallery on campus, but he just wasn't into it. He kept asking me to bring him back here. When I told him we couldn't, he got angry and started going off about me being a slave or something. I finally said enough...and broke it off," she replied quietly, bowing her head.

I reached over and touched her hand. "I'm so sorry..."

"He was using me...wanting to get closer to David. He wanted proof, to reveal what he was, but instead I saw what Ben was," she replied as red tears trickled down her cheek.

I glanced around, trying to find something to wipe up the red mess, but there wasn't a tissue in sight. I patted her hand and told her I'd be right back, running to the hall bathroom and grabbing tissue from there. She was calm when I re-entered with them in hand. As I wiped her cheeks, she looked up at me, the red from the tears and irritation accentuating her light green eyes.

"I should have known there was an ulterior motive. What a jerk," I mumbled, switching tissues.

"I thought after erasing his memory at the park and feeding him the new story, he would have dropped this witch hunt. Instead, it seems to have made it worse. He has this vendetta against David."

I quickly glanced toward the stairs and then back at her. "Does he know about this?"

She lowered her eyes. "Yes, he does. He was using me as well, but not like Ben."

I felt a little relieved and a whole lot angry. "I'll have a talk...with both of them."

She sighed and gave me a hug. "Thank you for being here. I'm excited about the next couple of days. Maybe David will let us have some time together," she commented, perking up.

I smiled and collected the bloody tissues. "That'd be nice," I replied, getting up and heading over to the trashcan.

Oddly, as I entered the kitchen my stomach growled. I glanced at the clock on the microwave and realized I hadn't eaten lunch. Looking in the refrigerator, I pulled out a couple items to make a salad and threw them together in a bowl. I sat at the island and began to eat, Madeline coming in shortly after and joining me.

"Oh yeah, I guess it's dinnertime," she remarked, sitting across from me. Is she going to watch me like David does?

I finished what I was chewing and glanced over my shoulder. "What's taking him so long?" I asked.

She looked up at the ceiling and then at me. "He's on his way now. He was talking with Cary."

I nodded and went back to eating. He showed up a moment later, surprised to find us in the kitchen. "I was hungry," I replied with a slight smile. I was still angry with him for what he was doing behind my back.

"That's what it's there for," he stated, sitting next to me.

I looked at him as he smiled at me, but I wasn't smiling. "So Madeline broke up with Ben today," I casually commented, stabbing the remaining pieces of lettuce.

He jerked his head in her direction and she shrugged. "You were right," she responded.

"I know what you were trying to do," I remarked, and he tried to interrupt me, but I continued without acknowledging him, "and I know he was doing the same thing, but it's not right. You're playing with emotions," I lectured as I indicated to her, "and lives."

His eyes dropped and he faced forward, shaking his head and pursing his lips. "I was trying to help us, protect us. I asked Madeline to convince him to give her another chance, using her to find out what his suspicions were about us," he replied and then raised his eyes to mine. "But I advised her to break up with him after our double date. He was getting too close, and it was becoming dangerous," he explained.

"Unfortunately, I couldn't," she added. "By that point, I was starting to really like him."

"So why couldn't you just let him in?" I asked, pushing the bowl away from me.

"I don't trust him," he responded firmly.

"Neither do I," she agreed.

I looked between the two of them and sighed. "Fair enough, but it's still wrong."

"I did what I had to. I caught him eavesdropping the night of the party…on our conversation in the library," he defended.

I thought back to that night and how both of them had acted. It all made sense now – they weren't trying to work it out, they were manipulating each other. "Don't worry. I'm going to have a nice, long conversation with Ben once I'm back home," I grumbled.

David turned to me and took my hands in his, gazing into my eyes. "Please forgive me, Megan. I shouldn't have done it."

I paused, trying to decipher what was going on behind those emerald eyes. "Is there anything else I should know?" I asked quietly.

"No, nothing else," he replied without hesitation.

I stood up and put my arms around him as I gave him a kiss. "I forgive you, but no more duplicity, please," I whispered in his ear. He nodded and I went over to Madeline, giving her a hug as well. "I'm sorry you were dragged into this. They shouldn't have played with your emotions like that."

"It's okay...I agreed to it. I just didn't expect Ben to be so aggressive about going after David."

"Never underestimate the power of puppy love," I replied, grabbing my bowl and cleaning it in the sink. I glanced out the window, watching the rain fall at a slant. I dried each piece and then returned them to their appropriate places. "So, what should we do now?" I asked, leaning against the sink and looking from one downtrodden face to the other. "Something fun?"

Madeline perked up suddenly, a smile on hers. "We could go out...to a club or something."

David shot her a look, narrowing his eyes. "I'm not sure that's a good idea," he responded.

I came over to the island and leaned on it, looking from one to the other as they stared each other down. "I don't know...I think it's a good idea."

She smiled. "Maybe we can see if Cary will go, too!"

"Now you're going too far. He can't be around that many people. Besides, you're only seventeen, Megan. You have to be at least eighteen to get into a club."

"I'm sure either of you could charm my way in," I reasoned with a grin.

"And this is the kind of exposure Cary needs. He'll do fine; I'll make sure of it," she argued.

He looked at me with disappointment in his eyes as he contemplated whether to agree or not. "All right, but only for a little while."

"Deal," she agreed, booking it from the room.

"I'll go change," I commented as I started to walk away, but he caught my arm.

"This is dangerous. I don't think you understand that."

"I do understand and it'll be fine. Come on…we all need to have some fun," I replied, trying to pry his fingers from me.

He sighed and let go. "I'll be waiting in the BMW," he commented flatly as he left the room.

I don't like him like this, but after what he did, I really don't care. Maybe clubbing will brighten everyone's mood. I went to my room and changed into a short dress, applied a little makeup, slipped on heels, and grabbed my purse. I met Madeline and Cary in the hall, she grinning wide and clenching onto him for dear life while he looked as apathetic as ever.

"David's in the car," I stated as I led the way toward the garage.

As I was opening the door, my phone rang. I told them to go ahead while I answered it. "Hey Megan. How are things?" Dad asked. Another day of checking on me.

"Good. I'm getting ready to go to a movie with my friends," I lied. My bad habits were starting up again.

"A double date, a sleepover, and now movies with friends…I'm glad you're at least keeping occupied."

"I have to have something to pass the time," I commented.

"Is David joining you?" he asked.

"No, he's working. But we have Ben and Justin," I replied, digging deeper and deeper. "So how's everything down there?"

"Good. We just got back to the house after spending the day on the yacht. A storm came up and forced us to dock."

"It's been raining here since yesterday," I remarked as I peeked around the door. David was glaring at me, still grumpy. "Uh oh, they're giving me *that* look," I commented, using that as a way to get off the phone.

"Well, I'll let you go." It worked. I said goodbye and hung up.

I closed the door and dashed down the stairs, running to the car. Climbing in the front seat, I was barely able to shut the door before David whipped out of the garage. He sped down the slick drive and nearly collided with the gate as it opened. Still upset.

Madeline gabbed in the back, thinking someone was listening to her, but all of us were preoccupied with other things. David was focused on the road, I was focused on him, and Cary was probably translating sci-fi movie quotes into binary code. But she didn't seem to care that no one responded to her. She was happy just to talk.

I reached over and touched David's arm, trying to get him to look at me. When he didn't, I decided to try to have a conversation. "Can you believe Madeline talked Cary into coming? That was a total shock," I commented as low as I could, so neither could hear me.

He took the downtown off ramp and sped through the damp, bumpy streets, still not looking at me or saying a word. Fine. I can play that game, too. I faced forward and crossed my arms, staying completely quiet as I stared out the side window and focused on the jazz music playing on the radio. He can go sulk in a corner all night while I dance with any and everyone. I've never been to a club and I was determined to enjoy it with or without him.

He parked on a dark side street and we all got out, looking around. Without a word, he started down the sidewalk and we followed, walking several blocks to our unknown destination. I didn't bother holding his hand or arm since he was being so cold and instead just walked beside him. Madeline jabbered the whole way, but at least it broke the tense silence between us.

We turned a corner, and directly in front of us stood an unassuming building with blacked out windows and a sign at the top that was difficult to read. She finally stopped chattering and stared at it, a little dismayed. I guess she expected somewhere better, but he decided on an older club, probably because they'd be more lax about my age or wouldn't even card.

A large man stood at the door as we walked up, no line or crowd outside. David pulled money out of his wallet and handed it to the man who hadn't bothered to acknowledge us. He took one look and opened the door, allowing us to enter. That was easy.

We walked down a dark tunnel, the music muted and rattling the walls as lights occasionally stretched along the ceiling. I stayed close to David, taking hold of his arm as we trudged through the narrow hallway. When we came to the end, the room opened up.

The song playing was thumping and lights were dancing everywhere. From the looks of the outside, I was surprised to see so many people inside, crammed like sardines in a can. Madeline held tight to Cary and I did the same with David as we pushed our way through the crowd.

When we found a decent spot, she started dancing around a frozen Cary. I had to laugh at his expression, completely bewildered and scared, as she whirled and jumped, looking comfortable and at home in such a place. David took hold of my wrist and started walking, patting him on the shoulder as we passed. I think I might have glimpsed a smile on his lips.

We stopped not far from them, and he stood waiting for me to do something. I started swaying to the beat and then danced more and more as it flowed through me. He put his hand on my hip and danced with me, a smile growing across his lips. Okay, that took a lot less time than I expected.

More often than not, women tried to maneuver their way between him and me, but it was David who turned them away. I noticed every once in a while, the same would happen to Cary, but Madeline was fierce and kept a lot of them at bay. She herself was popular with the guys, but she was too focused on him to bother.

It was hot in there, so it didn't take long to get sticky and dehydrated. David went to check on Madeline and Cary while I hit the bar for a drink – non-alcoholic, of course. As I waited for my order, some man started hitting on me. I politely declined his advances, saying I was waiting for my boyfriend, but he remained persistent. Again, I declined and as soon as my drink was ready, I rushed away.

I sipped it as I pushed through the crowd toward David and the others. "Having fun?" Madeline asked as I walked up.

"Yeah, but I'm not sure I'll do this again," I replied, taking another sip. David had a relieved look on his face as he put his arm around me.

She went back to dancing with a stoic Cary but was interrupted by a tall guy trying to cut in. Thinking it wasn't a big deal, she danced with him for a little while, but then turned back to Cary, remembering what she promised. I finished my drink and set it on a nearby table, resuming my dance with David.

"This is fun," I commented to him, resting my arm on his shoulder as I did a cha-cha.

He smiled and my heart fluttered. "Yes, it is, surprisingly."

I smiled back and then checked on Madeline and Cary, feeling obligated to do so. She was having a blast, and I think I might have seen a slight smile on his face. This was good for him; good for all of us, really. I turned my attention back to David, feeling content.

Everything was going fine until the guy from the bar found me, more drunk than he was before. "Hey baby, why don't you ditch this pretty boy and come dance with me?" he slurred as he grabbed my wrist.

"No, I'm not interested. Please let go," I snapped, jerking away.

It didn't take long for David to get between us. "You should leave," he growled.

"I'm not leaving!" he yelled as he swayed. "Not without her," he demanded, pointing at me.

David glared at him for a moment, considering the many things he could do to him, but then stepped back. My harasser turned to me, smiling triumphantly and thinking he won just as Madeline slipped into place and smiled at him. His attention off me and now on her, David took my arm and we joined Cary, letting her handle the drunk.

"You will go to the pay phone over there and call a cab. Go directly home and get in bed," she instructed. He repeated what she said and then disappeared. She waited a moment and then joined us. "See, no one gets hurt or exposed," she commented, passing between us and resuming her dance with Cary.

We stayed a little longer and then I finally told David I was ready to go. My body was tired and drained. He let Cary and Madeline know, and we all exited the club. She was still so full of energy as we walked to the car, dancing to inaudible music. As I held David, I just looked at her and rolled my eyes.

"Oh come on, Megan. You can't be tired!" she exclaimed.

"Oh yes, I can. It's late and I'm not a creature of the night," I replied. David and Madeline laughed and even Cary chuckled quietly. "Glad you find my humanity so amusing," I grumbled as I climbed in the front seat.

I didn't remember the drive back to the house. It was as if we were sitting at a light in town and then magically transported to the garage. I opened my eyes to a bright light and David staring at me. I must have fallen asleep. He helped me out and carried me into the house, setting my weary body on the loveseat in the grand salon.

"You need to eat," he commented from the kitchen as he sifted through items in the cabinets and fridge. He grabbed something and walked over, handing it to me. "Drink," he commanded.

I took a sip of the cold soda, letting it burn down my throat. I heard him throwing something together at the stove but I didn't bother looking. I took another sip, letting it sit in my mouth until it warmed and then swallowed. Another sip and I was feeling better.

I got up and joined him, sitting at the island. He turned and pushed a plate of food toward me. "Your sugar was low; that's why you felt tired and weak. Eat," he ordered.

I stuck my fork into a carrot coin and put it in my mouth, repeating the motions with the rest of the food and feeling rejuvenated with each bite. "You'll make a great doctor," I smiled, cutting a piece of meat. I poked it with my fork and held it in the air, staring at it. "How come you never chose that profession before?"

He sat beside me and watched as I brought it to my lips. "I didn't think I was strong enough to be around humans so consistently."

"That makes sense. Hospitals don't need a vampire running around causing more problems," I teased. He didn't find it funny. "I'm kidding," I clarified, setting my fork down. I was full and feeling more like myself.

He took the plate and scraped the remains into the trashcan, then took it to the sink and washed it with the other dishes. I remained at the island, waiting for him to say something, but he never did so I got up and went into the grand salon.

"Where did Cary and Madeline go?" I asked, looking around.

"Hunting," he replied without looking at me.

"Together? Do you think..."

He stopped what he was doing and stared at the sink and then out the window. "Wouldn't that be funny..." he muttered.

He put the dishes away and turned out the lights, leaving the Tiffany floor lamp in the grand salon casting a dim glow. He strolled into the room and took a seat next to me on the couch. Reaching up, he touched my cheek and I leaned into it. I closed my eyes and remained completely still. I could feel him moving closer, his breath on my skin and then his lips on it.

"It's getting late. You should go to bed," he whispered, kissing my neck.

"But…I'm not…tired anymore," I replied breathlessly.

"Then what do you want to do?" he asked softly, his lips on my chin.

"This…this is…good…"

They found mine and we kissed, gentle at first and then becoming more intense. My hands moved down his arms and when I reached his elbows, I dropped them and slipped them under his shirt, caressing his body with my fingertips. I forgot how good he felt. I moved closer, getting on my knees and forcing him to lie back.

I kissed down his neck to his chest, unbuttoning his shirt so I could continue, but he stopped me. I looked at him as he lifted my chin, sitting up as he leaned me back and kissed down my neck. He paused at the top of my chest, placing his hand over my heart, and then he bent over me, lowering his head to it. As he did, he removed his hand and placed his ear over it, resting there.

My pulse quickened as did my breathing. He tried to calm me but only made things worse. Then he sat back and smiled. "You get excited too easily," he commented, his fingers gliding from my cheek down my neck.

"What do you expect? Your head was just on my chest."

"I only wanted to listen to your heart…much like you listen to my breathing."

"Still…it's a sensitive place."

His fingers traced my neckline. "I know," he replied with a grin.

"Why do you do it then?"

"I like your reaction, the affect I have on you."

"So you like control," I surmised, getting on my knees again and leaning into him, "and power," I continued, putting my knee between his legs and getting closer to his face, my hand on his chest as I pushed him back, "making me do what you want me to do," I whispered with my lips on his neck. He remained calm. Darn it, it isn't working.

I moved to his chin, my lips caressing his cool skin. Still no response. I stopped above his mouth and he smiled, his teeth bright in the dull light. He knew what I was trying. I lifted my eyes and smirked. Pressing my lips to his, he closed his eyes as I gently kissed him. Then I stopped and sat up.

"I think I'll go to bed now," I stated, faking a yawn and standing up.

"Oh, no you won't," he responded, grabbing my wrist and pulling me toward him so I was lying on top of him. He held me to his lips, refusing to let me up.

"Oops! Are we interrupting something?" Madeline asked, surprising us.

He let go and I rolled off the loveseat, hitting the floor with a thud. He laughed as he sat up and extended his hand, helping me to my feet. "No, not at all," he replied, still chuckling.

I narrowed my eyes at him and then turned to Madeline and Cary who were standing at the entrance to the grand salon. Both were smiling. "Did you two have a nice time?" I inquired, trying to get the attention off David and me.

"If you think killing a defenseless animal could be 'nice', then yes, it was a blast," replied Cary, saying more words than I've ever heard him say.

She took a seat across from us and looked from me to David. "I guess we don't need to ask if you two had fun," she commented slyly.

He smiled at her and turned to me. "So are you ready for bed now?"

My face burned. "Yeah, I think so."

We said good night to them and then headed out of the room. Walking down the hall and crossing the foyer, my face was still hot. "That was so embarrassing," I whispered loudly, burying my head in his shoulder.

He rubbed my arm and laughed quietly. "It's nothing to be embarrassed about. We were only kissing and nothing more," he rationalized as he opened the bedroom door for me. He flipped on the light, and I went to the bathroom to get changed. When I came out, he was standing beside the bed waiting for me. "Would you like me to stay until you fall asleep?"

"Yes, I would. Tonight should be no different than any other night," I replied, slipping under the covers.

He sat next to me, scooting back to the headboard. I gave him a kiss and then laid my arm across his stomach as I rested my head on his chest, getting comfortable. He turned out the light and rubbed my shoulder as I closed my eyes. I wasn't really tired yet, but I needed to try to sleep.

What will I do tomorrow? The rain had tapered off and they were calling for partly cloudy skies, so David will be sleeping. I can't leave unless I ask for his keys…no I'll hang around here, maybe swim, walk around the woods, sit by the lake. Hopefully, I can waste enough of the day doing that. Maybe I'll call Ben and set up a meeting for Thursday.

The more I thought, the more tired I became. I moved, trying to find a more comfortable position. As if reading my mind, David turned on his side and faced me. I nestled into the bed, letting it envelop me, and nuzzled against his chest. This was how I wanted to fall asleep. Concentrating on his breathing, I let myself slowly drift away.

It took a moment to realize I was at David's the following morning. When it finally registered, I sighed happily. It was comforting knowing he was right upstairs, with me, but not.

It was fairly early, the sun shining brightly outside and pouring through the sheer curtains. It was funny how the guest room was nothing like the other bedrooms in the house. It was airy and open, letting the sunshine in instead of shunning it away.

I climbed out of bed, stretched, and headed to the bathroom to get my day going. After my shower, I dressed in jean shorts and a baby doll tee and headed to the kitchen to make breakfast. The house was so quiet and empty…and not warm or welcoming.

I tried not to make too much noise as I fixed my meal, not sure if I'd really disturb them or not. As I plated my food, I looked out the window and decided to eat on the terrace. It was much nicer outside in the fresh air, hearing the birds sing and the water lapping the shore in the distance. It was beautiful here, almost like I was somewhere far away from Richmond.

After I finished eating, I stayed outside and enjoyed the sunshine and serenity. It was a shame David could never experience this. As I let the sun soak into my skin, I thought about becoming like him. To have to give up friends, family…the sun. Would I ever be ready?

The choice was becoming more difficult the more I thought about it. I love David and want to be with him forever, but that really means forever. It's not like years on earth and eternity in the afterlife. And if I choose not to, I'll grow old while he stays the same. He won't want to be with me when my skin starts to sag and my hair turns white. And by then, I won't want to be changed.

Of course, I may not make it to becoming old and gray. My mother died young and her mother did as well. Who knows how far back it goes. Who's to say the same fate won't befit me? My dad's genes aren't that strong in me.

Damned if I do and damned if I don't.

I hate being alone. I always think of the worst things when I am and then I get upset. I looked up at the house toward David's room. The windows were all covered, not an ounce of light able to seep in. I could sneak in there and try to talk to him, but how coherent would he really be? I could call Claire, but that won't work because she's not in on the secret.

No one. I had no one to talk to about my dilemma.

I sighed as I grabbed my dishes and headed inside to clean them. I needed to get my mind off this because if I didn't, it'd hound me all day. As I washed, I thought about what to do next, finally coming up with something as I dried them.

After replacing the dishes in the cabinet and drawers, I went back to my room and put on tennis shoes, figuring a walk around the property would distract me. I slipped out the terrace door, leaving it unlocked so I could get back in, and jogged down the stairs. Stopping at the pool, I checked the water temperature. A little cool, but the day would only be getting hotter.

I shut the gate and paused on the path, figuring out which way I should go. Choosing left, I headed into the woods and took my time enjoying my little hike. When I reached the fence, I followed it a bit and then turned and headed across to the other side of the property. It was overgrown throughout, and I regretted wearing shorts as vines and briars whipped at my shins, but I was no longer thinking about my problem.

I crossed the drive and when I reached the fence on the other side, I decided to follow it to the lake. When I finally got there, I was ready for a break. Hot and sweaty, I sat on the dock, removed my socks and shoes, and put my scratched-up legs into the water. It stung at first, but soon the coolness relieved it. I leaned back on my palms and rested.

Hearing an approaching boat, I looked up to see it slowing down in front of me. I made eye contact with the driver and then went back to sunbathing. The man on the boat never said a word, just sped off. A couple minutes later, another boat passed with music blaring, but they never slowed. By the third boat, I decided it was time to go in. The lake was much more popular today. I grabbed my shoes and socks and dashed up the path to the house.

When I got to the patio, I rinsed my feet off at a spigot and headed inside. I looked around – still empty, still quiet. I went to the kitchen and threw something together for lunch and then tried to find a TV. I had to break this silence and hear some human voices.

I finally found one hidden under a cabinet. It was small, but it'd do. I turned it on and found a good channel, then sat at the island and watched it as I ate. It was a talk show, but at least it was an entertaining topic – makeovers. I finished the show and then cleaned, putting everything back as it was before heading to the guest room to change into a bathing suit.

While I was changing, my phone rang. "Hello?" I answered as I applied sun block.

"Hey Megan! Where are you? I've been trying to get in touch with you all morning. I went by the house and you weren't there, but your car was," Claire answered, exasperated.

Crap. I didn't think about what would happen if my friends came over. "Oh, I…I'm out," I replied.

"Where? Can I meet you? Justin's doing some family thing today and I'm all alone."

"Well…I'm actually at David's…I mean with David," I quickly corrected.

"Oh…okay. Well, I'll let you get back to what you were doing," she replied, dejected.

I felt bad for her. "What about Erin? Is she available?"

"No, she's in some sports camp this week."

"Oh. I'm really sorry. I'll make it up to you. Why don't we do something later in the week?" I asked, hoping to raise her spirits.

"Yeah, okay. I'll call you," she replied, a little happier.

"Just relax today…take a day for yourself," I encouraged.

She was quiet. "You know, that's not a bad idea. I think I'll go shopping and maybe get a mani-pedi," she decided, much perkier.

"Sounds ideal. I'll talk to you later," I remarked and hung up.

Grabbing a towel, I threw it over my arm and left the room, heading to the basement to get to the pool this time. I went out and laid my things on a lounge chair. I dove in and came up gasping – it was a lot colder than I expected. The sun touching the surface only warmed the top.

I swam a little while longer and then decided to hop in the hot tub. I sat in it for several minutes and when I was heated up enough, I dove back into the pool. I even sat out and tanned for a while. One last swim and I was ready to go in. I dried off and went inside, jogging up the stairs to the terrace door.

Locking it, I went to my room and hopped in the shower. I cranked up the hot water and stood there for a long time enjoying the warmth. When I had enough, I washed up and got out, then dried and went into the room, glancing at the clock as I passed it. Still several more hours before David wakes. As I slipped on my jean shorts from earlier, I thought about what we could do tonight.

I tucked both phones into my pockets, figuring I needed to have them on me in case I decided to wander again. I brushed my hair and put it in a braid, then grabbed my top. As I pulled it over my head, I smiled, happy that David was in my life and I was safe.

Then suddenly, everything went dark.

# Chapter 36
## An Unfortunate Trip

I wasn't sure what happened in the moments that followed. I wasn't unconscious or asleep but completely aware of everything. Darkness surrounded me and I couldn't move, being restrained by something. And that something didn't speak or make a sound, giving no explanation as to what they wanted or why they were doing this.

It moved slowly through the dark, dragging me along a corridor and then down stairs. I tried to scream, make some sort of noise to alert someone, but couldn't. A cold, leathery hand clasped tight to my mouth and a single arm constricted my body like a python does its prey. I kicked, trying to get loose, but it was no use.

As my eyes began to gradually adjust, I realized we were in a tunnel. It was fairly narrow, barely able to fit our two bodies, and tall. A sliver in the wall nearby provided just enough light to see some details. Maybe I could see who had me. I jerked, trying again to get free and catch a glimpse of my captor, but to no avail.

"You might as well calm down. I don't want to have to give you a concussion," a female voice hissed in my ear. She moved from behind me and paused to look around as she held me to the wall. I fought even harder, thinking I had a chance. "This would be a lot easier if you would stop thrashing," she growled.

I couldn't see her face, but I saw the glint of her eyes. Without warning, she dropped me to the floor, splaying me on my stomach against the hard ground. Sitting on my legs, she pulled my arms back and tied them together.

"Who are you? Where are you taking me?" I shouted, panicked.

She cackled, and a chill went through me as she tied my feet. Leaning forward, she forced a gag in my mouth. "You should have trusted your instincts, believed what you saw," she whispered in my ear, kissing my cheek with her icy lips before picking me up and throwing my bound body over her shoulder.

Odette.

I screamed, but the gag prevented any sound from coming out. My mind raced as I tried to comprehend what was going on. How was she out during the day? How did she get in the house? Where were we? What does she plan to do with me?

A dim glow cut the darkness as she opened a door and pushed aside a curtain. We were out of the tunnel and entering a room, one with a screen and rows of chairs – David's theater. He has secret passages in his house? So he wasn't joking…

The brilliance of the game room nearly blinded me as we exited. The sun shined bright outside, glistening off the pool water and reflecting into the room as the light scattered on the walls and ceiling. She set me down, leaning my constrained body against the patio doors and resting for a moment. Quickly turning away, she squatted on the floor and breathed heavy like she had just run a marathon.

*Tired, Odette? Why might that be?* I mentally asked, giving her a smug look.

It was now apparent how she could move about in the daylight. She was dressed in a heavy, black, floor-length cloak with a hood that completely covered her face. The sleeves were extra long, but she was wearing elbow length gloves for good measure. No light could touch her.

"Ready to go, love?" she asked, peeking out of the darkness of her hood as she reached up and pulled down a mask. Only her eyes showed, burning into mine. "Oh, and thank you for leaving the door unlocked. It made it that much easier to get in," she continued, her voice muffled slightly.

Great. I'm the cause of my own demise. I tried again to yell through the gag, but all that came out were grunts. She laughed as she grabbed me and threw my struggling body over her shoulder once again before heading out the door into the sunshine.

She jogged up the side and around the garage to a waiting car parked in the shadows. Could Brian be in it? I glanced inside as we passed, but the windows were too dark to see anything.

She opened the trunk and dropped me inside, her eyes grinning as she started to shut it, but then stopped. "Oh, I almost forgot," she commented as she reached into my pockets and took my phones. She slammed the trunk and I was left alone in the dark. I felt the car lurch forward and speed down the road. It slowed and then sped off again.

Was this it? My decision made for me?

No, I can't give up.

I glanced around, trying to find something to help me. They always said to break out a taillight to alert the police or other drivers, but my hands were behind my back and my feet were tied together. If we stopped, I could kick the trunk and signal to anyone nearby that I was in there. But how soon before that happened? I didn't even know my destination.

Thinking some more, I decided to at least attempt to get my hands in front of me instead of leaving them behind me. I had seen in movies how they did it, and I had nothing better to do than try. I curled into a fetal position and then slowly uncurled as I moved my legs through my arms. I pointed my toes and arched my back, bringing them around my feet. Thank God for ballet and gymnastics.

It felt better, but I was still tied up in a trunk. The car sped on, never seeming to stop. I continued to look for something to loosen my ropes, finding a sharp piece of metal sticking out of the side panel. I rubbed the rope against it, hoping for an easy slice through, but it was too thick. I refused to give up, though, figuring if I had some of it cut it'd be better than nothing.

As I worked, the sound of the tires on asphalt changed to the grinding of dirt. Are we there already? I sawed even faster. We traveled along that road for a while and then the car stopped suddenly. I halted what I was doing and dropped my arms as I listened. Silence. What was going on?

Hearing a muffled voice, I moved to the back of the trunk and concentrated on it, trying to make out what was being said. "But Brian, I have to stop…I'm exhausted. She took a lot out of me and the sun is so bright here," Odette whined. "As soon as it goes down and I feed, I'll get on the road and travel all night without stopping, unless for gas. Okay…I will…okay…I love you." And then there was silence again.

So Brian isn't here, but she's taking me to him. And she has to feed before she does, which means I'll have an opportunity to escape…unless she plans to feed on me. No, Brian wouldn't allow that. He'll want me whole and alive.

A door slammed suddenly and then the trunk opened. I looked up, blinded by a sunbeam hitting my face as it shone between the tree branches. "We had to make an unexpected stop," Odette huffed as she reached in and pulled me out.

As she swung me around, I took in my surroundings. We were in the woods, deep, parked in an overgrown driveway off a dirt road. She was taking me into a house, small, rundown, and boarded up. It was old and had a small porch that was falling off it, but nothing else distinguishable. There were no other houses within view.

The door creaked loudly as she forced it open and rushed inside, slamming it behind us. The room was all open, no dividers at all. Kitchen, dining room, living room, and bedroom – all one big room. The only thing that was separate was the bathroom.

She took me over to what I assumed was the living room and dropped me on a dusty rug in front of the fireplace. She removed her cloak and then crouched down beside me and stared. Leaning close, she ran her long, sharp nails down my cheek and grinned.

"You *are* beautiful. I can see why Brian is so interested in you. Well, and the fact that you belong to David," she muttered, cackling. I tried to say something, but the gag prevented me. "Oh, right. I guess I can remove that now. No one will hear you scream out here," she commented as she untied it and pulled it away.

I breathed deep and coughed, dust getting in my lungs, and then looked up at her with pleading eyes. "Why are you doing this?" I questioned, wiggling myself toward her.

She stood and gazed down at me like I was a filthy rodent. "Because Brian wants you. I'm not sure for what yet...maybe just to kill you or make you a vampire like he did me, though that could backfire like it did before," she replied, the last part under her breath as she dropped to the dilapidated couch.

"He...he made you?" I asked, astonished. I wonder if David knew that.

"Yes. He chose me because he wanted to be with me forever."

"Really..." I responded, surprised Brian could commit to anyone that long.

"Really," she replied, a bit offended. "He told me so the first night he drank from me."

"Are you sure that wasn't just his way of getting you to give in to him?"

"I don't have to defend our love to you," she growled and then closed her eyes and took a deep breath. She opened them a moment later and then looked at me and tilted her head. "What do you know anyway? David doesn't even care enough about you to change you. He probably hasn't even tasted your blood yet."

Something about her tone and look infuriated me. "No, he hasn't, but he does have plans to change me, just not now," I snapped back. "At least he has the decency to give me a choice."

She remained calm, still smiling. "Oh, I had a choice, as if I needed one. I knew we were meant to be from the moment I first saw him," she continued, looking at the fireplace as she reminisced. Then she turned back to me, glaring. "He saved me," she remarked sharply.

"How romantic," I commented.

"At least he told me what he was rather than keep it a secret," she scoffed.

She was trying to make me upset, but it wasn't going to work. I knew David's reason for not telling me initially and I accepted it. She flipped her hair and smirked, thinking she got the better of me. My eyes caught the glimmer of a necklace around her neck.

"Is that from your dear, sweet Brian?" I asked, pointing to it.

"Yes, thanks to one of our most recent victims," she grinned maliciously. "She wasn't going to need it anymore."

"Do you get gifts like that from him frequently – jewelry from dead women?"

She narrowed her eyes. "Not everyone is as rich as your boyfriend," she hissed.

I scooted closer. "Do you really believe Brian loves you?"

"Of course he does," she growled.

"So you're not threatened by the fact he wants me, that we'll be competing for his affection?" I egged.

I could see the hate and rage consuming her as it twisted her face. She raised her hand to slap me but stopped midair and grinned. "No, I'm not threatened. There's something bigger planned for you," she replied calmly as she lowered it. Lying back, she grabbed her cloak and closed her eyes. "Now shut up or I'll gag you again. I need sleep," she grumbled, covering herself.

This is my opportunity. Once she's out, I probably have an hour or two before she'll wake again. I need to find my phones. If I can get at least one, I can call David and let him know what's going on. But first, I need to figure out how I'm going to look for them. Hopping around will be too loud, as will scooting across the floor. I could roll, but then I won't be able to see anything and will get dizzy. My last option is to crawl on my elbows and knees.

Deciding the latter was best, I quietly got up and crawled toward the kitchen area. Halfway across the room, I had to stop because my elbows felt raw. I balled up and rested a moment, then pressed on, bearing the pain.

There was a counter jutting out from the wall by the door. I got to my feet and glanced around, seeing if I could find the phones. On a broken-down bed in the corner was a large purse, new and not at all dusty. It had to be hers. Hopefully, the phones were in it.

I slowly kneeled and crawled toward it, stopping to rest once more and then forcing myself to hurry. I reached it and rested my elbows on the tattered bedspread. Grabbing the purse, I dragged it toward me as I glanced back at Odette to make sure she was still sleeping. The coast clear, I started my search.

I reached inside and felt around for anything that could be a phone, pulling it out to check. Makeup compact, wallet, her phone…but no sign of mine. I checked the outer pockets and finally found the one David gave me. If any, this would be the one I wanted to call from. I glanced over my shoulder again as I slipped it into my pocket and then put all of her things back into the purse.

As I moved away from the bed, I noticed something bright red on the bedspread. I looked at my elbows and cursed, then anxiously glanced her way. Would she smell the blood? I dropped to the floor and quickly scooted across it on my knees, holding them close to my side. I was almost at the kitchen when she suddenly sat up, her fangs bared.

"Where do you think you're going?" she snarled, jumping over the couch and racing toward me.

I fell back and glanced behind me. "The bathroom," I replied as she stood over me and stared at the drying blood on my elbows.

She closed her eyes and inhaled, then opened them, their color almost red. "Well go!" she shouted, grabbing my arm and forcing me to my feet. She kicked the door open and pushed me in, nearly making me fall flat on my face. I caught myself and went to shut it, but she stopped it with her foot. "Ah ah ahh. Leave it open," she commanded.

I unbuttoned my shorts and shimmied them off, sitting on the nasty stool and going, though it was difficult with her standing there watching me. I pulled my shorts back on, making sure not to lose or expose the phone. As I buttoned them, my other phone rang, still in her purse.

Her face lit up as she glanced over at it and then at me. "Looks like you have a caller," she taunted as she went to the bed and pulled it out. Hopefully, she doesn't notice the other one missing. She looked at the screen. "Unknown…hmm, who might that be?" she questioned as she answered it. "Oops! Too late," she teased and then slipped it into her pocket.

"That might have been my dad. If I don't call him back, he'll get concerned and may call the police. May I check?" I asked as nicely as I could, putting my bound hands out expectantly.

She laughed. "Do you think I'm stupid?" she questioned, shoving them away. Then it rang again. "Ooo…could that be Daddy? Let's find out," she grinned maliciously as she answered it. "Hello? Oh, Mr. Caldwell…yes, I'm a friend of Megan…oh just hanging out with her today…well, um, she's tied up at the moment," she smirked as she looked me up and down. "Uh huh…uh huh…okay. I'll give her the message. It was nice talking to you. Bye," she responded and then hung up. "Oh, I hope I didn't get you in trouble."

"You evil witch!" I yelled as I tried to hit her, but she stopped me.

"You should learn to control your temper," she lectured, slipping the phone back into her pocket and holding tight to my arm. Dragging me into the living room, she forced me down onto a chair and then went back to lying on the couch with the cloak over her. "No disturbances, no sounds," she shouted from underneath. I glared at her even though she couldn't see me, but I hoped she felt it.

Sighing, I hung my head and then lifted it a moment later to glance around the room. It had a few pieces of old, cobwebby furniture and crooked pictures of people long forgotten still on the wall. What a dump. How in the world did she find this place or know about it? A victim maybe or a safe house?

I turned my attention back to the black lump on the dingy couch. She was still, blending into the furniture. I watched her for several minutes and she never moved. Good, she was asleep again. I carefully pulled the phone out of my pocket and looked at the time. There was no way David would get the call if I tried now. It was still another hour until sunset.

I returned the phone and sat back, awaiting dusk. Hopefully Odette still planned to hunt before hitting the road. Resisting my blood must have been difficult. She was fiercely loyal to Brian.

With nothing better to do, I busied myself with mental games while I waited. I even sang quietly to break the silence. I tried not to think negatively about my predicament, keeping completely upbeat. David will find me and punish her and Brian.

The room started getting dimmer as the sun began its descent. David would be awake soon. They'd all be awake soon. The last rays of light faded from the cracks in the boarded up windows and in the dark, I noticed her stirring. I really wanted her to sleep a little longer.

Not a moment later, she threw off the cape and scrambled to her feet, looking for me. "I was good. I didn't move," I commented and she growled.

I heard a match strike and then a small light appeared as she lit an oil lamp. As the flame brightened, the light danced on her face and made her expression demonic. "I'm not turning it up anymore. This is all you need; we won't be staying long," she grumbled, staring at me as she set it on the mantle above the fireplace.

"Yes, we don't want to keep dear Brian waiting," I replied sarcastically.

She rushed at me, grabbing my throat. "I should just feed on you," she growled, moving close to my neck as her fingers glided down it. She seized my bound hands and held them up, glancing over my elbows and smelling them again. She closed her eyes for a moment, then stared at me. "But Brian wants the first taste," she continued, dropping my arms.

Lucky me.

"I'll be nearby, so don't bother trying to run away," she stated as she walked toward the door. "I will find you and catch you if you do."

"Better get enough to last you through the night and into morning. It's a long trip," I shouted as she slammed the door, shaking the frail house and dropping debris from the walls and ceiling.

I waited a minute or two, then pulled out the phone again. Waking it, I pressed David's number. I leaned over and listened, waiting. Come on…pick up. It continued to ring. No answer. I ended the call and started to cry.

No, I can't give up. I pulled his number back up and tried again. I waited as the phone rang once, twice…

"Megan? Where are you?" he answered, worry in his voice.

"Oh…I'm so glad you picked up," I sobbed. "Odette…Odette kidnapped me. She's planning to take me to Brian."

He was quiet. "Do you know where you are?" he asked, trying poorly to hide his anger.

"No…I'm in some old boarded up house in the middle of the woods."

"Where's Odette?" he growled as I heard a door slam.

"She's out hunting. David, please hurry, she could be back at any moment," I begged, starting to get frantic. "She talked to my dad, told him I couldn't talk to him. He's probably worried or angry. Oh God, what do I do?"

His voice calmed. "It will be all right. We'll be there shortly. And I'll call your father. Just stay calm. When she comes back, act as if nothing has changed, all right?"

I sucked up the tears and took a deep breath. "Okay," I whispered.

"We'll be there soon, I promise. I love you, Megan," he responded, his voice soothing.

"I love you, too," I replied, trying not to cry again. I ended the call and slipped the phone back in my pocket. Taking several deep breaths, I calmed my sobs. I wouldn't let Odette see me like this.

I wiped my eyes on my arms and blew the moisture away, leaving no trace of tears. Then I sat patiently waiting for her to return. It was quiet in the house, but the sounds of the crickets and other creatures seeped through the broken windows and cracked walls. There was a scratching nearby and I feared she was back, but when I looked, it turned out to be a rat.

The flame was getting lower. I hope she was having a hard time finding something to feed on. Maybe she had to travel farther away. Good, it just buys me more time. I glanced around the room, seeing if there was anything I could use to free or defend myself in case David didn't arrive soon enough. In the corner was a splintered chair, and I wondered if a stake through the heart would kill her. Probably not, since you have to have a heart to begin with.

I continued to wait, looking around the dilapidated shack wondering when she'd arrive. It felt like I had been alone a long time. Maybe something happened to her.

Unfortunately, no sooner had I thought it, she burst through the door with renewed energy and strength. She stood just inside the doorframe, licking her lips and grinning manically. Not good.

"Ready to go, love?" she asked, jumping at me.

I flattened myself against the chair, startled, but then smiled. "I think so, but I'm really going to miss this lovely cabin and all the fun we've had together in it," I replied, looking around the dump.

She smiled back, her fangs still extended as she leaned on the arms of the chair and got right in my face. "You're so brave...but you won't be for long," she snarled, grabbing the collar of my shirt and pulling me up.

A loud bang on the roof interrupted her as pieces of the ceiling fell to the floor next to us. She released me and turned her head, following the creaking as something ran above us. Then there was silence. She looked around, a slight glimpse of fear in her eyes as she listened. Nothing. Then there was another loud bang, off to the side this time, and another on the opposite side of the room.

"Don't move. I'll be right back," she sneered, patting my cheek.

Dashing through the doorway, she disappeared into the darkness. I watched the barren opening, waiting for something to happen, but only found blackness. I listened for a sound, any sound, but only the quiet of the woods filled my ears. Seconds passed like minutes as I waited for some sign of anything. No sound, no sign of Odette, nothing.

I hung my head and shut my eyes, trying not to cry in case she returned. I sighed and then looked up toward the door one last time. Emptiness...and then David appeared. My heart nearly burst from my chest as he rushed toward me. He kissed me several times before kneeling in front of me and getting to work on the knots at my feet. I couldn't speak. I just smiled and cried, happy he found me. He reached up and touched my cheek, a softness in his expression.

"I'm here now...it's all right," he comforted.

He went back to working on the knot, finally getting it loose. I glanced at the door and then at him as he looked up at me and smiled. "Where's Odette?" I asked, trying to touch him with my bound hands.

"Cary and Madeline have her," he replied coldly. And that was all he said. I didn't ask any more questions; I just waited patiently to be free.

And when I was, I wrapped my arms around him and buried my head in his chest. He gently lifted me and cradled my body in his arms, walking toward the door. As he passed the mantle, he took the lamp and tossed it on the couch. Over his shoulder, I watched the fire spread and consume it before jumping from one chair to another. We were out the door by the time it overtook the entire room.

As his steps picked up pace, I tucked my head until he stopped. We were at his car, parked quite a distance from the house. He carefully set me in the front seat and was in his before I knew it. He started the car and slowly drove down the dirt road.

"How did you find me?" I asked, glancing back at the house engulfed in flames.

"The phone I gave you has a GPS tracker," he replied, turning onto a main road. All I could see now was billowing smoke coming from the woods. Sirens howled in the distance as we sped away.

"So where are we?" I inquired looking around, not recognizing anything.

"North Carolina."

She took me across state lines in an hour! I tried to fathom it. "H-how did she dri-" I started to ask, but he interrupted, knowing what I was thinking.

"We can be a blur, an indistinct blip on a radar that's there one second and gone the next."

That's good to know. I sat up in the seat and got comfortable, staring out the window. We were now on a major highway, driving faster than I had ever been. I tried not to look at the fuzzy cars and scenery.

"Did you call my dad?"

"I told him you were cleaning earlier and didn't hear the phone over your music."

"I'm sure I'll hear about that later. And what about Odette?"

"He asked. I told him she just stopped by for a moment."

"Did he ask why you were calling and not me?"

"Of course. I explained that you asked me to call while you cleaned up. He didn't like the idea but accepted it. You'll want to call him as soon as you can."

Maybe delaying it until tomorrow would be a good idea. "I don't know. He'll probably yell at me. Maybe tomorrow."

"You should call him when we get back to the house," he insisted.

I rolled my eyes. "Fine, I will."

"How are you feeling?" he asked, glancing over at me. "Are you all right?"

I gripped the armrest tightly. "Just worry about the road and not me," I immediately replied and he did, smiling. Once he was focused, I responded, "I'm okay…just a little shook up."

"That's understandable," he agreed, weaving between cars that almost seemed to be standing still.

"So aren't you curious?" I asked, leaning forward and turning my head to him.

He looked at me and I made a face, causing him to return his attention to the road. "Curious about what?"

"How she did it?"

"Yes, I am."

"Your secret passages. One comes out in the guest room?"

He pursed his lips. "Yes, through the closet. How very clever of her…or Brian," he replied, mumbling the last part.

"And she wore a heavy cloak to shield her from the sun," I continued.

"This was well thought out," he commented.

When he didn't say anymore, I moved closer to him, placing my hand on his arm. "Do you have any idea why Brian wants me so badly?"

He was quiet, glancing briefly out the side window, then ahead of him. "No, but I will find out."

I looked out the window, the blurry images making my eyes tired. Classical piano played softly from the radio, adding to my lethargy. I returned my attention to him, wanting to say something, but he seemed preoccupied with piecing together what happened today. I rested my head on his shoulder instead and closed my eyes, enjoying the cool night air blowing around me and diluting his aroma. He kissed my forehead occasionally, and I drifted in and out of sleep for the remainder of the trip.

I felt the familiarity of the turns and opened my eyes, sitting back. "We're home," I remarked quietly as I gazed out the window at the buildings and shops of Chesterfield, all dark. It was late.

"Do you need to stop for anything?" he asked, caressing my cheek.

"Nothing's open," I replied, scanning the shopping centers as we passed them.

He smiled. "There's always something open – gas stations, a few fast food restaurants…" he responded.

"No, we're close to the house. I'll wait."

He continued driving farther into the county, where the electrical lights of town faded and natural light abounded. I gazed out the window at the clear sky and the multitude of stars in the black canopy. It was gorgeous. I turned to him and smiled.

"Thank you," I whispered, placing my hand on his.

He pulled into his driveway and then looked at me. "For what?"

"Rescuing me."

"Don't thank me for that," he responded quietly, driving along the winding road through the darkened woods.

"Why?"

He parked in the garage and turned off the car, sitting silent for a moment. "It's my duty to protect you," he replied.

He climbed out before I could respond and was at my door in no time. Taking his hand, I rose and then led the way into the house. I immediately went to the kitchen, feeling famished, and searched the refrigerator for something. I settled on a sandwich, sitting at the island as I assembled it.

He sat beside me and watched as I ate, which I hated. Or maybe he wasn't watching me eat since I hadn't started yet. It was more like he was inspecting me, making sure no hair was out of place. I shrugged it off and lifted my sandwich, taking a bite. Suddenly, he grabbed my elbow.

"What did she do to you?" he asked, examining the wound and then lifting my other arm and checking it before dashing out of the room. He reappeared a moment later with a large first aid kit.

I put my food down and finished chewing. "Umm…she didn't do this," I replied, pointing to my elbows. "I did…when I crawled across the floor to get to her purse."

He lifted one side up and cleaned it, removing bits of dirt and wood. Once he was satisfied, he applied ointment and a bandage and then repeated with the other arm. "What about your legs?" he asked, raising his eyes briefly from his work.

"That was me, too. I took a walk around your property after breakfast. It's so overgrown," I explained, continuing to eat. "No, the most I got from Odette were bumps and bruises from her dropping me. I guess she was told to keep me in pristine condition."

He pulled a stool up and gently lifted one of my legs, inspecting it. Taking a cloth, he soaked it in antiseptic and dabbed it onto my skin, and I flinched at the coldness. He apologized and then repeated with the other side. When he was done, he left my legs resting on his lap, staring at them as he ran his fingers up and down my shins.

"What's going to happen to her?" I asked suddenly.

He looked up and furrowed his brow. "She will be punished."

"How?"

"You don't need to worry about that," he replied, leaning over and kissing my shins.

I wasn't worried, just curious. "All right, I won't," I stated, smiling at him as I finished my dinner. I'm sure whatever it is will be just.

"It's good to see you smile," he commented as he gently lowered my legs and brought his chair closer, "after the ordeal you went through today," he continued, placing his hands on my thighs and leaning toward me.

He gazed into my eyes and gently kissed my lips. But when he tried to move away, I slipped my hand into his hair and pulled him back to me, kissing with more passion. Moving closer, he continued as he stood and placed his cool hands on my burning face. I was trying to be strong, trying not to break down, though I wanted to. But I had been so worried, so fearful that I'd never make it back home. Tears began to stream from my eyes and he stopped, wiping the moisture from my cheeks.

"Don't cry," he whispered in my ear as he folded me into his comforting arms.

He held me for several minutes as I calmed and then released me when the sobbing ceased. He kissed the side of my face and then my neck, shoulder, down my arm, and ended at my hand. Looking up at me, he smiled, but all too soon it faded. He glanced over his shoulder at the door as Madeline and Cary entered.

She came running up to me and gave me a hug. "How are you doing?" she asked, doing a similar head to toe examination. David joined Cary in the doorway, talking quietly with him. I watched them, wondering what was going on. She tried to distract me, apparently not wanting me to hear or know what they were discussing. "Are you okay?" she asked, blocking my view.

"Yeah, much better. What's going on?" I inquired, trying to look around her.

"Oh, just going over the information we got out of Odette," she answered. "Hey! Let's go sit in the grand salon and talk," she exclaimed, grabbing my arm and dragging me out of the room.

"So what did you find out?" I questioned, sitting on the loveseat.

"Absolutely nothing. Brian only told her what he needed her to know and left the rest for her to make up on her own. We have no idea what his motives were."

"So this interrogation and sentencing…is it normal procedure among your kind?" I inquired, recalling the hierarchy of vampires in the books I've read.

She glanced toward David, not sure what to tell me. "Umm, well…in the clan I belonged to before living here, we had to punish two members for crimes against the family…and yeah, it was similar."

"So you don't have a judge and jury to decide if someone's guilty or not?"

"No, there's no higher power that dictates guilt or innocence. We police our own. There are very few of us in a given area and our total numbers are in the thousands, not billions like humans."

Very different from what authors come up with. I suppose they believe everyone, supernatural or not, needs to have law and order to prevent chaos. "So how is he going to punish her?"

She looked toward the kitchen, watching a heated exchange between Cary and him. "Umm…we're not sure yet," she replied, avoiding my eyes.

"Is that what they're arguing about?" I questioned, indicating to the guys.

She hesitated. "Umm, yeah," she responded, glancing their way. It grew quiet in the next room. She turned her attention back to me, smiling. "What did you do today, other than get kidnapped?"

"Hung around the house, took a walk, hung out on the dock, went swimming. Nothing exciting."

"Was it a sunny day?" she asked with bright eyes.

"Yes, with clear blue skies and a soft summer breeze," I smiled.

She closed them and sighed contentedly. "I remember those days…the warm sunshine on my skin, the smell of honeysuckle in the air, the quiet babbling of the brook near my house playing a soothing summer song with the cicadas and birds as I stretched out on its bank in the thick, green grass and watched the clouds shift and change from one creation to another…"

"It sounds lovely," I commented.

"It was," she replied quietly, looking away. While she silently reflected, I leaned on the arm of the loveseat and closed my eyes for just a second and then yawned. A lassitude loomed over me. "You should go to bed," she recommended, gently touching my arm. "It's been a long, tiring day and it's late."

I yawned again. "Yeah…but I need to call my dad first," I responded, standing up.

"Oh…you might need this," she commented, reaching in her pocket and pulling out a phone, my phone, before handing it to me. "We confiscated it from Odette and realized it wasn't hers."

I looked down at it in my hands. "Thank you," I replied. Good, now I won't have to explain to my dad what happened to it when he gets home. I walked into the kitchen and up to David. "I'm going to the guest room to call my dad and then crawl in bed," I informed him.

He reached up and cupped my chin in his hand. "All right. I'll be there soon," he whispered, pulling me toward him and kissing my lips softly. I wanted more, but he pulled away.

Sighing as I left the room, I glanced over my shoulder and watched as Madeline joined Cary and him. Walking the long way around, I took my time ambling down the hall, trying to eavesdrop, but realized it was no use as I passed the now closed door. Sighing again, I continued across the foyer to the guest room.

Pushing the door open, a shiver ran through me as I thought about the earlier events of the day. I entered and immediately backed up against a wall, hyperventilating. It was too fresh in my mind. And even though I knew Odette was restrained, I couldn't stay in this room tonight. I grabbed what I needed and dashed out the door.

I met David in the foyer as he was on his way downstairs. "Megan, is something wrong?" he asked, touching my shoulder. Madeline and Cary passed, and he nodded to them as they continued down the steps.

"I…I can't stay in there tonight. It's too…too…" I responded, trying to find the words.

"I understand. You can stay in my room instead," he offered, leading me upstairs. Then he smiled, "I won't need it until morning anyway."

He followed me all the way to his door, stopping there. "Don't be too long," I requested, gazing into his eyes.

"I won't," he replied, leaning in and kissing me. "Don't forget to call your father," he reminded as we parted.

I held up my phone and smiled weakly as I opened the door and flipped on the lights. As I entered the room, I turned and slowly closed it, gazing at David's gentle smile as I did. When just a sliver of his face remained in the crack, his soft expression hardened as he turned away and quickly disappeared. I dropped my head and rested it against the frame a moment as it clicked shut. I felt better being in his room, but I didn't want to be alone. Turning around, I headed to his bed and sat at the foot staring at the phone in my hands.

It was after midnight. I might wake Dad or Vanessa if I call now. But then again, he may be waiting for my call. Regardless, I need to do it, for Dad and for myself. I need to escape this world unknown to other humans and pretend for a while that it doesn't exist.

I unlocked the phone and searched for the number he gave me for the house down there. Swallowing hard, I braced myself for the tongue-lashing I was going to receive as I hit the button.

"Hello?" Dad answered after the first ring.

"Hey, Dad. Sorry I'm calling so late," I apologized immediately, trying to sound normal.

"Why *are* you calling so late?" he asked, not sounding happy at all.

"I tried once, but you never answered. Then David and I watched a movie, and I fell asleep during it. After he left, I realized I hadn't called you and…here we are," I lied, hoping he bought it.

He was quiet for several seconds. "Why was he at the house while you showered?"

I knew that would be an issue. "He came over early, just as I was finishing up. Before heading out to dinner, I wanted to clean up, so he waited in the family room while I did. Since I was in a hurry, I asked him to call you to respond to your earlier call and to make sure you knew he wasn't *with* me." It didn't make a lot of sense and he'd probably see right through it, but it was worth a try.

Another pause and then a sigh. "You could have just as easily called me, Megan. I wouldn't have kept you long."

I felt bad. "I know and I'm sorry. I just thought it'd be easier," I replied timidly, hanging my head and nibbling at my lip.

"It's okay. So how often have you had David over while we've been away?" he asked, changing the subject quickly.

"Umm…not much. He's been busy with work and school."

"What about anyone else?"

"Well, just Claire and Melissa. And Ben stopped by."

"Melissa…is she the one I talked to earlier today?"

I clenched my teeth, remembering Odette's conversation with him. "Yeah."

"I don't like you having so many people over while we're gone."

"It's just been those four," I defended but unsure why. Melissa was made up.

"This Melissa girl, is she one of the ones that live with David?"

"No, that's Madeline."

"Oh, is she a classmate then? I don't think I've ever heard you talk about her."

"Yeah, she is. I've mentioned her a couple times. We worked on a biology project together," I replied, digging my hole deeper and deeper. I needed to talk about something else before I said too much.

"Oh, yeah…now I remember her. She came to the house once?" he asked, hoping to not sound as though he didn't listen to me.

"Umm hmm, she did. So how's everything down there?" I inquired, changing the subject as quickly as he had.

"Good. Vanessa's sleeping, turning in early for once. Weather's been great. Only a couple more days, then it's back to the old grind."

"I'm sure you're looking forward to it, if I know you."

He laughed and I smiled, enjoying its pleasant sound. "Yes, you do. I've been secretly calling work to see how things are going and to find out what cases we've gotten."

"Dad! It's your honeymoon!" I exclaimed as I stood and walked around the room, wanting to move about. "The firm will not fall apart if you're not there."

"I know, I know," he replied sheepishly. "I can't help it. Luckily, there hasn't been anything too exciting, so my mind has been focused on being here rather than up there."

"That's a plus," I muttered.

There was muffled talking, then he came back on. "Well, I have to go. I've enjoyed talking to you, but Vanessa's calling me to come to bed. You should get some sleep, too. Love you," he commented hastily.

"Love you, too," I responded and hung up, sitting in a chair by one of the windows. Back to reality.

I glanced over my shoulder out into the yard, noticing dark figures moving among the trees. Was that David, Madeline, and Cary taking care of Odette? Dashing across the room, I quickly shut off the light in hopes of being able to see what was going on better in the dark. I fumbled my way back to the window and looked for them, but they were gone. Plopping down on the cushion, I sat on my legs and let out a frustrated sigh.

I stood after a moment, feeling my way to the bed and around to the lamp on the table beside it. I turned it on and sat on the mattress, staring at the wall. Why did I ever think I could catch them? The whole point of doing it without me seeing was to keep me out of it. I sighed again and got up, heading to the bathroom to get cleaned up and changed.

Fresh and comfortable, I climbed into bed and got under the covers. His scent surrounded me, and my head instantly began to swim. I should give in and go to sleep, but I really wanted to see David before I did. Avoiding the fog taking over, I sat up and glanced around for something to do while I waited. Several books lay on top of the bedside table, and I scanned the titles to see if there was anything interesting. Finding one, I slipped it out from under the others and opened it to the first chapter.

I was on the third one by the time my eyelids began to droop and the words blurred. I shut the book and returned it, turning off the light before lying on my side and cuddling into David's comforter. I closed my eyes and inhaled, breathing in his aroma and welcoming the foggy feeling I got sometimes when I was close to him. It didn't take long to fall asleep.

A cool hand against my warm cheek woke me from my slumber. I jumped, propping myself up on my elbows as I looked around. "It's just me, Megan," David whispered, leaning in and giving me a kiss.

"David..." I responded drowsily as I rolled toward him, laying my head on his chest. "What time is it?"

He rubbed my back and kissed the top of my head. "Late...or early. Depending on how you want to look at it," he replied, his voice low.

"Did you...take care of Odette?" I asked, trying to stay conscious.

"There is no need to worry about her anymore. Sleep..." he whispered, lifting my chin up to him and kissing me again.

My head spun as I tried to recover from the kiss. But I was too tired to fight it. Giving up, I pulled the comforter over my shoulders and nestled into his arm.

# Chapter 37
## Confirmation

"Aaaaaaaaaaaaaaaa!"

I sat up straight in bed, darkness all around me. Feeling next to me, I found David lying above the covers and nudged him. "David...David. I think I heard a scream..." I whispered, leaning over him.

He touched my cheek without faltering. "Megan, it's nothing. Go back to sleep," he replied softly, his hand slowly sliding down as it dropped to the bed.

With my eyes closed, I sat back and listened. Silence. I strained my ears to hear beyond the room. Everything was still and quiet.

Maybe I imagined it. I stared at the curtains surrounding the bed, trying to remember if I was dreaming of anything before I woke. When nothing came to mind, I disregarded what I heard. Curling up under the covers, I held him and quickly fell back asleep.

Waking several hours later, I gently kissed David before carefully slipping out of the curtains. I tried not to trip over anything in the darkness as I walked around the bed to the door. Quietly opening it, I was blinded momentarily by the bright light shining down the hall from the large window at the staircase. I quickly ducked out without letting too much of it in and shut the door tightly before scurrying down the stairs.

I stopped on the lower landing and admired the beauty of the glass and light. The sun shined brilliantly through the window, causing the many facets to sparkle and cast a multitude of rainbows onto the dark wood below my bare feet. The warmth emanating from it enticed me to stay, but I couldn't. Instead, I turned and continued down the stairs to the guest room.

I opened the door and paused. Glancing around, I waited for panic to overtake me, but I didn't feel the fear I felt last night. I continued into the room, grabbing a few things from my bag and heading into the bathroom to go through my usual morning routine.

My stomach growled as I fixed my hair, telling me it was time for lunch. I tidied up the room and then headed into the kitchen to find something to eat. Throwing several items together quickly, I sat at the island and ate while watching the weather report for a moment. Clouds would be moving into the area late in the afternoon, but it was unclear if they'd bring rain. Maybe David would get to have an early evening with me.

I flipped the channel to something else, enjoying the sound more than anything. Losing interest in the images on TV, I glanced out the grand salon windows and enjoyed the serene view. Caught up in the beauty, an overwhelming urge to get outside came over me. I quickly finished my food, cleaned my dishes, and put them away before rushing out the terrace door.

A burst of warm air hit me as I exited the house and I slowly descended the stairs to the patio, taking in the sights and sounds of summer. It was a glorious day and every creature expressed it as they called, chirped, and sang its praises. I continued through the gate and down the path as if being pulled by an unknown force. I felt happy, relieved, and safe once again.

I was almost at the lake when I looked down and noticed my shoelace was untied. To prevent anymore bumps, cuts, or bruises, I decided it'd be wise to fix it before continuing on. As I stood up, something through the woods caught my eye. With only time to kill, I ventured toward it, curious what I might find.

Coming upon a clearing near the water's edge, I glanced around at the small beach. How did I never notice it before? The dock and David's boat were to my left, so I surely would have seen it on my trips down to the lake.

Several freshly cut trees were stacked neatly at the edge of the wooded area. The stumps remained, circling a single tree that was left behind. Why would David clear all the other trees, but leave this one? I walked toward it and stopped dead in my tracks.

At the foot of the lone pine was an ashen figure curled into a ball, its hands covering its head. Was this some strange art piece by Madeline? I moved closer, crouching beside it and inspecting it in detail. A rope wrapped around both the figure and the tree as if it was purposely being held captive there.

Staring at the odd sculpture, I couldn't help feeling there was something eerily familiar about it. Its form, style, and overall appearance made me think I should know who it was, but I had no clue. Spotting something around its neck, I leaned closer. I made out a thin chain with something dangling from it.

Wanting to get a better look at it, I reached in, but as soon as my fingers came in contact with the surface of the figure, it collapsed into a pile of ash. I fell back and stared at it in shock. As the realization hit me, I gasped.

That wasn't a sculpture Madeline made – it was Odette! It was her scream I heard this morning as the sun came up. They put her to death!

How could they do that to her? I expected exile or torture, but not death! She was just a puppet, a pawn.

Wait...why was I defending her?

Maybe because I felt sorry for her. She hadn't done anything to deserve my sympathy and her punishment was just, but seeing her remains as they were got to me. She was in such pain. Her last moments must have been terrifying.

But still, she kidnapped me and was taking me to Brian who planned to do God knows what. She killed countless people. She was arrogant, nasty, and rude. David had given them, her, fair warning and she didn't care. She had it coming to her.

Will Brian know she was murdered? If he does, what will he do about it? Will he take David seriously and back off or will he become more aggressive now that his love, his creation, was dead?

I dug the necklace out of the ash and walked away from the execution site, not looking back as I headed toward the dock. David will know I found her. And he will know that what they did might bring a terrible tragedy our way.

Walking out onto the dock, I stopped and stared at the lake. It was peaceful and not a soul was on the water or anywhere around. I sat and stretched my legs out, leaning back on my hands as I continued to gaze. I cleared my mind and relaxed.

That was where I stayed for the remainder of the day, enjoying the peace and solitude I had before all hell broke loose. The clouds mentioned on the weather report this morning started moving in as predicted, covering the sun and the sky for as far as I could see. One enormous, gray blanket.

David would be waking soon, but I didn't bother moving. He'll find me, I know he will. So I stayed there, watching the water reflect the sky in a near mirror image.

I pulled the necklace out of my pocket and flipped the filigree butterfly over in my fingers several times. It came from a victim of Brian, and now Odette's the victim. A cursed trinket.

"I'm surprised to see you down here," David commented as he came up behind me. He crouched down and reached over my shoulder, taking my chin in his cool hand and tilting my head back. He smiled and then kissed me.

Upside-down kisses being as awkward as they are, I turned so we were as we should be. He moved his hand to my neck and I placed mine on his shoulder, steadying myself. I started to get lost in him, but then all my thoughts and questions from earlier nagged at me and I had to break away.

He sat next to me, a curious expression of why I stopped so abruptly in his eyes. I looked away. "I found Odette," I revealed as I held up the necklace.

"What was left of her," he replied casually, taking it from me. "She died at dawn as the sun came over the trees," he continued, moving so he was across from me.

"I didn't think you would kill her."

"Megan…I warned her and Brian twice; there wasn't going to be a third time."

"So what do you plan to do with him, being that he's the mastermind behind the whole thing?"

"I haven't decided yet, but I do not plan to hunt him down. I have to be here for you."

I knit my brow as I finally looked at him. "Did you know he made Odette?"

"What?" he questioned, stunned.

"She told me in the shack. She said maybe he'd change me like he did her…"

Now it was David who couldn't look me in the eye. "This is not good," he mumbled as he stared at the smooth planks underneath him.

"Why?" I asked, moving closer.

His eyes met mine. "He has a connection to her. He'll know she's dead," he responded and then paused. "I had hoped he wouldn't find out for at least another day, giving me time to prepare."

"So neither of them ever told you?"

"No…Brian said he found her, a fledgling needing help since her maker deserted her. How could he," he growled, standing up and pacing as he clenched the necklace. Then he stopped and launched it into the sky.

I stood and watched as it flew through the air far over the lake. It came down and broke the calm surface, sinking to the depths, never to curse anyone again. It was gone and so was Odette. But the ripples from it spread out and soon reached us, an omen of what was to come. David would not get away with killing her. There would be repercussions.

He was quiet, looking out over the water as the final ripples gradually faded. I came up behind him and put my arms around his body, resting my head between his shoulder blades and listening to him breathe. After a moment, he turned and held me in his arms.

"Everything will be fine. We'll be ready whenever he shows, if he does," he whispered.

I know he'll do whatever it takes to keep me safe. Then it hit me. "Make me one of you," I suggested, looking at him.

"What?" he questioned, furrowing his brow. "No…I can't," he replied, sadness in his eyes as he caressed my warm skin.

I could feel the heat burning in my cheeks as I started to get angry. That's it? He can't even consider it for just a moment? "Why? Are you not able to do it? Don't know how? Don't really want to? Why?" I asked, pushing away.

"You're not thinking this through…"

"I have! I don't want to grow old while you stay young or possibly end up like my mom, dying too early in a hospital bed!" I shouted.

"The timing's not right. You're too young and too many questions would be asked. Your family and friends would wonder…"

"So what! I'd have a better chance fighting Brian if he came after me. And maybe if you changed me, he wouldn't be interested in trying to take me from you," I argued.

But David just stood there, stoic.

I let out a frustrated sigh and started up the path. I need to get away, talk to someone else. Maybe Madeline will agree with me. I glanced back briefly, finding him unmoving on the dock. Why wasn't he trying to keep me from leaving?

I continued my angry trek up the path when suddenly I felt something catch my arm. I turned to him standing there, a firm grip on me. His head was down and as he lifted it, I noticed his eyes rimmed in red. "*I'm* not ready," he admitted through clenched teeth.

"Why?" I asked, turning to him.

He hesitated. "I don't want you to lose your humanity yet."

"Is that because you want me to stay fragile and helpless so you can always rescue me?"

"You've proven you are far from fragile and helpless, Megan. It's not that."

"Then what is it?" I asked, frustrated and near tears.

He moved closer, reaching up and caressing my cheek. "Your innocence."

"My innocence?"

He sighed. "What you go through to become like me…will change you. You see the world differently…you become different," he whispered, looking at me sadly and brushing my hair behind my ear. "I'm not ready to see you like that."

"I won't always be like that. Look at you and Madeline…"

"It takes a long time to get back to the way you were as a human, if ever. Some can't overcome it. But if you do, you're still not the same. You are constantly fighting that demon, that darkness, inside you."

"I won't let that happen to me," I responded.

"You won't have a choice."

I wanted to tell him he was wrong, that I'm stronger than he thinks, but it seemed like a never-ending, pointless argument. I was so mad and hurt, I couldn't contain the tears any longer. "Don't you love me enough to go through with it?"

He took me into his arms and held me close. "I love you more than anything, Megan. You brought that very real emotion out of me," he replied, kissing me. "And if you want it, I will do it, but the time has to be right...for both of us."

I was ready to argue, ready to get my point across, but I hesitated, thinking of how to do it. If I change now, I could help by fighting and defending rather than being the damsel in distress. I want to be useful not useless.

But then what happens once it's all over? I can't go back to my old life. And not doing so will create too many questions. Dad would launch an investigation into where I disappeared to or try to find out what happened to me, inevitably discovering a truth I don't want him to know. I could cover it up by pretending to die, but it'd be too heartbreaking for everyone and then I could never come back.

As much as I hated to admit it, David was right.

"Okay...I'll wait," I responded with a sigh. "But I don't want to be thirty when you feel the time is right," I added, smiling at him. He gave a soft smile back as we continued up the path to the house. "Now we need to figure out what to do about Brian."

"No *we* don't. Madeline, Cary, and I will devise a plan."

"Don't you think I should be involved, since he'll be coming after me, too?"

He thought for a moment, standing at the foot of the terrace stairs. "All right. *We* will discuss it together. After you," he offered, moving out of the way.

"Thank you," I replied, starting up the stairs.

As I reached the top, I glanced into the house. Cary and Madeline stared at me from their seats in the grand salon, awaiting our arrival. She gave a small smile as I opened the door.

"Come sit by me," she invited, patting the loveseat.

I glanced at David and he indicated I should, so I took my place next to her as he sat across from us. Cary was sitting beside him, leaning forward and resting his arms on his knees. "So what's the plan?" he asked.

"I don't have one yet. This is why we're meeting," David answered, sitting back in the chair looking so debonair.

"Do you think he'll call?" Madeline asked, looking between them. Neither responded. "I guess our whole plan of forcing Odette to make an excuse as to why she wasn't there last night won't hold up anymore."

"I just can't believe he lied to you! And now look at the mess we're in!" Cary exclaimed, sitting back and turning toward the window. Rain began to pelt it, streaming down the panes.

I was lost. "Umm...how do..." I started, looking at David as I pointed to the other two.

"Yes, they know," he responded softly. "But not because Brian told them. He lied to them as well. They both lied," he stated, his voice getting deeper.

"Do we know what the weather is in Baton Rouge? He may still be sleeping," she commented, pulling out her phone. I watched as she quickly checked it. "Sunny and hot," she announced.

"We still have time then. He'll probably call me directly. But if he calls either of you, take his side. We want him to believe it was me alone that executed Odette. That way he feels free to confide in one of you, and we can get an idea of what he's planning. Cary, it will most likely be you since he knows how close I've been to Madeline," David explained.

"Should I report back to you with any information?" he inquired.

"Yes. Keep your guard up, though. Brian is quite cunning."

"What if he decides to come up here?" she asked.

"We'll take turns watching Megan and her family. He has never been invited into the house, so he's unable to enter. And Megan, you need to make sure no one ever lets him in."

"Okay. I'm not concerned as much about my dad as I am about Vanessa. He really gets a hold on her," I replied, fidgeting.

"Do we plan to capture him?" she inquired, sitting on the edge of her seat. She looked excited about this whole ordeal.

"If we can, but it won't be easy. He's a lot older than Odette and has more experience getting away. He'll be harder to kill as well," David informed us, glancing at me.

"So what do we do now?" she asked, looking at each of us.

"We wait," he replied.

We sat quietly for several minutes. Then Madeline broke the silence. "Anyone for billiards or a card game?" she inquired.

"Yes, please" I replied. "I need the distraction."

"I'll join you," David agreed, standing up and offering his hand to me.

Cary looked like he was still contemplating it. "Come on, it'll be fun," she encouraged.

"Okay, let's go," he conceded, taking her hand.

We headed downstairs and each sat in a chair at the card table, opting to do that rather than play a game of billiards I'd undoubtedly lose. "What shall we play first?" I asked, looking around the table at my vampire friends. "Nothing that gives me a disadvantage," I added, tapping my temple.

They all smiled, and Madeline pulled out the cards and chips. "What about poker to start us off?"

All in agreement, she dealt the cards while Cary passed out the chips. We each looked at our hand and changed out the ones that were no good. My new hand was decent, so I slipped several chips into the center. I sat back and watched as David, Madeline, and Cary exchanged glances. In order, they each pushed their chips into the pile, one extravagantly more than the other. I looked at my cards again, feeling less sure about what I had.

"I fold," I announced, giving up.

"Me, too," Madeline followed.

David and Cary stared each other down, adding more chips to the pile. "All right, show them," Cary requested, finally giving in.

He laid his out and David laughed as he laid his down. "Two pair."

"You're too good at bluffing. I had a royal flush and you won with two pair!" he exclaimed.

"Years of experience," David replied, gathering up the cards and shuffling them. "Another game?" he asked, looking at each of us. We played a couple more rounds and then decided to move on to something else since he kept winning.

Blackjack – a game of chance. David couldn't possibly be that lucky. But as an added precaution, we made him the dealer so he couldn't win at all. The first couple of rounds, I did horribly, but as it progressed, I improved and even won some.

Through all the games and fun, my eyes couldn't help but wander occasionally to the patio doors, watching the pool and woods darken as night crept in. Any time now, we'll get a call from Brian. But as I continued to watch it grow darker, all phones were silent.

I paused for dinner while they continued to play. Then when I was done, we switched games again, laughing and having fun until a phone finally rang – David's. All eyes were on him as he stood and pulled it out, answering it as he left the room.

Seeing her still and quiet, my eyes shifted to Madeline as she stared off into space. After a moment, she closed her eyes and they began to twitch. Then suddenly, they opened.

"What's wrong?" I asked, grabbing her arm.

She looked angry. "He's blocking me out!" she fumed.

"You can do that?" I inquired, thinking all along that they could read each other's minds whenever they felt like it.

"Sure we can. You think we're an open book?" Cary replied, chuckling as he shuffled the cards. I'm liking him more and more as he warms up. "Another game?"

I looked around for David, but he was nowhere nearby. "All right, go ahead," I told him, waving my hand above the table.

Madeline was still distracted, trying again and getting more and more aggravated. "Why won't he let me listen in? We need to know what's going on, too."

"Maybe it's part of the plan – the less we know, the better," Cary replied, dealing them out.

I picked up my hand and looked at it. We were back to playing poker, but without the chips. She let out a frustrated sigh and picked up her cards. I exchanged a few and looked at my new hand. Not bad. They exchanged their cards and then looked at each other.

As I readied to show mine, my cell phone rang. Cary and Madeline both looked at me, curious. "It's probably my dad," I responded to their inquiring gazes. I laid my cards face up and answered the phone as I headed to the other side of the room.

"Did you have a good day?" Dad asked.

"Yeah, it was great," I replied, bothered. "Why have you been calling me every day, sometimes twice? You never used to do this."

"I'm just worried about you. It's been a long time since I've left you home alone."

"You left me home alone like two years ago and you called every other day…is this because of David?" I asked, realizing what's changed.

"No…not at all. Can't I worry?"

"I'm responsible, you know that," I replied, looking up to see David sitting at the table. He didn't look angry. "Everything's fine and will be. Enjoy your last evening in paradise and call me tomorrow afternoon when you're boarding the plane," I instructed.

"So there's nothing to worry about?"

I looked at David and his eyes caught mine and he smiled. "Nothing at all. I have to go, but I'll talk to you tomorrow."

"Okay, talk to you then," he replied and hung up. He didn't sound happy with our discussion, but that was the least of my worries at the moment.

I joined the group at the table and grabbed my new stack of cards, glancing at them. "So…what did I miss?" I asked, switching several out.

"Brian's not coming!" Madeline blurted out. "We don't have to worry about him."

"That's…great. What a relief," I replied, but why didn't it feel like it?

Noticing my hesitation, David excused both of us and led me away. Heading upstairs, we said nothing to each other as Cary and Madeline's laughter echoed behind us. When we reached the main floor, he stopped and turned to me, gently touching my chin and kissing me.

"What was that for?" I asked, smiling softly.

"To do just that," he replied, smiling back.

"So…what are we doing up here?" I asked, looking around.

"Not here," he responded, taking my hand and leading me to the library. He turned on the lights as we entered and indicated for me to sit on one of the leather couches. As I did, he followed. He held my hands in his and gazed into my eyes. "You don't have to worry. Brian relented. You're safe."

"I know…" I replied quietly, staring at my fidgeting hands.

He lifted my chin so I was looking at him. "Then why are you not happy?" he asked, concerned.

"I don't know. There's something nagging at me…telling me this isn't over. I…I just don't believe him."

He stared at me for a long time without saying anything. "You should trust your instinct," he finally replied. "It's your defense mechanism, for survival."

I felt better with the assurance that he trusted my intuition. I turned my back to him, lying against his chest as he put his arms around me and kissed my cheek. Staring at the wood paneled ceiling, I let out a soft sigh.

"What did he have to say?" I asked after several minutes of silence.

He didn't respond immediately. "He was angry about Odette's death…" he began and then paused. "He said this was a test, to see how far I would go for you. With her execution, he realized I would do anything to protect you," he continued, looking down at me. His fingers grazed my cheek and jaw as he slipped them under my chin and tilted it up. My eyes met his and my heart fluttered lightly. "Anything and everything," he whispered, kissing me.

I slipped my hand into his hair and gripped it, parting my lips. He turned and I rolled onto the couch as his body hovered over mine, a knee between my legs and an arm supporting him. With his free hand, he reached up and slipped it along my jaw, tilting my face away. His lips brushed my cheek and chin and then travelled down to my throat.

He kissed my anxious skin and made my heart thump. I felt his breath flow over my flesh as his lips parted. Pressing them to it, I lurched and gasped, excited by this new sensation. He moved away slightly, placing his lips on a new area of skin. I reacted the same and he paused, his breathing heavy. One more time and then I felt his fangs.

He turned his head away, controlling his urge, and I did the same, closing my eyes and letting my heart calm and blush wane. After a moment, I felt a soft kiss on my lips and before I opened my eyes, he was gone. I sat up and looked his way, finding him leaning on the arm at the other end, staring ahead. Then his eyes shifted to me and he smirked. The blush returned and I looked away.

"I think it's time you go to bed," he whispered.

"I think that's a good idea," I agreed, standing.

Exiting the library, we headed to the guest room. He turned out the light and got into his normal bedtime position as I slipped under the comforter. I rested my head on his chest and laid my arm across his stomach. Closing my eyes, I let out a contented breath as slumber came on instantaneously. I was more tired than I thought.

I was nearly asleep when he spoke. "I'll be by your house around eight-thirty tomorrow evening," he stated softly.

"Okay," I replied with a yawn. "I'll let myself out in the morning…wait, how will I get home?" I asked, drowsily looking up at him.

He kissed me and smiled. "I had Madeline pick up your car. It's parked out front."

"Oh…thank you…" I responded as I drifted away.


I wasn't alone.

I wasn't even in the right room.

This room was completely dark even though it was morning.

My arm over David, I realized I was in his bed. I sat up and leaned over, nudging him gently. "David…David," I whispered.

"Yes, Megan?" he asked quietly, rolling toward me.

"How…how did I get up here?" I questioned, trying to find him in the dark.

"I brought you up here," he answered, pausing as he tried to stay awake. "You were talking in your sleep and thrashing quite a bit. It was getting close to dawn…and I didn't want you to wake from a bad dream alone."

How considerate of him. I wonder what I was dreaming about.

"Thank you," I responded, leaning over to kiss him. I couldn't see a thing, but he knew what I was trying and found me instead. "I'm going to get my things together and head home. I'll see you tonight," I whispered, kissing him again before climbing out of the bed.

Feeling my way around the room, I found the door and slipped out without letting a lot of light in. The sun was shining just as brightly through the window as it had yesterday. But it was higher in the sky, which meant I slept a lot later than I expected. I rushed into the guest room and started gathering my things.

Glancing at my phone, I saw it was already after eleven. It didn't look as though Dad had called yet, so they hadn't left. Good, I still had time. I quickly tidied the room and then went into the bathroom to wash up, brush my teeth, and fix my hair. I grabbed all the toiletries I brought with me and headed back into the room.

I slipped them in the bag and pulled out an outfit. After changing, I stuffed the clothes I wore last night in with the others and put my shoes on. I headed to the door, giving the room a once over before leaving. Dropping the bag in the foyer, I went to the kitchen to empty the refrigerator and cabinets. I was sure David wouldn't mind since the food would go bad anyway.

Searching for bags, I finally found some in the pantry. I opened several and set them on the island, loading the items into each. When everything was packed away, I cleaned up the kitchen and even wiped down the inside of the refrigerator. I hauled the bags into the foyer and then went back to check the room over one last time.

Feeling satisfied with the way I was leaving his house, I headed out to my car with all my things. I locked the front door and jogged down the stairs, taking one last look before climbing in. Driving down the thick, tree-lined road, I took a deep breath and let it out.

Back to my normal teenage life.

I didn't think much about anything on my trip home, listening to music and singing along. I was happy and content, not worried about anything or feeling any kind of impending doom. Everything seemed right with the world at this moment.

I pulled in the driveway and parked beside my dad's car, getting out and dashing to the house. Unlocking the front door, I propped it open and ran out to get my things. On my second run back, I nearly collided with Ben carrying a couple of the bags.

"Oh, hey! What are you doing here?" I asked, surprised, but continued to the car to grab what was left.

"I've been waiting out here all night for you," he replied, following me. "Where have you been?"

I slammed the door and rushed toward the house. "Out," I responded as he kept close behind me.

"Out where?" he inquired as we entered the kitchen, setting the bags on the counter and peeking inside. "Not shopping…some of these groceries have been opened."

I slapped it shut and blocked him from looking anymore. "It's none of your business. Why are you here?"

He pulled out one of the stools and took a seat. "Madeline broke up with me…"

"Yeah, I heard," I muttered in irritation as I put the food away.

"You did? What am I saying…of course you did," he realized, answering his own question.

"Yes, I do talk to Madeline outside of my relationship with David," I replied as I finished unloading. Dad's going to be surprised when he sees all of the expensive, organic foods I brought home. I put the bags away under the island to use another time and pulled a stool around to the other side, sitting across from Ben. "So what is it you so desperately need to talk to me about regarding this break-up?" I asked as calmly as I could, laying my hands on the counter and staring at him.

He hesitated, looking away. "I think she might be in trouble…might have been forced to break up with me," he answered quietly.

I rolled my eyes and sighed loudly. "She is in no danger whatsoever. And believe me, if she was, she can more than take care of herself."

He turned and looked into my eyes. "Were you at David's last night?"

I could feel my face flush as the anger rose in me. "That is none of your business," I snapped.

"It's not smart, Megan. He's not who you think he is…"

I shot up, knocking the stool over and letting it clatter loudly on the hardwood floor. "I know exactly who he is and what he is!" I exclaimed, moving closer to him. "Geez, Ben! Stop being so protective and jealous! I'm not incompetent! I can think on my own and fend for myself!" I yelled. He jerked back, a look of utter shock on his face. Frustrated, I headed into the family room and sat on the couch. "Why can't you just accept him like everyone else and drop this ridiculous witch hunt?"

He slowly stood and walked cautiously toward me. "What do you mean you know exactly who and *what* he is?"

Crap, I slipped up. I rubbed my face and rested it in my hands. What am I going to tell him? Nothing will sound any better, but I'm not going to reveal that David is a vampire.

A hand alighted on my shoulder, and I looked up to see Ben standing before me. "What *is* David?" he asked, looking down at me with eyes intense and fearful.

"My boyfriend," I snapped.

"No, there's something more. You know something dark…something secret about him," he pushed.

"There's nothing dark or secret about him. What you see is what you get."

"Someone not like us, someone not normal. Maybe not even human…"

I looked down at my hands, trying not to give anything away. He's getting too close to the truth. "You're crazy, Ben," I commented, shaking my head.

"What power does he have over Madeline…over you?" he inquired, kneeling in front of me and trying to look in my eyes.

I sat back and crossed my arms, glaring at him. "There is no power. She's her own person, making her own decisions, same as me."

"Then why does she act so weird around him, always looking to him for approval or permission?"

I tried to think of a good excuse. "He's like a big brother to her. And she's new at this…dating. She lived a sheltered life before coming here," I explained, hoping he bought it.

He sat next to me and thought about it for a moment. "Okay, I'll give her that," he replied and then paused. "But that doesn't explain why she wouldn't take me to their house. She's hiding something about David and you know it," he accused.

My temper took over and I shot off the cushion. "Get out," I growled.

He looked at me, stunned. "Wh-what?"

"I want you to leave," I rephrased, wondering if he understood that. His expression remained fixed. "Wh-why?"

"You're accusing my boyfriend of things even after I told you specifically there's nothing. I'm done, Ben. I tried. I tried to prove to you that he's not a bad guy. And if you only knew what he's done for me, you'd change your tune. But no. You're too blind. You only see one thing and it's wrong. So I'm done. If you can't accept him, I don't want you around," I asserted.

He gawked at me, absolutely bewildered. "I...I don't know..." he replied quietly as he hung his head.

I crossed my arms tightly over my chest and narrowed my eyes at him. "Well then go home and think about it." He stared at the floor for several minutes, and I started to get more irritated. "Ben!" I snapped.

He looked up at me with mournful eyes and sighed. "You're right...I am blinded. I couldn't see that he makes you happy. I'm sorry, Megan, for being wrong about him. I accept David as your boyfriend," he responded.

The anger vanished as quick as it came and I sat down beside him, taking his hand in mine. "I didn't really want to lose you as a friend, but I just can't keep fighting with you over this," I admitted.

"I know. I'm a jealous idiot."

"Yes, you are," I smiled, removing my hand.

He stared outside for a moment and then looked at me. "Sooo...do you think I have a chance at getting back with Madeline?" he asked.

"Not at all. She's pretty pissed with you. You used her and that really hurt."

He dropped his head. "Oh," was all he said.

I sighed and glanced out the window. The yard was hazy from the heat and it made me glad to be indoors with the air conditioner. I turned back to Ben, finding him staring at me.

"Can I ask you just one thing before we put all of this behind us and start over?" he inquired.

"And what would that be?" I questioned, hoping whatever it was wouldn't start another fight.

"I stayed outside in my mom's car all night waiting for you, concerned about you. At least answer this – where were you?"

"You already know the answer," I responded, not wanting to go into detail.

"You know your dad would never approve," he commented.

"There are a lot of things I do he wouldn't approve and that's why I don't tell him," I retorted as I stood.

"David's a bad influence on you."

"No, he's not. It is all me, my own doing."

"I never took you for a bad girl," he responded with a smile as he stood. "I'm loving you more and more."

"Well, I'm taken," I replied, leading him to the door.

"If it ever happens to end, I'm here for you."

"I know. And you always will be."

"Yep, no getting rid of me," he agreed with a boyish grin.

"So we're good? The past is in the past?"

"Yep…but you're not expecting me to become best friends with him, are you?"

"No, I'll be happy if you're just friendly and not trying to make him out as some kind of horror movie villain."

"All right, I can do that," he smiled as he stepped outside.

"I'm glad to hear it," I remarked as I followed him.

"So what are you doing with the rest of your day?" he asked as he started down the steps.

"I'm going to enjoy the peace while I can, before Dad and Vanessa arrive," I remarked.

"Good luck," he responded, giving a smile as he glanced over his shoulder on his way to the car.

He climbed in and waved to me, starting it and pulling away. As soon as he was gone, I went back into the house and fixed something quick for lunch since I skipped breakfast. While I ate, I unforwarded the house phone and checked my phone for messages. Still nothing from Dad and Vanessa.

I sat on the couch and turned on the TV but didn't really watch it. I just wanted the sound of something living, artificial or not, that wouldn't argue with me. Staring at my phone, I contemplated what I should do next. I could call Dad, but then he'd get after me for lecturing him last night. I could take a nap, but I wasn't tired, not physically at least. I could call Claire and see what she was up to, but then I realized I didn't want another guest after Ben's visit. So I decided my best bet was to loaf.

And that was what I did for the rest of the day. Around six, I hopped off the couch and checked the cabinets for dinner ideas. Of course, that depended heavily on when Dad and Vanessa would be arriving. Why hadn't they called yet?

Deciding to go ahead and fix something large, I grabbed several items and got to work. I popped my concoction in the oven and went back to the couch to loaf some more until the food was ready. I checked it several times and when it was done, I took it out and set it on the counter to cool. I'd give Dad and Vanessa a little while longer and if I didn't hear from them, I'd go ahead and eat.

Half an hour passed, and I decided I wasn't going to wait any longer. I fixed myself a plate and went back to the couch, enjoying my delicious dinner alone. After I finished, I put the food back in the oven to keep warm. As I cleaned the dishes, I faintly heard the doorbell ring. I glanced at the clock and headed to the door.

"Hello, David," I greeted as I let him in. "I'm so glad you're here. It's nice to finally have some human company," I commented as I shut it.

He grinned mischievously. "If you consider me that," he responded, giving me a soft kiss. "Your father and stepmother haven't arrived yet?" he inquired.

"No, and I haven't heard from them either. I guess Dad's trying to make me worry after what I said last night."

"What did you tell him?"

"That it wasn't necessary to call me every day."

"I see," he replied as he followed me to the family room. "What did you find to do all day?" he asked, probably wondering if I sat out in the sun again.

"Nothing for most of it. But it didn't start out that way," I responded as I sat.

"What happened?" he questioned as he took a seat beside me.

"Ben. He apparently slept in his car last night waiting for me to come home. He surprised me as I unloaded my things, helping bring them in."

"At least he helped," he commented, trying to find something positive to say. "What did he want?"

"To talk to me about the break up and you."

"He still has a problem with me," he responded, more as a statement.

"Oh, I reamed him out. But by the end of our discussion, he agreed to play nice."

"Do you believe him?"

"I think I do."

"I hope you're right," he replied, staring at me. "Did he tell you what he thinks I am?"

"Not outright, but he has a broad idea. I don't think he knows exactly."

He looked away and then back at me. "But you say he's no longer a threat."

"Correct."

He paused, contemplating. "All right. I'll play nice, too," he replied with a smile creeping across his lips as he poked my side.

"What was that for?" I asked, poking him back.

He poked me again, this time in the ribs, and I giggled. He tried again and I slapped his hand. I jabbed my finger into his side and he actually chuckled as if it really tickled. Too funny – I never expected that. I jabbed him again, loving the uninhibited laugh he let out when I did, but then he grabbed my hand and tickled me. He made me laugh so hard I couldn't breathe. I climbed onto his lap and grabbed his hands to gain control, restraining him as residual giggles spilled from my lips.

My laughter and breathing were erratic, but as I gazed into his eyes, so stunning and bright green, both calmed. Focusing on me, the smile slowly faded from his lips as he leaned closer and kissed me. They were cool against mine and his breath beckoned me. Slipping my fingers into his soft hair, I clenched it as I pulled him closer and parted my lips. Without a fight, he went along with it. At least for a little while.

I never heard anything, but he must have. He turned his head slightly and whispered my name, trying to get my attention as I kissed his cheek and neck. Ignoring him, I returned to his lips to keep him from talking. He tried to push me away, but I resisted. I was determined not to stop, no matter what. Finally resorting to using his unnatural strength, he pried me away and held me at arm's length. I was panting heavily as I stared at him, wondering what was so important.

That's when the front door opened, and Dad and Vanessa entered.

# Chapter 38

## Resolutions

"Dad…I can explain," I contended as I quickly hopped off my boyfriend and ran toward him. David remained, his hand perfectly placed over his mouth to cover the smirk hiding beneath it. Somehow he found this amusing. "We weren't doing anything bad, just kissing," I tried to explain, my cheeks burning with embarrassment having to even admit that to him.

Vanessa gave a knowing look as she headed upstairs to put her things away while Dad stood in the hall, arms crossed and glaring at me. He turned and headed toward the living room and I followed. He wasn't going to yell at me in front of David, no matter how angry he was.

"What is he doing here?" he asked in a loud whisper, turning on me in the foyer.

I looked at him, bewildered. "This is when he usually comes over. And you never called to let me know when you got on the plane, so I couldn't tell you he'd be here," I answered angrily.

"After our conversation last night, I figured you'd rather not hear from me. And now I know why."

"Dad, it's not what you think…"

"What do you suppose I'm going to think? I come home from my honeymoon to find my teenage daughter on her college boyfriend's lap looking flustered," he replied, his voice a little louder as he indicated toward the family room.

Vanessa came down the stairs at that moment and smiled at me. "It's always fun to come back from a trip to drama at home," she commented, leaning on the banister.

"Not now, Vanessa," Dad responded wearily. "Why don't you go in the kitchen and find something for dinner."

"It's in the oven," I stated, leaning on the back of the loveseat. She huffed and left.

Dad paced back and forth and then sat on the bottom step. "Megan, Megan, Megan," he muttered as he shook his head. I waited for him to say something else, but he just sighed and held his head.

Knowing my father was preoccupied trying to swallow the fact that his little girl was no longer little or a girl, my attention turned to Vanessa now that she was loose and my boyfriend was unattended. I watched as she headed for the kitchen but was distracted by him sitting on the sofa. He glanced over the back at me and raised a brow, then turned to her as she spoke.

"Hi, David. How have you been?" she asked as she leaned over the back of the other half of the sofa, making sure her cleavage was showing.

"Very well, thank you," he replied, keeping his eyes at her eye level. "Did you have a pleasant honeymoon?"

"Yes, I did. Very pleasurable," she answered as she ran her fingers along her neckline and to her chest.

I glanced at Dad, wondering if he was seeing any of this, but he wasn't. His head was buried in his hands. Poor guy. I should console him, but what was going on in the family room was of more interest to me right now. I returned to them, catching David glance at me again. He smiled and then looked at Vanessa.

"The tropical climate seems to agree with you. You have a *glow* about you," he commented, looking at her and then cutting his eyes to me.

She giggled like a schoolgirl. "Aren't you sweet," she replied, moving closer.

Dad looked up. Needing to distract him from her obvious flirting with my boyfriend, I rushed to Dad's side and blocked his view. "I'm sorry I disappointed you," I apologized, putting my arm around him.

His attention solely on me, his face softened. "You haven't disappointed me, Megan. I guess I still have a problem with my little girl growing up. It hit me pretty hard when we talked last night and then seeing you tonight…"

"It's okay, Dad. You know I'll always be your Nut-Meg," I whispered, kissing his cheek. "Now why don't you get some dinner? I'm sure you're looking forward to a delicious home-cooked meal," I commented, helping him up.

"That does sound good," he replied, heading toward the kitchen.

Vanessa stopped flirting the moment we entered, joining us in the nook. I went to the oven and pulled the food out, setting it on the counter. "Still warm," I informed them as I opened the lid and stepped away.

"You're not eating?" Vanessa questioned as I sat on the couch next to David.

"No, we ate before you got here," I replied, looking at him and smiling. "Well, I guess you should be going," I remarked as I patted his hand.

"Yes, it's getting late," he responded, standing up. "Mrs. Caldwell…Mr. Caldwell," he commented as he bowed his head slightly to each before leaving the room. I guess he figured it best not to say too much.

I followed him to the door and paused at it. Briefly glancing back, I noticed Dad looking our way. "Well, I'll see you tomorrow then," I announced as I started to open the door.

David stopped me and leaned in close. "I'll come by in an hour," he whispered in my ear before gently kissing my lips. With a grin, he slipped through the doorway and disappeared.

I shut and locked it, pausing a moment before turning around and joining Dad and Vanessa in the nook. My cheeks felt hot all over again. Tucking my head, I sat and tried not to look at them immediately. I really didn't want to make small talk; I just wanted to go to my room and eagerly await David's arrival. But if I said I was going to bed now, they'd get suspicious, so I stayed.

Finally feeling the flush disappear from my cheeks, I looked up. "Did you have a good time?" I asked Vanessa as she took a bite of food.

She chewed slowly and then answered. "It was a blast. We had gorgeous weather the whole time, except that one day. We stayed inside most of it," she commented, seductively glancing at my dad and taking his hand in hers. He smiled slightly and continued eating.

Okay, that's too much. Not wanting to hear any more about it, I excused myself and went to watch TV. When I heard the dishes clattering in the sink, I hopped up and offered to take care of them since they needed to recuperate from their flight. She didn't argue as she dashed up the stairs. He lingered behind for a moment, wanting to say or ask something, but then turned and followed her.

I finished the dishes and packed the leftovers away before turning off the TV and lights and heading upstairs myself. It wouldn't be long before David arrived. Pausing at my door, I glanced down the hall toward Dad's room. The door was shut and I could hear muffled talking.

Figuring it was nothing to worry myself over, I entered my room and got ready for bed. Randomly grabbing a book off the shelf, I flopped face down on the mattress and began reading. I wasn't far into it when there came a quiet knocking on the door.

"Come in," I called.

Dad poked his head in. "Just wanted to say good night," he announced quietly.

"Oh, okay. Good night," I replied, looking up at him. He stayed in the doorway, staring at me. "Anything else?" I asked, getting anxious since David would be here at any moment.

He looked down at the floor and played with the door handle. He was quiet for a long time and then finally spoke. "You are being safe, aren't you?"

"Safe about wh...Dad! I told you we're not doing that!" I responded, sitting up.

He looked around my room and then returned to me, staring as if he was trying to read my mind. "I believe you," he replied after a moment and backed out of the room, shutting the door behind him.

No sooner had it closed, I heard a click on the other side of the room. I glanced over my shoulder as David came up behind me and sat. He leaned in and softly kissed my lips. He was warmer.

"Perfect timing," he commented as he stretched out next to me.

"Too perfect. How much did you hear?"

"All of it," he replied, rolling to his side as I turned the light off and slid under the covers.

I rolled over and faced him. "Vanessa was in top form tonight," I commented, wanting to change the subject.

I could see his bright smile in the dark. "Yes, she was."

"It didn't help that you hadn't fed in a while."

"True. But I did it to have more time with you," he responded, caressing my arm. "Do you realize it was Vanessa who put the thought in your father's mind that we were doing more than kissing?"

"How do you know that?"

"Eavesdropping," he answered, his grin once again showing. "He trusts you, though."

"He should. It's not like I have a track record or anything."

"You are as pure as the new fallen snow," he commented, kissing me.

"How long do you plan to stay tonight?" I asked, hoping he wouldn't leave until close to dawn.

"I think it would be safest if I stay until you're asleep."

"What do you mean?"

"I have a feeling your father will be back to check on you."

"What gives you that idea?"

"He feels he's losing you," he replied, gently caressing my skin and running his fingers through a few strands of hair.

"I still have a whole school year left," I protested. "Besides, he knows that day will come eventually."

"Yes, but I think he feels it will be forever. And if you change, it will be."

I paused, contemplating. "Does it really have to be forever?" I asked, sitting up slightly.

He was quiet. "Your relationship will never be the same. You'll look different and act different and for the first several years, you really should stay away from humans."

"But I'll be strong...for them and myself. I'll resist the urge," I argued.

"You may be able to do that, but eventually you'll have to cut yourself off from your friends and family anyway. They'll notice you never change, that as they grow old, you remain the same."

"Can't I tell them then what I am?" I asked, trying to be hopeful of a solution.

"No. They can never know, no matter how much you trust them. It will get out some way or another. And you can't change any and everyone, even if they ask. This is not something we do for fun or to avoid death. There is a limit."

He was right. I'll have to cut contact with everyone I know and love, either initially or later down the line. "Are you trying to discourage me?"

He slipped his hand under my chin and tilted it up, giving me a gentle kiss on the lips. "Of course not. You are the one I want to share eternity with. But I do want you to understand this is a serious decision. Once you graduate, it'll be your choice how long you want to wait." I didn't realize I shed a tear until after it crossed the bridge of my nose. "Oh Megan, don't weep," he whispered as he wiped it away.

He moved closer, holding me in his arms. I buried my head in his chest and sucked back the tears that tried to escape. There was no sense in crying; it wasn't like this was going to happen tomorrow. He kissed my forehead and held me closer. The little bit of warmth radiating from him was comforting and soon I was able to relax and drift into sleep.

*I was in an open area, Dad to one side of me and David on the other. I glanced at them as they called to me, both wanting me to choose them. But I had to choose one or the other; I couldn't have both.*

*At first, I joined my dad, choosing humanity over immortality. As I took his hand, I was transported through time. I watched as I tried to continue dating David, but as the years passed, I realized it was impossible. We broke up and I settled into a life with another human, starting a family and living in mediocrity. But even though I loved the man I married, I loved David more and still longed to be with him.*

*He watched from afar as I grew older, still the same person I met in the cemetery that night so long ago. And he continued to watch helplessly as I was stricken with the disease that took my mother and grandmother, unable to do anything because I refused. I had lived a long enough life and I accepted my fate. But as I lay in bed at home breathing my final breaths, his name was last on my lips before I gave into death.*

*Everything went black and then suddenly I was back at the beginning of the dream, standing between David and my father again. This time I chose David. I ran into his arms and kissed him, glancing back at my father. He smiled as he faded into a fog and when I returned my gaze to David, I wasn't sad. Tilting my head to the side, I gave myself to him.*

*No one seemed to think anything of my change, none the wiser to what happened to me. David and I were happy and safe. But twenty years down the road, people began to notice that we still looked like we did when we were young. It was then he informed me it was time to go. Knowing we had to protect my loved ones and ourselves, I didn't fight.*

*The images that came up after that were of me secretly visiting my dying father and attending his funeral, then the same for my friends. I was sad, but I also knew it was part of life, their life and not mine. My life was eternal, with David. The final images that flew by were of him and me standing together watching the world change around us as we stayed the same, with no end in sight.*

I woke the next morning, the conversation and dream from last night weighing heavily on my mind. I climbed out of bed and went out onto the balcony, lounging on the chaise as I watched the animals move about. The morning was warm with no humidity, allowing me to sit comfortably and mull over the dream and its meaning.

I was obviously weighing my options – what would happen if I chose this over that. Looking back, it seemed the option of choosing David outweighed remaining human. But what if the dream was wrong and I wasn't fated to end up like my mother? Could I still have a happy life as a human with or without David, or would it still end the same? I sighed, not sure what to do.

"Morning, Meg. What are you doing out here?" Dad asked, startling me. I was so deep in thought I didn't realize he was there until he spoke.

"Oh…just enjoying the pleasant morning," I replied with a soft smile.

I sat up and slipped over, making room for him. He sat and stared at me, reaching up after a moment to push a loose strand of hair behind my ear. He cupped my chin in his hand and lifted my face, then dropped it and looked away.

"Dad, what's wrong?" I inquired.

He looked at me briefly, and I noticed his eyes reddening. He quickly stood and went to the balcony doors. "You're growing up and I have to accept that. You'll be starting college next year. After that comes a career and then marriage and a family of your own," he answered, his back to me as he leaned in the doorway.

I joined him, watching his face as he took in my room. "I'm not leaving forever. I'll be coming back to visit."

He wiped his eyes. "I know…I just have this feeling that once you walk out the door, I'll never see you again."

How uncanny. "You will, I promise," I assured him, though I wasn't sure how I'd pull it off if I chose David.

He turned and gave me a big hug, kissing the top of my head. "I never thought time would pass so quickly," he whispered, kissing my head again.

I hugged back, holding him and treasuring every bit of it. It's been a long time since he hugged me like this. I sighed, enjoying one more second and then wriggled loose.

"So what are your plans today?" I asked, hoping to divert the conversation.

He wiped his eyes again as he sat on the edge of my bed. "I'm going into the office for a little while. Vanessa took off the rest of the week," he replied. I could care less what she was doing. "Why? Do you have other plans?" he inquired eagerly.

"No, well, I was going to see if Claire wanted to hang out. I owe her a day."

"Oh," he responded quietly. By the looks of it, it seemed he was hoping we could do something together.

"Why don't you and I do something this weekend?" I offered. "Like a movie or maybe even a game?"

He perked up. "Just the two of us?"

"Yep. I'll look online today to see if there's anything good."

He stood and gave me another hug. "I'd like that very much," he responded, then released me and smiled. "Well, I better get ready. I'll see you around dinner time," he remarked as he headed out the door, happier than a moment ago. He was assured and at peace.

But I wasn't.

The conversation and dream still disturbed me. I tried to distract myself while showering, setting my iPod and portable speakers up on the vanity and blaring the music, but it couldn't drown out my thoughts. I needed a bigger distraction. After I got dressed and fixed my hair, I called Claire.

"What's up?" she answered.

"I'm free today and wondered if you want to hang out."

"That'd be awesome! Justin has to work. What do you want to do?"

"I know it's nice outside and all, but do you want to go to the mall?" I asked, thinking that would be good.

"I hoped you were going to ask that. I'm just not up to laying in the sun or swimming today."

"Good...so I'll pick you up in fifteen minutes?" I inquired, slipping my shoes on.

"Nope, I'll be there in ten," she replied and hung up.

I grabbed my purse and dashed down the stairs, veering into the kitchen. I didn't have long and needed to grab something quick to tide me over until we had lunch. Vanessa sat on the couch watching TV in her robe. She lazily glanced my way and then returned to watching the screen. Talk shows, of course.

"What's your hurry?" she asked snidely, flipping the channel.

"Claire's picking me up and we're going to hang out at the mall," I replied, finishing a granola bar. "Dad knows," I added for good measure.

She looked back at me and smiled. "Have fun, *sweetie*."

I rolled my eyes and headed for the door. "See you around dinner," I shouted back as I opened it and walked out.

Sitting on the steps, I waited impatiently for Claire to arrive. It was getting warmer, and I didn't want to be out in the heat too long. The rising humidity wouldn't be kind to my hair. Plus, I didn't want to get all sticky and sweaty. Luckily, she pulled in the drive moments later, honking the horn as she waved at me. I hopped up and rushed to the car, climbing in it.

"This is a rare treat," I commented as she backed out.

"Yeah, I thought it'd be nice of me."

But I soon regretted it. Her driving is like her car – messy and all over the place. She whipped in and out of traffic and jabbered on and on, not paying enough attention to the road for my taste. I couldn't even tell you what she talked about because I was too busy looking out for her and fearing for my life.

As soon as she parked, I jumped out and breathed a heavy sigh, thankful we made it in one piece. I didn't know if I could handle the trip home with her. I might have to call Dad to pick me up later.

She smiled as we headed into the mall, taking my arm in hers and patting my hand. "Oh, it wasn't that bad," she commented as we entered.

And she was right, mainly for the fact it kept my mind off my dream. As we shopped and joked, I stayed distracted, enjoying the lightness of not having such a weight on my shoulders. When we went to lunch, however, I had enough downtime for it all to come back.

We separated – I wanted Italian and she wanted Chinese – which gave me that time alone I was trying to avoid. After grabbing my food, I took a seat at a table in the food court and waited for her to join me. The feeling from this morning and the added issue of my father and his fear hounded me. Poking at my food, I tried to think of something else but couldn't. I glanced around looking for Claire and found her still waiting to order.

Maybe I could hold off until I was twenty-nine. I'll look mature and yet still pass as being younger. And David and I won't look too odd together. That'll be a good time for us to move on as well. Claire will probably be married with kids…

"Megan…hello?" she called, and I snapped out of my daze.

"Sorry," I apologized, moving my purse out of the seat she wanted to sit in.

"So as I was saying…" she began, continuing whatever subject we left off on before splitting up. I didn't pay attention to the rest, playing with my food and continuing to dissect the dream. "What do you think?"

"Umm…think of what?"

"My plans for my date tomorrow with Justin. Were you listening to anything I said?"

I sighed and openly admitted, "No, not really…"

She reached over and touched my hand resting on the table. "Is something wrong? You've had this sudden mood change."

I looked at her, the concern genuine in her eyes. I want to tell her, but I can't. "It's nothing…just lost in thought."

She gave me a 'yeah right' glare. "Come on, something's bothering you. I'm your best friend; you can tell me," she coaxed.

I gave her a long look, my forehead creased as I tried to decide what to do. How can I tell her without *telling* her? I thought a moment longer and came up with the best analogy I could. "I have a dilemma. Dad wants me to stay local, go to a college not too far away so he can see me often. He's become very clingy since he came back from his honeymoon."

"Okay. What's the problem? David goes to VCU…you could live in the dorms so you don't have to deal with the step-witch on a daily basis and we can still hang out," she helpfully offered.

"I know…but what if David wants to move away, maybe go to another school?"

"Like where?"

"I don't know. Maybe up north, back home."

"You could still be boyfriend and girlfriend. Haven't you ever heard of a long distance relationship?"

"Yeah, but they rarely work out."

"Well, then tell him he can't go too far away."

I looked down at my food and played with it. "What if I want to go with him?"

She gave me a bewildered look. "Are you two that serious?"

"I want to be with him forever, and he feels the same about me," I replied, not exaggerating at all.

"Wow…when's the wedding?" she asked and I jerked my head toward her, my eyes wide. "I'm just kidding," she responded and I relaxed. "So what about us?"

"Us who?" I inquired, taking a bite of my now cold food.

"Your friends. Are you just going to leave and forget us?"

I smiled as I put my arm around her. "Of course not. How could I forget you?" Great. Claire, like my dad this morning, was making this whole thing that much harder.

I was quick to change the subject after that, not wanting to dwell on a decision I have yet to make. I felt a little better at least, being able to kind of get it off my chest without revealing anything. I still didn't have any answers, though. In time, they would come.

Inviting her to tell me again about her plans for her date, I listened attentively this time as we finished eating. Of course, she was happy to repeat it and I was glad to hear it. And as we returned to shopping, I helpfully suggested outfits and accessories for her date.

We exited the mall with a couple bags each. Claire bought a new outfit, earrings, and perfume, and I picked up an outfit and two dresses I thought David might like on me. I've enjoyed wearing scooping necklines around him lately for the attention and figured a couple more wouldn't hurt. As I sat in the car, I braced myself for the ride home, realizing I forgot to call to be picked up.

I didn't open my eyes or release my grip from the seat until she announced our arrival. I sighed, glad I made it back in one piece, and turned to her. "Thanks for hanging out with me today. It was lots of fun."

"Sure was. I hope David likes what you bought. Maybe you can model it for him," she commented, raising her brows up and down as I climbed out of the car.

I grinned as I poked my head in the window. "Are you going to model your new clothes for Justin?"

"Maybe," she replied with a wide grin, which was a definite yes.

"See you later, Claire," I laughed as I straightened up. I went up to the porch and unlocked the front door, turning to wave at her as I headed inside. She backed out of the drive and sped around the corner.

Not bothering to let Vanessa know I was home, I dashed up the stairs to my room. I hung my purchases on the closet door and went over to my laptop. I had enough time to look online for something to do with Dad. Checking movies first, I didn't find anything appropriate for the both of us. Looking up sporting events was even harder.

I finally settled on a Richmond Kickers game on Saturday, seven o'clock at the University of Richmond. I liked soccer and Dad would go to any sporting event just to see it live. I purchased the tickets and printed the receipt for pick up at the ticket booth.

Grabbing an envelope, I folded the receipt in thirds and slipped it inside. I sealed it and wrote 'Dad' on the front, drawing an ornamental line underneath. Sticking it in my back pocket, I glanced at the clock and figured it was time to get dinner started. I jogged down the stairs and headed into the kitchen, seeing Vanessa still on the couch, still in her robe.

Checking the cabinets, I had a hard time deciding what to make. With what we had, I chose to go with bruschetta chicken. All the commotion of preparation and cooking got her attention.

"Hey, you're home. Buy anything cute?" she asked, curious if it was anything she'd want to wear.

"A couple of dresses and an outfit. Nothing spectacular," I replied, downplaying their appeal.

"Cool," she responded and returned to the TV. I shook my head and went back to cooking.

Dad came in as I was finishing up. "Mmm…smells good," he commented as he went over to Vanessa and kissed her. "Have you been sitting here all day?" I heard him quietly ask her.

"It's my honeymoon," she replied.

He shook his head disapprovingly and then joined me in the kitchen. I smiled as I set the food on the island. "Oh, here Dad," I remarked as I pulled the envelope out of my pocket.

"What's this?" he inquired as he opened it. "Aww, Meg. Thank you," he responded as he looked at the receipt and then gave me a hug.

"One for you and one for me, this Saturday," I stated. "And dinner's ready," I added.

Sitting at the nook table, we ate and talked about how each of us spent our day. Dad came back to work just in time, getting an interesting case he was excited about. My day of shopping was definitely not as intriguing, and Vanessa's was the most boring, which she openly admitted, but she did have a lot to tell us about the programs she watched and the fascinating lives of the people on them.

I took care of the dishes and leftovers and then joined them on the couch for some TV. Right on time, the doorbell rang and I jumped up to get it. I let David in and led him back to the family room to sit with us. Dad wasn't too happy that Vanessa was still in a robe and David was seeing her that way. She, however, was pleased to show her entire thigh to him, not that he looked.

I snuggled into his arm as we sat on the sofa and watched a movie. It was nice being all together and not fighting or bickering. I looked at him and smiled and then looked at my dad and smiled. I may not be able to have both of them forever, but I have both of them now.

When the movie was over, David didn't linger, saying good night and leaving. I returned to the family room as Dad and Vanessa were getting up to go to bed. Guess it was time I go, too, then.

Dad thanked me again as we paused at the top of the stairs and then said good night and headed to his room as I turned into mine. David was lying on the bed staring at the ceiling as usual, waiting for me. I grabbed nightclothes and changed in the bathroom.

"I see you went shopping," he commented, indicating toward the closet as I came out.

I grinned. "Yes, I did. Would you like to see them…on me?" I asked hesitantly.

He raised his left brow and sat up. "All right," he responded with his delicious smirk.

I bit my lip, still smiling as I grabbed them off the door and ducked into the closet. I put on the outfit first – a billowy top with cap sleeves and a low-cut neck paired with plaid seersucker shorts. Strutting out, I stopped in front of the door, struck a pose as I tried not to laugh, and then did a turn and headed back to the closet.

I slipped on one of the dresses next. The scooping neckline was held up with spaghetti straps and the calf length skirt flowed out like something from the fifties. It was light and airy, very summery. I slowly opened the door and slinked out, posing closer to him and then heading back. I laughed to myself as I changed out of that dress and into the next one, thinking about his amused expression.

The last dress I put on was chocolate in color, strapless, and form fitting with a straight skirt that hit mid-thigh. I was a little more nervous to come out in it than the others. I wasn't used to wearing such short, tight clothes. I paused at the door, my hand on it while I eased my nerves.

As I edged out, I saw David's face change from amusement to awe. I slowly strolled toward him, blushing as I smiled softly, and paused at the bed. He remained still, drinking me in.

Feeling more embarrassed with his stare, I turned to head back to the closet, but he stopped me. Standing, he slipped his arm around my waist and held my body close to his, making my heart thump as he kissed me. First my lips, then my chin, on down my neck to the top of my chest and then up the other side, returning to my lips.

This is the attention I enjoy. "I see you like this one," I breathed as he kissed my neck again and I closed my eyes.

"You're more exposed...vulnerable," he replied quietly, running his finger along the top of the dress while barely touching my skin, "and you look amazing."

Stepping back and sitting on the bed, he pulled me down with him. I sat sideways on his lap and wrapped my arms around his neck, continuing to kiss him. One of his hands slid to my waist while the other held the side of my bare thigh. Feeling him touch the exposed skin made my pulse race and I knew what that led to. I felt the sharp scrape on my lip and slowly pulled back.

"I better get out of this before something bad happens," I whispered.

He kissed my neck and then let me go, smirking as I walked away. Glancing over my shoulder, I gave him a final look before slipping back into the closet. As soon as I was inside, I fell against the wall and took a deep breath.

That was intense.

After composing myself, I changed back into my original outfit and hung the clothes up. Yep, I'd say he definitely liked the new stuff. I came out and found him lying on his back with his hands behind his head, staring at the ceiling as before. He looked over at me and grinned, making my heart race all over again. I slowly walked over to the bed and crawled on it, sitting on my knees beside him. He sat up, leaning his arm on his knee, and looked at me.

"Feeling better now?" he asked, his lips curling into another smile.

"No, my heart's still racing," I answered, taking his hand and placing it on my chest. I held mine over it and watched him.

He closed his eyes and stayed completely still. I bit my lower lip and gradually leaned closer, continuing to hold his hand against my pounding heart. He was so handsome and I longed to kiss him. I moved even closer, inches from his lips. There was no reaction from him. My pulse gained speed as I placed my lips on his and parted them. He slowly raised his other hand and placed it on my cheek, responding to my advances.

As it slid to my neck, his fingers tilted my jaw up while my hand gradually dropped. He kissed my throat and my breath came out in short, quick pants. I could feel him smile against my skin. Then he released my chin and pressed his cheek to mine.

"That always seems to get you," he whispered and then sat back, still grinning.

"It's a sensitive spot," I replied, covering my neck with both hands.

He removed them and caressed it delicately with his fingers. "It's one of my favorite spots."

I blushed, tucking my head. "I better...lie down," I responded quietly as I scooted back to the headboard and put my legs under the covers.

I turned out the light before resting my head on the pillow. He lay next to me, gazing into my eyes. My lids felt heavy suddenly. "No discussion about your day or plans for tomorrow?" he asked.

Gradually opening them, I found him still staring at me. "Not tonight," I whispered. "I'm too tired."

He kissed my cheek and rolled to his back, staring at the ceiling again. I closed my eyes and let my body relax. As if he knew what I had been thinking about all day, he whispered in my ear, "When the time comes, the choice will not be as difficult as it is now."

I wanted to respond but fell asleep before I could.

Friday was like any other day of my summer vacation. I did some cleaning and went to the pool, but mostly avoided Vanessa. Forgetting to mention it the night before, I had to keep reminding myself all day to tell David I'd be going out Saturday evening with my dad. So to make up for the possibility of him wanting to do something then, I planned for us to go out tonight. When he arrived at his usual time, we left immediately.

"Where are we going?" he asked as I climbed in my car and unlocked the doors.

"I thought we'd go on the canal walk," I replied after he climbed inside.

He didn't ask any more questions as I drove into the city, making comments only to my reply about how I spent my day. But on our walk over to the canal, he was quiet. Being a pleasant summer night, a lot of people were out enjoying it. The soft burbling of conversations from other visitors seemed loud in his silence as we joined them.

Walking arm in arm in the lamplight, David looked at me and smiled. "What is the reason for this lovely evening stroll?" he asked finally.

I glanced at him and then at the darkened scenery around us. "I won't be home until after ten tomorrow night, so you can just meet me in my room."

He stopped. "Where will you be?"

"The other day, Dad was so upset about his little girl growing up that I planned for us to do something together. So we're going to a game," I explained. "I forgot to mention it to you yesterday."

He resumed walking. "That's nice of you. He'll appreciate it," he responded, not at all upset.

"So you're not mad?"

He laughed and several people looked at us. "Of course I'm not. You're spending time with your father. This is good for both of you."

Putting his arm around my shoulder, he pulled me close and kissed me. We continued our walk to the end and turned back around. Every once in a while, he smiled and nodded at people passing us. As usual, the women stared in awe as the men pulled them closer.

It was pleasant, not a lot of talking, just taking in the scenery and the night. The sky was full of stars even though we couldn't see the full extent of them thanks to the city lights. But it was nice regardless just being there with him.

When we arrived back home, he put on the usual show that he was leaving, kissing me at the door and then disappearing. I popped into the family room and told them about my evening, receiving envious glares from Vanessa. Feeling I wasted enough time, I said good night and headed up to my room to a waiting David. This time when I entered, he was at my laptop, searching the internet for something. He closed the site and shut the lid before I could see.

I dipped into the bathroom to change and then joined him when I was done, climbing into bed. I turned out the light and rested my head on his chest. But I wasn't as tired as last night.

"What were you looking up on my computer?" I asked.

"Where you will be tomorrow night," he replied, rubbing my back.

"Why would you need to know that?"

"Just in case…"

I sat up. "Don't you trust me?"

"Of course I trust you. I like to know so I can watch over you, make sure you don't get into any trouble."

"I appreciate it, but I'll be with my dad."

"I'll protect you from other things."

"Like what?"

"Well, there's still the chance that Brian may show up, as you felt. Then there may be other supernatural beings."

"Really," I responded sarcastically, lying back down and resting my chin on his chest. "Why would they be after me?"

His smile brightened up the darkness. "You know about us. You'll be a target either out of curiosity or torment."

"Oh. Well, make sure you don't let my dad see you," I responded, not taking his remark seriously.

"He won't."

I put my head down and listened to his breathing. My body relaxed and I let my mind open. Soon I could feel myself slowly drifting away.

"I'll see you at bedtime tomorrow evening. Have a good time at the game," he whispered in my ear before I was completely out.

I woke the next morning in a great mood. I showered, dressed, and then headed downstairs to make breakfast for everyone. Dad was the first to come in, smelling the frying bacon and the brewing coffee.

"This is a pleasant surprise," he commented, grabbing a cup and pouring some. He sat at the island and opened the paper I retrieved off the porch.

"It's best to start your day off with a hearty breakfast," I proclaimed as I flipped the French toast.

A robed Vanessa entered then and sat next to him, stealing his coffee and taking a sip. She made a disgusted face when she realized it was black. "Why are you so chipper this morning?" she asked, grabbing a cup and filling it. She added sugar and flavored creamer and then sat down.

"Well, it's a beautiful morning, I slept well last night, and I get to spend the evening with my dad," I answered as I fixed a plate and slipped it in front of him.

I pulled the syrup out of the fridge and grabbed utensils for all of us. Asking her what she wanted, I fixed another plate and set it in front of her, then fixed mine and sat across from them. We made idle conversation as we ate, discussing plans for the day.

After the meal, Vanessa headed upstairs to shower and get ready to go out and Dad stayed with me. He helped wash the dishes and clean up, spending a little quality time with me until she called him. I can only guess what she wanted him to do.

I finished up and went into the family room, turning on the TV. Finding nothing worthwhile, I went over to the bookcase and picked out a book. Stretching out on the couch, I read while I waited for further instruction on what I should do today.

Dad came in, dressed in khaki slacks and a polo shirt, and sat next to me. "We'll be gone most of the day. If you don't mind, wash a load of clothes and vacuum the main areas."

"No problem. See you when you get back," I replied, returning to my book.

He kissed the top of my head and left, meeting Vanessa at the door. It clicked and I was relieved by the sudden silence. I read for a couple hours and then set about doing the chores I was assigned. Once they were done, I returned to the couch and resumed my reading until they got home, finishing the book as they came in to greet me.

"I need to change and then we can head out to dinner," Dad commented as he stood behind the sofa. Vanessa glanced over from the kitchen, giving a pouty look as she did. "Sorry, honey. This is our night. Order in if you can't find anything good," he suggested as she stuck her head in the fridge, searching for something to eat.

He left the room as I put the book away, following him upstairs even though I didn't need to change or even freshen up. Instead, I sat at my desk and wrote a note for David, laying it on the bed before grabbing my purse and heading downstairs to wait for Dad. When he finally came down, he was dressed more casual for the game, in jeans and a t-shirt. He went into the kitchen, gave Vanessa a peck on the lips, and then we headed out.

We had a pleasant dinner at a restaurant near the university. He asked about my plans for college, but I didn't have much to tell him since I still hadn't decided on anything. "Time is running out. You need to make a decision soon," he told me.

Little does he know how true his statement really is. "I know. I'll work on it soon," I replied.

We headed to the game, finding our seats easily. We had a nice spot near the field on the sidelines. Dad enjoyed himself, but throughout the first half of the game, I couldn't help scanning the crowd for David or some random supernatural being planning an attack. Was he really being serious?

At half time, I excused myself, saying I had to use the restroom. When I was far enough away, I called him. "Are you looking for me?" he asked, humor in his smooth voice.

I hesitated, looking around. "Nooo," I replied.

"Well, you won't find me," he responded. "How is everything going?"

"I miss you," I replied, "but Dad's having a good time."

"You'll see me soon. You better get back now; your father is looking for you."

"Okay. See you shortly," I responded and hung up.

I headed back to my seat and glanced around one more time, but still didn't see him. He was good. "You almost missed the kick-off," Dad commented as I sat. "Everything okay?"

"Yeah, everything's fine," I replied, turning my attention to the game.

This time I watched it, enjoying the excitement and even yelling a couple times. I caught him smiling at me occasionally during the remainder of the second half, happy I was sharing this with him. And I was happy I could share it with him. I felt a stronger, better bond with him, something I had been missing the last four years.

As the game came to a close, we sat on the edge of our seats watching as the Kickers fought for control of the ball. The game was tied and everyone was cheering for another goal. As the clock wound down, all eyes were on the forwards as they rushed down the field with the ball. The whole stadium erupted into cheers of victory as the Kickers scored the final goal of the game, winning three to two.

All the way to the car, Dad and I avidly discussed the game and how close and exciting it was. And what a different experience it had been for both of us. Neither of us had gone to a soccer game outside of the ones for school.

Not ready to call it quits yet, we stopped at a little ice cream shop and enjoyed a sundae each to finish off our night. Dad was quiet, watching me eat. His expression was soft and kind, like he was seeing me as a little girl again in pigtails and a jumper. Then he sighed and looked down at his melting dessert.

"Thank you for doing this," he commented, flipping his toppings around.

"No problem, I had a great time. We should do it again," I replied.

He looked up with bright eyes. "All right. But next time, I pick."

"Deal."

I honestly had a fun evening, but I couldn't wait to get back to see David. We pulled in the driveway and I rushed up to the house, not waiting for Dad. I opened the door and ran to the family room to briefly let Vanessa know we were home. She was on the couch watching TV where I thought she'd be.

"Did you have fun?" she asked, not looking at me.

"Yeah, loads," I replied. "Well, good night," I continued hurriedly as I turned to leave.

"Wait," she requested and I stopped. Dad was just entering the house. "What's with this note you wrote your boyfriend?" she inquired, holding up a folded piece of paper between her fingers.

I glanced toward the door as Dad slipped upstairs. "What were you doing in my room?" I questioned, snatching it.

"Oh, I went in there to return something and saw it sitting on the bed," she replied casually. "Now why would you leave it out like that?" she asked suspiciously.

"I…I planned to give it to him, if he happened to come by tonight."

She glared at me. "Oh you know damn well he plans to come by tonight," she snarled. "So how often does he sneak into your room after you say you're going to bed?"

I should have known I wouldn't be able to fool her, but I still wasn't going to admit anything. "Never. He goes home or to work."

"Oh, please. I used to do the same thing, having boys visit me or sneaking out. You may fool your dad, but you're not fooling me."

"Well, as I've said before, I'm not like you. You're completely wrong."

"Okay then…I want to go to your room with you right now," she demanded as she stood. "Come on, let's go. You were so anxious to get up there a moment ago," she snapped, grabbing my arm and dragging me along.

"That's because I'm tired," I defended falsely. I was anxious to see him, but now I hope he isn't here.

We climbed the stairs and at the top, turned toward my room. She grabbed the handle and before I could stop her, she threw open the door. "Aha!" she exclaimed.

I was too worried to look, but when I saw her mouth agape, I scanned the room. I didn't see anything out of the ordinary. "See, he's not here," I retorted, trying to push her out of the room.

She turned and I almost fell. "No, no. He's hiding here somewhere," she commented as she searched under the bed and in my closet. Then she headed to the balcony.

She threw open the French doors and pushed through the curtains only to re-enter a moment later. "See. I was telling the truth. Now get out of my room!" I shouted as I shoved her, shutting the door and locking it.

I went over to the bed and dropped to the floor, covering my face with my hands. I can't believe she did that – oh wait, yes I can. I pulled the note out of my pocket and unfolded it. It was a good thing I left it pretty vague or else she would have had more fuel. I tore it up into tiny pieces and clenched them in my fist.

"Is everything all right?" David asked quietly over my shoulder.

I jumped. "Oh, you scared me!" I answered, throwing my hand to my chest. He was lying on his stomach across the bed, resting his chin on his hands as he looked down at me, a mischievous smile on his face. I was momentarily mesmerized by him, but quickly shook myself out of it. "Just Vanessa being a witch," I replied finally.

The smile faded and he looked up suddenly, quickly hopping off the bed. "Your father is coming," he stated as he dropped to the floor.

"What are you doing?" I whispered loudly.

"Hiding under the bed. You should unlock the door before he tries to enter," he instructed quietly.

I popped up and rushed to it, unlocking it as I heard Dad approaching. I tossed the remains of the letter in the trash and sat on the edge of the bed, slipping my shoes off and putting my hair in a bun as he knocked. "Come in," I invited.

"Hey, Meg. Vanessa said you two had a fight. What happened?" he asked as he entered and sat next to me.

"She came in my room without permission while I was gone," I answered.

"Well, that is wrong. I'll have a talk with her about it."

I felt something touch my heel and I kicked. "Thanks Dad," I replied as I crossed my ankles and glared at the floor.

"Well, you're getting older and should have some privacy. She needs to respect that."

This time, it tickled the bottom of my foot. I jerked and stifled a giggle but couldn't keep from smiling. I quickly covered my mouth and kicked back, hitting David's hand for sure. "Exactly," I agreed, clearing my throat. "Well, I'm really tired and I'm sure you are, too," I commented as I hugged him. "Good night, Dad."

"Good night," he replied as he stood and headed to the door, glancing at me before shutting it behind him.

As soon as I knew he was far enough down the hall, I hopped off the bed and got on my hands and knees. Lifting up the bed skirt, I stared right into the face of a grinning David. "You could have gotten me in trouble!" I whispered loudly as he pulled himself out from underneath, his grin disappearing into darkness.

He tried not to laugh. "I apologize. I shouldn't have done that, but it was too tempting."

"You should be sorry," I growled as I got to my feet and went to the bathroom to change. It was best to get in bed before Dad or Vanessa decided to come back.

The room was dark when I came out, and it took a moment for my eyes to adjust. I walked around the bed and climbed under the comforter. David leaned over and gently touched my face, kissing me. Even though I was upset with him, it felt good to be in his arms once more. We continued kissing a little longer and then he sat back. I rolled over and rested my head on his chest, getting comfortable.

"So, did you see anything unusual tonight?" I asked sardonically, slipping my hand under his shirt.

He kissed the side of my head. "Nothing at all. My mere presence must have scared them away."

"You're so full of yourself," I chuckled, running my fingers over his body. His skin was like fine, sculpted marble, cool and smooth.

I lifted my head and pulled his shirt up. "What are you doing?" he questioned softly.

I placed the side of my face against his chest. "I want to be closer to you," I replied.

Turning my head slightly, I kissed it. I relished being that near to him, smelling his skin and feeling the coolness on my cheek and lips. I traveled down his torso to his stomach and then raised my body slightly, hovering above him as a strange desire came over me. Grazing his abs, I intended to go further, but then he stopped me.

"Megan, no," he whispered, grabbing my shoulders and pulling me back.

I sat up, feeling embarrassed as I turned my back to him and wrapped my arms around my legs. "I'm sorry. I…I don't know what came over me," I whispered.

He moved behind me and kissed the back of my neck, resting his chin on my shoulder. "It's not you. It's the effect I have on you."

I kept my head bowed. "Is this normal?"

"With me it is, unfortunately. Part of my allure is that you will want me, desire me," he replied, kissing the side of my neck. I sighed. "But you have your own alluring qualities," he offered.

I lifted my head and looked over my shoulder, meeting his eyes. "You're joking."

He pulled the covers back and indicated for me to lie on my side. I hesitated at first and then gave in. Lying behind me, he put his arm around me and placed his hand over my heart. His body was against mine, shaped perfectly with it. Being that close sent a sensation through me I hadn't felt in a while and it started my heart beating faster.

He leaned in close to my ear, his lips nearly touching the lobe. "You do," he responded quietly. He moved his head slightly, his lips caressing my neck and shoulder, and whispered, "Your skin." His hand moved from above my heart to the top of my breasts. My cheeks grew warm, but I remained still. "Your innocence," he continued, moving his hand back to my heart. "But of course the most alluring quality…" he purred as he pressed his lips to my neck, holding them there for a moment before slowly lifting them off and breathing, "is your heartbeat."

My body felt electrified with his words. He gently kissed my neck several times, moving up to my jaw. Placing his fingers on my chin, he turned my face toward his, leaning over and kissing me softly at first and then parting his lips as it intensified. Breaking away, he moved down my neck again, his fangs scraping across my skin.

"See…you have a similar effect on me," he commented, lying back and resting his head on the pillow behind me.

My chest heaved and heart pounded. I never realized how much I affected him. Of course, that little demonstration had quite an effect on me. Well, at least we both wanted each other, though in different ways.

As I gradually calmed, he returned his hand to above my heart and I placed mine over it, squeezing softly. Feeling better, I closed my eyes and relaxed. "I love you, David," I whispered, bringing his hand to my lips and kissing it before replacing it.

"And I you, Megan," he replied softly, kissing the back of my neck.

I smiled as I slowly drifted off to sleep.

# Chapter 39
## Back to Normal

The rest of June flew by as we settled into a routine. Having Vanessa in the house all the time was no treat, but I had to learn to live with it, at least until I was out of high school. Most of the time, there was peace. David came by every night, hanging out for at least an hour and then leaving, only to be back before I went to bed.

Things were settling into a pattern of normalcy. I spent time with my friends during the day, my family in the evening, and David after dark. Life was great.

One night at the beginning of July, David and I went out to the gazebo to enjoy the warm summer evening before a storm. We sat on the swing and didn't talk, listening to the crickets and frogs serenade us. The smell of rain was heavy in the air and lightning periodically illuminated distant skies.

I watched the house as Dad paused at the patio doors, looking our way, and then continuing into the family room. Once he was out of view, David leaned in and placed his cool hand on my cheek, kissing me softly. His lips were equally as cool, but on a hot summer's night like this, I welcomed it.

I put my arms around his neck and threw my legs over his as I snuggled against his chest. "This is nice," I commented, twisting a lock of his hair around my finger.

"Yes, it is," he replied, watching the house.

Dad walked past the doors again, glancing our way as he did. He continued into the kitchen and stopped at the sink, his head down as he did something at it. Before he left, he looked up and at us. I felt a twinge of guilt.

I dropped my legs and faced forward, folding my hands on my lap. "So, are you doing anything special for the holiday?" I asked, figuring I'd start a conversation so we didn't look suspicious.

"What holiday?" he inquired, looking at me as he reached over and took my warm hand in his cold one.

"Fourth of July…Independence Day. It's this weekend."

"Oh, right…no. Do you have plans?" he questioned with a grin.

"Not really…"

He looked at the house again and then at me. "What about a cookout at my house? You, your father, and Vanessa can come over. If you like, you can even invite Claire, Erin, Ben, and their families," he suggested.

I looked at him and laughed. "Are you serious?"

"It would help with my façade."

I continued laughing. "Okay, but at this late notice, I don't know how many will be able to make it."

"As soon as you have a head count, let me know so I can purchase supplies," he responded, continuing to hold onto my hand as he stood and slowly raised me off the bench. "We should go inside. The clouds are moving in and it'll rain soon."

We walked arm in arm back to the house, arriving at the patio door just as it began falling. I smiled at him as I pulled the handle. Entering first, I led the way to the family room and stood before Dad and Vanessa.

"Hey, do we have any plans for this weekend?" I asked, holding his hand behind my back as he stood slightly behind me.

Dad looked at Vanessa and she looked at him and shrugged. He returned to me and replied, "Nothing that I know of. Why?"

"David has invited us to his house for a cookout Saturday," I responded, glancing back at him and smiling. "Are we able to go?" I inquired.

They looked at each other again. "We would be delighted to come," Vanessa answered this time, smiling broadly at him.

"What time?" Dad asked. "And would you like us to bring anything?"

David stepped to my side. "Let's say seven and no, I'll provide everything." I looked at him, a little surprised he was planning it for so early.

"Fabulous! I can't wait," Vanessa grinned.

"He's also inviting my friends and their families," I commented, putting my arm around his waist.

"That'll be nice. I'm sure Ben's sisters and Claire's brother will love it there," Dad responded, watching his expression.

"I'm sure they will," he agreed, smiling slightly.

"Well, I guess you better get going," I remarked to him, walking around the sofa.

"Good night, Mr. and Mrs. Caldwell," he stated as we left the room.

Grabbing an umbrella, we headed out the door and as we stepped off the porch, I opened it. Huddling together, we strolled to his car as the rain fell steadily around us. He opened the door and stood behind it while I stood on the other side, trying to make sure both of us remained covered. He leaned on it as he stared at me, a smirk on his lips.

"I know you're dying to ask," he commented.

"Of course I am. Are you crazy? That's too early!" I responded, trying not to be too loud.

"I already know what the weather will be for Saturday – cloudy in the afternoon and into evening with no threat of rain."

"Oh…aren't you so well prepared. Wait…have you been planning this?"

"Not really. It was just a thought," he replied with a mischievous grin. That gave it away.

I leaned in closer. "So you're not going to mind having the terror twins and the monster running amok in your house and yard?"

"Who?"

I forgot he wasn't well-versed with my friends' families. "Ben's little sisters and Claire's younger brother," I explained.

"Not at all. I think it'll be good for them. Besides, I could always get Cary to corral them," he commented with a half-smile.

I smacked him. "You're evil."

"No, I'm not," he responded as he leaned in and kissed me. "You should get back inside…your father is watching," he whispered as he shifted his eyes to the house. "See you later."

He kissed me again and then climbed in the car. I dashed toward the house as he pulled out of the driveway. From the dry porch, I shook out the umbrella as I watched him leave. Once he was out of view, I turned to go inside, meeting my father at the door as I opened it.

"What were you two talking about?" he asked as I entered.

"I was trying to get it across to him what he was getting into," I replied as I passed him, giving him a kiss on the cheek. "'Night Daddy," I said before heading up the stairs to my room.

I changed into nightclothes and grabbed a pad and pencil, flopping down on my bed. Flipping the notebook open, I thought of who he was inviting and listed them out. I glanced at the clock, trying to decide if I wanted to call anyone tonight. Claire would be up.

I grabbed my phone and dialed her number. She answered on the second ring. "Any plans for this weekend?" I asked, cutting to the chase.

"No, not really. Justin talked about going to some firework show, but I don't know."

"How about a cookout…at David's?"

"Other than the holiday, what's the occasion?"

"None. He just thought it'd be nice to invite friends over. He'd like your whole family to come."

She was quiet, which was unusual for her. "Are you serious? Again, what's the occasion?"

I laughed. "He wants to get to know everyone better," I lied, helping with his 'façade'.

"Ooo…you two are serious. Do I hear wedding bells in the near future?"

"Claire, be serious. I have to graduate high school first. Then college."

"I am serious. I will be your maid of honor, right?"

"Of course you will…when I decide to get married. Now, back to the cookout. Can you and your family come?"

"Wait, let me ask," she responded before putting the phone down. I heard her door open and the faint sound of her running down the stairs.

While I waited, I looked over the list and made sure to add Justin. There's no doubt he'd be coming. I shook my head. And she jokes about me being so serious in a relationship – her and Justin are practically joined at the hip.

"Megan…yeah, we can come," she replied, suddenly coming on the phone. "Mom's excited to meet your man. What time and do we need to bring anything?" she asked.

"Great! Umm…seven and no, David has everything covered."

"Is he inviting Ben and his family?"

"Yeah, he is. And don't worry. I've talked to both of them and they're going be civil."

"David wasn't the problem," she remarked.

"He was more than you know." There was silence on the other end. "Claire?"

"Sorry, call waiting. It's Justin. He's invited, too, right?"

"Of course. Should I put him down?"

"Yeah, but I'll ask him. If you don't hear from me, he's coming. Talk to you later," she responded quickly and hung up.

I looked at the list. So that's five for Claire. I glanced at the clock again. I didn't feel right calling Erin this late, but I probably could call Ben. This will be interesting. I haven't talked to him since our resolution.

Rolling over to my back, I dialed his number and waited for him to pick up. He should be home from work. It rang for the fourth time and I prepared to leave a message when his voice came on the line.

"Hey Ben. Long time," I greeted sheepishly.

"Been busy?"

"Yeah…you?"

"Of course. I've been trying to get as many hours as possible. So what's up with the late night call?" he asked, cutting the niceties.

"It's not *that* late," I replied defensively, glancing at the clock. Well for summer, it wasn't. "I wanted to see if you and your family had any plans for Saturday?"

"Fourth of July? Setting off fireworks in the street, as I do every year for the twins," he responded wearily.

"Would you like to come to a cookout instead…at David's?" He was quiet for a long time. "Ben?"

"Will Madeline be there?"

Oh, I forgot about her and him. "Yes, she will. But there won't be any hard feelings. I think she's moved on."

"Really? Who?"

"Do you remember Cary from the end of school party?"

"Antisocial Cary? She's dating him?" he asked, astonished.

They were a rather odd couple, but opposites do attract. "Yeah. They have more in common than you think."

"Good for her. She deserves better than someone jealous and hung up on a girl who only wants to be friends."

"Ben…I am not coming to your pity party. You'll find the right girl, maybe in college, and you'll forget all about me."

"So what time should we be there?" he asked, ignoring my comment.

"Seven."

"And he doesn't mind the twins coming?"

"Not at all. Hey, you've seen his place – they'll have a blast."

"Okay…anything's better than burning my fingers on matches and sparklers. I'll tell my mom tomorrow. See you Saturday."

All right. So that's four for Ben, bringing the total to twelve. I just need to call Erin tomorrow and I'll have my count for David by that evening, hopefully. I glanced at the clock for the last time and placed the pad on the bedside table. Turning off the light, I crawled under my covers.

David is late. Maybe he's hunting. Or maybe he's shopping for the cookout. I giggled quietly, imagining him strolling around the supermarket with a cart buying food. Once I had amused myself enough with that thought, I rolled over and stared at the balcony doors.

I was tired, but I didn't want to fall asleep before he showed up. Sitting up, I turned on the light and scanned the room for something to keep me awake. Hopping out of bed, I grabbed a book and read it while waiting.

I was deep into it when a warm hand caressed my bare leg. I lowered the book and turned toward David as he sat on the edge by me. He smiled and leaned in, kissing me softly.

"Still awake I see," he whispered.

"Yes, waiting for you," I replied. "I made some calls, and so far I have a total of twelve people coming to your cookout. I haven't talked to Erin, but I will tomorrow."

"How many are in her family?"

"Well, if her older brothers come, it'll be five, but they probably won't."

"I'll plan on enough food for twenty. Whatever is left over, your friends and family can take home."

I fidgeted with the pages of the open book on my lap. "Ben was hesitant about coming."

"That is to be expected. Was it because of me?"

"More so concern about seeing Madeline, but I told him she had moved on."

He laughed quietly. "That she has," he responded, leaning in and kissing me again. He removed the book and set it on the bedside table. "Well, I'm here and you can go to sleep now," he stated, lying beside me.

I kissed him and then rested my head on his chest. Sighing contently, I breathed in his aroma and welcomed the fog creeping into my mind. Soon my eyes drooped and I drifted off to sleep.

I called Erin the next day about the cookout and she declined. Her family was leaving on their vacation and wouldn't be back until the following Friday. She was disappointed she was going to miss all the fun, but not too much – they were headed to the Caribbean. I wished her a safe trip and hung up.

That evening, I told David the count was still at twelve. Luckily, he hadn't picked up the food yet. We took over the living room since Dad and Vanessa were watching TV in the family room. Sitting at either end of the loveseat facing each other, he watched as I doodled on the pad I brought just in case he needed me to jot anything down for him.

"I'm going tonight to pick up groceries. Madeline is currently getting decorations," he mentioned and then paused. "I probably should have had her pick up the food instead," he remarked, thinking that decision over. She'd undoubtedly go overboard, especially knowing kids would be there.

"Did you give her a limit?" I asked, glancing up from my scribbles.

He gave me a perplexed look. "Should I have?"

I laughed. "So you gave her a blank check and told her to have fun?"

"Not a blank check, but yes."

"You are seriously going to regret this," I laughed again.

He quickly pulled out his phone and dialed her number. "If you haven't already gathered, I've never done this before," he stated as he waited for her to pick up. I smiled as I shook my head, returning to doodling while imagining what she bought. "Madeline...I failed to mention to keep the decorations under three hundred...you what? I wasn't thinking of going to that extent...I understand, but...but...umm hmm...all right, five hundred more...thank you," he responded and hung up.

I tried not to laugh at him again as he wiped his face and grumbled. "So she already blew through three hundred dollars," I commented, stifling a giggle.

He propped his head on his hand and stared at me, pursing his lips. "She bought fireworks. I wasn't planning on that."

"Why not? It's the Fourth of July. Hey, you could shoot them off in the clearing by the lake," I helpfully suggested, remembering where the trees had been cut for Odette's execution.

He smiled and shook his head. "You're enjoying this, aren't you?"

"Just a little. Don't worry, it'll be over before you know it," I grinned.

"Not soon enough. Remind me never to do this again."

"No problem."

He glanced toward the kitchen and then looked at me. "What do you usually serve at a cookout?"

"I forgot this is a pretty modern concept. Umm…it depends. Some people cook burgers and hotdogs, others do barbeque chicken and steak."

He thought about that for a moment. "What would you like?"

"Steak, definitely, but you might want to pick up hotdogs for the kids," I suggested.

He sighed. "I should be going," he commented as he stood. "Would you like to join me? I could use your help."

I smiled up at him before standing. "I would love to, but you know how my dad is about letting me go out late with you."

"I could always *persuade* him into letting you go," he proposed with a smirk.

"No, you can't. But you can call me if you need anything," I replied, leading him to the door.

He raised his hand to Dad and Vanessa as I opened it, then leaned in and kissed me. "Expect plenty of calls," he teased, grinning mischievously.

"Don't keep me up all night."

"Why not? You'll have all day to sleep."

I rolled my eyes and then leaned my head against the door. "Will you be by later?"

"Of course, but it may be much later," he replied, a slight smile on his lips.

"Okay. Well, have fun," I responded. I moved closer and was just about to kiss him when my dad purposely coughed in the other room. "Bye," I whispered, kissing him quickly before closing the door.

I glared at Dad as I entered the family room and sat in his favorite chair. Vanessa was stretched out on the couch, her head on his lap and her interest only in what was on TV. Good, I wasn't in the mood to hear her snarky remarks. I watched the remaining bit of the movie with them and then headed up to bed.

The other phone rang as soon as I entered my room. "Yes, David," I answered as I crossed the room and pulled out pajamas.

"The store I planned to go to is closed. I'm placing my order online to be delivered around six. Could you come over early to accept it?"

I slipped my shorts off, pinning the phone between my shoulder and ear. "I think so. What's so special about this store?"

"They sell the best beef in the area, all organic and grain-fed. What are you doing?" he asked as I slipped on a pair of silky shorts.

"Changing," I replied before putting the phone down and slipping on my shirt. He said something, and it was probably good I didn't hear him. I picked it back up and sat on the edge of my bed, crisscrossing my legs. "You don't have to go to that extent, David. Regular beef from Martin's or Kroger will be fine."

"What else should I order? They have quite an extensive menu," he inquired, ignoring me.

I fixed my hair, the phone wedged between my ear and shoulder again. I thought about what would be at an upscale cookout. "Hmm…corn on the cob, green beans, baked potatoes…actually, don't worry about that. I'll pick that before I come over. You just worry about the meat."

"I'll bring money to cover it when I come over tonight."

"No, that's okay. It won't be much. So does this mean you'll be over sooner now that you don't have to spend all night shopping?" I asked, hopeful.

"I would have, but Madeline conned me into helping her. I'll be over as soon as I can. Try not to fall asleep before I get there," he replied.

"All right. See you soon," I responded and hung up.

I shook my head and sighed, thinking about David and Madeline working on decorating. This will be interesting, to say the least. It's amazing the extent he's going for my friends, family, and me. I smiled and shook my head again before lying back.

As I stared at the blue sky above me, I thought about the cookouts we used to have every summer. Our neighbors came, moseying in and out of the yard while Mom made sure everyone was taken care of and Dad cooked his famous burgers on the grill. My duty was to help them as needed. Then after the sun set, we would sit on the curb out front as Dad put on a spectacular firework show. I sat on Mom's lap and stared in wonder at the colorful sparks flying high into the air and then fizzing out on the pavement.

*Mom.*

I hadn't thought about or visited her in weeks and I felt guilty. My only excuse is I've been really busy…with David, with the wedding, with being kidnapped. She'll understand. And to make it up to her, I'll visit her before going to David's tomorrow.

My plans set, I rolled onto my side and stared at the balcony doors. It was quiet in the room, the sound of the TV and occasional comments from Dad or Vanessa carrying up the stairs. I couldn't make out much of what they were saying from where I was, but I did catch my boyfriend's name.

Curious, I turned out the light and quietly crept to my door, cracking it and sitting on the floor next to the opening. I could hear them a lot better now. They were watching the news, but Vanessa wasn't interested in it.

"I'm just saying it's intriguing that David's inviting us and Megan's friends and their families to a cookout. Don't you find that suspicious?" she asked.

"Maybe, or it could be for networking, getting to know people in this area."

"He's not running for office, Jack," she sneered.

"He has that huge house he built and is studying to be a doctor. Maybe he plans to open a practice here after he graduates."

"Isn't he working for the Medical Examiner? I don't think he plans to be the kind of doctor any living person would go to. No, I think he has an announcement to make," she hypothesized.

There was silence between them, the only noise coming from TV reporters blabbing on about the state of the economy and its effect on local businesses. Then Dad spoke up. "What kind of announcement?"

"Oh I don't know…maybe engagement?"

They were silent again and then Dad laughed. "No, neither are ready for that. Besides, David would have asked my permission first."

"What makes you think that?"

"Haven't you noticed how old-fashioned he is? His gestures, mannerisms, and even the way he talks sometimes. It's like he was raised by Victorian re-enactors."

That's too funny. Dad noticed and yet has never said anything to me about it. David needs to work on his presence if it's that obvious. I leaned my head against the doorframe and continued listening.

"Do you think we should bring something even though he said not to?" she asked.

"Maybe wine or champagne for the adults," he suggested. Did they really want to promote that?

"A couple bottles won't hurt," she commented. Guess so…

"Are we eavesdropping?" David's voice softly spoke in my ear, making me jump out of my skin.

"Geez! Can't you warn me?" I whispered loudly, staring at him as I held my chest.

The thin sliver of light from the cracked door cut down his face, highlighting his gorgeous green eyes. He was crouched on the floor, grinning at me like the Cheshire cat. I stood, quietly shutting the door, and then walked over to the bed. Sitting on the edge, I switched on the bedside lamp as he gracefully stood upright and joined me.

"What was so interesting to make you leave your bed?" he asked, leaning back on his palms.

"They were talking about you," I replied, then started to laugh. "She thought the reason behind the cookout was an engagement proposal."

"Really?" he questioned, arching his brow.

"Dad knew better, though. He said you would ask his permission first."

He sat up and gazed into my eyes. "And I would."

I was lost in the deep green of them, like I was staring into a dense, ancient forest. Without thought, I leaned in and kissed him, closing my eyes as I did and coming out of the trance. Breaking away, I looked down at my hands and fidgeted with them.

"So how did the decorating go?" I asked, distracting from my embarrassment.

"She went overboard, but the children will love it," he responded with a smile.

"Those kids are going to be overwhelmed with your place as it is. It's going to be interesting," I commented, glancing at him and trying not to get caught up in his eyes again

"You're right about that," he mumbled. "You should go to sleep now," he commented, reaching over and turning out the light. He stood and strolled to the other side of the bed, waiting for me.

Lying back, I slipped under the covers as he sat and leaned against the headboard next to me. I placed my arm across his stomach and rested my head on his chest. "All right. I'm going to sleep, but not because you told me to," I informed him.

"You can be so stubborn," he laughed quietly and then paused, smiling down at me. "Good night, Megan," he whispered as his kissed my cheek and rubbed my back.

Closing my eyes, I concentrated on his breathing and the feeling of his fingers caressing my spine. He brought his free arm around and placed his hand on my shoulder. His closeness made me feel safe and comfortable as his scent wrapped around me and caused my mind to become cloudy. It didn't take long to fall asleep after that.

I woke the next morning energized and full of purpose. There was a lot to do before tonight. After getting ready, I packed a small bag of necessities and as I picked up my phones to put in my purse, I noticed a small envelope under them. I opened it and removed the letter inside, unfolding it.

> *Megan,*
> *I know you said not to bother, but I insist.*
> *Have fun.*
> *David*

Folded up with the letter were his house key and a signed blank check. I shook my head and sighed as I slipped them into my purse. Fine – I'll use his money, but I'll be frugal. I grabbed the bag and headed downstairs. Dad was at the island, reading the paper and enjoying his morning coffee. He looked up as I walked in and furrowed his brow.

"You're up early for a Saturday," he commented, folding the paper.

"I have a lot of errands to run," I replied as I opened the refrigerator.

I pulled out cottage cheese and fresh berries and set them on the counter before grabbing a spoon and bowl. Sitting across from him, I emptied several spoonfuls of each into the bowl. As I took a bite, he stared at me with a displeased face. He was never a big fan of cottage cheese; he thought it looked like curdled milk.

"Where's Vanessa?" I asked after swallowing.

"Still in bed. So where are you off to?" he asked, looking over my attire.

"Oh, to the grocery store and then the cemetery," I replied, staring outside. It was a bright, beautiful day. I hope David was right about the weather later.

"The cemetery?"

I returned my attention to him. "Yeah, I was thinking about Mom last night and realized I hadn't visited her in a while. I'm going to the store to pick up flowers," I lied.

He hesitated, not sure if he wanted to ask or not. "Would you like some company?"

I smiled slightly to hide my chagrin. "It's okay. I'm used to going alone," I responded, finishing off my breakfast. "Well, I better get going," I commented as I rinsed my dishes and put them in the washer.

"Will you be home before we leave for the cookout?" he asked as I headed toward the archway.

"No, David wanted me to come by early and help set up," I responded, pausing under it. "Do you remember where the house is?"

"How could I forget," he commented with sadness in his voice. "See you around seven then."

Hopefully, he wasn't getting all nostalgic again. I tried to spend as much time with him as possible so he wouldn't get like this. Maybe it was the fact I was going to the cemetery and didn't want him to go. Or maybe it has to do with me going to David's early. Either way, he needed to learn to let me go sometimes.

Still, I felt guilty, so I went back into the room and gave him a peck on the cheek before leaving. Quickly grabbing my bags at the staircase and dashing out the door, I rushed to my car before he could stop me. I pulled out of the drive just as quickly and headed to my first destination – a florist.

Since I told Dad I was taking flowers to Mom, I had to make sure I did. Even though I doubt he would, I had to cover my tracks in case he decided to check up on me. He never went to the cemetery and it shocked me when he offered to come.

I pulled up to a little flower shop and bought a nice bouquet of Mom's favorites. This was the first time in a long time I was actually bringing her flowers. I usually reserved that for special occasions, but I think she deserved it today.

Their fragrance filled the car and my head, bringing thoughts of her as I drove. It reminded me of past springs in the garden, the perfume she wore on a summer evening outing, of her hair and skin when she hugged me. They had become my favorite flowers, too, because of her and the pleasant memories their aroma brought me.

Pulling through the gates of Hollywood Cemetery, my heart felt light and happy. Something felt right about visiting her today, like I was being called to do so. The trees were full and lush, providing plenty of shade to keep me cool as I crept along, passing all the familiar graves.

I continued around to the family crypt, stopping in front of it. Gently lifting the flowers off the seat, I stepped out of the car and paused to gaze at the amazing view she had. It was picturesque and peaceful, the water of the James rushing over the rocks below and the birds singing in the trees above. I always wanted to be buried here, with her and Dad.

But I wouldn't be.

My dilemma surfaced again. If I choose to change, I'll never be buried, doomed to walk the earth for eternity and never see my loved ones in the afterlife. Well, maybe not doomed – I'll be with David. I sighed and turned toward the crypt, opening the door and entering.

I laid the flowers in front of her plaque and sat next to her with my legs outstretched, leaning my head against the cool marble. I usually fell asleep and dreamed up conversations with her, but I wasn't the least bit tired. I really wanted to talk to her, though. I closed my eyes and concentrated, but I couldn't make contact. Finally, I decided just to say it.

"You were right, Mom…about David. But he's not a bad person. Well, he's not a person at all…he's a vampire," I confessed out loud, feeling oddly at ease with doing so. "And I love him."

Silence.

I closed my eyes, thinking hard. "He's leaving it up to me to choose if I want to be like him, when the time is right, but I can't decide. If I stay human, I'll lose him, but if I turn, I'll never see you or Dad or my friends again."

More silence.

I opened my eyes and looked up, sighing deeply. I pulled my knees to my chest and wrapped my arms around them. Bowing my head, tears pricked at my eyes. "Mom, what do I do?" I whispered, closing them again.

*Nut-Meg…don't get upset.*

The voice whispered on the wind, swirling around me in the crypt. I looked up, my eyes damp. There was no one there – not a specter, shadow, or orb.

"Momma?" I inquired softly.

*Yes?*

"Is it…is it really you?" I questioned, looking around. My heart filled with happiness knowing I could communicate with her.

*Yes, it is. Why are you crying?*

"I want to be with David, but I'm worried about what will happen afterward…with Dad and my friends…and you. Will I ever get to see or talk to you again?" I asked, still trying to find her.

*You'll see me again regardless. There's nothing to worry about.*

Her voice was distant and wispy. What do you mean?" I questioned.

*When you become numinous like us, you can see and communicate with beings you have never seen…or heard before.*

"How are you talking with me now?"

*It's taking…a great deal of power and I can't keep it up…much longer.*

"What about my friends? What about Dad?"

*That…will be…a little tougher.*

"Do you think I should go through with it?" I questioned, knowing my time was short.

*If you really…love him, then…yes. But wait…don't…rush…in…*

"Mom? Mom, your voice is fading."

*I know…I have to go. We'll…talk again. Thank you for…the flowers. I love you…Nut-Meg…*

"Mom?"

Silence again. She was gone.

I placed my hand on her plaque and held it there, the cool of the marble warming from my touch. Then suddenly it turned icy cold, but I didn't jerk away. I smiled, kissed her name, and stood.

"Thank you, Momma," I whispered before leaving the crypt.

I wiped my eyes as I stood outside, glancing around. After all these years, she finally made contact. I couldn't wait to tell David. I felt a happiness I hadn't felt in a long time as I climbed in my car. Slowly pulling around the circle, I glanced back at the crypt, smiled, and drove away.

# Chapter 40
## A Perfect Ending

Driving back into Chesterfield, I headed straight to the grocery store. I grabbed a cart and strolled down each aisle, picking up items I thought were necessary, but didn't require too much preparation. When I finished perusing the whole store, I headed to the cash register to check out. As the cashier scanned each item one by one, I proudly looked over my purchases.

I didn't go overboard but felt I picked up enough to satisfy the group and had a nice variety of sides. With the last item scanned, she announced the total – $157.32. I filled in what I needed and handed her the check. She processed it and gave me the receipt, which I tucked in my purse. No questions, no problems. Good.

On my walk to the car, I glanced at the sky. More clouds were moving in, but the sun still shined brightly in bursts. David's assuredness in the weather report was starting to worry me. But there was still time for it to get cloudier. I popped the trunk and loaded the groceries in the back and then left. It was five o'clock – perfect time to get to the house.

When I pulled up to the entrance, I entered the code and the gates creaked open. The woods were splotched with sunlight, occasionally fading in and out as clouds passed over the sun. As I neared the house, the light dimmed longer than it had all day. Maybe there would be enough coverage for him to wake.

Pulling around the circle, I parked in front of the door and stepped out as the sun broke through a large cloud. Guess not. I unlocked the front door and propped it open, making it easier to bring in the groceries. Unloading the bags onto the steps, I carried them two by two into the house.

It was quiet inside, no movement whatsoever. Of course, I didn't expect any. David, Madeline, and Cary would probably sleep until the sun completely disappeared and the threat of it coming back out had passed.

With the last few bags in hand, I shut the door and headed to the kitchen to fill the cabinets and refrigerator with my goodies. Once everything was put away, I decided to get to work on what I could prepare ahead of time while I waited for the meat delivery. David had a well-stocked kitchen for someone who never ate, but it served its purpose, especially for me on this occasion.

I picked up some fruit and a round watermelon with the intent of carving it out and making a fruit bowl. And seeing as I got everything done so proficiently, I had plenty of time to do it. I cut it into a basket shape, trying my best not to make too much of a mess, and then scooped all the meat out of it. I put it back in with other fruit, mixing it together to make a colorful, refreshing salad. After adding finishing touches, I covered it with clear wrap and slipped it into the refrigerator. Those garnishing classes I took with Dad several years ago really paid off.

As I wiped down the island, the intercom sounded for the gate. I answered it and buzzed the deliveryman through, heading out a moment later to meet him. Leaving the door ajar, I sat on the porch staring at the sky while waiting for him to arrive. It was becoming cloudier, but still not thick enough. I was getting anxious – there was only an hour left and the food still needed to be cooked.

I heard the rumbling of the truck in the distance and then spotted it lumbering toward the house. The driver slowed to a stop at the mouth of the circle and I could faintly see him through the windshield, his mouth agape as he leaned on the steering wheel and stared. I waved from the porch, but he didn't notice me, so I started jumping up and down and finally got his attention. Coming out of his stupor, he smiled and slowly pulled around, parking behind my car.

"This your house?" he asked as he stepped out.

"No, my boyfriend's," I replied, smiling politely. "So what can I help you with?" I inquired as I jogged down the steps.

He walked around to the back of the truck and opened the double doors. "It's heavy, all in one box, but I can handle it," he replied, pulling it out.

"Okay. Let me show you where to put it."

He followed me, staring up at the house and the door as I led him inside. As we entered the foyer, he spun around, taking it all in. I guided him down the hallway and opened the swinging door to the kitchen, feeling it best to go through that entrance rather than lead him around. Placing my hand on the cold granite counter, I indicated for him to set the carton on it.

"This is the biggest house I've ever seen," the man commented as he peeked into the grand salon.

"Yeah, it is huge. Do you have anything for me to sign?" I asked politely.

Not giving an immediate answer, he walked stiffly into the next room, his mouth gaping and eyes wide as he looked around. Guess not. I shrugged and opened the package, inspecting the contents to verify they arrived as ordered.

He came back around, still gawking, and pulled a piece of paper out of his back pocket. "Here," he replied, shoving it toward me.

He stumbled away again, over to the veranda, and stared out back while I glanced down at the paper. I couldn't believe the amount of money David was putting toward this cookout. I shook my head and added twenty-five percent for tip, signing my name. Taking the carbon copy, I walked over to give the man the top part.

"Having quite the party tonight," he remarked as he stared out the sunroom windows. My jaw dropped when I saw the extent of the decorating. Madeline went way overboard.

She had a variety of activities and playthings set up for the kids and there was American paraphernalia hanging everywhere. Tables lined the fence near the barbeque pit with patriotic tablecloths covering them. A couple of the bistro tables from the terrace were moved down to the pool area and decorated with red, white, or blue tablecloths and centerpieces. Oh boy...

"Yeah," I finally responded, handing him the piece of paper and smiling softly. "Oh, thanks for coming by on a holiday."

"You're welcome, young lady. Have fun and enjoy," he replied as I led him to the door.

As soon as he was gone, I shut and locked it and headed back to the kitchen to get the other items prepared. Glancing outside as I washed my hands, there was no sign of the sun in the sky. I smiled, a mixture of relief and excitement coming over me.

In high spirits and eager to get this party going, I hummed while I shucked the corn and worked on wrapping and poking potatoes. I found a large tray to set them on for easy transport outside. Opting for salad over green beans, I threw that together, covered it, and put it in the fridge. Now for the main course. Pulling the steak from the container, I sorted them out and prepared them for grilling, placing the varied sizes and cuts of meat on another large tray and covering it.

"I see you've made yourself quite at home in my kitchen," David commented, coming up behind me and kissing my neck.

"Oh!" I gasped, turning around and grinning. "Yes. I'm so glad you're awake," I responded, kissing him as I held my dirty hands in the air so I didn't touch him.

"The clouds came in a little later than predicted," he remarked and gave me another kiss. I twisted away and went to the sink to wash them, humming as I did. "You're in a good mood," he commented, leaning against the island as he watched me.

"Oh, just happy to be with you...and I talked to my mom today," I replied, glancing over my shoulder and smiling.

"I wondered when she would do that."

"You knew? Wait...what am I saying? How could I think you wouldn't know," I babbled as I dried my hands. "Have you ever talked to her?" I asked, flipping around to face him.

"No. She liked watching me from afar, not wanting to interfere."

"Not unless she had to, I guess."

"And she never did," he responded, smiling his crooked grin.

I leaned against the sink, looking at him. "How is it possible? Is there a reason why this is happening now?" I questioned.

"Your mind is open to the impossible," he explained, standing up and coming toward me. He pushed a stray strand behind my ear and smiled softly. "When you accepted that I exist, it unlocked a long dormant part of your human brain that made you more perceptive to other supernatural beings," he explained, caressing my cheek.

"She's visited me in my dreams before, but I thought that was more my mind creating her presence to soothe me," I commented, realizing that wasn't the case at all. "So all along, it really was her trying to talk to me," I stated, astonished I never picked up on it.

"What did you two talk about?" he asked, moving closer.

"You…of…of course," I stammered, looking into his eyes and getting caught up in them.

"What does she think about you and me…being together?" he inquired, his hand on my waist as he pulled me away from the counter.

My heart thumped hard, and I had to remind myself to breathe. "She…she doesn't seem to mind…"

I closed my eyes and inhaled slowly. He was right at my lips. "Does she think you should change?" he whispered, his brushing mine.

How does he know that's what we talked about? Am I that easy to read? "I…I…" I stuttered. He faded away from me and I opened my eyes, looking into his.

"Well?" he coerced.

My mind was foggy. "Umm…she said…" He stepped farther away, helping it to clear. "She said…as long as I love you…but she told me not to rush into it."

He smiled, approving her advice. "Very wise," he replied as he turned and looked at the counter. "You've been busy," he commented, changing the subject as he skimmed over my prep work.

"Yes, I have," I responded and then glanced at the clock. "And now I need you to get the grill going," I commanded, pushing him out of the kitchen.

He grinned and slipped out the terrace door only to come back several minutes later. "What shall I take?" he asked, reaching for a tray.

"That one and I'll bring this one," I replied as I handed him the meat and I took the corn and potatoes.

We headed down the stairs to the grill and set the trays on the counter by it. He opened the lid, dry heat bursting at us, and placed the vegetables on the upper rack since they'd take longer to cook. We were holding off on the steaks since they should be cooked to order, placing them in the small refrigerator sitting nearby. He closed the lid to the grill and turned to me, leaning against it.

"What now?" he asked, smiling, but then it waned. "Someone's here already," he remarked before dashing up the stairs.

I stayed on the patio and kept an eye on the food while I waited for him to return. In the meantime, I took in Madeline's handiwork up close. The decorations were much worse than what I had seen from above. Floatie toys bobbed on the surface of the pool and red, white, and blue streamers hung haphazardly from the arbors. It actually looked a little tacky. But I smiled, flattered by their attempt.

Hearing talking, I glanced up the steps to find Dad and Vanessa at the top. I shook my head as they started down them. I couldn't believe he let her out of the house in that – cut-off shorts that barely covered her butt and a mid-drift baring, skin-tight tank top. I bit my tongue and looked away, trying not to laugh at the two of them, like a rich tourist and a local prostitute.

"Wow! This is amazing!" she exclaimed as she reached the bottom, a bottle of wine in each hand. Of course she would be impressed. Dad, on the other hand, looked like he had the same expression I did when I first saw it.

"You can put the wine on the last table there," I pointed out as I opened the grill and checked the food. Everything looked good. Closing it, I excused myself and headed up the steps to bring the cold food out while David talked with them.

As I entered the house, I spied Madeline searching the cabinets. "What are you looking for?" I asked as I headed into the kitchen.

"I can't remember where I put the citronella. I need to set out some burners to ward off the other bloodsuckers," she joked.

"I think I saw them in here," I responded, opening a large cabinet in the corner.

"Oh, great!" she exclaimed, scooting to it. "So what do you think?"

"You went a little overboard, but the kids are going to love it," I commented, trying not to make her feel too bad. I'm sure she heard enough from my boyfriend.

"Thanks…David said it looked like a child who indulged in too many holiday sweets vomited all over the patio."

"It's not that bad," I laughed. "It's appropriate for the audience." She smiled up at me as I went to the sink to wash my hands again. As I glanced out the window, I noticed David heading down the path toward the lake. "Where is he disappearing to?" I inquired, looking down at her as she gathered several terra cotta bowls in her arms and stood.

"Oh…he's helping Cary setup the fireworks," she replied, grinning wide. "I'm so excited!" she squealed as she headed out the terrace door.

I shook my head and went to the refrigerator, pulling out the salad, dressings, watermelon, and drinks and setting them on the island. Then I grabbed the bag of paper goods and put it next to them. Taking what I could, I turned to leave and nearly ran into Dad.

"Need help?" he asked, holding my shoulders as he looked at my loaded arms.

"Yes," I replied with relief as I handed him what I was carrying. "They can go on the table closest to the gate," I instructed.

As I gathered some of the other items, the intercom sounded. I was the only one in the house at the time, so I dropped everything and ran to the receiver, buzzing them through. Abandoning my current duty, I went to the door and waited for the next guests to arrive. Thankfully, I didn't have long as Ben's mom pulled around the circle and parked next to Dad's car.

The twins threw open the door and took off as Ben chased after them, finally corralling and herding the yelling girls up the steps. His mom followed behind, trying not to gawk at the house. "Hi, Megan! Sorry we're a little early. Ben was anxious to get here," Ms. Galloway commented as she passed him and the struggling girls to give me a hug. He glared at her as he dragged the now screaming and thrashing twins to the door.

I crouched down to their level, looking at both of them, and they gradually calmed. "There's lots of fun stuff out back, but you have to be on your best behavior if you want to play with any of it," I told them in my sweetest voice.

They smiled at me and then looked angelically at Ben. "We'll behave. Can we go now?" they asked in unison.

He rubbed his temples and sighed. "Sure, but don't touch anything in the house on your way through," he sternly directed as he pushed them inside, looking back at me and mouthing a 'thank you'.

"So where's your boyfriend?" Ms. Galloway asked as we followed behind them. She paused in the foyer while I closed the door.

"Setting up the fireworks with his roommate, Cary," I commented as I led her down the hall to the grand salon.

"Oh, we're being treated to a show? How nice," she responded as she looked around. "This is quite a place he has here. What does he do again?"

"He's studying to be a doctor, but currently works for the Medical Examiner."

"They must pay well."

"No," I giggled. "He bought it with his inheritance," I responded, guiding her to the terrace door as she continued to take it all in. "Those who have arrived so far are out this way."

"Are your Dad and his new bride here?"

"Yep, by the pool," I pointed out. "I have to grab some things and then I'll be down."

She smiled softly before disappearing down the stairs. I slipped back into the kitchen and grabbed the last remaining items and then headed outside to finish setting up and check the food. As I came down the steps, I glanced around, curious if David was back. No sign of him yet.

I set the items on the table with the rest and went about spreading everything out, glancing around at everyone as I did. Ms. Galloway was talking with Dad and Vanessa, trying hard not to look aghast by her attire. The twins took no time stripping down to their suits and jumping in the pool while Ben stood on the side and watched them.

I finished organizing the buffet and headed over to him. "I'm sure they'll be fine," I whispered as I nudged him.

"It's a distraction," he replied, glancing at Madeline plugging in a string of lights.

I rolled my eyes and headed to the grill, checking on the corn and potatoes. They were finally done. I pulled them off and set them on the tray, placing it among the other food. Madeline came over just to pass by, and I gave her a perplexed look.

"More guests!" she exclaimed as she dashed up the stairs. It was a good thing they had such great hearing. I would have never heard the buzzer.

The grill was nice and hot and ready for the steaks, but I wasn't going to start them until David came back. I can cook a steak, but this was his house and his cookout; he should have the honor. I turned to head back into the house to get something when Claire and Justin came bounding down the stairs toward me, wide grins on their faces. Her parents and brother followed behind them, awestruck and not moving as fast.

"This is awesome!" Justin exclaimed, looking around. He wrapped his arms tight around Claire's waist, causing her to exhale forcefully, and kissed her cheek. "I can't wait to get in that pool again," he whispered to her.

She smiled hesitantly as her mom passed them and gave me a hug. "How are you, Megan? It seems like it's been ages since we talked," Mrs. James commented, her voice bright and playful. Mr. James smiled as he passed but didn't say a word as he headed straight for Dad. He was probably happy to see another adult male.

"I'm good. Enjoying my summer," I answered, smiling.

"So where's your man?" she asked, looking around. "I'm dying to meet him. Claire's told me so much about him."

"Down at the lake, setting up the fireworks," I replied, a twinge of sadness in my voice. "Hopefully, he'll be here soon. He has to get the steaks going," I continued, looking toward the path. "In the meantime, there are drinks at the end of the buffet, as well as snacks. Also, feel free to enjoy the pool and hot tub," I explained. She smiled and then searched for her husband.

When she found him, she strolled over, joining in the conversation with my father. I scanned the group, making sure everyone was here and content. Claire, Justin, the monster, and the twins were all in the pool, playing with the various items Madeline added, and having a great time. Ben sat on the edge watching them, and Madeline was bringing speakers from the basement outside. Now we were just waiting on David and Cary. Maybe I should go retrieve them.

I headed toward the gate. Just as I was about to open it, I noticed David strolling up. I stopped dead in my tracks and stared at him. There was something different about the way he looked, something winsome and mesmerizing about his lean body in his khaki pants and long-sleeve, button-down shirt that curved with his form.

It was an exceptionally warm evening, but he looked completely comfortable. His sleeves were rolled up to his elbows and the first several buttons of the moss-colored shirt were undone, showing the slightest bit of chest. He caught my stare and smiled, making my heart nearly leap out of my chest. My fingers nervously danced along the gate as he came closer, smiling as he paused to give me a kiss.

"Is everyone here?" he inquired softly in my ear as he entered the patio, his hand gliding along my waist to my back.

I was momentarily stunned but finally answered. "Y-yes, we're all here."

"Good. Would you like to introduce me to your friends' parents?" he asked as he looked around at the unfamiliar faces and then me.

"Okay," I replied bashfully. Slipping my arm under his, I clutched him as we walked up to the group of adults standing by the drink table. Composing myself, I cleared my throat and smiled politely. "Sorry to interrupt...I wanted to introduce you to my boyfriend and our host for this evening – David Archer," I announced, trying to sound calm, though being so close to him was making it hard.

He smiled and Mrs. James' started hyperventilating, as did Vanessa. Ben's mom, however, remained composed. How odd that she could resist his allure. Maybe it was from living without a man for so long.

"It is a pleasure to meet all of you," he greeted courteously with a slight bow of his head.

Claire's dad stuck out his hand immediately and he took it in his, shaking firmly. "Stanley James. Nice place you have here. If you're interested in buying other property, let me know," he greeted, abruptly handing him a card. Ever the salesman.

"Thank you, I'll consider it," David replied, glancing at it and then slipping it into his shirt pocket.

Mrs. James pushed her husband out of the way, sidling up to David. "It's so nice to finally meet you. Claire's told me so much about you," she cooed, touching his arm.

"I hope it was all good," he responded, smiling and patting her hand. She giggled as she flipped her hair and caressed her earrings.

Ms. Galloway took that opportunity to step in. "Hello. Sybil Galloway, Ben's mom. I've heard a lot about you as well," she commented, taking his hand.

The strangest thing happened then, unlike anything that happened with the other parents. The moment she touched him, her face went blank for a second and then she looked up at him and smiled nervously. Of course, he picked up on it immediately, cocking his head slightly to the side and smiling.

"I'm sure you have," he remarked.

She jerked her hand away and stepped back. "You're lucky to have someone like Megan," she responded, almost threateningly.

He disregarded her tone as he gazed at me and kissed my cheek. "I am *very* lucky," he replied. I tucked my head and blushed in response.

As I raised my eyes slightly, I saw everyone staring at us. Feeling uneasy with the unwanted attention from the group, I turned my head, my eyes meeting his, and whispered, "I...I think it's time to start grilling."

He nodded before focusing on the group. "Thank you for coming. It has been a pleasure talking with you, but I think we're all getting hungry," he stated as he released my arm. He slipped away, looking back at me and winking.

Ms. Galloway watched him for a moment, debating something, and then discreetly snuck away from the group and followed him as everyone resumed their conversation from before, adding in bits about my boyfriend. Once she caught up, she stopped him and started talking. Her expression was stern, but he remained calm and smiling. What were they discussing?

"What a pleasant young man," Mr. James remarked, bringing my attention back to the other parents. I nodded as he hooked his arm around his wife's and they turned to leave. She blinked as she looked at him, surprised he was there, and then she led him to the drink table.

Now only Dad and Vanessa remained. I tried not to look too distracted as they talked to me, but I wanted to know what was transpiring between David and Ms. Galloway. I listened and responded, but when I could, I snuck a glance. She kept her distance from him and when he moved closer to reply, she stepped back, almost scared. Did she know something? I briefly turned back to Dad and hoped Vanessa in particular didn't notice. Of course she was too caught up in herself to care.

"Hmph, he didn't say anything to me," she huffed as I glanced again at David. He was holding Ms. Galloway's hand this time, and she wasn't fearful, staring up at him as he talked to her.

"Honey, he didn't need to," Dad responded, not really acknowledging whether I was paying attention to them or not. But for good measure, I was. "He greeted us at the door, remember? And we see him practically every night," he continued as he started to leave.

As they walked away, she gave him a dirty look. He led her to the drink table to get her a glass of wine, probably hoping to pacify her. Good, now I can focus all my attention on David and Ms. Galloway. Curious how things were going, I searched for my boyfriend and found him at the grill, but Ben's mom was nowhere in sight. Did he do something to her?

"He's a keeper," a voice whispered by my ear, causing me to jump.

I jerked around and stared bewildered at Ms. Galloway's smiling face. "Oh! I thought you left," I exclaimed, holding my heart.

"I did, but I came back to tell you my impression of your boyfriend."

"Oh…" I responded, confused.

She smiled softly and took my hand. "I had a bad feeling about him at first, but after talking with him, I realized it was wrong," she commented, looking into my eyes.

"Oookay…" I responded hesitantly, not sure what to make of what she was saying.

"He's good for you, Megan," she remarked, watching him talk with Claire's dad as he grilled. This statement came as a shock to me coming from Ben's mom – the mother of the boy who was so suspicious of him. "Ben wasn't too thrilled about you dating him. He said David wasn't who he seemed," she continued and then leaned in closer. "But he's exactly who he seems," she finished, smiling at me.

I glanced at Ben sitting on the edge of the pool. "You know Ben still has a crush on me," I remarked.

She gazed at her son fondly. "Don't worry about him, he'll get over it. What you and David have is magical. The way he looks at you…the love in his eyes is genuine." She paused and sighed, looking at Ben again. "And he can't give you what David can."

I did my best to keep from looking surprised. How does she know what he can give me? Did David tell her? "Wh-what do you mean?"

"The kind of love you need," she responded enigmatically as she gently touched my shoulder. Then she leaned in close and whispered, "Your mother would approve."

I felt a tear slip down my cheek, and she smiled softly as she wiped it away and gave me a hug. She gave another gentle smile, cupping the side of my face before she turned and walked away, heading toward the pool to check on the twins. I looked over at David, happily grilling steaks, and thought about what she said. Then suddenly something cool touched me.

I jumped and jerked around to find Cary standing beside me, his hand on my shoulder. "How are you, Megan?" he asked, a pleasant grin on his lips. I never noticed before what a nice smile he had.

"A little confused, but otherwise good. You?" I replied, the shock wearing off.

"Great. I can't wait to set off the fireworks. I have a big show planned," he responded, scanning the crowd and stopping when he found Madeline.

She looked up and grinned at him as she hooked the last speaker up, turning on the stereo to test it. Pop music played in the background and everyone seemed to loosen up a little more. She swayed her hips to the beat, her mottled turquoise, scarf dress flowing around her as she beckoned him to join her. He looked at me and grinned before dashing around the pool and taking her into his arms. They really are cute together.

Which made me think...

I searched for Ben and found him sitting at a table all by himself, moping in a dark corner. With nothing better to do at the moment, I decided to go talk to him, maybe cheer him up. I grabbed two drinks and headed over, glancing back as David watched me. I smiled and he nodded curtly.

"Hey, Ben. I brought you a drink," I commented as I set it down on the table in front of him and took a seat.

"Thanks," he mumbled, playing with the cup.

"So why aren't you swimming or socializing?"

He looked around, avoiding me, and then took a sip. "There's no one worth socializing with," he muttered.

I leaned on the table. "You don't want to talk to Vanessa?" I asked, shifting my eyes to the side of the pool. She was leaning back, her back arched as she dangled her feet in the water. "I'm sure she'd looove to talk to you," I teased.

I got a grin out of him, though he tried hard not to. "I can't believe she wore what she did," he commented, finally looking at me.

"I know! I guess she wanted to impress all the hot, young guys."

He glanced at her and then at David. "Or one in particular," he mumbled. I narrowed my eyes and he apologized. "I'm sorry. I shouldn't have said that."

"It's okay. It's sad, but you're probably not too far from the truth. She might have also been hoping Brian was here."

"So how is old Brian doing settling into domestic life?"

I grimaced, instantly regretting bringing him up. I really wasn't in the mood to talk about him since I tried so hard to forget him. "Good. Living down in Baton Rouge. David hears from him occasionally," I responded, trying not to look like the conversation bothered me. "You know…I'm getting hungry. Let's go get our food," I suggested, quickly changing the subject.

I popped up and pushed the chair in as he slowly followed. "Not a bad idea," he agreed.

Noticing us walking over to the first table, David left the grill and strolled to the edge of the pool, calling to the twins and Claire's brother. They swam up without fear of this strange man and listened intently to what he said, answering the questions he asked. He smiled and then joined us, fixing plates for each of them.

Ben watched in amazement at how easily he balanced the three plates as he put the different requested items for each child on them. We waited for him to finish, figuring the kids should be taken care of first, and then grabbed our plates, napkins, and plasticware. A line soon began forming behind us.

As we fixed ours, David set the food on a table under the arbor and called the kids over. Without a fuss or whine, they climbed out of the pool and sat quietly in front of their meal, smiling as they ate. He smiled back and then headed our way. Ben looked at me and shrugged, as if to say, *Maybe he's not so bad after all, if kids can trust him.*

We waited patiently at the grill as he walked up. "How do you like your steak?" he asked Ben first.

He had a look on his face like he wanted to say one thing, but instead said something else. "Umm…medium well."

David checked one and then placed it on his plate. "And you?" he asked.

"Medium well is good for me, too," I replied as he placed it on my plate. "Are you going to join us?"

He glanced around. "As soon as everyone has their food, I will."

"We'll be over there," I informed him, pointing to a table under the arbor as we walked away.

Ben and I sat and I immediately cut into the tender, juicy steak. I was always amazed by David's cooking skills, for someone who never eats. Ben seemed to enjoy it as well, eating without saying a word. Halfway into our meal, Claire and Justin came over and sat, jabbering about everything as they began to eat. But then there was a sudden silence as they chewed slowly, savoring it.

I was just about finished when David finally joined us. "Would you like anything else?" he asked before sitting down. Claire and Justin shook their heads, still eating.

"No, I'm full," I replied.

"No thank you," Ben commented. "My compliments to the chef."

"Thank you," David responded, bowing his head, "but I can't take all the credit. It was a joint effort," he added, indicating toward me.

I blushed. "Well, I prepared the food. He cooked it."

"Aren't you going to eat, David?" Claire's mom asked, touching his shoulder and trembling as she paused on her way to check on her son.

"Not at this moment, but maybe later," he replied, smiling at her. She smiled back dumbly and then stumbled to the kids' table. He chuckled as he turned back to us. "There's about an hour before Cary plans to start the show. Anyone interested in a swim?"

"That sounds like a great idea," I replied, anxious to cool off.

"I could go for another dip," Claire seconded, smiling at Justin. He grimaced. "But after dessert," she added and he smiled.

"I would, but I forgot my trunks," Ben responded.

"You may borrow one of mine. We seem to be close to the same size," David replied, looking over him.

Ben hesitated and I urged him to go ahead. "Okay…thank you," he conceded.

"Follow me," David stated as he stood, and Ben did the same, following him up the terrace steps.

This seems to be going well.

Claire noticed and gave a thumbs up and a wink as they stood to get dessert. I mimicked her as I stood and headed in to change into my swimsuit. Grabbing my bag from beside the cabinet in the kitchen, I slipped into the guest room and put on my bikini. I wrapped a sarong around my waist and headed back down to the pool. Ben and David weren't out yet, but I decided not to wait.

Removing the sarong and laying it aside, I dove off the side of the pool into the deeper end. The cool water felt wonderful. I dunked under and swam toward the edge, popping up in time to see them exiting the basement. Hanging on the wall, I watched as they walked up.

What a huge difference between the two of them. David walked with confidence and fluidity and his skin radiated in the dim light. Everyone's eyes were on him. Ben, on the other hand, looked bland and indistinct in comparison and was visibly uncomfortable as he stumbled to a table to put his things down.

I was about to wave to them when I noticed the kids getting ready to jump in. Before they could, David stopped them. "It's adult swim," he told them gently. "Besides, you should wait half an hour or else your stomach will knot," he continued, smiling. They looked at him in wide-eyed wonder. He glanced up, looking for Madeline. When he found her, he signaled her to come over. "This is Madeline. She has a lot of fun games for you to play in the game room," he informed them, pointing toward the basement.

She took over then, leading them into the house singing a cute song as they went. Ben stared at him in amazement. "Okay, I think I might have to call you to babysit sometime. I can never get the twins to listen to me."

He smiled. "Younger siblings always have a problem listening to the older ones," he replied, trying not to make him feel bad.

Ben nodded knowingly and then jumped in the pool, sending a large splash over me. David dove in after him, barely making any at all, and swam up to me. The adults decided it was time for a swim as well, changing and entering the shallow end or hot tub. I glanced at Ben and then David, signaling them to follow me as I dove under the water and swam to the grotto.

I surfaced first and then David and Ben on either side of me. David held my hand underwater and watched as Ben shook out his ears. No sooner had we gotten settled, Justin and Claire joined us.

"Do you think our parents will come over here?" she asked, wiping her face.

"No, they like the shallow end so they can drink their wine and socialize," I replied.

"Good, we'll have some privacy then," she replied, relaxing and cuddling up to Justin.

"Man, can you believe it's July already?" he commented.

"I know! Soon it'll be August and then school starts after that and before you know it, we'll be graduating," she added.

"What does everyone plan to do after graduation?" David asked, looking around at my friends.

We glanced at each other and smiled. "College," we replied in unison.

"Have any of you decided on a school or applied yet?" he inquired. We collectively shook our heads.

"I'm staying here, starting out in community college," Claire answered first. "It's easier to get into the major colleges when you transfer in from community."

"I'm doing the same," Justin replied, smiling at her and then kissing her cheek.

"I found this great school in California I'm interested in, but it's expensive and too far away," Ben responded, sounding somewhat depressed.

"What do you plan to study?" David asked.

"Video game design," he replied. "It's always been a dream of mine."

"Have you checked any of the schools locally? You might be surprised at which ones offer that degree."

"It's been a couple years since I looked, but gaming *is* becoming more popular," he contemplated.

I smiled at David, happy he was trying to help him. "Yeah, VCU might even have a program now," I added.

David grinned at me. "Yes, I do believe I saw something like that advertised."

Ben smiled. "Oh, I don't know about living that close, but staying on this coast would be nice."

"So what about you, Megan? Have you decided yet?" Claire asked.

I looked at David and then at my friends. "I think I might go to VCU. I don't know that I'm ready to go too far away."

"Did you decide on a major?" Ben inquired.

"No, I'm still up in the air about that. Maybe over the course of the school year, it'll come to me."

"So David, do you plan to make Richmond your permanent home?" Claire asked, glancing briefly at me.

"I plan to stay as long as I feel necessary," he answered honestly.

"Why not permanently?" Justin questioned.

His lip curled at the corner into that mischievous grin I loved so much. "I like a change of scenery. I've moved around a lot in my life and become bored if I stay in one place too long."

Suddenly Madeline popped up out of the water, disrupting our focus on him and making several of us jump. "Oh, am I interrupting?" she asked as she hung on the wall next to him.

"No...did you need something?" he inquired.

"Cary is ready and waiting," she whispered and he nodded. She smiled at everyone before vanishing into the dim abyss.

"I guess it's time to gather everyone for the show," he stated before slipping into the water and disappearing as well. We continued to sit, looking at each other and wondering if we were supposed to follow. A moment later, he surfaced in front of us, making us jump again. "Are you coming?" he inquired with an arched brow.

Nodding, each of us slipped into the water and made our way out of the pool. The adults did the same as David informed them we were heading down to watch the fireworks. Before joining everyone, I grabbed my sarong and tied it around my hips.

Madeline led the way like some kind of pied piper with the children behind her and everyone else following as she sang a tune to entertain us. David hung back and waited for me to catch up, slipping his arm around my waist and giving me a kiss as we strolled down the path, keeping a bit of distance from the group.

Finally having some time alone with him, I asked, "What was that exchange you had with Ms. Galloway?"

He stared in front of us and then turned his face to me and grinned. "She saw what I was."

"What?" I asked, shocked he was so nonchalant about it. "How?"

He dropped back a little more. "She's a sensitive. When she touches someone, she gets a glimpse of what they are, but it's not concrete."

"So what did she see?"

"Death. But while that may be what I am, it's not *who* I am," he replied, and then he paused and turned to me. "I would never let you succumb to that. I would give my immortal life to save yours, Megan," he continued, gazing into my eyes with the deepest sincerity.

My heart thumped, and I couldn't move or speak. He slipped his hand under my jaw and leaned closer, giving me the softest kiss. I closed my eyes and reached up slowly, placing my arms around his neck and holding him as I kissed back.

He smiled as he gradually released me and moved away. "That is what I told her," he replied, urging me to walk.

I was silent as I thought about their conversation. "So she has supernatural powers. Does this mean Ben does, too?" I asked as we came closer to the group.

"It may not have matured in him yet or he may never get it. If he does, it could manifest itself in a different form."

"Did you know what she was when you met?"

"I don't have the ability to read another being that way, but I could tell she wasn't a normal human."

"Do you get that feeling from Ben?"

"No, but I am surprised he had an inkling of an idea of what I was so soon. Of course, he could have had help." I gave him a perplexed look. "From the twins," he indicated ahead of us.

"Wow...as long as I've known him and his family and I never noticed."

"I told you...we're all around you," he grinned. "And we've always been here. It's just that humans have turned a blind eye toward us, believing in the scientific rather than the mystical."

How true...

Ahead of us, the group stopped. I craned my neck to see what was going on and spotted Madeline directing everyone to find a place in the sand and get comfortable. I was a little confused – I thought the fireworks were being shot off from the clearing, but apparently that wasn't the case if we were sitting there. Seeing my puzzled look, David pointed farther down the lake.

Oh! Cary was shooting them off from another spot and the clearing would give us a better view of the whole sky! I felt dumb.

David sat in the sand, shirtless and still in his swim trunks, and looked up at me. I smiled and sat between his legs, leaning back against him. His body was cool, but it wasn't from the water or the walk. Regardless, it felt good on such a sultry, summer evening.

He kissed my cheek and then whispered in my ear, "I hope this is worth it."

I looked around at everyone anticipating the show and smiled. "It will be."

As soon as we were all settled and the children calmed, he glanced across the lake. Within seconds, the first rocket streamed into the sky, bursting in bold colors above us and showering down on the lake. It wasn't as big as the large, commercial displays, but it was just as good. The children ooo'd and ahhh'd as everyone else clapped.

The next one shot up and another quickly behind it, lighting the sky in red and blue, and then fizzling out. It continued like that for the next ten minutes, bright and striking, reflecting on the lake. Then came the grand finale.

I didn't know what to expect but was ready for anything. Several rockets shot into the sky, bursting at different intervals and in different colors as they filled the blackness with light so bright I winced. A couple more flew up after them and then it was silent. Everyone clapped and started back toward the house, all discussing the wonderful show and thanking David as they passed.

Being the last to get up, I stood and dusted off my bottom and turned to join the crowd when he caught my wrist and pulled me back down onto his lap. We were all alone on the sand. He gently touched my cheek and kissed me, making my head swim. Gazing into my eyes, he smiled at my face flushed with excitement.

"You were right," he whispered, kissing me again. "It *was* worth it."

I smiled contently and leaned against him, my arms around his neck as he rested on his elbows. The nattering voices faded, leaving only the sound of the gentle lapping water and the chirping of the frogs and crickets as we lounged, staring at the open sky now void of smoke and embers and splotched with shimmering stars.

Slowly turning his body, I slid off David's lap as he smiled down at me. As I lay on the sand staring up at him with the speckled black and gray sky behind him, I felt an overwhelming sense of euphoria. Bending his arms, he leaned closer and kissed me, my mind going blank as the world drifted away from us.

If time can just stop at this moment, I will never want for anything else. Everything is so perfect. There is nothing I have to fear, no decision I need to rush into, no relationships I need to relinquish. And I'm here in David's arms, where I want to stay.

But time wouldn't give us that satisfaction. Faint voices calling my name gradually crescendoed as they neared and I knew I had to go. And he knew it, too. He smiled as he helped me to my feet and I sighed, wishing for a few more minutes of heaven and knowing I couldn't have it.

We strolled arm in arm in devoted silence toward the beckoning calls while I gazed admiringly at him. He is mine and I am his and always will be. I could never give my heart to anyone else.

Closing in on the voices, I paused and turned, wanting just a moment more to be with him before we had to part. I would see him again soon, but it wouldn't be the same as being here in his arms under this starlit sky. I gazed into his eyes and he leaned in, pressing his lips to mine and knowing this was what I longed for. I savored the brevity of this moment and wished for it to last forever.

And though it won't now, someday it will.

# About the Author

Linette Kasper is an avid writer of young adult supernatural fantasy. She is currently working on the sequel to her debut novel, *Daimon*. Though Northern Virginia is where she rests her head, Richmond is where her dreams manifest into elaborate tales. She enjoys long walks in old cemeteries and trying to stop time frame by frame.

Discover more about Linette by following her on Facebook and Instagram or by checking out www.authorlinettekasper.com.

Made in the USA
Middletown, DE
13 December 2022

18394221R10328